GREAT TALES OF HORROR & THE SUPERNATURAL

GREAT TALES OF HORROR & THE SUPERNATURAL

Introduction by
STEPHEN KING

Compiled by
BILL PRONZINI, BARRY N. MALZBERG
& MARTIN H. GREENBERG

GALAHAD BOOKS

Published in 1985 by
Galahad Books
149 Madison Avenue
New York, New York 10016
Abridged from the Arbor House Treasury
of Horror and the Supernatural
By arrangement with Arbor House Publishing Co.,
a division of The Hearst Corporation

Library of Congress Catalog Card Number: 85-080467
ISBN: 0-88365-699-X

Printed in the United States of America

ACKNOWLEDGMENTS

The following pages constitute an extension of the copyright page.

"Pickman's Model" by H.P. Lovecraft, copyright © 1927 by Popular Fiction Publishing Co.; copyright © 1939, 1945 by August Derleth and Donald Wandrei. First published in *Weird Tales*. Reprinted by permission of Arkham House Publishers, Inc., Sauk City, Wisconsin 53583.

"Yours Truly, Jack the Ripper" by Robert Bloch, copyright © 1943 by Weird Tales for *Weird Tales*, July 1943. Copyright © 1971 by Robert Bloch. Reprinted by permission of the author and the author's agents, Scott Meredith Literary Agency, Inc., 845 Third Avenue, New York, New York 10022.

"The Screaming Laugh" by Cornell Woolrich, copyright © 1938 by Street and Smith Publications, Inc. Copyright renewed 1966 by The Conde Nast Publications, Inc. Originally published in *Clues*. Reprinted by permission of the Scott Meredith Literary Agency, Inc., 845 Third Avenue, New York, New York 10022, agents for the author's estate.

A Rose for Emily" by William Faulkner, copyright © 1930 and renewed 1958 by William Faulkner. Reprinted from *Collected Stories of William Faulkner*, by William Faulkner, by permission of Random House, Inc.

"Bianca's Hands" by Theodore Sturgeon, from *E Pluribus Unicorn*. Copyright © 1947 by Consolidated Press (London). Reprinted by permission of Kirby McCauley, Ltd.

"The Girl with the Hungry Eyes" by Fritz Leiber, copyright © 1949 by Avon Book Co. First published in *The Girl with the Hungry eyes and Other Stories*. Reprinted by permission of the author.

"Shut a Final Door" by Truman Capote, copyright © 1947 by Truman Capote. Reprinted from *Selected Writings of Truman Capote*, by Truman Capote, by permission of Random House, Inc.

"Come and Go Mad" by Fredric Brown, copyright © 1949 by *Weird Tales*; copyright renewed by Fredric Brown. Reprinted by permission of the Scott Meredith Literary Agency, Inc., 845 Third Avenue, New York, New York 10022, agents for the author's estate.

"The Scarlet King" by Evan Hunter, copyright © 1954 by Evan Hunter. Reprinted by permission of the William Morris Agency, Inc., on behalf of the author.

"Sticks" by Karl Edward Wagner, copyright © 1974 by Stuart David Schiff for *Whispers* #3. Reprinted by permission of Kirby McCauley, Ltd.

"Sardonicus" by Ray Russell, copyright © 1960 by Ray Russell. First appeared in *Playboy*. Reprinted by permission of the author.

"A Teacher's Rewards" by Robert Phillips, copyright © 1970 by the Vanguard Press, Inc. Originally appeared in *The Land of Lost Content,* and reprinted by permission of the author.

"The Roaches" by Thomas M. Disch, copyright © 1965 by Bruce-Royal Publishing Co. Originally appeared in *Escapade,* and reprinted by permission of the author.

"The Jam" by Henry Slesar, copyright © 1959 by HMH Publishing Co. From *Playboy.* Reprinted by permission of the author.

"Black Wind" by Bill Pronzini, copyright © 1979 by Bill Pronzini. First published in *Ellery Queen's Mystery Magazine.* Reprinted by permission of the author.

"The Road to Mictlantecutli" by Adobe James, copyright © 1965 by Knight Publishing Corporation, Los Angeles, California. Reprinted by permission of the author and his agents, London Management, London.

"Passengers" by Robert Silverberg, copyright © 1969 by Damon Knight. Originally published in *Orbit 4* and reprinted by permission of the author.

"The Explosives Expert" by John Lutz, copyright © 1968 by HSD Publications, Inc. Originally appeared in *Alfred Hitchcock's Mystery Magazine* and reprinted by permission of the author.

"Call First" by Ramsey Campbell, copyright © 1975 by Kirby McCauley. Reprinted by permission of Kirby McCauley, Ltd., agents for the author.

"The Fly" by Arthur Porges, copyright © 1952 by Fantasy House, Inc. From *The Magazine of Fantasy & Science Fiction.* Reprinted by permission of the author and the author's agents, Scott Meredith Literary Agency, Inc., 845 Third Avenue, New York, New York 10022.

"Namesake" by Elizabeth Morton, copyright © 1980 by Ultimate Publications, Inc. Originally appeared in *Amazing* and reprinted by permission of the author.

"Camps" by Jack Dann, copyright © 1979 by Jack Dann. Originally appeared in the May 1979 *Magazine of Fantasy & Science Fiction* and reprinted by permission of the author.

"You Know Willie" by Theodore R. Cogswell, copyright © 1957 by Fantasy House, Inc. First published in *The Magazine of Fantasy & Science Fiction* and reprinted by permission of the author.

"The Mindworm" by Cyril M. Kornbluth, copyright © 1950 by Cyril M. Kornbluth; renewed. Originally appeared in *Worlds Beyond* and reprinted by permission of Robert P. Mills, Ltd., agents for the author's estate.

"Warm" by Robert Sheckley, copyright © 1953 by Galaxy Publications, Inc. Originally appeared in *Galaxy* for June 1953 and reprinted by permission of the author.

"Transfer" by Barry N. Malzberg, copyright © 1975 by Ultimate Publications, Inc. Originally appeared in *Fantastic*. Reprinted by permission of the author.

"The Doll" by Joyce Carol Oates, copyright © 1980 by Joyce Carol Oates. First published in *Epoch*. Reprinted by permission of the author.

"If Damon Comes" by Charles L. Grant, copyright © 1978 by Charles L. Grant. Originally appeared in *Year's Best Horror Stories* #6 and reprinted by permission of the author.

"The Oblong Room" by Edward D. Hoch, copyright © 1967 by Fiction Publishing Company. Originally published in *The Saint* and reprinted by permission of the author.

"The Party" by William F. Nolan, copyright © 1967 by HMH Publishing Co. Originally appeared in *Playboy*. Reprinted by permission of the author.

"The Crate" by Stephen King, copyright © 1979 by Stephen King. Reprinted by permission of the author and the author's agents, Kirby McCauley, Ltd.

TO Cornell George Hopley-Woolrich
1903–1968

Contents

10 Contents

Introduction

I

FIRST OF ALL (and this is fundamental), you have my cheerful permission to shoot me if I fall into a classic crouching posture and begin to defend the horror story, your right to read it or the right of any writer—those represented in this volume, those not and those yet unborn—to tell such tales. I have been writing professionally since the age of eighteen and writing full-time since the age of twenty-five, and the bulk of what I've written has been classified as horror fiction (the story "The Crate," which the editors have kindly included in the present volume, is a pretty good case in point), so this defense posture comes naturally to me, as I think it comes to any writer who has been asked certain questions at cocktail parties over and over (and they are always asked by people who believe they are asking them for the first time). These questions include such gems as: *Where do you get your ideas? What kind of dreams do you have? Are you as weird as the stuff you write about?* There are others, but I won't bore you. The question that really causes the writer of horror fiction (or tales of the supernatural) to fall into this automatic defense posture isn't really a question at all but a veiled editorial comment. It is usually phrased like this: *Gee, I loved your last book* (or story), *but when are you going to write something serious?*

I hope that this book, coupled with the two or three other important volumes of short supernatural tales that have been published in the postwar era (if that phrase hasn't become at long last outdated), will make that posture of defense a little less necessary. If it proves anything, it proves that the tale of horror and/or the supernatural *is* serious, *is* important, *is* necessary . . . not only to those human beings who read to think, but to those vast numbers of readers who read to feel; the volume may even go a certain distance toward proving the idea that, as this mad century races toward its conclusion—a conclusion which seems ever more ominous and ever more absurd—it may be the most important and useful form of fiction which the moral writer may command.

Consider, if you will, "The Jolly Corner" by Henry James. It is

11

probably the most difficult tale in the volume you hold, both because of James's prose, which manages to be both intellectual and passionate, and because James's approach is so rational, so calm and so cerebral. But for all of that, the watchspring at the center of this story is so black and chilling, so plausibly insane, that the reader is swept away on a flood of terrifying conjecture. The main character has left America for England as a young man, on a whim, really, but with one thing and another (not the least of which is his love for the British culture, we may infer, knowing James's life), he does not return until he is a man approaching the furthest limits of middle age. He revisits his boyhood home in New York and gradually develops an obsession concerning this place, the "jolly corner" of his childhood, which is more suited to the protagonist in a Poe story than one in a tale by James. He begins to wonder what sort of man he would have become if he had remained in New York, and—little by little, as it always happens in the best fiction of the *outré* and the terrible—he becomes convinced that a ghost lives in the jolly corner. Not the ghost of a dead man, mind you, but the ghost of *himself as he might have been* had he stayed. His stalking of this ghost—this dopplegänger, if you will—is chilling indeed . . . the more chilling because this essentially mad quest is couched in the sanest prose imaginable. Your editors say that James's theme, the quest for self, is the undercurrent of all twentieth-century literature, and of course they are right (at least they are right if we restrict the discussion to American and, to a lesser degree, British literature), but James's story is placed in a context of such horror and such alienation that the reader is left cold, stunned and reeling. Such a story does not need to be defended; it needs to be cried from the rooftops. It begs to be read! And this is the most *difficult* story in the volume, the most intellectual, the most bloodless. If such a tale can cause a *frisson* of terror, then imagine the other delights that await you here. But . . . wait a minute, okay?

The word *frisson* itself, the French for that half-horrid, half-delightful shiver up the spine which the best tales of terror allow us to feel, has become debased by the critics of a genre which has become more and more to be regarded as popular entertainment and no more. The word, once reserved for such moments as that when the ghost of Hamlet's father appears to the guards of the watch, is now applied to such moments as when the Lutz's toilet overflows with black goop in *The Amityville Horror* or when the little girl in *The Exorcist* pukes pea soup all over the priest who is examining her. It has become too easy, that word. In the cheap coinage of a society which overflows with thousands of books each year and hundreds of lame ghost stories in which all the chains sound like plastic and all of the moans sound like chords played on a Moog synthesizer, the word has beome synonymous with *escape*, as in *escape reading*, as in *pop lit*, as in *masscult*, as in *junk reading*.

It seems important to me, in a book of this kind, to point out one fact at the outset, before the first spirit walks and before the first crypt door yawns wide: the tale of horror and the supernatural *is* an escape, but the reader must never believe that it is only an escape outward, into a kind of never-never land (that world, if you will, which is inhabited by heroes invented by Alistair MacLean, Ian Fleming, Phyllis Whitney, Sidney Sheldon, or Judith Krantz—books to be read while waiting for planes, in washaterias or under hairdryers); the tale of terror and supernatural is also an escape *inward*, toward the very center of our perceived humanity. The best tales of terror deal with questions of memory and mortality, and the fact that they so often haunt us after the lights are out, laughing ominously in the dark with teeth grown wondrously sharp and long, only proves the truth and the practicality of their vision.

This is not defense but warning: you must not come to tales such as these with your guard down. They will entertain you, they will rouse both your anger and your amusement (in one of them, for instance, you will encounter a man who laughs himself to death . . . but in the end it's not so funny, oh no, not at all), but they will not comfort you. One would be tempted to prescribe, so: "One to be taken each night, at bedtime, against the dreams which may come," but the healthy mind is best not prescribed for, and the spirit of a sane man or woman is its own best physician. So . . . take as many as seem required, morning, noon or in that ditch of dreams we call the night. But be careful. The journey is not outward but inward. There are no heroes charging tanks here, and no beautiful Hollywood starlets taking off their clothes; if that's what you came for, you've wandered into the wrong dream factory. Here there are only the quiet tickings of your worst dreams, those ones you've had wide awake at three in the morning, when the only light was the waxing-and-waning glow of your cigarette, when the only sound was the wind outside. These stories are the best of the best, and to read them is to turn inward and backward.

Some of them have their comforts, but none of them is safe . . . which is to say, they mirror life as we know it.

II

It came to me, reading these stories through and thinking of what I might say about them (said reading and thinking took place during a span of still, subzero days in January of this year . . . the perfect climate for stories of the insane and unnatural), that what I really wanted to talk about most of all was the *voice* of the horror story. By voice I think (although I am not sure) that I mean those things which are called *style* and *tone* in the composition manuals. Words do not matter a great deal on this subject anyway, I suppose; rhetoricians will define until their teeth drop out and their noses fall off, but what they all mean is the way the story would sound if we were actually inside the writer's head, hearing the tale unfold. We are talking about rhythms and cadences; possibly even the expressions we sense might be on the writer's face as certain words or developments come together in his or her mind. We are talking about something which is so much a throwback that it is almost atavistic; the tale not written down in a book but the tale told over a fire while the wind whips the trees outside or moans its way down a sterile drywash. To talk of style and tone is to speak of voice, I think, and to talk about voice is to bring the art of telling a tale back to the oral tradition, a place where the tale of terror is uniquely at home.

A friend of mine, a fine suspense novelist named David Morrell (and my definition of a suspense tale would simply be "a story in which the horrors are technically possible"), once wrote to me in a letter that, grotesque as it might seem to the outside world, he found himself actually *grinning* as he wrote passages of extreme terror or inventing scenes of surpassing gruesomeness. I responded in kind, actually relieved that someone else had shared this perverse experience, and immediately began to notice how many tales of terror share this one trait: the voice which powers them impresses us with a kind of ominous jocularity. I am not saying that this voice can be detected in all tales of horror and the supernatural (I do not detect it, for instance, in Truman Capote's grim tale of a heel brought to heel, "Shut a Final

Door," which you will find in this collection), but it is there in a remarkable number of them.

In the Poe classic, "The Tell-Tale Heart," the murdering narrator tells his story in a kind of cackling frenzy, laughing as he explains how cleverly he got rid of the old man's body by cutting it up in the tub and putting the pieces under the floorboards (and I quite consciously ripped the device off in my own story, "The Crate," where the narrator laughs uncontrollably as he pushes his bitch of a wife under the stairs where she is awaited by a monster of such ferocity that it is really a cartoon). That Poe story is not in this book (which is just as well, since most readers in the genre have it by heart), but another Poe tale, "Hop Frog," less known but just as chilling, is here. The protagonist of the story, quite appropriately to the thesis, is a jester. And if this hump-backed fellow's final jest is rather horrible—it involves a chain, a pulley, and a torch . . . but I'll say no more—it is also rather funny, in a rather twisted way.

Another story, Ambrose Bierce's "The Middle Toe of the Right Foot," also tells the tale of a joke gone horribly awry, and other examples in the genre abound, but these are plots more than voice. Yet in the work of Robert Bloch, represented here by "Yours Truly, Jack the Ripper," we find this same dangerous jocularity (Bloch, who is fond of telling interviewers that he really has the heart of a small boy—"I keep it in a jar on my desk"—is a wonderful after-dinner speaker who made his living for a while in the forties by writing one-liners). "Sardonicus," by Ray Russell, is, in addition to being perhaps the finest example of the modern gothic ever written, the story of a man who cannot stop smiling. In "The Hand," the normally sober Theodore Dreiser constantly offers interjections ("Think of that!" or "Imagine it!") that call to mind the ejaculations of Kurt Vonnegut ("Hi-ho," "So it goes," "And so on" and so on). And Thomas M. Disch's "The Roaches," which is surely one of the most horrible stories in this collection, is also blackly hilarious. Such a voice is simply unavailable to us outside of this contrary, cross-grained, morbid genre.

Other examples abound. In a Dennis Etchison story, "The Late Shift," we discover that the night clerks in all of those Seven-Elevens and Piggly-Wigglys and Stop-N-Go's are reanimated corpses. In J. G. Ballard's novel *Concrete Island*, a car-crash victim finds himself unable to get across the four lanes of M-15 traffic outside of London and so takes up permanent residence on the highway median. In Bram Stoker's *Dracula* (you will find Stoker represented here by "The Squaw," one of the three best short stories of horror that Irish gentleman ever wrote—and one which has its own grimly ironic strain of humor), Van Helsing goes into a fit of hysterical laughter after Lucy Westenra's funeral, and offers a stupefied John Seward a memorable soliloquy on King Laugh, "who come," Van Helsing says, "when he come, friend John . . . doubt it not!"

Anyone who has ever attended the theater has contemplated those Siamese twins Comedy and Tragedy, who are exactly alike save for the fact that the mouth of one curves up while the mouth of the other curves down. Anyone who has studied neoclassic tragedy even slightly will remember that humor was considered an integral part of tragedy, the light which illuminated even more fully the essential horror of the situation.

The long-running popularity of tales such as these attest to their entertainment value, but just because the reader is entertained is no reason to suppose that the writer has not been entertained also. In fact, the reverse is usually true—what has entertained the reader has first entertained the writer tenfold.

One way—a rather unimaginative one—to explain why the voice of the horror tale is so often grimly ironic or outright funny (and if you find nothing funny in a story such as "Squire Toby's Will," where the alcoholic old squire comes back as a bulldog with a white body and a black head, then I humbly submit that there is something seriously out of order with your funnybone) is to say that "it starts being funny when it stops being us." There's some truth to this, of course; it explains why we laugh when a guy gets a pie in the face or slips on a banana peel, for instance, and forms the basis for what we call "slapstick" . . . a form of humor which is closely allied to horror, we may realize if we stop to closely consider it.

But the "somebody else, not me" doctrine is not a very ennobling one, and if we try to apply it to the horror genre, it yields depressing results: it says, in effect, that we can be entertained by horrible happenings as long as they are not happening to us. This conclusion puts the horror tale on a level with public executions, and this is a level where some critics claim it rightly belongs . . . but this is a little like saying that there is no humor but slapstick humor. As there are other levels to humor, so are there other levels to its Siamese twin, horror.

At one time or another, all of us have come in contact with that romantic idea (ideal?) of the man or woman who is so brave that he/she "laughs at death." In a sense, this is exactly what the tale of horror does, and seen in that light it becomes a concept of peculiar nobility. "You know not when King Laugh come," Van Helsing says in Stoker's great novel, but to be able to laugh in the face of terror and the unknown surmounts humanity: such an ability is nearly godlike. Taken another step, the simple ability to make such tales a part of our popular entertainment suggests something more vital and more human than simple intellectual achievement—it suggests that even our emotions are capable of a peculiar sort of exaltation (is that too strong a word? it seems so, and yet I suspect it is not). The very fact that humor and horror are so closely allied suggests to me that we are very special animals indeed. It suggests that the horror story is the final existential development, and one uniquely suited for times when terrorists may be concocting nuclear bombs in basements and when national governments are underwriting, enthusiastically or not, killer viruses so potent that a teaspoonful may be enough to destroy a fifth of the world's population. The horror tale, taken in moderation, does not dull the sensibilities, but the ability to be entertained by the prospect of the trap, the drop or a night spent alone in the dark, is something almost unsuspected outside of this genre, which is so full of dark humor and sick jokes with teeth.

Just ask Eleazar Hunt, from Cornell Woolrich's "The Screaming Laugh," how incompatible the two are.

III

I think we've said most of it now—the most important point perhaps being that the stories you are about to read are unique not only because they are some of the best, but because they take the most stringent dictum of popular literature, "amuse the reader," to its darkest and outermost limits—but I'll finish by repeating an observation that I've made in other places: namely, that few people read introductions. Of course if you are a student and this book forms a part of your course work, and if your instructor has assigned these introductory pages, you are no doubt grimly slogging you way through to the end and wishing that I would hurry up and get out of your way. The author of an introduction to such a volume as this is like an after-dinner speaker, who is more heartily applauded for finishing than for whatever it was he had to say. Like an after-dinner speaker, I find the urge to drone on for another ten pages (or another hundred!) almost undeniable, but I will manage.

Suffice it to say, then, that tales of horror and the supernatural have been one of the few channels (outside of attending the church of your choice) which people have had since those times in the cave in which to explore the great mysteries of mortality, memory and survival, and perhaps the only channel which we can explore without taking up some particular badge of faith which blinds us to all the other possibilities. We can explore such essentially pagan concepts as werewolvery, vampirism and the dead who walk. We are able to deal with our own deaths on a "worst-case" basis (if, for instance, we can deal with "The Girl with the Hungry Eyes" in Fritz Leiber's powerful tale of psychosexual vampirism, we may find it a little easier to deal with the more mundane vampires of our own lives, whether they be cancer, diabetes or plain old garden-variety neurosis) and to remember our own pasts, both personal and racial. If we are so certain of our own civilization, we might consider the grim satisfaction we derive from the jester's revenge in Poe's "Hop Frog," or consider the cold grue we feel upon concluding Charles L. Grant's "If Damon Comes" or Karl Edward Wagner's "Sticks."

The tale of horror and the supernatural fulfills one more valuable human function. Besides showing us where the taboo lines of our society lie, they emphasize the light by marking out that spot where the darkness takes over. The best tales in the genre make one point over and over again—that the rational world both within us and without us is small, that our understanding is smaller yet, and that much of the universe in which we exist is, so far as we are able to tell, chaotic. So the horror story makes us appreciate our own well-lighted corner of that chaotic universe, and perhaps allows a moment of warm and grateful wonder that we should be allowed to exist in that fragile space of light at all.

So I recommend this wonderful batch of red-eyed and brimstone-smelling terrors to you with unreserved enthusiasm. They have, paradoxically, warmed a cold January weekend for me by frosting my bones and chilling my blood, a trick that our caveman ancestors might well have understood as they listened to one of their own tell about the thing that chased him home through the trees after the dark of night had fallen. Such a thing might still be out there, these forebears of ours might have thought, looking nervously at the gruesome drawings on the cave walls, and the next night one of us—me, even—might not escape. But for tonight the fire is warm, warmer for the chill around the heart, and brighter for the darkness outside where anything—any *thing*—might roam the night.

And here they are, my friends, like a ghostly crew astride skeletal horses. There is a certain oblong room which you will visit with Edward D. Hoch. William F. Nolan wants you to put on a funny hat, grab yourself a noisemaker and accompany him to a particularly nasty party. You've a date with Henry Slesar in a tunnel under a river, where you and he will experience the dubious delights of "The Jam." You'll meet a damned artist named Pickman and a girl named Bianca; you'll circle the world from Mictlantecutli to Germany to the house or the apartment building just up the street. One story, a brilliant tale by the late Fredric Brown, is titled "Come and Go Mad," but readers of horror stories stretching back a hundred generations (or a thousand!) have often discovered that such tales are one way to stay sane in a mad universe.

We're at the edge of the light now, and I think I'll leave you here to find your own way.

You have only to turn the page and step into the dark.

Bangor, Maine
January 5, 1981

GREAT TALES OF
HORROR &
THE
SUPERNATURAL

I
Grandmasters

Hop Frog

EDGAR ALLAN POE

This is a story of recrimination and vengeance by not only the finest American writer of horror fiction but probably the finest American writer of his century. Poe's reputation is not undimmed, but in recent decades his categorization as "the first detective story writer," "the first American writer of the supernatural" or "the first tragic figure in American fiction" has detracted from his true range and stature. Nowhere did the vision of a writer and the condition of his milieu so fuse as it did with Poe; he was in many ways the American nineteenth-century, and "Hop Frog"—the details of its chronology aside—is a major statement of the land of dreams just before (or during) its first encounter with the terrible engines of detail and circumstance.

I never knew anyone so keenly alive to a joke as the king was. He seemed to live only for joking. To tell a good story of the joke kind, and to tell it well, was the surest road to his favor. Thus it happened that his seven ministers were all noted for their accomplishments as jokers. They all took after the king, too, in being large, corpulent, oily men, as well as inimitable jokers. Whether people grow fat by joking, or whether there is something in fat itself which predisposes to a joke, I have never been quite able to determine; but certain it is that a lean joker is a *rara avis in terris*.

About the refinements, or, as he called them, the "ghosts" of wit, the king troubled himself very little. He had an especial admiration for *breadth* in a jest, and would often put up with *length*, for the sake of it. Overniceties wearied him. He would have preferred Rabelais' *Gargantua* to the *Zadig* of Voltaire: and, upon the whole, practical jokes suited his taste far better than verbal ones.

At the date of my narrative, professing jesters had not altogether gone out of fashion at court. Several of the great Continental "powers" still retained their "fools," who wore motley, with caps and bells, and who were expected to be always ready with sharp witticisms, at a moment's notice, in consideration of the crumbs that fell from the royal table.

Our king, as a matter of course, retained his "fool." The fact is, he *required* something in the way of folly—if only to counterbalance the heavy wisdom of the seven wise men who were his ministers—not to mention himself.

His fool, or professional jester, was not *only* a fool, however. His value was trebled in the eyes of the king, by the fact of his being also a dwarf and a cripple. Dwarfs were as common at court, in those days, as fools; and many monarchs would have found it difficult to get through their days (days are rather longer at court than elsewhere) without both a jester to laugh *with*, and a dwarf to laugh *at*. But, as I have already observed, your jesters, in ninety-nine cases out of a hundred, are fat, round and unwieldy—so that it was no small source of self-gratulation with our king that, in Hop-Frog (this was the fool's name), he possessed a triplicate treasure in one person.

I believe the name "Hop-Frog" was *not* that given to the dwarf by his sponsors at baptism, but it was conferred upon him, by general consent of the seven ministers, on account of his inability to walk as other men do. In fact, Hop-Frog could only get along by a sort of interjectional gait—something between a leap and a wriggle—a movement that afforded illimitable amusement, and of course consolation, to the king, for (notwithstanding the protuberance of his stomach and a constitutional swelling of the head) the king, by his whole court, was accounted a capital figure.

But although Hop-Frog, through the distortion of his legs, could move only with great pain and difficulty along a road or floor, the prodigious muscular power which nature seemed to have bestowed upon his arms by way of compensation for deficiency in the lower limbs, enabled him to perform many feats of wonderful dexterity, where trees or ropes were in question, or anything else to climb. At such exercises he certainly much more resembled a squirrel, or a small monkey, than a frog.

I am not able to say, with precision, from what country Hop-Frog originally came. It was from some barbarous region, however, that no person ever heard of—a vast distance from the court of our king. Hop-Frog, and a young girl very little less dwarfish than himself (although of exquisite proportions, and a marvelous dancer), had been forcibly carried off from their respective homes in adjoining provinces, and sent as presents to the king, by one of his ever-victorious generals.

Under these circumstances, it is not to be wondered at that a close intimacy arose between the two little captives. Indeed, they soon became sworn friends. Hop-Frog, who, although he made a great deal of sport, was by no means popular, had it not in his power to render Trippetta many services; but *she*, on account of her grace and exquisite beauty (although a dwarf), was universally admired and petted; so she possessed much influence; and never failed to use it, whenever she could, for the benefit of Hop-Frog.

On some grand state occasion—I forget what—the king determined to have a masquerade; and whenever a masquerade, or anything of that kind, occurred at our court, then the talents both of Hop-Frog and Trippetta were sure to be called into play. Hop-Frog, in especial, was so inventive in the way of getting up pageants, suggesting novel characters and arranging costume, for masked balls, that nothing could be done, it seems, without his assistance.

The night appointed for the *fête* had arrived. A gorgeous hall had been fitted up, under Trippetta's eye, with every kind of device which could possible give *éclat* to a masquerade. The whole court was in a fever of expectation. As for costumes and characters, it might well be supposed that everybody had come to a decision on such points. Many had made up their minds (as to what roles they should assume) a week, or even a month, in advance; and in fact, there was not a particle of indecision anywhere—except in the case of the king and his seven ministers. Why *they* hesitated I never could tell, unless they did it by way of a joke. More probably, they found it difficult, on account of being so fat, to make up their minds. At all events, time flew; and, as a last resort, they sent for Trippetta and Hop-Frog.

When the two little friends obeyed the summons of the king, they found him sitting at his wine with the seven members of his cabinet council; but the monarch appeared to be in a very ill humor. He knew that Hop-Frog was not fond of wine; for it excited the poor cripple almost to madness; and madness is no comfortable feeling. But the king loved his practical jokes, and took pleasure in forcing Hop-Frog to drink and (as the king called it) "to be merry."

"Come here, Hop-Frog," said he, as the jester and his friend entered the room; "swallow this bumper to the health of your absent friends [here Hop-Frog sighed] and then let us have the benefit of your invention. We want characters—*characters*, man—something novel—

out of the way. We are wearied with this everlasting sameness. Come, drink! The wine will brighten your wits."

Hop-Frog endeavored, as usual, to get up a jest in reply to these advances from the king; but the effort was too much. It happened to be the poor dwarf's birthday, and the command to drink to his "absent friends" forced the tears to his eyes. Many large, bitter drops fell into the goblet as he took it, humbly, from the hand of the tyrant.

"Ah! ha! ha! ha!" roared the latter, as the dwarf reluctantly drained the beaker. "See what a glass of good wine can do! Why, your eyes are shining already!"

Poor fellow! His large eyes *gleamed*, rather than shone; for the effect of wine on his excitable brain was not more powerful than instantaneous. He placed the goblet nervously on the table, and looked round upon the company with a half-insane stare. They all seemed highly amused at the success of the king's "*joke*."

"And now to business," said the prime minister, a *very* fat man.

"Yes," said the king. "Come, Hop-Frog, lend us your assistance. Characters, my fine fellow; we stand in need of characters—all of us—ha! ha! ha!" and as this was seriously meant for a joke, his laugh was chorused by the seven.

Hop-Frog also laughed, although feebly and somewhat vacantly.

"Come, come," said the king, impatiently, "have you nothing to suggest?"

"I am endeavoring to think of something *novel*," replied the dwarf, abstractedly, for he was quite bewildered by the wine.

"Endeavoring!" cried the tyrant, fiercely; "what do you mean by *that*? Ah, I perceive. You are sulky, and want more wine. Here, drink this!" and he poured out another goblet full and offered it to the cripple, who merely gazed at it, gasping for breath.

"Drink, I say!" shouted the monster, "or by the fiends—"

The dwarf hesitated. The king grew purple with rage. The courtiers smirked. Trippetta, pale as a corpse, advanced to the monarch's seat and, falling on her knees before him, implored him to spare her friend.

The tyrant regarded her for some moments, in evident wonder at her audacity. He seemed quite at a loss what to do or say—how most becomingly to express his indignation. At last, without uttering a syllable, he pushed her violently from him, and threw the contents of the brimming goblet in her face.

The poor girl got up as best she could, and, not daring even to sigh, resumed her position at the foot of the table.

There was a dead silence for about half a minute, during which the falling of a leaf, or of a feather, might have been heard. It was interrupted by a low, but harsh and protracted *grating* sound which seemed to come at once from every corner of the room.

"What—what—*what* are you making that noise for?" demanded the king, turning furiously to the dwarf.

The latter seemed to have recovered, in great measure, from his intoxication, and looking fixedly but quietly into the tyrant's face, merely ejaculated:

"I—I? How could it have been me?"

"The sound appeared to come from without," observed one of the courtiers. "I fancy it was the parrot at the window, whetting his bill upon his cage-wires."

"True," replied the monarch, as if much relieved by the suggestion; "but, on the honor of a knight, I could have sworn that it was the gritting of this vagabond's teeth."

Hereupon the dwarf laughed (the king was too confirmed a joker to object to anyone's laughing), and displayed a set of large, powerful and very repulsive teeth. Moreover, he avowed his perfect willingness to swallow as much wine as desired. The monarch was pacified; and having drained another bumper with no very perceptible ill effect, Hop-Frog entered at once, and with spirit, into the plans for the masquerade.

"I cannot tell what was the association of ideas," observed he, very tranquilly and as if he had never tasted wine in his life, "but *just after* your majesty had struck the girl and thrown the wine in her face—*just after* your majesty had done this, and while the parrot was making that odd noise outside the window there came into my mind a capital diversion—one of my own country frolics—often enacted among us, at our masquerades: but here it will be new altogether. Unfortunately, however, it requires a company of eight persons, and—"

"Here we *are*!" cried the king, laughing at his acute discovery of the coincidence; "eight to a fraction—I and my seven ministers. Come! what is the diversion?"

"We call it," replied the cripple, "the Eight Chained Ourang-Outangs, and it really is excellent sport if well enacted."

"*We* will enact it," remarked the king, drawing himself up, and lowering his eyelids.

"The beauty of the game," continued Hop-Frog, "lies in the fright it occasions among the women."

"Capital!" roared in chorus the monarch and his ministry.

"I will equip you as ourang-outangs," proceeded the dwarf; "leave all that to me. The resemblance shall be so striking, that the company of masqueraders will take you for real beasts—and of course they will be as much terrified as astonished."

"Oh, this is exquisite!" exclaimed the king. "Hop-Frog! I will make a man of you."

"The chains are for the purpose of increasing the confusion by their jangling. Your are supposed to have escaped, *en masse*, from your keepers. Your majesty cannot conceive the *effect* produced, at a masquerade, by eight chained ourang-outangs, imagined to be real ones by most of the company; and rushing in with savage cries, among the crowd of delicately and gorgeously habited men and women. The *contrast* is inimitable."

"It *must* be," said the king; and the council arose hurriedly (as it was growing late), to put in execution the scheme of Hop-Frog.

His mode of equipping the party as ourang-outangs was very simple, but effective enough for his purposes. The animals in question had, at the epoch of my story, very rarely been seen in any part of the civilized world; and as the imitations made by the dwarf were sufficiently beast like and more than sufficiently hideous, their truthfulness to nature was thus thought to be secured.

The king and his ministers were first encased in tight-fitting stock-ingette shirts and drawers. They were then saturated with tar. At this stage of the process, some one of the party suggested feathers; but the suggestion was at once overruled by the dwarf,who soon convinced the eight, by ocular demonstration, that the hair of such a brute as the ourang-outang was much more efficiently represented by *flax*. A thick coating of the latter was accordingly plastered upon the coating of tar. A long chain was now procured. First, it was passed about the waist of the king, *and tied*; then about another of the party, and also tied; then about all successively, in the same manner. When this chaining arrangement was complete, and the party stood as far apart from each other as possible, they formed a circle; and to make all things appear natural, Hop-Frog passed the residue of the chain, in two diameters, at right angles, across the circle, after the fashion adopted, at the present day, by those who capture chimpanzees, or other large apes, in Borneo.

The grand saloon in which the masquerade was to take place was a circular room, very lofty, and receiving the light of the sun only through a single window at top. At night (the season for which the apartment was especially designed) it was illuminated principally by a large chandelier, depending by a chain from the center of the skylight, and lowered, or elevated, by means of a counterbalance as usual; but (in order not to look unsightly) this latter passed outside the cupola and over the roof.

The arrangements of the room had been left to Trippetta's superintendence; but, in some particulars, it seems, she had been guided by the calmer judgment of her friend the dwarf. At his suggestion it was that, on this occasion, the chandelier was removed. Its waxen drippings (which, in weather so warm, it was quite impossible to prevent) would have been seriously detrimental to the rich dresses of the guests, who, on account of the crowded state of the saloon, could not *all* be expected to keep from out its center—that is to say, from under the chandelier. Additional sconces were set in various parts of the hall, out of the way; and a flambeau, emitting sweet odor, was placed in the right hand of each of the Caryatides that stood against the wall—some fifty or sixty all together.

The eight ourang-outangs, taking Hop-Frogs advice, waited patiently until midnight (when the room was thoroughly filled with masqueraders) before making their appearance. No sooner had the clock ceased striking, however, than they rushed, or rather rolled in, all together—for the impediments of their chains caused most of the party to fall, and all to stumble as they entered.

The excitement among the masqueraders was prodigious, and filled the heart of the king with glee. As had been anticipated, there were not a few of the guests who supposed the ferocious-looking creatures to be beasts of *some* kind in reality, if not precisely ourang-outangs. Many of the women swooned with affright; and had not the king taken the precaution to exclude all weapons from the saloon, his party might soon have expiated their frolic in their blood. As it was, a general rush was made for the doors; but the king had ordered them to be locked immediately upon his entrance; and, at the dwarf's suggestion, the keys had been deposited with *him*.

While the tumult was at its height, and each masquerader attentive only to his own safety (for, in fact, there was much *real* danger from the pressure of the excited crowd), the chain by which the chandelier ordinarily hung, and which had been drawn up on its removal, might have been seen very gradually to descend, until its hooked extremity came within three feet of the floor.

Soon after this, the king and his seven friends having reeled about the hall in all directions, found themselves, at length, in its center, and of course, in immediate contact with the chain. While they were thus situated, the dwarf, who had followed noiselessly at their heels, inciting them to keep up the commotion, took hold of their own chain at the intersection of the two portions which crossed the circle diametrically and at right angles. Here, with the rapidity of thought, he inserted the hook from which the chandelier had been wont to depend; and, in an instant, by some unseen agency, the chandelier chain was drawn so far upward as to take the hook out of reach, and, as an inevitable consequence, to drag the ourang-outangs together in close connection, and face to face.

The masqueraders, by this time, had recovered, in some measure, from their alarm; and, beginning to regard the whole matter as a well-contrived pleasantry, set up a loud shout of laughter at the predicament of the apes.

"Leave them to *me!*" now screamed Hop-Frog, his shrill voice making itself easily heard through all the din. "Leave them to *me*. I fancy *I* know them. If I can only get a good look at them, *I* can soon tell who they are."

Here, scrambling over the heads of the crowd, he managed to get to the wall; when, seizing a flambeau from one of the Caryatides, he returned, as he went, to the center of the room—leaped, with the agility of a monkey, upon the king's head—and thence clambered a few feet up the chain—holding down the torch to examine the group of ourang-outangs, and still screaming: "*I* shall soon find out who they are!"

And now, while the whole assembly (the apes included) were convulsed with laughter, the jester suddenly uttered a shrill whistle; when the chain flew violently up for about thirty feet—dragging with it the dismayed and struggling ourang-outangs, and leaving them suspended in mid-air between the skylight and the floor. Hop-Frog, clingling to the chain as it rose, still maintained his relative position in respect to the eight maskers, and still (as if nothing were the matter) continued to thrust his torch down toward them, as though endeavoring to discover who they were.

So thoroughly astonished was the whole company at this ascent that a dead silence, of about a minute's duration, ensued. It was broken by just such a low, harsh, *grating* sound, as had before attracted the attention of the king and his councillors when the former threw the wine in the face of Trippetta. But, on the present occasion, there could be no question as to where the sound issued. It came from the fanglike teeth of the dwarf, who ground them and gnashed them as he foamed at the mouth, and glared, with an expression of maniacal rage, into the upturned countenances of the king and his seven companions.

"Ah, ha!" said at length the infuriated jester. "Ah, ha! I begin to see who these people *are*, now!" Here, pretending to scrutinize the king more closely, he held the flambeau to the flaxen coat which enveloped him and which instantly burst into a sheet of vivid flame. In less than half a minute the whole eight ourang-outangs were blazing fiercely, amid the shrieks of the multitude who gazed at them from below, horror-stricken, and without the power to render them the slightest assistance.

At length the flames, suddenly increasing in virulence, forced the jester to climb higher up the chain, to be out of their reach; and, as he made his movement, the crowd again sank, for a brief instant, into silence. The dwarf seized his opportunity, and once more spoke:

"I now see *distinctly*," he said, "what manner of people these maskers are. They are a great king and his seven privy-councillors—a king who does not scruple to strike a defenseless girl, and his seven councillors who abet him in the outrage. As for myself, I am simply Hop-Frog, the jester—and *this is my last jest*."

Owing to the high combustibility of both the flax and the tar to which it adhered, the dwarf had scarcely made an end of his brief speech before the work of vengeance was complete. The eight corpses swung in their chains, a fetid, blackened, hideous and indistinguishable mass. The cripple hurled his torch at them, clambered leisurely to the ceiling, and disappeared through the skylight.

It is supposed that Trippetta, stationed on the roof of the saloon, had been the accomplice of her friend in his fiery revenge and that, together, they effected their escape to their own country; for neither was seen again.

Rappaccini's Daughter

NATHANIEL HAWTHORNE

This is one of the earliest of American horror stories, penned during the same period in the 1840's when Poe produced some of his finest arabesques; its first book appearance was in Hawthorne's collection Mosses from an Old Manse *(1846). As a work of literature, "Rappaccini's Daughter" is a brilliant portrayal of madness and evil that emphasizes Hawthorne's preoccupation with Puritan symbolism and allegory. But it is also a classic weird tale, and offers more than a few* frissons de horreur *for the connoisseur.*

We do not remember to have seen any translated specimens of the productions of M. de l'Aubépine—a fact the less to be wondered at, as his very name is unknown to many of his own countrymen as well as to the student of foreign literature. As a writer, he seems to occupy an unfortunate position between the Transcendentalists (who, under one name or another, have their share in all the current literature of the world) and the great body of pen-and-ink men who address the intellect and sympathies of the multitude. If not too refined, at all events too remote, too shadowy and unsubstantial in his modes of development to suit the taste of the latter class, and yet too popular to satisfy the spiritual or metaphysical requistions of the former, he must necessarily find himself without an audience, except here and there an individual or possibly an isolated clique. His writings, to do them justice, are not altogether destitute of fancy and originality; they might have won him greater reputation but for an inveterate love of allegory, which is apt to invest his plots and characters with the aspect of scenery and people in the clouds, and to steal away the human warmth out of his conceptions. His fictions are sometimes historical, sometimes of the present day, and sometimes, so far as can be discovered, have little or no reference either to time or space. In any case, he generally contents himself with a very slight embroidery of outward manners—the faintest possible counterfeit of real life—and endeavors to create an interest by some less obvious peculiarity of the subject. Occasionally a breath of Nature, a raindrop of pathos and tenderness, or a gleam of humor, will find its way into the midst of his fantastic imagery, and make us feel as if, after all, we were yet within the limits of our native Earth. We will only add to this very cursory notice that M. de l'Aubépine's productions, if the reader chance to take them in precisely the proper point of view, may amuse a leisure hour as well as those of a brighter man; if otherwise, they can hardly fail to look excessively like nonsense.

Our author is voluminous; he continues to write and publish with as much praiseworthy and indefatigable prolixity as if his efforts were crowned with the brilliant success that so justly attends those of Eugène Sue. His first appearance was by a collection of stories in a long series of volumes entitled *Contes deux fois racontées*. The titles of some of his more recent works (we quote from memory) are as follows: "Le Voyage Céleste à Chemin de Fer," 3 tom., 1838; "Le nouveau Pére Adam et la nouvelle Mére Eve," 2 tom., 1839; "Roderic; ou le Serpent à l'estomac," 2 tom., 1840; "Le Culte du Feu," a folio volume of ponderous research into the religion and ritual of the old Persian Ghebers, published in 1841; "La Soirée du Château en Espagne," 1 tom., 8vo, 1842; and "L'Artiste du Beau; ou le Papillon Mécanique," 5 tom., 4to, 1843. Our somewhat wearisome perusal of this starling catalogue of volumes has left behind it a certain personal affection and sympathy, though by no means admiration, for M. de l'Aubépine; and we would fain do the little in our power towards introducing him favorably to the American public. The ensuing tale is a translation of his "Beatrice; ou la Belle Empoisonneuse," recently published in *La Revue Anti-Aristocratique*. This journal, edited by the Comte de Bearhaven, has for some years past led the defense of liberal principles and popular rights with a faithfulness and ability worthy of all praise.

A young man, named Giovanni Guasconti, came, very long ago, from the more southern region of Italy, to pursue his studies at the University of Padua. Giovanni, who had but a scant supply of gold ducats in his pocket, took lodgings in a high and gloomy chamber of an old edifice which looked not unworthy to have been the palace of a Paduan noble, and which, in fact, exhibited over its entrance the armorial bearings of a family long since extinct. The young stranger, who was not unstudied in the great poem of his country, recollected that one of the ancestors of this family, and perhaps an occupant of this very mansion, had been pictured by Dante as a partaker of the immortal agonies of his Inferno. These reminiscences and associations, together with the tendency to heartbreak natural to a young man for the first time out of his native sphere, caused Giovanni to sigh heavily as he looked around the desolate and ill-furnished apartment.

"Holy Virgin, signor!" cried old Dame Lisabetta, who, won by the youth's remarkable beauty of person, was kindly endeavoring to give the chamber a habitable air, "what a sigh was that to come out of a young man's heart! Do you find this old mansion gloomy? For the love of heaven, then, put your head out of the window, and you will see as bright sunshine as you have left in Naples."

Guasconti mechanically did as the old woman advised, but could not quite agree with her that the Paduan sunshine was as cheerful as that of southern Italy. Such as it was, however, it fell upon a garden beneath the window and expended its fostering influences on a variety of plants, which seemed to have been cultivated with exceeding care.

"Does this garden belong to the house?" asked Giovanni.

"Heaven forbid, signor, unless it were fruitful of better pot herbs than any that grow there now," answered old Lisabetta. "No; that garden is cultivated by the own hands of Signor Giacomo Rappaccini, the famous doctor, who, I warrant him, has been heard of as far as Naples. It is said that he distills these plants into medicines that are as potent as a charm. Oftentimes you may see the signor doctor at work, and perchance the signora, his daughter, too, gathering the strange flowers that grow in the garden."

The old woman had now done what she could for the aspect of the chamber; and, commending the young man to the protection of the saints, took her departure.

Giovanni still found no better occupation than to look down into the garden beneath his window. From its appearance, he judged it to be one of those botanic gardens which were of earlier date in Padua than elsewhere in Italy or in the world. Or, not improbably, it might once have been the pleasure place of an opulent family; for there was the ruin of a marble fountain in the center, sculptured with rare art, but so woefully shattered that it was impossible to trace the original design from the chaos of remaining fragments. The water, however, continued to gush and sparkle into the sunbeams as cheerfully as ever. A little gurgling sound ascended to the young man's window, and made him feel as if the fountain were an immortal spirit that sung its song unceasingly and without heeding the vicissitudes around it, while one century embodied it in marble and another scattered the perishable garniture on the soil. All about the pool into which the water subsided grew various plants, that seemed to require a plentiful supply of moisture for the nourishment of gigantic leaves, and, in some instances, flowers gorgeously magnificent. There was one shrub in particular, set in a marble vase in the midst of the pool, that bore a profusion of purple blossoms, each of which had the luster and richness of a gem; and the whole together made a show so resplendent that it seemed enough to illuminate the garden, even had there been no sunshine. Every portion of the soil was peopled with plants and herbs, which, if less beautiful, still bore tokens of assiduous care, as if all had their individual virtues, known to the scientific mind that fostered them. Some were placed in urns, rich with old carving, and others in common garden pots; some crept serpentlike along the ground or climbed on high, using whatever means of ascent was offered them. One plant had wreathed itself round a statue of Vertumnus, which was thus quite veiled and shrouded in a drapery of hanging foliage, so happily arranged that it might have served a sculptor for a study.

While Giovanni stood at the window, he heard a rustling behind a screen of leaves, and became aware that a person was at work in the garden. His figure soon emerged into view, and showed itself to be that of no common laborer, but a tall, emaciated, sallow, and sickly looking man, dressed in a scholar's garb of black. He was beyond the middle term of life, with gray hair, a thin, gray beard, and a face singularly marked with intellect and cultivation, but which could never, even in his more youthful days, have expressed much warmth of heart.

Nothing could exceed the intentness with which this scientific gardener examined every shrub which grew in his path: it seemed as if he was looking into their inmost nature, making observations in regard to their creative essence, and discovering why one leaf grew in this shape and another in that, and wherefore such and such flowers differed among themselves in hue and perfume. Nevertheless, in spite of this deep intelligence on his part, there was no approach to intimacy between himself and these vegetable existences. On the contrary, he avoided their actual touch or the direct inhaling of their odors with a caution that impressed Giovanni most disagreeably; for the man's demeanor was that of one walking among malignant influences, such as savage beasts, or deadly snakes or evil spirits, which, should he allow them one moment of license, would wreak upon him some terrible

fatality. It was strangely frightful to the young man's imagination to
see this air of insecurity in a person cultivating a garden, that most
simple and innocent of human toils, and which had been alike the joy
and labor of the unfallen parents of the race. Was this garden, then,
the Eden of the present world? And this man, with such a perception
of harm in what his own hands caused to grow—was he the Adam?

The distrustful gardener, while plucking away the dead leaves or
pruning the too luxuriant growth of the shrubs, defended his hands
with a pair of thick gloves. Nor were these his only armor. When, in his
walk through the garden, he came to the magnificent plant that hung
its purple gems beside the marble fountain, he placed a kind of mask
over his mouth and nostrils, as if all this beauty did but conceal a
deadlier malice; but, finding his task still too dangerous, he drew back,
removed the mask and called loudly, but in the infirm voice of a
person affected with inward disease:

"Beatrice! Beatrice!"

"Here am I, my father. What would you?" cried a rich and youthful
voice from the window of the opposite house—a voice as rich as a
tropical sunset, and which made Giovanni, though he knew not why,
think of deep hues of purple or crimson and of perfumes heavily
delectable. "Are you in the garden?"

"Yes, Beatrice," answered the gardener, "and I need your help."

Soon there emerged from under a sculptured portal the figure of a
young girl, arrayed with as much richness of taste as the most splendid
of the flowers, beautiful as the day, and with a bloom so deep and vivid
that one shade more would have been too much. She looked redun-
dant with life, health and energy; all of which attributes were bound
down and compressed, as it were, and girdled tensely, in their luxu-
riance, by her virgin zone. Yet Giovanni's fancy must have grown
morbid while he looked down into the garden; for the impression
which the fair stranger made upon him was as if here were another
flower, the human sister of those vegetable ones, as beautiful as they,
more beautiful than the richest of them, but still to be touched only
with a glove, nor to be approached without a mask. As Beatrice came
down the garden path, it was observable that she handled and inhaled
the odor of several of the plants which her father had most sedulously
avoided.

"Here, Beatrice," said the latter, "see how many needful offices
require to be done to our chief treasure. Yet, shattered as I am, my life

might pay the penalty of approaching it so closely as circumstances demand. Henceforth, I fear, this plant must be consigned to your sole charge."

"And gladly will I undertake it," cried again the rich tones of the young lady, as she bent toward the magnificent plant and opened her arms as if to embrace it. "Yes, my sister, my splendor, it shall be Beatrice's task to nurse and serve thee; and thou shalt reward her with thy kisses and perfumed breath, which to her is as the breath of life."

Then, with all the tenderness in her manner that was so strikingly expressed in her words, she busied herself with such attentions as the plant seemed to require; and Giovanni, at his lofty window, rubbed his eyes and almost doubted whether it were a girl tending her favorite flower, or one sister performing the duties of affection to another. The scene soon terminated. Whether Dr. Rappaccini had finished his labors in the garden, or that his watchful eye had caught the stranger's face, he now took his daughter's arm and retired. Night was already closing in; oppressive exhalations seemed to proceed from the plants and steal upward past the open window; and Giovanni, closing the lattice, went to his couch and dreamed of a rich flower and beautiful girl. Flower and maiden were different, and yet the same, and fraught with some strange peril in either shape.

But there is an influence in the light of morning that tends to rectify whatever errors of fancy, or even of judgment, we may have incurred during the sun's decline, or among the shadows of the night, or in the less wholesome glow of moonshine. Giovanni's first movement, on starting from sleep, was to throw open the window and gaze down into the garden which his dreams had made so fertile of mysteries. He was surprised and a little ashamed to find how real and matter-of-fact an affair it proved to be, in the first rays of the sun which gilded the dewdrops that hung upon leaf and blossom, and, while giving a brighter beauty to each rare flower, brought everything within the limits of ordinary experience. The young man rejoiced that, in the heart of the barren city, he had the privilege of overlooking this spot of lovely and luxuriant vegetation. It would serve, he said to himself, as a symbolic language to keep him in communion with Nature. Neither the sickly and thought-worn Dr. Giacomo Rappaccini, it is true, nor his brilliant daughter was now visible; so that Giovanni could not determine how much of the singularity which he attributed to both was due to their own qualities and how much to his wonder-working fancy; but he was inclined to take a most rational view of the whole matter.

In the course of the day, he paid his respects to Signor Pietro Baglioni, professor of medicine in the university, a physician of eminent repute, to whom Giovanni had brought a letter of introduction. The professor was an elderly personage, apparently of genial nature, and habits that might almost be called jovial. He kept the young man to dinner, and made himself very agreeable by the freedom and liveliness of his conversation, especially when warmed by a flask or two of Tuscan wine. Giovanni, conceiving that men of science, inhabitants of the same city, must needs be on familiar terms with one another, took an opportunity to mention the name of Dr. Rappaccini. But the professor did not respond with so much cordiality as he had anticipated.

"Ill would it become a teacher of the divine art of medicine," said Professor Pietro Baglioni, in answer to a question of Giovanni, "to withhold due and well-considered praise of a physician so eminently skilled as Rappaccini; but, on the other hand, I should answer it but scantily to my conscience were I to permit a worthy youth like yourself, Signor Giovanni, the son of an ancient friend, to imbibe erroneous ideas respecting a man who might hereafter chance to hold your life and death in his hands. The truth is, our worshipful Dr. Rappaccini has as much science as any member of the faculty—with perhaps one single exception—in Padua, or all Italy; but there are certain grave objections to his professional character."

And what are they?" asked the young man.

"Has my friend Giovanni any disease of body or heart that he is so inquisitive about physicians?" said the professor, with a smile. "But as for Rappaccini, it is said of him—and I, who know the man well, can answer for its truth—that he cares infinitely more for science than for mankind. His patients are interesting to him only as subjects for some new experiment. He would sacrifice human life, his own among the rest, or whatever else was dearest to him, for the sake of adding so much as a grain of mustard seed to the great heap of his accumulated knowledge."

"Methinks he is an awful man indeed," remarked Guasconti, mentally recalling the cold and purely intellectual aspect of Rappaccini. "And yet, worshipful professor, is it not a noble spirit? Are there many men capable of so spiritual a love of science?"

"God forbid," answered the professor, somewhat testily, "at least, unless they take sounder views of the healing art than those adopted by Rappaccini. It is his theory that all medicinal virtues are comprised within those substances which we term vegetable poisons. These he cultivates with his own hands, and is said even to have produced new varieties of poison, more horribly deleterious than Nature, without the assistance of this learned person, would ever have plagued the world withal. That the signor doctor does less mischief is undeniable. Now and then, it must be owned, he has effected, or seemed to effect, a marvelous cure; but, to tell you my private mind, Signor Giovanni, he should receive little credit for such instances of success—they being probably the work of chance—but should be held strictly accountable for his failures, which may justly be considered his own work."

The youth might have taken Baglioni's opinions with many grains of allowance had he known that there was a professional warfare of long continuance between him and Dr. Rappaccini, in which the latter was generally thought to have gained the advantage. If the reader be inclined to judge for himself, we refer him to certain black-letter tracts on both sides, preserved in the medical department of the University of Padua.

"I know not, most learned professor," returned Giovanni, after musing on what had been said of Rappaccini's exclusive zeal for science, "I know not how dearly this physician may love his art; but surely there is one object more dear to him. He has a daughter."

"Aha!" cried the professor, with a laugh. "So now our friend Giovanni's secret is out. You have heard of this daughter, whom all the young men in Padua are wild about, though not half a dozen have ever had the good hap to see her face. I know little of the Signora Beatrice save that Rappaccini is said to have instructed her deeply in his science, and that, young and beautiful as fame reports her, she is already qualified to fill a professor's chair. Perchance her father destines her for mine! Other absurd rumors there be, not worth talking about or listening to. So now, Signor Giovanni, drink off your glass of Lachryma."

Guasconti returned to his lodgings somewhat heated with the wine he had quaffed, and which caused his brain to swim with strange fantasies in reference to Dr. Rappaccini and the beautiful Beatrice. On his way, happening to pass by a florist's, he bought a fresh bouquet of flowers.

Ascending to his chamber, he seated himself near the window, but within the shadow thrown by the depth of the wall, so that he could look down into the garden with little risk of being discovered. All beneath his eye was a solitude. The strange plants were basking in the sunshine, and now and then nodding gently to one another, as if in acknowledgment of sympathy and kindred. In the midst, by the shattered fountain, grew the magnificent shrub, with its purple gems clustering all over it; they glowed in the air, and gleamed back again out of the depths of the pool, which thus seemed to overflow with colored radiance from the rich reflection that was steeped in it. At first, as we have said, the garden was a solitude. Soon, however—as Giovanni had half-hoped, half-feared would be the case—a figure appeared beneath the antique sculptured portal, and came down between the rows of plants, inhaling their various perfumes as if she were one of those beings of old classic fable that lived upon sweet odors. On again beholding Beatrice, the young man was even startled to perceive how much her beauty exceeded his recollection of it; so brilliant, so vivid, was its character, that she glowed amid the sunlight, and, as Giovanni whispered to himself, positively illuminated the more shadowy intervals of the garden path. Her face being now more revealed than on the former occasion, he was struck by its expression of simplicity and sweetness—qualities that had not entered into his idea of her character, and which made him ask anew what manner of mortal she might be. Nor did he fail again to observe, or imagine, an analogy between the beautiful girl and the gorgeous shrub that hung its gemlike flowers over the fountain—a resemblance which Beatrice seemed to have indulged a fantastic humor in heightening, both by the arrangement of her dress and the selection of its hues.

Approaching the shrub, she threw open her arms, as with a passionate ardor, and drew its branches into an intimate embrace—so intimate that her features were hidden in its leafy bosom and her glistening ringlets all intermingled with the flowers.

"Give me thy breath, my sister," exclaimed Beatrice, "for I am faint with common air. And give me this flower of thine, which I separate with gentlest fingers from the stem and place it close beside my heart."

With these words, the beautiful daughter of Rappaccini plucked one of the richest blossoms of the shrub, and was about to fasten it in her bosom. But now, unless Giovanni's draughts of wine had bewildered his senses, a singular incident occurred. A small orange-colored reptile, of the lizard or chameleon species, chanced to be creeping along the path, just at the feet of Beatrice. It appeared to Giovanni—but, at the distance from which he gazed, he could scarcely have seen anything so minute—it appeared to him, however, that a drop or two of moisture from the broken stem of the flower descended upon the lizard's head. For an instant the reptile contorted itself violently, and then lay motionless in the sunshine. Beatrice observed this remarkable phenomenon, and crossed herself, sadly, but without surprise; nor did she therefore hesitate to arrange the fatal flower in her bosom. There it blushed, and almost glimmered with the dazzling effect of a precious stone, adding to her dress and aspect the one appropriate charm which nothing else in the world could have supplied. But Giovanni, out of the shadow of his window, bent forward and shrank back, and murmured and trembled.

"Am I awake? Have I my senses?" said he to himself. "What is this being? Beautiful shall I call her, or inexpressibly terrible?"

Beatrice now strayed carelessly through the garden, approaching closer beneath Giovanni's window, so that he was compelled to thrust his head quite out of its concealment in order to gratify the intense and painful curiousity which she excited. At this moment, there came a beautiful insect over the garden wall; it had, perhaps, wandered through the city, and found no flowers or verdure among those antique haunts of men until the heavy perfumes of Dr. Rappaccini's shrubs had lured it from afar. Without alighting on the flowers, this winged brightness seemed to be attracted by Beatrice, and lingered in the air and fluttered about her head. Now, here it could not be but that Giovanni Guasconti's eyes deceived him. Be that as it might, he fancied that, while Beatrice was gazing at the insect with childish delight, it grew faint and fell at her feet; its bright wings shivered; it was dead—from no cause that he could discern, unless it were the atmosphere of her breath. Again Beatrice crossed herself and sighed heavily as she bent over the dead insect.

An impulsive movement of Giovanni drew her eyes to the window. There she beheld the beautiful head of the young man—rather a Grecian than an Italian head, with fair, regular features, and a glistening of gold among his ringlets—gazing down upon her like a being that hovered in mid-air. Scarcely knowing what he did, Giovanni threw down the bouquet which he had hitherto held in his hand.

"Signora," said he, "these are pure and healthful flowers. Wear them for the sake of Giovanni Guasconti."

"Thanks, signor," replied Beatrice, with her rich voice, that came forth as it were like a gush of music, and with a mirthful expression half-childish and half-woman like. "I accept your gift, and would fain recompense it with this precious purple flower; but if I toss it into the air, it will not reach you. So Signor Guasconti must even content himself with my thanks."

She lifted the bouquet from the ground, and then, as if inwardly ashamed at having stepped aside from her maidenly reserve to respond to a stranger's greeting, passed swiftly homeward through the garden. But few as the moments were, it seemed to Giovanni, when she was on the point of vanishing beneath the sculptured portal, that his beautiful bouquet was already beginning to wither in her grasp. It was an idle thought; there could be no possibility of distinguishing a faded flower from a fresh one at so great a distance.

For many days after this incident, the young man avoided the window that looked into Dr. Rappaccini's garden, as if something ugly and monstrous would have blasted his eyesight had he been betrayed into a glance. He felt conscious of having put himself, to a certain extent, within the influence of an unintelligible power by the communication which he had opened with Beatrice. The wisest course would have been, if his heart were in any real danger, to quit his lodgings and Padua itself at once; the next wiser, to have accustomed himself, as far as possible, to the familiar and daylight view of Beatrice—thus bringing her rigidly and systematically within the limits of ordinary experience. Least of all, while avoiding her sight, ought Giovanni to have remained so near this extraordinary being that the proximity and possibility even of intercourse should give a kind of substance and reality to the wild vagaries which his imagination ran riot continually in producing. Guasconti had not a deep heart—or, at all events, its depths were not sounded now; but he had a quick fancy, and an ardent southern temperament, which rose every instant to a higher fever pitch. Whether or no Beatrice possessed those terrible attributes, that fatal breath, the affinity with those so beautiful and deadly flowers which were indicated by what Giovanni had witnessed, she had at least instilled a fierce and subtle poison into his system. It was not love, although her rich beauty was a madness to him; nor horror, even while he fancied her spirit to be imbued with the same baneful essence that seemed to pervade her physical frame; but a wild offspring of both love and horror that had each parent in it, and burned like one and shivered like the other. Giovanni knew not what to dread; still less did he know what to hope; yet hope and dread kept a continual warfare in his breast, alternately vanquishing one another and starting up afresh to renew the contest. Blessed are all simple emotions, be they dark or bright! It is the lurid intermixture of the two that produces the illuminating blaze of the infernal regions.

Sometimes he endeavored to assuage the fever of his spirit by a rapid walk through the streets of Padua or beyond its gates: his footsteps kept time with the throbbings of his brain, so that the walk was apt to accelerate itself to a race. One day he found himself arrested; his arm seized by a portly personage, who had turned back on recognizing the young man and expended much breath in overtaking him.

"Signor Giovanni! Stay, my young friend!" cried he. "Have you forgotten me? That might well be the case if I were as much altered as yourself."

It was Baglioni, whom Giovanni had avoided ever since their first meeting, from a doubt that the professor's sagacity would look too deeply into his secrets. Endeavoring to recover himself, he stared forth wildly from his inner world into the outer one and spoke like a man in a dream.

"Yes; I am Giovanni Guasconti. You are Professor Pietro Baglioni. Now let me pass!"

"Not yet, not yet, Signor Giovanni Guasconti," said the professor, smiling, but at the same time scrutinizing the youth with an earnest glance. "What! Did I grow up side by side with your father, and shall his son pass me like a stranger in these old streets of Padua? Stand still, Signor Giovanni; for we must have a word or two before we apart."

"Speedily, then, most worshipful professor, speedily," said Giovanni, with feverish impatience. "Does not your worship see that I am in haste?"

Now, while he was speaking, there came a man in black along the street, stooping and moving feebly like a person in inferior health. His face was all overspread with a most sickly and sallow hue, but yet so pervaded with an expression of piercing and active intellect that an observer might easily have overlooked the merely physical attributes and have seen only this wonderful energy. As he passed, this person exchanged a cold and distant salutation with Baglioni, but fixed his eyes upon Giovanni with an intentness that seemed to bring out whatever was within him worthy of notice. Nevertheless, there was a peculiar quietness in the look, as if taking merely a speculative, not a human, interest in the young man.

"It is Dr. Rappaccini!" whispered the professor when the stranger had passed. "Has he ever seen your face before?"

"Not that I know," answered Giovanni, starting at the name.

"He *has* seen you! He must have seen you!" said Baglioni, hastily. "For some purpose or other, this man of science is making a study of you. I know that look of his! It is the same that coldly illuminates his face as he bends over a bird, a mouse or a butterfly, which, in pursuance of some experiment, he has killed by the perfume of a flower; a look as deep as Nature itself, but without Nature's warmth of love. Signor Giovanni, I will stake my life upon it, you are the subject of one of Rappaccini's experiments!"

"Will you make a fool of me?" cried Giovanni, passionately. "*That*, signor professor, were an untoward experiment."

"Patience! Patience!" replied the imperturbable professor. "I tell thee, my poor Giovanni, that Rappaccini has a scientific interest in thee. Thou has fallen into fearful hands! And the Signora Beatrice—what part does she act in this mystery?"

But Guasconti, finding Baglioni's pertinacity intolerable, here broke away, and was gone before the professor could seize his arm. He looked after the young man intently and shook his head.

"This must not be," said Baglioni to himself. "The youth is the son of my old friend, and shall not come to any harm from which the arcana of medical science can preserve him. Besides, it is too insufferable an impertinence in Rappaccini, thus to snatch the lad out of my own hands, as I may say, and make use of him for his infernal experiments. This daughter of his! It shall be looked to. Perchance, most learned Rappaccini, I may foil you where you little dream of it!"

Meanwhile Giovanni had pursued a circuitous route, and at length found himself at the door of his lodgings. As he crossed the threshold, he was met by old Lisabetta, who smirked and smiled, and was evidently desirous to attract his attention; vainly, however, as the ebullition of his feelings had momentarily subsided into a cold and dull vacuity. He turned his eyes full upon the withered face that was puckering itself into a smile, but seemed to behold it not. The old dame, therefore, laid her grasp upon his cloak.

"Signor! Signor!" whispered she, still with a smile over the whole breadth of her visage, so that it looked not unlike a grotesque carving in wood, darkened by centuries. "Listen, signor! There is a private entrance into the garden!"

"What do you say?" exclaimed Giovanni, turning quickly about, as if an inanimate thing should start into feverish life. "A private entrance into Dr. Rappaccinni's garden?"

"Hush! Hush! Not so loud!" whispered Lisabetta, putting her hand over his mouth. "Yes; into the worshipful doctor's garden, where you may see all his fine shrubbery. Many a young man in Padua would give gold to be admitted among those flowers."

Giovanni put a piece of gold into her hand.

"Show me the way," said he.

A surmise, probably excited by his conversation with Baglioni, crossed his mind that his interposition of old Lisabetta might perchance be connected with the intrigue, whatever were its nature, in which the professor seemed to suppose that Dr. Rappaccini was involving him. But such a suspicion, though it disturbed Giovanni, was inadequate to restrain him. The instant that he was aware of the possibility of approaching Beatrice, it seemed an absolute necessity of his existence to do so. It mattered not whether she were angel or demon; he was irrevocably within her sphere, and must obey the law that whirled him onward, in ever-lessening circles, toward a result which he did not attempt to foreshadow; and yet, strange to say, there came across him a sudden doubt whether this intense interest on his part were not delusory; whether it were really of so deep and positive a nature as to justify him in now thrusting himself into an incalculable position; whether it were not merely the fantasy of a young man's brain, only slightly or not at all connected with his heart.

He paused, hesitated, turned half-about, but again went on. His withered guide led him along several obscure passages, and finally undid a door, through which, as it was opened, there came the sight and sound of rustling leaves, with the broken sunshine glimmering among them. Giovanni stepped forth, and, forcing himself through the entanglement of a shrub that wreathed its tendrils over the hidden entrance, stood beneath his own window in the open area of Dr. Rappaccini's garden.

How often is it the case that, when impossibilities have come to pass and dreams have condensed their misty substance into tangible realities, we find ourselves calm, and even coldy self-possessed, amid circumstances which it would have been a delirium of joy or agony to anticipate! Fate delights to thwart us thus. Passion will choose his own time to rush upon the scene, and lingers sluggishly behind when an appropriate adjustment of events would seem to summon his appearance. So was it now with Giovanni. Day after day, his pulses had throbbed with feverish blood at the improbable idea of an interview with Beatrice, and of standing with her, face to face, in this very garden, basking in the Oriental sunshine of her beauty, and snatching from her full gaze the mystery which he deemed the riddle of his own existence. But now there was a singular and untimely equanimity within his breast. He threw a glance around the garden to discover if Beatrice or her father were present, and, perceiving that he was alone, began a critical observation of the plants.

The aspect of one and all of them dissatisfied him; their gorgeousness seemed fierce, passionate and even unnatural. There was hardly an individual shrub which a wanderer, straying by himself through a forest, would not have been startled to find growing wild, as if an unearthly face had glared at him out of the thicket. Several also would have shocked a delicate instinct by an appearance of artificialness indicating that there had been such commixture and, as it were, adultery of various vegetable species that the production was no longer of God's making, but the monstrous offspring of man's depraved fancy, glowing with only an evil mockery of beauty. They were probably the result of experiment, which in one or two cases had succeeded in mingling plants individually lovely into a compound possessing the questionable and ominous character that distinguished the whole growth of the garden. In fine, Giovanni recognized but two or three plants in the collection, and those of a kind that he well knew to be poisonous. While busy with these contemplations, he heard the rustling of a silken garment, and, turning, beheld Beatrice emerging from beneath the sculptured portal.

Giovanni had not considered with himself what should be his deportment; whether he should apologize for his intrusion into the garden, or assume that he was there with the privity, at least, if not by the desire, of Dr. Rappaccini or his daughter; but Beatrice's manner placed him at his ease, though leaving him still in doubt by what agency he had gained admittance. She came lightly along the path and met him near the broken fountain. There was surprise in her face, but brightened by a simple and kind expression of pleasure.

"You are a connoisseur in flowers, signor," said Beatrice, with a smile, alluding to the bouquet which he had flung her from the window. "It is no marvel, therefore, if the sight of my father's rare collection has tempted you to take a nearer view. If he were here, he could tell you many strange and interesting facts as to the nature and habits of these shrubs; for he has spent a lifetime in such studies, and this garden is his world!"

"And yourself, lady," observed Giovanni, "if fame says true, you likewise are deeply skilled in the virtues indicated by these rich blossoms and these spicy perfumes. Would you deign to be my instructress, I should prove an apter scholar than if taught by Signor Rappaccini himself."

"Are there such idle rumors?" asked Beatrice, with the music of a pleasant laugh. "Do people say that I am skilled in my father's science of plants? What a jest is there! No; though I have grown up among these flowers, I know no more of them than their hues and perfume; and sometimes methinks I would fain rid myself of even that small knowledge. There are many flowers here, and those not the least brilliant, that shock and offend me when they meet my eye. But pray, signor, do not believe these stories about my science. Believe nothing of me save what you see with your own eyes."

"And must I believe all that I have seen with my own eyes?" asked Giovanni, pointedly, while the recollection of former scenes made him shrink. "No, signora; you demand too little of me. Bid me believe nothing save what comes from your own lips."

It would appear that Beatrice understood him. There came a deep flush to her cheek; but she looked full into Giovanni's eyes, and responded to his gaze of uneasy suspicion with a queenlike haughtiness.

"I do so bid you, signor," she replied. "Forget whatever you may have fancied in regard to me. If true to the outward senses, still it may be false in its essence; but the words of Beatrice Rappaccini's lips are true from the depths of the heart outward. Those you may believe."

A fervor glowed in her whole aspect and beamed upon Giovanni's consciousness like the light of truth itself; but while she spoke, there was a fragrance in the atmosphere around her, rich and delightful, though evanescent, yet which the young man, from an undefinable reluctance scarcely dared to draw into his lungs. It might be the odor of the flowers. Could it be Beatrice's breath which thus embalmed her words with a strange richness, as if by steeping them in her heart? A faintness passed like a shadow over Giovanni and flitted away; he seemed to gaze through the beautiful girl's eyes into her transparent soul, and felt no more doubt or fear.

The tinge of passion that had colored Beatrice's manner vanished; she became gay, and appeared to derive a pure delight from her communion with the youth not unlike what the maiden of a lonely island might have felt conversing with a voyager from the civilized world. Evidently her experience of life had been confined within the limits of that garden. She talked now about matters as simple as the daylight or summer clouds, and now asked questions in reference to the city, or Giovanni's distant home, his friends, his mother, and his sisters—questions indicating such seclusion, and such lack of familiarity with modes and forms, that Giovanni responded as if to an infant. Her spirit gushed out before him like a fresh rill that was just catching its first glimpse of the sunlight and wondering at the reflections of earth and sky which were flung into its bosom. There came thoughts, too, from a deep source, and fantasies of a gemlike brilliancy, as if diamonds and rubies sparkled upward among the bubbles of the fountain. Ever and anon there gleamed across the young man's mind a sense of wonder that he should be walking side by side with the being who had so wrought upon his imagination, whom he had idealized in such hues of terror, in whom he had positively witnessed such manifestations of dreadful attributes—that he should be conversing with Beatrice like a brother, and should find her so human and so maidenlike. But such reflections were only momentary; the effect of her character was too real not to make itself familiar at once.

In this free intercourse, they had strayed through the garden, and now, after many turns among its avenues, were come to the shattered fountain, beside which grew the magnificent shrub, with its treasury of glowing blossoms. A fragrance was diffused from it which Giovanni recognized as identical with that which he had attributed to Beatrice's breath, but incomparably more powerful. As her eyes fell upon it, Giovanni beheld her press her hand to her bosom as if her heart were throbbing suddenly and painfully.

"For the first time in my life," murmured she, addressing the shrub, "I had forgotten thee."

"I remember, signora," said Giovanni, "that you once promised to reward me with one of these living gems for the bouquet which I had the happy boldness to fling to your feet. Permit me now to pluck it as a memorial of this interview."

He made a step toward the shrub with extended hand; but Beatrice darted forward, uttering a shriek that went through his heart like a dagger. She caught his hand and drew it back with the whole force of her slender figure. Giovanni felt her touch thrilling through his fibers.

"Touch it not!" exclaimed she, in a voice of agony. "Not for thy life! It is fatal!"

Then, hiding her face, she fled from him and vanished beneath the sculptured portal. As Giovanni followed her with his eyes, he beheld the emaciated figure and pale intelligence of Dr. Rappaccini, who had been watching the scene, he knew not how long, within the shadow of the entrance.

No sooner was Guasconti alone in his chamber than the image of Beatrice came back to his passionate musings, invested with all the witchery that had been gathering around it ever since his first glimpse of her, and now likewise imbued with a tender warmth of girlish womanhood. She was human; her nature endowed with all gentle and feminine qualities; she was worthiest to be worshipped; she was capable, surely, on her part, of the height and heroism of love. Those tokens which he had hitherto considered as proofs of a frightful peculiarity in her physical and moral system were now either forgotten, or, by the subtle sophistry of passion transmitted into a golden crown of enchantment, rendering Beatrice the more admirable by so much as she was the more unique. Whatever had looked ugly was now beautiful; or, if incapable of such a change, it stole away and hid itself among those shapeless half-ideas which throng the dim region beyond the daylight on our perfect consciousness. Thus did he spend the night, nor fell asleep until the dawn had begun to awaken the slumbering flowers in Dr. Rappaccini's garden, whither Giovanni's dreams doubtless led him. Up rose the sun in his due season, and, flingling his beams upon the young man's eyelids, awoke him to a sense of pain. When thoroughly aroused, he became sensible of a burning and tingling agony in his hand—in his right hand—the very hand which Beatrice had grasped in her own when he was on the point of plucking one of the gemlike flowers. On the back of that hand there was now a purple print like that of four small fingers, and the likeness of a slender thumb upon his wrist.

Oh, how stubbornly does love—or even that cunning semblance of love which flourishes in the imagination, but strikes no depth of root into the heart—how stubbornly does it hold its faith until the moment comes when it is doomed to vanish into thin mist! Giovanni wrapped a handkerchief about his hand and wondered what evil thing had stung him, and soon forgot his pain in a reverie of Beatrice.

After the first interview, a second was in the inevitable course of what we call fate. A third; a fourth; and a meeting with Beatrice in the garden was no longer an incident in Giovanni's daily life, but the whole space in which he might be said to live; for the anticipation and memory of that ecstatic hour made up the remainder. Nor was it otherwise with the daughter of Rappaccini. She watched for the youth's appearance, and flew to his side with confidence as unreserved as if they had been playmates from early infancy—as if they were such playmates still. If, by any unwonted chance, he failed to come at the appointed moment, she stood beneath the window and sent up the rich sweetness of her tones to float around him in his chamber and echo and reverberate throughout his heart: "Giovanni! Giovanni! Why tarriest thou? Come down!" And down he hastened into that Eden of poisonous flowers.

But, with all this intimate familiarity, there was still a reserve in Beatrice's demeanor, so rigidly and invariably sustained that the idea of infringing it scarcely occurred to his imagination. By all appreciable signs, they loved; they had looked love with eyes that conveyed the holy secret from the depths of one soul into the depths of the other, as if it were too sacred to be whispered by the way; they had even spoken love in those gushes of passion when their spirits darted forth in articulated breathlike tongues of long-hidden flame; and yet there had been no seal of lips, no clasp of hands, nor any slightest caress such as love claims and hallows. He had never touched one of the gleaming ringlets of her hair; her garment—so marked was the physical barrier between them—had never been waved against him by a breeze. On the few occasions when Giovanni had seemed tempted to overstep the limit, Beatrice grew so sad, so stern, and withal wore such a look of desolate separation, shuddering at itself, that not a spoken word was requisite to repel him. At such times, he was startled at the horrible suspicions that rose, monsterlike, out of the caverns of his heart and stared him in the face; his love grew thin and faint as the morning mist; his doubts alone had substance. But, when Beatrice's face brightened again after the momentary shadow, she was transformed at once from the mysterious, questionable being whom he had watched with so much awe and horror; she was now the beautiful and unsophisticated girl whom he felt that his spirit knew with a certainty beyond all other knowledge.

A considerable time had now passed since Giovanni's last meeting with Baglioni. One morning, however, he was disagreeably surprised by a visit from the professor, whom he had scarcely thought of for whole weeks, and would willingly have forgotten still longer. Given up as he had long been to pervading excitement, he could tolerate no companions except upon condition of their perfect sympathy with his present state of feeling. Such sympathy was not to be expected from Professor Baglioni.

The visitor chatted carelessly for a few moments about the gossip of the city and the university, and then took up another topic.

"I have been reading an old classic author lately," said he, "and met with a story that strangely interested me. Possibly you may remember it. It is of an Indian prince, who sent a beautiful woman as a present to Alexander the Great. She was as lovely as the dawn and gorgeous as the sunset; but what especially distinguished her was a certain rich perfume in her breath—richer than a garden of Persian roses. Alexander, as was natural to a youthful conqueror, fell in love at first sight with this magnificent stranger; but a certain sage physician, happening to be present, discovered a terrible secret in regard to her."

"And what was that?" asked Giovanni, turning his eyes downward to avoid those of the professor.

"That this lovely woman," continued Baglioni, with emphasis, "had been nourished with poisons from her birth upward, until her whole nature was so imbued with them that she herself had become the deadliest poison in existence. Poison was her element of life. With that rich perfume of her breath she blasted the very air. Her love would have been poison—her embrace death. Is not this a marvelous tale?"

"A childish fable," answered Giovanni, nervously starting from his chair. "I marvel how your worship finds time to read such nonsense among your graver studies."

"By the by," said the professor, looking uneasily about him, "what singular fragrance is this in your apartment? Is it the perfume of your gloves? It is faint, but delicious; and yet, after all, by no means agreeable. Were I to breathe it long, methinks it would make me ill. It is like the breath of a flower; but I see no flowers in the chamber."

"Nor are there any," replied Giovanni, who had turned pale as the professor spoke, "nor, I think, is there any fragrance except in your worship's imagination. Odors being a sort of element combined of the sensual and the spiritual, are apt to deceive us in this manner. The recollection of a perfume, the bare idea of it, may easily be mistaken for a present reality."

"Ay, but my sober imagination does not often play such tricks," said

Baglioni, "and, were I to fancy any kind of odor, it would be that of some vile apothecary drug wherewith my fingers are likely enough to be imbued. Our worshipful friend Rappaccini, as I have heard, tinctures his medicaments with odors richer than those of Araby. Doubtless, likewise, the fair and learned Signora Beatrice would minister to her patients with draughts as sweet as a maiden's breath; but woe to him that sips them!"

Giovanni's face evinced many contending emotions. The tone in which the professor alluded to the pure and lovely daughter of Rappaccini was a torture to his soul; and yet the intimation of a view of her character opposite to his own gave instantaneous distinctness to a thousand dim suspicions, which now grinned at him like so many demons. But he strove hard to quell them and to respond to Baglioni with a true lover's perfect faith.

"Signor professor," said he, "you were my father's friend; perchance, too, it is your purpose to act a friendly part towards his son. I would fain feel nothing towards you save respect and deference; but I pray you to observe, signor, that there is one subject on which we must not speak. You know not the Signora Beatrice. You cannot, therefore, estimate the wrong—the blasphemy, I may even say—that is offered to her character by a light or injurious word."

"Giovanni! My poor Giovanni," answered the professor, with a calm expression of pity, "I know this wretched girl far better than yourself. You shall hear the truth in respect to the poisoner Rappaccini and his poisonous daughter; yes, poisonous as she is beautiful. Listen; for, even should you do violence to my gray hairs, it shall not silence me. That old fable of the Indian woman has become a truth by the deep and deadly science of Rappaccini and in the person of the lovely Beatrice."

Giovanni groaned and hid his face.

"Her father," continued Baglioni, "was not restrained by natural affection from offering up his child in this horrible manner as the victim of his insane zeal for science; for, let us do him justice, he is as true a man of science as ever distilled his own heart in an alembic. What, then, will be your fate? Beyond a doubt you are selected as the material of some new experiment. Perhaps the result is to be death; perhaps a fate more awful still. Rappaccini, with what he calls the interest of science before his eyes, will hesitate at nothing."

"It is a dream," muttered Giovanni to himself. "Surely it is a dream."

"But," resumed the professor, "be of good cheer, son of my friend. It is not yet too late for rescue. Possibly we may even succeed in bringing back this miserable child within the limits of ordinary nature, from which her father's madness has estranged her. Behold this little silver vase! It was wrought by the hands of the renowned Benvenuto Cellini, and is well worthy to be a love gift to the fairest dame in Italy. But its contents are invaluable. One little sip of this antidote would have rendered the most virulent poisons of the Borgias innocuous. Doubt not that it will be as efficacious against those of Rappaccini. Bestow the vase, and the precious liquid within it, on your Beatrice, and hopefully await the result."

Baglioni laid a small, exquisitely wrought silver vial on the table and withdrew, leaving what he had said to produce its effect upon the young man's mind.

"We will thwart Rappaccini yet," thought he, chuckling to himself, as he descended the stairs. "But, let us confess the truth of him, he is a wonderful man—a wonderful man indeed; a vile empiric, however, in his practice, and therefore not to be tolerated by those who respect the good old rules of the medical profession."

Throughout Giovanni's whole acquaintance with Beatrice, he had occasionally, as we have said, been haunted by dark surmises as to her character; yet so thoroughly had she made herself felt by him as a simple, natural, most affectionate and guileless creature, that the image now held up by Professor Baglioni looked as strange and incredible as if it were not in accordance with his own original conception. True, there were ugly recollections connected with his first glimpses of the beautiful girl; he could not quite forget the bouquet that withered in her grasp, and the insect that perished amid the sunny air, by no ostensible agency save the fragrance of her breath. These incidents, however, dissolving in the pure light of her character, had no longer the efficacy of facts, but were acknowledged as mistaken fantasies, by whatever testimony of the senses they might appear to be substantiated. There is something truer and more real than what we can see with the eyes and touch with the finger. On such better evidence had Giovanni founded his confidence in Beatrice, though rather by the necessary force of her high attributes than by any deep and generous faith on his part. But now his spirit was incapable of sustaining itself at the height to which the early enthusiasm of passion had exalted it; he fell down, groveling among earthly doubts, and defiled therewith the pure whiteness of Beatrice's image. Not that he gave her up; he did but distrust. He resolved to institute some decisive test that should satisfy him, once for all, whether there were those dreadful peculiarities in her physical nature which could not be supposed to exist without some corrersponding monstrosity of soul. His eyes, gazing down afar, might have deceived him as to the lizard, the insect and the flowers; but if he could witness, at the distance of a few paces, the sudden blight of one fresh and healthful flower in Beatrice's hand, there would be room for no further question. With this idea, he hastened to the florist's and purchased a bouquet that was still gemmed with the morning dewdrops.

It was now the customary hour of his daily interview with Beatrice. Before descending into the garden, Giovanni failed not to look at his figure in the mirror—a vanity to be expected in a beautiful young man, yet, as displaying itself at that troubled and feverish moment, the token of a certain shallowness of feeling and insincerity of character. He did gaze, however, and said to himself that his features had never before possessed so rich a grace, nor his eyes such vivacity, nor his cheeks so warm a hue of superabundant life.

"At least," thought he, "her poison has not yet insinuated itself into my system. I am no flower to perish in her grasp."

With that thought, he turned his eyes on the bouquet, which he had never once laid aside from his hand. A thrill of indefinable horror shot through his frame on perceiving that those dewy flowers were already beginning to droop; they wore the aspect of things that had been fresh and lovely yesterday. Giovanni grew white as marble, and stood motionless before the mirror, staring at his own reflection there as at the likeness of something frightful. He remembered Baglioni's remark about the fragrance that seemed to pervade the chamber. It must have been the poison in his breath! Then he shuddered—shuddered at himself. Recovering from his stupor, he began to watch with curious eye a spider that was busily at work hanging its web from the antique cornice of the apartment, crossing and recrossing the artful system of interwoven lines—as vigorous and active a spider as ever dangled from an old ceiling. Giovanni bent towards the insect, and emitted a deep, long breath. The spider suddenly ceased its toil; the web vibrated with a tremor originating in the body of the small artisan. Again Giovanni sent forth a breath, deeper, longer and imbued with a venomous feeling out of his heart; he knew not whether he were wicked, or only desperate. The spider made a convulsive grip with his limbs and hung dead across the window.

"Accursed! Accursed!" muttered Giovanni, addressing himself. "Hast thou grown so poisonous that this deadly insect perishes by thy breath?"

At that moment, a rich, sweet voice came floating up from the garden.

"Giovanni! Giovanni! It is past the hour! Why tarriest thou? Come down!"

"Yes," muttered Giovanni again. "She is the only being whom my breath may not slay! Would that it might!"

He rushed down, and in an instant was standing before the bright and loving eyes of Beatrice. A moment ago, his wrath and despair had been so fierce that he could have desired nothing so much as to wither her by a glance; but with her actual presence there came influences which had too real an existence to be at once shaken off: recollections of the delicate and benign power of her feminine nature, which had so often enveloped him in a religious calm; recollections of many a holy and passionate outgush of her heart, when the pure fountain had been unsealed from its depths and made visible in its transparency to his mental eye; recollections which, had Giovanni known how to estimate them, would have assured him that all this ugly mystery was but an earthly illusion, and that, whatever mist of evil might seem to have gathered over her, the real Beatrice was a heavenly angel. Incapable as he was of such high faith, still her presence had not utterly lost its magic. Giovanni's rage was quelled into an aspect of sullen insensibility. Beatrice, with a quick spiritual sense, immediately felt that there was a gulf of blackness between them which neither he nor she could pass. They walked on together, sad and silent, and came thus to the marble fountain and to its pool of water on the ground, in the midst of which grew the shrub that bore gemlike blossoms. Giovanni was affrightened at the eager enjoyment—the appetite, as it were—with which he found himself inhaling the fragrance of the flowers.

"Beatrice," asked he, abruptly, "whence came this shrub?"

"My father created it," answered she, with simplicity.

"Created it! Created it!" repeated Giovanni. "What mean you, Beatrice?"

"He is a man fearfully acquainted with the secrets of Nature," replied Beatrice, "and, at the hour when I first drew breath, this plant sprang from the soil, the offspring of his science, of his intellect, while I was but his earthly child. Approach it not!" continued she, observing with terror that Giovanni was drawing nearer to the shrub. "It has qualities that you little dream of. But I, dearest Giovanni, I grew up and blossomed with the plant and was nourished with its breath. It was my sister, and I loved it with a human affection; for, alas!—hast thou not suspected it?—there was an awful doom."

Here Giovanni frowned so darkly upon her that Beatrice paused and trembled. But her faith in his tenderness reassured her and made her blush that she had doubted for an instant.

"There was an awful doom," she continued, "the effect of my father's fatal love of science, which estranged me from all society of my kind. Until heaven sent thee, dearest Giovanni, oh, how lonely was thy poor Beatrice!"

"Was it a hard doom?" asked Giovanni, fixing his eyes upon her.

"Only of late have I known how hard it was," answered she, tenderly. "Oh, yes; but my heart was torpid, and therefore quiet."

Giovanni's rage broke forth from his sullen gloom like a lightening flash out of a dark cloud.

"Accursed one!" cried he, with venomous scorn and anger. "And, finding thy solitude wearisome, thou hast severed me likewise from all the warmth of life and enticed me into thy region of unspeakable horror!"

"Giovanni!" exclaimed Beatrice, turning her large, bright eyes upon his face. The force of his words had not found its way into her mind; she was merely thunderstruck.

"Yes, poisonous thing!" repeated Giovanni, beside himself with passion. "Thou hast done it! Thou hast blasted me! Thou hast filled my veins with poison! Thou has made me as hateful, as ugly, as loathsome and deadly a creature as thyself—a world's wonder of hideous monstrosity! Now, if our breath be happily as fatal to ourselves as to all others, let us join our lips in one kiss of unutterable hatred, and so die!"

"What has befallen me?" murmured Beatrice, with a low moan out of her heart. "Holy Virgin, pity me, a poor heartbroken child!"

"Thou—dost thou pray?" cried Giovanni, still with the same fiendish scorn. "Thy very prayers, as they come from thy lips, tain the atmosphere with death. Yes, yes; let us pray! Let us to church and dip our fingers in the holy water at the portal! They that come after us will perish as by a pestilence! Let us sign crosses in the air! It will be scattering curses abroad in the likeness of holy symbols!"

"Giovanni," said Beatrice, calmly, for her grief was beyond passion, "why dost thou join thyself with me thus in those terrible words? I, it is true, am the horrible thing thou namest me. But thou—what has thou to do, save with one other shudder at my hideous misery to go forth out of the garden and mingle with thy race, and forget that there ever crawled on earth such a monster as poor Beatrice?"

"Dost thou pretend ignorance?" asked Giovanni, scowling upon her. "Behold! This power have I gained from the pure daughter of Rappaccini."

There was a swarm of summer insects flitting through the air in search of the food promised by the flower odors of the fatal garden. They circled round Giovanni's head, and were evidently attracted towards him by the same influence which had drawn them for an instant within the sphere of several of the shrubs. He sent forth a breath among them, and smiled bitterly at Beatrice as at least a score of insects fell dead upon the ground.

"I see it! I see it!" shrieked Beatrice. "It is my father's fatal science! No, no, Giovanni; it was not I! Never! Never! I dreamed only to love thee and be with thee a little time, and so let thee pass away, leaving but thine image in mine heart; for, Giovanni, believe it, though my body be nourished with poison, my spirit is God's creature, and craves love as its daily food. But my father—he has united us in this fearful sympathy. Yes; spurn me, tread upon me, kill me! Oh, what is death after such words as thine? But it was not I. Not for a world of bliss would I have done it."

Giovanni's passion had exhausted itself in its outburst from his lips. There now came across him a sense, mournful, and not without tenderness, of the intimate and peculiar relationship between Beatrice and himself. They stood, as it were, in an utter solitude, which would be made none the less solitary by the densest throng of human life. Ought not, then, the desert of humanity around them to press this insulated pair closer together? If they should be cruel to one another, who was there to be kind to them? Besides, thought Giovanni, might there not still be a hope of his returning within the limits of ordinary nature, and leading Beatrice, the redeemed Beatrice, by the hand? Oh, weak, and selfish, and unworthy spirit, that could dream of an earthly union and earthly happiness as possible, after such deep love had been so bitterly wronged as was Beatrice's love by Giovanni's blighting words! No, no; there could be no such hope. She must pass heavily, with that broken heart, across the borders of time—she must bathe her hurts in some fount of paradise, and forget her grief in the light of immortality, and *there* be well.

But Giovanni did not know it.

"Dear Beatrice," said he, approaching her, while she shrank away as always at his approach, but now with a different impulse, "dearest Beatrice, our fate is not yet so desperate. Behold! there is a medicine, potent, as a wise physician has assured me, and almost divine in its efficacy. It is composed of ingredients the most opposite to those by which thy awful father has brought this calamity upon thee and me. It is distilled of blessed herbs. Shall we not quaff together, and thus be purified from evil?"

"Give it me!" said Beatrice, extending her hand to receive the little silver vial which Giovanni took from his bosom. She added, with a peculiar emphasis, "I will drink; but do thou await the result."

She put Bagilioni's antidote to her lips; and, at the same moment, the figure of Rappaccini emerged from the portal and came slowly towards the marble fountain. As he drew near, the pale man of science seemed to gaze with a triumphant expression at the beautiful youth and maiden, as might an artist who should spend his life in achieving a picture or a group of statuary and finally be satisfied with his success. He paused; his bent form grew erect with conscious power; he spread his hands over them in the attitude of a father imploring a blessing upon his children; but those were the same hands that had thrown poison into the stream of their lives. Giovanni trembled. Beatrice shuddered nervously, and pressed her hand upon her heart.

"My daughter," said Rappaccini, "thou art no longer lonely in the world. Pluck one of those precious gems from thy sister shrub and bid thy bridegroom wear it in his bosom. It will not harm him now. My science and the sympathy between thee and him have so wrought within his system that he now stands apart from common men, as thou dost, daughter of my pride and triumph, from ordinary women. Pass on, then, through the world, most dear to one another and dreadful to all besides!"

"My father," said Beatrice feebly, and still as she spoke she kept her hand upon her heart, "wherefore didst thou inflict this miserable doom upon thy child?"

"Miserable!" exclaimed Rappaccini. "What mean you, foolish girl? Dost thou deem it misery to be endowed with marvelous gifts against which no power nor strength could avail an enemy—misery, to be able to quell the mightiest with a breath—misery, to be as terrible as thou art beautiful? Wouldst thou, then, have preferred the condition of a weak woman, exposed to all evil and capable of none?"

"I would fain have been loved, not feared," murmured Beatrice, sinking down upon the ground. "But now it matters not. I am going, father, where the evil which thou hast striven to mingle with my being will pass away like a dream—like the fragrance of these poisonous flowers, which will no longer taint my breath among the flowers of Eden. Farewell, Giovanni! Thy words of hatred are like lead within my heart; but they, too, will fall away as I ascend. Oh, was there not, from the first, more poison in thy nature than in mine?"

To Beatrice—so radically had her earthly part been wrought upon by Rappaccini's skill—as poison had been life, so the powerful antidote was death; and thus the poor victim of man's ingenuity and of thwarted nature, and of the fatality that attends all such efforts of perverted wisdom, perished there, at the feet of her father and Giovanni. Just at that moment, Professor Pietro Baglioni looked forth from the window, and called loudly, in a tone of triumph mixed with horror, to the thunderstricken man of science:

"Rappaccini! Rappaccini! And is *this* the upshot of your experiment!"

Squire Toby's Will

J. SHERIDAN LE FANU

*No one wrote the nineteenth century ghost story better than J.
Sheridan Le Fanu, the renowned Irish novelist, short story writer and
poet. His work strongly influenced such subsequent masters of the
supernatural tale as M. R. James, Algernon Blackwood and H. Russell
Wakefield. This story of spectral vengeance is of of his finest—and
that makes it very good indeed.*

Many persons accustomed to travel the old York and London road,
in the days of stagecoaches, will remember passing, in the afternoon,
say, of an autumn day, in their journey to the capital, about three
miles south of the town of Applebury and a mile and a half before you
reach the old Angel Inn, a large black-and-white house, as those
old-fashioned cage-work habitations are termed, dilapidated and
weather-stained, with broad lattice windows glimmering all over in the
evening sun with little diamond panes, and thrown into relief by a
dense background of ancient elms. A wide avenue, now overgrown like
a churchyard with grass and weeds, and flanked by double rows of the
same dark trees, old and gigantic, with here and there a gap in their
solemn files, and sometimes a fallen tree lying across on the avenue,
leads up to the hall door.

Looking up its somber and lifeless avenue from the top of the
London coach, as I have often done, you are struck with so many signs
of desertion and decay—the tufted grass sprouting in the chinks of the
steps and window stones, the smokeless chimneys over which the
jackdaws are wheeling, the absence of human life and all its evidence,
that you conclude at once that the place is uninhabited and abandoned to decay. The name of this ancient house is Gylingden Hall.
Tall hedges and old timber quickly shroud the old place from view,
and about a quarter of a mile further on you pass, embowered in
melancholy trees, a small and ruinous Saxon chapel, which, time out
of mind, has been the burying place of the family of Marston, and
partakes of the neglect and desolation which brood over their ancient
dwelling place.

The grand melancholy of the secluded valley of Gylingden, lonely as an enchanted forest, in which the crows returning to their roosts among the trees, and the straggling deer who peep from beneath their branches, seem to hold a wild and undisturbed dominion, heightens the forlorn aspect of Gylingden Hall.

Of late years repairs have been neglected, and here and there the roof is stripped, and "the stitch in time" has been wanting. At the side of the house exposed to the gales that sweep through the valley like a torrent through its channel, there is not a perfect window left, and the shutters but imperfectly exclude the rain. The ceilings and walls are mildewed and green with damp stains. Here and there, where the drip falls from the ceiling, the floors are rotting. On stormy nights, as the guard described, you can hear the doors clapping in the old house, as far away as old Gryston bridge, and the howl and sobbing of the wind through its empty galleries.

About seventy years ago died the old squire, Toby Marston, famous in that part of the world for his hounds, his hospitality and his vices. He had done kind things, and he had fought duels: he had given away money and he had horse whipped people. He carried with him some blessings and a good many curses, and left behind him an amount of debts and charges upon the estates which appalled his two sons, who had no taste for business or accounts, and had never suspected, till that wicked, open-handed and swearing old gentleman died, how very nearly he had run the estates into insolvency.

They met in Gylingden Hall. They had the will before them, and lawyers to interpret, and information without stint, as to the encumbrances with which the deceased had saddled them. The will was so framed as to set the two brothers instantly at deadly feud.

These brothers differed in some points; but in one material characteristic they resembled one another, and also their departed father. They never went into a quarrel by halves, and once in, they did not stick at trifles.

The elder, Scroope Marston, the more dangerous man of the two, had never been a favorite of the old squire. He had no taste for the sports of the field and the pleasures of a rustic life. He was no athlete, and he certainly was not handsome. All this the squire resented. The young man, who had no respect for him, and outgrew his fear of his violence as he came to manhood, retorted. This aversion, therefore, in the ill-conditioned old man grew into positive hatred. He used to wish that d——d pippin-squeezing, humpbacked rascal Scroope out of the way of better men—meaning his younger son Charles; and in his cups would talk in a way which even the old and young fellows who followed his hounds, and drank his port, and could stand a reasonable amount of brutality, did not like.

Scroope Marston was slightly deformed, and he had the lean sallow face, piercing black eyes and black lank hair, which sometimes accompany deformity.

"I'm no feyther o' that hog-backed creature. I'm no sire of hisn, d——n him! I'd as soon call that tongs son o' mine," the old man used to bawl, in allusion to his son's long, lank limbs: "Charlie's a man, but that's a jack-an-ape. He has no good nature; there's nothing handy, nor manly, nor no one turn of a Marston in him."

And when he was pretty drunk, the old squire used to swear he should never "sit at the head o' that board; nor frighten away folk from Gylingden Hall wi' his d——d hatchet face—the black loon!"

Handsome Charlie was the man for his money. He knew what a horse was, and could sit to his bottle; and the lasses were all clean *mad* about him. He was a Marston every inch of his six foot two.

Handsome Charlie and he, however, had also had a row or two. The old squire was free with horsewhip as with his tongue, and on occasion when neither weapon was quite practicable, had been known to give a fellow "a tap o' his knuckles." Handsome Charlie, however, thought there was a period at which personal chastisement should cease; and one night, when the port was flowing, there was some allusion to Marion Hayward, the miller's daughter, which for some reason the old gentleman did not like. Being "in liquor," and having clearer ideas about pugilism than self-government, he struck out, to the surprise of all present, at handsome Charlie. The youth threw back his head scientifically, and nothing followed but the crash of a decanter on the floor. But the old squire's blood was up, and he bounced from his chair. Up jumped handsome Charlie, resolved to stand no nonsense. Drunken Squire Lilbourne, intending to mediate, fell flat on the floor, and cut his ear among the glasses. Handsome Charlie caught the thump which the old squire discharged at him upon his open hand, and catching him by the cravat, swung him with his back to the wall. They said the old man never looked so purple, nor his eyes so goggle before; and then handsome Charlie pinioned him tight to the wall by both arms.

"Well, I say—come, don't you talk no more nonsense o' that sort, and I won't lick you," croaked the old squire. "You stopped that un clever, you did. Didn't he? Come, Charlie, man, gie us your hand, I say, and sit down again, lad." And so the battle ended; and I believe it was the last time the squire raised his hand to handsome Charlie.

But those days were over. Old Toby Marston lay cold and quiet enough now, under the drip of the mighty ash tree within the Saxon ruin where so many of the old Marston race returned to dust, and were forgotten. The weather-stained top boots and leather breeches, the three-cornered cocked hat to which old gentlemen of that day still clung, and the well-known red waistcoat that reached below his hips, and the fierce pug face of the old squire, were now but a picture of memory. And the brothers between whom he had planted an irreconcilable quarrel were now in their new mourning suits, with the gloss still on, debating furiously across the table in the great oak parlor, which had so often resounded to the banter and coarse songs, the oaths and laughter of the congenial neighbors whom the old squire of Gylingden Hall loved to assemble there.

These young gentlemen, who had grown up in Gylingden Hall, were not accustomed to bridle their tongues, nor, if need be, to hesitate about a blow. Neither had been at the old man's funeral. His death had been sudden. Having been helped to his bed in that hilarious and quarrelsome state which was induced by port and punch, he was found dead in the morning—his head hanging over the side of the bed, and his face very black and swollen.

Now the squire's will despoiled his eldest son of Gylingden, which had descended to the heir time out of mind. Scroope Marston was furious. His deep stern voice was heard inveighing against his dead father and living brother, and the heavy thumps on the table with which he enforced his stormy recriminations resounded through the large chamber. Then broke in Charles's rougher voice, and then came a quick alternation of short sentences, and then both voices together in growing loudness and anger, and at last, swelling the tumult, the expostulations of pacific and frightened lawyers, and at last a sudden break up of the conference. Scroope broke out of the room, his pale furious face showing whiter against his long black hair, his dark fierce eyes blazing, his hands clenched, and looking more ungainly and deformed than ever in the convulsions of his fury.

Very violent words must have passed between them; for Charlie, though he was the winning man, was almost as angry as Scroope. The elder brother was for holding possession of the house, and putting his rival to legal process to oust him. But his legal advisers were clearly against it. So, with a heart boiling over with gall, up he went to London, and found the firm who had managed his father's business fair and communicative enough. They looked into the settlements, and found that Gylingden was expected. It was very odd, but so it was, specially excepted; so that the right of the old squire to deal with it by his will could not be questioned.

Notwithstanding all this, Scroope, breathing vengeance and aggression, and quite willing to wreck himself provided he could run his brother down, assailed handsome Charlie, and battered old Squire Toby's will in the Prerogative Court and also at common law, and the feud between the brothers was knit, and every month their exasperation was heightened.

Scroope was beaten, and defeat did not soften him. Charles might have forgiven hard words; but he had been himself worsted during the long campaign in some of those skirmishes, special motions and so forth, that constitute the episodes of a legal epic like that in which the Marston brothers figured as opposing combatants; and the blight of law costs had touched him, too, with the usual effect upon the temper of a man of embarrassed means.

Years flew, and brought no healing on their wings. On the contrary, the deep corrosion of this hatred bit deeper by time. Neither brother married. But an accident of a different kind befell the younger, Charles Marston, which abridged his enjoyments very materially.

This was a bad fall from his hunter. There were severe fractures, and there was concussion of the brain. For some time it was thought that he could not recover. He disappointed these evil auguries, however. He did recover, but changed in two essential particulars. He had received an injury in his hip, which doomed him never more to sit in the saddle. And the rollicking animal spirits which hitherto had never failed him, had now taken flight forever.

He had been for five days in a state of coma—absolute insensibility—and when he recovered consciousness he was haunted by an indescribable anxiety.

Tom Cooper, who had been butler in the palmy days of Gylingden Hall, under old Squire Toby, still maintained his post with old-fashioned fidelity, in these days of faded splendor and frugal housekeeping. Twenty years had passed since the death of his old master. He had grown lean, and stooped, and his face, dark with the peculiar brown of age, furrowed and gnarled, and his temper, except with his master, had waxed surly.

His master had visited Bath and Buxton, and came back, as he went, lame, and halting gloomily about with the aid of a stick. When the hunter was sold, the last tradition of the old life at Gylingden disappeared. The young squire, as he was still called, excluded by his mischance from the hunting field, dropped into a solitary way of life, and halted slowly and solitarily about the old place, seldom raising his eyes, and with an appearance of indescribable gloom.

Old Cooper could talk freely on occasion with his master; and one day he said, as he handed him his hat and stick in the hall:

"You should rouse yourself up a bit, Master Charles!"

"It's past rousing with me, old Cooper."

"It's just this, I'm thinking: there's something on your mind, and you won't tell no one. There's no good keeping it on your stomach. You'll be a deal lighter if you tell it. Come, now, what is it, Master Charlie?"

The squire looked with his round gray eyes straight into Cooper's eyes. He felt that there was a sort of spell broken. It was like the old rule of the ghost who can't speak till it is spoken to. He looked earnestly into old Cooper's face for some seconds, and sighed deeply.

"It ain't the first good guess you've made in your day, old Cooper, and I'm glad you've spoke. It's bin on my mind, sure enough, ever since I had that fall. Come in here after me, and shut the door."

The squire pushed open the door of the oak parlor, and looked round on the pictures abstractedly. He had not been there for some time, and, seating himself on the table, he looked again for a while in Cooper's face before he spoke.

"It's not a great deal, Cooper, but it troubles me, and I would not tell it to the parson nor the doctor; for God knows what they'd say, though there's nothing to signify in it. But you were always true to the family, and I don't mind if I tell you."

" 'Tis as safe with Cooper, Master Charles, is if 'twas locked in a chest, and sunk in a well."

"It's only this," said Charles Marston, looking down on the end of his stick, with which he was tracing lines and circles, "all the time I was lying like dead, as you thought, after the fall, I was with the old master." He raised his eyes to Coopers's again as he spoke, and with an awful oath he repeated—"I was with him, Cooper!"

"He was a good man, sir, in his way," repeated old Cooper, returning his gaze with awe. "He was a good master to me, and a good father to you, and I hope he's happy. May God rest him!"

"Well," said Squire Charles, "it's only this: the whole of that time I was with him, or he was with me—I don't know which. The upshot is, we were together, and I thought I'd never get out of his hands again, and all the time he was bullying me about some one thing; and if it was to save my life, Tom Cooper, by—from the time I waked I never could call to mind what it was; and I think I'd give that hand to know; and if you can think of anything it might be—for God's sake! Don't be afraid, Tom Cooper, but speak it out, for he threatened me hard, and it was surely him."

Here ensued a silence.

"And what did you think it might be yourself, Master Charles?" said Cooper.

"I hadn't thought of aught that's likely. I'll never hit on't—*never*. I thought it might happen he knew something about that d—— humpbacked villain, Scroope, that swore before Lawyer Gingham I made away with a paper of settlements—me and father; and, as I hope to be saved, Tom Cooper, there never was a bigger lie! I'd a had the law of him for them identical words, and cast him for more than he's worth; only Lawyer Gingham never goes into nothing for me since money grew scarce in Gylingden; and I can't change my lawyer, I owe him such a hatful of money. But he did, he swore he'd hang me yet for it. He said it in them identical words—he'd never rest till he *hanged* me for it, and I think it was, like enough, something about *that* the old master was troubled; but it's enough to drive a man mad. I *can't* bring it to mind—I can't remember a word he said, only he threatened awful, and looked—Lord a mercy on us!—frightful bad."

"There's no need he should. May the Lord a mercy on him!" said the old butler.

"No, of course; and you're not to tell a soul, Cooper—not a living soul, mind, that I said he looked bad, nor nothing about it."

"God forbid!" said old Cooper, shaking his head. "But I was thinking, sir, it might ha' been about the slight that's bin so long put on him by having no stone over him, and never a scratch o' a chisel to say who he is."

"Ay! Well, I didn't think o' that. Put on your hat, old Cooper, and come down wi' me; for I'll look after that, at any rate."

There is a by path leading by a turnstile to the park, and thence to the picturesque old burying place, which lies in a nook by the roadside, embowered in ancient trees. It was a fine autumnal sunset, and melancholy lights and long shadows spread their peculiar effects over the landscape as handsome Charlie and the old butler made their way slowly toward the place where handsome Charlie was himself to lie at last.

"Which of the dogs made that howling all last night?" asked the squire, when they had got on a little way.

" 'Twas a strange dog, Master Charlie, in front of the house; ours was all in the yard—a white dog wi' a black head, he looked to be, and he was smelling round them mounting steps the old master, God be wi' him! set up, the time his knee was bad. When the tyke got up atop of them, howlin' up at the windows, I'd like to shy something at him."

"Hullo! Is that like him?" said the squire, stopping short, and pointing with his stick at a dirty-white dog, with a large black head, which was scampering round them in a wide circle, half-crouching with that air of uncertainty and deprecation which dogs so well know how to assume.

He whistled the dog up. He was a large, half-starved bull dog.

"That fellow has made a long journey—thin as a whipping post, and stained all over, and his claws worn to the stumps," said the squire, musingly. "He isn't a bad dog, Cooper. My poor father liked a good bull dog, and knew a cur from a good' un."

The dog was looking up into the squire's face with the peculiar grim visage of his kind, and the squire was thinking irreverently how strong a likeness it presented to the character of his father's fierce pug features when he was clutching his horsewhip and swearing at a keeper.

"If I did right I'd shoot him. He'll worry the cattle, and kill our dogs," said the squire. "Hey, Cooper? I'll tell the keeper to look after him. That fellow could pull down a sheep, and he shan't live on my mutton."

But the dog was not to be shaken off. He looked wistfully after the squire, and after they had got a little way on, he followed timidly.

It was vain trying to drive him off. The dog ran round them in wide circles, like the infernal dog in *Faust*; only he left no track of thin flame behind him. These maneuvers were executed with a sort of beseeching air, which flattered and touched the object of this odd preference. So he called him up again, patted him and then and there in a manner adopted him.

The dog now followed their steps dutifully, as if he had belonged to handsome Charlie all his days. Cooper unlocked the little iron door, and the dog walked in close behind their heels, and followed them as they visited the roofless chapel.

The Marstons were lying under the floor of this little building in rows. There is not a vault. Each has his distinct grave closed in a lining of masonry. Each is surmounted by a stone kist, on the upper flag of which is enclosed his epitaph, except that of poor old Squire Toby. Over him was nothing but the grass and the line of masonry which indicate the site of the kist, whenever his family should afford him one like the rest.

"Well, it does look shabby. It's the elder brother's business; but if he won't, I'll see to it myself, and I'll take care, old boy, to cut sharp and deep in it, that the elder son having refused to lend a hand the stone was put there by the younger."

They strolled round this little burial ground. The sun was now below the horizon, and the red metallic glow from the clouds, still illuminated by the departed sun, mingled luridly with the twilight. When Charlie peeped again into the little chapel, he saw the ugly dog stretched upon Squire Toby's grave, looking at least twice his natural length, and performing such antics as made the young squire stare. If you have ever seen a cat stretched on the floor, with a bunch of Valerian, straining, writhing, rubbing its jaws in long-drawn caresses, and in the absorption of a sensual ecstasy, you have seen a phenomenon resembling that which handsome Charlie witnessed on looking in.

The head of the brute looked so large, its body so long and thin, and its joints so ungainly and dislocated, that the squire, with old Cooper beside him, looked on with a feeling of disgust and astonishment, which, in a moment or two more, brought the squire's stick down upon him with a couple of heavy thumps. The beast awakened from his ecstasy, sprang to the head of the grave, and there on a sudden, thick and bandy as before, confronted the squire, who stood at its foot, with a terrible grin, and eyes that glared with the peculiar green of canine fury.

The next moment the dog was crouching abjectly at the squire's feet.

"Well, he's a rum 'un!" said old Cooper, looking hard at him.

"I like him," said the squire.

"I don't," said Cooper.

"But he shan't come in here again," said the squire.

"I shouldn't wonder if he was a witch," said old Cooper, who remembered more tales of witchcraft than are now current in that part of the world.

"He's a good dog," said the squire, dreamily. "I remember the time I'd a given a handful for him—but I'll never be good for nothing again. Come along."

And he stooped down and patted him. So up jumped the dog and looked up in his face, as if watching for some sign, ever so slight, which he might obey.

Cooper did not like a bone in that dog's skin. He could not imagine what his master saw to admire in him. He kept him all night in the gun room, and the dog accompanied him in his halting rambles about the place. The fonder his master grew of him, the less did Cooper and the other servants like him.

"He hasn't a point of a good dog about him," Cooper would growl. "I think Master Charlie be blind. And old Captain (an old red parrot, who sat chained to a perch in the oak parlor, and conversed with himself, and nibbled at his claws and bit his perch all day)—old Captain, the only living thing, except one or two of us, and the squire himself, that remembers the old master, the minute he saw the dog, screeched as if he was struck, shakin' his feathers out quite wild, and drops down, poor old soul, a-hanging' by his foot, in a fit."

But there is no accounting for fancies, and the squire was one of those dogged persons who persist more obstinately in their whims the more they are opposed. But Charles Marston's health suffered by his lameness. The transition from habitual and violent exercise to such a life as his privation now consigned him to, was never made without a risk to health; and a host of dyspeptic annoyances, the existence of which he had never dreamed of before, now beset him in sad earnest. Among these was the now not unfrequent troubling of his sleep with dreams and nightmares. In these his canine favorite invariably had a part and was generally a central, and sometimes a solitary, figure. In these visions the dog seemed to stretch himself up the side of the squire's bed, and in dilated proportions to sit at his feet, with a horrible likeness to the pug features of old Squire Toby, with his tricks of wagging his head and throwing up his chin; and then he would talk to him about Scroope, and tell him "all wasn't straight," and that he "must make it up wi' Scroope," that he, the old squire, had "served him an ill turn," that "time was nigh up," and that "fair was fair," and he was "troubled where he was, about Scroope."

Then in his dream this semi-human brute would approach his face to his, crawling and crouching up his body, heavy as lead, till the face of the beast was laid on his, with the same odious caresses and stretchings and writhings which he had seen over the old squire's grave. Then Charlie would wake up with a gasp and a howl, and start upright in the bed, bathed in a cold moisture, and fancy he saw something white sliding off the foot of the bed. Sometimes he thought it might be the curtain with white lining that slipped down, or the coverlet disturbed by his uneasy turnings; but he always fancied, at such moments, that he saw something white sliding hastily off the bed; and always when he had been visited by such dreams the dog next morning was more than usually caressing and servile, as if to obliterate, by a more than ordinary welcome, the sentiment of disgust which the horror of the night had left behind it.

The doctor half-satisfied the squire that there was nothing in these dreams, which, in one shape or another, invariably attended forms of indigestion such as he was suffering from.

For a while, as if to corroborate this theory, the dog ceased altogether to figure in them. But at last there came a vision in which, more unpleasantly than before, he did resume his old place.

In his nightmare the room seemed all but dark; he heard what he knew to be the dog walking from the door round his bed slowly, to the side from which he always had come upon it. A portion of the room was uncarpeted, and he said he distinctly heard the peculiar tread of a dog, in which the faint clatter of the claws is audible. It was a light stealthy step, but at every tread the whole room shook heavily; he felt something place itself at the foot of his bed, and saw a pair of green eyes staring at him in the dark, from which he could not remove his own. Then he heard, as he thought, the old Squire Toby say—"The eleventh hour be passed, Charlie, and ye've done nothing—you and 'a done Scroope a wrong!" and then came a good deal more, and then—"The time's nigh up, it's going to strike." And with a long low growl, the thing began to creep up upon his feet; the growl continued, and he saw the reflection of the upturned green eyes upon the bed clothes, as it began slowly to stretch itself up his body towards his face.

With a loud scream, he waked. The light, which of late the squire was accustomed to have in his bed room, had accidentally gone out. He was afraid to get up, or even to look about the room for some time; so sure did he feel of seeing the green eyes in the dark fixed on him from some corner. He had hardly recovered from the first agony which nightmare leaves behind it, and was beginning to collect his thoughts, when he heard the clock strike twelve. And he bethought him of the words "the eleventh hour be passed—time's nigh up—it's going to strike!" and he almost feared that he would hear the voice reopening the subject.

Next morning the squire came down looking ill.

"Do you know a room, old Cooper," said he, "they used to call King Herod's chamber?"

"Aye, sir; the story of King Herod was on the walls o't when I was a boy."

"There's a closet off it—is there?"

"I can't be sure o' that; but 'tisn't worth your looking at, now; the hangings was rotten, and took off the walls, before you was born; and there's nou't there but some old broken things and lumber. I seed them put there myself by poor Twinks; he was blind of an eye, and footman afterwards. You'll remember Twinks? He died here, about the time o' the great snow. There was a deal o' work to bury him, poor fellow!"

"Get the key, old Cooper; I'll look at the room," said the squire.

"And what the devil can you want to look at it for?" said Cooper, with the old-world privilege of a rustic butler.

"And what the devil's that to you? But I don't mind if I tell you. I don't want that dog in the gun room, and I'll put him somewhere else; and I don't care if I put him there."

"A bulldog in a bedroom! Oons, sir! the folks 'ill say you're clean mad!"

"Well, let them; get you the key and let us look at the room."

"You'd shoot him if you did right, Master Charlie. You never heard what a noise he kept up all last night in the gun room, walking to and fro growling like a tiger in a show; and, say what you like, the dog's not worth his feed; he hasn't a point of a dog; he's a bad dog."

"I know a dog better than you—and he's a good dog!" said the squire, testily.

"If you was a judge of a dog you'd hang that 'un," said Cooper.

"I'm not a-going to hang him, so there's an end. Go you, and get the key; and don't be talking, mind, when you go down. I may change my mind."

Now this freak of visiting King Herod's room had, in truth, a totally different object from that pretended by the squire. The voice in his nightmare had uttered a particular direction, which haunted him, and would give him no peace until he had tested it. So far from liking that dog today, he was beginning to regard it with a horrible suspicion; and if old Cooper had not stirred his obstinate temper by seeming to dictate, I dare say he would have got rid of the inmate effectually before evening.

Up to the third story, long disused, he and old Cooper mounted. At the end of a dusty gallery, the room lay. The old tapestry, from which the spacious chamber had taken its name, had long given place to modern paper, and this was mildewed, and in some places hanging from the walls. A thick mantle of dust lay over the floor. Some broken chairs and boards, thick with dust, lay, along with other lumber, piled together at one end of the room.

They entered the closet, which was quite empty. The squire looked round, and you could hardly have said whether he was relieved or disappointed.

"No furniture here," said the squire, and looked through the dusty window. "Did you say anything to me lately—I don't mean this morning—about this room, or the closet—or anything—I forget—"

"Lor' bless you! Not I. I han't been thinkin' o' this room this forty year."

"Is there any sort of old furniture called a *buffet*—do you remember?" asked the squire.

"A buffet? Why, yes—to be sure—there was a buffet, sure enough, in this closet, now you bring it to my mind," said Cooper. "But it's papered over."

"And what is it?"

"A little cupboard in the wall," answered the old man.

"Ho—I see—and there's such a thing here, is there, under the paper? Show me whereabouts it was."

"Well—I think it was somewhere about here," answered he, rapping his knuckles along the wall opposite the window. "Ay, there it is," he added, as the hollow sound of a wooden door was returned to his knock.

The squire pulled the loose paper from the wall, and disclosed the doors of a small press, about two feet square, fixed in the wall.

"The very thing for my buckles and pistols, and the rest of my gimcracks," said the squire. "Come away, we'll leave the dog where he is. Have you the key of that little press?"

No, he had not. The old master had emptied and locked it up, and desired that it should be papered over, and that was the history of it.

Down came the squire, and took a strong turn-screw from his gun case; and quietly he reascended to King Herod's room, and, with little trouble, forced the door of the small press in the closet wall. There were in it some letters and canceled leases, and also a parchment deed which he took to the window and read with much agitation. It was a supplemental deed executed about a fortnight after the others, and previously to his father's marriage, placing Gylingden under strict settlement to the elder son, in what is called "tail male." Handsome Charlie, in his fraternal litigation, had acquired a smattering of technical knowledge, and he perfectly well knew that the effect of this would be not only to transfer the house and lands to his brother Scroope, but to leave him at the mercy of that exasperated brother, who might recover from him personally every guinea he had ever received by way of rent, from the date of his father's death.

It was a dismal, clouded day, with something threatening in its aspect, and the darkness, where he stood, was made deeper by the top of one of the huge old trees overhanging the window.

In a state of awful confusion he attempted to think over his position. He placed the deed in his pocket, and nearly made up his mind to destroy it. A short time ago he would not have hesitated for a moment under such circumstances; but now his health and his nerves were shattered, and he was under a supernatural alarm which the strange discovery of this deed had powerfully confirmed.

In this state of profound agitation he heard a sniffing at the closet door, and then an impatient scratch and a long low growl. He screwed his courage up, and, not knowing what to expect, threw the door open and saw the dog, not in his dream shape, but wriggling with joy, and crouching and fawning with eager submission; and then wandering about the closet, the brute growled awfully into the corners of it, and seemed in an unappeasable agitation.

Then the dog returned and fawned and crouched again at his feet.

After the first moment was over, the sensations of abhorrence and fear began to subside, and he almost reproached himself for requitting the affection of this poor friendless brute with the antipathy which he had really done nothing to earn.

The dog pattered after him down the stairs. Oddly enough, the sight of this animal, after the first revulsion, reassured him; it was, in his eyes, so attached, so good-natured and palpably so mere a dog.

By the hour of evening the squire had resolved on a middle course; he would not inform his brother of his discovery, nor yet would he destroy the deed. He would never marry. He was past that time. He would leave a letter, explaining the discovery of the deed, addressed to the only surviving trustee—who had probably forgotten everything about it—and having seen out his own tenure, he would provide that all should be set right after his death. Was not that fair? At all events it quite satisfied what he called his conscience, and he thought it a devilish good compromise for his brother; and he went out, towards sunset, to take his usual walk.

Returning in the darkening twilight, the dog, as usual attending him, began to grow frisky and wild, at first scampering round him in great circles, as before, nearly at the top of his speed, his great head between his paws as he raced. Gradually more excited grew the pace and narrow his circuit, louder and fiercer his continuous growl, and the squire stopped and grasped his stick hard, for the lurid eyes and grin of the brute threatened an attack. Turning round and round as the excited brute encircled him, and striking vainly at him with his stick, he grew at last so tired that he almost despaired of keeping him longer at bay; when on a sudden the dog stopped short and crawled up to his feet wriggling and crouching submissively.

Nothing could be more apologetic and abject; and when the squire dealt him two heavy thumps with his stick, the dog whimpered only, and writhed and licked his feet. The squire sat down on a prostrate tree; and his dumb companion, recovering his wonted spirits immediately, began to sniff and nuzzle among the roots. The squire felt in his breast pocket for the deed—it was safe; and again he pondered, in this loneliest of spots, on the question whether he should preserve it for restoration after his death to his brother, or destroy it forthwith. He began rather to lean toward the latter solution, when the long low growl of the dog not far off startled him.

He was sitting in a melancholy grove of old trees, that slants gently westward. Exactly the same odd effect of light I have before described—a faint red glow reflected downward from the upper sky, after the sun had set, now gave to the growing darkness a lurid uncertainty. This grove, which lies in a gentle hollow, owing to its circumscribed horizon on all but one side, has a peculiar character of loneliness.

He got up and peeped over a sort of barrier, accidentally formed of the trunks of felled trees laid one over the other, and saw the dog straining up the other side of it, and hideously stretched out, his ugly head looking in consequence twice the natural size. His dream was coming over him again. And now between the trunks the brute's ungainly head was thrust, and the long neck came straining through, and the body, twining after it like a huge white lizard; and as it came striving and twisting through, it growled and glared as if it would devour him.

As swiftly as his lameness would allow, the squire hurried from this solitary spot towards the house. What thoughts exactly passed through his mind as he did so, I am sure he could not have told. But when the dog came up with him it seemed appeased, and even in high good humor, and no longer resembled the brute that haunted his dreams.

That night, near ten o'clock, the squire, a good deal agitated, sent for the keeper, and told him that he believed the dog was mad, and that he must shoot him. He might shoot the dog in the gun room, where he was—a grain of shot or two in the wainscot did not matter, and the dog must not have a chance of getting out.

The squire gave the gamekeeper his double-barreled gun, loaded with heavy shot. He did not go with him beyond the hall. He placed his hand on the keeper's arm; the keeper said his hand trembled, and that he looked "as white as curds."

"Listen a bit!" said the squire under his breath.

They heard the dog in a state of high excitement in the room—growling ominously, jumping on the window stool and down again, and running round the room.

"You'll need to be sharp, mind—don't give him a chance—slip in edgeways, d'ye see? and give him both barrels!"

"Not the first mad dog I've knocked over, sir," said the man, looking very serious as he cocked the gun.

As the keeper opened the door, the dog had sprung into the empty grate. He said he "never see sich a stark, staring devil." The beast made a twist round, as if, he thought, to jump up the chimney—"but that wasn't to be done at no price"—and he made a yell—not like a dog—like a man caught in a mill-crank, and before he could spring at the keeper, he fired one barrel into him. The dog leaped towards him, and rolled over, receiving the second barrel in his head, as he lay snorting at the keeper's feet!

"I never seed the like; I never heard a screech like that!" said the keeper, recoiling. "It makes a fellow feel queer."

"Quite dead?" asked the squire.

"Not a stir in him, sir," said the man, pulling him along the floor by the neck.

"Throw him outside the hall door now," said the squire; "and mind you pitch him outside the gate tonight—old Cooper says he's a witch," and the pale squire smiled, "so he shan't lie in Gylingden."

Never was man more relieved than the squire, and he slept better for a week after this than he had done for many weeks before.

It behooves us all to act promptly on our good resolutions. There is a determined gravitation towards evil, which, if left to itself, will bear down first intentions. If at one moment of superstitious fear the squire had made up his mind to a great sacrifice, and resolved in the matter of that deed so strangely recovered to act honestly by his brother, that resolution very soon gave place to the compromise with fraud which so conveniently postponed the restitution to the period when further enjoyment on his part was impossible. Then came more tidings of Scroope's violent and minatory language, with always the same burthen—that he would leave no stone unturned to show that there had existed a deed which Charles had either secreted or destroyed, and that he would never rest till he had hanged him.

This of course was wild talk. At first it had only enraged him; but, with his recent guilty knowledge and suppression, had come fear. His danger was the existence of the deed, and little by little he brought himself to a resolution to destroy it. There were many falterings and recoils before he could bring himself to commit this crime. At length, however, he did it, and got rid of the custody of that which at any time might become the instrument of disgrace and ruin. There was relief in this, but also the new and terrible sense of actual guilt.

He had got pretty well rid of his supernatural qualms. It was a different kind of trouble that agitated him now.

But this night, he imagined, he was awakened by a violent shaking of his bed. He could see, in the very imperfect light, two figures at the foot of it, holding each a bedpost. One of these he half-fancied was his brother Scroope, but the other was the old squire—of that he was sure—and he fancied that they had shaken him up from his sleep. Squire Toby was talkng as Charlie wakened, and he heard him say:

"Put out of our own house by you! It won't hold for long. We'll come in together, friendly, and stay. Forewarned, wi' yer eyes open, ye did it; and now Scroope'll hang you! We'll hang you together! Look at me, you devil's limb."

And the old squire tremblingly stretched his face, torn with shot and bloody, and growing every moment more and more into the likeness of the dog, and began to stretch himself out and climb the bed over the footboard; and he saw the figure at the other side, little more than a black shadow, begin also to scale the bed; and there was instantly a dreadful confusion and uproar in the room, and such a gabbling and laughing; he could not catch the words; but, with a scream, he woke, and found himself standing on the floor. The phantoms and the clamor were gone, but a crash and ringing of fragments was in his ears. The great china bowl, from which for generations the Marstons of Gylingden had been baptized, had fallen from the mantelpiece, and was smashed on the hearthstone.

"I've bin dreamin' all night about Mr. Scroope, and I wouldn't wonder, old Cooper, if he was dead," said the squire, when he came down in the morning.

"God forbid! I was adreamed about him, too, sir: I dreamed he was dammin' and sinkin' about a hole was burnt in his coat, and the old master, God be wi' him! said—quite plain—I'd 'a swore 'twas himself—'Cooper, get up, ye d—— land-loupin' thief, and lend a hand to hang him—for he's a daft cur, and no dog o' mine.' 'Twas the dog shot over night, I do suppose, as was runnin' in my old head. I thought old master gied me a punch wi' his knuckles, and says I, wakenin' up, 'At yer service, sir'; and for a while I couldn't get it out o' my head, master was in the room still."

Letters from town soon convinced the squire that his brother Scroope, so far from being dead, was particularly active; and Charlie's attorney wrote to say, in serious alarm, that he had heard, accidentally, that he intended setting up a case, of a supplementary deed of settlement, of which he had secondary evidence, which would give him Gylingden. And at this menace handsome Charlie snapped his fingers, and wrote courageously to his attorney; abiding what might follow with, however, a secret foreboding.

Scroope threatened loudly now, and swore after his bitter fashion, and reiterated his old promise of hanging that cheat at last. In the midst of these menaces and preparations, however, a sudden peace proclaimed itself: Scroope died, without time even to make provisions for a posthumous attack upon his brother. It was one of those cases of disease of the heart in which death is as sudden as by a bullet.

Charlie's exultation was undisguised. It was shocking. Not, of course, altogether malignant. For there was the expansion consequent on the removal of a secret fear. There was also the comic piece of luck, that only the day before Scroope had destroyed his old will, which left to a stranger every farthing he possessed, intending in a day or two to execute another to the same person, charged with the express condition of prosecuting the suit against Charlie.

The result was that all his possessions went unconditionally to his brother Charles as his heir. Here were grounds for abundance of savage elation. But there was also the deep-seated hatred of half a life of mutual and persistent aggression and revilings; and handsome Charlie was capable of nursing a grudge, and enjoying a revenge with his whole heart.

He would gladly have prevented his brother's being buried in the old Gylingden chapel, where he wished to lie; but his lawyers doubted his power, and he was not quite proof against the scandal which would attend his turning back the funeral, which would, he knew, be attended by some of the country gentry and others, with an hereditary regard for the Marstons.

But he warned his servants that not one of them was to attend it; promising, with oaths and curses not to be disregarded, that any one of them who did so, should find the door shut in his face on his return.

I don't think, with the exception of old Cooper, that the servants cared for this prohibition, except as it balked a curiosity always strong in the solitude of the country. Cooper was very much vexed that the eldest son of the old squire should be buried in the old family chapel, and no sign of decent respect from Gylingden Hall. He asked his master whether he would not, at least, have some wine and refreshments in the oak parlor, in case any of the country gentlemen who paid this respect to the old family should come up to the house? But the squire only swore at him, told him to mind his own business, and ordered him to say, if such a thing happened, that he was out, and no preparations made, and, in fact, to send them away as they came. Cooper expostulated stoutly, and the squire grew angrier; and after a tempestuous scene, took his hat and stick and walked out, just as the funeral descending the valley from the direction of the Old Angel Inn came in sight.

Old Cooper prowled about disconsolately, and counted the carriages as well as he could from the gate. When the funeral was over, and they began to drive away, he returned to the hall, the door of which lay open, and as usual deserted. Before he reached it quite, a mourning coach drove up, and two gentlemen in black cloaks, and with crapes to their hats, got out, and without looking to the right or the left, went up the steps into the house. Cooper followed them slowly. The carriage had, he supposed, gone round to the yard, for, when he reached the door, it was no longer there.

So he followed the two mourners into the house. In the hall he found a fellow servant, who said he had seen two gentlemen, in black cloaks, pass through the hall, and go up the stairs without removing their hats, or asking leave of anyone. This was very odd, old Cooper thought, and a great liberty; so upstairs he went to make them out.

But he could not find them then, nor ever. And from that hour the house was troubled.

In a little time there was not one of the servants who had not something to tell. Steps and voices followed them sometimes in the passages, and tittering whispers, always minatory, scared them at the corners of the galleries, or from dark recesses; so that they would return panic-stricken to be rebuked by thin Mrs. Beckett, who looked on such stories as worse than idle. But Mrs. Beckett herself, a short time after, took a very different view of the matter.

She had herself begun to hear these voices, and with this formidable aggravation, that they came always when she was at her prayers, which she had been punctual in saying all her life, and utterly interrupted them. She was scared at such moments by dropping words and sentences, which grew, as she persisted, into threats and blasphemies.

These voices were not always in the room. They called, as she fancied, through the walls, very thick in that old house, from the neighboring apartments, sometimes on one side, sometimes on the other; sometimes they seemed to holloa from distant lobbies, and came muffled, but threateningly, through the long paneled passages.

As they approached they grew furious, as if several voices were speaking together. Whenever, as I said, this worthy woman applied herself to her devotions, these horrible sentences came hurrying towards the door, and, in panic, she would start from her knees, and all then would subside except the thumping of her heart against her stays, and the dreadful tremors of her nerves.

What these voices said, Mrs. Beckett never could quite remember one minute after they had ceased speaking; one sentence chased another away; gibe and menace and impious denunciation, each hideously articulate, were lost as soon as heard. And this added to the effect of these terrifying mockeries and invectives, that she could not, by any effort, retain their exact import, although their horrible character remained vividly present to her mind.

For a long time the squire seemed to be the only person in the house absolutely unconscious of these annoyances. Mrs. Beckett had twice made up her mind within the week to leave. A prudent woman, however, who has been comfortable for more than twenty years in a place, thinks oftener than twice before she leaves it. She and old Cooper were the only servants in the house who remembered the good old housekeeping in Squire Toby's day. The others were few, and such as could hardly be accounted regular servants. Meg Dobbs, who acted as housemaid, would not sleep in the house, but walked home, in trepidation, to her father's, at the gatehouse, under the escort of her little brother, every night. Old Mrs. Beckett, who was high and mighty with the makeshift servants of fallen Gylingden, let herself down all at once, and made Mrs. Kymes and the kitchenmaid move their beds into her large and faded room, and there, very frankly, shared her nightly terrors with them.

Old Cooper was testy and captious about these stories. He was already uncomfortable enough by reason of the entrance of the two muffled figures into the house, about which there could be no mistake. His own eyes had seen them. He refused to credit the stories of the women, and affected to think that the two mourners might have left the house and driven away, on finding no one to receive them.

Old Cooper was summoned at night to the oak parlor, where the squire was smoking.

"I say, Cooper," said the squire, looking pale and angry, "what for ha' you been frightenin' they crazy women wi' your plaguy stories? D—— me, if you see ghosts here it's no place for you, and it's time you should pack. I won't be left without servants. Here has been old Beckett, wi' the cook and the kitchenmaid, as white as pipeclay, all in a row, to tell me I must have a parson to sleep among them, and preach down the devil! Upon my soul, you're a wise old body, filling their heads wi' maggots! And Meg goes down to the lodge every night, afeared to lie in the house—all your doing, wi' your old wives' stories—ye withered old Tom o' Bedlam!"

"I'm not to blame, Master Charles. 'Tisn't along o' no stories o' mine, for I'm never done tellin' 'em it's all vanity and vapors. Mrs. Beckett'ill tell you that, and there's been many a wry word betwixt us on the head o't. Whate'er I may *think*," said old Cooper, significantly, and looked askance, with the sternness of fear in the squire's face.

The squire averted his eyes, and muttered angrily to himself, and turned away to knock the ashes out of his pipe on the hob, and then turning suddenly round upon Cooper again, he spoke, with a pale face, but not quite so angrily as before.

"I know you're no fool, old Cooper, when you like. Suppose there was such a thing as a ghost here, don't you see, it ain't to them snipe-headed women it'id go to tell its story. What ails you, man, that you should think aught about it, but just what I think? You had a good headpiece o' yer own once, Cooper, don't be you clappin' a goosecap over it, as my poor father used to say; d—— it old boy, you mustn't let 'em be fools, settin' one another wild wi' their blether, and makin' the folk talk what they shouldn't, about Gylingden and the family. I don't think ye'd like that, old Cooper, I'm sure ye wouldn't. The women has gone out o' the kitchen, make up a bit o' fire, and get your pipe. I'll go to you, when I finish this one, and we'll smoke a bit together, and a glass o' brandy and water."

Down went the old butler, not altogether unused to such condescensions in that disorderly and lonely household; and let not those who can choose their company, be too hard on the squire who couldn't.

When he had got things tidy, as he said, he sat down in that big old kitchen, with his feet on the fender, the kitchen candle burning in a great brass candlestick, which stood on the deal table at his elbow, with the brandy bottle and tumblers beside it, and Cooper's pipe also in readiness. And these preparations completed, the old butler, who had remembered other generations and better times, fell into rumination, and so, gradually, into a deep sleep.

Old Cooper was half-awakened by someone laughing low, near his head. He was dreaming of old times in the hall, and fancied one of "the young gentlemen" going to play him a trick, and he mumbled something in his sleep, from which he was awakened by a stern deep voice, saying, "You weren't at the funeral; I might take your life, I'll take your ear." At the same moment, the side of his head received a violent push, and he started to his feet. The fire had gone down, and he was chilled. The candle was expiring in the socket, and threw on the white wall long shadows, that danced up and down from the ceiling to the ground, and their black outlines he fancied resembled the two men in cloaks, whom he remembered with a profound horror.

He took the candle, with all the haste he could, getting along the passage, on whose walls the same dance of black shadows was continued, very anxious to reach his room before the light should go out. He was startled half out of his wits by the sudden clang of his master's bell, close over his head, ringing furiously.

"Ha, ha! There it goes—yes, sure enough," said Cooper, reassuring himself with the sound of his own voice, as he hastened on, hearing more and more distinct every moment the same furious ringing. "He's fell asleep, like me; that's it, and his lights is out, I lay you fifty—"

When he turned the handle of the door of the oak parlor, the squire wildly called, "Who's *there?*" in the tone of a man who expects a robber.

"It's me, old Cooper, all right, Master Charlie, you didn't come to the kitchen after all, sir."

"I'm very bad, Cooper; I don't know how I've been. Did you meet anything?" asked the squire.

"No," said Cooper.

They stared at one another.

"Come here—stay here! Don't you leave me! Look round the room, and say is all right; and gie us your hand, old Cooper, for I must hold it." The squire's was damp and cold, and trembled very much. It was not very far from daybreak now.

After a time he spoke again: "I 'a done many a thing I shouldn't; I'm not fit to go, and wi' God's blessin' I'll look to it—why shouldn't I? I'm as lame as old Billy—I'll never be able to do any good no more, and I'll give over drinking, and marry, as I ought to 'a done long ago—none o' yer fine ladies, but a good homely wench; there's Farmer Crump's youngest daughter, a good lass, and discreet. What for shouldn't I take her? She'd take care o' me, and wouldn't bring a head full o' romances here, and mantua-makers' trumpery, and I'll talk with the parson, and I'll do what's fair wi' everyone; and mind, I said I'm sorry for many a thing I 'a done."

A wild cold dawn had by this time broken. The squire, Cooper said, looked "awful bad," as he got his hat and stick, and sallied out for a walk, instead of going to his bed, as Cooper besought him, looking so wild and distracted, that it was plain his object was simply to escape from the house. It was twelve o'clock when the squire walked into the kitchen, where he was sure of finding some of the servants, looking as if ten years had passed over him since yesterday. He pulled a stool by the fire, without speaking a word, and sat down. Cooper had sent to Applebury for the doctor, who had just arrived, but the squire would not go to him. "If he wants to see me, he may come here," he muttered as often as Cooper urged him. So the doctor did come, charily enough, and found the squire very much worse than he had expected.

The squire resisted the order to get to his bed. But the doctor insisted under a threat of death, at which his patient quailed.

"Well, I'll do what you say—only this—you must let old Cooper and Dick Keeper stay wi' me. I mustn't be left alone, and they must keep awake o' nights; and stay a while, do *you*. When I get round a bit, I'll go and live in a town. It's dull livin' here, now that I can't do nou't, as I used, and I'll live a better life, mind ye; ye heard me say that, and I don't care who laughs, and I'll talk wi' the parson. I like 'em to laugh, hang 'em, it's a sign I'm doin' right, at last."

The doctor sent a couple of nurses from the County Hospital, not choosing to trust his patient to the management he had selected, and he went down himself to Gylingden to meet them in the evening. Old Cooper was ordered to occupy the dressing room, and sit up at night, which satisfied the squire, who was in a strangely excited state, very low, and threatened, the doctor said, with fever.

The clergyman came, an old, gentle, "book-learned" man, and talked and prayed with him late that evening. After he had gone the squire called the nurses to his bedside, and said:

"There's a fellow sometimes comes; you'll never mind him. He looks in at the door and beckons—a thin, humpbacked chap in mourning, wi' black gloves on; ye'll know him by his lean face, as brown as the wainscot: don't ye mind his smilin'. You don't go out to him, nor ask him in; he won't say nou't; and if he grows anger'd and looks awry at ye, don't be afeared, for he can't hurt ye, and he'll grow tired waitin', and go away; and for God's sake mind ye don't ask him in, nor go out after him!"

The nurses put their heads together when this was over, and held afterwards a whispering conference with old Cooper. "Law bless ye!—no, there's no madman in the house," he protested; "not a soul but what ye saw—it's just a trifle o' the fever in his head—no more."

The squire grew worse as the night wore on. He was heavy and delirious, talking of all sorts of things—of wine, and dogs, and lawyers; and then he began to talk, as it were, to his brother Scroope. As he did so, Mrs. Oliver, the nurse, who was sitting up alone with him, heard, as she thought, a hand softly laid on the door handle outside, and a stealthy attempt to turn it. "Lord bless us! Who's there?" she cried, and her heart jumped into her mouth as she thought of the hump-backed man in black, who was to put in his head smiling and beckoning—"Mr. Cooper! Sir! Are you there?" she cried. "Come here, Mr. Cooper, please—do, sir, quick!"

Old Cooper, called up from his doze by the fire, stumbled in from the dressing room, and Mrs. Oliver seized him tightly as he emerged.

"The man with the hump has been atryin' the door, Mr. Cooper, as sure as I am here." The squire was moaning and mumbling in his fever, understanding nothing, as she spoke. "No, no! Mrs. Oliver, ma'am, it's impossible, for there's no sich man in the house: what is Master Charlie sayin'?"

"He's saying *Scroope* every minute, whatever he means by that, and—and—hisht!—listen—there's the handle again," and, with a loud scream, she added—"Look at his head and neck in at the door!" and in her tremor she strained old Cooper in an agonizing embrace.

The candle was flaring, and there was a wavering shadow at the door that looked like the head of a man with a long neck, and a longish sharp nose, peeping in and drawing back.

"Don't be a d—— fool, ma'am!" cried Cooper, very white, and shaking her with all his might. "It's only the candle, I tell you—nothing in life but that. Don't you see?" and he raised the light. "And I'm sure there was no one at the door, and I'll try, if you let me go."

The other nurse was asleep on a sofa, and Mrs. Oliver called her up in a panic, for company, as old Cooper opened the door. There was no one near it, but at the angle of the gallery was a shadow resembling that which he had seen in the room. He raised the candle a little, and it seemed to beckon with a long hand as the head drew back. "Shadow from the candle!" exclaimed Cooper aloud, resolved not to yield to Mrs. Oliver's panic; and, candle in hand, he walked to the corner. There was nothing. He could not forbear peeping down the long gallery from this point, and as he moved the light, he saw precisely the same sort of shadow, a little further down, and as he advanced the same withdrawal, and beckon. "Gammon!" said he; "it is nou't but the candle." And on he went, growing half-angry and half-frightened at the persistency with which this ugly shadow—a literal shadow he was sure it was—presented itself. As he drew near the point where it now appeared, it seemed to collect itself, and nearly dissolve in the central panel of an old carved cabinet which he was now approaching.

In the center panel of this is a sort of boss carved into a wolf's head. The light fell oddly upon this, and the fugitive shadow seemed to be breaking up, and rearranging itself oddly. The eyeball gleamed with a point of reflected light, which glittered also upon the grinning mouth, and he saw the long, sharp nose of Scroope Marston, and his fierce eye looking at him, he thought, with a steadfast meaning.

Old Cooper stood gazing upon this sight, unable to move, till he saw the face, and the figure that belonged to it, begin gradually to emerge from the wood. At the same time he heard voices approaching rapidly up a side gallery, and Cooper, with a loud "Lord a mercy on us!" turned and ran back again, pursued by a sound that seemed to shake the old house like a mighty gust of wind.

Into his master's room burst old Cooper, half-wild with fear, and clapped the door and turned the key in a twinkling, looking as if he had been pursued by murderers.

"Did you hear it?" whispered Cooper, now standing near the dressing room door. They all listened, but not a sound from without disturbed the utter stillness of night. "God bless us! I doubt it's my old head that's gone crazy!" exclaimed Cooper.

He would tell them nothing but that he was himself "an old fool," to be frightened by their talk, and that "the rattle of a window, or the dropping o' a pin" was enough to scare him now; and so he helped himself through that night with brandy, and sat up talking by his master's fire.

The squire recovered slowly from his brain fever, but not perfectly. A very little thing, the doctor said, would suffice to upset him. He was not yet sufficiently strong to remove for change of scene and air, which were necessary for his complete restoration.

Cooper slept in the dressing room, and was now his only nightly attendant. The ways of the invalid were odd: he liked, half-sitting up in his bed, to smoke his churchwarden o' nights, and made old Cooper smoke, for company, at the fireside. As the squire and his humble friend indulged in it, smoking is a taciturn pleasure, and it was not until the master of Gylingden had finished his third pipe that he essayed conversation, and when he did, the subject was not such as Cooper would have chosen.

"I say, old Cooper, look in my face, and don't be afeared to speak out," said the squire, looking at him with a steady, cunning smile; "you know all this time, as well as I do, who's in the house. You needn't deny—hey?—Scroope and my father?"

"Don't you be talking like that, Charlie," said old Cooper, rather sternly and frightened, after a long silence, still looking in his face, which did not change.

"What's the good o' shammin', Cooper? Scroope's took the hearin' o' yer right ear—you know he did. He's looking angry. He's nigh took my life wi' this fever. But he's not done wi' me yet, and he looks awful wicked. Ye saw him—ye know ye did."

Cooper was awfully frightened, and the odd smile on the squire's lips frightened him still more. He dropped his pipe, and stood gazing in silence at his master, and feeling as if he were in a dream.

"If ye think so, ye should not be smiling like that," said Cooper, grimly.

"I'm tired, Cooper, and it's as well to smile as to'other thing; so I'll even smile while I can. You know what they mean to do wi' me. That's all I wanted to say. Now, lad, go on wi' yer pipe—I'm goin' asleep."

So the squire turned over in his bed, and lay down serenely, with his head on the pillow. Old Cooper looked at him, and glanced at the door, and then half-filled his tumbler with brandy, and drank it off, and felt better, and got to his bed in the dressing room.

In the dead of night he was suddenly awakened by the squire, who was standing, in his dressing gown and slippers, by his bed.

"I've brought you a bit o' present. I got the rents o' Hazelden yesterday, and ye'll keep that for yourself—it's a fifty—and give t'other to Nelly Carwell, tomorrow; I'll sleep the sounder; and I saw Scroope since; he's not such a bad 'un after all, old fellow! He's got a crape over his face—for I told him I couldn't bear it; and I'd do many a thing for him now. I never could stand shilly-shally. Good night, old Cooper!"

And the squire laid his trembling hand kindly on the old man's shoulder, and returned to his own room. "I don't half-like how he is. Doctor don't come half-often enough. I don't like that queer smile o' his, and his hand was as cold as death. I hope in God his brain's not a-turnin'!"

With these reflections, he turned to the pleasanter subject of his present, and at last fell asleep.

In the morning, when he went into the squire's room, the squire had left his bed. "Never mind; he'll come back, like a bad shillin'," thought old Cooper, preparing the room as usual. But he did not return. Then began an uneasiness, succeeded by a panic, when it began to be plain that the squire was not in the house. What had become of him? None of his clothes, but his dressing gown and slippers, were missing. Had he left the house, in his present sickly state, in that garb, and, if so, could he be in his right senses; and was there a chance of his surviving a cold, a damp night, so passed, in the open air?

Tom Edwards was up to the house, and told them that, walking a mile or so that morning, at four o'clock—there being no moon—along with Farmer Nokes, who was driving his cart to market, in the dark, three men walked, in front of the horse, not twenty yards before them, all the way from Gylingden Lodge to the burial ground, the gate of which was opened for them from within, and the three men entered, and the gate was shut. Tom Edwards thought they were gone in to make preparation for a funeral of some member of the Marston family. But the occurrence seemed to Cooper, who knew there was no such thing, horribly ominous.

He now commenced a careful search, and at last bethought him of the lonely upper story and King Herod's chamber. He saw nothing changed there, but the closet door was shut, and, dark as was the morning, something, like a large white knot sticking out over the door, caught his eye.

The door resisted his efforts to open it for a time; some great weight forced it down against the floor; at length, however, it did yield a little, and a heavy crash, shaking the whole floor, and sending an echo flying through all the silent corridors, with a sound like receding laughter, half-stunned him.

When he pushed open the door, his master was lying dead upon the floor. His cravat was drawn halter-wise tight round his throat, and had done its work well. The body was cold, and had been long dead.

In due course the coroner held his inquest, and the jury pronounced that "the deceased, Charles Marston, had died by his own hand, in a state of temporary insanity." But old Cooper had his own opinion about the squire's death, though his lips were sealed, and he never spoke about it. He went and lived for the residue of days in York, where there are still people who remember him, a taciturn and surly old man, who attended church regularly, and also drank a little, and was known to have saved some money.

The Squaw

BRAM STOKER

Dracula's author was no more a one-book person than Somerset Maugham or Mary Shelley, but the force and shaping power of his most famous work has, ironically, diminished the shape and dimensions of the ouevre. The Squaw, an archetypal revenge story, gains in power from its careful and cunning displacement of protagonist (who turns out to be other than what the opening implies) and has perhaps the most horrific ending of any in this book.

Nurnberg at the time was not so much exploited as it has been since then. Irving had not been playing *Faust*, and the very name of the old town was hardly known to the great bulk of the traveling public. My wife and I being in the second week of our honeymoon, naturally wanted someone else to join our party, so that when the cheery stranger, Elias P. Hutcheson, hailing from Isthmian City, Bleeding Culch, Maple Tree County, Neb., turned up at the station at Frankfort, and casually remarked that he was going on to see the most all-fired old Methusaleh of a town in Yurrup, and that he guessed that so much traveling alone was enough to send an intelligent, active citizen into the melancholy ward of a daft house, we took the pretty broad hint and suggested that we should join forces. We found, on comparing notes afterwards, that we had each intended to speak with some diffidence or hesitation so as not to appear too eager, such not being a good compliment to the success of our married life; but the effect was entirely marred by our both beginning to speak at the same instant—stopping simultaneously and then going on together again. Anyhow, no matter how, it was done; and Elias P. Hutcheson became one of our party. Straightway Amelia and I found the pleasant benefit; instead of quarreling, as we had been doing, we found that the restraining influence of a third party was such that we now took every opportunity of spooning in odd corners. Amelia declares that ever since she has, as the result of that experience, advised all her friends to take a friend on the honeymoon. Well, we "did" Nurnberg together, and much enjoyed the racy remarks of our transatlantic friend, who, from his quaint speech and his wonderful stock of adventures, might have stepped out of a novel. We kept for the last object of interest in the city to be visited the Burg, and on the day appointed for the visit strolled round the outer wall of the city by the eastern side.

The Burg is seated on a rock dominating the town, and an immensely deep fosse guards it on the northern side. Nurnberg has been happy in that it was never sacked; had it been it would certainly not be so spick-and-span perfect as it is at present. The ditch has not been used for centuries, and now its base is spread with tea gardens and orchards, of which some of the trees are of quite respectable growth. As we wandered round the wall, dawdling in the hot July sunshine, we often paused to admire the views spread before us, and in especial the great plain covered with towns and villages and bounded with a blue line of hills, like a landscape of Claude Lorraine. From this we always turned with new delight to the city itself, with its myriad of quaint old gables and acre wide red roofs dotted with dormer windows, tier upon tier. A little to our right rose the towers of the Burg, and nearer still, standing grim, the Torture Tower, which was, and is, perhaps, the most interesting place in the city. For centuries the tradition of the Iron Virgin of Nurnberg has been handed down as an instance of the horrors of cruelty of which man is capable; we had long looked forward to seeing it; and here at last was its home.

In one of our pauses we leaned over the wall of the moat and looked down. The garden seemed quite fifty or sixty feet below us, and the sun pouring into it with an intense, moveless heat like that of an oven. Beyond rose the gray, grim wall seemingly of endless height, and losing itself right and left in the angles of bastion and counterscarp. Trees and bushes crowned the wall, and above again towered the lofty houses on whose massive beauty time has only set the hand of approval. The sun was hot and we were lazy; time was our own, and we lingered, leaning on the wall. Just below us was a pretty sight—a great black cat lying stretched in the sun, whilst round her gamboled prettily a tiny black kitten. The mother would wave her tail for the kitten to play with, or would raise her feet and push away the little one as an encouragement to further play. They were just at the foot of the wall, and Elias P. Hutcheson, in order to help the play, stooped and took from the walk a moderate-sized pebble.

"See!" he said, "I will drop it near the kitten, and they will both wonder where it came from."

"Oh, be careful," said my wife; "you might hit the dear little thing!"

"Not me, ma'am," said Elias P. "Why, I'm as tender as a Maine cherry tree. Lor, bless ye, I wouldn't hurt the poor pooty little critter more'n I'd scalp a baby. An' you may bet your variegated socks on that! See, I'll drop it fur away on the outside so's not to go near her!" Thus saying, he leaned over and held his arm out at full length and dropped the stone. It may be that there is some attractive force which draws lesser matters to greater; or more probably that the wall was not plumb but sloped to its base—we not noticing the inclination from above; but the stone fell with a sickening thud that came up to us through the hot air, right on the kitten's head, and shattered out its little brains then and there. The black cat cast a swift upward glance, and we saw her eyes like green fire fixed an instant on Elias P. Hutcheson; and then her attention was given to the kitten, which lay still with just a quiver of her tiny limbs, whilst a thin red stream trickled from a gaping wound. With a muffled cry, such as a human being might give, she bent over the kitten licking its wound and moaning. Suddenly she seemed to realize that it was dead, and again threw her eyes up at us. I shall never forget the sight, for she looked the perfect incarnation of hate. Her green eyes blazed with lurid fire, and the white, sharp teeth seemed to almost shine through the blood which dabbled her mouth and whiskers. She gnashed her teeth, and her claws stood out stark and at full length on every paw. Then she made a wild rush up the wall as if to reach us, but when the momentum ended fell back, and further added to her horrible appearance for she fell on the kitten, and rose with her black fur smeared with its brains and blood. Amelia turned quite faint, and I had to lift her back from the wall. There was a seat close by in shade of a spreading plane tree, and here I placed her whilst she composed herself. Then I went back to Hutcheson, who stood without moving, looking down on the angry cat below.

As I joined him, he said:

"Wall, I guess that air the savagest beast I ever see—'cept once when an Apache squaw had an edge on a half-breed what they nicknamed 'Splinters' 'cos of the way he fixed up her papoose which he stole on a raid just to show that he appreciated the way they had given his mother the fire torture. She got that kinder look so set on her face that it jest seemed to grow there. She followed Splinters more'n three year till at last the braves got him and handed him over to her. They did say that no man, white or Injun, had ever been so long a-dying under the tortures of the Apaches. The only time I ever see her smile was when I wiped her out. I kem on the camp just in time to see Splinters pass in his checks, and he wasn't sorry to go either. He was a hard citizen, and though I never could shake with him after that papoose business—for it was bitter bad, and he should have been a white man, for he looked like one—I see he had got paid out in full. Durn me, but I took a piece of his hide from one of his skinnin posts an' had it made into a pocketbook. It's here now!" and he slapped the breast pocket of his coat.

Whilst he was speaking the cat was continuing her frantic efforts to get up the wall. She would take a run back and then charge up, sometimes reaching an incredible height. She did not seem to mind the heavy fall which she got each time but started with renewed vigor; and at every tumble her appearance became more horrible. Hutcheson was a kind-hearted man—my wife and I had both noticed little acts of kindness to animals as well as to persons—and he seemed concerned at the state of fury to which the cat had wrought herself.

"Wall, now!" he said, "I du declare that that poor critter seems quite desperate. There! There! Poor thing, it was all an accident—though that won't bring back your little one to you. Say! I wouldn't have had such a thing happen for a thousand! Just shows what a clumsy fool of a man can do when he tries to play! Seems I'm too darned slipper-handed to even play with a cat. Say colonel!"—it was a pleasant way he had to bestow titles freely—"I hope your wife don't hold no grudge against me on account of this unpleasantness? Why, I wouldn't have had it occur on no account."

He came over to Amelia and apologized profusely, and she with her usual kindness of heart hastened to assure him that she quite understood that it was an accident. Then we all went again to the wall and looked over.

The cat missing Hutcheson's face had drawn back across the moat, and was sitting on her haunches as though ready to spring. Indeed, the very instant she saw him she did spring, and with a blind unreasoning fury, which would have been grotesque, only that it was so frightfully real. She did not try to run up the wall, but simply launched herself at him as though hate and fury could lend her wings to pass straight through the great distance between them. Amelia, womanlike, got quite concerned, and said to Elias P. in a warning voice:

"Oh! You must be very careful. That animal would try to kill you if she were here; her eyes look like positive murder."

He laughed out jovially. "Excuse me, ma'am," he said, "but I can't help laughin'. Fancy a man that has fought grizzlies an' Injuns bein' careful of bein' murdered by a cat!"

When the cat heard him laugh, her whole demeanor seemed to change. She no longer tried to jump or run up the wall, but went quietly over, and sitting again beside the dead kitten began to lick and fondle it as though it were alive.

"See!" said I, "the effect of a really strong man. Even that animal in the midst of her fury recognizes the voice of a master, and bows to him!"

"Like a squaw!" was the only comment of Elias P. Hutcheson, as we moved on our way round the city fosse. Every now and then we looked over the wall and each time saw the cat following us. At first she had kept going back to the dead kitten, and then as the distance grew took it in her mouth and so followed. After a while, however, she abandoned this, for we saw her following all alone; she had evidently hidden the body somewhere. Amelia's alarm grew at the cat's persistence, and more than once she repeated her warning; but the American always laughed with amusement, till finally, seeing that she was beginning to be worried, he said:

"I say, ma'am, you needn't be skeered over that cat. I go heeled, I du!" Here he slapped his pistol pocket at the back of his lumbar region. "Why sooner'n have you worried, I'll shoot the critter, right here, an' risk the police interfern' with a citizen of the United States for carryin' arms contrary to reg'lations!" As he spoke he looked over the wall, but the cat, on seeing him, retreated, with a growl, into a bed of tall flowers, and was hidden. He went on: "Blest if that ar critter ain't got more sense of what's good for her than most Christians. I guess we've seen the last of her! You bet, she'll go back now to that busted kitten and have a private funeral of it all to herself!"

Amelia did not like to say more, lest he might, in mistaken kindness to her, fulfill his threat of shooting the cat: and so we went on and crossed the little wooden bridge leading to the gateway whence ran the steep paved roadway between the Burg and the pentagonal Torture Tower. As we crossed the bridge we saw the cat again down below us. When she saw us her fury seemed to return, and she made frantic efforts to get up the steep wall. Hutcheson laughed as he looked down at her, and said:

"Good-by, old girl. Sorry I in-jured your feelin's, but you'll get over it in time! So long!" And then we passed through the long, dim archway and came to the gate of the Burg.

When we came out again after our survey of this most beautiful old place which not even the well-intentioned efforts of the gothic restorers of forty years ago have been able to spoil—though their restoration was then glaring white—we seemed to have quite forgotten the unpleasant episode of the morning. The old lime tree with its great trunk gnarled with the passing of nearly nine centuries, the deep well cut through the heart of the rock by those captives of old, and the lovely view from the city wall whence we heard, spread over almost a full quarter of an hour, the multitudinous chimes of the city, had all helped to wipe out from our minds the incident of the slain kitten.

We were the only visitors who had entered the Torture Tower that morning—so at least said the old custodian—and as we had the place all to ourselves were able to make a minute and more satisfactory survey than would have otherwise been possible. The custodian, looking to us as the sole source of his gains for the day, was willing to meet our wishes in any way. The Torture Tower is truly a grim place, even now when many thousands of visitors have sent a stream of life, and the joy that follows life, into the place; but at the time I mention it wore its grimmest and most gruesome aspect. The dust of ages seemed to have settled on it, and the darkness and the horror of its memories seem to have become sentient in a way that would have satisfied the Pantheistic souls of Philo or Spinoza. The lower chamber where we entered was seemingly, in its normal state, filled with incarnate darkness; even the hot sunlight streaming in through the door seemed to be lost in the vast thickness of the walls, and only showed the masonry rough as when the builder's scaffolding had come down, but coated with dust and marked here and there with patches of dark stain which, if walls could speak, could have given their own dread memories of fear and pain. We were glad to pass up the dusty wooden staircase, the custodian leaving the outer door open to light us somewhat on our way; for to our eyes the one long-wick'd, evil-smelling candle stuck in a sconce on the wall gave an inadequate light. When we came up through the open trap in the corner of the chamber overhead, Amelia held on to me so tightly that I could actually feel her heart beat. I must say for my own part that I was not surprised at her fear, for this room was even more gruesome than that below. Here there was certainly more light, but only just sufficient to realize the horrible surroundings of the place. The builders of the tower had evidently intended that only they who should gain the top should have any of the joys of light and prospect. There, as we had noticed from below, were ranges of windows, albeit of medieval smallness, but elsewhere in the tower were only a very few narrow slits such as were habitual in places of medieval defense. A few of these only lit the chamber, and these so high up in the wall that from no part could the sky be seen through the thickness of the walls. In racks, and leaning in disorder against the walls, were a number of headsmen's swords, great double-handed weapons with broad blade and keen edge. Hard by were several blocks whereon the necks of the victims had lain, with here and there deep notches where the steel had bitten through the guard of flesh and shored into the wood. Round the chamber, placed in all sorts of irregular ways, were many implements of torture which made one's heart ache to see—chairs full of spikes which gave instant and excruciating pain; chairs and couches with dull knobs whose torture was seemingly less, but which, though slower, were equally efficacious; racks, belts, boots, gloves, collars, all made for compressing at will; steel baskets in which the head could be slowly crushed into a pulp if necessary; watchmen's hooks with long handle and knife that cut at resistance—this a specialty of the old Nurnberg police system; and many, many other devices for man's injury to man. Amelia grew quite pale with the horror of the things, but fortunately did not faint, for being a little overcome she sat down on a torture chair, but jumped up again with a shriek, all tendency to faint gone. We both pretended that it was the injury done to her dress by the dust of the chair, and the rusty spikes which had upset her, and Mr. Hutcheson acquiesced in accepting the explanation with a kind-hearted laugh.

But the central object in the whole of this chamber of horrors was the engine known as the Iron Virgin, which stood near the center of the room. It was a rudely shaped figure of a woman, something of the bell order, or, to make a closer comparison, of the figure of Mrs. Noah in the children's ark, but without that slimness of waist and perfect *rondeur* of hip which marks the aesthetic type of the Noah family. One would hardly have recognized it as intended for a human figure at all had not the founder shaped on the forehead a rude semblance of a woman's face. This machine was coated with rust without, and covered with dust; a rope was fastened to a ring in the front of the figure, about where the waist should have been, and was drawn through a pulley, fastened on the wooden pillar which sustained the flooring above. The custodian pulling this rope showed that a section of the front was hinged like a door at one side; we then saw that the engine was of considerable thickness, leaving just room enough inside for a man to be placed. The door was of equal thickness and of great weight, for it took the custodian all his strength, aided though he was by the contrivance of the pulley, to open it. This weight was partly due to the fact that the door was of manifest purpose hung so as to throw its weight downwards, so that it might shut of its own accord when the strain was released. The inside was honeycombed with rust—nay more, the rust alone that comes through time would hardly have eaten so deep into the iron walls; the rust of the cruel stains was deep indeed! It was only, however, when we came to look at the inside of the door that the diabolical intention was manifest to the full. Here were several long spikes, square and massive, broad at the base and sharp at the points, placed in such a position that when the door should close the upper ones would pierce the eyes of the victim, and the lower ones his heart and vitals. The sight was too much for poor Amelia, and this time she fainted dead off, and I had to carry her down the stairs, and place her on a bench outside till she recovered. That she felt it to the quick was afterwards shown by the fact that my eldest son bears to this day a rude birthmark on his breast, which has, by family consent, been accepted as representing the Nurnberg Virgin.

When we got back to the chamber we found Hutcheson still opposite the Iron Virgin; he had been evidently philosophizing, and now gave us the benefit of his thought in the shape of a sort of exordium.

"Wall, I guess I've been learnin' somethin' here while madam has been gettin' over her faint. 'Pears to me that we're a long way behind the times on our side of the big drink. We uster think out on the plains that the Injun could give us points in tryin' to make a man oncomfortable; but I guess your old medieval law-and-order party could raise him every time. Splinters was pretty good in his bluff on the squaw, but this here young miss held a straight flush all high on him. The points of them spikes air sharp enough still, though even the edges air eaten out by what uster be on them. It'd be a good thing for our Indian section to get some specimens of this here play-toy to send round to the Reservations jest to knock the stuffin' out of the bucks, and the squaws too, by showing them as how old civilization lays over them at their best. Guess but I'll get in that box a minute jest to see how it feels!"

"Oh no! No!" said Amelia. "It is too terrible!"

"Guess, ma'am, nothing's too terrible to the explorin' mind. I've been in some queer places in my time. Spent a night inside a dead horse while a prairie fire swept over me in Montana territory—an' another time slept inside a dead buffler when the Comanches was on the warpath an' I didn't keer to leave my kyard on them. I've been two days in a caved-in tunnel in the Billy Broncho gold mine in New Mexico, an' was one of the four shut up for three parts of a day in the caisson what slid over on her side when we was settin' the foundations of the Buffalo Bridge. I've not funked an odd experience yet, an' I don't propose to begin now!"

We saw that he was set on the experiment, so I said: "Well, hurry up, old man, and get through it quick!"

"All right, general," said he, "but I calculate we ain't quite ready yet. The gentlemen, my predecessors, what stood in that thar canister, didn't volunteer for the office—not much! And I guess there was some ornamental tyin' up before the big stroke was made. I want to go into this thing fair and square, so I must get fixed up proper first. I dare say this old galoot can rise some string and tie me up accordin' to sample?"

This was said interrogatively to the old custodian, but the latter, who understood the drift of his speech, though perhaps not appreciating to the full the niceties of dialect and imagery, shook his head. His protest was, however, only formal and made to be overcome. The American thrust a gold piece into his hand, saying, "Take it, pard! It's your pot; and don't be skeer'd. This ain't no necktie party that you're asked to assist in!" He produced some thin frayed rope and proceeded to bind our companion with sufficient strictness for the purpose. When the upper part of his body was bound, Hutcheson said:

"Hold on a moment, judge. Guess I'm too heavy for you to tote into the canister. You jest let me walk in, and then you can wash up regardin' my legs!"

Whilst speaking he had backed himself into the opening which was just enough to hold him. It was a close fit and no mistake. Amelia looked on with fear in her eyes, but she evidently did not like to say anything. Then the custodian completed his task by tying the

American's feet together so that he was now absolutely helpless and fixed in his voluntary prison. He seemed to really enjoy it, and the incipient smile which was habitual to his face blossomed into actuality as he said:

"Guess this here Eve was made out of the rib of a dwarf! There ain't much room for a full-grown citizen of the United States to hustle. We uster make our coffins more roomier in Idaho territory. Now, judge, you jest begin to let this door down, slow, on to me. I want to feel the same pleasure as the other jays had when those spikes began to move toward their eyes!"

"Oh no! No! No!" broke in Amelia hysterically. "It is too terrible! I can't bear to see it!—I can't! I can't!"

But the American was obdurate. "Say, colonel," said he, "Why not take madame for a little promenade? I wouldn't hurt her feelin's for the world; but now that I am here, havin' kem eight thousand miles, wouldn't it be too hard to give up the very experience I've been pinin' an' pantin' fur? A man can't get to feel like canned goods every time! Me and the judge here'll fix up this thing in no time, an' then you'll come back, an' we'll all laugh together!"

Once more the resolution that is born of curiosity triumphed, and Amelia stayed holding tight to my arm and shivering whilst the custodian began to slacken slowly inch by inch the rope that held back the iron door. Hutcheson's face was positively radiant as his eyes followed the first movement of the spikes.

"Wall!" he said, "I guess I've not had enjoyment like this since I left Noo York. Bar a scrap with a French sailor at Wapping—an' that warn't much of a picnic neither—I've not had a show fur real pleasure in this dod-rotted Continent, where there ain't no b'ars nor no Injuns, an' where nary man goes heeled. Slow there, judge! Don't you rush this business! I want a show for my money this game—I du!"

The custodian must have had in him some of the blood of his predecessors in that ghastly tower, for he worked the engine with a deliberate and excruciating slowness which after five minutes, in which the outer edge of the door had not moved half as many inches, began to overcome Amelia. I saw her lips whiten, and felt her hold upon my arm relax. I looked around an instant for a place whereon to lay her, and when I looked at her again found that her eye had become fixed on the side of the Virgin. Following its direction I saw the black cat crouching out of sight. Her green eyes shown like danger lamps in the gloom of the place, and their color was heightened by the blood which still smeared her coat and reddened her mouth. I cried out:

"The cat! Look out for the cat!" for even then she sprang out before the engine. At this moment she looked like a triumphant demon. Her eyes blazed with ferocity, her hair bristled out till she seemed twice her normal size, and her tail lashed out about as does a tiger's when the quarry is before it. Elias P. Hutcheson when he saw her was amused, and his eyes positively sparkled with fun as he said:

"Darned if the squaw hain't got on all her war paint! Jest give her a shove off if she comes any of her tricks on me, for I'm so fixed everlastingly by the boss, that durn my skin if I can keep my eyes from her if she wants them! Easy there, judge! Don't you slack that ar rope or I'm euchered!"

At this moment Amelia completed her faint, and I had to clutch hold of her round the waist or she would have fallen to the floor. Whilst attending to her I saw the black cat crouching for a spring, and jumped up to turn the creature out.

But at that instant, with a sort of hellish scream, she hurled herself, not as we expected at Hutcheson, but straight at the face of the custodian. Her claws seemed to be tearing wildly as one sees in the Chinese drawings of the dragon rampart, and as I looked I saw one of them light on the poor man's eye, and actually tear through it and down his cheek, leaving a wide band of red where the blood seemed to spurt from every vein.

With a yell of sheer terror which came quicker than even his sense of pain, the man leaped back, dropping as he did so the rope which held back the iron door. I jumped for it, but was too late, for the cord ran like lightning through the pulley block, and the heavy mass fell forward from its own weight.

As the door closed I caught a glimpse of our poor companion's face. He seemed frozen with terror. His eyes stared with a horrible anguish as if dazed, and no sound came from his lips.

And then the spikes did their work. Happily the end was quick, for when I wrenched open the door they had pierced so deep that they had locked in the bones of the skull through which they had crushed and actually tore him—it—out of his iron prison till, bound as he was, he fell at full length with a sickly thud upon the floor, the face turning upward as he fell.

I rushed to my wife, lifted her up and carried her out, for I feared for her very reason if she should wake from her faint to such a scene. I laid her on the bench outside and ran back. Leaning against the wooden column was the custodian moaning in pain whilst he held his reddening handkerchief to his eyes. And sitting on the head of the poor American was the cat, purring loudly as she licked the blood which trickled through the gashed socket of his eyes.

I think no one will call me cruel because I seized one of the old executioner's swords and shore her in two as she sat.

The Jolly Corner

HENRY JAMES

Here it is again; the central theme of Henry James which became, soon enough, the undercurrent of the modern vision in literature: the shift of levels, alternation of the fantastic and real, disturbing intersection, eventual fusion. The Turn of the The Screw accomplishes this stunningly at near-novel length; "The Jolly Corner," a less well-known but no less terrifying story, does so in less than a third of that. Like Poe, but through a different prism, James anticipated not only the century but its aftermath: the abandonment of intellectual belief in the theory of causality.

I

"Everyone asks me what I 'think' of everything," said Spencer Brydon; "and I make answer as I can—begging or dodging the question, putting them off with any nonsense. It wouldn't matter to any of them really," he went on, "for, even were it possible to meet in that stand-and-deliver way so silly a demand on so big a subject, my 'thoughts' would still be almost altogether about something that concerns only myself." He was talking to Miss Staverton, with whom for a couple of months now he had availed himself of every possible occasion to talk; this disposition and this resource, this comfort and support, as the situation in fact presented itself, having promptly enough taken the first place in the considerable array of rather unattenuated surprises attending his so strangely belated return to America. Everything was somehow a surprise; and that might be natural when one had so long and so consistently neglected everything, taken pains to give surprises so much margin for play. He had given them more than thirty years—thirty-three, to be exact; and they now seemed to him to have organized their performance quite on the scale of that license. He had been twenty-three on leaving New York—he was fifty-six today: unless indeed he were to reckon as he had sometimes, since his repatriation, found himself feeling; in which case he would have lived longer than is often allotted to man. It would have taken a century, he repeatedly said to himself, and said also to Alice Staverton, it would have taken a longer absence and a more averted mind than those even of which he had been guilty, to pile up the differences, the newnesses, the queernesses, above all the bignesses, for the better or the worse, that at present assaulted his vision wherever he looked.

The great fact all the while however had been the incalculability; since he *had* supposed himself, from decade to decade, to be allowing, and in the most liberal and intelligent manner, for brilliancy of change. He actually saw that he had allowed for nothing; he missed what he would have been sure of finding, he found what he would never have imagined. Proportions and values were upside-down; the ugly things he had expected, the ugly things of his faraway youth, when he had too promptly waked up to a sense of the ugly—these uncanny phenomena placed him rather, as it happened, under the charm; whereas the "swagger" things, the modern, the monstrous, the famous things, those he had more particularly, like thousands of ingenuous inquirers every year, come over to see, were exactly his sources of dismay. They were as so many set traps for displeasure, above all for reaction, of which his restless tread was constantly press-ing the spring. It was interesting, doubtless, the whole show, but it would have been too disconcerting hadn't a certain finer truth saved the situation. He had distinctly not, in this steadier light, come over *all* for the monstrosities; he had come, not only in the last analysis but quite on the face of the act, under an impulse with which they had nothing to do. He had come—putting the thing pompously—to look at his "property," which he had thus for a third of a century not been within four thousand miles of; or, expressing it less sordidly, he had yielded to the humor of seeing again his house on the jolly corner, as he usually, and quite fondly, described it—the one in which he had first seen the light, in which various members of his family had lived and had died, in which the holidays of his overschooled boyhood had been passed and the few social flowers of his chilled adolescence gathered, and which, alienated then for so long a period, had, through the successive deaths of his two brothers and the termination of old arrangements, come wholly into his hands. He was the owner of another, not quite so "good"—the jolly corner having been, far from back, superlatively extending and consecrated; and the value of the pair represented his main capital, with an income consisting, in these later years, of their respective rents which (thanks precisely to their original excellent type) had never been depressingly low. He could live in "Europe," as he had been in the habit of living, on the product of these flourishing New York leases, and all the better since, that of the second structure, the mere number in its long row, having within a twelvemonth fallen in, renovation at a high advance had proved beautifully possible.

These were items of property indeed, but he had found himself since his arrival distinguishing more than ever between them. The house within the street, two bristling blocks westward, was already in course of reconstruction as a tall mass of flats; he had acceded, some time before, to overtures for this conversion—in which, now that it was going forward, it had been not the least of his astonishments to find himself able, on the spot, and though without a previous ounce of such experience, to participate with a certain intelligence, almost with a certain authority. He had lived his life with his back so turned to such concerns and his face addressed to those of so different an order that he scarce knew what to make of this lively stir, in a compartment of his mind never yet penetrated, of a capacity for business and a sense for construction. These virtues, so common all round him now, had been dormant in his own organism—where it might be said of them perhaps that they had slept the sleep of the just. At present, in the splendid autumn weather—the autumn as least was a pure boon in the terrible place—he loafed about his "work" undeterred, secretly agitated; not in the least "minding" that the whole proposition, as they said, was vulgar and sordid, and ready to climb ladders, to walk the plank, to handle materials and look wise about them, to ask questions, in fine, and challenge explanations and really "go into" figures.

It amused, it verily quite charmed him; and, by the same stroke, it amused, and even more, Alice Staverton, though perhaps charming her perceptibly less. She wasn't however going to be better off for it, as *he* was—and so astonishingly much: nothing was now likely, he knew, even to make her better off than she found herself, in the afternoon of life, as the delicately frugal possessor and tenant of the small house in Irving Place to which she had subtly managed to cling through her almost unbroken New York career. If he knew the way to it now better than to any other address among the dreadful multiplied numberings which seemed to him to reduce the whole place to some vast ledger page, overgrown, fantastic, of ruled and crisscrossed lines and figures—if he had formed, for his consolation, that habit, it was really not a little because of the charm of his having encountered and recognized, in the vast wilderness of the wholesale, breaking through the mere gross generalization of wealth and force and success, a small still scene where items and shades, all delicate things, kept the sharpness of the notes of a high voice perfectly trained, and where economy hung about like the scent of a garden. His old friend lived with one maid and herself dusted her relics and trimmed her lamps and polished her silver; she stood off, in the awful modern crush, when she could, but she sallied forth and did battle when the challenge was really to "spirit," the spirit she after all confessed to, proudly and a little shyly, as to that of the better time, that of *their* common, their quite far away and antediluvian social period and order. She made use of the street cars when need be, the terrible things that people scrambled for as the panic-stricken at sea scramble for the boats; she affronted, inscrutably, under stress, all the public concussions and ordeals; and yet, with that slim mystifying grace of her appearance, which defied you to say if she were a fair young woman who looked older through trouble, or fine smooth older one who looked young through successful indifference; with her precious reference, above all, to memories and histories into which he could enter, she was as exquisite for him as some pale pressed flower (a rarity to begin with), and, failing other sweetnesses, she was a sufficient reward of his effort. They had communities of knowledge, "their " knowledge (this discriminating possessive was always on her lips) of presences of the other age, presences all overlaid, in his case, by the experience of a man and the freedom of a wanderer, overlaid by pleasure, by infidelity, by passages of life that were strange and dim to her, just by "Europe" in short, but still unobscured, still exposed and cherished, under that pious visitation of the spirit from which she had never been diverted.

She had come with him one day to see how his "apartment house" was rising; he had helped her over gaps and explained to her plans, and while they were there had happened to have, before her, a brief but lively discussion with the man in charge, the representative of the building firm that had undertaken his work. He had found himself quite "standing-up" to this personage over a failure on the latter's part to observe some detail of one of their noted conditions, and had so lucidly argued his case that, besides ever so prettily flushing, at the time, for sympathy in his triumph, she had afterwards said to him (though to a slightly greater effect of irony) that he had clearly for too many years neglected a real gift. If he had but stayed at home he would have anticipated the inventor of the skyscraper. If he had but stayed at home he would have discovered his genius in time really to start some new variety of awful architectual hare and run it till it burrowed in the gold mine. He was to remember these words, while the weeks elapsed, for the small silver ring they had sounded over the queerest and deepest of his own lately most disguised and most muffled vibrations.

It had begun to be present to him after the first fortnight, it had broken out with the oddest abruptness, this particular wanton wonderment: it met him there—and this was the image under which he himself judged the matter, or at least, not a little, thrilled and flushed with it—very much as he might have been met by some strange figure, some unexpected occupant, at a turn of one of the dim passages of an empty house. The quaint analogy quite hauntingly remained with him, when he didn't indeed rather improve it by a still intenser form: that of his opening a door behind which he would have made sure of finding nothing, a door into a room shuttered and void, and yet so coming, with a great suppressed start, on some quite erect confronting presence, sometimes planted in the middle of the place and facing him through the dusk. After that visit to the house in construction he walked with his companion to see the other and always so much the better one, which in the eastward direction formed one of the corners, the "jolly" one precisely, of the street now so generally dishonored and disfigured in its westward reaches, and of the comparatively conservative avenue. The avenue still had pretensions, as Miss Staverton said, to decency; the old people had mostly gone, the old names were unknown, and here and there an old association seemed to stray, all vaguely, like some very aged person, out too late, whom you might meet and feel the impulse to watch or follow, in kindness, for safe restoration to shelter.

They went in together, our friends; he admitted himself with his key, as he kept no one there, he explained, preferring, for his reasons, to leave the place empty, under a simple arrangement with a good woman living in the neighborhood and who came for a daily hour to open windows and dust and sweep. Spencer Brydon had his reasons and was growingly aware of them; they seemed to him better each time he was there, though he didn't name them all to his companion, any more than he told her as yet how often, how quite absurdly often, he himself came. He only let her see for the present, while they walked through the great blank rooms, that absolute vacancy reigned and that, from top to bottom, there was nothing but Mrs. Muldoon's broomstick, in the corner, to tempt the burglar. Mrs. Muldoon was then on the premises, and she loquaciously attended the visitors, preceding them from room to room and pushing back shutters and throwing up sashes—all to show them, as she remarked, how little there was to see. There was little indeed to see in the great gaunt shell where the main dispositions and the general apportionment of space, the style of an age of ampler allowances, had nevertheless for its master their honest pleading message, affecting him as some good old servant's, some lifelong retainer's appeal for a character, or even for a retiring pension; yet it was also a remark of Mrs. Muldoon's that, glad as she was to oblige him by her noonday round, there was a request she greatly hoped he would never make of her. If he should wish her for any reason to come in after dark she would just tell him, if he "plased," that he must ask it of somebody else.

The fact that there was nothing to see didn't militate for the worthy woman against what one *might* see, and she put it frankly to Miss Staverton that no lady could be expected to like, could she? "scraping up to thim top storys in the ayvil hours." The gas and electric light were off the house, and she fairly evoked a gruesome vision of her march through the great gray rooms—so many of them as there were too!—with her glimmering taper. Miss Staverton met her honest glare with a smile and the profession that she herself certainly would recoil from such an adventure. Spencer Brydon meanwhile held his peace—for the moment; the question of the "evil" hours in his old home had already become too grave for him. He had begun some time since to "crape," and he knew just why a packet of candles addressed to that pursuit had been stowed by his own hand, three weeks before, at the back of a drawer of the fine old sideboard that occupied, as a "fixture," the deep recess in the dining room. Just now he laughed at his companions—quickly however changing the subject; for the reason that, in the first place, his laugh struck him even at that moment as starting the odd echo, the conscious human resonance (he scarce knew how to qualify it) that sounds made while he was there alone sent back to his ear or his fancy; and that, in the second, he imagined Alice Staverton for the instant on the point of asking him, with a divination, if he ever so prowled. There were divinations he was unprepared for, and he had at all events averted inquiry by the time Mrs. Muldoon had left them, passing on to other parts.

There was happily enough to say, on so consecrated a spot, that could be said freely and fairly; so that a whole train of declarations was precipitated by his friend's having herself broken out, after a yearning look round: "But I hope you don't mean they want you to pull *this* to pieces!" His answer came, promptly, with his reawakened wrath: it was of course exactly what they wanted, and what they were "at" him for, daily, with the iteration of people who couldn't for their life understand a man's liability to decent feelings. He had found the place, just as it stood and beyond that he could express, an interest and a joy. There were values other than the beastly rent values, and in short, in short—! But it was thus Miss Staverton took him up. "In short you're to make so good a thing of your skyscraper that, living in luxury on *those* ill-gotten gains, you can afford for a while to be sentimental here!" Her smile had for him, with the words, the particular mild irony with which he found half her talk suffused; an irony without bitterness and that came, exactly, from her having so much imagination—not, like the cheap sarcasms with which one heard most people, about the world of "society," bid for the reputation of cleverness, from nobody's really having any. It was agreeable to him at this very moment to be sure that when he had answered, after a brief demur, "Well yes: so, precisely, you may put it!" her imagination would still do him justice. He explained that even if never a dollar were to come to him from the other house he would nevertheless cherish this one; and he dwelt, further, while they lingered and wandered, on the fact of the stupefaction he was already exciting, the positive mystification he felt himself create.

He spoke of the value of all he read into it, into the mere sight of the walls, mere shapes of the rooms, mere sound of the floors, mere feel, in his hand, of the old silverplated knobs of the several mahogany doors, which suggested the pressure of the palms of the dead; the seventy years of the past in fine that these things represented, the annals of nearly three generations, counting his grandfather's, the one that had ended there, and the impalpable ashes of his long-extinct youth, afloat in the very air like microscopic motes. She listened to everything; she was a woman who answered intimately but who utterly didn't chatter. She scattered abroad therefore no cloud of words; she could assent, she could agree, above all she could encourage, without doing that. Only at the last she went a little further than he had done himself. "And then how do you know? You may still, after all, want to live here." It rather indeed pulled him up, for it wasn't what he had been thinking, at least in her sense of the words. "You mean I may decide to stay on for the sake of it?"

"Well, *with* such a home—!" But, quite beautifully, she had too much tact to dot so monstrous an *i*, and it was precisely an illustration of the way she didn't rattle. How could any one—of any wit—insist on anyone else's "wanting" to live in New York?

"Oh," he said, "I *might* have lived here (since I had my opportunity early in life); I might have put in here all these years. Then everything would have been different enough—and, I dare say, 'funny' enough. But that's another matter. And then the beauty of it—I mean of my perversity, of my refusal to agree to a 'deal'—is just in the total absence of a reason. Don't you see that if I had a reason about the matter at all it would *have* to be the other way, and would then be inevitably a reason of dollars? There are no reasons here *but* of dollars. Let us therefore have none whatever—not the ghost of one."

They were back in the hall then for departure, but from where they stood the vista was large, through an open door, into the great square main saloon, with its almost antique felicity of brave spaces between windows. Her eyes came back from that reach and met his own a moment. "Are you very sure the 'ghost' of one doesn't, much rather, serve—?"

He had a positive sense of turning pale. But it was as near as they were then to come. For he made answer, he believed, between a glare and a grin: "Oh ghosts—of course the place must swarm with them! I should be ashamed of it if it didn't. Poor Mrs. Muldoon's right, and it's why I haven't asked her to do more than look in."

Miss Staverton's gaze again lost itself, and things she didn't utter, it was clear, came and went in her mind. She might even for the minute, off there in the fine room, have imagined some element dimly gathering. Simplified like the death mask of a handsome face, it perhaps produced for her just then an effect akin to the stir of an expression in the "set" commemorative plaster. Yet whatever her impression may have been she produced instead a vague platitude. "Well, if it were only furnished and lived in—!"

She appeared to imply that in case of its being still furnished he might have been a little less opposed to the idea of a return. But she passed straight into the vestibule, as if to leave her words behind her, and the next moment he had opened the house door and was standing with her on the steps. He closed the door and, while he repocketed his key, looking up and down, they took in the comparatively harsh actuality of the avenue, which reminded him of the assault of the outer light of the desert on the traveler emerging from an Egyptian tomb. But he risked before they stepped into the street his gathered answer to her speech. "For me it *is* lived in. For me it *is* furnished." At which it was easy for her to sigh "Ah yes—!" all vaguely and discreetly; since his parents and his favorite sister, to say nothing of other kin, in numbers, had run their course and met their end there. That represented, within the walls, ineffaceable life.

It was a few days after this that, during an hour passed with her again, he had expressed his impatience of the too flattering curiosity—among the people he met—about his appreciation of New York. He had arrived at none at all that was socially producible, and as for that matter of his "thinking" (thinking the better or the worse of anything there) he was wholly taken up with one subject of thought. It was mere vain egoism, and it was moreover, if she liked, a morbid obsession. He found all things come back to the question of what he personally might have been, how he might have led his life and "turned out," if he had not so, at the outset, given it up. And confessing for the first time to the intensity within him of this absurd speculation—which but proved also, no doubt, the habit of too selfishly thinking—he affirmed the impotence there of any other source of interest, any other native appeal. "What would it have made of me, what would it have made of me? I keep forever wondering, all idiotically; as if I could possibly know! I see what it has made of dozens of others, those I meet, and it positively aches within me, to the point of exasperation, that it would have made something of me as well. Only I can't make out *what*, and the worry of it, the small rage of curiosity never to be satisfied, brings back what I remember to have felt, once or twice, after judging best, for reasons, to burn some important letter unopened. I've been sorry, I've hated it—I've never known what was in the letter. You may of course say it's a trifle—!"

"I don't say it's a trifle," Miss Staverton gravely interrupted.

She was seated by her fire, and before her, on his feet and restless, he turned to and fro between this intensity of his idea and a fitful and unseeing inspection, through his single eyeglass, of the dear little old objects on her chimney-piece. Her interruption made him for an instant look at her harder. "I shouldn't care if you did!" he laughed, however; "and it's only a figure, at any rate, for the way I now feel. *Not* to have followed my perverse young course—and almost in the teeth of my father's curse, as I may say; not to have kept it up, so, 'over there,' from that day to this, without a doubt or a pang; not, above all, to have liked it, to have loved it, so much, loved it, no doubt, with such an abysmal conceit of my own preference: some variation from *that*, I say, must have produced some different effect for my life and for my 'form.' I should have stuck here—if it had been possible; and I was too young, at twenty-three, to judge, *pour deux sous*, whether it *were* possible. If I had waited I might have seen it was, and then I might have been, by staying here, something nearer to one of these types who have been hammered so hard and made so keen by their conditions. It isn't that I admire them so much—the question of any charm in them, or of any charm, beyond that of the rank money passion, exerted by their conditions *for* them, has nothing to do with the matter: it's only a question of what fantastic, yet perfectly possible, development of my own nature I mayn't have missed. It comes over me that I had then a strange *alter ego* deep down somewhere within me, as the full-blown flower is in the small tight bud, and that I just took the course, I just transferred him to the climate, that blighted him for once and forever."

"And you wonder about the flower," Miss Staverton said. "So do I, if you want to know; and so I've been wondering these several weeks. I believe in the flower," she continued, "I felt it would have been quite splendid, quite huge and monstrous."

"Monstrous above all!" her visitor echoed; "and I imagine, by the same stroke, quite hideous and offensive."

"You don't believe that," she returned; "if you did you wouldn't wonder. You'd know, and that would be enough for you. What you feel—and what I feel *for* you—is that you'd have had power."

"You'd have liked me that way?" he asked.

She barely hung fire. "How should I not have liked you?"

"I see. You'd have liked me, have preferred me, a billionare!"

"How should I not have liked you?" she simply again asked.

He stood before her still—her question kept him motionless. He took it in, so much there was of it; and indeed his not otherwise meeting it testified to that. "I know at least what I am," he simply went on; "the other side of the medal's clear enough. I've not been edifying—I believe I'm thought in a hundred quarters to have been barely decent. I've followed strange paths and worshipped strange gods; it must have come to you again and again—in fact you've admitted to me as much—that I was leading, at any time these thirty years, a selfish frivolous scandalous life. And you see what it has made of me."

She just waited, smiling at him. "You see what it has made of *me*."

"Oh you're a person whom nothing can have altered. You were born to be what you are, anywhere, anyway: you've the perfection nothing else could have blighted. And don't you see how, without my exile, I shouldn't have been waiting till now—?" But he pulled up for the strange pang.

"The great thing to see," she presently said, "seems to me to be that it has spoiled nothing. It hasn't spoiled your being here at last. It hasn't spoiled this. It hasn't spoiled your speaking—" She also however faltered.

He wondered at everything her controlled emotion might mean. "Do you believe then—too dreadfully!—that I *am* as good as I might ever have been?"

"Oh no! Far from it!" With which she got up from her chair and was nearer to him. "But I don't care," she smiled.

"You mean I'm good enough?"

She considered a little. "Will you believe it if I say so? I mean will you let that settle your question for you?" And then as if making out in his face that he drew back from this, that he had some idea which, however absurd, he couldn't yet bargain away: "Oh you don't care either—but very differently: you don't care for anything but yourself."

Spencer Brydon recognized it—it was in fact what he had absolutely professed. Yet he importantly qualified. "*He* isn't myself. He's the just so totally other person. But I do want to see him," he added. "And I can. And I shall."

Their eyes met for a minute while he guessed from something in hers that she divined his strange sense. But neither of them otherwise expressed it, and her apparent understanding, with no protesting shock, no easy derision, touched him more deeply than anything yet, constituting for his stifled perversity, on the spot, an element that was like breathable air. What she said however was unexpected. "Well, *I've* seen him."

"You—?"

"I've see him in a dream."

"Oh a 'dream'—!" It let him down.

"But twice over," she continued. "I saw him as I see you now."

"You've dreamed the same dream—?"

"Twice over," she repeated. "The very same."

This did somehow a little speak to him, as it also gratified him. "You dream about me at that rate?"

"Ah about *him*!" she smiled.

His eyes again sounded her. "Then you know all about him."

And as she said nothing more: "What's the wretch like?"

She hestitated, and it was as if he were pressing her so hard that, resisting for reasons of her own, she had to turn away. "I'll tell you some other time!"

II

It was after this that there was most of a virtue for him, most of a cultivated charm, most of a preposterous secret thrill, in the particular form of surrender to his obsession and of address to what he more and more believed to be his privilege. It was what in these weeks he was living for—since he really felt life to begin but after Mrs. Muldoon had retired from the scene and, visiting the ample house from attic to cellar, making sure he was alone, he knew himself in safe possession and, as he tacitly expressed it, let himself go. He sometimes came twice in the twenty-four hours; the moments he liked best were those of gathering dusk, of the short autumn twilight; this was the time of which, again and again, he found himself hoping most. Then he could, as seemed to him, most intimately wander and wait, linger and listen, feel his fine attention, never in his life before so fine, on the pulse of the great vague place: he preferred the lampless hour and only wished he might have prolonged each day the deep crepuscular spell. Later—rarely much before midnight, but then for a considerable vigil—he watched with his glimmering light; moving slowly, holding it high, playing it far, rejoicing above all, as much as he might, in open vistas, reaches of communication between rooms and by passages; the long straight chance or show, as he would have called it, for the revelation he pretended to invite. It was a practice he found he could perfectly "work" without exciting remark; no one was in the least the wiser for it; even Alice Staverton, who was moreover a well of discretion, didn't quite fully imagine.

He let himself in and let himself out with the assurance of calm proprietorship; and accident so far favored him that, if a fat avenue "officer" had happened on occasion to see him entering at eleven-thirty, he had never yet, to the best of his belief, been noticed as emerging at two. He walked there on the crisp November nights, arrived regularly at the evening's end; it was as easy to do this after dining out as to take his way to a club or to his hotel. When he left his club, if he hadn't been dining out, it was ostensibly to go to his hotel; and when he left his hotel, if he had spent a part of the evening there, it was ostensibly to go to his club. Everything was easy in fine; everything conspired and promoted: there was truly even in the strain of his experience something that glossed over, something that salved and simplified, all the rest of consciousness. He circulated, talked, renewed, loosely and pleasantly, old relations—met indeed, so far as he could, new expectations and seemed to make out on the whole that in spite of the career, of such different contacts, which he had spoken of to Miss Staverton as ministering so little, for those who might have watched it, to edification, he was positively rather liked than not. He was a dim secondary social success—and all with people who had truly not an idea of him. It was all mere surface sound, this murmur of their welcome, this popping of their corks—just as his gestures of response were the extravagant shadows, emphatic in proportion as they meant little, of some game of *ombres chinoises*. He projected himself all day, in thought, straight over the bristling line of hard unconscious heads and into the other, the real, the waiting life; the life that, as soon as he had heard behind him the click of his great house door, began for him, on the jolly corner, as beguilingly as the slow opening bars of some rich music follows the tap of the conductor's wand.

He always caught the first effect of the steel point of his stick on the old marble of the hall pavement, large black-and-white squares that he remembered as the admiration of his childhood and that had then made in him, as he now saw, for the growth of an early conception of style. This effect was the dim reverberating tinkle as of some far-off bell hung who should say where?—in the depths of the house, of the past, of that mystical other world that might have flourished for him had he not, for weal or woe, abandoned it. On this impression he did ever the same thing; he put his stick noiselessly away in a corner—feeling the place once more in the likeness of some great glass bowl, all precious concave crystal, set delicately humming by the play of a moist finger round its edge. The concave crystal held, as it were, this mystical other world, and the indescribably fine murmur of its rim was the sigh there, the scarce audible pathetic wail to his strained ear, of all the old baffled forsworn possibilities. What he did therefore by this appeal of his hushed presence was to wake them into such measure of ghostly life as they might still enjoy. They were shy, all but unappeasably shy, but they weren't really sinister; at least they weren't as he had hitherto felt them—before they had taken the Form he so yearned to make them take, the Form he at moments saw himself in the light of fairly hunting on tiptoe, the points of his evening shoes, from room to room and from story to story.

That was the essence of his vision—which was all rank folly, if one would, while he was out of the house and otherwise occupied, but which took on the last verisimilitude as soon as he was placed and posted. He knew what he meant and what he wanted; it was as clear as the figure on a check presented in demand for cash. His *alter ego* "walked"—that was the note of his image of him, while his image of his motive for his own odd pastime was the desire to waylay him and meet him. He roamed, slowly, warily, but all restlessly, he himself did—Mrs. Muldoon had been right, absolutely, with her figure of their "craping;" and the presence he watched for would roam restlessly too. But it would be as cautious and as shifty; the conviction of its probable, in fact its already quite sensible, quite audible evasion of pursuit grew for him from night to night, laying on him finally a rigor to which nothing in his life had been comparable. It had been the theory of many superficially judging persons, he knew, that he was wasting that life in a surrender to sensations, but he had tasted of no pleasure so fine as his actual tension, had been introduced to no sport that demanded at once the patience and the nerve of this stalking of a creature more subtle, yet at bay perhaps more formidable, than any beast of the forest. The terms, the comparisons, the very practices of the chase positively came again into play; there were even moments when passages of his occasional experience as a sportsman, stirred memories, from his younger time, of moor and mountain and desert, revived for him—and to the increase of his keenness—by the tremendous force of analogy. He found himself at moments—once he had

placed his single light on some mantel shelf or in some recess
—stepping back into shelter or shade, effacing himself behind a door or
in an embrasure, as he had sought of old the vantage of rock and tree;
he found himself holding his breath and living in the joy of the instant,
the supreme suspense created by big game alone.

He wasn't afraid (though putting himself the question as he
believed gentlemen on Bengal tiger shoots or in close quarters with the
great bear of the Rockies had been known to confess to having put it);
and this indeed—since here at least he might be frank!—because of the
impression, so intimate and so strange, that he himself produced as yet
a dread, produced certainly a strain, beyond the liveliest he was likely
to feel. They fell for him into categories, they fairly became familiar,
the signs, for his own perception, of the alarm his presence and his
vigilance created; though leaving him always to remark, portentously,
on his probably having formed a relation, his probably enjoying a
consciousness, unique in the experience of man. People enough, first
and last, had been in terror apparitions, but who had ever before so
turned the tables and become himself, in the apparitional world, an
incalculable terror? He might have found this sublime had he quite
dared to think of it; but he didn't too much insist, truly, on that side of
his privilege. With habit and repetition he gained to an extraordinary
degree the power to penetrate the dusk of distances and the darkness
of corners, to resolve back into their innocence the treacheries of
uncertain light, the evil-looking forms taken in the gloom by mere
shadows, by accidents of the air, by shifting effects of perspective;
putting down his dim luminary he could still wander on without it,
pass into other rooms and, only knowing it was there behind him in
case of need, see his way about, visually project for his purpose a
comparative clearness. It made him feel, this acquired faculty, like
some monstrous stealthy cat; he wondered if he would have glared at
these moments with large shining yellow eyes, and what it mightn't
verily be, for the poor hard-pressed *alter ego*, to be confronted with
such a type.

He liked however the open shutters; he opened everywhere those
Mrs. Muldoon had closed, closing them as carefully afterwards, so that
she shouldn't notice: he liked—oh this he did like, and above all in the
upper rooms!—the sense of the hard silver of the autumn stars through
the window panes, and scarcely less the flare of the street lamps below,
the white electric luster which it would have taken curtains to keep

out. This was human actual social; this was of the world he had lived in, and he was more at his ease certainly for the countenance, coldly general and impersonal, that all the while and in spite of his detachment it seemed to give him. He had support of course mostly in the rooms at the wide front and the prolonged side; it failed him considerably in the central shades and the parts at the back. But if he sometimes, on his rounds, was glad of his optical reach, so none the less often the rear of the house affected him as the very jungle of his prey. The place was there more subdivided; a large "extension" in particular, where small rooms for servants had been multiplied, abounded in nooks and corners, in closets and passages, in the ramifications especially of an ample back staircase over which he leaned, many a time, to look far down—not deterred from his gravity even while aware that he might, for a spectator, have figured some solemn simpleton playing at hide-and-seek. Outside in fact he might himself make that ironic *rapprochement;* but within the walls, and in spite of the clear windows, his consistency was proof against the cynical light of New York.

It had belonged to the idea of the exasperated consciousness of his victim to become a real test for him; since he had quite put it to himself from the first that, oh distinctly! he could "cultivate" his whole perception. He had felt it as above all open to cultivation—which indeed was but another name for his manner of spending his time. He was bringing it on, bringing it to perfection, by practice; in consequence of which it had grown so fine that he was now aware of impressions, attestations of his general postulate, that couldn't have broken upon him at once. This was the case more specifically with a phenomenon at last quite frequent for him in the upper rooms, the recognition—absolutely unmistakable, and by a turn dating from a particular hour, his resumption of his campaign after a diplomatic drop, a calculated absence of three nights—of his being definitely followed, tracked at a distance carefully taken and to the express end that he should the less confidently, less arrogantly, appear to himself merely to pursue. It worried, it finally quite broke him up, for it proved, of all the conceivable impressions, the one least suited to his book. He was kept in sight while remaining himself—as regards the essence of his position—sightless, and his only recourse then was in abrupt turns, rapid recoveries of ground. He wheeled about, retracing his steps, as if he might so catch in his face at least the stirred air of

some other quick revolution. It was indeed true that his fully dis-
localized thought of these maneuvers recalled to him Pantaloon, at
the Christmas farce, buffeted and tricked from behind by ubiquitous
Harlequin; but it left intact the influence of the conditions themselves
each time he was reexposed to them, so that in fact this association,
had he suffered it to become constant, would on a certain side have
but ministered to his intenser gravity. He had made, as I have said, to
create on the premises the baseless sense of a reprieve, his three
absences; and the result of the third was to confirm the aftereffect of
the second.

On his return, that night—the night succeeding his last
intermission—he stood in the hall and looked up the staircase with a
certainty more intimate than any he had yet known. "He's *there*, at
the top, and waiting—not, as in general, falling back for disappearance.
He's holding his ground, and it's the first time—which is a proof, isn't
it? that something has happened for him." So Brydon argued with his
hand on the banister and his foot on the lowest stair; in which position
he felt as never before the air chilled by his logic. He himself turned
cold in it, for he seemed of a sudden to know what now was involved.
"Harder pressed?—yes, he takes it in, with its thus making clear to him
that I've come, as they say, 'to stay.' He finally doesn't like and can't
bear it, in the sense, I mean, that his wrath, his menaced interest, now
balances with his dread. I've hunted him till he has 'turned': that, up
there, is what has happened—he's the fanged or the antlered animal
brought at last to bay." There came to him, as I say—but determined
by an influence beyond my notation!—the acuteness of this certainty;
under which however the next moment he had broken into a sweat
that he would as little have consented to attribute to fear as he would
have dared immediately to act upon it for enterprise. It marked
nonetheless a prodigious thrill, a thrill that represented sudden dismay,
no doubt, but also represented, and with the self-same throb, the
strangest, the most joyous, possibly the next minute almost the
proudest, duplication of consciousness.

"He has been dodging, retreating, hiding, but now, worked up to
anger, he'll fight"—this intense impression made a single mouthful, as
it were, of terror and applause. But what was wondrous was that the
applause, for the felt fact, was so eager, since, if it was his other self he
was running to earth, this ineffable identity was thus in the last resort
not unworthy of him. It bristled there—somewhere near at hand,

however unseen still—as the hunted thing, even as the trodden worm of the adage *must* at last bristle; and Brydon at this instant tasted probably of a sensation more complex than had ever before found itself consistent with sanity. It was as if it would have shamed him that a character so associated with his own should triumphantly succeed in just skulking, should to the end not risk the open, so that the drop of this danger was, on the spot, a great lift of the whole situation. Yet with another rare shift of the same subtlety he was already trying to measure by how much more he himself might now be in peril of fear; so rejoicing that he could, in another form, actively inspire that fear, and simultaneously quaking for the form in which he might passively know it.

The apprehension of knowing it must after a little have grown in him, and the strangest moment of his adventure perhaps, the most memorable or really most interesting, afterwards, of his crisis, was the lapse of certain instants of concentrated conscious *combat*, the sense of a need to hold on to something, even after the manner of a man slipping and slipping on some awful incline; the vivid impulse, above all, to move, to act, to charge, somehow and upon something—to show himself, in a word, that he wasn't afraid. The state of "holding on" was thus the state to which he was momentarily reduced; if there had been anything, in the great vacancy, to seize, he would presently have been aware of having clutched it as he might under a shock at home have clutched the nearest chair back. He had been surprised at any rate—of this he *was* aware—into something unprecedented since his original appropriation of the place; he had closed his eyes, held them tight, for a long minute, as with that instinct of dismay and that terror of vision. When he opened them the room, the other contiguous rooms, extraordinarily, seemed lighter—so light, almost, that at first he took the change for day. He stood firm, however that might be, just where he had paused; his resistance had helped him—it was as if there were something he had tided over. He knew after a little what this was—it had been in the imminent danger of flight. He had stiffened his will against going; without this he would have made for the stairs, and it seemed to him that, still with his eyes closed, he would have descended them, would have known how, straight and swiftly, to the bottom.

Well, as he had held out, here he was—still at the top, among the more intricate upper rooms and with the gauntlet of the others, of all the rest of the house, still to run when it should be his time to go. He would go at his time—only at his time: didn't he go every night very much at the same hour? He took out his watch—there was light for that: it was scarcely a quarter past one, and he had never withdrawn so soon. He reached his lodgings for the most part at two—with his walk of a quarter of an hour. He would wait for the last quarter—he wouldn't stir till then; and he kept his watch there with his eyes on it, reflecting while he held it that this deliberate wait, a wait with an effort, which he recognized, would serve perfectly for the attestation he desired to make. It would prove his courage—unless indeed the latter might most be proved by his budging at last from his place. What he mainly felt now was that, since he hadn't scuttled, he had his dignities—which had never in his life seemed so many—all to preserve and to carry aloft. This was before him in truth as a physical image, an image almost worthy of an age of greater romance. That remark indeed glimmered for him only to glow the next instant with a finer light; since what age of romance, after all, could have matched either the state of his mind or, "objectively," as they said, the wonder of his situation? The only difference would have been that, brandishing his dignities over his head as in a parchment scroll, he might then—that is in the heroic time—have proceeded downstairs with a drawn sword in his other grasp.

At present, really, the light he had set down on the mantel of the next room would have to figure his sword; which utensil, in the course of a minute, he had taken the requisite number of steps to possess himself of. The door between the rooms was open, and from the second another door opened to a third. These rooms, as he remembered, gave all three upon a common corridor as well, but there was a fourth, beyond them, without issue save through the preceding. To have moved, to have heard his step again, was appreciably a help; though even in recognizing this he lingered once more a little by the chimney-piece on which his light had rested. When he next moved, just hesitating where to turn, he found himself considering a circumstance that, after his first and comparatively vague apprehension of it, produced in him the start that often attends some pang of recollection, the violent shock of having ceased happily to forget. He had come into sight of the door in which the brief chain of communication ended and which he now surveyed from the nearer threshold, the one not directly facing it. Placed at some distance to the left of this point, it would have admitted him to the last room of the four, the room without other approach or egress, had it not, to his intimate conviction, been closed *since* his former visitation, the matter probably of a quarter of an hour before. He stared with all his eyes at the wonder of the fact, arrested again where he stood and again holding his breath while he sounded its sense. Surely it had been *subsequently* closed—that is it had been on his previous passage indubitably open!

He took it full in the face that something had happened between—that he couldn't not have noticed before (by which he meant on his original tour of all the rooms that evening) that such a barrier had exceptionally presented itself. He had indeed since that moment undergone an agitation so extraordinary that it might have muddled for him any earlier view; and he tried to convince himself that he might perhaps then have gone into the room and, inadvertently, automatically, on coming out, have drawn the door after him. The difficulty was that this exactly was what he never did; it was against his whole policy, as he might have said, the essence of which was to keep vistas clear. He had them from the first, as he was well aware, quite on the brain: the strange apparition, at the far end of one of them, of his baffled "prey" (which had become by so sharp an irony so little the term now to apply!) was the form of success his imagination had most cherished, projecting into it always a refinement of beauty. He had known fifty times the start of perception that had afterwards dropped; had fifty times gasped to himself "There!" under some fond brief hallucination. The house, as the case stood, admirably lent itself; he might wonder at the taste, the native architecture of the particular time, which could rejoice so in the multiplication of doors—the opposite extreme to the modern, the actual almost complete proscription of them; but it had fairly contributed to provoke this obsession of the presence encountered telescopically, as he might say, focused and studied in diminishing perspective and as by a rest for the elbow.

It was with these considerations that his present attention was charged—they perfectly availed to make what he saw portentous. He *couldn't*, by any lapse, have blocked that aperture; and if he hadn't, if it was unthinkable, why what else was clear but that there had been another agent? Another agent?—he had been catching, as he felt, a moment back, the very breath of him; but when had he been so close as in this simple, this logical, this completely personal act? It was so logical, that is, that one might have *taken* it for personal; yet for what did Brydon take it, he asked himself, while, softly panting, he felt his eyes almost leave their sockets. Ah this time at last they *were*, the two, the opposed projections of him, in presence; and this time, as much as one would, the question of danger loomed. With it rose, as not before, the question of courage—for what he knew the blank face of the door to say to him was "Show us how much you have!" It stared, it glared back at him with that challenge; it put to him the two alternatives: should he just push it open or not? Oh to have this consciousness was to *think*—and to think, Brydon knew, as he stood there, was, with the lapsing moments, not to have acted! Not to have acted—that was the misery and the pang—was even still not to act; was in fact *all* to feel the thing in another, in a new and terrible way. How long did he pause and how long did he debate? There was presently nothing to measure it; for his vibration had already changed—as just by the effect of its intensity. Shut up there, at bay, defiant, and with the prodigy of the thing palpably provably *done*, thus giving notice like some stark signboard—under that accession of accent the situation itself had turned; and Brydon at last remarkably made up his mind on what it had turned to.

It had turned altogether to a different admonition; to a supreme hint, for him, of the value of discretion! This slowly dawned, no doubt—for it could take its time; so perfectly, on his threshold, had he been stayed, so little as yet had he either advanced or retreated. It was the stangest of all things that now when, by his taking ten steps and applying his hand to the latch, or even his shoulder and his knee, if necessary, to a panel, all the hunger of his prime need might have been met, his high curiosity crowned, his unrest assuaged—it was amazing, but it was also exquisite and rare, that insistence should have, at a touch, quite dropped from him. Discretion—he jumped at that; and yet not, verily, at such a pitch, because it saved his nerves or his skin, but because, much more valuably, it saved the situation. When I say he "jumped" at it I feel the consonance of this term with the fact that—at the end indeed of I know not how long—he did move again, he crossed straight to the door. He wouldn't touch it—it seemed now that he might *if* he would: he would only just wait there a little, to show, to prove, that he wouldn't. He had thus another station, close to the thin partition by which revelation was denied him; but with his eyes bent and his hands held off in a mere intensity of stillness. He listened as if there had been something to hear, but this attitude, while it lasted, was his own communication. "If you won't then—good: I spare you and I give up. You affect me as by the appeal positively for pity: you convince me that for reasons rigid and sublime—what do I know?—we both of us should have suffered. I respect them then, and, though moved and privileged as, I believe, it has never been given to man, I retire, I renounce—never, on my honor, to try again. So rest forever—and let *me*!"

That, for Brydon was the deep sense of this last demonstration—solemn, measured, directed, as he felt it to be. He brought it to a close, he turned away; and now verily he knew how deeply he had been stirred. He retraced his steps, taking up his candle, burnt, he observed, well-nigh to the socket, and marking again, lighten it as he would, the distinctness of his footfall; after which, in a moment, he knew himself at the other side of the house. He did here what he had not yet done at these hours—he opened half a casement, one of those in the front, and let in the air of the night; a thing he would have taken at any time previous for a sharp rupture of his spell. His spell was broken now, and it didn't matter—broken by his concession and his surrender, which made it idle henceforth that he should ever come back. The empty street—its other life so marked even by the great lamplit vacancy—was within call, within touch; he stayed there as to be in it again, high above it though he was still perched; he watched as for some comforting common fact, some vulgar human note, the passage of a scavenger or a thief, some nightbird however base. He would have blessed that sign of life; he would have welcomed positively the slow approach of his friend the policeman, whom he had hitherto only sought to avoid, and was not sure that if the patrol had come into sight he mightn't have felt the impulse to get into relation with it, to hail it, on some pretext, from his fourth floor.

The pretext that wouldn't have been too silly or too compromising, the explanation that would have saved his dignity and kept his name, in such a case, out of the papers, was not definite to him: he was so occupied with the thought of recording his discretion—as an effect of the vow he had just uttered to his intimate adversary—that the importance of this loomed large and something had overtaken all ironically his sense of proportion. If there had been a ladder applied to the front of the house, even one of the vertiginous perpendiculars employed by painters and roofers and sometimes left standing overnight, he would have managed somehow, astride of the windowsill, to compass by outstretched leg and arm that mode of descent. If there had been some such uncanny thing as he had found in his room at hotels, a workable fire-escape in the form of notched cable or a canvas shoot, he would have availed himself of it as a proof—well, of his present delicacy. He nursed that sentiment, as the question stood, a little in vain, and even—at the end of he scarcely knew, once more, how long—found it, as by the action on his mind of the failure of response of the outer world, sinking back to vague anguish. It seemed to him he had waited an age for some stir of the great grim hush; the life of the town was itself under a spell—so unnaturally, up and down the whole prospect of known and rather ugly objects, the blankness and the silence lasted. Had they ever, he asked himself, the hard-faced houses, which had begun to look livid in the dim dawn, had they ever spoken so little to any need of his spirit? Great builded voids, great crowded stillnesses put on, often, in the heart of cities, for the small hours, a sort of sinister mask, and it was of this large collective negation that Brydon presently became conscious—all the more that the break of day was, almost incredibly, now at hand, proving to him what a night he had made of it.

He looked again at his watch, saw what had become of his time values (he had taken hours for minutes—not, as in other tense situations, minutes for hours) and the strange air of the streets was but the weak, the sullen flush of a dawn in which everything was still locked up. His choked appeal from his own open window had been the sole note of life, and he could but break off at last as for a worse despair. Yet while so deeply demoralized he was capable again of an impulse denoting—at least by his present measure—extraordinary resolution; of retracing his steps to the spot where he had turned cold with the extinction of his last pulse of doubt as to there being in the place another presence than his own. This required an effort strong enough to sicken him; but he had his reason, which overmastered for the moment everything else. There was the whole of the rest of the house to traverse, and how should he screw himself to that if the door he had seen closed were at present open? He could hold to the idea that the closing had practically been for him an act of mercy, a chance offered him to descend, depart, get off the ground and never again profane it. This conception held together, it worked; but what it meant for him depended now clearly on the amount of forbearance his recent action, or rather his recent inaction, had engendered. The image of the "presence," whatever it was, waiting there for him to go—this image had not yet been so concrete for his nerves as when he stopped short of the point at which certainty would have come to him. For, with all his resolution, or more exactly with all his dread, he did stop short—he hung back from really seeing. The risk was too great and his fear too definite: it took at this moment an awful specific form.

He knew—yes, as he had never known anything—that, *should* he see the door open, it would all too abjectly be the end of him. It would mean that the agent of his shame—for his shame was the deep abjection—was once more at large and in general possession; and what glared him thus in the face was the act that this would determine for him. It would send him straight about to the window he had left open, and by that window, be long ladder and dangling rope as absent as they would, he saw himself uncontrollably insanely fatally take his way to the street. The hideous chance of this he at least could avert; but he could only avert it by recoiling in time from assurance. He had the whole house to deal with, this fact was still there; only he now knew that uncertainty alone could start him. He stole back from where he had checked himself—merely to do so was suddenly like safety—and, making blindly for the greater staircase, left gaping rooms and sounding passages behind. Here was the top of the stairs, with a fine large dim descent and three spacious landings to mark off. His instinct was all for mildness, but his feet were harsh on the floors, and strangely, when he had in a couple of minutes become aware of this, it counted somehow for help. He couldn't have spoken, the tone of his voice would have scared him, and the common conceit or resource of "whistling in the dark" (whether literally or figuratively) have appeared basely vulgar; yet he liked nonetheless to hear himself go, and when he had reached his first landing—taking it all with no rush, but quite steadily—that stage of success drew from him a gasp of relief.

The house, withal, seemed immense, the scale of space again inordinate; the open rooms, to no one of which his eyes deflected, gloomed in their shuttered state like mouths of caverns; only the high skylight that formed the crown in the deep well created for him a medium in which he could advance, but which might have been, for queerness of color, some watery underworld. He tried to think of something noble, as that his property was really grand, a splendid possession; but this nobleness took the form too of the clear delight with which he was finally to sacrifice it. They might come in now, the builders, the destroyers—they might come as soon as they would. At the end of two flights he had dropped to another zone, and from the middle of the third, with only one more left, he recognized the influence of the lower windows, of half-drawn blinds, of the occasional gleam of street lamps, of the glazed spaces of the vestibule. This was the bottom of the sea, which showed an illumination of its own and which he even saw paved—when at a given moment he drew up to sink a long look over the banisters—with the marble squares of his childhood. By that time indubitably he felt, as he might have said in a commoner cause, better; it had allowed him to stop and draw breath, and the ease increased with the sight of the old black-and-white slabs. But what he most felt was that now surely, with the element of impunity pulling him as by hard firm hands, the case was settled for what he might have seen above had he dared that last look. The closed door, blessedly remote now, was still closed—and he had only in short to reach that of the house.

He came down further, he crossed the passage forming the access to the last flight; and if here again he stopped an instant it was almost for the sharpness of the thrill of assured escape. It made him shut his eyes—which opened again to the straight slope of the remainder of the stairs. Here was impunity still, but impunity almost excessive; inasmuch as the side lights and the high fan tracery of the entrance were glimmering straight into the hall; an appearance produced, he the next instant saw, by the fact that the vestibule gaped wide, that the hinged halves of the inner door had been thrown far back. Out of that again the *question* sprang at him, making his eyes, as he felt, half-start from his head, as they had done, at the top of the house, before the sign of the other door. If he had left that one open, hadn't he left this one closed, and wasn't he now in *most* immediate presence of some inconceivable occult activity? It was as sharp, the question, as a knife in his side, but the answer hung fire still and seemed to lose itself in the vague darkness to which the thin admitted dawn, glimmering archwise over the whole outer door, made a semicircular margin, a cold silvery nimbus that seemed to play a little as he looked—to shift and expand and contract.

It was as if there had been something within it, protected by indistinctness and corresponding in extent with the opaque surface behind, the painted panels of the last barrier to his escape, of which the key was in his pocket. The indistinctness mocked him even while he stared, affected him as somehow shrouding or challenging certitude, so that after faltering an instant on his step he let himself go with the sense that here *was* at last something to meet, to touch, to take, to know—something all unnatural and dreadful, but to advance upon which was the condition for him either of liberation or of supreme defeat. The penumbra, dense and dark, was the virtual screen of a figure which stood in it as still as some image erect in a niche or as some black-vizored sentinel guarding a treasure. Brydon was to know afterwards, was to recall and make out, the particular thing he had believed during the rest of his descent. He saw, in its great gray glimmering margin, the central vagueness diminish, and he felt it to be taking the very form toward which, for so many days, the passion of his curiosity had yearned. It gloomed, it loomed, it was something, it was somebody, the prodigy of a personal presence.

Rigid and conscious, spectral yet human, a man of his own substance and stature waited there to measure himself with his power to dismay. This only could it be—this only till he recognized, with his advance, that what made the face dim was the pair of raised hands that covered it and in which, so far from being offered in defiance, it was buried as for dark deprecation. So Brydon, before him, took him in; with every fact of him now, in the higher light, hard and acute—his planted stillness, his vivid truth, his grizzled bent head and white masking hands, his queer actuality of evening dress, of dangling double eyeglass, of gleaming silk lappet and white linen, of pearl button and gold watch guard and polished shoe. No portrait by a great modern master could have presented him with more intensity, thrust him out of his frame with more art, as if there had been "treatment," of the consummate sort, in his every shade and salience. The revulsion, for our friend, had become, before he knew it, immense—this drop, in the act of apprehension, to the sense of his adversary's inscrutable maneuver. That meaning at least, while he gaped, it offered him; for he could but gape at his other self in this other anguish, gape as a proof that *he*, standing there for the achieved, the enjoyed, the triumphant life, couldn't be faced in his triumph. Wasn't the proof in the splendid covering hands, strong and completely spread?—so spread and so intentional that, in spite of a special verity that surpassed every other, the fact that one of these hands had lost two fingers, which were reduced to stumps, as if accidentally shot away, the face was effectually guarded and saved.

"Saved," though, *would* it be?—Brydon breathed his wonder till the
very impunity of his attitude and the very insistence of his eyes
produced, as he felt, a sudden stir which showed the next instant as a
deeper portent, which the head raised itself, the betrayal of a braver
purpose. The hands, as he looked, began to move, to open; then, as if
deciding in a flash, dropped from the face and left it uncovered and
presented. Horror, with the sight, had leaped into Brydon's throat,
gasping there in a sound he couldn't utter; for the bared identity was
too hideous as *his*, and his glare was the passion of his protest. The
face, *that* face, Spencer Brydon's?—he searched it still, but looking
away from it in dismay and denial, falling straight from his height of
sublimity. It was unknown, inconceivable, awful, disconnected from
any possibility—! He had been "sold," he inwardly moaned, stalking
such game as this: the presence before him was a presence, the horror
within him a horror, but the waste of his nights had been only grotesque and the success of his adventure an irony. Such an identity fitted
his at *no* point, made its alternative monstrous. A thousand times yes,
as it came upon him nearer now—the face was the face of a stranger. It
came upon him nearer now, quite as one of those expanding fantastic
images projected by the magic lantern of childhood; for the stranger,
whoever he might be, evil, odious, blatant, vulgar, had advanced as for
aggression, and he knew himself give ground. Then harder pressed still,
sick with the force of his shock, and falling back as under the hot
breath and the roused passion of a life larger than his own, a rage of
personality before which his own collapsed, he felt the whole vision
turn to darkness and his very feet give way. His head went round; he
was going; he had gone.

III

What had next brought him back, clearly—though after how
long?—was Mrs. Muldoon's voice, coming to him from quite near,
from so near that he seemed presently to see her as kneeling on the
ground before him while he lay looking up at her; himself not wholly
on the ground, but half-raised and upheld—conscious, yes, of tenderness of support and, more particularly, of a head pillowed in extraordinary softness and faintly refreshing fragrance. He considered, he
wondered, his wit but half at his service; then another face intervened,

bending more directly over him, and he finally knew that Alice Staverton had made her lap an ample and perfect cushion to him, and that she had to this end seated herself on the lowest degree of the staircase, the rest of his long person remaining stretched on his old black-and-white slabs. They were cold, these marble squares of his youth; but *he* somehow was not, in this rich return of consciousness—the most wonderful hour, little by little, that he had ever known, leaving him, as it did, so gratefully, so abysmally passive, and yet as with a treasure of intelligence waiting all round him for quiet appropriation; dissolved, he might call it, in the air of the place and producing the golden glow of a late autumn afternoon. He had come back, yes—come back from further away than any man but himself had ever traveled; but it was strange how with this sense what he had come back *to* seemed really the great thing, and as if his prodigious journey had been all for the sake of it. Slowly but surely his consciousness grew, his vision of his state thus completing itself: he had been miraculously *carried* back—lifted and carefully borne as from where he had been picked up, the uttermost end of an interminable gray passage. Even with this he was suffered to rest, and what had now brought him to knowledge was the break in the long mild motion.

It had brought him to knowledge, to knowledge—yes, this was the beauty of his state; which came to resemble more and more that of a man who has gone to sleep on some news of a great inheritance, and then, after dreaming it away, after profaning it with matters strange to it, has waked up again to serenity of certitude and has only to lie and watch it grow. This was the drift of his patience—that he had only to let it shine on him. He must moreover, with intermissions, still have been lifted and borne; since why and how else should he have known himself, later on, with the afternoon glow intenser, no longer at the foot of his stairs—situated as these now seemed at that dark other end of his tunnel—but on a deep windowbench of his high saloon, over which had been spread, couch fashion, a mantle of soft stuff lined with gray fur that was familiar to his eyes and that one of his hands kept fondly feeling as for its pledge of truth. Mrs. Muldoon's face had gone, but the other, the second he had recognized, hung over him in a way that showed how he was still propped and pillowed. He took it all in, and the more he took it the more it seemed to suffice: he was as much at peace as if he had had food and drink. It was the two women who had found him, on Mrs. Muldoon's having plied, at her usual hour, her latchkey—and on her having above all arrived while Miss Staverton still lingered near the house. She had been turning away, all anxiety, from worrying the vain bell-handle—her calculation having been of the hour of the good woman's visit; but the latter, blessedly, had come up while she was still there, and they had entered together. He had then lain, beyond the vestibule, very much as he was lying now—quite, that is, as he appeared to have fallen, but all so wondrously without bruise or gash; only in a depth of stupor. What he most took in, however, at present, with the steadier clearance, was that Alice Staverton had for a long unspeakable moment not doubted he was dead.

"It must have been that I *was*." He made it out as she held him. "Yes—I can only have died. You brought me literally to life. Only," he wondered, his eyes rising to her, "only, in the name of all the benedictions, how?"

It took her but an instant to bend her face and kiss him, and something in the manner of it, and in the way her hands clasped and locked his head while he felt the cool charity and virtue of her lips, something in all this beatitude somehow answered everything. "And now I keep you," she said.

"Oh keep me, keep me!" he pleaded while her face still hung over him: in response to which it dropped again and stayed close, clingingly close. It was the seal of their situation—of which he tasted the impress for a long blissful moment in silence. But he came back. "Yet how did you know—?"

"I was uneasy. You were to have come, you remember—and you had sent no word."

"Yes, I remember—I was to have gone to you at one today." It caught on to their "old" life and relation—which were so near and so far. "I was still out there in my strange darkness—where was it, what was it? I must have stayed there so long." He could but wonder at the depth and the duration of his swoon.

"Since last night?" she asked with a shade of fear for her possible indiscretion.

"Since this morning—it must have been; the cold dim dawn of today. Where have I been," he vaguley wailed, "where have I been?" He felt her hold him close, and it was if this helped him now to make in all security his mild moan. "What a long dark day!"

All in her tenderness she had waited a moment. "In the cold dim dawn?" she quavered.

But he had already gone on piecing together the parts of the whole prodigy. "As I didn't turn up you came straight—?"

She barely cast about. "I went first to your hotel—where they told me of your absence. You had dined out last evening and hadn't been back since. But they appeared to know you had been at your club."

"So you had the idea of *this*—?"

"Of what?" she asked in a moment.

"Well—of what has happened."

"I believed at least you'd have been here. I've known, all along," she said, "that you've been coming."

" 'Known' it—?"

"Well, I've believed it. I said nothing to you after that talk we had a month ago—but I felt sure. I knew you *would*," she declared.

"That I'd persist, you mean?"

"That you'd see him."

"Ah but I didn't!" cried Brydon with his long wail. "There's somebody—an awful beast; whom I brought, too horribly, to bay. But it's not me."

At this she bent over him again, and her eyes were in his eyes. "No—it's not you." And it was as if, while her face hovered, he might have made out in it, hadn't it been so near, some particular meaning blurred by a smile. "No, thank heaven," she repeated—"it's not you! Of course it wasn't to have been."

"Ah but it *was*," he gently insisted. And he stared before him now as he had been staring for so many weeks. "I was to have known myself."

"You couldn't!" she returned consolingly. And then reverting, and as if to account further for what she had herself done, "But it wasn't only *that*, that you hadn't been at home," she went on. "I waited till the hour at which we had found Mrs. Muldoon that day of my going with you; and she arrived, as I've told you, while, failing to bring anyone to the door, I lingered in my despair on the steps. After a little, if she hadn't come, by such a mercy, I should have found means to hunt her up. But it wasn't," said Alice Staverton, as if once more with her fine intention—"it wasn't only that."

His eyes, as he lay, turned back to her. "What more then?"

She met it, the wonder she had stirred. "In the cold dim dawn, you say? Well, in the cold dim dawn of this morning I too saw you."

"Saw *me*—?"

"Saw *him*," said Alice Staverton. "It must have been at the same moment."

He lay an instant taking it in—as if he wished to be quite reasonable. "At the same moment?"

"Yes—in my dream again, the same one I've named to you. He came back to me. Then I knew it for a sign. He had come to you."

At this Brydon raised himself; he had to see her better. She helped him when she understood his movement, and he sat up, steadying himself beside her there on the windowbench and with his right hand grasping her left. "*He* didn't come to me."

"You came to yourself," she beautifully smiled.

"Ah I've come to myself now—thanks to you, dearest. But this brute, with his awful face—this brute's a black stranger. He's none of *me*, even as I *might* have been," Brydon sturdily declared.

But she kept the clearness that was like the breath of infallibility. "Isn't the whole point that you'd have been different?"

He almost scowled for it. "As different as *that*—?"

Her look again was more beautiful to him than the things of this world. "Haven't you exactly wanted to know *how* different? So this morning," she said, "you appeared to me."

"Like *him*?"

"A black stranger!"

"Then how did you know it was I?"

"Because, as I told you weeks ago, my mind, my imagination, had worked so over what you might, what you mightn't have been—to show you, you see, how I've thought of you. In the midst of that you came to me—that my wonder might be answered. So I knew," she went on; "and believed that, since the question held you too so fast, as you told me that day, you too would see for yourself. And when this morning I again saw I knew it would be because you had—and also then, from the first moment, because you somehow wanted me. *He* seemed to tell me of that. So why," she strangely smiled, "shouldn't I like him?"

It brought Spencer Brydon to his feet. "You 'like' that horror—?"

"I *could* have liked him. And to me," she said, "he was no horror. I had accepted him."

" 'Accepted'—?" Brydon oddly sounded.

"Before, for the interest of his difference—yes. And as *I* didn't disown him, as *I* knew him—which you at last, confronted with him in his difference, so cruelly didn't, my dear—well, he must have been, you see, less dreadful to me. And it may have pleased him that I pitied him."

She was beside him on her feet, but still holding his hand—still with her arm supporting him. But though it all brought for him thus a dim light, "You 'pitied' him?" he grudgingly, resentfully asked.

"He has been unhappy; he has been ravaged," she said.

"And haven't I been unhappy? Am not I—you've only to look at me!—ravaged?"

"Ah I don't say I like him *better*," she granted after a thought. "But he's grim, he's worn—and things have happened to him. He doesn't make shift, for sight, with your charming monocle."

"No"—it struck Brydon: "I couldn't have sported mine 'downtown.' They'd have guyed me there."

"His great convex pince-nez—I saw it, I recognized the kind—is for his poor ruined sight. And his poor right hand—!"

"Ah!" Brydon winced—whether for his proved identity or for his lost fingers. Then, "He has a million a year," he lucidly added. "But he hasn't you."

"And he isn't—no, he isn't—*you!*" she murmured as he drew her to his breast.

"Man Overboard!"

WINSTON CHURCHILL

This little known short short by the man widely believed to be the greatest statesman of our century first appeared in an 1898 issue of The Harmsworth Magazine. (Churchill contributed a fair amount of short fiction to this and other popular magazines of the period, a fact about his life of which most people are unaware.) That he knew and understood the brief tale of terror is amply demonstrated in the pages which follow.

It was a little after half-past nine when the man fell overboard. The mail steamer was hurrying through the Red Sea in the hope of making up the time which the currents of the Indian Ocean had stolen. The night was clear, though the moon was hidden behind clouds. The warm air was laden with moisture. The still surface of the waters was only broken by the movement of the great ship, from whose quarter the long, slanting undulations struck out, like the feathers from an arrow shaft, and in whose wake the froth and air bubbles churned up by the propeller trailed in a narrowing line to the darkness of the horizon.

There was a concert on board. All the passengers were glad to break the monotony of the voyage, and gathered around the piano in the companion-house. The decks were deserted. The man had been listening to the music and joining in the songs. But the room was hot, and he came out to smoke a cigarette and enjoy a breath of the wind which the speedy passage of the liner created. It was the only wind in the Red Sea that night.

The accommodation-ladder had not been unshipped since leaving Aden, and the man walked out on to the platform, as on to a balcony. He leaned his back against the rail and blew a puff of smoke into the air reflectively. The piano struck up a lively turn, and a voice began to sing the first verse of "The Rowdy Dowdy Boys." The measured pulsations of the screw were a subdued but additional accompaniment. The man knew the song. It had been the rage at all the music halls, when he had started for India seven years before. It reminded him of the brilliant and busy streets he had not seen for so long, but was soon to see again. He was just going to join in the chorus, when the railng, which had been insecurely fastened, gave way suddenly with a snap, and he fell backwards into the warm water of the sea amid a great splash.

For a moment he was physically too much astonished to think. Then he realized that he must shout. He began to do this even before he rose to the surface. He achieved a hoarse, inarticulate, half-choked scream. A startled brain suggested the word "Help!" and he bawled this out lustily and with frantic effort six or seven times without stopping. Then he listened.

> Hi! hi! clear the way
> For the Rowdy Dowdy Boys.

The chorus floated back to him across the smooth water, for the ship had already passed completely by. And as he heard the music a long stab of terror drove through his heart. The possibility that he would not be picked up dawned for the first time on his consciousness. The chorus started again—

> Then—I—say—boys,
> Who's for a jolly spree?
> Rum—tum—tiddley—um,
> Who'll have a drink with me?

"Help! help! help!" shrieked the man, in desperate fear.

> Fond of a glass now and then,
> Fond of a row or noise;
> Hi! hi! clear the way
> For the Rowdy Dowdy Boys!

The last words drawled out faint and fainter. The vessel was steaming fast. The beginning of the second verse was confused and broken by the ever-growing distance. The dark outline of the great hull was getting blurred. The stern light dwindled.

Then he set out to swim after it with furious energy, pausing every dozen strokes to shout long wild shouts. The disturbed waters of the sea began to settle again to their rest. The widening undulations became ripples. The aerated confusion of the screw fizzed itself upwards and out. The noise of motion and the sounds of life and music died away.

The liner was but a single fading light on the blackness of the waters and a dark shadow against the paler sky.

At length full realization came to the man, and he stopped swimming. He was alone—abandoned. With the understanding his brain reeled. He began again to swim, only now instead of shouting he prayed—mad, incoherent prayers, the words stumbling into one another.

Suddenly a distant light seemed to flicker and brighten. A surge of joy and hope rushed through his mind. They were going to stop—to turn the ship and come back. And with the hope came gratitude. His prayer was answered. Broken words of thanksgiving rose to his lips. He stopped and stared after the light—his soul in his eyes. As he watched it, it grew gradually but steadily smaller. Then the man knew that his fate was certain. Despair succeeded hope. Gratitude gave place to curses. Beating the water with his arms, he raved impotently. Foul oaths burst from him, as broken as his prayers—and as unheeded.

The fit of passion passed, hurried by increasing fatigue. He became silent—silent as was the sea, for even the ripples were subsiding into the glassy smoothness of the surface. He swam on mechanically along the track of the ship, sobbing quietly to himself, in the misery of fear. And the stern light became a tiny speck, yellower but scarcely bigger than some of the stars, which here and there shone between the clouds.

Nearly twenty minutes passed, and the man's fatigue began to change to exhaustion. The overpowering sense of the inevitable pressed upon him. With the weariness came a strange comfort. He need not swim all the long way to Suez. There was another course. He would die. He would resign his existence since he was thus abandoned. He threw up his hands impulsively and sank. Down, down he went through the warm water. The physical death took hold of him and he began to drown. The pain of that savage grip recalled his anger. He fought with it furiously. Striking out with arms and legs he sought to get back to the air. It was a hard struggle, but he escaped victorious and gasping to the surface. Despair awaited him. Feebly splashing with his hands he moaned in bitter misery—

"I can't—I must. O God! Let me die."

The moon, then in her third quarter, pushed out from behind the concealing clouds and shed a pale, soft glitter upon the sea. Upright in the water, fifty yards away, was a black triangular object. It was a fin. It approached him slowly.

His last appeal had been heard.

The Hand

THEODORE DREISER

Between the publication of his two most famous works, Sister
Carrie *(1900) and* An American Tragedy *(1925), Theodore Dreiser was
occasionally forced by economic pressures to abandon full-time writing and take editorial jobs. (His books did not sell well because of their
controversial subject matter, more often than not relating to sexual
topics which were considered taboo in the pre-Prohibition era.) One
of these editorial positions, from 1907 to 1910, was as editor-in-chief of
Butterick Publications, a line of magazines which included the pulp,*
Adventure. *During his tenure there he further supplemented his income by writing and publishing a small number of "popular" stories.
"The Hand" is among the best of these—a powerful tale of greed and
vengeance from beyond the grave that, in theme at least, is reminis-
cent of B. Traven's* The Treasure of the Sierra Madre.

I

Davidson could distinctly remember that it was between two and
three years after the grisly event in the Monte Orte range—the sickening and yet deserved end of Mersereau, his quondam partner and
fellow adventurer—that anything to be identified with Merserau's
malice toward him, and with Mersereau's probable present existence
in the spirit world, had appeared in his life.

He and Mersereau had worked long together as prospectors, inves-
tors, developers of property. It was only after they had struck it rich in
the Klondike that Davidson had grown so much more apt and shrewd
in all commercial and financial matters, whereas Mersereau had
seemed to stand still—not to rise to the splendid opportunities which
then opened to him. Why, in some of those later deals it had not been
possible for Davidson even to introduce his old partner to some of the
moneyed men he had to deal with. Yet Mersereau had insisted, as his
right, if you please, on being "in on" everything—everything!

Take that wonderful Monte Orte property, the cause of all the
subsequent horror. He, Davidson—not Mersereau—had discovered or

heard of the mine, and had carried it along, with old Besmer as a tool or decoy—Besmer being the ostensible factor—until it was all ready for him to take over and sell or develop. Then it was that Mersereau, having been for so long his partner, demanded a full half—a third, at least—on the ground that they had once agreed to work together in all these things.

Think of it! And Mersereau growing duller and less useful and more disagreeable day by day, and year by year! Indeed, toward the last he had threatened to expose the trick by which jointly, seven years before, they had possessed themselves of the Skyute Pass mine; to drive Davidson out of public and financial life, to have him arrested and tried—along with himself, of course. Think of that!

But he had fixed him—yes, he had, damn him! He had trailed Mersereau that night to old Besmer's cabin on the Monte Orte, when Besmer was away. Mersereau had gone there with the intention of stealing the diagram of the new field, and had secured it, true enough. A thief he was, damn him. Yet, just as he was making safely away, as he thought, he, Davidson, had struck him cleanly over the ear with that heavy rail-bolt fastened to the end of a walnut stick, and the first blow and done for him.

Lord, how the bone above Mersereau's ear had sounded when it cracked! And how bloody one side of that bolt was! Mersereau hadn't had time to do anything before he was helpless. He hadn't died instantly, though, but had turned over and faced him, Davidson, with that savage, scowling face of his and those blazing animal eyes.

Lying half-propped up on his left elbow, Mersereau had reached out toward him with that big, rough, bony right hand of his—the right with which he always boasted of having done so much damage on this, that and the other occasion—had glared at him as much as to say:

"Oh, if I could only reach you just for a moment before I go!"

Then it was that he, Davidson, had lifted the club again. Horrified as he was, and yet determined that he must save his own life, he had finished the task, dragging the body back to an old fissure behind the cabin and covering it with branches, a great pile of pine fronds, and as many as one hundred and fifty boulders, great and small, and had left his victim. It was a sickening job and a sickening sight, but it had to be.

Then, having finished he slipped dismally away, like a jackal, thinking of that hand in the moonlight, held up so savagely, and that look. Nothing might have come of that either, if he hadn't been inclined to brood on it so much, on the fierceness of it.

No, nothing had happened. A year had passed, and if anything had been going to turn up it surely would have by then. He, Davidson, had gone first to New York, later to Chicago, to dispose of the Monte Orte claim. Then, after two years, he had returned here to Mississippi, where he was enjoying comparative peace. He was looking after some sugar property which had once belonged to him, and which he was now able to reclaim and put in charge of his sister as a home against a rainy day. He had no other.

But that body back there! That hand uplifted in the moonlight—to clutch him if it could! Those eyes.

II—JUNE, 1905

Take that first year, for instance, when he had returned to Gatchard in Mississippi, whence both he and Mersereau had originally issued. After looking after his own property he had gone out to a tumble-down estate of his uncle's in Issaqueena County—a leaky, old, slope-roofed house where, in a bedroom on the top floor, he had had his first experience with the significance or reality of the hand.

Yes, that was where first he had really seen it pictured in that curious, unbelievable way; only who would believe that it was Mersereau's hand? They would say it was an accident, chance, rain dropping down. But the hand had appeared on the ceiling of that room just as sure as anything, after a heavy rain storm—it was almost a cyclone—when every chink in the old roof had seemed to leak water.

During the night, after he had climbed to the room by way of those dismal stairs with their great landing and small glass oil-lamp he carried, and had sunk to rest, or tried to, in the heavy, wide, damp bed, thinking, as he always did those days, of the Monte Orte and Merse-reau, the storm had come up. As he had listened to the wind moaning outside he had heard first the scratch, scratch, scratch, of some limb, no doubt, against the wall—sounding, or so it seemed in his feverish unrest, like some one penning an indictment against him with a worn, rusty pen.

And then, the storm growing worse, and in a fit of irritation and self-contempt at his own nervousness, he had gone to the window, but just as lightning struck a branch of the tree nearest the window and so very near him, too—as though someone, something, was seeking to strike him—(Mersereau?) and as though he had been lured by that scratching. God! He had retreated, feeling that it was meant for him.

But that big, knotted hand painted on the ceiling by the dripping water during the night! There it was, right over him when he awoke, outlined or painted as if with wet, gray whitewash against the wretched but normally pale blue of the ceiling when dry. There it was—a big, open hand just like Mersereau's as he had held it up that night—huge, knotted, rough, the fingers extended as if tense and clutching. And, if you will believe it, near it was something that looked like a pen—an old, long-handled pen—to match that scratch, scratch, scratch!

"Huldah," he had inquired of the old black mammy who entered in the morning to bring him fresh water and throw open the shutters, "what does that look like to you up there—that patch on the ceiling where the rain came through?"

He wanted to reassure himself as to the character of the thing he saw—that it might not be a creation of his own feverish imagination, accentuated by the dismal character of this place.

" 'Pears t' me mo' like a big han' 'an anythin' else, Marse Davi'son," commented Huldah, pausing and staring upward. "Mo' like a big fist, kinda. Dat air's a new drip come las' night, I reckon. Dis here ole place ain' gonna hang togethah much longah, less'n some repairin' be done mighty quick now. Yassir, dat air's a new drop, sho's yo' bo'n, en it come on'y las' night. I hain't never seed dat befo'."

And then he had inquired, thinking of the fierceness of the storm:

"Huldah, do you have many such storms up this way?"

"Good gracious, Marse Davi'son, we hain't seed no sech blow en—en come three years now. I hain't seed no sech lightnin' en I doan't know when."

Wasn't that strange, that it should all come on the night, of all nights, when he was there? And no such other storm in three years!

Huldah stared idly, always ready to go slow and rest, if possible, whereas he had turned irritably. To be annoyed by ideas such as this! To always be thinking of that Monte Orte affair! Why couldn't he forget it? Wasn't it Mersereau's own fault? He never would have killed the man if he hadn't been forced to it.

And to be haunted in this way, making mountains out of mole hills, as he thought then! It must be his own miserable fancy—and yet Mersereau had looked so threateningly at him. That glance had boded something; it was too terrible not to.

Davidson might not want to think of it, but how could he stop? Mersereau might not be able to hurt him any more, at least not on this earth; but still, couldn't he? Didn't the appearance of this hand seem to indicate that he might? He was dead, of course. His body, his skeleton, was under that pile of rocks and stones, some of them as big as washtubs. Why worry over that, and after two years? And still—

That hand on the ceiling!

III—DECEMBER, 1905

Then, again, take that matter of meeting Pringle in Gatchard just at that time, within the same week. It was due to Davidson's sister. She had invited Mr. and Mrs. Pringle in to meet him one evening, without telling him that they were spiritualists and might discuss spiritualism.

Clairvoyance, Pringle called it, or seeing what can't be seen with material eyes, and clairaudience, or hearing what can't be heard with material ears, as well as materialization, or ghosts, and table-rapping, and the like. Table-rapping—that damned tap-tapping that he had been hearing ever since!

It was Pringle's fault, really. Pringle had persisted in talking. He, Davidson, wouldn't have listened, except that he somehow became fascinated by what Pringle said concerning what he had heard and seen in his time. Mersereau must have been at the bottom of that, too.

At any rate, after he had listened, he was sorry, for Pringle had had time to fill his mind full of those awful facts or ideas which had since harassed him so much—all that stuff about drunkards, degenerates and weak people generally being followed about by vile, evil spirits and used to effect those spirits' purposes or desires in this world. Horrible!

Wasn't it terrible? Pringle—big, mushy creature that he was, sickly and stagnant like a springless pool—insisted that he had even seen clouds of these spirits about drunkards, degenerates, and the like, in streetcars, on trains, and about vile corners at night. Once, he said, he had seen just one evil spirit—think of that!—following a certain man all the time, at his left elbow—a dark, evil, red-eyed thing, until finally the man had been killed in a quarrel.

Pringle described their shapes, these spirits, as varied. They were small, dark, irregular clouds, with red or green spots somewhere for eyes, changing in form and becoming longish or round like a jellyfish, or even like a misshapen cat or dog. They could take any form at will—even that of a man.

Once, Pringle declared, he had seen as many as fifty about a drunkard who was staggering down a street, all of them trying to urge him into the nearest saloon, so that they might reexperience in some vague way the sensation of drunkenness, which at some time or other they themselves, having been drunkards in life, had enjoyed!

It would be the same with a drug fiend, or indeed with any one of weak or evil habits. They gathered about such an one like flies, their red or green eyes glowing—attempting to get something from them, perhaps, if nothing more than a little sense of their old earth life.

The whole thing was so terrible and disturbing at the time, particularly that idea of men being persuaded or influenced to murder, that he, Davidson, could stand it no longer, and got up and left. But in his room upstairs he meditated on it, standing before his mirror. Suddenly—would he ever forget it—as he was taking off his collar and tie, he had heard that queer tap, tap, tap, right on his dressing table or under it, and for the first time, when, Pringle said, ghosts made when table-rapping in answer to a call, or to give warning of their presence.

Then something said to him, almost as clearly as if he heard it:

This is me, Mersereau, come back at last to get you! Pringle was just an excuse of mine to let you know I was coming, and so was that hand in that old house, in Issaqueena County. It was mine! I will be with you from now on. Don't think I will ever leave you!

It had frightened and made him half-sick, so wrought up was he. For the first time he felt cold chills run up and down his spine—the creeps. He felt as if someone were standing over him—Mersereau, of course—only he could not see or hear a thing, just that faint tap at first, growing louder a littler later, and quite angry when he tried to ignore it.

People did live, then, after they were dead, especially evil people—people stronger than you, perhaps. They had the power to come back, to haunt, to annoy you if they didn't like anything you had done to them. No doubt Mersereau was following him in the hope of revenge, there in the spirit world, just outside this one, close at his heels, like that evil spirit attending the other man whom Pringle had described.

IV—FEBRUARY, 1906

Take that case of the hand impressed on the soft dough and plaster of Paris, described in an article that he had picked up in the dentist's office out there in Pasadena—Mersereau's very hand, so far as he could judge. How about that for a coincidence, picking up the magazine with that disturbing article about psychic materialization in Italy, and later in Berne, Switzerland, where the scientists were gathered to investigate that sort of thing? And just when he was trying to rid himself finally of the notion that any such thing could be!

According to that magazine article, some old crone over in Italy—spiritualist, or witch, or something—had got together a crowd of experimentalists or professors in an abandoned house on an almost deserted island off the coast of Sardinia. There they had conducted experiments with spirits, which they called materialization, getting the impression of the fingers of a hand, or of a whole hand and arm, or of a face, on a plate of glass covered with soot, the plate being locked in a small safe on the center of a table about which they sat!

He, Davidson, couldn't understand, of course, how it was done, but done it was. There in that magazine were half a dozen pictures, reproductions of photographs of a hand, an arm, and a face—or a part of one, anyhow. And if they looked like anything, they looked exactly like Mersereau's! Hadn't Pringle, there in Gatchard, Miss., stated spirits could move anywhere, over long distances, with the speed of light. And would it be any trick for Mersereau to appear there at Sardinia, and then engineer this magazine into his presence, here in Los Angeles? Would it? It would not. Spirits were free and powerful *over there*, perhaps.

There was not the least doubt that these hands, these partial impressions of a face, were those of Mersereau. Those big knuckles! That long, heavy, humped nose and big jaw! Whose else could they be?—they were Mersereau's, intended, when they were made over there in Italy, for him, Davidson, to see later here in Los Angeles. Yes, they were! And looking at that sinister face reproduced in the magazine, it seemed to say, with Mersereau's old coarse sneer:

You see? You can't escape me! I'm showing you how much alive I am over here, just as I was on earth. And I'll get you yet, even if I have to go farther than Italy to do it!

It was amazing, the shock he took from that. It wasn't just that alone, but the persistence and repetition of this hand business. What could it mean? Was it really Mersereau's hand? As for the face, it wasn't all there—just the jaw, mouth, cheek, left temple, and a part of the nose and eye; but it was Mersereau's all right. He had gone clear over there into Italy somewhere, in a lone house on an island, to get this message of his undying hate back to him. Or was it just spirits, evil spirits, bent on annoying him because he was nervous and sensitive now?

V—OCTOBER, 1906

Even now crowded hotels and new buildings weren't the protection he had at first hoped and thought they would be. Even there you weren't safe—not from a man like Mersereau. Take that incident there in Los Angeles, and again in Seattle, only two months ago now, when Mersereau was able to make that dreadful explosive or crashing sound, as if one had burst a huge paper bag full of air, or upset a china closet full of glass and broken everything, when as a matter of fact nothing at all had happened. It had frightened him horribly the first two or three times, believing as he did that something fearful had happened. Finding that it was nothing—or Mersereau—he was becoming used to it now; but other people, unfortunately, were not.

He would be—as he had been that first time—sitting in his room perfectly still and trying to amuse himself, or not to think, when suddenly there would be that awful crash. It was astounding! Other people heard it, of course. They had in Los Angeles. A maid and a porter had come running the first time to inquire, and he had had to protest that he had heard nothing. They couldn't believe it at first, and had gone to the other rooms to look. When it happened the second time, the management had protested, thinking it was a joke he was playing; and to avoid the risk of exposure he had left.

After that he could not keep a valet or nurse about him for long. Servants wouldn't stay and managers of hotels wouldn't let him remain when such things went on. Yet he couldn't live in a house or apartment alone, for there the noises and atmospheric conditions would be worse than ever.

VI—JUNE, 1907

Take that last old house he had been in—but never would be in again!—at Anne Haven. There he actually visualized the hand—a thing as big as a washtub at first, something like smoke or shadow in a black room moving about over the bed and everywhere. Then, as he lay there, gazing at it spellbound, it condensed slowly, and he began to feel it. It was now a hand of normal size—there was no doubt of it in the world—going over him softly, without force, as a ghostly hand must, having no real physical strength, but all the time with a strange, electric, secretive something about it, as if it were not quite sure of itself, and not quite sure that he was really there.

The hand, or so it seemed—God!—moved right up to his neck and began to feel over that as he lay there. Then it was that he guessed just what it was that Mersereau was after.

It was just like a hand, the fingers and thumb made into a circle and pressed down over his throat, only it moved over him gently at first, because it really couldn't do anything yet, not having the material strength. But the intention! The sense of cruel, savage determination that went with it!

And yet, if one went to a nerve specialist or doctor about all this, as he did afterwards, what did the doctor say? He had tried to describe how he was breaking down under the strain, how he could not eat or sleep on account of all these constant tappings and noises; but the moment he even began to hint at his experiences, especially the hand or the noises, the doctor exclaimed:

"Why, this is plain delusion! You're nervously run down, that's all that ails you—on the verge of pernicious anemia, I should say. You'll have to watch yourself as to this illusion about spirits. Get it out of your mind. There's nothing to it!"

Wasn't that just like one of these nerve specialists bound up in their little ideas of what they knew or saw, or thought they saw?

VII—NOVEMBER, 1907

And now take this very latest development at Battle Creek recently where he had gone trying to recuperate on the diet there. Hadn't Mersereau, implacable demon that he was, developed this latest trick of making his food taste queer to him—unpallatable or with an odd odor?

He, Davidson, knew it was Mersereau, for he felt him beside him at the table whenever he sat down. Besides, he seemed to hear something—clairaudience was what they called it, he understood—he was beginning to develop that, too, now. It was Mersereau of course saying in a voice which was more like a memory of a voice than anything real—the voice of some one you could remember as having spoken in a certain way, say, ten years or more ago:

I've fixed it so you can't eat anymore, you—

There followed a long list of vile expletives, enough in itself to sicken one.

Thereafter, in spite of anything he could do to make himself think to the contrary, knowing that the food was all right, really, Davidson found it to have an odor or a taste which disgusted him, and which he could not overcome, try as he would. The management assured him that it was all right as he knew it was—for others. He saw them eating it. But he couldn't—had to get up and leave, and the little he could get down he couldn't retain, or it wasn't enough for him to live on. God, he would die, this way! Starve, as he surely was doing by degrees now.

And Mersereau always seeming to be standing by. Why, if it weren't for fresh fruit on the stands at times, and just plain, fresh-baked bread in bakers' windows, which he could buy and eat quickly, he might not be able to live at all. It was getting to that pass!

VIII—AUGUST, 1908

That wasn't the worst, either, bad as all that was. The worst was the fact that under the strain of all this he was slowly but surely breaking down, and that in the end Mersereau might really succeed in driving him out of life here—to do what, if anything, to him there? What? It was such an evil pack by which he was surrounded, now, those who lived just on the other side and hung about the earth, vile, debauched creatures, as Pringle had described them, and as Davidson had come to know for himself, fearing them and their ways so much, and really seeing them at times.

Since he had come to be so weak and sensitive, he could see them for himself—vile things that they were, swimming before his gaze in the dark whenever he chanced to let himself be in the dark, which was not often—friends of Mersereau, no doubt, and inclined to help him just for the evil of it.

For this long time now Davidson had taken to sleeping with the light on, wherever he was, only tying a handkerchief over his eyes to keep out some of the glare. Even then he could see them—queer, misshapen things, for all the world like wavy, stringy jellyfish or coils of thick, yellowish black smoke, moving about, changing in form at times, yet always looking dirty or vile, somehow, and with those queer, dim, reddish or greenish glows for eyes. It was sickening!

IX—October, 1908

Having accomplished so much, Mersereau would by no means be content to let him go. Davidson knew that! He could talk to him occasionally now, or at least could hear him and answer back, if he chose, when he was alone and quite certain that no one was listening.

Mersereau was always saying, when Davidson would listen to him at all—which he wouldn't often—that he would get him yet, that he would make him pay, or charging him with fraud and murder.

"*I'll choke you yet!*" The words seemed to float in from somewhere, as if he were remembering that at some time Mersereau had said that in his angry, savage tone—not as if he heard it; and yet he was hearing it, of course.

I'll choke you yet! You can't escape! You may think you'll die a natural death, but you won't and that's why I'm poisoning your food to weaken you. You can't escape! I'll get you, sick or well, when you can't help yourself, when you're sleeping. I'll choke you, just as you hit me with that club. That's why you're always seeing and feeling this hand of mine! I'm not alone. I've nearly had you many a time already, only you have managed to wriggle out so far, jumping up, but some day you won't be able to—see? Then—

The voice seemed to die away at times, even in the middle of a sentence, but at the other times—often, often—he could hear it completing the full thought. Sometimes he would turn on the thing and exclaim:

"Oh, go to the devil!" or, "Let me alone!" or, "Shut up!" Even in a closed room and all alone, such remarks seemed strange to him, addressed to a ghost; but he couldn't resist at times, annoyed as he was. Only he took good care not to talk if anyone was about.

It was getting so that there was no real place for him outside of an asylum, for often he would get up screaming at night—he had to, so sharp was the clutch on his throat—and then always, wherever he was, a servant would come in and want to know what was the matter. He would have to say that it was a nightmare—only the management always requested him to leave after the second or third time, say, or after an explosion or two. It was horrible!

He might as well apply to a private asylum or sanatarium now, having all the money he had, and explain that he had delusions—delusions! Imagine!—and ask to be taken care of. In a place like that they wouldn't be disturbed by his jumping up and screaming at night, feeling that he was being choked, as he was, or by his leaving the table because he couldn't eat the food, or by his talking back to Mersereau, should they chance to hear him, or by the noises when they occurred.

They could assign him a special nurse and a special room, if he wished—only he didn't wish to be too much alone. They could put him in charge of someone who would understand all these things, or to whom he could explain. He couldn't expect ordinary people, or hotels catering to ordinary people, to put up with him any more. Mersereau and his friends made too much trouble.

He must go and hunt up a good place somewhere where they understood such things, or at least tolerated them, and explain, and then it would all pass for the hallucinations of a crazy man—though as a matter of fact, he wasn't crazy at all. It was all too real, only the average or so-called normal person couldn't see or hear as he could —hadn't experienced what he had.

X—DECEMBER, 1908

"The trouble is, doctor, that Mr. Davidson is suffering from the delusion that he is pursued by evil spirits. He was not committed here by any court, but came of his own accord about four months ago, and we let him wander about here at will. But he seems to be growing worse, as time goes on.

"One of his worst delusions, doctor, is that there is one spirit in particular who is trying to choke him to death. Dr. Major, our superintendent, says he has incipient tuberculosis of the throat, with occasional spasmodic contractions. There are small lumps or callouses here and there as though caused by outside pressure and yet our nurse assures us that there is no such outside irritation. He won't believe that: but whenever he tries to sleep, especially in the middle of the night, he will jump up and come running out into the hall, insisting that one of these spirits, which he insists are after him, is trying to choke him to death. He really seems to believe it, for he comes out coughing and choking and feeling at his neck as if someone has been trying to strangle him. He always explains the whole matter to me as being the work of evil spirits and asks me to not pay any attention to him unless he calls for help or rings his call bell; and so I never think anything more of it now unless he does.

"Another of his ideas is that these same spirits do something to his food—put poison in it, or give it a bad odor or taste, so that he can't eat it. When he does find anything he can eat, he grabs it and almost swallows it whole, before, as he says, the spirits have time to do anything to it. Once, he says, he weighed more than two hundred pounds, but now he only weights one hundred and twenty. His case is exceedingly strange and pathetic, doctor!

"Dr. Major insists that it is purely a delusion, that so far as being choked is concerned, it is the incipient tuberculosis, and that his stomach trouble comes from the same thing; but by association of ideas, or delusion, he thinks someone is trying to choke him and poison his food, when it isn't so at all. Dr. Major says that he can't imagine what could have started it, but whenever he begins to ask him questions, Mr. Davidson refuses to talk, and gets up and leaves.

"One of the peculiar things about his idea of being choked, doctor, is that when he is merely dozing he always wakes up in time, and has the power to throw it off. He claims that the strength of these spirits is not equal to his own when he is awake, or even dozing, but when he's asleep their strength is greater and that then they may injure him. Sometimes, when he has had a fright like this, he will come out in the hall and down to my desk there at the lower end, and ask if he mayn't sit there by me. He says it calms him. I always tell him yes, but it won't be five minutes before he'll get up and leave again, saying that he's being annoyed or that he won't be able to contain himself if he stays any longer, because of the remarks being made over his shoulder or in his ear.

"Often he'll say: 'Did you hear that, Miss Liggett? It's astonishing, the low, vile things that man can say at times!' When I say, 'No, I didn't hear,' he always says, 'I'm so glad!' "

"No one has ever tried to relieve him of this by hypnotism, I suppose?"

"Not that I know of, doctor. Dr. Major may have tried it. I have only been here three months."

"Tuberculosis is certainly the cause of the throat trouble, as Dr. Major says, and as for the stomach trouble, that comes from the same thing—natural enough under the circumstances. We may have to resort to hypnotism a little later. I'll see. In the meantime you'd better caution all who come in touch with him never to sympathize, or even seem to believe in anything he imagines is being done to him. It will merely encourage him in his notions. And get him to take his medicine regularly; it won't cure, but it will help. Dr. Major has asked me to give special attention to his case, and I want the conditions as near right as possible."

"Yes, sir."

XI—JANUARY, 1909

The trouble with these doctors was that they really knew nothing of anything save what was on the surface, the little they had learned at a medical college or in practice, chiefly how certain drugs, tried by their predecessors in certain cases, were known to act. They had no imagination whatever, even when you tried to tell them.

Take that latest young person who was coming here now in his good clothes and with his car, fairly bursting with his knowledge of what he called psychiatrics, looking into Davidson's eyes so hard and smoothing his temples and throat—massage, he called it—saying that he had incipient tuberculosis of the throat and stomach trouble, and utterly disregarding the things which he, Davidson, could personally see and hear! Imagine the fellow trying to persuade him, at this late date, that all that was wrong with him was tuberculosis, that he didn't see Mersereau standing right beside him at times, bending over him, holding up that hand and telling him how he intended to kill him yet—that it was all an illusion!

Imagine saying that Mersereau couldn't actually seize him by the throat when he was asleep, or nearly so, when Davidson himself, looking at his throat in the mirror, could see the actual fingerprints —Mersereau's—for a moment or so afterward. At any rate, his throat, was red and sore from being clutched as Mersereau of late was able to clutch him! And that was the cause of these lumps. And to say, as they had said at first, that he himself was making them by rubbing and feeling his throat, and that it was tuberculosis!

Wasn't it enough to make one want to quit the place? If it weren't for Miss Liggett and Miss Koehler, his private nurse, and their devoted care, he would. That Miss Koehler was worth her weight in gold, learning his ways as she had, being so uniformly kind, and bearing with his difficulties so genially. He would leave her something in his will.

To leave this place and go elsewhere, though, unless he could take her along, would be folly. And anyway, where else would he go? Here at least were other people, patients like himself, who could understand and could sympathize with him—people who weren't convinced as were these doctors that all that he complained of was mere delusion. Imagine! Old Rankin, the lawyer, for instance, who had suffered untold persecution from one living person and another, mostly politicians, was convinced that this, Davidson's, troubles were genuine, and liked to hear about them, just as did Miss Koehler. These two did not insist, as the doctors did, that he had slow tuberculosis of the throat, and could live a long time and overcome his troubles if he would. They were merely companionable at such times as Mersereau would give him enough peace to be sociable.

The only real trouble, though, was that he was growing so weak from lack of sleep and food—his inability to eat the food which his enemy bewitched and to sleep at night on account of the choking—that he couldn't last much longer. This new physician whom Dr. Major had called into consultation in regard to his case was insisting that along with his throat trouble he was suffering from acute anemia, due to long undernourishment, and that only a solution of strychnine injected into the veins would help him. But as to Mersereau poisoning his food—not a word would he hear. Besides, now that he was practically bedridden, not able to jump up as freely as before, he was subject to a veritable storm of bedevilment at the hands of Mersereau. Not only could he see—especially towards evening, and in the very early hours of the morning—Mersereau hovering about him like a black shadow, a great, bulky shadow—yet like him in outline, but he could feel his enemy's hand moving over him. Worse, behind or about him he often saw a veritable cloud of evil creatures, companions or tools of Mersereau's who were there to help him and who kept swimming about like fish in dark waters, and seemed to eye the procedure with satisfaction.

When food was brought to him, early or late, and in whatever form, Mersereau and they were there, close at hand, as thick as flies, passing over and through it in an evident attempt to spoil it before he could eat it. Just to see them doing it was enough to poison it for him. Besides, he could hear their voices urging Mersereau to do it.

"That's right—poison it!"

He can't last much longer!"

"Soon he'll be weak enough so that when you grip him he will really die!"

It was thus that they actually talked—he could hear them.

He also heard vile phrases addressed to him by Mersereau, the iterated and reiterated words *murderer* and *swindler* and *cheat* there in the middle of the night. Often, although the light was still on, he saw as many as seven dark figures, very much like Mersereau's, although different, gathered close about him—like men in consultation—evil men. Some of them sat upon his bed, and it seemed as if they were about to help Mersereau to finish him, adding their hands to his.

Behind them again was a complete circle of those evil, swimming things with green and red eyes, always watching—helping probably. He had actually felt the pressure of the hand to grow stronger of late, when they were all there. Only, just before he felt he was going to faint, and because he could not spring up any more, he invariably screamed or gasped a choking gasp and held his finger on the button which would bring Miss Koehler. Then she would come, lift him up and fix his pillows. She also always assured him that it was only the inflammation of his throat, and rubbed it with alcohol, and gave him a few drops of something internally to ease it.

After all this time, and in spite of anything he could tell them, they still believed, or pretended to believe, that he was suffering from tuberculosis, and that all the rest of this was delusion, a phase of insanity!

And Mersereau's skeleton still out there on the Monte Orte!

And Mersereau's plan, with the help of others, of course, was to choke him to death: there was no doubt of that now; and yet they would believe after he was gone that he had died of tuberculosis of the throat. Think of that.

XII—Midnight of february 10, 1909

The Ghost of Mersereau (*bending over Davidson*): "Softly! Softly! He's quite asleep! He didn't think we could get him—that I could! But this time—yes. Miss Koehler is asleep at the end of the hall and Miss Liggett can't come, can't hear. He's too weak now. He can scarcely move or groan. Strengthen my hand, will you! I will grip him so tight this time that he won't get away! His cries won't help him this time! He can't cry as he once did! Now! Now!"

A Cloud of Evil Spirits (*swimming about*): "Right! Right! Good! Good! Now! Ah!"

Davidson (*waking, choking, screaming and feebly striking out*): "Help! Help! He-l-p! Miss—Miss—H—e—l—p!"

Miss Liggett (*dozing heavily in her chair*): "Everything is still. No one restless. I can sleep." (Her head nods.)

The Cloud of Evil Spirits: "Good! Good! Good! His soul at last! Here it comes! He couldn't escape this time! Ah! Good! Good! Now!"

Mersereau (*to Davidson*): "You murderer! At last! At last!"

XIII—3 a.m. of February 17, 1909

Miss Koehler (*at the bedside, distressed and pale*): "He must have died some time between one and two, doctor. I left him at one o'clock, comfortable as I could make him. He said he was feeling as well as could be expected. He's been very weak during the last few days, taking only a little gruel. Between half-past one and two I thought I heard a noise, and came to see. He was lying just as you see here, except that his hands were up to his throat, as if it were hurting or choking him. I put them down for fear they would stiffen that way. In trying to call one of the other nurses just now, I found that the bell was out of order, although I know it was all right when I left, because he always made me try it. So he may have tried to ring."

Dr. Major (*turning the head and examining the throat*): "It looks as if he had clutched his throat rather tightly this time, I must say. Here is the mark of his thumb on this side and of his four fingers on the other. Rather deep for the little strength he had. Odd that he should have imagined that someone else was trying to choke him, when he was always pressing at his own neck! Throat tuberculosis is very painful at times. That would explain the desire to clutch at his throat."

Miss Liggett: "He was always believing that an evil spirit was trying to choke him, doctor."

Dr. Major: "Yes, I know—association of ideas. Dr. Scain and I agree as to that. He had a bad case of chronic tuberculosis of the throat, with accompanying malnutrition, due to the effect of the throat on the stomach; and his notion about evil spirits pursuing him and trying to choke him was simply due to an innate tendency on the part of the subconscious mind to join things together—any notion, say, with any pain. If he had had a diseased leg, he would have imagined that evil spirits were attempting to saw it off, or something like that. In the same way the condition of his throat affected his stomach, and he imagined that the spirits were doing something to his food. Make out a certificate showing acute tuberculosis of the esophagus as the cause, with delusions of persecution as his mental condition. While I am here we may as well look in on Mr. Baff."

The Valley of the Spiders

H.G. WELLS

*Spiders, perhaps, have terrified more people than any other type of
creature, large or small. The spiders in this classic tale of "cauld grue"
are extra-large and therefore extra-terrifying; in their own way they are
as awesome as the better-known Martians in* The War of the Worlds.
*H. G. Wells wrote horror every bit as well as he wrote science fiction.
He did, indeed.*

Towards midday the three pursuers came abruptly round a bend in
the torrent bed upon the sight of a very broad and spacious valley. The
difficult and winding trench of pebbles along which they had tracked
the fugitives for so long expanded to a broad slope, and with a common impulse the three men left the trail, and rode to a low eminence
set with olive-dun trees, and there halted, the two others, as became
them, a little behind the man with the silver-studded bridle.

For a space they scanned the great expanse below them with eager
eyes. It spread remoter and remoter, with only a few clusters of sere
thorn bushes here and there, and the dim suggestions of some now
waterless ravine to break its desolation of yellow grass. Its purple
distances melted at last into the bluish slopes of the further hills—hills
it might be of a greener kind—and above them invisibly supported,
and seeming indeed to hang in the blue, were the snow-clad summits
of mountains—that grew larger and bolder to the north-westward as
the sides of the valley drew together. And westward the valley opened
until a distant darkness under the sky told where the forests began.
But the three men looked neither east nor west, but only steadfastly
across the valley.

The gaunt man with the scarred lip was the first to speak
"Nowhere," he said, with a sigh of disappointment in his voice. "But
after all, they had a full day's start."

"They don't know we are after them," said the little man on the
white horse.

"*She* would know," said the leader bitterly, as if speaking to himself.

"Even then they can't go fast. They've got no beast but the mule, and all today the girl's foot has been bleeding—"

The man with the silver bridle flashed a quick intensity of rage on him. "Do you think I haven't seen that?" he snarled.

"It helps, anyhow," whispered the little man to himself.

The gaunt man with the scarred lip stared impassively.

"They can't be over the valley, " he said. "If we ride hard—"

He glanced at the white horse and paused.

"Curse all white horses!" said the man with the silver bridle and turned to scan the beast his curse included.

The little man looked down between the melancholy ears of his steed.

"I did my best," he said.

The two others stared again across the valley for a space. The gaunt man passed the back of his hand across the scarred lip.

"Come up!" said the man who owned the silver bridle, suddenly. The little man started and jerked his rein, and the horse hooves of the three made a multitudinous faint pattering upon the withered grass as they turned back towards the trail. . . .

They rode cautiously down the long slope before them, and so came through a waste of prickly twisted bushes and strange dry shapes of horny branches that grew amongst the rocks, into the level below. And there the trail grew faint, for the soil was scanty, and the only herbage was this scorched dead straw that lay upon the ground. Still, by hard scanning, by leaning beside the horse's neck and pausing ever and again, even these white men could contrive to follow after their prey.

There were trodden places, bent and broken blades of the coarse grass, and ever and again the sufficient intimation of a footmark. And once the leader saw a brown smear of blood where the half-caste girl may have trod. And at that under his breath he cursed her for a fool.

The gaunt man checked his leader's tracking, and the little man on the white horse rode behind, a man lost in a dream. They rode one after another, the man with the silver bridle led the way, and they spoke never a word. After a time it came to the little man on the white horse that the world was very still. He started out of his dream. Besides the minute noises of their horses and equipment, the whole great valley kept the brooding quiet of a painted scene.

Before him went his master and his fellow, each intently leaning forward to the left, each impassively moving with the paces of his horse; their shadows went before them—still, noiseless, tapering attendants; and nearer a crouched cool shape was his own. He looked about him. What was it had gone? Then he remembered the reverberation from the banks of the gorge and the perpetual accompaniment of shifting, jostling pebbles. And, moreover—? There was no breeze. That was it! What a vast, still place it was, a monotonous afternoon slumber. And the sky open and blank, except for a somber veil of haze that had gathered in the upper valley.

He straightened his back, fretted with his bridle, puckered his lips to whistle, and simply sighed. He turned in his saddle for a time, and stared at the throat of the mountain gorge out of which they had come. Blank! Blank slopes on either side, with never a sign of a decent beast or tree—much less a man. What a land it was! What a wilderness! He dropped again into his former pose.

It filled him with a momentary pleasure to see a wry stick of purple black flash out into the form of a snake, and vanish amidst the brown. After all, the infernal valley *was* alive. And then, to rejoice him still more, came a breath across his face, a whisper that came and went, the faintest inclination of a stiff black-antlered bush upon a crest, the first intimations of a possible breeze. Idly he wetted his finger, and held it up.

He pulled up sharply to avoid a collision with the gaunt man, who had stopped at fault upon the trail. Just at that guilty moment he caught his master's eye looking towards him.

For a time he forced an interest in the tracking. Then, as they rode on again, he studied his master's shadow and hat and shoulder appearing and disappearing behind the gaunt man's nearer contours. They had ridden four days out of the very limits of the world into this desolate place, short of water, with nothing but a strip of dried meat under their saddles, over rocks and mountains, where surely none but these fugitives had ever been before—for *that!*

And all this was for a girl, a mere willful child! And the man had whole cityfuls of people to do his basest bidding—girls, women! Why in the name of passionate folly *this* one in particular? asked the little man, and scowled at the world, and licked his parched lips with a blackened tongue. It was the way of the master, and that was all he knew. Just because she sought to evade him. . . .

His eye caught a whole row of high-plumed canes bending in unison, and then the tails of silk that hung before his neck flapped and fell.

The breeze was growing stronger. Somehow it took the stiff stillness out of things—and that was well.

"Hullo!" said the gaunt man.

All three stopped abruptly.

"What?" asked the master. "What?"

"Over there," said the gaunt man, pointing up the valley.

"What?"

"Something coming towards us."

And as he spoke a yellow animal crested a rise and came bearing down upon them. It was a big wild dog, coming before the wind, tongue out, at a steady pace, and running with such an intensity of purpose that he did not seem to see the horsemen he approached. He ran with his nose up, following, it was plain, neither scent nor quarry. As he drew nearer the little man felt for his sword. "He's mad," said the gaunt rider.

"Shout!" said the little man and shouted.

The dog came on. Then when the little man's blade was already out, it swerved aside and went panting by them and past. The eyes of the little man followed its flight. "There was no foam," he said. For a space the man with the silver-studded bridle stared up the valley. "Oh, come on!" he cried at last. "What does it matter?" and jerked his horse into movement again.

The little man left the insoluble mystery of a dog that fled from nothing but the wind, and lapsed into profound musings on human character. "Come on!" he whispered to himself. "Why should it be given to one man to say 'Come on!' with that stupendous violence of effect. Always, all his life, the man with the silver bridle has been saying that. If *I* said it—!" thought the little man. But people marvelled when the master was disobeyed even in the wildest things. This half-caste girl seemed to him, seemed to everyone, mad—blasphemous almost. The little man, by way of comparison, reflected on the gaunt rider with the scarred lip, as stalwart as his master, as brave and, indeed, perhaps braver, and yet for him there was obedience, nothing but to give obedience duly and stoutly. . . .

Certain sensations of the hands and knees called the little man back to more immediate things. He became aware of something. He rode up beside his gaunt fellow. "Do you notice the horses? " he said in an undertone.

The gaunt face looked interrogation.

"They don't like this wind," said the little man, and dropped behind as the man with the silver bridle turned upon him.

"It's all right," said the gaunt-faced man.

They rode on again for a space in silence. The foremost two rode downcast upon the trail, the hindmost man watched the haze that crept down the vastness of the valley, nearer and nearer, and noted how the wind grew in strength moment by moment. Far away on the left he saw a line of dark bulks—wild hog perhaps, galloping down the valley, but of that he said nothing, nor did he remark again upon the uneasiness of the horses.

And then he saw first one and then a second great white ball, a great shining white ball like a gigantic head of thistledown, that drove before the wind athwart the path. These balls soared high in the air, and dropped and rose again and caught for a moment, and hurried on and passed, but at the sight of them the restlessness of the horses increased.

Then presently he saw that more of these drifting globes—and then soon very many more—were hurrying towards him down the valley.

They became aware of a squealing. Athwart the path a huge boar rushed, turning his head but for one instant to glance at them, and then hurtling on down the valley again. And at that, all three stopped and sat in their saddles, staring into the thickening haze that was coming upon them.

"If it were not for this thistledown—" began the leader.

But now a big globe came drifting past within a score of yards of them. It was really not an even sphere at all, but a vast, soft, ragged, filmy thing, a sheet gathered by the corners, an aerial jellyfish, as it were, but rolling over and over as it advanced, and trailing long, cobwebby threads and streamers that floated in its wake.

"It isn't thistledown," said the little man.

"I don't like the stuff," said the gaunt man.

And they looked at one another.

"Curse it!" cried the leader. "The air's full of it up there. If it keeps on at this pace long, it will stop us altogether.

An instinctive feeling, such as lines out a herd of deer at the approach of some ambiguous thing, prompted them to turn their horses to the wind, ride forwards for a few paces, and stare at that advancing multitude of floating masses. They came on before the wind with a sort of smooth swiftness, rising and falling noiselessly, sinking to earth, rebounding high, soaring—all with a perfect unanimity, with a still, deliberate assurance.

Right and left of the horsemen the pioneers of this strange army passed. At one that rolled along the ground, breaking shapelessly and trailing out reluctantly into long grappling ribbons and bands, all three horses began to shy and dance. The master was seized with a sudden, unreasonable impatience. He cursed the drifting globes roundly. "Get on!" he cried; "get on! What do these things matter? How *can* they matter? Back to the trail!" He fell swearing at his horse and sawed the bit across its mouth.

He shouted aloud with rage. "I will follow that trail, I tell you," he cried. "Where is the trail!"

He gripped the bridle of his prancing horse and searched amidst the grass. A long and clinging thread fell across his face, a gray streamer dropped about his bridle arm, some big, active thing with many legs ran down the back of his head. He looked up to discover one of those gray masses anchored as it were above him by these things and flapping out ends as a sail flaps when a boat comes about—but noiselessly.

He had an impression of many eyes, of a dense crew of squat bodies, of long, many-jointed limbs hauling at their mooring ropes to bring the thing down upon him. For a space he stared up, reining in his prancing horse with the instinct born of years of horsemanship. Then the flat of a sword smote his back, and a blade flashed overhead and cut the drifting balloon of spider web free, and the whole mass lifted softly and drove clear and away.

"Spiders!" cried the voice of the gaunt man. "The things are full of big spiders! Look, my lord!"

The man with the silver bridle still followed the mass that drove away.

"Look, my lord!"

The master found himself staring down at a red smashed thing on the ground that, in spite of partial obliteration, could still wriggle unavailing legs. Then when the gaunt man pointed to another mass that bore down upon them, he drew his sword hastily. Up the valley now it was like a fog bank torn to rags. He tried to grasp the situation.

"Ride for it!" the little man was shouting. "Ride for it down the valley."

What happened then was like the confusion of a battle. The man

with the silver bridle saw the little man go past him slashing furiously
at imaginary cobwebs, saw him cannon into the horse of the gaunt
man and hurl it and its rider to earth. His own horse went a dozen
paces before he could rein it in. Then he looked up to avoid imaginary
dangers, and then back again to see a horse rolling on the ground, the
gaunt man standing and slashing over it at a rent and fluttering mass of
gray that streamed and wrapped about them both. And thick and fast
as thistledown on waste land on a windy day in July, the cobweb
masses were coming on.

The little man had dismounted, but he dared not release his horse.
He was endeavoring to lug the struggling brute back with the strength
of one arm, while with the other he slashed aimlessly. The tentacles of
a second gray mass had entangled themselves with the struggle, and
this second gray mass came to its moorings, and slowly sank.

The master set his teeth, gripped his bridle, lowered his head and
spurred his horse forward. The horse on the ground rolled over, there
was blood and moving shapes upon the flanks, and the gaunt man
suddenly leaving it, ran forward towards his master, perhaps ten paces.
His legs were swathed and encumbered with gray; he made ineffectual
movements with his sword. Gray streamers waved from him; there was
a thin veil of gray across his face. With his left hand he beat at
something on his body, and suddenly he stumbled and fell. He struggled to rise, and fell again, and suddenly, horribly, began to howl,
"Oh—ohoo, ohooh!"

The master could see the great spiders upon him, and others upon
the ground.

As he strove to force his horse nearer to this gesticulating screaming
gray object that struggled up and down, there came a clatter of hooves,
and the little man, in act of mounting, swordless, balanced on his belly
athwart the white horse, and clutching its mane, whirled past. And
again a clinging thread of gray gossamer swept across the master's face.
All about him and over him, it seemed this drifting, noiseless cobweb
circled and drew nearer him. . . .

To the day of his death he never knew just how the event of that
moment happened. Did he, indeed, turn his horse, or did it really of its
own accord stampede after its fellow? Suffice it that in another second
he was galloping full tilt down the valley with his sword whirling
furiously overhead. And all about him on the quickening breeze, the

spiders' airships, their air bundles and air sheets, seemed to him to hurry in a conscious pursuit.

Clatter, clatter, thud, thud—the man with the silver bridle rode, heedless of his direction, with his fearful face looking up now right, now left, and his sword arm ready to slash. And a few hundred yards ahead of him, with a tail of torn cobweb trailing behind him, rode the little man on the white horse, still but imperfectly in the saddle. The reeds bent before them, the wind blew fresh and strong, over his shoulder the master could see the webs hurrying to overtake. . . .

He was so intent to escape the spiders' webs that only as his horse gathered together for a leap did he realize the ravine ahead. And then he realized it only to misunderstand and interfere. He was leaning forward on his horse's neck and sat up and back all too late.

But if in his excitement he had failed to leap, at any rate he had not forgotten how to fall. He was horseman again in mid-air. He came off clear with a mere bruise upon his shoulder, and his horse rolled, kicking spasmodic legs, and lay still. But the master's sword drove its point into the hard soil, and snapped clean across, as though Chance refused him any longer as her Knight, and the splintered end missed his face by an inch or so.

He was on his feet in a moment, breathlessly scanning the onrushing spider webs. For a moment he was minded to run, and then thought of the ravine, and turned back. He ran aside once to dodge one drifting terror, and then he was swiftly clambering down the precipitous sides, and out of the touch of the gale.

There under the lee of the dry torrent's steeper banks he might crouch, and watch these strange, gray masses pass and pass in safety till the wind fell, and it became possible to escape. And there for a long time he crouched, watching the strange, gray, ragged masses trail their streamers across his narrowed sky.

Once a stray spider fell into the ravine close beside him—a full foot it measured from leg to leg, and its body was half a man's hand—and after he had watched its monstrous alacrity of search and escape for a little while, and tempted it to bite his broken sword, he lifted up his iron heeled boot and smashed it into a pulp. He swore as he did so, and for a time sought up and down for another.

Then presently, when he was surer these spider swarms could not drop into the ravine, he found a place where he could sit down, and sat and fell into deep thought and began after his manner to gnaw his knuckles and bite his nails. And from this he was moved by the coming of the man with the white horse.

He heard him long before he saw him, as a clattering of hooves, stumbling footsteps, and a reassuring voice. Then the little man appeared, a rueful figure, still with a tail of white cobweb trailing behind him. They approached each other without speaking, without salutation. The little man was fatigued and shamed to the pitch of hopeless bitterness, and came to a stop at last, face to face with his seated master. The latter winced a little under his dependent's eye. "Well?" he said at last, with no pretense of authority.

"You left him!"

"My horse bolted."

"I know. So did mine."

He laughed at his master mirthlessly.

"I say my horse bolted," said the man who once had a silver-studded bridle.

"Cowards both," said the little man.

The other gnawed his knuckle through some meditative moments, with his eyes on his inferior.

"Don't call me a coward," he said at length.

"You are a coward like myself."

"A coward possibly. There is a limit beyond which every man must fear. That I have learnt at last. But not like yourself. That is where the difference comes in."

"I never could have dreamt you would have left him. He saved your life two minutes before. . . . Why are you our lord?"

The master gnawed his knuckles again, and his countenance was dark.

"No man calls me a coward," he said. "No. . . . A broken sword is better than none. . . . One spavined white horse cannot be expected to carry two men a four days' journey. I hate white horses, but this time it cannot be helped. You begin to understand me? . . . I perceive that you are minded, on the strength of what you have seen and fancy, to taint my reputation. It is men of your sort who unmake kings. Besides which—I never liked you."

"My lord!" said the little man.

"No," said the master. "*No!*"

He stood up sharply as the little man moved. For a minute perhaps they faced one another. Overhead the spiders' balls went driving.

There was a quick movement among the pebbles; a running of feet, a cry of despair, a gasp and a blow. . . .

Towards nightfall the wind fell. The sun set in a calm serenity, and the man who had once possessed the silver bridle came at last very cautiously and by an easy slope out of the ravine again; but now he led the white horse that once belonged to the little man. He would have gone back to his horse to get his silver-mounted bridle again, but he feared night and a quickening breeze might still find him in the valley, and besides he disliked greatly to think he might discover his horse all swathed in cobwebs and perhaps unpleasantly eaten.

And as he thought of those cobwebs and of all the dangers he had been through, and the manner in which he had been preserved that day, his hand sought a little reliquary that hung about his neck, and he clasped it for a moment with heartfelt gratitude. As he did so his eyes went across the valley.

"I was hot with passion," he said, "and now she has met her reward. They also, no doubt—"

And behold! Far away out of the wooded slopes across the valley, but in the clearness of the sunset distinct and unmistakable, he saw a little spire of smoke.

At that his expression of serene resignation changed to an amazed anger. Smoke? He turned the head of the white horse about, and hesitated. And as he did so a little rustle of air went through the grass about him. Far away upon some reeds swayed a tattered sheet of gray. He looked at the cobwebs; he looked at the smoke.

"Perhaps, after all, it is not them," he said at last.

But he knew better.

After he had stared at the smoke for some time, he mounted the white horse.

As he rode, he picked his way amidst stranded masses of web. For some reason there were many dead spiders on the ground, and those that lived feasted guiltily on their fellow. At the sound of his horse's hooves they fled.

Their time had passed. From the ground, without either a wind to carry them or a winding sheet ready, these things, for all their poison, could do him no evil.

He flicked with his belt at those he fancied came too near. Once, where a number ran together over a bare place, he was minded to

dismount and trample them with his boots, but this impulse he over-
came. Ever and again he turned in his saddle, and looked back at the
smoke.

"Spiders," he muttered over and over again. "Spiders! Well, well
.... The next time I must spin a web."

The Middle Toe of the Right Foot

AMBROSE BIERCE

The work of Ambrose Bierce has been called, among other things over the past hundred years, "paranoid," "malevolent," "morbid" and "venomous"—which may be true assessments, in that these were all undeniable facets of Bierce's character. But it is also true that Bierce was a master of style and plot, particularly when it came to exercises in horror and the supernatural, and that he knew whereof he wrote in those stories dealing with the spectres which haunt the human mind. "The Middle Toe of the Right Foot" is perhaps his best and most cynical tale of this type—and a thunderingly good chiller in the bargain.

I

It is well-known that the old Manton house is haunted. In all the rural district near about, and even in the town of Marshall, a mile away, not one person of unbiased mind entertains a doubt of it; incredulity is confined to those opinionated persons who will be called "cranks" as soon as the useful word shall have penetrated the intellectual demesne of the Marshall *Advance*. The evidence that the house is haunted is of two kinds: the testimony of disinterested witnesses who have had ocular proof, and that of the house itself. The former may be disregarded and ruled out on any of the various grounds of objection which may be urged against it by the ingenious; but facts within the observation of all are material and controlling.

In the first place, the Manton house has been unoccupied by mortals for more than ten years, and with its outbuildings is slowly falling into decay—a circumstance which in itself the judicious will hardly venture to ignore. It stands a little way off the loneliest reach of the Marshall and Harriston road, in an opening which was once a farm and is still disfigured with strips of rotting fence and half-covered with brambles overrunning a stony and sterile soil long unacquainted with the plow. The house itself is in tolerably good condition, though badly weather-stained and in dire need of attention from the glazier, the smaller male population of the region having attested in the manner of its kind its disapproval of dwelling without dwellers. It is two stories in height, nearly square, its front pierced by a single doorway flanked on each side by a window boarded up to the very top. Corresponding windows above, not protected, serve to admit light and rain to the rooms of the upper floor. Grass and weeds grow pretty rankly all about, and a few shade trees, somewhat the worse for wind, and leaning all in one direction, seem to be making a concerted effort to run away. In short, as the Marshall town humorist explained in the columns of the *Advance*, "The proposition that the Manton house is badly haunted is the only logical conclusion from the premises." The fact that in this dwelling Mr. Manton thought it expedient one night some ten years ago to rise and cut the throats of his wife and two small children, removing at once to another part of the country, has no doubt done its share in directing public attention to the fitness of the place for supernatural phenomena.

To this house, one summer evening, came four men in a wagon. Three of them promptly alighted, and the one who had been driving hitched the team to the only remaining post of what had been a fence. The fourth remained seated in the wagon. "Come," said one of his companions, approaching him, while the others moved away in the direction of the dwelling—"this is the place."

The man addressed did not move. "By God!" he said harshly, "this is a trick, and it looks to me as if you were in it."

"Perhaps I am," the other said, looking him straight in the face and speaking in a tone which had something of contempt in it. "You will remember, however, that the choice of place was with your own assent left to the other side. Of course if you are afraid of spooks—"

"I am afraid of nothing," the man interrupted with another oath, and sprang to the ground. The two then joined the others at the door, which one of them had already opened with some difficulty, caused by rust of lock and hinge. All entered. Inside it was dark, but the man who had unlocked the door produced a candle and matches and made a light. He then unlocked a door on their right as they stood in the passage. This gave them entrance to a large, square room that the candle but dimly lighted. The floor had a thick carpeting of dust, which partly muffled their footfalls. Cobwebs were in the angles of the walls and depended from the ceiling like strips of rotting lace, making undulatory movements in the disturbed air. The room had two windows in adjoining sides, but from neither could anything be seen except the rough inner surfaces of boards a few inches from the glass. There was no fireplace, no furniture; there was nothing: besides the cobwebs and the dust, the four men were the only objects there which were not a part of the structure.

Strange enough they looked in the yellow light of the candle. The one who had so reluctantly alighted was especially spectacular—he might have been called sensational. He was of middle age, heavily built, deep chested and broad shouldered. Looking at his figure, one would have said that he had a giant's strength; at his features, that he would use it like a giant. He was clean shaven, his hair rather closely cropped and gray. His low forehead was seamed with wrinkles above the eyes, and over the nose these became vertical. The heavy black brows followed the same law, saved from meeting only by an upward turn at what would otherwise have been the point of contact. Deeply sunken beneath these, glowed in the obscure light a pair of eyes of uncertain color, but obviously enough too small. There was something forbidding in their expression, which was not bettered by the cruel mouth and wide jaw. The nose was well enough, as noses go; one does not expect much of noses. All that was sinister in the man's face seemed accentuated by an unnatural pallor—he appeared altogether bloodless.

The appearance of the other men was sufficiently commonplace: they were such persons as one meets and forgets that he met. All were younger than the man described, between whom and the eldest of the others, who stood apart, there was apparently no kindly feeling. They avoided looking at each other.

"Gentlemen," said the man holding the candle and keys, "I believe everything is right. Are you ready, Mr. Rosser?"

The man standing apart from the group bowed and smiled.

"And you, Mr. Grossmith?"

The heavy man bowed and scowled.

"You will be pleased to remove your outer clothing."

Their hats, coats, waistcoats and neckwear were soon removed and thrown outside the door, in the passage. The man with the candle now nodded, and the fourth man—he who had urged Grossmith to leave the wagon—produced from the pocket of his overcoat two long, murderous-looking bowie-knives, which he drew now from their leather scabbards.

"They are exactly alike," he said, presenting one to each of the two principals—for by this time the dullest observer would have understood the nature of this meeting. It was to be a duel to the death.

Each combatant took a knife, examined it critically near the candle and tested the strength of blade and handle across his lifted knee. Their persons were then searched in turn, each by the second of the other.

"If it is agreeable to you, Mr. Grossmith," said the man holding the light, "you will place yourself in that corner."

He indicated the angle of the room farthest from the door, whither Grossmith retired, his second parting from him with a grasp of the hand which had nothing of cordiality in it. In the angle nearest the door Mr. Rosser stationed himself, and after a whispered consultation his second left him, joining the other near the door. At that moment the candle was suddenly extinguished, leaving all in profound darkness. This may have been done by a draught from the opened door; whatever the cause, the effect was startling.

"Gentlemen," said a voice which sounded strangely unfamiliar in the altered condition affecting the relations of the senses—"gentlemen, you will not move until you hear the closing of the outer door."

A sound of trampling ensued, then the closing of the inner door; and finally the outer one closed with a concussion which shook the entire building.

A few minutes afterward a belated farmer's boy met a light wagon which was being driven furiously toward the town of Marshall. He declared that behind the two figures on the front seat stood a third, with its hands upon the bowed shoulders of the others, who appeared to struggle vainly to free themselves from its grasp. This figure, unlike the others, was clad in white, and had undoubtedly boarded the wagon as it passed the haunted house. As the lad could boast a considerable former experience with the supernatural thereabouts his word had the weight justly due to the testimony of an expert. The story (in connection with the next day's events) eventually appeared in the *Advance*, with some slight literary embellishments and a concluding intimation that the gentlemen referred to would be allowed the use of the paper's columns for their version of the night's adventure. But the privilege remained without a claimant.

II

The events that led up to this "duel in the dark" were simple enough. One evening three young men of the town of Marshall were sitting in a quiet corner of the porch of the village hotel, smoking and discussing such matters as three educated young men of a Southern village would naturally find interesting. Their names were King, Sancher and Rosser. At a little distance, within easy hearing, but taking no part in the conversation, sat a fourth. He was a stranger to the others. They merely knew that on his arrival by the stagecoach that afternoon he had written in the hotel register the name Robert Grossmith. He had not been observed to speak to anyone except the hotel clerk. He seemed, indeed, singularly fond of his own company—or, as the *personnel* of the *Advance* expressed it, "grossly addicted to evil associations." But then it should be said in justice to the stranger that the *personnel* was himself of a too convivial disposition fairly to judge one differently gifted, and had, moreover, experienced a slight rebuff in an effort at an "interview."

"I hate any kind of deformity in a woman," said King, "whether natural or—acquired. I have a theory that any physical defect has its correlative mental and moral defect."

"I infer, then," said Rosser, gravely, "that a lady lacking the moral advantage of a nose would find the struggle to become Mrs. King an arduous enterprise."

"Of course you may put it that way," was the reply; "but, seriously, I once threw over a most charming girl on learning quite accidentally that she had suffered amputation of a toe. My conduct was brutal if you like, but if I had married that girl I should have been miserable for life and should have made her so."

"Whereas," said Sancher, with a light laugh, "by marrying a gentleman of more liberal views she escaped with a parted throat."

"Ah, you know to whom I refer. Yes, she married Manton, but I don't know about his liberality; I'm not sure but he cut her throat because he discovered that she lacked that excellent thing in woman, the middle toe on the right foot."

"Look at that chap!" said Rosser in a low voice, his eyes fixed upon the stranger.

That chap was obviously listening intently to the conversation.

"Damn his impudence!" muttered King—"what ought we to do?"

"That's an easy one," Rosser replied, rising. "Sir," he continued, addressing the stranger, "I think it would be better if you would remove your chair to the other end of the veranda. The presence of gentlemen is evidently an unfamiliar situation to you."

The man sprang to his feet and strode forward with clenched hands, his face white with rage. All were now standing. Sancher stepped between the belligerents.

"You are hasty and unjust," he said to Rosser; "this gentleman has done nothing to deserve such language."

But Rosser would not withdraw a word. By the custom of the country and the time there could be but one outcome to the quarrel.

"I demand the satisfaction due to a gentleman," said the stranger, who had become more calm. "I have not an acquaintance in this region. Perhaps you, sir," bowing to Sancher, "will be kind enough to represent me in this matter."

Sancher accepted the trust—somewhat reluctantly it must be confessed, for the man's appearance and manner were not at all to his liking. King, who during the colloquy had hardly removed his eyes from the stranger's face and had not spoken a word, consented with a nod to act for Rosser, and the upshot of it was that, the principals having retired, a meeting was arranged for the next evening. The nature of the arrangements has been already disclosed. The duel with knives in a dark room was once a commoner feature of Southwestern life than it is likely to be again. How thin a veneering of "chivalry" covered the essential brutality of the code under which such encounters were possible we shall see.

III

In the blaze of a midsummer noonday the old Manton house was hardly true to its traditions. It was of the earth, earthy. The sunshine caressed it warmly and affectionately, with evident disregard of its bad reputation. The grass greening all the expanse in its front seemed to grow, not rankly, but with a natural and joyous exuberance, and the weeds blossomed quite like plants. Full of charming lights and shadows and populous with pleasant-voiced birds, the neglected shade trees no longer struggled to run away, but bent reverently beneath their burdens of sun and song. Even in the glassless upper windows was an expression of peace and contentment, due to the light within. Over the stony fields the visible heat danced with a lively tremor incompatible with the gravity which is an attribute of the supernatural.

Such was the aspect under which the place presented itself to Sheriff Adams and two other men who had come out from Marshall to look at it. One of these men was Mr. King, the sheriff's deputy; the other, whose name was Brewer, was a brother of the late Mrs. Manton. Under a beneficent law of the state relating to property which has been for a certain period abandoned by an owner whose residence cannot be ascertained, the sheriff was legal custodian of the Manton farm and appurtenances thereunto belonging. His present visit was in mere perfunctory compliance with some order of a court in which Mr. Brewer had an action to get possession of the property as heir to his deceased sister. By a mere coincidence, the visit was made on the day after the night that Deputy King had unlocked the house for another and very different purpose. His presence now was not of his own choosing: he had been ordered to accompany his superior and at the moment could think of nothing more prudent than simulated alacrity in obedience to the command.

Carelessly opening the front door, which to his surprise was not locked, the sheriff was amazed to see, lying on the floor of the passage into which it opened, a confused heap of men's apparel. Examination showed it to consist of two hats, and the same number of coats, waistcoats and scarves, all in a remarkably good state of preservation, albeit somewhat defiled by the dust in which they lay. Mr. Brewer was equally astonished, but Mr. King's emotion is not of record. With a new and lively interest in his own actions the sheriff now unlatched and pushed open a door on the right, and the three entered. The room was apparently vacant—no; as their eyes became accustomed to the dimmer light something was visible in the farthest angle of the wall. It was a human figure—that of a man crouching close in the corner. Something in the attitude made the intruders halt when they had barely passed the threshold. The figure more and more clearly defined itself. The man was upon one knee, his back in the angle of the wall, his shoulders elevated to the level of his ears, his hand before his face, palms outward, the fingers spread and crooked like claws; the white face turned upward on the retracted neck had an expression of unutterable fright, the mouth half-open, the eyes incredibly expanded. He was stone dead. Yet with the exception of a bowie-knife, which had evidently fallen from his own hand, not another object was in the room.

In thick dust that covered the floor were some confused footprints near the door and along the wall through which it opened. Along one of the adjoining walls, too, past the boarded-up windows, was the trail made by the man himself in reaching his corner. Instinctively in approaching the body the three men followed that trail. The sheriff grasped one of the outthrown arms; it was as rigid as iron, and the application of a gentle force rocked the entire body without altering the relation of its parts. Brewer, pale with excitement, gazed intently into the distorted face. "God of mercy!" he suddenly cried, "it is Manton!"

"You are right," said King, with an evident attempt at calmness: "I knew Manton. He then wore a full beard and his hair long, but this is he."

He might have added: "I recognized him when he challenged Rosser. I told Rosser and Sancher who he was before we played him this horrible trick. When Rosser left this dark room at our heels, forgetting his outer clothing in the excitement, and driving away with us in his shirt-sleeves—all through the discreditable proceedings we knew whom we were dealing with, murderer and coward that he was!"

But nothing of this did Mr. King say. With his better light he was trying to penetrate the mystery of the man's death. That he had not once moved from the corner where he had been stationed; that his posture was that of neither attack nor defense; that he had dropped his weapon; that he had obviously perished of sheer horror of something he *saw*—these were circumstances which Mr. King's disturbed intelligence could not rightly comprehend.

Groping in intellectual darkness for a clue to his maze of doubt, his gaze, directed mechanically downward in the way of one who ponders momentous matters, fell upon something which, there, in the light of day and in the presence of living companions, affected him with terror.

In the dust of years that lay thick upon the floor—leading from the door by which they had entered, straight across the room to within a yard of Manton's crouching corpse—were three parallel lines of footprints—light but definite impressions of bare feet, the outer ones those of small children, the inner a woman's. From the point at which they ended they did not return; they pointed all one way. Brewer, who had observed them at the same moment, was leaning forward in an attitude of rapt attention, horribly pale.

"Look at that!" he cried, pointing with both hands at the nearest print of the woman's right foot, where she had apparently stopped and stood. "The middle toe is missing—it was Gertrude!"

Gertrude was the late Mrs. Manton, sister to Mr. Brewer.

Pickman's Model

H. P. LOVECRAFT

*No writer since Poe has had more influence on the field of maca-
bre fiction than Howard Phillips Lovecraft. His tales of
Cthulhu—malevolent beings from another dimension bent on invad-
ing our world and destroying mankind—have inspired dozens of writers
(among them August Derleth, Robert Bloch, Henry Kuttner and J.
Ramsey Campbell) to perpetuate the mythos with tales of their own.
However, Lovecraft also wrote other types of horror and supernatural
stories, some of the best of which are Poesque in design and effect.
"Pickman's Model" is such a story. Considered by some to be
Lovecraft's most potent nightmare, it numbers among its virtues one
of the most shuddersome surprise twists in all of weird fiction.*

You needn't think I'm crazy, Eliot—plenty of others have queerer
prejudices than this. Why don't you laugh at Oliver's grandfather,
who won't ride in a motor? If I don't like that damned subway, it's my
own business; and we got here more quickly anyhow in the taxi. We'd
have had to walk up the hill from Park Street if we'd taken the car.

I know I'm more nervous than I was when you saw me last year, but
you don't need to hold a clinic over it. There's plenty of reason, God
knows, and I fancy I'm lucky to be sane at all. Why the third degree?
You didn't use to be so inquisitive.

Well, if you must hear it, I don't know why you shouldn't. Maybe
you ought to, anyhow, for you kept writing me like a grieved parent
when you heard I'd begun to cut the Art Club and keep away from
Pickman. Now that he's disappeared I go around to the club once in a
while, but my nerves aren't what they were.

No, I don't know what's become of Pickman, and I don't like to
guess. You might have surmised I had some inside information when I
dropped him—and that's why I don't want to think where he's gone.
Let the police find what they can—it won't be much, judging from the
fact that they don't know yet of the old North End place he hired
under the name of Peters. I'm not sure that I could find it again
myself—not that I'd ever try, even in broad daylight! Yes, I do know, or

am afraid I know, why he maintained it. I'm coming to that. And I think you'll understand before I'm through why I don't tell the police. They would ask me to guide them, but I couldn't go back there even if I knew the way. There was something there—and now I can't use the subway or (and you may as well have your laugh at this, too) go down into cellars any more.

I should think you'd have known I didn't drop Pickman for the same silly reasons that fussy old women like Dr. Reid or Joe Minot or Rosworth did. Morbid art doesn't shock me, and when a man has the genius Pickman had I feel it an honor to know him, no matter what direction his work takes. Boston never had a greater painter than Richard Upton Pickman. I said it at first and I say it still, and I never swerved an inch, either, when he showed that "Ghoul Feeding." That, you remember, was when Minot cut him.

You know, it takes profound art and profound insight into Nature to turn out stuff like Pickman's. Any magazine-cover hack can splash paint around wildly and call it a nightmare or a Witches' Sabbath or a portrait of the devil, but only a great painter can make such a thing really scare or ring true. That's because only a real artist knows the actual anatomy of the terrible or the physiology of fear—the exact sort of lines and proportions that connect up with latent instincts or hereditary memories of fright, and the proper color contrasts and lighting effects to stir the dormant sense of strangeness. I don't have to tell you why a Fuseli really brings a shiver while a cheap ghost-story frontispiece merely makes us laugh. There's something those fellows catch—beyond life—that they're able to make us catch for a second. Doré had it. Sime has it. Angarola of Chicago has it. And Pickman had it as no man ever had it before or—I hope to heaven—ever will again.

Don't ask me what it is they see. You know, in ordinary art, there's all the difference in the world between the vital, breathing things drawn from Nature or models and the artificial truck that commercial small fry reel off in a bare studio by rule. Well, I should say that the really weird artist has a kind of vision which makes models, or summons up what amounts to actual scenes from the spectral world he lives in. Anyhow, he manages to turn out results that differ from the pretender's mince-pie dreams in just about the same way that the life painter's results differ from the concoctions of a correspondence-school cartoonist. If I had ever seen what Pickman saw—but no! Here, let's have a drink before we get any deeper. Gad, I wouldn't be alive if I'd ever seen what that man—if he was a man—saw!

You recall that Pickman's forte was faces. I don't believe anybody since Goya could put so much of sheer hell into a set of features or a twist of expression. And before Goya you have to go back to the medieval chaps who did the gargoyles and chimeras on Notre Dame and Mont Saint-Michel. They believed all sorts of things—and maybe they saw all sorts of things, too, for the Middle Ages had some curious phases. I remember your asking Pickman yourself once, the year before you went away, wherever in thunder he got such ideas and visions. Wasn't that a nasty laugh he gave you? It was partly because of that laugh that Reid dropped him. Reid, you know, had just taken up comparative pathology, and was full of pompous "inside stuff" about the biological or evolutionary significance of this or that mental or physical symptom. He said Pickman repelled him more and more every day, and almost frightened him toward the last—that the fellow's features and expression were slowly developing in a way he didn't like; in a way that wasn't human. He had a lot of talk about diet, and said Pickman must be abnormal and eccentric to the last degree. I suppose you told Reid, if you and he had any correspondence over it, that he'd let Pickman's paintings get on his nerves or harrow up his imagination. I know I told him that myself—then.

But keep in mind that I didn't drop Pickman for anything like this. On the contrary, my admiration for him kept growing; for that "Ghoul Feeding" was a tremendous achievement. As you know, the club wouldn't exhibit it, and the Museum of Fine Arts wouldn't accept it as a gift; and I can add that nobody would buy it, so Pickman had it right in his house till he went. Now his father has it in Salem—you know Pickman comes of old Salem stock, and had a witch ancestor hanged in 1692.

I got into the habit of calling on Pickman quite often, especially after I began making notes for a monograph on weird art. Probably it was his work which put the idea into my head, and anyhow, I found him a mine of data and suggestions when I came to develop it. He showed me all the paintings and drawings he had about; including some pen-and-ink sketches that would, I verily believe, have got him kicked out of the club if many of the members had seen them. Before long I was pretty nearly a devotee, and would listen for hours like a schoolboy to art theories and philosophic speculations wild enough to qualify him for the Danvers asylum. My hero worship, coupled with the fact that people generally were commencing to have less and less to do with him made him get very confidential with me; and one evening he hinted that if I were fairly close-mouthed and none too squeamish, he might show me something rather unusual—something a bit stronger than anything he had in the house.

"You know," he said, "there are things that won't do for Newbury Street—things that are out of place here, and that can't be conceived here, anyhow. It's my business to catch the overtones of the soul, and you won't find those in a parvenu set of artificial streets on made land. Back Bay isn't Boston—it isn't anything yet, because it's had no time to pick up memories and attract local spirits. If there are any ghosts here, they're the tame ghosts of a salt marsh and a shallow cove; and I want human ghosts—the ghosts of beings highly organized enough to have looked on hell and known the meaning of what they saw.

"The place for an artist to live is the North End. If any aesthete were sincere, he'd put up with the slums for the sake of the massed traditions. God, man! Don't you realize that places like that weren't merely *made*, but actually *grew*? Generation after generation lived and felt and died there, and in days when people weren't afraid to live and feel and die. Don't you know there was a mill on Copp's Hill in 1632, and that half the present streets were laid out by 1650? I can show you houses that have stood two centuries and a half and more; houses that have witnessed what would make a modern house crumble into powder. What do moderns know of life and the forces behind it? You call the Salem witchcraft a delusion, but I'll wager my four-times-great-grandmother could have told you things. They hanged her on Gallows Hill, with Cotton Mather looking sanctimoniously on. Mather, damn him, was afraid somebody might succeed in kicking free of this accursed cage of monotony—I wish someone had laid a spell on him or sucked his blood in the night!

"I can show you a house he lived in, and I can show you another one he was afraid to enter in spite of all his fine bold talk. He knew things he didn't dare put into that stupid *Magnalia* or that puerile *Wonders of the Invisible World*. Look here, do you know the whole North End once had a set of tunnels that kept certain people in touch with each other's houses, and the burying ground, and the sea? Let them prosecute and persecute above ground—things went on every day that they couldn't reach, and voices laughed at night that they couldn't place!

"Why, man, out of ten surviving houses built before 1700 and not moved since I'll wager that in eight I can show you something queer in the cellar. There's hardly a month that you don't read of workmen finding bricked-up arches and wells leading nowhere in this or that old place as it comes down—you could see one near Henchman Street from the elevated last year. There were witches and what their spells summoned; pirates and what they brought in from the sea; smugglers; privateers—and I tell you, people knew how to live, and how to enlarge the bounds of life, in the old time! This wasn't the only world a bold and wise man could know—faugh! And to think of today in contrast, with such pale pink brains that even a club of supposed artists get shudders and convulsions if a picture goes beyond the feelings of a Beacon Street tea table!

"The only saving grace of the present is that it's too damned stupid to question the past very closely. What do maps and records and guidebooks really tell of the North End? Bah! At a guess I'll guarantee to lead you to thirty or forty alleys and networks of alleys north of Prince Street that aren't suspected by ten living beings outside of the foreigners that swarm them. And what do those dagoes know of their meaning? No, Thurber, these ancient places are dreaming gorgeously and overflowing with wonder and terror and escapes from the commonplace, and yet there's only one living soul to understand or profit by them. Or rather, there's only one living soul—for I haven't been digging around in the past for nothing!

"See here, you're interested in this sort of thing. What if I told you that I've got another studio up there, where I can catch the night spirit of antique horror and paint things that I couldn't even think of in Newbury Street? Naturally I don't tell those cursed old maids at the club—with Reid, damn him, whispering even as it is that I'm a sort of monster bound down the toboggan of reverse evolution. Yes, Thurber, I decided long ago that one must paint terror as well as beauty from life, so I did some exploring in places where I had reason to know terror lives.

"I've got a place that I don't believe three living Nordic men besides myself have ever seen. It isn't so very far from the elevated as distance goes, but it's centuries away as the soul goes. I took it because of the queer old brick well in the cellar—one of the sort I told you about. The shack's almost tumbling down, so that nobody else would live there, and I'd hate to tell you how little I pay for it. The windows are boarded up, but I like that all the better, since I don't want daylight for what I do. I paint in the cellar, where the inspiration is thickest, but I've other rooms furnished on the ground floor. A Sicilian owns it, and I've hired it under the name of Peters.

"Now if you're game, I'll take you there tonight. I think you'd enjoy the pictures, for as I said, I've let myself go a bit there. It's no vast tour—I sometimes do it on foot, for I don't want to attract attention with a taxi in such a place. We can take the shuttle at the South Station for Battery Street, and after that the walk isn't much."

Well, Eliot, there wasn't much for me to do after that harangue but to keep myself from running instead of walking for the first vacant cab we could sight. We changed to the elevated at the South Station, and at about twelve o'clock had climbed down the steps at Battery Street and struck along the old waterfront past Constitution Wharf. I didn't keep track of the cross streets, and can't tell you yet which it was we turned up, but I know it wasn't Greenough Lane.

When we did turn, it was to climb through the deserted length of the oldest and dirtiest alley I ever saw in my life, with crumbling-looking gables, broken small-paned windows, and archaic chimneys that stood out half-disintegrated against the moonlit sky. I don't believe there were three houses in sight that hadn't been standing in Cotton Mather's time—certainly I glimpsed at least two with an overhang, and once I thought I saw a peaked roof line of the almost forgotten pregambrel type, though antiquarians tell us there are none left in Boston.

From that alley, which had a dim light, we turned to the left into an equally silent and still narrower alley with no light at all: and in a minute made what I think was an obtuse-angled bend toward the right in the dark. Not long after this Pickman produced a flashlight and revealed an antediluvian ten-paneled door that looked damnably worm-eaten. Unlocking it, he ushered me into a barren hallway with what was once splendid dark oak paneling—simple, of course, but thrillingly suggestive of the time of Andros and Phipps and the Witchcraft. Then he took me through a door on the left, lighted an oil lamp, and told me to make myself at home.

Now, Eliot, I'm what the man in the street would call fairly "hard-boiled," but I'll confess that what I saw on the walls of that room gave me a bad turn. They were his pictures, you know—the ones he couldn't paint or even show in Newbury Street—and he was right when he said he had "let himself go." Here—have another drink—I need one anyhow!

There's no use in my trying to tell you what they were like, because the awful, the blasphemous horror, and the unbelievable loathsomeness and moral foetor came from simple touches quite beyond the power of words to classify. There was none of the exotic technique you see in Sidney Sime, none of the trans-Saturnian landscapes and lunar fungi that Clark Ashton Smith uses to freeze the blood. The backgrounds were mostly old churchyards, deep woods, cliffs by the sea, brick tunnels, ancient paneled rooms, or simple vaults of masonry. Copp's Hill Burying Ground, which could not be many blocks away from this very house, was a favorite scene.

The madness and monstrosity lay in the figures in the foreground—for Pickman's morbid art was preeminently one of demoniac portraiture. These figures were seldom completely human, but often approached humanity in varying degree. Most of the bodies, while roughly bipedal, had a forward slumping, and a vaguely canine cast. The texture of the majority was a kind of unpleasant rubberiness. Ugh! I can see them now! Their occupations—well, don't ask me to be too precise. They were usually feeding—I won't say on what. They were sometimes shown in groups in cemeteries or underground passages, and often appeared to be in battle over their prey—or rather, their treasure trove. And what damnable expressiveness Pickman sometimes gave the sightless faces of this charnel booty! Occasionally the things were shown leaping through open windows at night, or squatting on the chests of sleepers, worrying at their throats. One canvas showed a ring of them baying about a hanged witch on Gallows Hill, whose dead face held a close kinship to theirs.

But don't get the idea that it was all this hideous business of theme and setting which struck me faint. I'm not a three-year-old kid, and I'd seen much like this before. It was the *faces*, Eliot, those accursed *faces*, that leered and slavered out of the canvas with the very breath of life! By God, man, I verily believe they *were* alive! That nauseous wizard had waked the fires of hell in pigment, and his brush had been a nightmare-spawning wand. Give me that decanter, Eliot!

There was one thing called "The Lesson"—heaven pity me, that I ever saw it! Listen—can you fancy a squatting circle of nameless dog-like things in a churchyard teaching a small child how to feed like themselves? The price of a changeling, I suppose—you know the old myth about how the weird people leave their spawn in cradles in exchange for the human babes they steal. Pickman was showing what happens to those stolen babes—how they grow up—and then I began to see a hideous relationship in the faces of the human and nonhuman figures. He was, in all his gradations of morbidity between the frankly nonhuman and the degradedly human, establishing a sardonic linkage and evolution. The dog-things were developed from mortals!

And no sooner had I wondered what he made of their own young as left with mankind in the form of changelings, than my eye caught a picture embodying that very thought. It was that of an ancient Puritan interior—a heavily beamed room with lattice windows, a settle, and clumsy seventeenth-century furniture, with the family sitting about while father read from the Scriptures. Every face but one showed nobility and reverence, but that one reflected the mockery of the pit. It was that of a young man in years, and no doubt belonged to a supposed son of that pious father, but in essence it was the kin of the unclean things. It was their changeling—and in a spirit of supreme irony Pickman had given the features a very perceptible resemblance to his own.

By this time Pickman had lighted a lamp in an adjoining room and was politely holding open the door for me; asking me if I would care to see his "modern studies." I hadn't been able to give him much of my opinions—I was too speechless with fright and loathing—but I think he fully understood and felt highly complimented. And now I want to assure you again, Eliot, that I'm no mollycoddle to scream at anything which shows a bit of departure from the usual. I'm middle-aged and decently sophisticated, and I guess you saw enough of me in France to know I'm not easily knocked out. Remember, too, that I'd just about recovered my wind and gotten used to those frightful pictures which turned colonial New England into a kind of annex of hell. Well, in spite of all this, that next room forced a real scream out of me, and I had to clutch at the doorway to keep from keeling over. The other chamber had shown a pack of ghouls and witches overrunning the world of our forefathers, but this one brought the horror right into our own daily life!

Gad, how that man could paint! There was a study called "Subway

Accident," in which a flock of the vile things were clambering up from some unknown catacomb through a crack in the floor of the Boylston Street subway and attacking a crowd of people on the platform. Another showed a dance on Copp's Hill among the tombs with the background of today. Then there were any number of cellar views, with monsters creeping in through holes and rifts in the masonry and grinning as they squatted behind barrels or furnaces and waited for their first victim to descend the stairs.

One disgusting canvas seemed to depict a vast cross-section of Beacon Hill, with antlike armies of the mephitic monsters squeezing themselves through burrows that honeycombed the ground. Dances in the modern cemeteries were freely pictured, and another conception somehow shocked me more than all the rest—a scene in an unknown vault, where scores of the beasts crowded about one who held a well-known Boston guidebook and was evidently reading aloud. All were pointing to a certain passage, and every face seemed so distorted with epileptic and reverberant laughter that I almost thought I heard the fiendish echoes. The title of the picture was, "Holmes, Lowell, and Longfellow Lie Buried in Mount Auburn."

As I gradually steadied myself and got readjusted to this second room of deviltry and morbidity, I began to analyze some of the points in my sickening loathing. In the first place, I said to myself, these things repelled because of the utter inhumanity and callous cruelty they showed in Pickman. The fellow must be a relentless enemy of all mankind to take such glee in the torture of brain and flesh and the degradation of the mortal tenement. In the second place, they terrified because of their very greatness. Their art was the art that convinced—when we saw the pictures we saw the demons themselves and were afraid of them. And the queer part was, that Pickman got none of his power from the use of selectiveness or bizarrerie. Nothing was blurred, distorted, or conventionalized; outlines were sharp and lifelike, and details were almost painfully defined. And the faces!

It was not any mere artist's interpretation that we saw; it was pandemonium itself, crystal clear in stark objectivity. That was it, by heaven! The man was not a fantaisiste or romanticist at all—he did not even try to give us the churning, prismatic ephemera of dreams, but coldly and sardonically reflected some stable, mechanistic, and well-established horror-world which he saw fully, brilliantly, squarely and unfalteringly. God knows what that world can have been, or where he ever glimpsed the blasphemous shapes that loped and trotted and crawled through it; but whatever the baffling source of his images, one thing was plain. Pickman was in every sense—in conception and in execution—a thorough, painstaking and almost scientific *realist*.

My host was now leading the way down cellar to his actual studio, and I braced myself for some hellish effects among the unfinished canvases. As we reached the bottom of the damp stairs he turned his flashlight to a corner of the large open space at hand, revealing the circular brick curb of what was evidently a great well in the earthen floor. We walked nearer, and I saw that it must be five feet across, with walls a good foot thick and some six inches above the ground level—solid work of the seventeenth century, or I was much mistaken. That, Pickman said, was the kind of thing he had been talking about—an aperture of the network of tunnels that used to undermine the hill. I noticed idly that it did not seem to be bricked up, and that a heavy disc of wood formed the apparent cover. Thinking of the things this well must have been connected with if Pickman's wild hints had not been mere rhetoric, I shivered slightly; then turned to follow him up a step and through a narrow door into a room of fair size, provided with a wooden floor and furnished as a studio. An acetylene gas outfit gave the light necessary for work.

The unfinished pictures on easels or propped against the walls were as ghastly as the finished ones upstairs, and showed the painstaking methods of the artist. Scenes were blocked out with extreme care, and penciled guide lines told of the minute exactitude which Pickman used in getting the right perspective and proportions. The man was great—I say it even now, knowing as much as I do. A large camera on a table excited my notice, and Pickman told me that he used it in taking scenes for backgrounds, so that he might paint them from photographs in the studio instead of carting his outfit around the town for this or that view. He thought a photograph quite as good as an actual scene or model for sustained work, and declared he employed them regularly.

There was something very disturbing about the nauseous sketches and half-finished monstrosities that leered around from every side of the room, and when Pickman suddenly unveiled a huge canvas on the side away from the light I could not for my life keep back a loud scream—the second I had emitted that night. It echoed and echoed through the dim vaultings of that ancient and nitrous cellar, and I had to choke back a flood of reaction that threatened to burst out as hysterical laughter. Merciful Creator! Eliot, but I don't know how much was real and how much was feverish fancy. It doesn't seem to me that earth can hold a dream like that!

It was a colossal and nameless blasphemy with glaring red eyes, and it held in bony claws a thing that had been a man, gnawing at the head as a child nibbles at a stick of candy. Its position was a kind of crouch, and as one looked one felt that at any moment it might drop its present prey and seek a juicier morsel. But damn it all, it wasn't even the fiendish subject that made it such an immortal fountainhead of all panic—not that, nor the face with its pointed ears, bloodshot eyes, flat nose and drooling lips. It wasn't the scaly claws nor the mould-caked body nor the half-hooved feet—none of these, though any one of them might well have driven an excitable man to madness.

It was the technique, Eliot—the cursed, the impious, the unnatural technique! As I am a living being, I never elsewhere saw the actual breath of life so fused into a canvas. The monster was there—it glared and gnawed and gnawed and glared—and I knew that only a suspension of Nature's laws could ever let a man paint a thing like that without a model—without some glimpse of the netherworld which no mortal unsold to the Fiend has ever had.

Pinned with a thumbtack to a vacant part of the canvas was a piece of paper now badly curled up—probably, I thought, a photograph from which Pickman meant to paint a background as hideous as the nightmare it was to enhance. I reached out to uncurl and look at it, when suddenly I saw Pickman start as if shot. He had been listening with peculiar intensity ever since my shocked scream had waked unaccustomed echoes in the dark cellar, and now he seemed struck with a fright which, though not comparable to my own, had in it more of the physical than of the spiritual. He drew a revolver and motioned me to silence, then stepped out into the main cellar and closed the door behind him.

I think I was paralyzed for an instant. Imitating Pickman's listening, I fancied I heard a faint scurrying sound somewhere, and a series of squeals or beats in a direction I couldn't determine. I thought of huge rats and shuddered. Then there came a subdued sort of clatter which somehow set me all in gooseflesh—a furtive, groping kind of clatter, though I can't attempt to convey what I mean in words. It was like heavy wood falling on stone or brick—wood on brick—what did that make me think of?

It came again, and louder. There was a vibration as if the wood had fallen farther than it had fallen before. After that followed a sharp grating noise, a shouted gibberish from Pickman, and the deafening discharge of all six chambers of a revolver, fired spectacularly as a lion tamer might fire in the air for effect. A muffled squeal or squawk, and a thud. Then more wood and brick grating, a pause, and the opening of the door—at which I'll confess I started violently. Pickman reappeared with his smoking weapon, cursing the bloated rats that infested the ancient well.

"The deuce knows what they eat, Thurber," he grinned, "for those archaic tunnels touched graveyard and witch-den and seacoast. But whatever it is, they must have run short, for they were devilish anxious to get out. Your yelling stirred them up, I fancy. Better be cautious in these old places—our rodent friends are the one drawback, though I sometimes think they're a positive asset by way of atmosphere and color."

Well, Eliot, that was the end of the night's adventure. Pickman had promised to show me the place, and heaven knows he had done it. He led me out of the tangle of alleys in another direction, it seems, for when we sighted a lamp post we were in a half-familiar street with monotonous rows of mingled tenement blocks and old houses. Charter Street, it turned out to be, but I was too flustered to notice just where we hit it. We were too late for the elevated, and walked back downtown through Hanover Street. I remember that walk. We switched from Tremont up Beacon, and Pickman left me at the corner of Joy, where I turned off. I never spoke to him again.

Why did I drop him? Don't be impatient. Wait till I ring for coffee. We've had enough of the other stuff, but I for one need something. No—it wasn't the paintings I saw in that place; though I'll swear they were enough to get him ostracized in nine-tenths of the homes and clubs of Boston, and I guess you won't wonder now why I have to steer clear of subways and cellars. It was—something I found in my coat the next morning. You know, the curled-up paper tacked to that frightful canvas in the cellar; the thing I thought was a photograph of some scene he meant to use as a background for that monster. That last scare had come while I was reaching to uncurl it, and it seems I had vacantly crumpled it into my pocket. But here's the coffee—take it black, Eliot, if you're wise.

Yes, that paper was the reason I dropped Pickman; Richard Upton Pickman, the greatest artist I have ever known—and the foulest being that ever leaped the bounds of life into the pits of myth and madness. Eliot—old Reid was right. He wasn't strictly human. Either he was born in strange shadow, or he'd found a way to unlock the forbidden gate. It's all the same now, for he's gone—back into the fabulous darkness he loved to haunt. Here, let's have the chandelier going.

Don't ask me to explain or even conjecture about what I burned. Don't ask me, either, what lay behind the molelike scrambling Pickman was so keen to pass off as rats. There are secrets, you know, which might have come down from old Salem times, and Cotton Mather tells even stranger things. You know how damned lifelike Pickman's paintings were—how we all wondered where he got those faces.

Well—that paper wasn't a photograph of any background, after all. What it showed was simply the monstrous being he was painting on that awful canvas. It was the model he was using—and its background was merely the wall of the cellar studio in minute detail. But by God, Eliot, *it was a photograph from life.*

Yours Truly, Jack the Ripper

ROBERT BLOCH

Robert Bloch has been scaring the bejammers out of people for more than forty-five years, and he is still going strong. Although he will always be remembered for Psycho, *he has produced an enormous body of first-rate work in the horror genre, some of which has been adapted by others for films and television. He won a Hugo Award for his fantasy, "That Hell-Bound Train," in 1959. The present selection proves that his reputation is well-deserved.*

I looked at the stage Englishman. He looked at me.

"Sir Guy Hollis?" I asked.

"Indeed. Have I the pleasure of addressing John Carmody, the psychiatrist?"

I nodded. My eyes swept over the figure of my distinguished visitor. Tall, lean, sandy-haired—with the traditional tufted moustache. And the tweeds. I suspected a monocle concealed in a vest pocket, and wondered if he'd left his umbrella in the outer office.

But more than that, I wondered what the devil had impelled Sir Guy Hollis of the British Embassy to seek out a total stranger here in Chicago.

Sir Guy didn't help matters any as he sat down. He cleared his throat, glanced around nervously, tapped his pipe against the side of the desk. Then he opened his mouth.

"Mr. Carmody," he said, "have you ever heard of—Jack the Ripper?"

"The murderer?" I asked.

"Exactly. The greatest monster of them all. Worse than Springheel Jack or Crippen. Jack the Ripper. Red Jack."

"I've heard of him," I said.

"Do you know his history?"

"I don't think we'll get any place swapping old wives' tales about famous crimes of history."

He took a deep breath.

"This is no old wives' tale. It's a matter of life or death."

190

He was so wrapped up in his obsession he even talked that way. Well—I was willing to listen. We psychiatrists get paid for listening.

"Go ahead," I told him. "Let's have the story."

Sir Guy lit a cigarette and began to talk.

"London, 1888," he began. "Late summer and early fall. That was the time. Out of nowhere came the shadowy figure of Jack the Ripper—a stalking shadow with a knife, prowling through London's East End. Haunting the squalid dives of Whitechapel, Spitalfields. Where he came from no one knew. But he brought death. Death in a knife.

"Six times that knife descended to slash the throats and bodies of London's women. Drabs and alley sluts. August 7th was the date of the first butchery. They found her lying there with thirty-nine stab wounds. A ghastly murder. On August 31st, another victim. The press became interested. The slum inhabitants were more deeply interested still.

"Who was this unknown killer who prowled in their midst and struck at will in the deserted alleyways of nighttown? And what was more important—when would he strike again?

"September 8th was the date. Scotland Yard assigned special deputies. Rumors ran rampant. The atrocious nature of the slayings was the subject for shocking speculation.

"The killer used a knife—expertly. He cut throats and removed—certain portions—of the bodies after death. He chose victims and settings with a fiendish deliberation. No one saw him or heard him. But watchmen making their gray rounds in the dawn would stumble across the hacked and horrid thing that was the Ripper's handiwork.

"Who was he? What was he? A mad surgeon? A butcher? An insane scientist? A pathological degenerate escaped from an asylum? A deranged nobleman? A member of the London police?

"Then the poem appeared in the newspapers. The anonymous poem, designed to put a stop to speculations—but which only aroused public interest to a further frenzy. A mocking little stanza:

> I'm not a butcher, I'm not a Yid
> Nor yet a foreign skipper,
> But I'm your own true loving friend,
> Yours truly—Jack the Ripper.

"And on September 30th, two more throats were slashed open. There was silence, then, in London for a time. Silence, and a nameless fear. When would Red Jack strike again? They waited through October. Every figment of fog concealed his phantom presence. Concealed it well—for nothing was learned of the Ripper's identity, or his purpose. The drabs of London shivered in the raw wind of early November. Shivered, and were thankful for the coming of each morning's sun.

"November 9th. They found her in her room. She lay there very quietly, limbs neatly arranged. And beside her, with equal neatness, were laid her breasts and heart. The Ripper had outdone himself in execution.

"Then, panic. But needless panic. For though press, police, and populace alike waited in sick dread, Jack the Ripper did not strike again.

"Months passed. A year. The immediate interest died, but not the memory. They said Jack had skipped to America. That he had committed suicide. They said—and they wrote. They've written ever since. But to this day no one knows who Jack the Ripper was. Or why he killed. Or why he stopped killing."

Sir Guy was silent. Obviously he expected some comment from me.

"You tell the story well," I remarked. "Though with a slight emotional bias."

"I suppose you want to know why I'm interested?" he snapped.

"Yes. That's exactly what I'd like to know."

"Because," said Sir Guy Hollis, "I am on the trail of Jack the Ripper now. I think he's here—in Chicago!"

"Say that again."

"Jack the Ripper is alive, in Chicago, and I'm out to find him."

He wasn't smiling. It wasn't a joke.

"See here," I said. "What was the date of these murders?"

"August to November, 1888."

"1888? But if Jack the Ripper was an able-bodied man in 1888, he'd surely be dead today! Why look, man—if he were merely born in that year, he'd be fifty-seven years old today!"

"Would he?" smiled Sir Guy Hollis. "Or should I say, 'Would she?' Because Jack the Ripper may have been a woman. Or any number of things."

"Sir Guy," I said. "You came to the right person when you looked me up. You definitely need the services of a psychiatrist."

"Perhaps. Tell me, Mr. Carmody, do you think I'm crazy?"

I looked at him and shrugged. But I had to give him a truthful answer.

"Frankly—no."

"Then you might listen to the reasons I believe Jack the Ripper is alive today."

"I might."

"I've studied these cases for thirty years. Been over the actual ground. Talked to officials. Talked to friends and acquaintances of the poor drabs who were killed. Visited with men and women in the neighborhood. Collected an entire library of material touching on Jack the Ripper. Studied all the wild theories or crazy notions.

"I learned a little. Not much, but a little. I won't bore you with my conclusions. But there was another branch of inquiry that yielded more fruitful return. I have studied unsolved crimes. Murders.

"I could show you clippings from the papers of half the world's greatest cities. San Francisco. Shanghai. Calcutta. Omsk. Paris. Berlin. Pretoria. Cairo. Milan. Adelaide.

"The trail is there, the pattern. Unsolved crimes. Slashed throats of women. With the peculiar disfigurations and removals. Yes, I've followed a trail of blood. From New York westward across the continent. Then to the Pacific. From there to Africa. During the World War of 1914-18 it was Europe. After that, South America. And since 1930, the United States again. Eighty-seven such murders—and to the trained criminologist, all bear the stigma of the Ripper's handiwork.

"Recently there were the so-called Cleveland torso slayings. Remember? A shocking series. And finally, two recent deaths in Chicago. Within the past six months. One out on South Dearborn. The other somewhere up in Halsted. Same type of crime, same technique. I tell you, there are unmistakable indications in all these affairs—indications of the work of Jack the Ripper!"

"A very tight theory," I said. "I'll not question your evidence at all, or the deductions you draw. You're the criminologist, and I'll take your word for it. Just one thing remains to be explained. A minor point, perhaps, but worth mentioning."

"And what is that?" asked Sir Guy.

"Just how could a man of, let us say, eighty-five years commit these crimes? For if Jack the Ripper was around thirty in 1888 and lived, he'd be eighty-five today."

"Suppose he didn't get any older?" whispered Sir Guy.

"What's that?"

"Suppose Jack the Ripper didn't grow old? Suppose he is still a young man today?

"It's a crazy theory, I grant you," he said. "All the theories about the Ripper are crazy. The idea that he was a doctor. Or a maniac. Or a woman. The reasons advanced for such beliefs are flimsy enough. There's nothing to go by. So why should my notion be any worse?"

"Because people grow older," I reasoned with him. "Doctors, maniacs and women alike."

"What about—*sorcerers?*"

"Sorcerers?"

"Necromancers. Wizards. Practicers of Black Magic."

"What's the point?"

"I studied," said Sir Guy. "I studied everything. After a while I began to study the dates of the murders. The pattern those dates formed. The rhythm. The solar, lunar, stellar rhythm. The sidereal aspect. The astrological significance.

"Suppose Jack the Ripper didn't murder for murder's sake alone? Suppose he wanted to make—a sacrifice?"

"What kind of a sacrifice?"

Sir Guy shrugged. "It is said that if you offer blood to the dark gods they grant boons. Yes, if a blood offering is made at the proper time—when the moon and the stars are right—and with the proper ceremonies—they grant boons. Boons of youth. Eternal youth."

"But that's nonsense!"

"No. That's—Jack the Ripper."

I stood up. "A most interesting theory," I told him. "But why do you come here and tell it to me? I'm not an authority on witchcraft. I'm not a police official or criminologist. I'm a practicing psychiatrist. What's the connection?"

Sir Guy smiled.

"You are interested, then?"

"Well, yes. There must be some point."

"There is. But I wished to be assured of your interest first. Now I can tell you my plan."

"And just what is that plan?"

Sir Guy gave me a long look.

"John Carmody," he said, "you and I are going to capture Jack the Ripper."

2

That's the way it happened. I've given the gist of that first interview in all its intricate and somewhat boring detail, because I think it's important. It helps to throw some light on Sir Guy's character and attitude. And in view of what happened after that—

But I'm coming to those matters.

Sir Guy's thought was simple. It wasn't even a thought. Just a hunch.

"You know the people here," he told me. "I've inquired. That's why I came to you as the ideal man for my purpose. You number amongst your acquaintances many writers, painters, poets. The so-called intelligentsia. The lunatic fringe from the near north side.

"For certain reasons—never mind what they are—my clues lead me to infer that Jack the Ripper is a member of that element. He chooses to pose as an eccentric. I've a feeling that with you to take me around and introduce me to your set, I might hit upon the right person."

"It's all right with me," I said. "But just how are you going to look for him? As you say, he might be anybody, anywhere. And you have no idea what he looks like. He might be young or old. Jack the Ripper—a Jack of all trades? Rich man, poor man, begger man, thief, doctor, lawyer—how will you know?"

"We shall see." Sir Guy sighed heavily. "But I must find him. At once."

"Why the hurry?"

Sir Guy sighed again. "Because in two days he will kill again."

"Are you sure?"

"Sure as the stars. I've plotted this chart, you see. All of the murders correspond to certain astrological rhythm patterns. If, as I suspect, he makes a blood sacrifice to renew his youth, he must murder within two days. Notice the pattern of his first crimes in London. August 7th. Then August 31st. September 8th. September 30th. November 9th. Intervals of twenty-four days, nine days, twenty-two days—he killed two this time—and then forty days. Of course there were crimes in between. There had to be. But they weren't discovered and pinned on him.

"At any rate, I've worked out a pattern for him, based on all my data. And I say that within the next two days he kills. So I must seek him out, somehow, before then."

"And I'm still asking you what you want me to do."

"Take me out," said Sir Guy. "Introduce me to your friends. Take me to parties."

"But where do I begin? As far as I know, my artistic friends, despite their eccentricities, are all normal people."

"So is the Ripper. Perfectly normal. Except on certain nights." Again that faraway look in Sir Guy's eyes. "Then he becomes an ageless pathological monster, crouching to kill."

"All right," I said. "All right. I'll take you."

We made our plans. And that evening I took him over to Lester Baston's studio.

As we ascended to the penthouse roof in the elevator I took the opportunity to warn Sir Guy.

"Baston's a real screwball," I cautioned him. "So are his guests. Be prepared for anything and everything."

"I am." Sir Guy Hollis was perfectly serious. He put his hand in his trousers pocket and pulled out a gun.

"What the—" I began.

"If I see him I'll be ready," Sir Guy said. He didn't smile, either.

"But you can't go running around at a party with a loaded revolver in your pocket, man!"

"Don't worry, I won't behave foolishly."

I wondered. Sir Guy Hollis was not, to my way of thinking, a normal man.

We stepped out of the elevator, went toward Baston's apartment door.

"By the way," I murmured, "just how do you wish to be introduced? Shall I tell them who you are and what you are looking for?"

"I don't care. Perhaps it would be best to be frank."

"But don't you think that the Ripper—if by some miracle he or she is present—will immediately get the wind up and take cover?"

"I think the shock of the announcement that I am hunting the

Ripper would provoke some kind of betraying gesture on his part," said Sir Guy.

"It's a fine theory. But I warn you, you're going to be in for a lot of ribbing. This is a wild bunch."

Sir Guy smiled.

"I'm ready," he announced. "I have a little plan of my own. Don't be shocked at anything I do."

I nodded and knocked on the door.

Baston opened it and poured out into the hall. His eyes were as red as the maraschino cherries in his Manhattan. He teetered back and forth regarding us very gravely. He squinted at my square-cut homburg hat and Sir Guy's moustache.

"Aha," he intoned. "The Walrus and the Carpenter."

I introduced Sir Guy.

"Welcome," said Baston, gesturing us inside with over-elaborate courtesy. He stumbled after us into the garish parlor.

I stared at the crowd that moved restlessly through the fog of cigarette smoke.

It was the shank of the evening for this mob. Every hand held a drink. Every face held a slightly hectic flush. Over in one corner the piano was going full blast, but the imperious strains of the *March* from *The Love for Three Oranges* couldn't drown out the profanity from the crap game in the other corner.

Prokofieff had no chance against African polo, and one set of ivories rattled louder than the other.

Sir Guy got a monocle-full right away. He saw LaVerne Gonnister, the poetess, hit Hymie Kralik in the eye. He saw Hymie sit down on the floor and cry until Dick Pool accidentally stepped on his stomach as he walked through to the dining room for a drink.

He heard Nadia Vilinoff, the commercial artist, tell Johnny Odcutt that she thought his tattooing was in dreadful taste, and he saw Barclay Melton crawl under the dining room table with Johnny Odcutt's wife.

His zoological observations might have continued indefinitely if Lester Baston hadn't stepped to the center of the room and called for silence by dropping a vase on the floor.

"We have distinguished visitors in our midst," bawled Lester, waving his empty glass in our direction. "None other than the Walrus and the Carpenter. The Walrus is Sir Guy Hollis, a something-or-other from the British Embassy. The Carpenter, as you all know, is our own John Carmody, the prominent dispenser of libido liniment."

He turned and grabbed Sir Guy by the arm, dragging him to the middle of the carpet. For a moment I thought Hollis might object, but a quick wink reassured me. He was prepared for this.

"It is our custom, Sir Guy," said Baston, loudly, "to subject our new friends to a little cross-examination. Just a little formality at these very formal gatherings, you understand. Are you prepared to answer questions?"

Sir Guy nodded and grinned.

"Very well," Baston muttered. "Friends—I give you this bundle from Britain. Your witness."

Then the ribbing started. I meant to listen, but at that moment Lydia Dare saw me and dragged me off into the vestibule for one of those Darling-I-waited-for-your-call-all-day routines.

By the time I got rid of her and went back, the impromptu quiz session was in full swing. From the attitude of the crowd, I gathered that Sir Guy was doing all right for himself.

Then Baston himself interjected a question that upset the apple-cart.

"And what, may I ask, brings you to our midst tonight? What is your mission, oh Walrus?"

"I'm looking for Jack the Ripper."

Nobody laughed.

Perhaps it struck them all the way it did me. I glanced at my neighbors and began to *wonder.*

LaVerne Gonnister. Hymie Kralik. Harmless. Dick Pool. Nadia Vilinoff. Johnny Odcutt and his wife. Barclay Melton. Lydia Dare. All harmless.

But what a forced smile on Dick Pool's face! And that sly, self-conscious smirk that Barclay Melton wore!

Oh, it was absurd, I grant you. But for the first time I saw these people in a new light. I wondered about their lives—their secret lives beyond the scenes of parties.

How many of them were playing a part, concealing something?

Who here would worship Hecate and grant that horrid goddess the dark boon of blood?

Even Lester Baston might be masquerading.

The mood was upon us all, for a moment. I saw questions flicker in the circle of eyes around the room.

Sir Guy stood there, and I could swear he was fully conscious of the situation he'd created, and enjoyed it.

I wondered idly just what was *really* wrong with him. Why he had this odd fixation concerning Jack the Ripper. Maybe he was hiding secrets, too. . . .

Baston, as usual, broke the mood. He burlesqued it.

"The Walrus isn't kidding, friends," he said. He slapped Sir Guy on the back and put his arm around him as he orated. "Our English cousin is really on the trail of the fabulous Jack the Ripper. You all remember Jack the Ripper, I presume? Quite a cut-up in the old days, as I recall. Really had some ripping good times when he went out on a tear.

"The Walrus has some idea that the Ripper is still alive, probably prowling around Chicago with a Boy Scout knife. In fact—" Baston paused impressively and shot it out in a rasping stage whisper—"in fact, he has reason to believe that Jack the Ripper might even be right here in our midst tonight."

There was the expected reaction of giggles and grins. Baston eyed Lydia Dare reprovingly. "You girls needn't laugh," he smirked. "Jack the Ripper might be a woman, too, you know. Sort of a Jill the Ripper."

"You mean you actually suspect one of us?" shrieked LaVerne Gonnister, simpering up to Sir Guy. "But that Jack the Ripper person disappeared ages ago, didn't he? In 1888?"

"Aha!" interrupted Baston. "How do you know so much about it, young lady? Sounds suspicious! Watch her, Sir Guy—she may not be as young as she appears. These lady poets have dark pasts."

The tension was gone, the mood was shattered, and the whole thing was beginning to degenerate into a trivial party joke. The man who had played the *March* was eyeing the piano with a *scherzo* gleam in his eye that augured ill for Prokofieff. Lydia Dare was glancing at the kitchen, waiting to make a break for another drink.

Then Baston caught it.

"Guess what?" he yelled. "The Walrus has a gun."

His embracing arm had slipped and encountered the hard outline of the gun in Sir Guy's pocket. He snatched it out before Hollis had the opportunity to protest.

I stared hard at Sir Guy, wondering if this thing had carried far enough. But he flicked a wink my way and I remembered he had told me not to be alarmed.

So I waited as Baston broached a drunken inspiration.

"Let's play fair with our friend the Walrus," he cried. "He came all the way from England to our party on this mission. If none of you is willing to confess, I suggest we give him a chance to find out—the hard way."

"What's up?" asked Johnny Odcutt.

"I'll turn out the lights for one minute. Sir Guy can stand here with his gun. If anyone in this room is the Ripper he can either run for it or take the opportunity to—well, eradicate his pursuer. Fair enough?"

It was even sillier than it sounds, but it caught the popular fancy. Sir Guy's protests went unheard in the ensuing babble. And before I could stride over and put in my two cents' worth, Lester Baston had reached the light switch.

"Don't anybody move," he announced, with fake solemnity. "For one minute we will remain in darkness—perhaps at the mercy of a killer. At the end of that time, I'll turn up the lights again and look for bodies. Choose your partners, ladies and gentlemen."

The lights went out.

Somebody giggled.

I heard footsteps in the darkness. Mutterings.

A hand brushed my face.

The watch on my wrist ticked violently. But even louder, rising above it, I heard another thumping. The beating of my heart.

Absurd. Standing in the dark with a group of tipsy fools. And yet there was real terror lurking here, rustling through the velvet blackness.

Jack the Ripper prowled in darkness like this. And Jack the Ripper had a knife. Jack the Ripper had a madman's brain and a madman's purpose.

But Jack the Ripper was dead, dead and dust these many years—by every human law.

Only there are no human laws when you feel yourself in the darkness, when the darkness hides and protects and the outer mask slips off your face and you feel something welling up within you, a brooding shapeless purpose that is brother to the blackness.

Sir Guy Hollis shrieked.

There was a grisly thud.

Baston put the lights on.

Everybody screamed.

Sir Guy Hollis lay sprawled on the floor in the center of the room. The gun was still clutched in his hand.

I glanced at the faces, marveling at the variety of expressions human beings can assume when confronting horror.

All the faces were present in the circle. Nobody had fled. And yet Sir Guy Hollis lay there.

LaVerne Gonnister was wailing and hiding her face.

"All right."

Sir Guy rolled over and jumped to his feet. He was smiling.

"Just an experiment, eh? If Jack the Ripper *were* among those present, and thought I had been murdered, he would have betrayed himself in some way when the lights went on and he saw me lying there.

"I am convinced of your individual and collective innocence. Just a gentle spoof, my friends."

Hollis stared at the goggling Baston and the rest of them crowding in behind him.

"Shall we leave, John?" he called to me. "It's getting late, I think."

Turning, he headed for the closet. I followed him. Nobody said a word.

It was a pretty dull party after that.

3

I met Sir Guy the following evening as we agreed, on the corner of Twenty-Ninth and South Halsted.

After what had happened the night before, I was prepared for almost anything. But Sir Guy seemed matter-of-fact enough as he stood huddled against a grimy doorway and waited for me to appear.

"Boo!" I said, jumping out suddenly. He smiled. Only the betraying gesture of his left hand indicated that he'd instinctively reached for his gun when I startled him.

"All ready for our wild-goose chase?" I asked.

"Yes." He nodded. "I'm glad that you agreed to meet me without asking questions," he told me. "It shows you trust my judgment." He took my arm and edged me along the street slowly.

"It's foggy tonight, John," said Sir Guy Hollis. "Like London."

I nodded.

"Cold, too, for November."

I nodded again and half-shivered my agreement.

"Curious," mused Sir Guy. "London fog and November. The place and the time of the Ripper murders."

I grinned through darkness. "Let me remind you, Sir Guy, that this isn't London, but Chicago. And it isn't November, 1888. It's over fifty years later."

Sir Guy returned my grin, but without mirth. "I'm not so sure, at that," he murmured. "Look about you. Those tangled alleys and twisted streets. They're like the East End. Mitre Square. And surely they are as ancient as fifty years, at least."

"You're in the black neighborhood of South Clark Street," I said shortly. "And why you dragged me down here I still don't know."

"It's a hunch," Sir Guy admitted. "Just a hunch on my part, John. I want to wander around down here. There's the same geographical conformation in these streets as in those courts where the Ripper roamed and slew. That's where we'll find him, John. Not in the bright lights, but down here in the darkness. The darkness where he waits and crouches."

"Isn't that why you brought a gun?" I asked. I was unable to keep a trace of sarcastic nervousness from my voice. All this talk, this incessant obsession with Jack the Ripper, got on my nerves more than I cared to admit.

"We may need a gun," said Sir Guy, gravely. "After all, tonight is the appointed night."

I sighed. We wandered on through the foggy, deserted streets. Here and there a dim light burned above a gin-mill doorway. Otherwise, all was darkness and shadow. Deep, gaping alleyways loomed as we proceeded down a slanting side street.

We crawled through that fog, alone and silent, like two tiny maggots floundering within a shroud.

"Can't you see there's not a soul around these streets?" I said.

"He's bound to come," said Sir Guy. "He'll be drawn here. This is what I've been looking for. A *genius loci*. An evil spot that attracts evil. Always, when he slays, it's in the slums.

"You see, that must be one of his weaknesses. He has a fascination for squalor. Besides, the women he needs for sacrifice are more easily found in the dives and stewpots of a great city."

"Well, let's go into one of the dives or stewpots," I suggested. "I'm cold. Need a drink. This damned fog gets into your bones. You Britishers can stand it, but I like warmth and dry heat."

We emerged from our sidestreet and stood upon the threshold of an alley.

Through the white clouds of mist ahead, I discerned a dim blue light, a naked bulb dangling from a beer sign above an alley tavern.

"Let's take a chance," I said. "I'm beginning to shiver."

"Lead the way," said Sir Guy. I led him down the alley passage. We halted before the door of the dive.

"What are you waiting for?" he asked.

"Just looking in," I told him. "This is a rough neighborhood, Sir Guy. Never know what you're liable to run into. And I'd prefer we didn't get into the wrong company. Some of these places resent white customers."

"Good idea, John."

I finished my inspection through the doorway. "Looks deserted," I murmured. "Let's try it."

We entered a dingy bar. A feeble light flickered above the counter and railing, but failed to penetrate the further gloom of the back booths.

A gigantic black lolled across the bar. He scarcely stirred as we came in, but his eyes flicked open quite suddenly and I knew he noted our presence and was judging us.

"Evening," I said.

He took his time before replying. Still sizing us up. Then, he grinned.

"Evening, gents. What's your pleasure?"

"Gin," I said. "Two gins. It's a cold night."

"That's right, gents."

He poured, I paid, and took the glasses over to one of the booths. We wasted no time in emptying them.

I went over to the bar and got the bottle. Sir Guy and I poured ourselves another drink. The big man went back into his doze, with one wary eye half-open against any sudden activity.

The clock over the bar ticked on. The wind was rising outside, tearing the shroud of fog to ragged shreds. Sir Guy and I sat in the warm booth and drank our gin.

He began to talk, and the shadows crept up about us to listen.

He rambled a great deal. He went over everything he'd said in the office when I met him, just as though I hadn't heard it before. The poor devils with obsessions are like that.

I listened very patiently. I poured Sir Guy another drink. And another.

But the liquor only made him more talkative. How he did run on! About ritual killings and prolonging the life unnaturally—the whole fantastic tale came out again. And of course, he maintained his un-yielding conviction that the Ripper was abroad tonight.

I suppose I was guilty of goading him.

"Very well," I said, unable to keep the impatience from my voice. "Let us say that your theory is correct—even though we must overlook every natural law and swallow a lot of superstition to give it any credence.

"But let us say, for the sake of argument, that you are right. Jack the Ripper was a man who discovered how to prolong his own life through making human sacrifices. He did travel around the world as you believe. He is in Chicago now and is planning to kill. In other words, let us suppose that everything you claim is gospel truth. So what?"

"What do you mean, 'so what'?" said Sir Guy.

"I mean—so what?" I answered him. "If all this is true, it still doesn't prove that by sitting down in a dingy gin-mill on the South Side, Jack the Ripper is going to walk in here and let you kill him, or turn him over to the police. And come to think of it, I don't even know now just what you intend to *do* with him if you ever did find him."

Sir Guy gulped his gin. "I'd capture the bloody swine," he said. "Capture him and turn him over to the government, together with all the papers and documentary evidence I've collected against him over a period of many years. I've spent a fortune investigating this affair, I tell you, a fortune! His capture will mean the solution of hundreds of unsolved crimes, of that I am convinced."

In vino veritas. Or was all this babbling the result of too much gin? It didn't matter. Sir Guy Hollis had another. I sat there and wondered what to do with him. The man was rapidly working up to a climax of hysterical drunkenness.

"That's enough," I said, putting out my hand as Sir Guy reached for the half-emptied bottle again. "Let's call a cab and get out of here. It's getting late and it doesn't look as though your elusive friend is going to put in his appearance. Tomorrow, if I were you, I'd plan to turn all those papers and documents over to the FBI. If you're so convinced of the truth of your theory, they are competent to make a very thorough investigation, and find your man."

"No." Sir Guy was drunkenly obstinate. "No cab."

"But let's get out of here anyway," I said, glancing at my watch. "It's past midnight."

He sighed, shrugged, and rose unsteadily. As he started for the door, he tugged the gun free from his pocket.

"Here, give me that!" I whispered. "You can't walk around the street brandishing that thing."

I took the gun and slipped it inside my coat. Then I got hold of his right arm and steered him out of the door. The black man didn't look up as we departed.

We stood shivering in the alleyway. The fog had increased. I couldn't see either end of the alley from where we stood. It was cold. Damp. Dark. Fog or no fog, a little wind was whispering secrets to the shadows at our backs.

Sir Guy, despite his incapacity, still stared apprehensively at the alley, as though he expected to see a figure approaching.

Disgust got the better of me.

"Childish foolishness," I snorted. "Jack the Ripper, indeed! I call this carrying a hobby too far."

"Hobby?" He faced me. Through the fog I could see his distorted face. "You call this a hobby?"

"Well, what is it?" I grumbled. "Just why else are you so interested in tracking down this mythical killer?"

My arm held his. But his stare held me.

"In London," he whispered. "In 1888 . . . one of those nameless drabs the Ripper slew . . . was my mother."

"What?"

"Later I was recognized by my father, and legitimatized. We swore to give our lives to find the Ripper. My father was the first to search. He died in Hollywood in 1926—on the trail of the Ripper. They said he was stabbed by an unknown assailant in a brawl. But I knew who that assailant was.

"So I've taken up his work, do you see, John? I've carried on. And I will carry on until I do find him and kill him with my own hands."

I believed him then. He wouldn't give up. He wasn't just a drunken babbler any more. He was as fanatical, as determined, as relentless as the Ripper himself.

Tomorrow he'd be sober. He'd continue the search. Perhaps he'd turn those papers over to the FBI. Sooner or later, with such persistence—and with his motive—he'd be successful. I'd always known he had a motive.

"Let's go," I said, steering him down the alley.

"Wait a minute," said Sir Guy. "Give me back my gun." He lurched a little. "I'd feel better with the gun on me."

He pressed me into the dark shadows of a little recess.

I tried to shrug him off, but he was insistent.

"Let me carry the gun, now, John," he mumbled.

"All right," I said.

I reached into my coat, brought my hand out.

"But that's not a gun," he protested. "That's a knife."

"I know."

I bore down on him swiftly.

"John!" he screamed.

"Never mind the 'John,' " I whispered, raising the knife. "Just call me . . . Jack."

The Screaming Laugh

CORNELL WOOLRICH

Woolrich wrote codified nightmares; the consistency, unity and darkness of his vision has perhaps never been truly understood in his own country as it is on the continent, where he is considered a major American writer and where his The Bride Wore Black *was the basis of one of Truffaut's most successful films noir. Of the short stories he turned out for the pulp magazines in the 1930's and 1940's, perhaps none was as terrifying as "The Screaming Laugh," whose final pages plunge into a horror so inexpressible that, perhaps, it is only the indirection which saves us (and Woolrich himself) from going all the way.*

A call came into constabulary headquarters, at the county seat, about seven one morning. It was from Milford Junction, a local doctor named Johnson reporting the death of one Eleazar Hunt some time during the night. Just a routine report, as required by law.

"And have you ascertained the causes?" asked the sheriff.

"Yes, I just got through examining him. I find he had burst a blood vessel—laughing too hard. Nothing out of the usual about it, but of course that's for you to decide."

"Well, I'll send a man over to check." The sheriff turned to Al Traynor, one of the members of his constabulary, who had just come in. "Drive down Milford Junction way, Al. Local resident near there, name of Eleazar Hunt, died from laughing too hard. Look things over just for the record."

"Laughing too hard?" Traynor looked at him when he heard that. Then he shrugged. "Well, I suppose if you've got to go, it's better to go laughing than crying."

He returned to his car and started off for Milford Junction. It was about three-quarters of an hour's drive by the new state highway that had been completed only two or three years before, although the hamlet itself wasn't directly on this, had to be reached by a dirt feeder road that branched off it. The Hunt place was about half a mile on the

207

other side of it, near a point where the highway curved back again to rejoin the short cut, cutting a corner off the late Mr. Hunt's acreage.

The white-painted farmhouse with its green shutters gleamed dazzlingly in the early morning sunshine. Peach trees, bursting into bloom before it, hid the roof and cast blue shade on the ground. A wire fence at the back enclosed a poultry yard, and beyond that were hen houses, a stall from which a black-and-white cow looked plaintively forth, a toolshed, a roofed well, a vegetable garden. It was an infinitely pleasant-looking little property, and if death had struck there at all, there was no outward sign.

There was a coupé standing in the road before the house, belonging to the doctor who had reported the death, presumably. Traynor coasted up behind it, braked, got out and went in through the gate. He had to crouch to pass under some of the low-hanging peach boughs. There was a cat sunning itself on the lower doorstep. He reached down to tickle it and a man came around the corner of the house just then, stood looking at him.

He was sunburned, husky and about thirty. He wore overalls and was carrying an empty millet sack in his hand. Judging by the commotion audible at the back, he had just finished feeding the poultry. His eyes were shrewd and lidded in a perpetual squint that had nothing to do with the sun.

"You the undertaker already?" he wanted to know.

"Sheriff's office," snapped Traynor, none too pleased at the comparison. "You work here?"

"Yep. Hired man."

"How long?"

" 'Bout six months."

"What's your name?"

"Dan Fears."

"He keep anybody else on?"

Fears answered indirectly, with a scornful gesture toward the back. "Not enough to keep one man busy as it is. Tend one cow and pick up a few eggs."

It occurred to Traynor if there was that little to do, why hadn't the cow been led out to pasture by now and the poultry fed earlier? He went on in, stepping high over the cat. She looked indolently upward at his heel as it passed over her.

A shaggy, slow-moving man was coming toward the screen door to meet Traynor as he pushed through it with a single cursory knock at its frame. Johnson was a typical country doctor, of a type growing scarcer by the year. You could tell by looking at him that he'd never hurried or got excited in his life. You could surmise that he'd never refused a middle-of-the-night call from miles away in the dead of winter either. He was probably highly competent, in spite of his misleading rusticity.

"Hello, son." He nodded benignly. "You from the sheriff's office? I was just going back to my own place to make out the death certificate."

"Can I see him?"

"Why, shore. Right in here." The doctor parted a pair of old-fashioned sliding doors and revealed the "front parlor" of the house. Across the top of each window was stretched a valance of faded red plush, ending in a row of little plush balls. On a table stood an oil lamp—there was no electricity this far out—with a frosted glass dome and a lot of little glass prisms dangling from it.

There was an old-fashioned reclining chair with an adjustable back near the table and lamp. Just now it was tilted only slightly, at a comfortable reading position. It was partly covered over with an ordinary bedsheet, like some furniture is in summertime, only the sheet bulged in places and a clawlike hand hung down from under it, over the arm of the chair. Traynor reached down, turned back the upper edge of the sheet. It was hard not to be jolted. The face was a cartoon of frozen hilarity. It wasn't just that death's-head grimace that so often, because of bared teeth, faintly suggests a grin. It was the real thing. It was Laughter, permanently photographed in death. The eyes were creased into slits; you could see the dried but still faintly glistening saline traces of the tears that had overflowed their ducts down alongside his nose. The mouth was a vast upturned crescent full of yellowish horse teeth. The whole head was thrown stiffly back at an angle of uncontrollable risibility. It was uncanny only because it was so motionless, so silent, so permanent.

"You found him just like this?"

"Shore. Had to examine him, of course, but rigor had already set in, so I figger nothing I did disturbed him much." Johnson chuckled inside himself, gave Traynor a humorously reproachful look. "Why, son, you don't think this is one of *those* things? Shame on you!"

He saw that he hadn't convinced the younger man by his raillery.

"Why, I examined him thoroughly, son," he protested gently. "I know my business as well as the next man. I tell you not a finger was laid on this man. Nothing's happened to him but what I said. He burst a blood vessel from laughing too hard. Course, if you want me to perform a complete autopsy, send his innards and the contents of his stomach down to the state laboratory—" It was said with an air of paternal patience, as if he were humoring a headstrong boy.

"I'm not discrediting your competence, doctor. What's this?" Traynor picked up a little booklet, lying open tent-shaped on the table. *Joe Miller's Joke Book*, it said on the cover, and the copyright was 1892.

"That's what he was reading. That's what got him, I reckon. Found it lying on the floor under his right hand. Fell from his fingers at the moment of death, I guess."

"Same page?"

"Same one it's open at now. You want to find the exact joke he was reading when he passed away, that what you're aiming at, son?" More of that paternal condescension.

Traynor evidently did, or at least an approximation of what type of killing humor this was. He stopped doing anything else and stood there stock-still for five minutes, conscientiously reading every joke on the two open pages, about a dozen altogether. The first one read:

Pat: Were you calm and collected when the explosion occurred?
Mike: I wuz calm and Murphy wuz collected.

The others were just about as bad, some even staler.

"Do me a favor, doc," he said abruptly, passing the booklet over. "Read these for yourself."

"Ph, now, here—" protested Johnson, with a rueful glance at the still form in the chair, but he went ahead and did what Traynor requested.

Traynor watched his expression closely. He'd only just met the man, but he could already tell he was full of a dry sort of humor. But not a gleam showed, his face never changed from first to last; it became, if anything, sort of mournful.

"D'you see what I mean?" was all Traynor said, taking the booklet back and tossing it aside.

Johnson shook his head. "No two people have the same sense of humor, remember that, son. What's excruciatingly funny to one man goes right over another's head. Likely, these jokes were new to him, not mossbacked like they are to you and me."

"Did you know him at all, doc?"

"Just to say howdy to on the road."

"Ever see him smile much?"

"Can't say I did. But there's nothing funny about saying howdy. What is it you're driving at, son?"

Traynor didn't answer. He went over to the corpse, unbuttoned its shirt, and scrutinized the underarms and ribs with exhaustive intentness.

The doctor just stood looking on. "You won't find any marks of violence, son. I've been all over that."

Next Traynor squatted down by the feet, drew up one trousers leg to the knees, then the other. Johnson by this time, it was plain to see, considered him a bad case of dementia detectivis. Traynor seemed to see something at last; he smiled grimly. All Johnson could see were a pair of shanks encased in wool socks, supported by garters. Patent garters, sold by the million, worn by the million.

"Found something suspicious?" he asked, but without conviction, it was easy to see.

"Suspicious isn't the word," Traynor murmured low. "Damning."

"Damning whom—and of what?" said Johnson dryly.

Again Traynor didn't answer.

He hurriedly unlaced both of Hunt's shoes, dropped them off. Then he unfastened one garter and stripped the sock off his foot. Turned it inside out and peered at the sole. Peered at the sole of the foot itself too. He stripped the other one off and went through the same proceeding. Johnson, meanwhile, was shaking his head disapprovingly, as if his patience were being overtaxed.

"You are the most pee-culiar young fellow I ever hope to meet," he sighed.

Traynor balled up the two socks, and thrust one into each pocket of his coat, garter and all. They were black—fortunately. He flipped the sheet back over the bared feet, concealing them. A little wisp of something rose in the air as he did so, disturbed by the draft of his doing that, fluttered, winged downward again. A little bit of fluff, it seemed to be. He went after it, nevertheless, retrieved it, took an envelope out of his pocket, and thrust it in.

Johnson was past even questioning his actions by now; he was convinced they were unaccountable by all rational standards, anyway. "Would you care to talk to Mrs. Hunt?" he asked.

"Yes, I sure would," Traynor said curtly.

Johnson went out to the hall, called respectfully up the stairs:

"Mrs. Hunt, honey."

She was very ready to come down, Traynor noticed. Her footsteps began to descend almost before the words were out of the doctor's mouth. As though she'd been poised right up above at the head of the staircase, waiting for the summons.

He couldn't help a slight start of surprise as she came into sight. He had expected someone near Hunt's own age. She was about twenty-eight, the buxom blonde type. "Second wife," Traynor thought.

She had reached the bottom by now, and the doctor introduced them.

"This is Mr. Traynor of the sheriff's office."

"How do you do?" she said mournfully. But her eyes were clear, so she must have stopped crying some time before. "Did you want to talk to me?"

"Just to ask you the main facts, that's all."

"Oh. Well, let's go outdoors, huh? It—it sort of weighs you down in here." She glanced toward the partly open parlor doors, glanced hurriedly away again.

They went outside, began to stroll aimlessly along the front of the house, then around the corner and along the side. He could see Fears out there in the sun, beyond the poultry yard, hoeing the vegetable patch. Fears turned his head, looked over his shoulder at them as they came into sight, then looked down again. Hunt's widow seemed unaware of his existence.

"Well," she was saying, "all I can tell you is, I went upstairs to bed about ten o'clock last night, left him down there reading by the lamp. I'm a sound sleeper, and before I knew it, it was daybreak and the roosters woke me up. I saw he'd never come up to bed. I hurried down, and there he was just like I'd left him, lamp still lit and all, only the book had fallen out of his hand. He had this broad grin on his face and—"

"He did?" he interrupted.

"Yes. Isn't it spooky?" She shuddered. "Did you see it?"

"I did. And spooky," he said slowly, "is a very good word for it."

If he meant anything by that, she seemed to miss it completely.

She wound up the little there was left of her story. "I tried to wake him, and when I couldn't, I knew what it was. I called to Fears, but he was out back someplace, so I ran all the way down the road to Dr. Johnson's house myself and brought him back."

"Did he usually stay down alone like that, nights, and read?"

"Yes. Only in the beginning, when I first married him, he used to read things like mail order catalogues and such. Well, I'd tried to liven him up a little lately. I bought that joke book for him and left it lying around, tried to coax him to read it. He wouldn't have any part of it at first, pretending not to be interested, but I think on the sly he began to dip into it after I'd go upstairs at nights. He wasn't used to laughing and he got a stitch or something, I guess. Maybe he was ashamed to have me catch him at it and tried to hold it in—and that's what happened to him."

They were lingering under the parlor windows. He'd stopped un-noticeably, so she had too, perforce. He was gazing blankly around, eyes on the treetops, the fleecy clouds skimming by, everywhere but the right place. He'd seen something on the ground, and the job was to retrieve it right under her eyes without letting her see him do it.

"Do you mind?" he said, and took out a package of cigarettes. It was crumpled from being carried around on his person for days, and in trying to shake one out, he lost nearly the whole contents. He bent down and picked them up again one by one, with a fine disregard for hygiene, and each time something else as well. It was very neatly done. It went over her head completely.

They turned around and went slowly back to the front of the house again. As they were rounding the corner once more, Traynor looked back. He saw Fears raise his head and look after them at that moment. "Very allergic to my being here," Traynor thought to himself.

Johnson came out of the door.

"The undertaker's here."

And he looked questioningly at Traynor; the latter nodded his permission for removal.

She said, "Oh, I'd better get upstairs; I don't want to—see him go," and hurriedly ran inside.

Traynor didn't hang around to watch, either. He drifted back around the side of the house again. He let himself through the poultry yard, and out at the far side of it, where Fears was puttering around. He approached him with a fine aimlessness, like a man who has nothing to do with himself and gravitates toward the nearest person in sight to kill time chatting.

"He had a nice place here," he remarked.

Fears straightened, leaned on his hoe, drew his sleeve across his forehead. "No money in it, though." He was looking the other way, off from Traynor.

"What do you figure she'll do, keep on running it herself now that he's gone?"

The question should have brought the other's head around toward him, at least. It didn't. Fears spat reflectively, still kept looking stubbornly away from him.

"I don't think she's cut out for it, don't think she'd make a go of it."

There's something in this direction, away from where he's looking, that he doesn't want me to notice, Traynor told himself. He subtly jockeyed himself around so that he could look behind him without turning his entire head.

There was a toolshed there. Implements were stacked up against the wall at the back of it. The door was open and the sun shone sufficiently far in to reveal them. It glinted from the working edges of shovels, rakes, spades. But he noted a trowel with moist clayey soil drying out along its wedge; it was drying to a dirty gray white color.

"That looks like the well," he thought. Aloud he said: "Sun's getting hotter by the minute. Think I'll have a drink."

Fears dropped the hoe handle, stooped and got it again.

"I'd advise you to get it from the kitchen," he said tautly. "Well's all stirred up and muddy, 'pears like part of the sides must have crumbled. Have to 'low it to settle."

"Oh, I'm not choosy," Traynor remarked, strolling toward it. It hadn't rained in weeks. He shifted around to the far side of the structure, where he could face Fears while he pretended to dabble with the chained drinking cup.

There could be no mistaking it, the man was suddenly tense, rigid, out there in the sun, even while he went ahead stiffly hoeing. Every play of his shoulders and arms was forced. He wasn't even watching what he was doing, his hoe was damaging some tender young shoots.

Traynor didn't bother getting his drink after all. He knew all he needed to know now. What's Fears been up to down there that he don't want me to find out about?—Traynor wondered. And more important still, did it have anything to do with Eleazar Hunt's death? He couldn't answer the first—yet—but he already had more than a sneaking suspicion that the answer to the second was yes.

He sauntered back toward the tiller.

"You're right," he admitted; "it's all soupy."

With every step that took him farther away from the well rim, he could see more and more of the apprehension lift from Fears. It was almost physical, the way he seemed to straighten out, loosen up there under his eyes, until he was all relaxed again.

"Told you so," Fears muttered, and once again he wiped his forehead with a great wide sweep of the arm. But it looked more like relief this time than sweat.

"Well, take it easy." Traynor drifted lethargically back toward the front of the house once more. He knew Fears's eyes were following him every step of the way; he could almost feel them boring into the back of his skull. But he knew that if he turned and looked, the other would lower his head too quickly for him to catch him at it, so he didn't bother.

Hunt's body had been removed now and Dr. Johnson was on the point of leaving. They walked out to the roadway together toward their cars.

"Well, son," the doctor wanted to know, "still looking for something ornery in this or are you satisfied?"

"Perfectly satisfied now," Traynor assured him grimly, but he didn't say in which way he meant it. "Tell the truth, doc," he added. "Did you ever see a corpse grin that broadly before?"

"There you go again," sighed Johnson. "Well, no, can't say I have. But there is such a thing as cadaveric spasm, you know."

"There is," Traynor agreed. "And this isn't it. In fact this is so remarkable I'm going to have it photographed before I let the undertaker put a finger to him. I'd like to keep a record of it."

"Shucks," the doctor scoffed as he got in his coupé. "Why, I bet there never was a normal decease yet that couldn't be made to 'pear unnatural if you tried hard enough."

"And there never was an unnatural one yet," Traynor answered softly, that couldn't be made to appear normal—if you were willing to take things for granted."

After he had arranged for the photographs to be taken, he dropped in at the general store. A place like that, he knew, was the nerve center, the telephone exchange, of the village, so to speak. The news of Eleazar Hunt's death had spread by now, and the cracker barrel brigade were holding a postmortem. Traynor, who was not known by sight to anyone present, for his duties had not brought him over this way much, did not identify himself for fear of making them self-conscious in the presence of the law. He hung around, trying to make up his mind between two brands of plug tobacco, neither of which he intended buying, meanwhile getting an earful.

"Waal," said one individual, chewing a straw, "guess we'll never know now whether he actually did git all that money from the highway commission folks claim he did, for slicin' off a corner of his propitty to run that new road through."

"He always claimed he didn't. Not a penny of it ever showed up in the bank. My cousin works there and he'd be the first one to know it if it did."

"They say he tuck and hid it out at his place, that's why. Too mean to trust the bank, and he didn't want people thinking he was rich."

An ancient of eighty stepped forth, right angled over a hickory stick, and tapped it commandingly to gain the floor. "Shows ye it don't pay to teach an old dog new tricks! I've knowed Eleazar Hunt since he was knee-high to a grasshopper, and this is the first time I ever heard tell of him even smiling, let alone laughing fit to kill like they claim he done. Exceptin' just once, but that were beyond his control and didn't count."

"When was that?" asked Traynor, chiming in carefully casual. He knew by experience the best way to bring out these villagers' full narrative powers was to act bored stiff.

The old man fastened on him eagerly, glad of an audience. "Why, right in here where we're standing now, 'bout two years ago. Him and me was both standing up to the counter to git waited on, and Andy took me first and asked me what I wanted. So I raised this here stick of mine to point up at the shelf and without meaning to, I grazed Eleazar's side with the tip of it—I can't see so good any more, you know. Well, sir, for a minute I couldn't believe my ears. Here he was, not only laughing, but giggling like a girl, clutching at his ribs and shying away from me. Then the minute he got free of the stock, he changed right back to his usual self, mouth turned down like a horse-shoe, snapped, 'Careful what you're doing, will you!' Ticklish, that's all it was. Some's more so than others."

"Anyone else see that but you?"

"I saw it," said the storekeeper. "I was standing right behind the counter when it happened. I never knew that about him until then myself. Funny mixture, to be ticklish with a glum disposition like he had."

"And outside of that, you say you never saw him smile?"

"Not even as a boy!" declared the old man vehemently.

"*She* was livening him up, though, lately," qualified the store-keeper. "Heard she was making right smart progress too."

"Who told you?" asked Traynor, lidding his eyes.

"Why, she did herself."

Traynor just nodded to himself. Buildup beforehand, he was thinking.

"Yes, and that's what killed him!" insisted the garrulous old man. "Way I figger it, he'd never used them muscles around the mouth that you shape smiles with and so they'd gone useless on him from lack of practice. Just like if you don't use your right arm for fifty years, it withers on you. Then she comes along and starts him to laughing at joke books and whatnot, and the strain was too much for him. Like I said before, you can't teach an old dog new tricks! These old codgers that marry young chickens!"

All Traynor did, after the old man had stumped out with an accu-rate shot at the brass receptacle inside the door, was get his name from the storekeeper and jot it down in his notebook, without letting anyone see him do it. The ancient one just might come in handy as a witness, if a murder trial was to come up—provided of course that he lasted that long.

"Well, how does it look?" the sheriff asked Traynor when he finally got back to headquarters.

"It doesn't look good," was the grim answer. "It was murder."

The sheriff drew in his breath involuntarily. "Got any evidence?" he said finally.

His eyes opened wide in astonishment as a small joke book, a handful of chicken feathers, and a pair of black socks with garters still attached, descended upon his desk. "What've these got to do with it?" he asked in stupefaction. "You don't mean to tell me—this is your evidence, do you?"

"It certainly is," said Traynor gloomily. "It's all the evidence there is or ever will be. This, and photographs I've had taken of his face. It's the cleverest thing that was ever committed under the sun. But not quite clever enough."

"Well, don't you think you'd better at least tell me what makes you so sure? What did you see?"

"All right," said Traynor irritably, "here's what I saw—and I know you're going to say right away it didn't amount to a row of pins. I saw a dead man with a broad grin on his face, too broad to be natural. I saw chicken feathers lying scattered around the ground—"

"It's a poultry farm, after all; they raise chickens there."

"But their tips are all bent over at right angles to the quill; show me the chicken that can do that to itself. And they were lying *outside* the wired enclosure, under the window of the room in which the dead man was."

"And?" said the sheriff, pointing to the socks.

"A few fibers of the same chicken feathers, adhering to the soles. The socks are black, luckily! I could see them with my naked eye."

"But isn't it likely that this Hunt might potter around in his stocking feet, even outdoors—where there are chicken feathers lying around?"

"Yes. But these fibers are on the linings of the socks, not the outsides of the soles. I reversed them pulling them off his feet."

"Anything else?"

"Not directly bearing on the commission of the murder itself, but involved in it. I saw a trowel with white clay drying on its edges, and a pair of thick gauntlets, used for spraying something on the peach trees, hanging up in the toolshed. Now tell me all this is no good to us."

"It certainly isn't!" declared the sheriff emphatically. "Why, I'd be laughed out of office if I moved against anyone on the strength of evidence such as this. You're talking in riddles, man! I can't make anything out of this. You not only haven't told me whom you suspect, but you haven't even given me the method used, or the motive."

Traynor drummed his fingertips on the desk. "And yet I'm dead sure. I'm as sure of it right now as if I'd seen it with my own eyes. I can give you the method right now, but what's the use? You'd only laugh at me, I can tell by the look on your face. I could name the motive and the suspects too, but until I've got the one, there's no use bringing in the others; there wouldn't be enough to hold them on."

"Well"—his superior shrugged, turning up his palms—"what do you want me to do?"

"Very little," muttered Traynor, "except lend me a waterproof pocket flashlight, if you've got one. And stick around till I come back; I've got an idea I won't be coming alone. There might be matters discussed that you'd be interested in."

"Where'll you be in the meantime?" the sheriff called after him as he pocketed the light and headed for the door.

"Down in Eleazar Hunt's well," was the cryptic answer. "And not because I'm thirsty, either."

Traynor coasted to a noiseless stop, well down the road from the Hunt place and out of sight of it, at about ten thirty that night. He snapped off his headlights, got out, examined the torch the sheriff had lent him to make sure it was in good working order, then cut across into the trees on foot, and made his way along under them parallel to the road but hidden from it.

There were no lights showing by the time he'd come in sight of the house. Death or no death, people in the country retire early. He knew there was no dog on the place so he didn't hesitate in breaking cover and skirting the house around to the back. The story was Hunt had been too stingy to keep one, begrudging the scraps it would have required to feed it. His sour face, was the general verdict, was enough to frighten away any trespasser.

He found the poultry yard locked, but his business wasn't with that; he detoured around the outside of it in the pale moonlight, treading warily in order not to make his presence known. He played his light briefly on the toolshed door; it was closed but not locked, fortunately. He eased it open, caught up the trowel and rope ladder he had noticed yesterday morning, and hurried over to the well with them. He mightn't need the trowel, but he took it with him to make sure. The clay, incidentally, had been carefully scraped off it now—but too late to do Fears any good; the damage had already been done.

Traynor clamped the iron hooks on the end of the ladder firmly to the rim of the well, paid it out all the way down the shaft until he heard it go in with a muffled splash. It sounded deeper than he enjoyed contemplating, but if Fears had gone down in there, dredging, then he could do it too.

He clicked his light on, tucked it firmly under his left armpit, straddled the well guard, and started climbing down, trowel wedged in his coat pocket. The ladder pivoted lightly from side to side under his weight, but so long as it didn't snarl up altogether, that was all right. He stopped every few rungs to play the light around the shaft in a circle. Nothing showed above the water line, any more than it had yesterday morning, but that trowel hadn't had clay on it, and the water hadn't been all muddied up, for nothing.

The water hit him unexpectedly and he jolted at the knifelike cold of it. He knew he couldn't stay in it very long without numbing, but he kept going down rung by rung. It came up his legs, hit his kidneys, finally rose above the light under his arm. That was waterproof, didn't go out. He stretched one leg downward off the ladder, feeling for the bottom. No bottom; the shaft seemed to go to China. One sure thing was, *he* couldn't—and keep on breathing.

He explored the wall of the well under the water line with his free hand, all around him and down as far as he could reach. The clay was velvet smooth, unmarred. Another rung—they were widely spaced—would take his head under, and he didn't like to risk it; he was already beginning to get numb all over.

Then suddenly the leg that he was using for a depth finder struck something like a plank. But across the shaft, behind him. He'd attached the ladder to the wrong side of the well rim. Still, it was fairly accessible; the circumference of the bore wasn't unduly large. He adjusted his leg to its height and got his heel on it. Tested its sustaining powers and it didn't crumble in spite of the fact that it must have been waterlogged for years. It was evidently inserted solidly into the clay, like a sort of shelf, more of it bedded than actually protruding. Still it was a risky thing to trust oneself to; he had an idea it was meant more for a marker than to be used to stand on. He turned his body outward to face it, got across to it without mishap, but bringing the ladder with him over his shoulder as a precaution. He was mostly under water during the whole maneuver, and rapidly chilling to the bone. That Fears before him had been through all this without some good, all powerful reason, he refused to believe.

He found a large cavity on that side of the well almost at once. It was just a few inches above the plank, a large square recess gouged out of the compact clay. It was, as far as his waterlogged fingertips could make out, a large empty biscuit tin wedged in flush with the well wall, open end outward. A sort of handmade but nonetheless efficient safe deposit box, so to speak.

But the important thing was that he could feel a heavy rubbery bulk resting within it. Flat, pouch-shaped. He drew this out, teeth chattering as the water momentarily rose into his nostrils, and finding it was too bulky to wedge into his pocket, tucked it into his submerged waistband, not caring to run the risk of bringing it up under his arm and perhaps dropping it to the bottom of the well just as he neared the top. The trowel, which he found he had not needed after all, he tossed over his shoulder into watery oblivion. The light, though it hampered him the way he kept it pinned against his side, he retained because it was not his but the sheriff's.

He renewed his grip on the transported ladder, took his feet off the scaffolding, and let the ladder swing back with him to its original side of the well. He didn't feel the slight collision at all, showing how thoroughly numbed he was by now, and showing what a risk he was running every moment of having his hold on it automatically relax and drop him into the depths. Nor could he tell the difference when his body was finally clear of the water. Meaning he'd better get out of there fast.

But it was twice as slow getting up as it had been getting down. He couldn't tell, through shoes and all, when each successive rung was firmly fixed under the arches of his feet, he kept making idiotic pawing gestures with his whole leg each time before it would finally catch on. That should have looked very funny, but not down there where he was.

Finally the cloying dampness of the air began to lift a little and he knew he must be nearing the top. Then a whiff of draught, that he would never have felt if he'd been dry, struck through his drenched clothes like ice-cold needles, and that proved it. His teeth were tapping together like typewriter keys.

There was something else, some faint warning that reached him. Not actually heard so much as sensed. As if someone's breath were coming down the shaft from just over his head, slightly amplified as if by a sounding board. He acted on it instantly, more from instinct than actual realization of danger. Unsheathed the light from under his arm and pointed it upward. He was closer to the top than he'd thought, scarcely a yard below it. The beam illumined Fears's face, bent low above him, contorted into a maniacal grimace of impending destruction, both arms high over his head wielding something. It looked like the flat of a shovel, but there was not time to find out, do anything but get out of its way. It came hissing down in a big arc against the well shaft. It would have smashed his skull like an egg, ground the fragments into the clay—great whipcords of straining muscle stood out on the arms wielding it—but he swerved his body violently sidewise off the ladder, hanging on just by one hand and one foot, and it cycloned by, missing him by fractions of inches, and battered into the clay with a pulpy whack.

Fears had been in too much of a hurry; if he'd let him get up a single rung higher, so that his head showed above the well rim, nothing could have saved him from being brained by the blow. The torch, of course, went skittering down into oblivion with a distant *plink!* The shovel followed it a second later; Fears didn't trouble to bring it up again from striking position, let go of it, perhaps under the mistaken impression that it had served its purpose and the only reason the victim didn't topple was that his stunned body had become tangled in the ropes.

Traynor could feel the ladder jar under him as his would-be destroyer sought to detach the hooks that clasped the well rim and throw the whole structure snaking down to the bottom. The very weight of his own body, on the inside, pinning it down close to the shaft, defeated the first try, gave him an added second's grace. To free the hooks, Fears had to raise the climber's whole weight first, ladder and all, to get enough slack into it.

There wasn't enough time to finish climbing out. Traynor vaulted up one more rung with the agility of desperation, so that his head cleared the shaft rim; he flung up his arm and caught Fears's lowered head, bent down to his task, toward him in a riveted headlock that was like a drowning man's. Fears gave a muffled howl of dismay, tried to arch his slumped back against it. There was a brief equipoise, then gravity and their combined topheavy positions had their way. Fears came floundering over into the mouth of the well, nearly broke Traynor's back by the shift of weight to the other side of him, tore him off his own precarious foothold, and they both went plunging sickeningly down off the ladder together. Their two yells of approaching destruction blended hollowly into one.

Numb and half-frozen as Traynor already was, the shock of submersion was evidently less for him than for Fears, plunging in with his pores wide open and possibly overheated from hurrying out to the well from a warm bed. Traynor had been in the water once already, felt it less than he would have the first time. The way people condition their bodies to frigid water by wetting themselves before they dive off a board, for instance.

He never touched bottom, even now. He came up alone—the fall must have loosened the bear hug he'd had on the other man—struck out wildly all around him, aware that if he went down again— The radius of the confining wall was luckily narrow. He contacted the ladder, sealed his hands to it in a hold that blow torches couldn't have pried off, got on it again, and quickly pulled himself up above the water.

He waited there a minute, willing to stretch out a hand, but unable to do more than that. Fears never came up. Not a sound broke the inky black silence around Traynor but the slow heave of the disturbed water itself. The shock had either made the man lose consciousness or he'd struck his head against his own shovel at the bottom. If there was a bottom, which Traynor was beginning to doubt.

Go in again after him and try to find him, he couldn't. He got the warning from every cramped muscle in his body, and his restricted lungs and pounding heart. It meant his own sure death, inevitably. There are times one can tell. He wasn't even sure that he could get up any more, unaided.

But he finally did, tottering painfully rung by rung and feeling as if he'd been doing this all night. He flung himself across the well rim, crawled clear of it on his belly like some half-drowned thing, then turned over on his back and did nothing else much but just breathe. Gusts of uncontrollable shivering swept over him every once in a while. Finally he sat up, pulled off his soaked coat, shirt, and even undershirt, and began beating himself all over the body with them to bring back the circulation.

It was only when he'd started it going again that he remembered to feel for the rubber pouch that had cost two lives so far, and nearly a third—his own. If he'd lost it down there, he'd had all his trouble for nothing. But instead of falling out, it had slipped down under his waistband and become wedged in the top of one trousers leg, too bulky to go any farther. There wasn't enough sensation left in his leg to tell him it was there until he'd pried it out with both hands.

"Money," he murmured, when he'd finally stripped it open and examined it. He turned his head and looked toward that sinister black opening in the ground. "I thought it was that. It almost always is."

There were seventy-five thousand dollars in it, so well protected they weren't even damp after three years' immersion.

He put on his coat and made his way back toward the house. One of the upper story window sashes eased up and a voice whispered cautiously down in the stillness:

"Did you get him, Dan?"

"No, Dan didn't get him, Mrs. Hunt," he answered in full speaking tone. "Put on something and come down; I'm taking you in to the sheriff's office with me. And don't keep me waiting around down here; I'm chilled to the bone."

The sheriff awoke with a start when Traynor thrust open his office door and ushered Mrs. Hunt in ahead of him.

"Here's one," he said, "and the other one's at the bottom of the well with the rest of the slimy things where he belongs. Sit down, Mrs. Hunt, while I run through the facts for the benefit of my superior here.

"I'll begin at the beginning. The state built a spanking fine concrete highway that sliced off a little corner of Eleazar Hunt's property. He had the good luck—or bad luck, as it now turns out to have been—to collect seventy-five thousand dollars for it. Here it is." He threw down the waterlogged package. "There's your motive. First of all, it got him a second wife, almost before he knew it himself. Then, through the wife, it got him a hired man. Then, through the hired man *and* the wife, it got him—torture to the death."

He turned to the prisoner, who was sitting nervously shredding her handkerchief. "You want to tell the rest of it, or shall I? I've got it on the tip of my tongue, you know—and I've got it straight."

"I'll tell it," she said dully. "You seem to know it anyway."

"How'd you catch on he was hypersensitive to tickling?"

"By accident. I was sitting on the arm of his chair one evening, trying to vamp it out of him—where the money was, you know. I happened to tickle him under the chin, and he jumped a mile. Dan saw it happen and that gave him the idea. He built it up to me for weeks. 'If he was tied down,' he said, 'in one place so he couldn't get away from it, he couldn't hold out against it very long, he'd have to tell you. It'd be like torture, but it wouldn't hurt him.' It sounded swell, so I gave in."

"But, honest, I didn't know Dan meant to kill him. He was the one did it. I didn't! I thought he only meant for us to take the money and lam, and leave El tied up."

"Never mind that; go ahead."

"Dan had it all thought out beautiful. He had me go around the village first building it up that I was getting El to laugh and liven up. He even had me buy the joke book at the general store. Then last night about ten thirty when El was sitting by the lamp reading some seed catalogues, I gave the signal and Dan came up behind him with rope and pillows from the bed and insect spray gauntlets. He held him while I put the gauntlets on him—they're good thick buckram, you know—so no rope burns would show from his struggles, and then he tied his hands to the arms of the chair, over the gauntlets. The pillows we used over his waist and thighs, for the same reason, to deaden the ropes. Then he let the chair back down nearly flat, and he took off El's shoes and socks, and brought in a handful of chicken feathers from the yard, and squatted down in front of him like an Indian, and started to slowly stroke the soles of his feet back and forth. It was pretty awful to watch and listen to: I hadn't thought it would be. But that screaming laugh! Tickling doesn't sound bad, you know.

"Every time Dan blunted a feather, he'd throw it away and start in using a new one. And he said in his sleepy way: 'Care to tell us where it is now? No? Wa-al, mebbe you know best.' I wanted to bring him water once, but Dan wouldn't let me, said that would only help him hold out longer.

"El was such a stubborn fool. He didn't once say he didn't have the money, he only said he'd see us both in hell before he told us where it was. He fainted away, the first time, about twelve. After that he kept getting weaker all the time, couldn't laugh any more, just heave his ribs.

"Finally he gave in, whispered it was in a tin box plastered into the well, below the water line. He told us there was a rope ladder he'd made himself to get down there, hidden in the attic. Dan lowered himself down, and got it out, brought it up, and counted it. I wanted to leave right way, but he talked me out of it. He said: 'We'll only give ourselves away if we do that. We know where it is now. Let's leave it there a mite longer; he mayn't live *as long as you'd expect*.' I see now what he meant; I still didn't then. Well, I listened to him; he seemed to have the whole thing lined up so cleverly. He climbed back with it and left it down there. Then we went back to the house. I went upstairs, and I no sooner got there than I heard El start up this whimpering and cooing again, like a little newborn baby. I quickly ran down to try and stop him, but it was too late. Just as I got there, El overstrained himself and suddenly went limp. That little added extra bit more killed him, and Dan Fears had known it would, that's why he did it!

"I got frightened, but he told me there was nothing to worry about, everything was under control, and they'd never tumble in a million years. We took the ropes and pillows and gauntlets off him, of course, and no marks were left. We raised the chair back to reading position, and dropped the joke book by his hand, and I put on his shoes and socks. The only thing was, after he'd been dead a little while, his face started to relapse to that sour, scowly look he always had all his life, and that didn't match the joke book. Well, Dan took care of that too. He waited until just before he was starting to stiffen, and then he arranged the lips and mouth with his hands so it looked like he'd been laughing his head off; and they hardened and stayed that way. Then he sent me out to fetch the doctor." She hung her head. "It seemed so perfect. I don't know how it is it fell through."

"How did you catch on so quick, Al?" the sheriff asked Traynor, while they were waiting for a stenographer to come and take down her confession.

"First of all, the smile. You could see his features had been rearranged after death. Before rigor sets in, there's a relaxation to the habitual expression. Secondly, the jokes were no good. Fears may have thought a sour puss wouldn't match them, but it would have matched them lots better than the one they gave him. Thirdly, when I hitched up the cuffs of his trousers, I saw that his socks had been put on wrong, as if in a hurry by someone who wasn't familiar with things like that—therefore presumably it was a woman. The garter clasps were fastened at the insides of the calves, but the original indentations still showed on the outsides. Fourthly, the bent chicken feathers. I still didn't quite get it, though, until I learned this afternoon at the general store that he was supersensitive to tickling. That gave me the whole picture, intact. I'd already seen the clay on the trowel, and Fears did his level best to keep me away from the well, so it didn't take much imagination to figure where the money was hidden. The marks of the ropes may not have shown on his hands, but the gauntlets were scarred by their friction, I could see that plainly even by the light of the torch when I went back to the toolshed tonight.

"It was pretty good, I'll give it that. If they'd only left his face alone. I don't think my suspicions would have been awakened in the first place. They spoiled it by overdoing it; just a mere inference of how he'd died wasn't enough—they had guilty consciences, so they wanted to make sure of getting their point across, hitting the onlooker in the eye with it. And that was the one thing he'd never had in life—a sense of humor. The joke wasn't really in the book after all. The joke was on them."

A Rose for Emily

WILLIAM FAULKNER

William Faulkner won the Nobel Prize, two Pulitzer Prizes, and wrote (among many others) such novels as The Sound and the Fury *(1929),* As I Lay Dying *(1930) and the masterful* Sanctuary *(1931). So what is he doing in a horror treasury, you ask? Well for one thing, he wrote about violence, decay, abnormality and eternal truths. And for another thing, he wrote this story.*

When Miss Emily Grierson died, our whole town went to her funeral: the men through a sort of respectful affection for a fallen monument, the women mostly out of curiosity to see the inside of her house, which no one save an old manservant—a combined gardener and cook—had seen in at least ten years.

It was a big, squarish frame house that had once been white, decorated with cupolas and spires and scrolled balconies in the heavily lightsome style of the seventies, set on what had once been our most select street. But garages and cotton gins had encroached and obliterated even the august names of that neighborhood; only Miss Emily's house was left, lifting its stubborn and coquettish decay above the cotton wagons and the gasoline pumps—an eyesore among eyesores. And now Miss Emily had gone to join the representatives of those august names where they lay in the cedar-bemused cemetery among the ranked and anonymous graves of Union and Confederate soldiers who fell at the battle of Jefferson.

Alive, Miss Emily had been a tradition, a duty, and a care; a sort of hereditary obligation upon the town, dating from that day in 1894 when Colonel Sartoris, the mayor—he who fathered the edict that no Negro woman should appear on the streets without an apron—remitted her taxes, the dispensation dating from the death of her father on into perpetuity. Not that Miss Emily would have accepted charity. Colonel Sartoris invented an involved tale to the effect that Miss Emily's father had loaned money to the town, which the town, as a matter of business, preferred this way of repaying. Only a man of

Colonel Sartoris's generation and thought could have invented it, and only a woman could have believed it.

When the next generation, with its more modern ideas, became mayors and aldermen, this arrangement created some little dissatisfaction. On the first of the year they mailed her a tax notice. February came, and there was no reply. They wrote her a formal letter, asking her to call at the sheriff's office at her convenience. A week later the mayor wrote her himself, offering to call or to send his car for her, and received in reply a note on paper of an archaic shape, in a thin, flowing calligraphy in faded ink, to the effect that she no longer went out at all. The tax notice was also enclosed, without comment.

They called a special meeting of the Board of Aldermen. A deputation waited upon her, knocked at the door through which no visitor had passed since she ceased giving china-painting lessons eight or ten years earlier. They were admitted by the old Negro into a dim hall from which a stairway mounted into still more shadow. It smelled of dust and disuse—a close, dank smell. The Negro led them into the parlor. It was furnished in heavy, leather-covered furniture. When the Negro opened the blinds of one window, they could see that the leather was cracked; and when they sat down, a faint dust rose sluggishly about their thighs, spinning with slow motes in the single sun ray. On a tarnished gilt easel before the fireplace stood a crayon portrait of Miss Emily's father.

They rose when she entered—a small, fat woman in black, with a thin gold chain descending to her waist and vanishing into her belt, leaning on an ebony cane with a tarnished gold head. Her skeleton was small and spare; perhaps that was why what would have been merely plumpness in another was obesity in her. She looked bloated, like a body long submerged in motionless water, and of that pallid hue. Her eyes, lost in the fatty ridges of her face, looked like two small pieces of coal pressed into a lump of dough as they moved from one face to another while the visitors stated their errand.

She did not ask them to sit. She just stood in the door and listened quietly until the spokesman came to a stumbling halt. Then they could hear the invisible watch ticking at the end of the gold chain.

Her voice was dry and cold. "I have no taxes in Jefferson. Colonel Sartoris explained it to me. Perhaps one of you can gain access to the city records and satisfy yourselves."

"But we have. We are the city authorities, Miss Emily. Didn't you get a notice from the sheriff, signed by him?"

"I received a paper, yes," Miss Emily said. "Perhaps he considers himself the sheriff . . . I have no taxes in Jefferson."

"But there is nothing on the books to show that, you see. We must go by the—"

"See Colonel Sartoris. I have no taxes in Jefferson."

"But, Miss Emily—"

"See Colonel Sartoris." (Colonel Sartoris had been dead almost ten years.) "I have no taxes in Jefferson. Tobe!" The Negro appeared. "Show these gentlemen out."

II

So she vanquished them, horse and foot, just as she had vanquished their fathers thirty years before about the smell. That was two years after her father's death and a short time after her sweetheart—the one we believed would marry her—had deserted her. After her father's death she went out very little; after her sweetheart went away, people hardly saw her at all. A few of the ladies had the temerity to call, but were not received, and the only sign of life about the place was the Negro man—a young man then—going in and out with a market basket.

"Just as if a man—any man—could keep a kitchen properly," the ladies said; so they were not surprised when the smell developed. It was another link between the gross, teeming world and the high and mighty Griersons.

A neighbor, a woman, complained to the mayor, Judge Stevens, eighty years old.

"But what will you have me do about it, madam?" he said.

"Why, send her word to stop it," the woman said. "Isn't there a law?"

"I'm sure that won't be necessary," Judge Stevens said. "It's probably just a snake or a rat that nigger of hers killed in the yard. I'll speak to him about it."

The next day he received two more complaints, one from a man who came in diffident deprecation. "We really must do something about it, judge. I'd be the last one in the world to bother Miss Emily, but we've got to do something." That night the Board of Aldermen met—three graybeards and one younger man, a member of the rising generation.

"It's simple enough," he said. "Send her word to have her place cleaned up. Give her a certain time to do it in, and if she don't . . ."

"Dammit, sir," Judge Stevens said, "will you accuse a lady to her face of smelling bad?"

So the next night, after midnight, four men crossed Miss Emily's lawn and slunk about the house like burglars, sniffing along the base of the brickwork and at the cellar openings while one of them performed a regular sowing motion with his hand out of a sack slung from his shoulder. They broke open the cellar door and sprinkled lime there, and in all the outbuildings. As they recrossed the lawn, a window that had been dark was lighted and Miss Emily sat in it, the light behind her, and her upright torso motionless as that of an idol. They crept quietly across the lawn and into the shadow of the locusts that lined the street. After a week or two the smell went away.

That was when people had begun to feel really sorry for her. People in our town, remembering how Old Lady Wyatt, her great-aunt, had gone completely crazy at last, believed that the Griersons held themselves a little too high for what they really were. None of the young men were quite good enough to Miss Emily and such. We had long thought of them as a tableau: Miss Emily a slender figure in white in the background, her father a spraddled silhouette in the foreground, his back to her and clutching a horsewhip, the two of them framed by the back-flung front door. So when she got to be thirty and was still single, we were not pleased exactly, but vindicated; even with insanity in the family she wouldn't have turned down all of her chances if they had really materialized.

When her father died, it got about that the house was all that was left to her; and in a way, people were glad. At last they could pity Miss Emily. Being left alone, and a pauper, she had become humanized. Now she too would know the old thrill and the old despair of a penny more or less.

The day after his death all the ladies prepared to call at the house and offer condolence and aid, as is our custom. Miss Emily met them at the door, dressed as usual and with no trace of grief on her face. She told them that her father was not dead. She did that for three days, with the ministers calling on her, and the doctors, trying to persuade her to let them dispose of the body. Just as they were about to resort to law and force, she broke down, and they buried her father quickly.

We did not say she was crazy then. We believed she had to do that. We remembered all the young men her father had driven away, and we knew that with nothing left, she would have to cling to that which had robbed her, as people will.

III

She was sick for a long time. When we saw her again, her hair was cut short, making her look like a girl, with a vague resemblance to those angels in colored church windows—sort of tragic and serene.

The town had just let the contracts for paving the sidewalks, and in the summer after her father's death they began the work. The construction company came with niggers and mules and machinery, and a foreman named Homer Barron, a Yankee—a big, dark, ready man, with a big voice and eyes lighter than his face. The little boys would follow in groups to hear him cuss the niggers, and the niggers singing in time to the rise and fall of picks. Pretty soon he knew everybody in town. Whenever you heard a lot of laughing anywhere about the square, Homer Barron would be in the center of the group. Presently we began to see him and Miss Emily on Sunday afternoons driving in the yellow-wheeled buggy and the matched team of bays from the livery stable.

At first we were glad that Miss Emily would have an interest, because the ladies all said, "Of course a Grierson would not think seriously of a Northerner, a day laborer." But there were still others, older people, who said that even grief could not cause a real lady to forget *noblesse oblige*—without calling it *noblesse oblige*. They just said, "Poor Emily. Her kinsfolk should come to her." She had some kin in Alabama; but years ago her father had fallen out with them over the estate of Old Lady Wyatt, the crazy woman, and there was no communication between the two families. They had not even been represented at the funeral.

And as soon as the old people said, "Poor Emily," the whispering began. "Do you suppose it's really so?" they said to one another. "Of course it is. What else could . . ." This behind their hands; rustling of craned silk and satin behind jalousies closed upon the sun of Sunday afternoon as the thin, swift clop-clop-clop of the matched team passed: "Poor Emily."

She carried her head high enough—even when we believed that she was fallen. It was as if she demanded more than ever the recognition of her dignity as the last Grierson; as if it had wanted that touch of earthiness to reaffirm her imperviousness. Like when she bought the rat poison, the arsenic. That was over a year after they had begun to say "Poor Emily," and while the two female cousins were visiting her.

"I want some poison," she said to the druggist. She was over thirty then, still a slight woman, though thinner than usual, with cold, haughty black eyes in a face the flesh of which was strained across the temples, and about the eye-sockets as you imagine a lighthouse-keeper's face ought to look. "I want some poison," she said.

"Yes, Miss Emily. What kind? For rats and such? I'd recom—"

"I want the best you have. I don't care what kind."

The druggist named several. "They'll kill anything up to an elephant. But what you want is—"

"Arsenic," Miss Emily said. "Is that a good one?"

"Is . . . arsenic? Yes, ma'am. But what you want—"

"I want arsenic."

The druggist looked down at her. She looked back at him, erect, her face like a strained flag. "Why, of course," the druggist said. "If that's what you want. But the law requires you to tell what you are going to use it for."

Miss Emily just stared at him, her head tilted back in order to look him eye for eye, until he looked away and went and got the arsenic and wrapped it up. The Negro delivery boy brought her the package; the druggist didn't come back. When she opened the package at home there was written on the box, under the skull and bones: "For rats."

IV

So the next day we all said, "She will kill herself"; and we said it would be the best thing. When she had first begun to be seen with Homer Barron, we had said, "She will marry him." Then we said, "She will persuade him yet," because Homer himself had remarked—he liked men, and it was known that he drank with the younger men in the Elks' Club—that he was not a marrying man. Later we said, "Poor

Emily" behind the jalousies as they passed on Sunday afternoon in the glittering buggy, Miss Emily with her head high and Homer Barron with his hat cocked and a cigar in his teeth, reins and whip in a yellow glove.

Then some of the ladies began to say that it was a disgrace to the town and a bad example to the younger people. The men did not want to interfere, but at last the ladies forced the Baptist minister—Miss Emily's people were Episcopal—to call upon her. He would never divulge what happened during that interview, but he refused to go back again. The next Sunday they again drove about the streets, and the following day the minister's wife wrote to Miss Emily's relations in Alabama.

So she had blood kin under her roof again and we sat back to watch developments. At first nothing happened. Then we were sure that they were to be married. We learned that Miss Emily had been to the jeweler's and ordered a man's toilet set in silver, with the letter H. B. on each piece. Two days later we learned that she had bought a complete outfit of men's clothing, including a nightshirt, and we said, "They are married." We were really glad. We were glad because the two female cousins were even more Grierson than Miss Emily had ever been.

So we were not surprised when Homer Barron—the streets had been finished some time since—was gone. We were a little disappointed that there was not a public blowing-off, but we believed that he had gone on to prepare for Miss Emily's coming, or to give her a chance to get rid of the cousins. (By that time it was a cabal, and we were all Miss Emily's allies to help circumvent the cousins.) Sure enough, after another week they departed. And, as we had expected all along, within three days Homer Barron was back in town. A neighbor saw the Negro man admit him at the kitchen door at dusk one evening.

And that was the last we saw of Homer Barron. And of Miss Emily for some time. The Negro man went in and out with the market basket, but the front door remained closed. Now and then we would see her at a window for a moment, as the men did that night when they sprinkled the lime, but for almost six months she did not appear on the streets. Then we knew that this was to be expected too; as if that quality of her father which had thwarted her woman's life so many times had been too virulent and too furious to die.

When we next saw Miss Emily, she had grown fat and her hair was turning gray. During the next few years it grew grayer and grayer until it attained an even pepper-and-salt iron gray, when it ceased turning. Up to the day of her death at seventy-four it was still that vigorous iron gray, like the hair of an active man.

From that time on her front door remained closed, save for a period of six or seven years, when she was about forty, during which she gave lessons in china-painting. She fitted up a studio in one of the downstairs rooms, where the daughters and granddaughters of Colonel Sartoris's contemporaries were sent to her with the same regularity and in the same spirit that they were sent to church on Sundays with a twenty-five-cent piece for the collection plate. Meanwhile her taxes had been remitted.

Then the newer generation became the backbone and the spirit of the town, and the painting pupils grew up and fell away and did not send their children to her with boxes of color and tedious brushes and pictures cut from the ladies' magazines. The front door closed upon the last one and remained closed for good. When the town got free postal delivery, Miss Emily alone refused to let them fasten the metal numbers above her door and attach a mailbox to it. She would not listen to them.

Daily, monthly, yearly we watched the Negro grow grayer and more stooped, going in and out with the market basket. Each December we sent her a tax notice, which would be returned by the post office a week later, unclaimed. Now and then we would see her in one of the downstairs windows—she had evidently shut up the top floor of the house—like the carven torso of an idol in a niche, looking or not looking at us, we could never tell which. Thus she passed from generation to generation—dear, inescapable, impervious, tranquil and perverse.

And so she died. Fell ill in the house filled with dust and shadows, with only a doddering Negro man to wait on her. We did not even know she was sick; we had long since given up trying to get any information from the Negro. He talked to no one, probably not even to her, for his voice had grown harsh and rusty, as if from disuse.

She died in one of the downstairs rooms, in a heavy walnut bed with a curtain, her gray head propped on a pillow yellow and mouldy with age and lack of sunlight.

V

The Negro met the first of the ladies at the front door and let them in, with their hushed, sibilant voices and their quick, curious glances, and then he disappeared. He walked right through the house and out the back and was not seen again.

The two female cousins came at once. They held the funeral on the second day, with the town coming to look at Miss Emily beneath a mass of bought flowers, with the crayon face of her father musing profoundly above the bier and the ladies sibilant and macabre; and the very old men—some in their brushed Confederate uniforms—on the porch and the lawn, talking of Miss Emily as if she had been a contemporary of theirs, believing that they had danced with her and courted her perhaps, confusing time with its mathematical progression, as the old do, to whom all the past is not a diminishing road but, instead, a huge meadow which no winter ever quite touches, divided from them now by the narrow bottleneck of the most recent decade of years.

Already we knew that there was one room in that region above stairs which no one had seen in forty years, and which would have to be forced. They waited until Miss Emily was decently in the ground before they opened it.

The violence of breaking down the door seemed to fill this room with pervading dust. A thin, acrid pall as of the tomb seemed to lie everywhere upon this room decked and furnished as for a bridal: upon the valance curtains of faded rose color, upon the rose-shaded lights, upon the dressing table, upon the delicate array of crystal and the man's toilet things backed with tarnished silver, silver so tarnished that the monogram was obscured. Among them lay a collar and tie, as if they had just been removed, which, lifted, left upon the surface a pale crescent in the dust. Upon a chair hung the suit, carefully folded; beneath it the two mute shoes and the discarded socks.

The man himself lay in the bed.

For a long while we just stood there, looking down at the profound and fleshless grin. The body had apparently once lain in the attitude of an embrace, but now the long sleep that outlasts love, that conquers even the grimace of love, had cuckolded him. What was left of him, rotted beneath what was left of the nightshirt, had become inextricable from the bed in which he lay; and upon him and upon the pillow beside him lay that even coating of the patient and biding dust.

Then we noticed that in the second pillow was the indentation of a head. One of us lifted something from it, and leaning forward, that faint and invisible dust dry and acrid in the nostrils, we saw a long strand of iron gray hair.

Bianca's Hands

THEODORE STURGEON

*One of the giants of the science fiction of the 1940's and 1950's,
Theodore Sturgeon has examined love in all its permutations and
combinations throughout his career. A gentle, sensitive man, it is
difficult to think of him as a candidate for inclusion in a horror
anthology—but then again, love and horror are by no means mutually
exclusive emotions, as "Bianca's Hands" vividly illustrates.*

Bianca's mother was leading her when Ran saw her first. Bianca was
squat and small, with dank hair and rotten teeth. Her mouth was
crooked and it drooled. Either she was blind or she just didn't care
about bumping into things. It didn't really matter because Bianca was
an imbecile. Her hands . . . .

They were lovely hands, graceful hands, hands as soft and smooth
and white as snowflakes, hands whose color was lightly tinged with
pink like the glow of Mars on snow. They lay on the counter side by
side, looking at Ran. They lay there half-closed and crouching, each
pulsing with a movement like the panting of a field creature, and they
looked. Not watched. Later, they watched him. Now they looked.
They did, because Ran felt their united gaze, and his heart beat
strongly.

Bianca's mother demanded cheese stridently. Ran brought it to her
in his own time while she berated him. She was a bitter woman, as any
woman has a right to be who is wife of no man and mother to a
monster. Ran gave her the cheese and took her money and never
noticed that it was not enough, because of Bianca's hands. When
Bianca's mother tried to take one of the hands it scuttled away from
the unwanted touch. It did not lift from the counter, but ran on its
fingertips to the edge and leaped into a fold of Bianca's dress. The
woman took the unresisting elbow and led Bianca out.

Ran stayed there at the counter unmoving, thinking of Bianca's
hands. Ran was strong and bronze and not very clever. He had never
been taught about beauty and strangeness, but he did not need that

238

teaching. His shoulders were wide, and his arms were heavy and thick, but he had great soft eyes and thick lashes. They curtained his eyes now. He was seeing Bianca's hands again dreamily. He found it hard to breathe. . . .

Harding came back. Harding owned the store. He was a large man whose features barely kept his cheeks apart. He said, "Sweep up, Ran. We're closing early today." Then he went behind the counter, squeezing past Ran.

Ran got the broom and swept slowly.

"A woman bought cheese," he said suddenly. "A poor woman with very old clothes. She was leading a girl. I can't remember what the girl looked like, except—who was she?"

"I saw them go out," said Harding. "The woman is Bianca's mother, and the girl is Bianca. I don't know their other name. They don't talk to people much. I wish they wouldn't come in here. Hurry up, Ran."

Ran did what was necessary and put away his broom. Before he left he asked, "Where do they live, Bianca and her mother?"

"On the other side. A house on no road, away from people. Good night, Ran."

Ran went from the shop directly over to the other side, not waiting for his supper. He found the house easily, for it was indeed away from the road, and stood rudely by itself. The townspeople had cauterized the house by wrapping it in empty fields.

Harshly, "What do you want?" Bianca's mother asked as she opened the door.

"May I come in?"

"What do you want?"

"May I come in?" he asked again. She made as if to slam the door, and then stood aside. "Come."

Ran went in and stood still. Bianca's mother crossed the room and sat under an old lamp, in the shadow. Ran sat opposite her, on a three-legged stool. Bianca was not in the room.

The woman tried to speak, but embarrassment clutched at her voice. She withdrew into her bitterness, saying nothing. She kept peeping at Ran, who sat quietly with his arms folded and the uncertain light in his eyes. He knew she would speak soon, and he could wait.

"Ah, well. . . ." She was silent after that, for a time, but now she had forgiven him his intrusion. Then, "It's a great while since anyone came to see me; a great while . . . it was different before. I was a pretty girl—"

She bit her words off, and her face popped out of the shadows, shriveled and sagging as she leaned forward. Ran saw that she was beaten and cowed and did not want to be laughed at.

"Yes," he said gently. She sighed and leaned back so that her face disappeared again. She said nothing for a moment, sitting looking at Ran, liking him.

"We were happy, the two of us," she mused, "until Bianca came. He didn't like her, poor thing, he didn't, no more than I do now. He went away. I stayed by her because I was her mother. I'd go away myself, I would, but people know me, and I haven't a penny—not a penny. . . . They'd bring me back to her, they would, to care for her. It doesn't matter much now, though, because people don't want me any more than they want her, they don't. . . ."

Ran shifted his feet uneasily, because the woman was crying. "Have you room for me here?" he asked.

Her head crept out into the light. Ran said swiftly, "I'll give you money each week and I'll bring my own bed and things." He was afraid she would refuse.

She merged with the shadows again. "If you like," she said, trembling at her good fortune. "Though why you'd want to . . . still, I guess if I had a little something to cook up nice, and a good reason for it, I could make someone real cozy here. But—*why?*" She rose. Ran crossed the room and pushed her back into the chair. He stood over her, tall.

"I never want you to ask me that," he said, speaking very slowly. "Hear?"

She swallowed and nodded. "I'll come back tomorrow with the bed and things," he said.

He left her there under the lamp, blinking out of the dimness, folded round and about with her misery and her wonder.

People talked about it. People said, "Ran has moved to the house of Bianca's mother." "It must be because—" "Ah," said some, "Ran was always a strange boy. It must be because—" "Oh, *no!*" cried others, appalled. "Ran is such a good boy. He wouldn't—"

Harding was told. He frightened the busy little woman who told him. He said, "Ran is very quiet, but he is honest, and he does his work. As long as he comes here in the morning and earns his wage, he can do what he wants, where he wants, and it is not my business to stop him." He said this so very sharply that the little woman dared not say anything more.

Ran was very happy, living there. Saying little, he began to learn about Bianca's hands.

He watched Bianca being fed. Her hands would not feed her, the lovely aristocrats. Beautiful parasites they were, taking their animal life from the heavy squat body that carried them, and giving nothing in return. They would lie one on each side of her plate, pulsing, while Bianca's mother put food into the distinterested drooling mouth. They were shy, those hands, of Ran's bewitched gaze. Caught out there naked in the light and open of the tabletop, they would creep to the edge and drop out of sight—all but four rosy fingertips clutching the cloth.

They never lifted from a surface. When Bianca walked, her hands did not swing free, but twisted in the fabric of her dress. And when she approached a table or the mantelpiece and stood, her hands would run lightly up and leap, landing together, resting silently, watchfully, with that pulsing peculiar to them.

They cared for each other. They would not touch Bianca herself, but each hand groomed the other. It was the only labor to which they would bend themselves.

Three evenings after he came, Ran tried to take one of the hands in his. Bianca was alone in the room, and Ran went to her and sat beside her. She did not move, nor did her hands. They rested on a small table before her, preening themselves. This, then, was when they really began watching him. He felt it, right down to the depths of his enchanted heart. The hands kept stroking each other, and yet they knew he was there, they knew of his desire. They stretched themselves before him, archly, languorously, and his blood pounded hot. Before he could stay himself he reached and tried to grasp them. He was strong, and his move was sudden and clumsy. One of the hands seemed to disappear, so swiftly did it drop into Bianca's lap. But the other—

Ran's thick fingers closed on it and held it captive. It writhed, all but tore itself free. It took no power from the arm on which it lived, for Bianca's arms were flabby and weak. Its strength, like its beauty, was intrinsic, and it was only by shifting his grip to the puffy forearm that Ran succeeded in capturing it. So intent was he on touching it, holding it, that he did not see the other hand leap from the idiot girl's lap, land crouching at the table's edge. It reared back, fingers curling spiderlike, and sprang at him, fastening on his wrist. It clamped down agonizingly, and Ran felt bones give and crackle. With a cry he released the girl's arm. Her hands fell together and ran over each other, feeling for any small scratch, any tiny damage he might have done them in his passion. And as he sat there clutching his wrist, he saw the hands run to the far side of the little table, hook themselves over the edge, and, contracting, draw her out of her place. She had no volition of her own—ah, but her hands had! Creeping over the walls, catching obscure and precarious holds in the wainscoting, they dragged the girl from the room.

And Ran sat there and sobbed, not so much from the pain in his swelling arm, but in shame for what he had done. They might have been won to him in another, gentler way. . . .

His head was bowed; yet suddenly he felt the gaze of those hands. He looked up swiftly enough to see one of them whisk around the doorpost. It had come back, then, to see. . . . Ran rose heavily and took himself and his shame away. Yet he was compelled to stop in the doorway, even as had Bianca's hands. He watched covertly and saw them come into the room dragging the unprotesting idiot girl. They brought her to the long bench where Ran had sat with her. They pushed her on to it, flung themselves to the table, and began rolling and flattening themselves most curiously about. Ran suddenly realized that there was something of his there, and he was comforted, a little. They were rejoicing, drinking thirstily, reveling in his tears.

Afterward for nineteen days, the hands made Ran do penance. He knew them as inviolate and unforgiving; they would not show themselves to him, remaining always hidden in Bianca's dress or under the supper table. For those nineteen days Ran's passion and desire grew. More—his love became true love, for only true love knows reverence—and the possession of the hands became his reason for living, his goal in the life which that reason had given him.

Ultimately they forgave him. They kissed him coyly when he was not looking, touched him on the wrist, caught and held him for one sweet moment. It was at table . . . a great power surged through him, and he gazed down at the hands, now returned to Bianca's lap. A strong muscle in his jaw twitched, swelled and fell. Happiness like a golden light flooded him; passion spurred him, love imprisoned him, reverence was the gold of the golden light. The room wheeled and whirled about him, and forces unimaginable flickered through him. Battling with himself, yet lax in the glory of it, Ran sat unmoving, beyond the world, enslaved and yet possessor of all. Bianca's hands flushed pink, and if ever hands smiled to each other, then they did.

He rose abruptly, flinging his chair from him, feeling the strength of his back and shoulders. Bianca's mother, by now beyond surprise, looked at him and away. There was that in his eyes which she did not like, for to fathom it would disturb her, and she wanted no trouble. Ran strode from the room and outdoors, to be by himself that he might learn more of this new thing that had possessed him.

It was evening. The crooked bending skyline drank the buoyance of the sun, dragged it down, sucking greedily. Ran stood on a knoll, his nostrils flaring, feeling the depth of his lungs. He sucked in the crisp air, and it smelled new to him, as though the sunset shades were truly in it. He knotted the muscles of his thighs and stared at his smooth, solid fists. He raised his hands high over is head and, stretching, sent out such a great shout that the sun sank. He watched it, knowing how great and tall he was, how strong he was, knowing the meaning of longing and belonging. And then he lay down on the clean earth, and he wept.

When the sky grew cold enough for the moon to follow the sun beyond the hills, and still an hour after that, Ran returned to the house. He struck a light in the room of Bianca's mother, where she slept on a pile of old clothes. Ran sat beside her and let the light wake her. She rolled over to him and moaned, opened her eyes, and shrank from him. "Ran . . . what do you want?"

"Bianca. I want to marry Bianca."

Her breath hissed between her gums. "No!" It was not a refusal but astonishment. Ran touched her arm impatiently. Then she laughed.

"To—marry—Bianca. It's late, boy. Go back to bed, and in the morning you'll have forgotten this thing, this dream."

"I've not been to bed," he said patiently, but growing angry. "Will you give me Bianca, or not?"

She sat up and rested her chin on her withered knees. "You're right to ask me, for I'm her mother. Still and all—Ran, you've been good to us, Bianca and me. You're—you are a good boy, but—forgive me, lad, but you're something of a fool. Bianca's a monster. I say it though I am what I am to her. Do what you like, and never a word will I say. You should have known. I'm sorry you asked me, for you have given me the memory of speaking so to you. I don't understand you; but do what you like, boy."

It was to have been a glance, but it became a stare as she saw his face. He put his hands carefully behind his back, and she knew he would have killed her else.

"I'll—marry her, then?" he whispered.

She nodded, terrified. "As you like, boy."

He blew out the light and left her.

Ran worked hard and saved his wages and made one room beautiful for Bianca and himself. He built a soft chair and a table that was like an altar for Bianca's sacred hands. There was a great bed, and heavy cloth to hide and soften the walls, and a rug.

They were married, though marrying took time. Ran had to go far afield before he could find one who would do what was necessary. The man came far and went again afterward, so that none knew of it, and Ran and his wife were left alone. The mother spoke for Bianca, and Bianca's hand trembled frighteningly at the touch of the ring, writhed and struggled and then lay passive, blushing and beautiful. But it was done. Bianca's mother did not protest, for she didn't dare. Ran was happy, and Bianca- ·well, nobody cared about Bianca.

After they were married Bianca followed Ran and his two brides into the beautiful room. He washed Bianca and used rich lotions. He washed and combed her hair and brushed it many times until it shone, to make her more fit to be with the hands he had married. He never touched the hands, though he gave them soaps and creams and tools with which they could groom themselves. They were pleased. Once one of them ran up his coat and touched his cheek and made him exultant.

He left then and returned to the shop with his heart full of music. He worked harder than ever, so that Harding was pleased and let him go home early. He wandered the hours away by the bank of a brook, watching the sun on the face of the chuckling water. A bird came to circle him, flew unafraid through the aura of gladness about him. The delicate tip of a wing brushed his wrist with the touch of the first secret kiss from the hands of Bianca. The singing that filled him was part of the nature of laughing, the running of water, the sound of the wind in the reeds by the edge of the stream. He yearned for the hands, and he knew he could go now and clasp them and own them; instead he stretched out on the bank and lay smiling, all lost in the sweetness and poignance of waiting, denying desire. He laughed for pure joy in a world without hatred, held in the stainless palms of Bianca's hands.

As it grew dark he went home. All during that nuptial meal Bianca's hands twisted about one of his while he ate with the other, and Bianca's mother fed the girl. The fingers twined about each other and about his own, so that three hands seemed to be wrought of one flesh, to become a thing of lovely weight at his arm's end. When it was quite dark they went to the beautiful room and lay where he and the hands could watch, through the window, the clean, bright stars swim up out of the forest. The house and the room were dark and silent. Ran was so happy that he hardly dared to breathe.

A hand fluttered up over his hair, down his cheek, and crawled into the hollow of his throat. Its pulsing matched the beat of his heart. He opened his own hands wide and clenched his fingers, as though to catch and hold this moment.

Soon the other hand crept up and joined the first. For perhaps an hour they lay there passive with their coolness against Ran's warm neck. He felt them with his throat, each smooth convolution, each firm small expanse. He concentrated, with his mind and his heart on his throat, on each part of the hands that touched him, feeling with all his being first one touch and then another, though the contact was there unmoving. And he knew it would be soon now, soon.

As if at a command, he turned on his back and dug his head into the pillow. Staring up at the vague dark hangings on the wall, he began to realize what it was for which he had been working and dreaming so long. He put his head back yet farther and smiled, waiting. This would be possession, completion. He breathed deeply, twice, and the hands began to move.

The thumbs crossed over his throat, and the fingertips settled one by one under his ears. For a long moment they lay there, gathering strength. Together, then, in perfect harmony, each cooperating with the other, they became rigid, rock-hard. Their touch was still light upon him, still light . . . no, now they were passing their rigidity to him, turning it to a contraction. They settled to it slowly, their pressure measured and equal. Ran lay silent. He could not breathe now, and did not want to. His great arms were crossed on his chest, his knotted fists under his armpits, his mind knowing a great peace. Soon, now. . . .

Wave after wave of engulfing, glorious pain spread and receded. He saw color impossible, without light. He arched his back, up, up . . . the hands bore down with all their hidden strength, and Ran's body bent like a bow, resting on feet and shoulders. Up, up. . . .

Something burst within him—his lungs, his heart—no matter. It was complete.

There was blood on the hands of Bianca's mother when they found her in the morning in the beautiful room, trying to soothe Ran's neck. They took Bianca away, and they buried Ran, but they hanged Bianca's mother because she tried to make them believe Bianca had done it, Bianca, whose hands were quite dead, drooping like brown leaves from her wrists.

The Girl with the Hungry Eyes

FRITZ LEIBER

"There are vampires and vampires," the narrator of this little nightmare says, "and the ones that suck blood aren't the worst." The truth of those words will become evident to you, just as they became evident to him, when you meet "The Girl with the Hungry Eyes"—perhaps the most scarifying of all the macabre creations of award-winning fantasist Fritz Leiber. And there can be no higher praise for any story, considering such other Leiber masterpieces as "Smoke Ghost," "The Hound" and Conjure Wife.

All right, I'll tell you why the Girl gives me the creeps. Why I can't stand to go down town and see the mob slavering up at her on the tower, with that pop bottle or pack of cigarettes or whatever it is beside her. Why I hate to look at magazines any more because I know she'll turn up somewhere in a brassière or a bubble bath. Why I don't like to think of millions of Americans drinking in that poisonous half-smile. It's quite a story—more story than you're expecting.

No, I haven't suddenly developed any long-haired indignation at the evils of advertising and the national glamour-girl complex. That'd be a laugh for a man in my racket, wouldn't it? Though I think you'll agree there's something a little perverted about trying to capitalize on sex that way. But it's okay with me. And I know we've had the Face and the Body and the Look and what not else, so why shouldn't someone come along who sums it all up so completely, that we have to call her the Girl and blazon her on all the billboards from Times Square to Telegraph Hill?

But the Girl isn't like any of the others. She's unnatural. She's morbid. She's unholy.

Oh, these are modern times, you say, and the sort of thing I'm hinting at went out with witchcraft. But you see I'm not altogether sure myself what I'm hinting at, beyond a certain point. There are vampires and vampires, and not all of them suck blood.

And there were the murders, if they were murders. Besides, let me ask you this. Why, when America is obsessed with the Girl, don't we find out more about her? Why doesn't she rate a *Time* cover with a droll biography inside? Why hasn't there been a feature in *Life* or *The Post*? A profile in the *New Yorker*? Why hasn't *Charm* or *Mademoiselle* done her career saga? Not ready for it? Nuts!

Why haven't the movies snapped her up? Why hasn't she been on "Information, Please"? Why don't we see her kissing candidates at political rallies? Why isn't she chosen queen of some sort of junk or other at a convention?

Why don't we read about her tastes and hobbies, her views of the Russian situation? Why haven't the columnists interviewed her in a kimono on the top floor of the tallest hotel in Manhattan and told us who her boy friends are?

Finally—and this is the real killer—why hasn't she ever been drawn or painted?

Oh, no she hasn't. If you knew anything about commercial art you'd know that. Every blessed one of those pictures was worked up from a photograph. Expertly? Of course. They've got the top artists on it. But that's how it's done.

And now I'll tell you the why of all that. It's because from the top to the bottom of the whole world of advertising, news and business, there isn't a solitary soul who knows where the Girl came from, where she lives, what she does, who she is, even what her name is.

You heard me. What's more, not a single solitary soul ever sees her—except one poor damned photographer, who's making more money off her than he ever hoped to in his life and who's scared and miserable as hell every minute of the day.

No, I haven't the faintest idea who he is or where he has his studio. But I know there has to be such a man and I'm morally certain he feels just like I said.

Yes, I might be able to find her, if I tried. I'm not sure though—by now she probably has other safeguards. Besides, I don't want to.

Oh, I'm off my rocker, am I? That sort of thing can't happen in the Era of the Atom? People can't keep out of sight that way, not even Garbo?

Well I happen to know they can, because last year I was that poor damned photographer I was telling you about. Yes, last year, when the Girl made her first poisonous splash right here in this big little city of ours.

Yes, I know you weren't here last year and you don't know about it. Even the Girl had to start small. But if you hunted through the files of the local newspapers, you'd find some ads, and I might be able to locate you some of the old displays—I think Lovelybelt is still using one of them. I used to have a mountain of photos myself, until I burned them.

Yes, I made my cut off her. Nothing like what that other photographer must be making, but enough so it still bought this whiskey. She was funny about money. I'll tell you about that.

But first picture me then. I had a fourth-floor studio in that rathole the Hauser Building, not far from Ardleigh Park.

I'd been working at the Marsh-Mason studios until I'd gotten my bellyful of it and decided to start in for myself. The Hauser Building was awful—I'll never forget how the stairs creaked—but it was cheap and there was a skylight.

Business was lousy. I kept making the rounds of all the advertisers and agencies, and some of them didn't object to me too much personally, but my stuff never clicked. I was pretty near broke. I was behind on my rent. Hell, I didn't even have enough money to have a girl.

It was one of those dark, gray afternoons. The building was very quiet—I'd just finished developing some pix I was doing on speculation for Lovelybelt Girdles and Budford's Pool and Playground. My model had left. A Miss Leon. She was a civics teacher at one of the high schools and modeled for me on the side, just lately on speculation, too. After one look at the prints, I decided that Miss Leon probably wasn't just what Lovelybelt was looking for—or my photography either. I was about to call it a day.

And then the street door slammed four storys down and there were steps on the stairs and she came in.

She was wearing a cheap, shiny black dress. Black pumps. No stockings. And except that she had a gray cloth coat over one of them, those skinny arms of hers were bare. Her arms are pretty skinny, you know, or can't you see things like that any more?

And then the thin neck, the slightly gaunt, almost prim face, the tumbling mass of dark hair, and looking out from under it the hungriest eyes in the world.

That's the real reason she's plastered all over the country today, you know—those eyes. Nothing vulgar, but just the same they're looking at you with a hunger that's all sex and something more than sex. That's what everybody's been looking for since the Year One—something a little more than sex.

Well, boys, there I was, alone with the Girl, in an office that was getting shadowy, in a nearly empty building. A situation that a million male Americans have undoubtedly pictured to themselves with various lush details. How was I feeling? Scared.

I know sex can be frightening. That cold heart-thumping when you're alone with a girl and feel you're going to touch her. But if it was sex this time, it was overlaid with something else.

At least I wasn't thinking about sex.

I remember that I took a backward step and that my hand jerked so that the photos I was looking at sailed to the floor.

There was the faintest dizzy feeling like something was being drawn out of me. Just a little bit.

That was all. Then she opened her mouth and everything was back to normal for a while.

"I see you're a photographer, mister," she said. "Could you use a model?"

Her voice wasn't very cultivated.

"I doubt it," I told her, picking up the pix. You see, I wasn't impressed. The commercial possibilities of her eyes hadn't registered on me yet, by a long shot. "What have you done?"

Well, she gave me a vague sort of story and I began to check her knowledge of model agencies and studios and rates and what not and pretty soon I said to her, "Look here, you never modeled for a photographer in your life. You just walked in here cold."

Well, she admitted that was more or less so.

All along through our talk I got the idea she was feeling her way, like someone in a strange place. Not that she was uncertain of herself, or of me, but just of the general situation.

"And you think anyone can model?" I asked her pityingly.

"Sure," she said.

"Look," I said, "a photographer can waste a dozen negatives trying to get one halfway human photo of an average woman. How many do you think he'd have to waste before he got a real catchy, glamourous photo of her?"

"I think I could do it," she said.

Well, I should have kicked her out right then. Maybe I admired the cool way she stuck to her dumb little guns. Maybe I was touched by her underfed look. More likely I was feeling mean on account of the way my pictures had been snubbed by everybody and I wanted to take it out on her by showing her up.

"Okay, I'm going to put you on the spot," I told her. "I'm going to try a couple of shots of you. Understand it's strictly on spec. If somebody should ever want to use a photo of you, which is about one chance in two million, I'll pay you regular rates for your time. Not otherwise."

She gave me a smile. The first. "That's swell by me," she said.

Well, I took three or four shots, close-ups of her face since I didn't fancy her cheap dress, and at least she stood up to my sarcasm. Then I remembered I still had the Lovelybelt stuff and I guess the meanness was still working in me because I handed her a girdle and told her to go behind the screen and get into it and she did, without getting flustered as I'd expected, and since we'd gone that far, I figured we might as well shoot the beach scene to round it out, and that was that.

All this time I wasn't feeling anything particular one way or the other, except every once in a while I'd get one of those faint dizzy flashes and wonder if there was something wrong with my stomach or if I could have been a bit careless with my chemicals.

Still, you know, I think the uneasiness was in me all the while.

I tossed her a card and pencil. "Write your name and address and phone," I told her and made for the darkroom.

A little later she walked out. I didn't call any good-bys. I was irked because she hadn't fussed around or seemed anxious about her poses, or even thanked me, except for that one smile.

I finished developing the negatives, made some prints, glanced at them, decided they weren't a great deal worse than Miss Leon. On an impulse I slipped them in with the pictures I was going to take on the rounds next morning.

By now I'd worked long enough, so I was a bit fagged and nervous, but I didn't dare waste enough money on liquor to help that. I wasn't very hungry. I think I went to a cheap movie.

I didn't think of the Girl at all, except maybe to wonder faintly why in my present womanless state I hadn't made a pass at her. She had seemed to belong to a—well, distinctly more approachable social strata than Miss Leon. But then, of course, there were all sorts of arguable reasons for my not doing that.

Next morning I made the rounds. My first step was Munsch's

Brewery. They were looking for a "Munsch Girl." Papa Munsch had a
sort of affection for me, though he razzed my photography. He had a
good natural judgment about that, too. Fifty years ago he might have
been one of the shoe-string boys who made Hollywood.

Right now he was out in the plant pursuing is favorite occupation.
He put down the beaded schooner, smacked his lips, gabbled
something technical to someone about hops, wiped his fat hands on
the big apron he was wearing, and grabbed my thin stack of pictures.

He was about halfway through, making noises with his tongue and
teeth, when he came to her. I kicked myself for even having stuck
her in.

"That's her," he said. "The photography's not so hot, but that's the
girl."

It was all decided. I wonder now why Papa Munsch sensed what the
Girl had right away, while I didn't. I think it was because I saw her first
in the flesh, if that's the right word.

At the time I just felt faint.

"Who is she?" he said.

"One of my new models." I tried to make it casual.

"Bring her out tomorrow morning," he told me. "And your stuff.
We'll photograph her here.

"Here, don't look so sick," he added. "Have some beer."

Well, I went away telling myself it was just a fluke, so that she'd
probably blow it tomorrow with her inexperience, and so on.

Just the same, when I reverently laid my next stack of pictures on
Mr. Fitch, of Lovelybelt's, rose-colored blotter, I had hers on top.

Mr. Fitch went through the motions of being an art critic. He
leaned over backwards, squinted his eyes, waved his long fingers, and
said, "Hmm. What do you think, Miss Willow? Here, in this light, of
course, the photograph doesn't show the bias cut. And perhaps we
should use the Lovelybelt Imp instead of the Angel. Still, the girl. . . .
Come over here, Binns." More finger-waving. "I want a married man's
reaction."

He couldn't hide the fact that he was hooked.

Exactly the same thing happened at Budford's Pool and Playground, except that Da Costa didn't need a married man's say-so.

"Hot stuff," he said, sucking his lips. "Oh boy, you photographers!"

I hot-footed it back to the office and grabbed up the card I'd given
her to put down her name and address.

It was blank.

I don't mind telling you that the next five days were about the worst I ever went through, in an ordinary way. When next morning rolled around and I still hadn't got hold of her, I had to start stalling.

"She's sick," I told Papa Munsch over the phone.

"She at a hospital?" he asked me.

"Nothing that serious," I told him.

"Get her out here then. What's a little headache?"

"Sorry, I can't."

Papa Munsch got suspicious. "You really got this girl?"

"Of course I have."

"Well, I don't know. I'd think it was some New York model, except I recognized your lousy photography."

I laughed.

"Well look, you get her here tomorrow morning, you hear?"

"I'll try."

"Try nothing. You get her out here."

He didn't know half of what I tried. I went around to all the model and employment agencies. I did some slick detective work at the photographic and art studios. I used up some of my last dimes putting advertisements in all three papers. I looked at high school yearbooks and at employee photos in local house organs. I went to restaurants and drugstores, looking at waitresses, and to dime stores and department stores, looking at clerks. I watched the crowds coming out of movie theaters. I roamed the streets.

Evenings, I spent quite a bit of time along Pick-Up Row. Somehow that seemed the right place.

The fifth afternoon I knew I was licked. Papa Munsch's deadline—he'd given me several, but this was it—was due to run out at six o'clock. Mr. Fitch had already canceled.

I was at the studio window, looking out at Ardleigh Park.

She walked in.

I'd gone over this moment so often in my mind that I had no trouble putting on my act. Even the faint dizzy feeling didn't throw me off.

"Hello," I said, hardly looking at her.

"Hello," she said.

"Not discouraged yet?"

"No." It didn't sound uneasy or defiant. It was just a statement.

I snapped a look at my watch, got up and said curtly. "Look here, I'm going to give you a chance. There's a client of mine looking for a girl of your general type. If you do a real good job you might break into the modeling business.

"We can see him this afternoon if we hurry," I said. I picked up my stuff. "Come on. And next time if you expect favors, don't forget to leave your phone number."

"Uh, uh," she said, not moving.

"What do you mean?" I said.

"I'm not going out to see any client of yours."

"The hell you aren't," I said. "You little nut, I'm giving you a break."

She shook her head slowly. "You're not fooling me, baby, you're not fooling me at all. They want me." And she gave me the second smile.

At the time I thought she must have seen my newspaper ad. Now I'm not so sure.

"And now I'll tell you how we're going to work," she went on. "You aren't going to have my name or address or phone number. Nobody is. And we're going to do all the pictures right here. Just you and me."

You can imagine the roar I raised at that. I was everything—angry, sarcastic, patiently explanatory, off my nut, threatening, pleading.

I would have slapped her face off, except it was photographic capital.

In the end all I could do was phone Papa Munsch and tell him her conditions. I knew I didn't have a chance, but I had to take it.

He gave me a really angry bawling out, said "no" several times and hung up.

It didn't worry her. "We'll start shooting at ten o'clock tomorrow," she said.

It was just like her, using that corny line from the movie magazines.

About midnight Papa Munsch called me up.

"I don't know what insane asylum you're renting this girl from," he said, "but I'll take her. Come round tomorrow morning and I'll try to get it through your head just how I want the pictures. And I'm glad I got you out of bed!"

After that it was a breeze. Even Mr. Fitch reconsidered and after taking two days to tell me it was quite impossible, he accepted the conditions too.

Of course you're all under the spell of the Girl, so you can't understand how much self-sacrifice it represented on Mr. Fitch's part when he agreed to forego supervising the photography of my model in the Lovelybelt Imp or Vixen or whatever it was we finally used.

Next morning she turned up on time according to her schedule, and we went to work. I'll say one thing for her, she never got tired and she never kicked at the way I fussed over shots. I got along okay, except I still had that feeling of something being shoved away gently. Maybe you've felt it just a little, looking at her picture.

When we finished I found out there were still more rules. It was about the middle of the afternoon. I started with her to get a sandwich and coffee.

"Uh, uh," she said. "I'm going down alone. And look, baby, if you ever try to follow me, if you ever so much as stick your head out of that window when I go, you can hire yourself another model."

You can imagine how all this crazy stuff strained my temper—and my imagination. I remember opening the window after she was gone—I waited a few minutes first—and standing there getting some fresh air and trying to figure out what could be behind it, whether she was hiding from the police, or was somebody's ruined daughter, or maybe had got the idea it was smart to be temperamental, or more likely Papa Munsch was right and she was partly nuts.

But I had my pictures to finish up.

Looking back it's amazing to think how fast her magic began to take hold of the city after that. Remembering what came after, I'm frightened of what's happening to the whole country—and maybe the world. Yesterday I read something in *Time* about the Girl's picture turning up on billboards in Egypt.

The rest of my story will help show you why I'm frightened in that big, general way. But I have a theory, too, that helps explain, though it's one of those things that's beyond that "certain point." It's about the Girl. I'll give it to you in a few words.

You know how modern advertising gets everybody's mind set in the same direction, wanting the same things, imagining the same things. And you know the psychologists aren't so skeptical of telepathy as they used to be.

Add up the two ideas. Suppose the identical desires of millions of people focused on one telepathic person. Say a girl. Shaped her in their image.

Imagine her knowing the hiddenmost hungers of millions of men.

Imagine her seeing deeper into those hungers than the people that had them, seeing the hatred and the wish for death behind the lust. Imagine her shaping herself in that complete image, keeping herself as aloof as marble. Yet imagine the hunger she might feel in answer to their hunger.

But that's getting a long way from the facts of my story. And some of those facts are darn solid. Like money. We made money.

That was the funny thing I was going to tell you. I was afraid the Girl was going to hold me up. She really had me over a barrel, you know.

But she didn't ask for anything but the regular rates. Later on I insisted on pushing more money at her, a whole lot. But she always took it with that same contemptuous look, as if she were going to toss it down the first drain when she got outside.

Maybe she did.

At any rate, I had money. For the first time in months I had money enough to get drunk, buy new clothes, take taxicabs. I could make a play for any girl I wanted to. I only had to pick.

And so of course I had to go and pick . . .

But first let me tell you about Papa Munsch.

Papa Munsch wasn't the first of the boys to try to meet my model but I think he was the first to really go soft on her. I could watch the change in his eyes as he looked at her pictures. They began to get sentimental, reverent. Mama Munsch had been dead for two years.

He was smart about the way he planned it. He got me to drop some information which told him when she came to work, and then one morning he came pounding up the stairs a few minutes before.

"I've got to see her, Dave," he told me.

I argued with him, I kidded him, I explained he didn't know just how serious she was about her crazy ideas. I even pointed out he was cutting both our throats. I even amazed myself by bawling him out.

He didn't take any of it in his usual way. He just kept repeating, "But, Dave, I've got to see her."

The street door slammed.

"That's her," I said, lowering my voice. "You've got to get out."

He wouldn't, so I shoved him in the darkroom. "And keep quiet," I whispered. "I'll tell her I can't work today."

I knew he'd try to look at her and probably come bustling in, but there wasn't anything else I could do.

The footsteps came to the fourth floor. But she never showed at the door. I got uneasy.

"Get that bum out of there!" she yelled suddenly from beyond the door. Not very loud, but in her commonest voice.

"I'm going up to the next landing," she said. "And if that fat-bellied bum doesn't march straight down to the street, he'll never get another picture of me except spitting in his lousy beer."

Papa Munsch came out of the darkroom. He was white. He didn't look at me as he went out. He never looked at her pictures in front of me again.

That was Papa Munsch. Now it's me I'm telling about. I talked around the subject with her, I hinted, eventually I made my pass.

She lifted my hand off her as if it were a damp rag.

"No, baby," she said. "This is working time."

"But afterwards . . ." I pressed.

"The rules still hold." And I got what I think was the fifth smile.

It's hard to believe, but she never budged an inch from that crazy line. I mustn't make a pass at her in the office, because our work was very important and she loved it and there mustn't be any distractions. And I couldn't see her anywhere else, because if I tried to, I'd never snap another picture of her—and all this with more money coming in all the time and me never so stupid as to think my photography had anything to do with it.

Of course I wouldn't have been human if I hadn't made more passes. But they always got the wet-rag treatment and there weren't any more smiles.

I changed. I went sort of crazy and light-headed—only sometimes I felt my head was going to burst. And I started to talk to her all the time. About myself.

It was like being in a constant delirium that never interfered with business. I didn't pay any attention to the dizzy feeling. It seemed natural.

I'd walk around and for a moment the reflector would look like a sheet of white-hot steel, or the shadows would seem like armies of moths, or the camera would be a big black coal car. But the next instant they'd come all right again.

I think sometimes I was scared to death of her. She'd seem the strangest, most horrible person in the world. But other times . . . .

And I talked. It didn't matter what I was doing—lighting her, posing her, fussing with props, snapping my pictures—or where she was—on the platform, behind the screen, relaxing with a magazine—I kept up a steady gab.

I told her everything I knew about myself. I told her about my first girl. I told her about my brother Bob's bicycle. I told her about running away on a freight, and the licking pa gave me when I came home. I told her about shipping to South America and the blue sky at night. I told her about Betty. I told her about my mother dying of cancer. I told her about being beaten up in a fight in an alley behind a bar. I told her about Mildred. I told her about the first picture I ever sold. I told her how Chicago looked from a sailboat. I told her about the longest drunk I was ever on. I told her about Marsh-Mason. I told her about Gwen. I told her about how I met Papa Munsch. I told her about hunting her. I told her about how I felt now.

She never paid the slightest attention to what I said. I couldn't even tell if she heard me.

It was when we were getting our first nibble from national advertisers that I decided to follow her when she went home.

Wait, I can place it better than that. Something you'll remember from the out-of-town papers—those maybe murders I mentioned. I think there were six.

I say "maybe" because the police could never be sure they weren't heart attacks. But there's bound to be suspicion when attacks happen to people whose hearts have been okay, and always at night when they're alone and away from home and there's a question of what they were doing.

The six deaths created one of those "mystery poisoner" scares. And afterwards there was a feeling that they hadn't really stopped, but were being continued in a less suspicious way.

That's one of the things that scares me now.

But at that time my only feeling was relief that I'd decided to follow her.

I made her work until dark one afternoon. I didn't need any excuses, we were snowed under with orders. I waited until the street door slammed, then I ran down. I was wearing rubber-soled shoes. I'd slipped on a dark coat she'd never seen me in, and a dark hat.

I stood in the doorway until I spotted her. She was walking by Ardleigh Park towards the heart of town. It was one of those warm fall nights. I followed her on the other side of the street. My idea for tonight was just to find out where she lived. That would give me a hold on her.

She stopped in front of a display window, of Everley's department store, standing back from the flow. She stood there looking in.

I remembered we'd done a big photograph of her for Everley's, to make a flat model for a lingerie display. That was what she was looking at.

At the time it seemed all right to me that she should adore herself, if that was what she was doing.

When people passed she'd turn away a little or drift back further into the shadows.

Then a man came by alone. I couldn't see his face very well, but he looked middle-aged. He stopped and stood looking in the window.

She came out of the shadows and stepped up beside him.

How would you boys feel if you were looking at a poster of the Girl and suddenly she was there beside you, her arm linked with yours?

This fellow's reaction showed plain as day. A crazy dream had come to life for him.

They talked for a moment. Then he waved a taxi to the curb. They got in and drove off.

I got drunk that night. It was almost as if she'd known I was following her and had picked that way to hurt me. Maybe she had. Maybe this was the finish.

But the next morning she turned up at the usual time and I was back in the delirium, only now with some new angles added.

That night when I followed her she picked a spot under a street-lamp, opposite one of the Munsch Girl billboards.

Now it frightens me to think of her lurking that way.

After about twenty minutes a convertible slowed down going past her, backed up, swung into the curb.

I was closer this time. I got a good look at the fellow's face. He was a little younger, about my age.

Next morning the same face looked up at me from the front page of the paper. The convertible had been found parked on a sidestreet. He had been in it. As in the other maybe-murders, the cause of death was uncertain.

All kinds of thoughts were spinning in my head that day, but there were only two things I knew for sure. That I'd got the first real offer from a national advertiser, and that I was going to take the Girl's arm and walk down the stairs with her when we quit work.

She didn't seem surprised. "You know what you're doing?" she said. "I know."

She smiled. "I was wondering when you'd get around to it."

I began to feel good. I was kissing everything good-by, but I had my arm around hers.

It was another of those warm fall evenings. We cut across into Ardleigh Park. It was dark there, but all around the sky was a sallow pink from the advertising signs.

We walked for a long time in the park. She didn't say anything and she didn't look at me, but I could see her lips twitching and after a while her hand tightened on my arm.

We stopped. We'd been walking across the grass. She dropped down and pulled me after her. She put her hands on my shoulders. I was looking down at her face. It was the faintest sallow pink from the glow in the sky. The hungry eyes were dark smudges.

I was fumbling with her blouse. She took my hand away, not like she had in the studio. "I don't want that," she said.

First I'll tell you what I did afterwards. Then I'll tell you why I did it. Then I'll tell you what she said.

What I did was run away. I don't remember all of that because I was dizzy, and the pink sky was swinging against the dark trees. But after a while I staggered into the lights of the street. The next day I closed up the studio. The telephone was ringing when I locked the door and there were unopened letters on the floor. I never saw the Girl again in the flesh, if that's the right word.

I did it because I didn't want to die. I didn't want the life drawn out of me. There are vampires and vampires, and the ones that suck blood aren't the worst. If it hadn't been for the warning of those dizzy flashes, and Papa Munsch and the face in the morning paper, I'd have gone the way the others did. But I realized what I was up against while there was still time to tear myself away. I realized that wherever she came from, whatever shaped her, she's the quintessence of the horror behind the bright billboard. She's the smile that tricks you into throwing away your money and your life. She's the eyes that lead you on and on, and then show you death. She's the creature you give everything for and never really get. She's the being that takes everything you've got and gives nothing in return. When you yearn towards her face on the billboards, remember that. She's the lure. She's the bait. She's the Girl.

And this is what she said, "I want you. I want your high spots. I want everything that's made you happy and everything that's hurt you bad. I want your first girl. I want that shiny bicycle. I want that licking. I want that pinhole camera. I want Betty's legs. I want the blue sky filled with stars. I want your mother's death. I want your blood on the cobblestones. I want Mildred's mouth. I want the first picture you sold. I want the lights of Chicago. I want the gin. I want Gwen's hands. I want your wanting me. I want your life. Feed me, baby, feed me."

Shut a Final Door

TRUMAN CAPOTE

This story by a twenty-three-year-old Truman Capote won first prize in the 1948 O. Henry Prize Stories annual collection. Although Capote went on to do a major body of work (his first novel Other Voices, Other Rooms *was published that year), "Shut a Final Door" is perhaps his peak accomplishment in short fiction, as swiftly, elegantly, perilously toward the end, it takes the sheer bottom out and leaves the reader, like the protagonist, nothing but the rhythms and implications of his own stricken heart.*

"Walter, listen to me; if everyone dislikes you, works against you, don't believe they do so arbitrarily: you create these situations for yourself."

Anna had said that, and, though his healthier side told him she intended nothing malicious (if Anna was not a friend, then who was?), he'd despised her for it, had gone around telling everybody how much he despised Anna, what a bitch she was: that woman! he said, don't trust that Anna: this plain-spoken act of hers—nothing but a cover-up for all her repressed hostility; terrible liar, too, can't believe a word she says: dangerous, my God! And naturally all he said went back to Anna, so that when he called about a play opening they'd planned attending together she told him: "Sorry, Walter, I can't afford you any longer: I understand you very well, and I have a certain amount of sympathy: it's very compulsive, your malice, and you aren't too much to blame, but I don't want ever to see you again because I'm not so well myself that I can afford it." But why? and what had he done? Well, sure, he'd gossiped about her, but it wasn't as though he'd meant it, and after all, as he said to Jimmy Bergman (now there was a two-face if ever there was one), what was the use of having friends if you couldn't discuss them objectively?

He said you said they said we said round and round. Round and round, like the paddle-bladed ceiling fan wheeling above; turning and turning, stirring stale air ineffectively, it made a watch-tick sound, counted seconds in the silence. Walter inched to a cooler part of the bed, and closed his eyes against the dark little room. At seven that evening he'd arrived in New Orleans, at seven thirty he'd registered in this hotel, an anonymous sidestreet place. It was August, and it was as though bonfires burned in the red night sky, and the unnatural Southern landscape, observed so assiduously from the train, and which, trying to sublimate all else, he retraced in memory, intensified a feeling of having traveled to the end, the falling off.

But why he was here in this stifling hotel in this faraway town he could not say. There was a window in the room, but he could not seem to get it open, and he was afraid to call the bellboy (what queer eyes that kid had!), and he was afraid to leave the hotel, for what if he got lost? and if he got lost, even a little, then he would be lost altogether. He was hungry; he hadn't eaten since breakfast, so he found some peanut-butter crackers left over from a package he'd bought in Saratoga, and washed them down with a finger of Four Roses, the last. It made him sick: he vomited in a wastebasket, collapsed back on the bed, and cried until the pillow was wet. After a while he just lay there in the hot room shivering, just lay there and watched the slow-turning fan; there was no beginning to its action, and no end: it was a circle.

An eye, the earth, the rings of a tree, everything is a circle, and all circles, Walter said, have a center. It was crazy for Anna to say what had happened was his own doing. If there was anything wrong with him really, then it had been made so by circumstances beyond his control, by, say, his churchly mother, or his father, an insurance official in Hartford, or his older sister, Cecile, who'd married a man forty years her senior: "I just wanted to get out of that house," that was her excuse, and, to tell the truth, Walter had thought it reasonable enough.

But he did not know where to begin thinking about himself, did not know where to find the center. The first telephone call? No, that had been only three days ago and, properly speaking, was the end, not the beginning. Well, he could start with Irving, for Irving was the first person he'd known in New York.

Now Irving was a sweet little Jewish boy with a remarkable talent for chess and not much else: he had silky hair, and pink baby cheeks, and looked about sixteen: actually he was twenty-three, Walter's age, and they'd met at a bar in the Village. Walter was alone and very lonesome in New York, and so when this sweet little Irving was friendly he decided maybe it would be a good idea to be friendly, too—because you never can tell. Irving knew a great many people, and everyone was very fond of him, and he introduced Walter to all his friends.

And there was Margaret. Margaret was more or less Irving's girl friend. She was only so-so looking (her eyes bulged, there was always a little lipstick on her teeth, she dressed like a child of ten), but she had a hectic brightness which Walter found attractive. He could not understand why she bothered with Irving at all. "Why do you?" he said, on one of the long walks they'd begun taking together in Central Park.

"Irving is sweet," she said, "and he loves me very purely, and who knows: I might just as well marry him."

"A damn fool thing to do," he said. "Irving could never be your husband because he's really your little brother. Irving is everyone's little brother."

Margaret was too bright not to see the truth in this. So one day when Walter asked if he might make love to her she said all right she didn't mind if he did. They made love often after that.

Eventually Irving heard about it, and one Monday there was a nasty scene in, curiously enough, the same bar where they'd met. There had been that evening a party in honor of Kurt Kuhnhardt (Kuhnhardt Advertising), Margaret's boss, and she and Walter had gone together, afterwards stopping by this bar for a nightcap. Except for Irving and a couple of girls in slacks the place was empty. Irving was sitting at the bar, his cheeks quite pink, his eyes rather glazed: he looked like a little boy playing grown-up, for his legs were too short to reach the stool's footrest; they dangled doll-like. The instant Margaret recognized him she tried to turn around and walk out, but Walter wouldn't let her. And anyway, Irving had seen them: never taking his eyes from them, he put down his whiskey, slowly climbed off the stool, and, with a kind of sad, ersatz toughness, strutted forward.

"Irving, dear—" said Margaret, and stopped, for he'd given her a terrible look.

His chin was trembling. "You go away," he said, and it was as though he were denouncing some childhood tormentor, "I hate you." Then, almost in slow motion, he swung out and, as if he clutched a knife, struck Walter's chest: it was not much of a blow, and when Walter did nothing but smile, Irving slumped against a jukebox, screaming: "Fight me, you damned coward; come on, and I'll kill you, I swear before God I will." So that was how they left him.

Walking home, Margaret began to cry in a soft tired way. "He'll never be sweet again," she said. And Walter said: "I don't know what you mean." "Oh yes you do," she told him, her voice a whisper, "yes you do; the two of us, we've taught him how to hate. Somehow I don't think he ever knew before."

Walter had been in New York now four months. His original capital of five hundred dollars had fallen to fifteen, and Margaret lent him money to pay his January rent at the Brevoort: why, she wanted to know, didn't he move some place cheaper? Well, he told her, it was better to have a good address. And what about a job? When was he going to start working? Or was he? Sure, he said, sure, as a matter of fact he thought about it a good deal. But he didn't intend fooling around with just any little jerkwater thing that came along: he wanted something good, something with a future, something in, say, advertising. All right, said Margaret, maybe she could help him; at any rate, she'd speak with her boss, Mr. Kuhnhardt.

The K.K.A., so-called, was a middle-sized agency, but, as such things go, very good, the best. Kurt Kuhnhardt, who'd founded it in 1925, was a curious man with a curious reputation: a lean, fastidious German, a bachelor, he lived in an elegant black house on Sutton Place, a house interestingly furnished with, among other things, three Picassos, a superb music box, South Sea Island masks, and a burly Danish youngster, the houseboy. He invited occasionally some one of his staff in to dinner, whoever was favorite at the moment, for he was continually selecting protégés: it was a dangerous position, these alliances being, as they were, whimsical and uncertain: the protégé found himself checking the want ads when, just the evening previous, he'd dined most enjoyably with his benefactor. During his second week at the K.K.A., Walter, who had been hired as Margaret's assistant, received a memorandum from Mr. Kuhnhardt asking him to lunch, and this, of course, excited him unspeakably.

"Killjoy?" said Margaret, straightening his tie, plucking lint off a lapel. "Nothing of the sort. It's just that—well, Kuhnhardt's wonderful to work for so long as you don't get too involved—or you're likely not to be working: period."

Walter knew what she was up to; she didn't fool him a minute; he felt like telling her so, too, but restrained himself: it wasn't time yet. One of these days, though, he was going to have to get rid of her, and soon. It was degrading, his working for Margaret. And besides, the tendency from now on would be to keep him down. But nobody could do that, he thought, looking into Mr. Kuhnhardt's sea blue eyes, nobody could keep Walter down.

"You're an idiot," Margaret told him. "My God, I've seen these little friendships of K.K.'s a dozen times, and they don't mean a damn; he used to palsy-walsy around with the switchboard operator: all K.K. wants is someone to play the fool. Take my word, Walter, there aren't any short cuts: what matters is how you do your job."

He said: "And have you complaints on that score? I'm doing as well as could be expected."

"It depends on what you mean by expected," she said.

One Saturday not long afterwards he made a date to meet her in Grand Central. They were going up to Hartford to spend the afternoon with his family, and for this she'd bought a new dress, new hat and shoes. But he did not show up. Instead, he drove out on Long Island with Mr. Kuhnhardt, and was the most awed of three hundred guests at Rosa Cooper's debut ball. Rosa Cooper (nee Kuppermann) was heiress to the Cooper Dairy Products: a dark, plump, pleasant child with an unnatural British accent, the result of four years at Miss Jewett's. She wrote a letter to a friend named Anna Stimson, who subsequently showed it to Walter: "Met the divinest man. Danced with him six times, a divine dancer. He is an Advertising Executive, and is terribly divinely good-looking. We have a date—dinner and the theater!"

Margaret did not mention the episode, nor did Walter. It was as though nothing had happened, except that now, unless there was office business to discuss, they never spoke, never saw each other. One afternoon, knowing she would not be at home, he went to her apartment and used a passkey given him long ago; there were things he'd left here, clothes, some books, his pipe; rummaging around collecting all this, he discovered a photograph of himself scrawled red with lipstick: it gave him for an instant the sensation of falling in a dream. He also came across the only gift he'd ever made her, a bottle of L'Heure Bleue, still unopened. He sat down on the bed, and, smoking a cigarette, stroked his hand over the cool pillow, remembering the way her head had lain there, remembering, too, how they used to lie here Sunday mornings reading the funnies aloud, Barney Google and Dick Tracy and Joe Palooka.

He looked at the radio, a little green box; they'd always made love to music, any kind, jazz, symphonies, choir programs: it had been their signal, for whenever she'd wanted him, she'd said, "Shall we listen to the radio, darling?" Anyway, it was finished, and he hated her, and that was what he needed to remember. He found the bottle of perfume again, and put it in his pocket: Rosa might like a surprise.

In the office the next day he stopped by the water cooler and Margaret was standing there. She smiled at him fixedly, and said: "Well, I didn't know you were a thief." It was the first overt disclosure of the hostility between them. And suddenly it occurred to Walter he hadn't in all the office a single ally. Kuhnhardt? He could never count on him. And everyone else was an enemy: Jackson, Einstein, Fisher, Porter, Capehart, Ritter, Villa, Byrd. Oh sure, they were all smart enough not to tell him point-blank, not so long as K.K.'s enthusiasm continued.

Well, dislike was at least positive, and the one thing he could not tolerate was vague relations, possibly because his own feelings were so indecisive, ambiguous: he was never certain whether he liked X or not. He needed X's love, but was incapable of loving. He could never be sincere with X, never tell him more than fifty percent of the truth. On the other hand, it was impossible for him to permit X these same imperfections: somewhere along the line Walter was sure he'd be betrayed. He was afraid of X, terrified. Once in high school he'd plagiarized a poem, and printed it in the school magazine; he could not forget its final line, *All our acts are acts of fear*. And when his teacher caught him out, had anything ever seemed to him more unjust?

He spent most of the early summer week ends at Rosa Cooper's Long Island place. The house was as a rule well-staffed with hearty Yale and Princeton undergraduates, which was irritating, for they were the sort of boys who, around Hartford, made green birds fly in his stomach, and seldom allowed him to meet them on their own ground. As for Rosa herself, she was a darling; everyone said so, even Walter.

But darlings are rarely serious, and Rosa was not serious about Walter. He didn't mind too much. He was able on these week ends to make a good many contacts: Taylor Ovington, Joyce Randolph (the starlet), E. L. McEvoy, a dozen or so people whose names cast considerable glare in his address book. One evening he went with Anna Stimson to see a film featuring the Randolph girl, and before they were scarcely seated everyone for aisles around knew she was a Friend of his, knew she drank too much, was immoral, and not nearly so pretty as Hollywood made her out to be. Anna told him he was an adolescent female. "You're a man in only one respect, sweetie," she said.

It was through Rosa that he'd met Anna Stimson. An editor on a fashion magazine, she was almost six feet tall, wore black suits, affected a monocle, a walking cane, and pounds of jingling Mexican silver. She'd been married twice, once to Buck Strong, the horse-opera idol, and she had a child, a fourteen-year-old son who'd had to be put away in what she called a "corrective academy."

"He was a nasty child," she said. "He liked to take potshots out the window with a .22, and throw things, and steal from Woolworth's: awful brat, just like you."

Anna was good to him, though, and in her less depressed, less malevolent moments listened kindly while he groaned out his problems, while he explained why he was the way he was: all his life some cheat had been dealing him the wrong cards. Attributing to Anna every vice but stupidity, he liked to use her as a kind of confessor: there was nothing he could tell her of which she might legitimately disapprove. He would say: "I've told Kuhnhardt a lot of lies about Margaret; I suppose that's pretty rotten, but she would do the same for me; and anyway my idea is not for him to fire her, but maybe transfer her to the Chicago office."

Or, "I was in a bookshop, and a man was standing there and we began talking: a middle-aged man, rather nice, very intelligent. When I went outside he followed, a little ways behind: I crossed the street, he crossed the street, I walked fast, he walked fast. This kept up six or seven blocks, and when I finally figured out what was going on I felt tickled, I felt like kidding him on. So I stopped at the corner and hailed a cab; then I turned around and gave this guy a long, long look, and he came rushing up, all smiles. And I jumped in the cab, and slammed the door and leaned out the window and laughed out loud: the look on his face, it was awful, it was like Christ. I can't forget it. And tell me, Anna, why did I do this crazy thing? It was like paying back all the people who've ever hurt me, but it was something else, too." He would tell Anna these stories, go home and go to sleep: his dreams were clear blue.

Now the problem of love concerned him, mainly because he did not consider it a problem. Nevertheless, he was conscious of being unloved: this knowledge was like an extra heart beating inside him. But there was no one. Anna, perhaps. Did Anna love him? "Oh," said Anna, "when was anything ever what it seemed to be? Now it's a tadpole, now it's a frog. It looks like gold but you put it on your finger and it leaves a green ring. Take my second husband: he looked like a nice guy, and turned out to be just another heel. Look around this very room: why, you couldn't burn incense in that fireplace, and those mirrors, they give space, they tell a lie. Nothing, Walter, is ever what it seems to be. Christmas trees are cellophane, and snow is only soap chips. Flying around inside us is something called the Soul, and when you die you're never dead; yes, and when we're alive we're never alive. And so you want to know if I love you? Don't be dumb, Walter, we're not even friends—"

Listen, the fan: turning wheels of whisper: he said you said they said we said round and round fast and slow while time recalled itself in endless chatter. Old broken fan breaking silence: August the third the third the third!

August the third, a Friday, and it was there, right in Winchell's column, his own name: "Big shot ad exec Walter Ranney and dairy heiress Rosa Cooper are telling intimates to start buying rice." Walter himself had given the item to a friend of a friend of Winchell's. He showed it to the counter boy at the Whelan's where he ate breakfast: "That's me," he said, "I'm the guy," and the look on the boy's face was good for his digestion.

It was late when he reached the office that morning, and as he walked down the aisle of desks a small gratifying flurry among the typists preceded him. No one said anything, however. Around eleven, after a pleasant hour of doing nothing but feel exhilarated, he went to the drugstore downstairs for a cup of coffee. Three men from the office, Jackson, Ritter and Byrd, were there, and when Walter came in Jackson poked Byrd, and Byrd poked Ritter, and all of them turned around. "Whatcha say, big shot?" said Jackson, a pink man prematurely bald, and the other two laughed. Acting as if he hadn't heard, Walter stepped quickly into a phone booth: "Bastards," he said pretending to dial a number. And finally, after waiting a long while for them to leave, he made a real call: "Rosa, hello, did I wake you up?"

"No."

"Say, did you see Winchell?"

"Yes."

Walter laughed. "Where do you suppose he gets that stuff?"

Silence.

"What's the matter? You sound kind of funny."

"Do I?"

"Are you mad or something?"

"Just disappointed."

"About what?"

Silence. And then: "It was a cheap thing to do Walter, pretty cheap."

"I don't know what you mean."

"Good-by, Walter."

On the way out he paid the cashier for a cup of coffee he'd forgotten to have. There was a barbershop in the building. He said he wanted a shave; no—make it a haircut; no—a manicure; and suddenly, seeing himself in the mirror, where his face reflected as pale almost as the barber's bib, he knew he did not know what he wanted. Rosa had been right, he was cheap. He'd always been willing to confess his faults, for, by admitting them, it was as if he made them no longer to exist. He went back upstairs, and sat at his desk, and felt as though he were bleeding inside, and wished very much to believe in God. A pigeon strutted on the ledge outside his window. For some time he watched the shimmering sunlit feathers, the wobbly sedateness of its movements; then, before realizing it, he'd picked up and thrown a glass paperweight: the pigeon climbed calmly upward, the paperweight careened like a giant raindrop: suppose, he thought, listening for a faraway scream, suppose it hits someone, kills them? But there was nothing. Only the ticking fingers of typists, a knocking at the door: "Hey, Ranney, K.K. wants to see you."

"I'm sorry," said Mr. Kuhnhardt, doodling with a gold pen. "And I'll write a letter for you, Walter. Any time."

Now in the elevator the enemy, all submerging with him, crushed Walter between them; Margaret was there wearing a blue hair ribbon: she looked at him, and her face was different from other faces, not vacant as theirs were, and sterile: here still was compassion. But as she looked at him, she looked through him, too. This is my dream: he must not allow himself to believe otherwise; and yet under his own arm he carried the dream's contradiction, a manila envelope stuffed with all the personals saved from his desk. When the elevator emptied into the lobby, he knew he must speak with Margaret, ask her to forgive him, beg her protection, but she was slipping swiftly toward an exit, losing herself among the enemy: I love you, he said, running after her, I love you, he said, saying nothing.

"Margaret! Margaret!"

She turned around. The blue hair ribbon matched her eyes, and her eyes, gazing up at him, softened, became rather friendly. Or pitying.

"Please," he said, "I thought we could have a drink together, go over to Benny's maybe. We used to like Benny's, remember?"

She shook her head. "I've got a date, and I'm late already."

"Oh."

"Yes—well, I'm late," she said, and began to run. He stood watching as she raced down the street, her ribbon streaming, shining in the darkening summer light. And then she was gone.

His apartment, a one-room walk-up near Gramercy Park, needed an airing, a cleaning, but Walter, after pouring a drink, said to hell with it and stretched out on the couch. What was the use? No matter what you did or how hard you tried, it all came finally to zero; everyday everywhere everyone was being cheated, and who was there to blame? It was strange, though; lying here sipping whiskey in the dusk graying room he felt calmer than he had for God knows how long. It was like the time he'd failed algebra and felt so relieved, so free: failure was definite, a certainty, and there is always peace in certainties. Now he would leave New York, take a vacation trip; he had a few hundred dollars, enough to last until fall.

And, wondering where he should go, he all at once saw, as if a film had commenced running in his head, silk caps, cherry-colored and lemon, and little wise-faced men wearing exquisite polka-dot shirts: closing his eyes, he was suddenly five years old, and it was delicious remembering the cheers, the hot dogs, his father's big pair of binoculars. Saratoga! Shadows masked his face in the sinking light. He turned on a lamp, fixed another drink, put a rhumba record on the phonograph, and began to dance, the soles of his shoes whispering on the carpet: he'd often thought that with a little training he could've been a professional.

Just as the music ended, the telephone rang. He simply stood there, afraid somehow to answer, and the lamplight, the furniture, everything in the room went quite dead. When at last he thought it had stopped, it commenced again; louder, it seemed, and more insistent. He tripped over a footstool, picked up the receiver, dropped and recovered it, said: "Yes?"

Long-distance: a call from some town in Pennsylvania, the name of which he didn't catch. Following a series of spasmic rattlings, a voice, dry and sexless and altogether unlike any he'd ever heard before, came through: "Hello, Walter."

"Who is this?"

No answer from the other end, only a sound of strong orderly breathing; the connection was so good it seemed as though whoever it was was standing beside him with lips pressed against his ear. "I don't like jokes: who is this?"

"Oh, you know me, Walter. You've known me a long time." A click, and nothing.

It was night and raining when the train reached Saratoga. He'd slept most of the trip, sweating in the hot dampness of the car, and dreamed of an old castle where only old turkeys lived, and dreamed a dream involving his father, Kurt Kuhnhardt, someone no-faced, Margaret and Rosa, Anna Stimson, and a queer fat lady with diamond eyes. He was standing on a long, deserted street; except for an approaching procession of slow, black, funeral-like cars there was no sign of life. Still, he knew, his eyes unseen observed his nakedness from every window, and he hailed frantically the first of the limousines; it stopped and a man, his father, invitingly held open the door: daddy, he yelled, running forward, and the great door slammed shut, mashing off his fingers, and his father, with a great belly laugh, leaned out the window to toss an enormous wreath of roses. In the second car was Margaret, in the third the lady with the diamond eyes (wasn't this Miss Casey, his old algebra teacher?), in the fourth Mr. Kuhnhardt and a new protégé, the no-faced creature. Each door opened, each closed, all laughed, all threw roses. The procession rolled smoothly away down the silent street. And with a terrible scream Walter fell among the mountain of roses: thorns tore wounds, and a sudden rain, a gray cloudburst, shattered the blooms, and washed pale blood bleeding over the leaves.

By the fixed stare of a woman sitting opposite he realized at once he'd yelled aloud in his sleep. He smiled at her sheepishly, and she looked away with, he imagined, some embarrassment. She was a cripple; on her left foot she wore a giant shoe. Later, in the Saratoga station, he helped her with her luggage, and they shared a taxi; there was no conversation: each sat in his corner looking at the rain, the blurred lights. In New York a few hours before he'd withdrawn from the bank all his savings, locked the door of his apartment, and left no messages; furthermore, there was in this town not a soul who knew him: it was a good feeling.

The hotel was filled; not to mention the racing crowd, there was, the desk clerk told him, a medical convention: no, sorry, he didn't know of a room anywhere. Maybe tomorrow.

So Walter found the bar. As long as he was going to stay up all night he might as well do it drunk. The bar, very large, very hot and noisy, was brilliant with summer-season grotesques: sagging silver-fox ladies, and little stunted jockeys, and pale loud-voiced men wearing cheap fantastic checks. After a couple of drinks, though, the noise seemed far away. Then, glancing around, he saw the cripple. She was alone at a table where she sat primly sipping crème de menthe. They exchanged a smile. Rising, Walter went to join her. "It's not like we were strangers," she said, as he sat down. "Here for the races, I suppose?"

"No," he said, "just a rest. And you?"

She pursed her lips. "Maybe you noticed I've got a clubfoot; oh, sure now, don't look surprised: you noticed, everybody does. Well, see," she said, twisting the straw in her glass, "see, my doctor's going to give a talk at this convention, going to talk about me and my foot on account of I'm pretty special. Gee, I'm scared. I mean I'm going to have to show off my foot."

Walter said he was sorry, and she said oh there was nothing to be sorry about; after all, she was getting a little vacation out of it, wasn't she? "And I haven't been out of the city in six years. It was six years ago I spent a week at the Bear Mountain Inn." Her cheeks were red, rather mottled, and her eyes, set too closely together, were lavender-colored, intense: they seemed never to blink. She wore a gold band on her wedding finger; play-acting, to be sure: it would not have fooled anybody.

"I'm a domestic," she said, answering a question. "And there's nothing wrong with that: it's honest and I like it. The people I work for have the cutest kid, Ronnie. I'm better to him than his mother, and he loves me more: he's told me so. That one, she stays drunk all the time."

It was depressing to listen to, but Walter, afraid suddenly to be alone, stayed and drank and talked in the way he'd once talked to Anna Stimson. Shh! she said at one point, for his voice had risen too high, and a good many people were staring. Walter said the hell with them, he didn't care; it was as if his brain were made of glass, and all the whiskey he'd drunk had turned into a hammer; he could feel the shattered pieces rattling in his head, distorting focus, falsifying shape; the cripple, for instance, seemed not one person, but several: Irving, his mother, a man named Bonaparte, Margaret, all those and others: more and more he came to understand experience is a circle of which no moment can be isolated, forgotten.

The bar was closing. They went Dutch on the check and, while waiting for change, neither spoke. Watching him with her unblinking lavender eyes, she seemed quite controlled, but there was going on inside, he could tell, some subtle agitation. When the waiter returned they divided the change, and she said: "If you want to, you can come to my room." A rashlike blush covered her face. "I mean, you said you didn't have any place to sleep—" Walter reached out and took her hand: the smile she gave him was touchingly shy.

Reeking with dime-store perfume, she came out of the bathroom wearing only a sleazy flesh-colored kimono, and the monstrous black shoe. It was then that he realized he could never go through with it. And he'd never felt so sorry for himself: not even Anna Stimson would ever have forgiven him this. "Don't look," she said, and there was a trembling in her voice, "I'm funny about anybody seeing my foot."

He turned to the window, where pressing elm leaves rustled in the rain, and lightning, too far off for sound, winked whitely. "All right," she said. Walter did not move.

"All right," she repeated anxiously. "Shall I put out the light? I mean, maybe you like to get ready—in the dark."

He came to the edge of the bed, and, bending down, kissed her cheek. "I think you're so very sweet, but—"

The telephone interrupted. She looked at him dumbly. "Jesus God," she said, and covered the mouthpiece with her hand, "it's long-distance! I'll bet it's about Ronnie! I'll bet he's sick, or—hello—what?—Ranney? Gee, no. You've got the wrong—"

"Wait," said Walter, taking the receiver. "This is me, this is Walter Ranney."

"Hello, Walter."

The voice, dull and sexless and remote, went straight to the pit of his stomach. The room seemed to seesaw, to buckle. A moustache of sweat sprouted on his upper lip. "Who is this?" he said so slowly the words did not connect coherently.

"Oh, you know me, Walter. You've known me a long time." Then silence: whoever it was had hung up.

"Gee," said the woman, "now how do you suppose they knew you were in my room; I mean—say, was it bad news? You look kind of—"

Walter fell across her, clutching her to him, pressing his wet cheek against hers. "Hold me," he said, discovering he could still cry. "Hold me, please."

"Poor little boy," she said patting his back. "My poor little boy: we're awfully alone in this world, aren't we?" And presently he went to sleep in her arms.

But he had not slept since, nor could he now, not even listening to the lazy lull of the fan; in its turning he could hear train wheels: Saratoga to New York, New York to New Orleans. And New Orleans he'd chosen for no special reason, except that it was a town of strangers, and a long way off. Four spinning fan blades, wheels and voices, round and round; and after all, as he saw it now, there was to this network of malice no ending, none whatever.

Water flushed down wall pipes, steps passed overhead, keys jangled in the hall, a news commentator rumbled somewhere beyond, next door a little girl said why? Why? WHY? Yet in the room there was a sense of silence. His feet shining in the transom light looked like amputated stone: the gleaming toenails were ten small mirrors all reflecting greenly. Sitting up, he rubbed sweat off with a towel; now more than anything the heat frightened him for it made him know tangibly his own helplessness. He threw the towel across the room, where landing on a lampshade it swung back and forth. At this moment the telephone rang. And rang. And it was ringing so loud he was sure all the hotel could hear. An army would be pounding at his door. So he pushed his face into the pillow, covered his ears with his hands, and thought: think of nothing things, think of wind.

Come and Go Mad

FREDRIC BROWN

One of the most terrifying of all phenomena is the human mind gone mad. But what is madness? And what is sanity? Is reality as we perceive it, or is it something else entirely—something beyond our wildest nightmares? These are the questions Frederic Brown, a master of the mordant and the bizarre, asks in this chilling novelette—and the answers he provides are fearful enough to drive one mad . . .

He had known it, somehow, when he had awakened that morning. He knew it more surely now, staring out of the editorial room window into the early afternoon sunlight slanting down among the buildings to cast a pattern of light and shadow. He knew that soon, perhaps even today, something important was going to happen. Whether good or bad he did not know, but he darkly suspected. And with reason; there are few good things that may unexpectedly happen to a man, things, that is, of lasting importance. Disaster can strike from innumerable directions, in amazingly diverse ways.

A voice said, "Hey, Mr. Vine," and he turned away from the window, slowly. That in itself was strange for it was not his manner to move slowly; he was a small, volatile man, almost catlike in the quickness of his reactions and his movements.

But this time something made him turn slowly from the window, almost as though he never again expected to see that chiaroscuro of an early afternoon.

He said, "Hi, Red."

The freckled copy boy said, "His Nibs wants to see ya."

"Now?"

"Naw. Atcher convenience. Sometimes next week, maybe. If yer busy, give him an apperntment."

He put his fist against Red's chin and shoved, and the copy boy staggered back in assumed distress.

He went over to the water cooler. He pressed his thumb on the button and water gurgled into the paper cup.

Harry Wheeler sauntered over and said, "Hiya, Nappy. What's up? Going on the carpet?"

He said, "Sure, for a raise."

He drank and crumpled the cup, tossing it into the wastebasket. He went over to the door marked PRIVATE and went through it.

Walter J. Candler, the managing editor, looked up from the work on his desk and said affably, "Sit down, Vine. Be with you in a moment," and then looked down again.

He slid into the chair opposite Candler, worried a cigarette out of his shirt pocket and lighted it. He studied the back of the sheet of paper of which the managing editor was reading the front. There wasn't anything on the back of it.

The M.E. put the paper down and looked at him. "Vine, I've got a screwy one. You're good on screwy ones."

He grinned slowly at the M.E. He said, "If that's a compliment, thanks."

"It's a compliment, all right. You've done some pretty tough things for us. This one's different. I've never yet asked a reporter to do anything I wouldn't do myself. *I* wouldn't do this, so I'm not asking you to."

The M.E. picked up the paper he'd been reading and then put it down again without even looking at it. "Ever hear of Ellsworth Joyce Randolph?"

"Head of the asylum? Hell yes, I've met him. Casually."

"How'd he impress you?"

He was aware that the managing editor was staring at him intently, that it wasn't too casual a question. He parried. "What do you mean? In what way? You mean is he a good Joe, is he a good politician, has he got a good bedside manner for a psychiatrist, or what?"

"I mean, how sane do you think he is?"

He looked at Candler and Candler wasn't kidding. Candler was strictly deadpan.

He began to laugh, and then he stopped laughing. He leaned forward across Candler's desk. "Ellsworth Joyce Randolph," he said. "You're talking about Ellsworth Joyce Randolph?"

Candler nodded. "Dr. Randolph was in here this morning. He told a rather strange story. He didn't want me to print it. He did want me to check on it, to send our best man to check on it. He said if we found it

was true we could print it in hundred and twenty line type in red ink."
Candler grinned wryly. "We could, at that."

He stumped out his cigarette and studied Candler's face. "But the
story itself is so screwy you're not sure whether Dr. Randolph himself
might be insane?"

"Exactly."

"And what's tough about the assignment?"

"The doc says a reporter could get the story only from the inside."

"You mean, go in as a guard or something?"

Candler said, "As something."

"Oh."

He got up out of the chair and walked over to the window, stood
with his back to the managing editor, looking out. The sun had moved
hardly at all. Yet the shadow pattern in the streets looked different,
obscurely different. The shadow pattern inside him was different, too.
This, he knew, was what had been going to happen. He turned around.
He said, "No. Hell no."

Candler shrugged imperceptibly. "Don't blame you. I haven't even
asked you to. I wouldn't do it myself."

He asked, "What does Ellsworth Joyce Randolph think is going on
inside his nut house? It must be something pretty screwy if it made
you wonder whether Randolph himself is sane."

"I can't tell you that, Vine. Promised him I wouldn't, whether or
not you took the assignment."

"You mean—even if I took the job I still wouldn't know what I was
looking for?"

"That's right. You'd be prejudiced. You wouldn't be objective.
You'd be looking for something, and you might think you found
it whether it was there or not. Or you might be so prejudiced
against finding it that you'd refuse to recognize it if it bit you in the
leg."

He strode from the window over to the desk and banged his fist
down on it.

He said, "God damn it, Candler, why *me*? You know what happened to me three years ago."

"Sure. Amnesia."

"Sure, amnesia. Just like that. But I haven't kept it any secret that I
never got *over* that amnesia. I'm thirty years old—or am I? My memory

goes back three years. Do you know what it feels like to have a blank wall in your memory only three years back?

"Oh, sure, I know what's on the other side of that wall. I know because everybody tells me. I know I started here as a copy boy ten years ago. I know where I was born and when and I know my parents are both dead. I know what they look like—because I've seen their pictures. I know I didn't have a wife and kids, because everybody who knew me told me I didn't. Get that part—everybody who knew me, not everybody I knew. I didn't know anybody.

"Sure, I've done all right since then. After I got out of the hospital—and I don't even remember the accident that put me there—I did all right back here because I still knew how to write news stories, even though I had to learn everybody's name all over again. I wasn't any worse off than a new reporter starting cold on a paper in a strange city. And everybody was as helpful as hell."

Candler raised a placating hand to stem the tide. He said, "Okay, Nappy. You said no, and that's enough. I don't see what all that's got to do with this story, but all you had to do was say no. So forget about it."

The tenseness hadn't gone out of him. He said, "You don't see what *that's* got to do with the story? You ask—or, all right, you don't ask, you suggest—that I get myself certified as a madman, go into an asylum as a patient. When—how much confidence could anyone have in his own mind when he can't remember going to school, can't remember the first time he met any of the people he works with every day, can't remember starting on the job he works at, can't remember—anything back of three years before?"

Abruptly he struck the desk again with his fist, and then looked foolish about it. He said, "I'm sorry. I didn't mean to get wound up about it like that."

Candler said, "Sit down."

"The answer's still no."

"Sit down, anyway."

He sat down and fumbled a cigarette out of his pocket, got it lighted.

Candler said, "I didn't even mean to mention it, but I've got to now. Now that you talked that way. I didn't know you felt like that about your amnesia. I thought that was water under the bridge.

"Listen, when Dr. Randolph asked me what reporter we had that could best cover it, I told him about you. What your background was. He remembered meeting you, too, incidentally. But he hadn't known you had amnesia."

"Is that why you suggested me?"

"Skip that till I make my point. He said that while you were there, he'd be glad to try one of the newer, milder forms of shock treatment on you, and that it might restore your lost memories. He said it would be worth trying."

"He didn't say it would work."

"He said it might; that it wouldn't do any harm."

He stubbed out the cigarette from which he'd taken only three drags. He glared at Candler. He didn't have to say what was in his mind; the managing editor could read it.

Candler said, "Calm down, boy. Remember I didn't bring it up until you yourself started in on how much that memory-wall bothered you. I wasn't saving it for ammunition. I mentioned it only out of fairness to you, after the way you talked."

"Fairness!"

Candler shrugged. "You said no. I accepted it. Then you started raving at me and put me in a spot where I had to mention something I'd hardly thought of at the time. Forget it. How's that graft story coming? Any new leads?"

"You going to put someone else on the asylum story?"

"No. You're the logical one for it."

"What *is* the story? It must be pretty woolly if it makes you wonder if Dr. Randolph is sane. Does he think his patients ought to trade places with his doctors, or what?"

He laughed. "Sure, you can't tell me. That's really beautiful double bait. Curiosity—and hope of knocking down that wall. So what's the rest of it? If I say yes instead of no, how long will I be there, under what circumstances? What chance have I got of getting out again? How do I get in?"

Candler said slowly, "Vine, I'm not sure any more I want you to try it. Let's skip the whole thing."

"Let's not. Not until you answer my questions, anyway."

"All right. You'd go in anonymously, so there wouldn't be any stigma attached if the story wouldn't work out. If it does, you can tell the whole truth—including Dr. Randolph's collusion in getting you in and out again. The cat will be out of the bag, then.

"You might get what you want in a few days—and you wouldn't stay on it more than a couple of weeks in any case."

"How many at the asylum would know who I was and what I was there for, besides Randolph?"

"No one," Candler leaned forward and held up four fingers of his left hand. "Four people would have to be in on it. You." He pointed to one finger. "Me." A second. "Dr. Randolph." The third finger. "And one other reporter from here."

"Not that I'd object, but why the other reporter?"

"Intermediary. In two ways. First, he'll go with you to some psychiatrist; Randolph will recommend one you can fool comparatively easily. He'll be your brother and request that you be examined and certified. You convince the psychiatrist you're nuts and he'll certify you. Of course it takes two doctors to put you away, but Randolph will be the second. Your alleged brother will want Randolph for the second one."

"All this under an assumed name?"

"If you prefer. Of course there's no real reason why it should be."

"That's the way I feel about it. Keep it out of the papers, of course. Tell everybody around here—except my—hey, in that case we couldn't make up a brother. But Charlie Doerr, in Circulation, is my first cousin and my nearest living relative. He'd do, wouldn't he?"

"Sure. And he'd have to be intermediary the rest of the way, then. Visit you at the asylum and bring back anything you have to send back."

"And if, in a couple of weeks, I've found nothing, you'll spring me?"

Candler nodded. "I'll pass the word to Randolph; he'll interview you and pronounce you cured, and you're out. You come back here, and you've been on vacation. That's all."

"What kind of insanity should I pretend to have?"

He thought Candler squirmed a little in his chair. Candler said, "Well—wouldn't this Nappy business be a natural? I mean, paranoia is a form of insanity which Dr. Randolph told me, hasn't any physical symptoms. It's just a delusion supported by a systematic framework of rationalization. A paranoiac can be sane in every way except one."

He watched Candler and there was a faint twisted grin on his lips. "You mean I should think I'm Napoleon?"

Candler gestured slightly. "Choose your own delusion. But—isn't that one a natural? I mean, the boys around the office always kidding you and calling you Nappy. And—" He finished weakly, "—and everything."

And then Candler looked at him squarely. "Want to do it?"

He stood up. "I think so. I'll let you know for sure tomorrow morning after I've slept on it, but unofficially—yes. Is that good enough?"

Candler nodded.

He said, "I'm taking the rest of the afternoon off; I'm going to the library to read up on paranoia. Haven't anything else to do anyway. And I'll talk to Charlie Doerr this evening. Okay?"

"Fine. Thanks."

He grinned at Candler. He leaned across the desk. He said, "I'll let you in on a little secret, now that things have gone this far. Don't tell anyone. I *am* Napoleon!"

It was a good exit line, so he went out.

II

He got his hat and coat and went outside, out of the air-conditioning and into the hot sunlight. Out of the quiet madhouse of a newspaper office after deadline, into the quieter madhouse of the streets on a sultry July afternoon.

He tilted his panama back on his head and ran his handkerchief across his forehead. Where was he going? Not to the library to bone up on paranoia; that had been a gag to get off for the rest of the afternoon. He'd read everything the library had on paranoia—and on allied subjects—over two years ago. He was an expert on it. He could fool any psychiatrist in the country into thinking that he was sane—or that he wasn't.

He walked north to the park and sat down on one of the benches in the shade. He put his hat on the bench beside him and mopped his forehead again.

He stared out at the grass, bright green in the sunlight, at the pigeons with their silly head-bobbing method of walking, at a red squirrel that came down one side of a tree, looked about him and scurried up the other side of the same tree.

And he thought back to the wall of amnesia of three years ago.

The wall that hadn't been a wall at all. The phrase intrigued him: a wall at all. Pigeons on the grass, alas. A wall at all.

It wasn't a wall at all; it was a shift, an abrupt change. A line had been drawn between two lives. Twenty-seven years of a life before the accident. Three years of a life since the accident.

They were not the same life.

But no one knew. Until this afternoon he had never even hinted the truth—if it *was* the truth—to anyone. He'd used it as an exit line in leaving Candler's office, knowing Candler would take it as a gag. Even so, one had to be careful; use a gag-line like that often, and people begin to wonder.

The fact that his extensive injuries from that accident had included a broken jaw was probably responsible for the fact that today he was free and not in an insane asylum. That broken jaw—it had been in a cast when he'd returned to consciousness forty-eight hours after his car had run head-on into a truck ten miles out of town—had prevented him from talking for three weeks.

And by the end of three weeks, despite the pain and the confusion that had filled him, he'd had a chance to think things over. He'd invented the wall. The amnesia, the convenient amnesia that was so much more believable than the truth as he knew it.

But *was* the truth as he knew it?

That was the haunting ghost that had ridden him for three years now, since the very hour when he had awakened to whiteness in a white room and a stranger, strangely dressed, had been sitting beside a bed the like of which had been in no field hospital he'd ever heard of or seen. A bed with an overhead framework. And when he looked from the stranger's face down at his own body, he saw that one of his legs and both of his arms were in casts and that the cast of the leg stuck upward at an angle, a rope running over a pully holding it so.

He'd tried to open his mouth to ask where he was, what had happened to him, and that was when he discovered the cast on his jaw.

He'd stared at the stranger, hoping the latter would have sense enough to volunteer the information and the stranger had grinned at him and said, "Hi, George. Back with us, huh? You'll be all right."

And there was something strange about the language—until he

placed what it was. English. Was he in the hands of the English? And it was a language, too, which he knew little of, yet he understood the stranger perfectly. And why did the stranger call him George?

Maybe some of the doubt, some of the fierce bewilderment, showed in his eyes, for the stranger leaned closer to the bed. He said, "Maybe you're still confused, George. You were in a pretty bad smash-up. You ran that coupé of yours head-on into a gravel truck. That was two days ago, and you're just coming out of it for the first time. You're all right, but you'll be in the hospital for a while, till all the bones you busted knit. Nothing seriously wrong with you."

And then waves of pain had come and swept away the confusion, and he had closed his eyes.

Another voice in the room said, "We're going to give you a hypo, Mr. Vine," but he hadn't dared open his eyes again. It was easier to fight the pain without seeing.

There had been the prick of a needle in his upper arm. And pretty soon there'd been nothingness.

When he came back again—twelve hours later, he learned afterwards—it had been to the same white room, the same strange bed, but this time there was a woman in the room, a woman in a strange white costume standing at the foot of the bed studying a paper that was fastened to a piece of board.

She smiled at him when she saw that his eyes were open. She said, "Good morning, Mr. Vine. Hope you're feeling better. I'll tell Dr. Holt that you're back with us."

She went away and came back with a man who was also strangely dressed, in roughly the same fashion as had been the stranger who had called him George.

The doctor looked at him and chuckled. "Got a patient, for once, who can't talk back to me. Or even write notes." Then his face sobered. "Are you in pain, though? Blink once if you're not, twice if you are."

The pain wasn't really very bad this time, and he blinked once. The doctor nodded with satisfaction. "That cousin of yours," he said, "has kept calling up. He'll be glad to know you're going to be back in shape to—well, to listen if not to talk. Guess it won't hurt you to see him a while this evening."

The nurse rearranged his bedclothing and then, mercifully, both she and the doctor had gone, leaving him alone to straighten out his chaotic thoughts.

Straighten them out? That had been three years ago, and he hadn't been able to straighten them out yet:

The startling fact that they'd spoken English and that he'd understood that barbaric tongue perfectly, despite his slight previous knowledge of it. How could an accident have made him suddenly fluent in a language which he had known but slightly?

The startling fact that they'd called him by a different name. "George" had been the name used by the man who'd been beside his bed last night. "Mr. Vine," the nurse had called him. George Vine, an English name, surely.

But there was one thing a thousand times more startling than either of those: It was what last night's stranger (could he be the "cousin" of whom the doctor had spoken?) had told him about the accident. "You ran that coupé of yours head-on into a gravel truck."

The amazing thing, the contradictory thing, was that he *knew* what a *coupé* was and what a *truck* was. Not that he had any recollection of having driven either, of the accident itself, or of anything beyond that moment when he'd been sitting in the tent after Lodi—but—but how could a picture of a coupé, something driven by a gasoline engine arise to his mind when such a concept had never been *in* his mind before.

There was that mad mingling of two worlds—the one sharp and clear and definite. The world he'd lived his twenty-seven years of life in, the world into which he'd been born twenty-seven years ago, on August 15th, 1769, in Corsica. The world in which he'd gone to sleep—it seemed like last night—in his tent at Lodi, as general of the army in Italy, after his first important victory in the field.

And then there was this disturbing world into which he had been awakened, this white world in which people spoke an English—now that he thought of it—which was different from the English he had heard spoken at Brienne, in Valence, at Toulon, and yet which he understood perfectly, which he knew instinctively that he could speak if his jaw were not in a cast. This world in which people called him George Vine, and in which, strangest of all, people used words that he did not know, could not conceivably know, and yet which brought pictures to his mind.

Coupé, truck. They were both forms of—the word came to his mind unbidden—automobiles. He concentrated on what an automobile was and how it worked, and the information was there. The cylinder block, the pistons driven by explosions of gasoline vapor, ignited by a spark of electricity from a generator—

Electricity. He opened his eyes and looked upward at the shaded light in the ceiling, and he knew, somehow, that it was an *electric* light, and in a general way he knew what electricity was.

The Italian Galvani—yes, he'd read of some experiments of Galvani, but they hadn't encompassed anything practical such as a light like that. And staring at the shaded light, he visualized behind it water power running dynamos, miles of wire, motors running generators. He caught his breath at the concept that came to him out of his own mind, or part of his own mind.

The faint, fumbling experiments of Galvani with their weak currents and kicking frogs' legs had scarcely foreshadowed the unmysterious mystery of that light up in the ceiling; and that was the strangest thing yet; part of his mind found it mysterious and another part took it for granted and understood in a general sort of way how it all worked.

Let's see, he thought, the electric light was invented by Thomas Alva Edison somewhere around— Ridiculous; he'd been going to say around 1900, and it was now only 1796!

And then the really horrible thing came to him and he tried—painfully, in vain—to sit up in bed. It *had* been 1900, his memory told him, and Edison had died in 1931—and a man named Napoleon Bonaparte had died a hundred and ten years before that, in 1821.

He'd nearly gone insane then.

And, sane or insane, only the fact that he could not speak had kept him out of a madhouse; it gave him time to think things out, time to realize that his only chance lay in pretending amnesia, in pretending that he remembered nothing of life prior to the accident. They don't put you in a madhouse for amnesia. They tell you who you are, let you go back to what they tell you your former life was. They let you pick up the threads and weave them, while you try to remember.

Three years ago he'd done that. Now, tomorrow, he was going to a psychiatrist and say that he was—Napoleon!

III

The slant of the sun was greater. Overhead a big bird of a plane droned by and he looked up at it and began laughing, quietly to himself—not the laughter of madness. True laughter because it sprang from the conception of Napoleon Bonaparte riding in a plane like that and from the overwhelming incongruity of that idea.

It came to him then that he'd never ridden in a plane that he remembered. Maybe George Vine had; at some time in the twenty-seven years of life George Vine had spent, he must have. But did that mean that *he* had ridden in one? That was a question that was part of the big question.

He got up and started to walk again. It was almost five o'clock; pretty soon Charlie Doerr would be leaving the paper and going home for dinner. Maybe he'd better phone Charlie and be sure he'd be home this evening.

He headed for the nearest bar and phoned; he got Charlie just in time. He said, "This is George. Going to be home this evening?"

"Sure, George. I was going to a poker game, but I called it off when I learned you'd be around."

"When you learned—oh, Candler talked to you?"

"Yeah. Say, I didn't know you'd phone me or I'd have called Marge, but how about coming out for dinner? It'll be all right with her, I'll call her now if you can."

He said, "Thanks, no, Charlie. Got a dinner date. And say, about that card game; you can go. I can get there about seven and we won't have to talk all evening; an hour'll be enough. You wouldn't be leaving before eight anyway."

Charlie said, "Don't worry about it; I don't much want to go anyway, and you haven't been out for a while. So I'll see you at seven, then."

From the phone booth, he walked over to the bar and ordered a beer. He wondered why he'd turned down the invitation to dinner; probably because, subconsciously, he wanted another couple of hours by himself before he talked to anyone, even Charlie and Marge.

He sipped his beer slowly, because he wanted to make it last; he had to stay sober tonight, plenty sober. There was still time to change his mind; he'd left himself a loophole, however small. He could still go to Candler in the morning and say he'd decided not to do it.

Over the rim of his glass he stared at himself in the back-bar mirror. Small, sandy-haired, with freckles on his nose, stocky. The small and stocky part fitted all right; but the rest of it! Not the remotest resemblance.

He drank another beer slowly, and that made it half-past five.

He wandered out again and walked, this time toward town. He walked past the *Blade* and looked up to the third floor and at the window he'd been looking out of when Candler had sent for him. He wondered if he'd ever sit by that window again and look out across a sunlit afternoon.

Maybe. Maybe not.

He thought about Clare. Did he want to see her tonight?

Well, no, to be honest about it, he didn't. But if he disappeared for two weeks or so without having even said good-by to her, then he'd have to write her off his books.

He'd better.

He stopped in at a drugstore and called her home. He said, "This is George, Clare. Listen, I'm being sent out of town tomorrow on an assignment; don't know how long I'll be gone. One of those things that might be a few days or a few weeks. But could I see you late this evening, to say so long?"

"Why sure, George. What time?"

"It might be after nine, but not much after. That be okay? I'm seeing Charlie first, on business; may not be able to get away before nine."

"Of course, George. Any time."

He stopped in at a hamburger stand, although he wasn't hungry, and managed to eat a sandwich and a piece of pie. That made it a quarter after six and, if he walked he'd get to Charlie's at just about the right time. So he walked.

Charlie met him at the door. With fingers on his lips, he jerked his head backward toward the kitchen where Marge was wiping dishes. He whispered, "I didn't tell Marge, George. It'd worry her."

He wanted to ask Charlie why it would, or should, worry Marge, but he didn't. Maybe he was a little afraid of the answer. It would have to mean that Marge was worrying about him already, and that was a bad sign. He thought he'd been carrying everything off pretty well for three years now.

Anyway, he couldn't ask because Charlie was leading him into the living room and the kitchen was within easy earshot, and Charlie was saying, "Glad you decided you'd like a game of chess, George. Marge is going out tonight; movie she wants to see down at the neighborhood show. I was going to that card game out of self-defense, but I didn't want to."

He got the chessboard and men out of the closet and started to set up a game on the coffee table.

Marge came in with a tray bearing tall cold glasses of beer and put it down beside the chessboard. She said, "Hi, George. Hear you're going away a couple of weeks."

He nodded. "But I don't know where. Candler—the managing editor—asked me if I'd be free for an out-of-town assignment and I said sure, and he said he'd tell me about it tomorrow."

Charlie was holding out clenched hands, a pawn in each, and he touched Charlie's left hand and got white. He moved pawn to king's fourth and, when Charlie did the same, advanced his queen's pawn.

Marge was fussing with her hat in front of the mirror. She said, "If you're not here when I get back, George, so long and good luck."

He said, "Thanks, Marge. 'By."

He made a few more moves before Marge came over, ready to go, kissed Charlie good-by, and then kissed him lightly on the forehead. She said, "Take care of yourself, George."

For a moment his eyes met her pale blue ones and he thought, she *is* worrying about me. It scared him a little.

After the door had closed behind her, he said, "Let's not finish the game, Charlie. Let's get to the brass tacks, because I've got to see Clare about nine. Dunno how long I'll be gone, so I can't very well not say good-by to her."

Charlie looked up at him. "You and Clare serious, George?"

"I don't know."

Charlie picked up his beer and took a sip. Suddenly his voice was brisk and businesslike. He said, "All right, let's sit on the brass tacks. We've got an appointment for eleven o'clock tomorrow morning with a guy named Irving, Dr. W. E. Irving, in the Appleton Block. He's a psychiatrist; Dr. Randolph recommended him.

"I called him up this afternoon after Candler talked to me; Candler had already phoned Randolph. I gave my right name. My story was this: I've got a cousin who's been acting queer lately and whom I wanted him to talk to. I didn't give the cousin's name. I didn't tell him in what way you'd been acting queer; I ducked the question and said I'd rather have him judge for himself without prejudice. I said I'd talked you into talking to a psychiatrist and that the only one I knew of was Randolph; that I'd called Randolph, who said he didn't do much private practice and recommended Irving. I told him I was your nearest living relative.

"That leaves the way open to Randolph for the second name on the certificate. If you can talk Irving into thinking you're really insane and he wants to sign you up, I can insist on having Randolph, whom I wanted in the first place. And this time, of course, Randolph will agree."

"You didn't say a thing about what kind of insanity you suspected me of having?"

Charlie shook his head. He said, "So, anyway, neither of us goes to work at the *Blade* tomorrow. I'll leave home the usual time so Marge won't know anything, but I'll meet you downtown—say, in the lobby of the Christina—at a quarter of eleven. And if you can convince Irving that you're committable—if that's the word—we'll get Randolph right away and get the whole thing settled tomorrow."

"And if I change my mind?"

"Then I'll call the appointment off. That's all. Look, isn't that all there is to talk over? Let's play this game of chess out; it's only twenty after seven."

He shook his head. "I'd rather talk, Charlie. One thing you forgot to cover, anyway. After tomorrow. How often you coming to see me to pick up bulletins for Candler?"

"Oh, sure, I forgot that. As often as visiting hours will permit—three times a week. Monday, Wednesday, Friday afternoons. Tomorrow's Friday, so if you get in, the first time I'll be able to see you is Monday."

"Okay. Say, Charlie, did Candler even hint to you at what the story is that I'm supposed to get in there?"

Charlie Doerr shook his head slowly. "Not a word. What is it? Or is it too secret for you to talk about?"

He stared at Charlie, wondering. And suddenly he felt that he couldn't tell the truth: that he didn't know either. It would make him look so silly. It hadn't sounded so foolish when Candler had given the reason—*a* reason, anyway—for not telling him, but it would sound foolish now.

He said, "If he didn't tell you, I guess I'd better not either, Charlie." And since that didn't sound too convincing, he added, "I promised Candler I wouldn't."

Both glasses of beer were empty by then, and Charlie took them into the kitchen for refilling.

He followed Charlie, somehow preferring the informality of the kitchen. He sat a-straddle of a kitchen chair, leaning his elbows on the back of it, and Charlie leaned against the refrigerator.

Charlie said, "Prosit!" and they drank, and then Charlie asked, "Have you got your story ready for Doc Irving?"

He nodded. "Did Candler tell you what I'm to tell him?"

"You mean, that you're Napoleon?" Charlie chuckled.

Did that chuckle ring true? He looked at Charlie, and he knew that what he was thinking was completely incredible. Charlie was square and honest as they came. Charlie and Marge were his best friends; they'd been his best friends for three years that he knew of. Longer than that, a hell of a lot longer, according to Charlie. But beyond those three years—that was something else again.

He cleared his throat because the words were going to stick a little. But he had to ask, he had to be sure. "Charlie, I'm going to ask you a hell of a question. Is this business on the up and up?"

"Huh?"

"It's a hell of a thing to ask. But—look, you and Candler don't think I'm crazy, do you? You didn't work this out between you to get me put away—or anyway examined—painlessly, without my knowing it was happening, till too late, did you?"

Charlie was staring at him. He said, "Jeez, George, you don't think I'd do a thing like that, do you?"

"No, I don't. But—you could think it was for my own good, and you might on that basis. Look, Charlie, if it *is* that, if you *think* that, let me point out that this isn't fair. I'm going up against a psychiatrist tomorrow to lie to him, to try to convince him that I have delusions. Not to be honest with him. And that would be unfair as hell, to me. You see that, don't you, Charlie?"

Charlie's face got a little white. He said slowly, "Before God, George, it's nothing like that. All I know about this is what Candler and you have told me."

"You think I'm sane, fully sane?"

Charlie licked his lips. He said, "You want it straight?"

"Yes."

"I never doubted it, until this moment. Unless—well, amnesia is a form of mental aberration, I suppose, and you've never got over that, but that isn't what you mean, is it?"

"No."

"Then, until right now—George, that sounds like a persecution complex, if you really meant what you asked me. A conspiracy to get you to— Surely you can see how ridiculous it is. What possible reason would either Candler or I have to get you to lie yourself into being committed?"

He said, "I'm sorry, Charlie. It was just a screwy momentary notion. No, I don't think that, of course." He glanced at his wristwatch. "Let's finish that chess game, huh?"

"Fine. Wait till I give us a refill to take along."

He played carelessly and managed to lose within fifteen minutes. He turned down Charlie's offer of a chance for revenge and leaned back in his chair.

He said, "Charlie, ever hear of chessmen coming in red and black?"

"N-no. Either black and white, or red and white, any I've ever seen. Why?"

"Well—" He grinned. "I suppose I oughtn't to tell you this after just making you wonder whether I'm really sane after all, but I've been having recurrent dreams recently. No crazier than ordinary dreams except that I've been dreaming the same things over and over. One of them is something about a game between the red and the black; I don't even know whether it's chess. You know how it is when you dream; things seem to make sense whether they do or not. In the dream I don't wonder whether the red-and-black business is chess or not; I know, I guess, or seem to know. But the knowledge doesn't carry over. You know what I mean?"

"Sure. Go on."

"Well, Charlie, I've been wondering if it just might have something to do with the other side of that wall of amnesia I've never been able to cross. This is the first time in my—well, not in my life, maybe, but in the three years I remember of it, that I've had recurrent dreams. I wonder if—if my memory may not be trying to get through.

"Did I ever have a set of red-and-black chessmen, for instance? Or, in any school I went to, did they have intramural basketball or baseball between red teams and black teams, or—or anything like that?"

Charlie thought for a moment before he shook his head. "No," he said, "nothing like that. Of course there's red and black in roulette—*rouge et noir*. And it's the two colors in a deck of playing cards."

"No, I'm pretty sure it doesn't tie in with cards or roulette. It's not—not like that. It's a game *between* the red and the black. They're the players, somehow. Think hard, Charlie; not about where you might have run into that idea, but where *I* might have."

He watched Charlie struggle and after a while he said, "Okay, don't sprain your brain, Charlie. Try this one. *The brightly shining.*"

"The brightly shining what?"

"Just that phrase, *the brightly shining*. Does it mean anything to you, at all?"

"No." ·

"Okay," he said. "Forget it."

IV

He was early and he walked past Clare's house, as far as the corner and stood under the big elm there, smoking the rest of his cigarette, thinking bleakly.

There wasn't anything to think about, really; all he had to do was say good-by to her. Two easy syllables. And stall off her questions as to where he was going, exactly how long he'd be gone. Be quiet and casual and unemotional about it, just as though they didn't mean anything in particular to each other.

It *had* to be that way. He'd known Clare Wilson a year and a half now, and he'd kept her dangling that long; it wasn't fair. This had to be the end, for her sake. He had about as much business asking a woman to marry him as—as a madman who thinks he's Napoleon!

He dropped his cigarette and ground it viciously into the walk with his heel, then went back to the house, up on the porch, and rang the bell.

Clare herself came to the door. The light from the hallway behind her made her hair a circlet of spun gold around her shadowed face.

He wanted to take her into his arms so badly that he clenched his fists with the effort to keep his arms down.

Stupidly, he said, "Hi, Clare. How's everything?"

"I don't know, George. How *is* everything? Aren't you coming in?"

She'd stepped back from the doorway to let him past and the light was on her face now, sweetly grave. She knew something was up, he thought; her expression and the tone of her voice gave that away.

He didn't want to go in. He said, "It's such a beautiful night, Clare. Let's take a stroll."

"All right, George." She came out onto the porch. "It is a fine night, such beautiful stars." She turned and looked at him. "Is one of them yours?"

He started a little. Then he stepped forward and took her elbow, guiding her down the porch steps. He said lightly, "All of them are mine. Want to buy any?"

"You wouldn't *give* me one? Just a teeny little dwarf star, maybe? Even one that I'd have to use a telescope to see?"

They were out on the sidewalk then, out of hearing of the house, and abruptly her voice changed, the playful note dropped from it, and she asked another question, "What's wrong, George?"

He opened his mouth to say nothing was wrong, and then closed it again. There wasn't any lie that he could tell her, and he couldn't tell her the truth, either. Her asking of that question, in that way, should have made things easier; it made them more difficult.

She asked another, "You mean to say good-by for—for good, don't you, George?"

He said, "Yes," and his mouth was very dry. He didn't know whether it came out as an articulate monosyllable or not, and he wetted his lips and tried again. He said, "Yes, I'm afraid so, Clare."

"Why?"

He couldn't make himself turn to look at her, he stared blindly ahead. He said, "I—I can't tell you, Clare. But it's the only thing I can do. It's best for both of us."

"Tell me one thing, George. Are you really going away? Or was that just—an excuse?"

"It's true. I'm going away; I don't know for how long. But don't ask me where, please. I can't tell you that."

"Maybe I can tell you, George. Do you mind if I do?"

He minded all right; he minded terribly. But how could he say so? He didn't say anything, because he couldn't say yes, either.

They were beside the park now, the little neighborhood park that was only a block square and didn't offer much in the way of privacy, but which did have benches. And he steered her—or she steered him; he didn't know which—into the park and they sat down on a bench. There were other people in the park, but not too near. Still he hadn't answered her question.

She sat very close to him on the bench. She said, "You've been worried about your mind, haven't you, George?"

"Well—yes, in a way, yes, I have."

"And your going away has something to do with that, hasn't it? You're going somewhere for observation or treatment, or both?"

"Something like that. It's not as simple as that, Clare, and I—I just can't tell you about it."

She put her hand on his hand, lying on his knee. She said, "I knew it was something like that, George. And I don't ask you to tell me anything about it.

"Just—just don't say what you meant to say. Say so long instead of good-by. Don't even write me, if you don't want to. But don't be noble and call everything off here and now, for my sake. At least wait until you've been wherever you're going. Will you?"

He gulped. She made it sound so simple when actually it was so complicated. Miserably he said, "All right, Clare. If you want it that way."

Abruptly she stood up. "Let's get back, George."

He stood beside her. "But it's early."

"I know, but sometimes—Well, there's a psychological moment to end a date, George. I know that sounds silly, but after what we've said, wouldn't it be—uh—anitclimactic—to—"

He laughed a little. He said, "I see what you mean."

They walked back to her home in silence. He didn't know whether it was happy or unhappy silence; he was too mixed up for that.

On the shadowed porch, in front of the door, she turned and faced him. "George," she said. Silence.

"Oh, damn you, George; quit being so *noble* or whatever you're being. Unless, of course, you *don't* love me. Unless this is just an elaborate form of—of runaround you're giving me. Is it?"

There were only two things he could do. One was run like hell. The other was what he did. He put his arms around her and kissed her. Hungrily.

When that was over, and it wasn't over too quickly, he was breathing a little hard and not thinking too clearly, for he was saying what he hadn't meant to say at all, "I love you, Clare. I love you; I love you so."

And she said, "I love you, too, dear. You'll come back to me, won't you?" And he said, "Yes. *Yes.*"

It was four miles or so from her home to his rooming house, but he walked, and the walk seemed to take only seconds.

He sat at the window of his room, with the light out, thinking, but the thoughts went in the same old circles they'd gone in for three years.

No new factor had been added except that now he was going to stick his neck out, way out, miles out. Maybe, just maybe, this thing was going to be settled one way or the other.

Out there, out his window, the stars were bright diamonds in the sky. Was one of them his star of destiny? If so, he was going to follow it, follow it even into the madhouse if it led there. Inside him was a deeply rooted conviction that this wasn't accident, that it wasn't coincidence that had led to his being asked to tell the truth under guise of falsehood.

His star of destiny.

Brightly shining? No, the phrase from his dreams did not refer to that; it was not an adjective phrase, but a noun, *The brightly shining*. What was *the brightly shining?*

And the red and the black? He'd thought of everything Charlie had suggested, and other things, too. Checkers, for instance. But it was not that.

The red and the black.

Well, whatever the answer was, he was running full-speed toward it now, not away from it.

After a while he went to bed, but it was a long time before he went to sleep.

V

Charlie Doerr came out of the inner office marked PRIVATE and put his hand out. He said, "Good luck, George. The doc's ready to talk to you now."

He shook Charlie's hand and said, "You might as well run along. I'll see you Monday, first visiting day."

"I'll wait here," Charlie said. "I took the day off work anyway, remember? Besides, maybe you won't have to go."

He dropped Charlie's hand, and stared into Charlie's face. He said slowly, "What do you mean, Charlie—maybe I won't have to go."

"Why—" Charlie looked puzzled. "Why, maybe he'll tell you you're all right, or just suggest regular visits to see him until you're straightened out, or—" Charlie finished weakly, "—or something."

Unbelievingly, he stared at Charlie. He wanted to ask, am I crazy or are you, but that sounded crazy under the circumstances. But he had to be sure, sure that Charlie just hadn't let something slip from his mind; maybe he'd fallen into the role he was supposed to be playing when he talked to the doctor just now. He asked, "Charlie, don't you remember that—" And even the rest of that question seemed insane for him to be asking, with Charlie staring blankly at him. The answer was in Charlie's face; it didn't have to be brought to Charlie's lips.

Charlie said again, "I'll wait, of course. Good luck, George."

He looked into Charlie's eyes and nodded, then turned and went through the door marked PRIVATE. He closed it behind him, meanwhile studying the man who had been sitting behind the desk and who had risen as he entered. A big man, broad shouldered, iron gray hair.

"Dr. Irving?"

"Yes, Mr. Vine. Will you be seated, please?"

He slid into the comfortable, padded armchair across the desk from the doctor.

"Mr. Vine," said the doctor, "a first interview of this sort is always a bit difficult. For the patient, I mean. Until you know me better, it will be difficult for you to overcome a certain reticence in discussing yourself. Would you prefer to talk, to tell things your own way, or would you rather I asked questions?"

He thought that over. He'd had a story ready, but those few words with Charlie in the waiting room had changed everything.

He said, "Perhaps you'd better ask questions."

"Very well." There was a pencil in Dr. Irving's hand and paper on the desk before him. "Where and when were you born?"

He took a deep breath. "To the best of my knowledge, in Corsica on August 15th, 1769. I don't actually remember being born, of course. I do remember things from my boyhood on Corsica, though. We stayed there until I was ten, and after that I was sent to school at Brienne."

Instead of writing, the doctor was tapping the paper lightly with the tip of the pencil. He asked, "What month and year is this?"

"August, 1947. Yes, I know that should make me a hundred and seventy-some years old. You want to know how I account for that. I don't. Nor do I account for the fact that Napoleon Bonaparte died in 1821."

He leaned back in the chair and crossed his arms, staring up at the

ceiling. "I don't attempt to account for the paradoxes or the dis-
crepancies. I recognize them as such. But according to my own
memory, and aside from logic pro or con, I was Napoleon for twenty-
seven years. I won't recount what happened during that time; it's all
down in the history books.

"But in 1796, after the battle of Lodi, while I was in charge of the
armies in Italy, I went to sleep. As far as I knew, just as anyone goes to
sleep anywhere, any time. But I woke up—with no sense whatever of
duration by the way—in a hospital in town here, and I was informed
that my name was George Vine, that the year was 1944, and that I was
twenty-seven years old.

"The twenty-seven years old part checked, and that was all. Absolutely all. I have no recollections of any parts of George Vine's life,
prior to his—my—waking up in the hospital after the accident. I know
quite a bit about his early life now, but only because I've been told.

"I know when and where he was born, where he went to school, and
when he started work at the *Blade*. I know when he enlisted in the
army and when he was discharged—late in 1943—because he
developed a trick knee after a leg injury. Not in combat, incidentally,
and there wasn't any 'psycho-neurotic' on my—his—discharge."

The doctor quit doodling with the pencil. He asked, "You've felt
this way for three years—and kept it a secret?"

"Yes. I had time to think things over after the accident, and yes, I
decided then to accept what they told me about my identity. They'd
have locked me up, of course. Incidentally, I've *tried* to figure out an
answer. I've studied Dunne's theory of time—even Charles Fort!" He
grinned suddenly. "Ever read about Casper Hauser?"

Dr. Irving nodded.

"Maybe he was playing smart the way I did. And I wonder how
many other amnesiacs pretended they didn't know what happened
prior to a certain date—rather than admit they had memories at
obvious variance with the facts."

Dr. Irving said slowly, "Your cousin informs me that you were a
bit—ah—'hepped' was his word—on the subject of Napoleon before
your accident. How do you account for that?"

"I've told you I don't account for any of it. But I can verify that fact,
aside from what Charlie Doerr says about it. Apparently I—the George
Vine I, if I was ever George Vine—was quite interested in Napoleon,
had read about him, made a hero of him, and had talked about him

quite a bit. Enough so that the fellows he worked with at the *Blade* nicknamed him 'Nappy.' "

"I notice you distinguish between yourself and George Vine. Are you or are you not he?"

"I have been for three years. Before that—I have no recollection of being George Vine. I don't think I was. I think—as nearly as I think anything—that *I*, three years ago, woke up in George Vine's body."

"Having done what for a hundred and seventy-some years?"

"I haven't the faintest idea. Incidentally, I don't doubt that this *is* George Vine's body, and with it I inherited his knowledge—except his personal memories. For example, I knew how to handle his job at the newspaper, although I didn't remember any of the people I worked with there. I have his knowledge of English, for instance, and his ability to write. I knew how to operate a typewriter. My handwriting is the same as his."

"If you think that you are not Vine, how do you account for that?"

He leaned forward. "I think part of me is George Vine, and part of me isn't. I think some transference has happened which is outside the run of ordinary human experience. That doesn't necessarily mean that it's supernatural—nor that I'm insane. *Does it?*"

Dr. Irving didn't answer. Instead, he asked, "You kept this secret for three years, for understandable reasons. Now, presumably for other reasons, you decide to tell. What are the other reasons? What has happened to change your attitude?"

It was the question that had been bothering him.

He said slowly, "Because I don't believe in coincidence. Because something in the situation itself has changed. Because I'm willing to risk imprisonment as a paranoiac to find out the truth."

"What in the situation has changed?"

"Yesterday it was suggested—by my employer—that I feign insanity for a practical reason. And the very kind of insanity which I have, if any. Surely, I will admit the possibility that I'm insane. But I can only operate on the theory that I'm not. You know that you're Dr. Willard E. Irving; you can only operate on that theory—but how do you *know* you are? Maybe you're insane, but you can only act as though you're not."

"You think your employer is part of a plot—ah—against you? You think there is a conspiracy to get you into a sanitarium?"

"I don't know. Here's what has happened since yesterday noon." He took a deep breath. Then he plunged. He told Dr. Irving the whole story of his interview with Candler, what Candler had said about Dr. Randolph, about his talk with Charlie Doerr last night and about Charlie's bewildering about-face in the waiting room.

When he was through he said, "That's all." He looked at Dr. Irving's expressionless face with more curiosity than concern, trying to read it. He added, quite casually, "You don't believe me, of course. You think I'm insane."

He met Irving's eyes squarely. He said, "You have no choice—unless you would choose to believe I'm telling you an elaborate set of lies to convince you I'm insane. I mean, as a scientist and as a psychiatrist, you cannot even admit the possibility that the things I believe—*know*—are objectively true. Am I not right?"

"I fear that you are. So?"

"So go ahead and sign your commitment. I'm going to follow this thing through. Even to the detail of having Dr. Ellsworth Joyce Randolph sign the second one."

"You make no objection?"

"Would it do any good if I did?"

"On one point, yes, Mr. Vine. If a patient has a prejudice against—or a delusion concerning—one psychiatrist, it is best not to have him under that particular psychiatrist's care. If you think Dr. Randolph is concerned in a plot against you, I would suggest that another one be named."

He said softly, "Even if I choose Randolph?"

Dr. Irving waved a deprecating hand, "Of course, if both you and Mr. Doerr prefer—"

"We prefer."

The iron gray head nodded gravely. "Of course you understand one thing; if Dr. Randolph and I decide you should go to the sanitarium, it will not be for custodial care. It will be for your recovery through treatment."

He nodded.

Dr. Irving stood. "You'll pardon me a moment? I'll phone Dr. Randolph."

He watched Dr. Irving go through a door to an inner room. He thought; there's a phone on his desk right there; but he doesn't want me to overhear the conversation.

He sat there very quietly until Irving came back and said, "Dr.

Randolph is free. And I phoned for a cab to take us there. You'll pardon me again? I'd like to speak to your cousin, Mr. Doerr."

He sat there and didn't watch the doctor leave in the opposite direction for the waiting room. He could have gone to the door and tried to catch words in the low-voiced conversation, but he didn't. He just sat there until he heard the waiting room door open behind him and Charlie's voice said, "Come on, George. The cab will be waiting downstairs by now."

They went down in the elevator and the cab was there. Dr. Irving gave the address.

In the cab, about half-way there, he said, "It's a beautiful day," and Charlie cleared his throat and said, "Yeah, it is." The rest of the way he didn't try it again and nobody said anything.

VI

He wore gray trousers and a gray shirt, open at the collar and with no necktie that he might decide to hang himself with. No belt, either, for the same reason, although the trousers buttoned so snugly around the waist that there was no danger of them falling off. Just as there was no danger of his falling out any of the windows; they were barred.

He was not in a cell, however; it was a large ward on the third floor. There were seven other men in the ward. His eyes ran over them. Two were playing checkers, sitting on the floor with a board on the floor between them. One sat in a chair, staring fixedly at nothing; two leaned against the bars of one of the open windows, looking out and talking casually and sanely. One read a magazine. One sat in a corner, playing smooth arpeggios on a piano that wasn't there at all.

He stood leaning against the wall, watching the other seven. He'd been here two hours now; it seemed like two years.

The interview with Dr. Ellsworth Joyce Randolph had gone smoothly; it had been practically a duplicate of his interview with Irving. And quite obviously, Dr. Randolph had never heard of him before.

He'd expected that, of course.

He felt very calm, now. For a while, he'd decided, he wasn't going to think, wasn't going to worry, wasn't even going to feel.

He strolled over and stood watching the checker game.

It was a sane checker game; the rules were being followed.

One of the men looked up and asked, "What's your name?"

It was a perfectly sane question; the only thing wrong with it was that the same man had asked the same question four times now within the two hours he'd been here.

He said, "George Vine."

"Mine's Bassington, Ray Bassington. Call me Ray. Are you insane?"

"No."

"Some of us are and some of us aren't. He is." He looked at the man who was playing the imaginary piano, "Do you play checkers?"

"Not very well."

"Good. We eat pretty soon now. Anything you want to know, just ask me."

"How do you get out of here? Wait, I don't mean that for a gag, or anything. Seriously, what's the procedure?"

"You go in front of the board once a month. They ask you questions and decide if you go or stay. Sometimes they stick needles in you. What you down for?"

"Down for? What do you mean?"

"Feeble-minded, manic-depressive, dementia praecox, involutional melancholia—"

"Oh. Paranoia, I guess."

"That's bad. Then they stick needles in you."

A bell rang somewhere.

"That's dinner," said the other checker player. "Ever try to commit suicide? Or kill anyone?"

"No."

"They'll let you eat at an A table then, with knife and fork."

The door of the ward was being opened. It opened outward and a guard stood outside and said, "All right." They filed out, all except the man who was sitting in the chair staring into space.

"How about him?" he asked Ray Bassington.

"He'll miss a meal tonight. Manic-depressive, just going into the depressive stage. They let you miss one meal; if you're not able to go to the next they take you and feed you. You a manic-depressive?"

"No."

"You're lucky. It's hell when you're on the downswing. Here, through this door."

It was a big room. Tables and benches were crowded with men in gray shirts and gray trousers, like his. A guard grabbed his arm as he went through the doorway and said, "There. That seat."

It was right beside the door. There was a tin plate, messy with food, and a spoon beside it. He asked, "Don't I get a knife and fork? I was told—"

The guard gave him a shove toward the seat. "Observation period, seven days. Nobody gets silverware till their observation period's over. Siddown."

He sat down. No one at his table had silverware. All the others were eating, several of them noisily and messily. He kept his eyes on his own plate, unappetizing as that was. He toyed with his spoon and managed to eat a few pieces of potato out of the stew and one or two of the chunks of meat that were mostly lean.

The coffee was in a tin cup and he wondered why until he realized how breakable an ordinary cup would be and how lethal could be one of the heavy mugs cheap restaurants use.

The coffee was weak and cool; he couldn't drink it.

He sat back and closed his eyes. When he opened them again there was an empty plate and an empty cup in front of him and the man at his left was eating very rapidly. It was the man who'd been playing the nonexistent piano.

He thought, if I'm here long enough, I'll get hungry enough to eat that stuff. He didn't like the thought of being there that long.

After a while a bell rang and they got up, one table at a time on signals he didn't catch, and filed out. His group had come in last; it went out first.

Ray Bassington was behind him on the stairs. He said, "You'll get used to it. What'd you say your name is?"

"George Vine."

Bassington laughed. The door shut on them and a key turned.

He saw it was dark outside. He went over to one of the windows and stared out through the bars. There was a single bright star that showed just above the top of the elm tree in the yard. *His* star? Well, he'd followed it here. A cloud drifted across it.

Someone was standing beside him. He turned his head and saw it was the man who'd been playing piano. He had a dark, foreign-looking face with intense black eyes; just then he was smiling, as though at a secret joke.

"You're new here, aren't you? Or just get put in this ward, which?"

"New. George Vine's the name."

"Baroni. Musician. Used to be, anyway. Now—let it go. Anything you want to know about the place?"

"Sure. How to get out of it."

Baroni laughed, without particular amusement but not bitterly either. "First, convince them you're all right again. Mind telling what's wrong with you—or don't you want to talk about it? Some of us mind, others don't."

He looked at Baroni, wondering which way he felt. Finally he said, "I guess I don't mind. I—think I'm Napoleon."

"Are you?"

"Am I what?"

"*Are* you Napoleon? If you aren't, that's one thing. Then maybe you'll get out of here in six months or so. If you really *are*—that's bad. You'll probably die here."

"Why? I mean, if I *am*, then I'm sane and—"

"Not the point. Point's whether they think you're sane or not. Way they figure, if you think you're Napoleon you're not sane. Q.E.D. You stay here."

"Even if I tell them I'm convinced I'm George Vine?"

"They've worked with paranoia before. And that's what they've got you for, count on it. And any time a paranoiac gets tired of a place, he'll try to lie his way out of it. They weren't born yesterday. They know that."

"In general, yes, but how—"

A sudden cold chill went down his spine. He didn't have to finish the question. *They stick needles in you—* It hadn't meant anything when Ray Bassington had said it.

The dark man nodded. "Truth serum," he said. "When a paranoiac reaches the stage where he's cured *if* he's telling the truth, they make sure he's telling it before they let him go."

He thought what a beautiful trap it had been that he'd walked into. He'd probably die here, now.

He leaned his head against the cool iron bars and closed his eyes. He heard footsteps walking away from him and knew he was alone.

He opened his eyes and looked out into the blackness; now the clouds had drifted across the moon, too.

Clare, he thought; *Clare*.

A trap.

But—if there was a trap, there must be a trapper.

He was sane or he was insane. If he was sane, he'd walked into a trap, and *if there was a trap, there must be a trapper, or trappers*.

If he was insane—

God, let it be that he *was* insane. That way everything made such sweetly simple sense, and someday he might be out of here, he might go back to working for the *Blade*, possibly even with a memory of all the years he'd worked there. Or that George Vine had worked there.

That was the catch. *He* wasn't George Vine.

And there was another catch. *He* wasn't insane.

The cool iron of the bars against his forehead.

After a while he heard the door open and looked around. Two guards had come in. A wild hope, reasonless, surged up inside him. It didn't last.

"Bedtime, you guys," said one of the guards. He looked at the manic-depressive sitting motionless on the chair and said, "Nuts. Hey, Bassington, help me get this guy in."

The other guard, a heavy-set man with hair close-cropped like a wrestler's, came over to the window.

"You. You're the new one in here. Vine, ain't it?"

He nodded.

"Want trouble, or going to be good?" Fingers of the guard's right hand clenched, the fist went back.

"Don't want trouble. Got enough."

The guard relaxed a little. "Okay, stick to that and you'll get along. Vacant bunk's in there." He pointed. "One on the right. Make it up yourself in the morning. Stay in the bunk and mind your own business. If there's any noise or trouble here in the ward, we come and take care of it. Our own way. You wouldn't like it."

He didn't trust himself to speak, so he just nodded. He turned and went through the door of the cubicle to which the guard had pointed. There were two bunks in there; the manic-depressive who'd been on the chair was lying flat on his back on the other, staring blindly up at the ceiling through wide-open eyes. They'd pulled his shoes off, leaving him otherwise dressed.

He turned to his own bunk, knowing there was nothing on earth he could do for the other man, no way he could reach him through the impenetrable shell of blank misery which is the manic-depressive's intermittent companion.

He turned down a gray sheet-blanket on his own bunk and found under it another gray sheet-blanket atop a hard but smooth pad. He slipped off his shirt and trousers and hung them on a hook on the wall at the foot of his bed. He looked around for a switch to turn off the light overhead and couldn't find one. But, even as he looked, the light went out.

A single light still burned somewhere in the ward room outside, and by it he could see to take his shoes and socks off and get into the bunk.

He lay very quiet for a while, hearing only two sounds, both faint and seeming far away. Somewhere in another cubicle off the ward someone was singing quietly to himself, a wordless monody; somewhere else someone else was sobbing. In his own cubicle, he couldn't hear even the sound of breathing from his roommate.

Then there was a shuffle of bare feet and someone in the open doorway said, "George Vine."

He said, "Yes?"

"Shhhh, not so loud. This is Bassington. Want to tell you about that guard; I should have warned you before. Don't ever tangle with him."

"I didn't."

"I heard; you were smart. He'll slug you to pieces if you give him half a chance. He's a sadist. A lot of guards are; that's why they're bughousers; that's what they call themselves, bughousers. If they get fired one place for being too brutal they get on at another one. He'll be in again in the morning; I thought I'd warn you."

The shadow in the doorway was gone.

He lay in the dimness, the almost-darkness, feeling rather than thinking. Wondering. Did mad people ever know that they were mad? Could they tell? Was every one of them sure, as he was sure—?

That quiet, still thing lying on the bunk near his, inarticularly suffering, withdrawn from human reach into a profound misery beyond the understanding of the sane—

"Napoleon Bonaparte!"

A clear voice, but had it been within his mind, or from without? He sat up on the bunk. His eyes pierced the dimness, could discern no form, no shadow, in the doorway.

He said, "Yes?"

VII

Only then, sitting up on the bunk and having answered "Yes," did he realize the name by which the voice had called him.

"Get up. Dress."

He swung his legs out over the edge of the bunk, stood up. He reached for his shirt and was slipping his arms into it before he stopped and asked, "Why?"

"To learn the truth."

"Who are you?" he asked.

"Do not speak aloud. I can hear you. I am within you and without. I have no name."

"Then *what* are you?" He said it aloud, without thinking.

"An instrument of The Brightly Shining."

He dropped the trousers he'd been holding. He sat down carefully on the edge of the bunk, leaned over and groped around for them.

His mind groped, too. Groped for he knew not what. Finally he found a question—*the* question. He didn't ask it aloud this time; he thought it, concentrated on it as he straightened out his trousers and thrust his legs in them.

"Am I mad?"

The answer—*No*—came clear and sharp as a spoken word, but had it been spoken? Or was it a sound that was only in his mind?

He found his shoes and pulled them on his feet. As he fumbled the laces into some sort of knots, he thought, "Who—what—is The Brightly Shining?"

"The Brightly Shining is *that which is Earth*. It is the intelligence of our planet. It is one of three intelligences in the solar system, one of many in the universe. Earth is one; it is called The Brightly Shining."

"I do not understand," he thought.

"You will. Are you ready?"

He finished the second knot. He stood up. The voice said, "Come. Walk silently."

It was as though he was being led through the almost-darkness, although he felt no physical touch upon him; he saw no physical presence beside him. But he walked confidently, although quietly on tiptoe, knowing he would not walk into anything nor stumble. Through the big room that was the ward, and then his outstretched hand touched the knob of a door.

He turned it gently and the door opened inward. Light blinded him. The voice said, "Wait," and he stood immobile. He could hear sound—the rustle of paper, the turn of a page—outside the door, in the lighted corridor.

Then from across the hall came the sound of a shrill scream. A chair scraped and feet hit the floor of the corridor, walking away toward the sound of the scream. A door opened and closed.

The voice said, "Come," and he pulled the door open the rest of the way and went outside, past the desk and the empty chair that had been just outside the door of the ward.

Another door, another corridor. The voice said, "Wait," the voice said, "Come"; this time a guard slept. He tiptoed past. Down steps.

He thought the question, "Where am I going?"

"Mad," said the voice.

"But you said I wasn't—" He'd spoken aloud and the sound startled him almost more than had the answer to his last question. And in the silence that followed the words he'd spoken there came—from the bottom of the stairs and around the corner—the sound of a buzzing switchboard, had someone said, "Yes? . . . Okay, doctor, I'll be right up." Footsteps and the closing of an elevator door.

He went down the remaining stairs and around the corner and he was in the front main hall. There was an empty desk with a switchboard beside it. He walked past it and to the front door. It was bolted and he threw the heavy bolt.

He went outside, into the night.

He walked quietly across cement, across gravel; then his shoes were on grass and he didn't have to tiptoe any more. It was as dark now as the inside of an elephant; he felt the presence of trees nearby and leaves brushed his face occasionally, but he walked rapidly, confidently, and his hand went forward just in time to touch a brick wall.

He reached up and he could touch the top of it; he pulled himself up and over it. There was broken glass on the flat top of the wall; he cut his clothes and his flesh badly, but he felt no pain, only the wetness of blood and the stickiness of blood.

He walked along a lighted road, he walked along dark and empty streets, he walked down a darker alley. He opened the back gate of a yard and walked to the back door of a house. He opened the door and went in. There was a lighted room at the front of the house; he could see the rectangle of light at the end of a corridor. He went along the corridor and into the lighted room.

Someone who had been seated at a desk stood up. Someone, a man, whose face he knew but whom he could not—

"Yes," said the man, smiling, "you know me, but you do not know me. Your mind is under partial control and your ability to recognize me is blocked out. Other than that and your analgesia—you are covered with blood from the glass on the wall, but you don't feel any pain—your mind is normal and you are sane."

"What's it all about?" he asked. "Why was I brought here?"

"Because you are sane. I'm sorry about that, because you can't be. It is not so much that you retained memory of your previous life, after you'd been moved. That happens. It is that you somehow know something of what you shouldn't—something of The Brightly Shining, and of the Game between the red and the black. For that reason—"

"For that reason, what?" he asked.

The man he knew and did not know smiled gently. "For that reason you must know the rest, so that you will know nothing at all. For everything will add to nothing. The truth will drive you mad."

"That I do not believe."

"Of course you don't. If the truth were conceivable to you, it would not drive you mad. But you cannot remotely conceive the truth."

A powerful anger surged up within him. He stared at the familiar face that he knew and did not know, and he stared down at himself; at the torn and bloody gray uniform, at his torn and bloody hands. The hands hooked like claws with the desire to kill—someone, the someone, whoever it was, who stood before him.

He asked, "What are you?"

"I am an instrument of The Brightly Shining."

"The same which led me here, or another?"

"One is all, all is one. Within the whole and its parts, there is no difference. One instrument is another and the red is the black and the black is the white and there is no difference. The Brightly Shining is the soul of the Earth. I use *soul* as the nearest word in your vocabulary."

Hatred was almost a bright light. It was almost something that he could lean into, lean his weight against.

He asked, "What is The Brightly Shining?" He made the words a curse in his mouth.

"Knowing will make you mad. You want to know?"

"Yes." He made a curse out of that simple, sibilant syllable.

The lights were dimming. Or was it his eyes? The room was

becoming dimmer, and at the same time receding. It was becoming a tiny cube of dim light, seen from afar and outside, from somewhere in the distant dark, ever receding, turning into a pinpoint of light, and within that point of light ever the hated Thing, the man—or was it a man?—standing beside the desk.

Into darkness, into space, up and apart from the Earth—a dim sphere in the night, a receding sphere outlined against the spangled blackness of eternal space, occulting the stars, a disc of black.

It stopped receding, and time stopped. It was as though the clock of the universe stood still. Beside him, out of the void, spoke the voice of the instrument of The Brightly Shining.

"Behold," it said. "The Being of Earth."

He beheld. Not as though an outward change was occurring, but an inward one, as though his senses were being changed to enable him to perceive something hitherto unseeable.

The ball that was Earth began to glow. Brightly to shine.

"You see the intelligence that rules Earth," said the voice. "The sum of the black and the white and the red, that are one, divided only as the lobes of a brain are divided, the trinity that is one."

The glowing ball and the stars behind it faded, and the darkness became deeper darkness and then there was dim light, growing brighter, and he was back in the room with the man standing at the desk.

"You saw," said the man whom he hated. "But you do not understand. You ask, *what* have you seen, *what* is The Brightly Shining? It is a group intelligence, the true intelligence of Earth, one intelligence among three in the solar system, one among many in the universe.

"What, then, is man? Men are pawns, in games of—to you —unbelievable complexity, between the red and the black, the white and the black, for amusement. Played by one part of an organism against another part, to while away an instant of eternity. There are vaster games, played between galaxies. Not with man.

"Man is a parasite peculiar to Earth, which tolerates his presence for a little while. He exists nowhere else in the cosmos, and he does not exist here for long. A little while, a few chessboard wars, which he thinks he fights himself— You begin to understand."

The man at the desk smiled.

"You want to know of yourself. Nothing is less important. A move was made, before Lodi. The opportunity was there for a move of the red; a stronger, more ruthless personality was needed; it was a turning point in history—which means in the game. Do you understand now? A pinch hitter was put in to become Napoleon."

He managed two words. "And then?"

"The Brightly Shining does not kill. You had to be put somewhere, some time. Long later a man named George Vine was killed in an accident; his body was still usable. George Vine had not been insane, but he had had a Napoleonic complex. The transference was amusing."

"No doubt." Again it was impossible to reach the man at the desk. The hatred itself was a wall between them. "Then George Vine is dead?"

"Yes. And you, because you knew a little too much, must go mad so that you will know nothing. Knowing the truth will drive you mad."

"No!"

The instrument only smiled.

VIII

The room, the cube of light, dimmed; it seemed to tilt. Still standing, he was going over backward, his position becoming horizontal instead of vertical.

His weight was on his back and under him was the soft-hard smoothness of his bunk, the roughness of a gray sheet-blanket. And he could move; he sat up.

Had he been dreaming? Had he really been outside the asylum? He held up his hands, touched one to the other, and they were wet with something sticky. So was the front of his shirt and the thighs and knees of his trousers.

And his shoes were on.

The blood was there from climbing the wall. And now the analgesia was leaving, and pain was beginning to come into his hands, his chest, his stomach and his legs. Sharp biting pain.

He said aloud, *"I am not mad. I am not mad."* Was he screaming it?

A voice said, "No. Not yet." Was it the voice that had been here in the room before? Or was it the voice of the man who had stood in the lighted room? Or had both been the same voice?

It said, "Ask, 'What is man?'"

Mechanically, he asked it.

"Man is a blind alley in evolution, who came too late to compete, who has always been controlled and played with by The Brightly Shining, which was old and wise before man walked erect.

"Man is a parasite upon a planet populated before he came, populated by a Being that is one and many, a billion cells but a single mind, a single intelligence, a single will—as is true of every other populated planet in the universe.

"Man is a joke, a clown, a parasite. He is nothing; he will be less."

"Come and go mad."

He was getting out of bed again; he was walking. Through the doorway of the cubicle, along the ward. To the door that led to the corridor; a thin crack of light showed under it. But this time his hand did not reach out for the knob. Instead he stood there facing the door, and it began to glow; slowly it became light and visible.

As though from somewhere an invisible spotlight played upon it, the door became a visible rectangle in the surrounding blackness; as brightly visible as the crack under it.

The voice said, "You see before you a cell of your ruler, a cell unintelligent in itself, yet a tiny part of a unit which is intelligent, one of a trillion units which make up *the* intelligence which rules the Earth—and you. And which Earthwide intelligence is one of a million intelligences which rule the universe."

"The *door?* I don't—"

The voice spoke no more; it had withdrawn, but somehow inside his mind was the echo of silent laughter.

He leaned closer and saw what he was meant to see. An ant was crawling up the door.

His eyes followed it, and numbing horror crawled apace, up his spine. A hundred things that had been told and shown him suddenly fitted into a pattern, a pattern of sheer horror. The black, the white, the red; the black ants, the white ants, the red ants; the players with men, separate lobes of a single group brain, the intelligence that was one. Man an accident, a parasite, a pawn; a million planets in the universe inhabited each by an insect race that was a single intelligence for the planet—and all the intelligences together were the single cosmic intelligence that was—*God!*

The one-syllable word wouldn't come.

He went mad, instead.

He beat upon the now-dark door with his bloody hands, with his knees, his face, with himself, although already he had forgotten why, had forgotten what he wanted to crush.

He was raving mad—dementia praecox, not paranoia—when they released his body by putting it into a straight-jacket, released it from frenzy to quietude.

He was quietly mad—paranoia, not dementia praecox—when they released him as sane eleven months later.

Paranoia, you see, is a peculiar affliction; it has no physical symptoms, it is merely the presence of a fixed delusion. A series of metrazol shocks had cleared up the dementia praecox and left only the fixed delusion that he was George Vine, a reporter.

The asylum authorities thought he was, too, so the delusion was not recognized as such and they released him and gave him a certificate to prove he was sane.

He married Clare; he still works at the *Blade*—for a man named Candler. He still plays chess with his cousin, Charlie Doerr. He still sees—for periodic checkups—both Dr. Irving and Dr. Randolph.

Which of them smiles inwardly? What good would it do you to know?

It doesn't matter. Don't you understand? Nothing matters!

II
Modern Masters

The Scarlet King

EVAN HUNTER

Evan Hunter is one of those enviable, not to mention brilliant, fiction writers who can create remarkable work in any form they choose. Several of his novels (The Blackboard Jungle; Last Summer; Sons; Love, Dad) *have been critically acclaimed bestsellers; one of his stories from* Playboy *was selected for inclusion in the prestigious* Best American Short Stories; *his 87th Precinct detective series, as Ed McBain, is not only the best of the police procedurals but ranks in the top ten on mystery fiction's all-time list. When he turns to horror fiction, as he did occasionally in the early 1950's, he is bound to produce a story both thematically powerful (for its psychological portrait of the ravages of war on the individual) and terrifying enough to raise the hackles on anyone's neck. Here, then, Evan Hunter in a macabre mood, with his tale of "The Scarlet King" . . .*

It was the little things that annoyed him, always the little things, those and of course the king of hearts.

If only these little things didn't bother him so, if only he could look at them dispassionately and say, "You don't bother me, you *can't* bother me," everything would be all right. But that wasn't the way it worked. They did bother him. They started by gnawing at his nerves, tiny little nibbles of annoyance until his nerves were frayed and ready to unravel. And then the restless annoyance spread to his muscles, until his face began to tic and his hands began to clench and unclench spasmodically. He could not control the tic or the unconscious spasms of his hands, and his inability to control them annoyed him even more until he was filled with a futile sort of frustrated rage, and it was always then that the king of hearts popped into his mind.

Even now, even just thinking about the things that annoyed him, he could see the king. It was not a one-eyed king like the king of diamonds, oh no. The king of hearts had two eyes, two eyes that stared up from the cynically sneering face on the card. The king held a sword in his hand, but the sword was hidden, oh so cleverly hidden, held aloft ready to strike, but only the hilt and a very small portion of the blade was visible, and the rest of the sword, the part that could tear and hack and rip, was hidden behind the king's head and crown.

He was a clever king, the king of hearts, and he was the cause of everything, of why the annoyances got out of hand occasionally, he was the cause, all right, he was the cause, that two-eyed clever louse, *why doesn't that girl upstairs stop playing that goddamned piano!*

Now just a minute, he told himself. Just get a grip, because if you don't get a grip, we're going to be in trouble. Now just forget that little rat is up there pounding those scales, up and down, up and down, *do, re, mi, fa, so, la, ti, do, ti, la, so* . . . .

Forget her!

Dammit, forget her!

He crossed the room, and slammed down the window, but he could still hear the monotonous sound of the little girl at the piano upstairs, a sound which seeped through the floorboards and dripped down the walls. He covered his ears with his cupped palms, but the sound leaked through his fingers, *do, re, mi, fa, so* . . .

Think of something else, he commanded himself.

Think of Tom.

It was nice of Tom to have loaned him the apartment. Tom was a good brother, one of the best. And it was very nice of him to have parted with the apartment so willingly, but of course he'd been going on a hunting trip anyway, so the apartment would be empty all weekend, and Tom couldn't possibly have known about the little girl upstairs and her goddamned piano. Tom knew that things were annoying him a lot, but he didn't know the half of it, God he'd turn purple if he knew the half of it, but even so he couldn't be blamed for that monotonous little girl upstairs.

He had seen the girl yesterday, walking with her mother in the little park across the street, a nice-looking little girl, and a pretty mother, and he had smiled and nodded his head, but that was before he knew the little girl was an aspiring impresario. Today, he had seen the mother leaving shortly before noon, heading across the park with the autumn wind lapping at her skirts. And shortly after that, the piano had started.

It was close to two o'clock now, and the mother still hadn't returned, and the piano had gone since noon, up and down those damn scales, when would she stop, wouldn't she ever stop practicing, how long does someone have to practice in order to . . .

We're back on that again, he thought, and that's dangerous. We have to forget the little annoyances because he just loves these little annoyances. When the annoyances get out of hand, he steps in with his leering face and the sword hidden behind his crown, so we can't let the annoyances get out of hand. So she's practicing a piano, what's so terrible about that? Isn't a little girl allowed to practice a piano? Isn't this a free country? Goddammit, didn't I fight to keep it free?

He didn't want to think about the fighting, either, but he had thought about it, and now it was full-blown in his mind, and he knew he could not shove it out of his mind until he had examined every facet of the living nightmare that had been with him since that day.

It had been a clear day, the weather in Korea surprisingly like the weather in New York, and it had been quiet all along the front, and everyone was talking about this being it, this being the end. He hadn't known whether or not to believe the rumors, but it had certainly felt like the end, not even a rifle shot since early the night before, the entire front as still and as complacent as a mountain lake.

He had sat in the foxhole with Scarpa, a New York boy he had known since his days at Fort Dix. They had played cutthroat poker all morning, and Scarpa had won heavily, pulling in the matchsticks which served as poker chips, each matchstick representing a dollar bill. They had taken a break for chow, and then they'd gone back to the game, and Scarpa kept winning, winning heavily, and Scarpa's good luck began to annoy him. He had lifted each newly dealt hand with a sort of desperate urgency, wanting to beat Scarpa now, wanting desperately to win. When Scarpa dealt him the ten, jack, queen, and ace of hearts, he had reached for his fifth card eagerly, hoping it was the king, hoping he could sit there smugly with a royal flush while Scarpa confidently bet into him.

The fifth card had been a four of clubs.

He was surprised to find his hands trembling. He looked across the mess kit that served as a table, and he discarded the four of clubs and said, "One card."

Scarpa looked up at him curiously.

"Two pair?" he asked, a slight smile on his face.

"Just give me one card, that's all."

"Sure," Scarpa said.

He dealt the card face down on the mess kit.

"I'm pat," Scarpa said, smiling.

He reached for the card. If Scarpa was pat, he was holding either a straight, a flush, or a full house. Or maybe he just had two pair and hadn't drawn for fear he'd give away his hand. That was not likely, though. If Scarpa thought he was playing against a man who already held two pair, he'd have taken a card, hoping to fill in one of the pair.

No. Scarpa was sitting with a straight, a flush, or a full house.

If he drew the king of hearts, he would beat Scarpa.

"Bet five bucks," Scarpa said.

He still did not pick up the face-down card. He threw ten match-sticks into the pot and said, "Raise you five."

"Without looking at your cards?" Scarpa asked incredulously.

"I'm raising five. Are you in this, or not?"

Scarpa smirked. "Sure. And since we're playing big time, let's kick it up another ten."

He looked across at Scarpa. He knew he should pick up the card and look at it, but there was something about Scarpa's insolent attitude that goaded him. He did not pick up the card.

"Let's put it all on this hand," he said bravely. "All that I owe you. Double or nothing."

"Without picking up that card?" Scarpa asked.

"Yes."

"You can't beat me without that fifth card. You know that, don't you?"

"Double or nothing," I said.

Scarpa shrugged. "Sure. Double or nothing. It's a deal. Pick up your card."

"Maybe I don't need the card, he said." "Maybe I'm sitting here with four of a kind."

Scarpa chuckled. "Maybe," he said. "But it better be a *high* four of a kind."

He felt his first twinge of panic then. He had figured Scarpa wrong. Scarpa was probably holding a low four of a kind, which meant he *had* to fill the royal flush now. A high straight wouldn't do the trick. It had to be the king of hearts.

He reached for the card, and lifted it.

He felt first a wild exultance, a sweeping sort of triumph that lashed at his body when he saw the king with his upraised, partially hidden sword. He lifted his head and opened his mouth, ready to shout, "A royal flush!" and then he saw the Mongol.

The Mongol was a big man, and he held a bigger sword, and for a moment he couldn't believe that what he was seeing was real. He looked back to the king of hearts, and he opened his mouth wide to shriek a warning to Scarpa, but the Mongol was lifting the sword, the biggest sword he'd ever seen in his life, and then the sword came down in a sweeping, glittering arc, and he saw pain register on Scarpa's face when the blade struck, and then his head parted in the center, like an apple under a sharp paring knife, and the blood squirted out of his eyes and his nose and his mouth.

He looked at Scarpa, and then he looked again at the Mongol, and he thought only *I had a royal flush, I had a royal flush*. He found his bayonet in his hand. He saw his arm swinging back, and then he hacked downward at the Mongol, and he saw the stripe of red appear on the side of the Mongol's neck, and he struck again, and again, until the Mongol's neck and shoulder was a gushing red tangle of ribbons. The Mongol collapsed into the foxhole, the length of him falling over the scattered cards. Alongside his body, the king of hearts smirked.

The CO couldn't understand how the Mongol had got through the lines. He reprimanded his men, and then he noticed the strange dazed expression on the face of the man who'd slain the Mongol. He sent him to the field hospital at once.

The medics called it shock, and they worked over him, and finally they made sense out of his gibberish, but not enough sense. They shipped him back to the States. The bug doctors talked to him, and they gave him occupational therapy, mystified when he refused to play cards with the other men. They had seen men affected by killing before. Not all men could kill. A man who could not kill was worthless to the army. They discharged him.

They had not known it was all because of that royal flush. They had not known how annoyed he'd been with Scarpa all that day, and how that red king of hearts, that scarlet king, was the key to unraveling all that annoyance.

Now, in the safety of his brother's apartment, he thought of that day again, and he thought of the Mongol's intrusion, and of how his triumph had been shattered by that intrusion. If only it had been different. If only he could have said, "I have a royal flush, Scarpa, you louse. Look at it! Look at it, and let me see that goddamned smirk vanish! Look at it, Scarpa!"

The Mongol had divided the smirk on Scarpa's face, but the king of hearts had lain there in the bottom of the foxhole, and nothing erased that superior smirk on his face, nothing, nothing.

It was bad. He knew that it was bad. You're not supposed to react this way. Normal people don't react this way. If a little girl is playing the piano, you let her play. *God, when is she going to stop!*

You don't start getting annoyed, not if you're normal. You don't let these things bother you until you can't control them any more.

Tom wouldn't let these little things annoy him. Tom was all right, and hadn't Tom been through a war? The big war, not the child's play in Korea, but had Tom ever seen a Mongol cavalry attack, with gongs sounding, and trumpets blaring, had Tom ever seen that, ever experienced the horrible stench of fear when you stood in the wake of the advancing horses?

Well, the Mongol he'd killed hadn't been on horseback, so he couldn't use that as an excuse. The Mongol was, in a way, a very vulnerable man, despite his hugeness and the size of his sword. The bayonet had split his skin just like any man's, and his blood had flown as red as the woman's in Baltimore.

I don't want to think about the woman in Baltimore, he told himself.

He looked up at the ceiling of the room, and he prayed *Please, little girl, please stop playing the piano. Please, please.*

Do, re, mi, fa, so, la, ti . . . .

The woman in Baltimore had been a nice old lady. Except for the way she smacked her lips. He had lived in the room across the hall from her, and she'd always invited him in for tea in the afternoon, and she'd served those very nice little cookies with chocolate trails of icing across their tops. He had liked the cookies and the tea, until he'd begun noticing the way the old lady smacked her lips. She had very withered, parched lips, and every time she sipped at her tea, she smacked them with a loud purse, and there was something disgusting about it, something almost obscene. It began to annoy him.

It began to annoy him the way Scarpa had annoyed him that day in the foxhole.

He tried to stay away from the old lady, but he couldn't. He wanted to go in there and say, "Can't you stop that goddamn vulgar smacking of your lips, you sanctimonious old hag?" That would have shut her up, all right. That would have shown her he wasn't going to take any more of her disgusting slurping.

But he could not bring himself to do it, and so she continued to annoy him, until his face began to tic, and his hands began to tremble, and one day he seized a knife from her kitchen drawer and hacked at her neck until her jugular vein split in a scarlet bubble of blood.

He had left Baltimore.

He had gone down to Miami and taken a job as a beach boy in one of the big hotels. He had always been a good swimmer, a man who should have been put in underwater demolition or something, not dumped into a foxhole with people who couldn't swim at all. He had been lucky in Baltimore because the old lady herself ran the boarding house in which he'd stayed. There was one other boarder, an old man who never left his room. The old lady was the only person who'd known his name, and she wasn't telling it to anyone, not any more.

But in Miami, faced with what he had done, afraid it might happen again, he took on an assumed name, a name he had forgotten now. Everyone called him by his assumed name, and he garnered fat tips from the sun-tanned people who lolled at the edge of the swimming pool. And all he'd had to do was arrange their beach chairs or get them a drink of orange juice every now and then. It was a good life, and he felt very warm and very healthy, and he thought for a while that he would forget all about the king of hearts and the Mongol and the old lady in Baltimore.

Until Carl began getting wise.

He hadn't liked Carl to begin with. Carl was one of these sinewy muscular guys who always put on a big show at the diving board, one of those characters who liked to swim the length of the pool six times underwater, and then brag about it later.

Carl's bragging began to get on his nerves. All right, Carl *was* a good swimmer, but he was good too!

It started one night while they were vacuuming out the bottom of the pool.

"I'm wasting my time in this dump," Carl said. "I should be working in a water show someplace."

"You're not that good," he'd answered.

Carl looked up. "What do you mean by that?"

"Just what I said. I've seen better swimmers."

"You have, huh?"

"Yes, I have."

"Who, for instance? Johnny Weissmuller?"

"No, I wasn't talking about Johnny Weissmuller. I've just seen better swimmers, that's all. Even I can swim better than you."

"You think so, huh?"

"Yes, I think so. In fact, I know so. I won a PAL medal when I was a kid. For swimming."

"You know what you can do with a PAL medal, don't you?" Carl asked.

"I'm only saying it because I want you to know you're not so hot, that's all."

"Kid, maybe you'd like to put your money where your mouth is, huh?"

"How do you mean?"

"A contest. Any stroke you call, or all of the strokes, if you like. We'll race across the pool. What do you say?"

"Any time," he answered.

"How much have you got to lose?"

"I'll bet you everything I've saved since I've been here."

"And how much is that?"

"About five hundred bucks."

"It's a bet," Carl said, and he extended his hand and sealed the bargain.

The bet disturbed him. Now that he had made it, he was not at all sure he *could* swim better than Carl, not at all sure. He thought about it, and the more he thought about it, the more annoyed he became, until finally the familiar tic and trembling broke out again, and he felt this frustrated rage within him. He wanted to call off the bet, tell Carl he'd seen better swimmers and even *he* was a better swimmer, but he saw no reason to have to prove it, so what the hell, why should he waste his time for a measly five hundred bucks? That's what he wanted to tell Carl, but he realized that would sound like chickening out, and he didn't know what to do, and his annoyance mounted, and back of it all was that scarlet king, and he hated that card with all his might, and his hatred spread to include Carl.

He could not go through with the match.

He stole a bread knife from the kitchen on the night before he was to swim, and he went to Carl's room. Carl was surprised to see him, and he was even more surprised when the knife began hacking at his neck and shoulder in even regular strokes until he collapsed lifeless and blood-spattered to the floor.

It was all because of the king of hearts. All because of that clever, sneaky character with the hidden sword.

The gas station attendant in Georgia, on the way up North, that had been the worst, because that man had annoyed him only a very little bit, haggling over the price of the gas, but he had hit him anyway, hit him with the sharp cleaving edge of a tire iron, knocked him flat to the concrete of his one-man filling station, and then hacked away at him until the man was unrecognizable.

And now, the little girl upstairs, pounding the piano, annoying him in the same way all the others had annoyed him, annoying, annoying until he would see red, and in that red, the king would take shape, leering.

If he could defeat the king, of course, he could defeat all the rest of them.

It was just a matter of looking the king straight in the eye, even when he was being terribly annoyed, looking him straight in the eye, and not allowing him to take hold. Why, of course, that was the ticket! What was he, anyway? Just a card, wasn't he? Couldn't he stare down a card? What was so difficult about that?

... *mi, fa, so, la, ti* ....

Shut up, you, he shouted silently at the ceiling. Just shut up! You don't know what trouble you're causing me. You don't know what I'm doing just to stop from ... from ... hurting you. Now just shut up. Just stop that goddamned pounding for a minute, while I find a deck of cards. There must be a deck of cards somewhere around here. Doesn't Tom play cards? Why sure, everyone plays cards.

He began looking through the apartment, the tic in his face working, his hands trembling, the piano thudding its notes through the floor upstairs, the notes slithering down the long walls of the apartment. When he found the deck in one of the night-table drawers, he ripped it open quickly, not looking at the label, not caring about anything but getting those cards in his hands, wanting only to stare down the king of hearts, wanting to win against the king, knowing if he could defeat the king, his troubles would all be over.

He shuffled the cards and put them face down on the table.

He was trembling uncontrollably now, and he looked up and this time he shouted aloud at the little girl and her piano.

"Shut up! This is important! Can't you shut up a minute?"

The little girl either hadn't heard him, or didn't care to stop practicing.

"You little louse," he whispered. "I'm doing this all for you, but you don't care, do you? I ought to come up there and just tell you that you stink, that's all, that you'll never play piano anyway, that I could play better piano with one hand tied behind my back, that's what I ought to do. But I'm being good to you. I'm going through all this trouble, trying to beat that red king, and all because of you, and do you give a damn?"

Viciously, he turned over the first card.

A ten of diamonds.

He felt a wave of relief spread over him. Doggedly, he turned the second card. A queen of clubs. Again the relief, but again he plunged on. A nine of hearts. A jack of spades. And then . . .

The king of hearts.

Upstairs the girl pounded at the piano, the scales dripping down the walls in slimy monotony. The tic in his face was wild now. He stared at the king, and his hands trembled on the table top, and he sought the evil eyes and the leering mouth, and the hidden sword, and he wanted to rush upstairs and stop the piano playing, but he knew if he could beat the king, if he could only beat the king . . .

He kept staring at the face of the card.

He did not move from the table. He kept staring at the card and listening to the *do, re, mi, fa* upstairs, and in a few moments, the tic stopped, and he could control his hands, and he felt a wild exultant rush of relief.

I've beat him, he thought, *I've really beat him! He can't harm me any more. That's the last king of hearts! The king is dead!*

And in his exultance, and in his triumph, he began turning over other cards, one after the other, burying the king, hiding him from sight forever, turning over nines and tens and an ace and a queen and . . .

The king of hearts.

His heart leaped.

The king of hearts!

But that couldn't . . . no, it couldn't be . . . he'd . . . the king was dead, he had stared it down, beaten it, buried it, but . . .

He stared at the card. It was the king of hearts, no doubt about it, the smirking face and the hidden sword, back again, back to plague him, oh God, oh God there was no escape, no escape at all, he had killed it and now it was back again, staring up at him, staring up with a *do, re, mi, fa* . . .

"Shut up!" he roared. "Goddammit, can't you shut up?"

He swept the cards from the table top, the frustrated rage mounting inside him again. He saw the box the cards had come in, and he swept that to the floor, too, not seeing the printed *Pinochle Playing Cards* on its face.

He went to the kitchen with his face ticcing and his hands trembling, listening to the piano upstairs. He took a meat cleaver from the kitchen drawer, and then sadly, resignedly, he went into the hallway and upstairs.

To the Mongol who was playing the piano.

Sticks

KARL EDWARD WAGNER

Dr. Karl Edward Wagner is a physician with a deep misunderstanding of human nature and human fears. Best known for his heroic fantasies featuring "Kane," his short fiction has been making a deep impression on the field of horror literature since the early 1970's. A noted authority on fantasy, he writes a monthly column for Fantasy Newsletter *and edits Carcosa Press, one of the leading small presses in the field. "Sticks is arguably his finest short story, and won the British August Derleth Fantasy Award in 1974.*

I

The lashed-together framework of sticks jutted from a small cairn alongside the stream. Colin Leverett studied it in perplexment—half a dozen odd lengths of branch, wired together at cross angles for no fathomable purpose. It reminded him unpleasantly of some bizarre crucifix, and he wondered what might lie beneath the cairn.

It was the spring of 1942—the kind of day to make the war seem distant and unreal, although the draft notice waited on his desk. In a few days Leverett would lock his rural studio, wonder if he would see it again—be able to use its pens and brushes and carving tools when he did return. It was good-by to the woods and streams of upstate New York, too. No fly rods, no tramps through the countryside in Hitler's Europe. No point in putting off fishing that troutstream he had driven past once, exploring back roads of the Otselic Valley.

Mann Brook—so it was marked on the old Geological Survey map—ran southeast of DeRuyter. The unfrequented country road crossed over a stone bridge old before the first horseless carriage, but Leverett's Ford eased across and onto the shoulder. Taking fly rod and tackle, he included pocket flask and tied an iron skillet to his belt. He'd work his way downstream a few miles. By afternoon he'd lunch on fresh trout, maybe some bullfrog-legs.

It was a fine clear stream, though difficult to fish as dense bushes hung out from the bank, broken with stretches of open water hard to

328

work without being seen. But the trout rose boldly to his fly, and Leverett was in fine spirits.

From the bridge the valley along Mann Brook began as fairly open pasture, but half a mile downstream the land had fallen into disuse and was thick with second growth evergreens and scrub-apple trees. Another mile, and the scrub merged with dense forest, which continued unbroken. The land here, he had learned, had been taken over by the state many years back.

As Leverett followed the stream he noted the remains of an old railroad embankment. No vestige of tracks or ties—only the embankment itself, overgrown with large trees. The artist rejoiced in the beautiful dry-wall culverts spanning the stream as it wound through the valley. To his mind it seemed eerie, this forgotten railroad running straight and true through virtual wilderness.

He could imagine an old wood-burner with its conical stack, steaming along through the valley dragging two or three wooden coaches. It must be a branch of the old Oswego Midland Rail Road, he decided, abandoned rather suddenly in the 1870's. Leverett, who had a memory for detail, knew of it from a story his grandfather told of riding the line in 1871 from Otselic to DeRuyter on his honeymoon. The engine had so labored up the steep grade over Crumb Hill that he got off to walk alongside. Probably that sharp grade was the reason for the line's abandonment.

When he came across a scrap of board nailed to several sticks set into a stone wall, his darkest thought was that it might read "No Trespassing." Curiously, though the board was weathered featureless, the nails seemed quite new. Leverett scarcely gave it much thought, until a short distance beyond he came upon another such contrivance. And another.

Now he scratched at the day's stubble on his long jaw. This didn't make sense. A prank? But on whom? A child's game? No, the arrangement was far too sophisticated. As an artist, Leverett appreciated the craftsmanship of the work—the calculated angles and lengths, the designed intricacy of the maddeningly inexplicable devices. There was something distinctly uncomfortable about their effect.

Leverett reminded himself that he had come here to fish and continued downstream. But as he worked around a thicket he again stopped in puzzlement.

Here was a small open space with more of the stick lattices and an arrangement of flat stones laid out on the ground. The stones—likely taken from one of the many dry-wall culverts—made a pattern maybe twenty by fifteen feet, that at first glance resembled a ground plan for a house. Intrigued, Leverett quickly saw that this was not so. If the ground plan were for anything, it would have to be for a small maze.

The bizarre lattice structures were all around. Sticks from trees and bits of board nailed together in fantastic array. They defied description; no two seemed alike. Some were only one or two sticks lashed together in parallel or at angles. Others were worked into complicated lattices of dozens of sticks and boards. One could have been a child's tree house—it was built in three planes, but was so abstract and useless that it could be nothing more than an insane conglomeration of sticks and wire. Sometimes the contrivances were stuck in a pile of stones or a wall, maybe thrust into the railroad embankment or nailed to a tree.

It should have been ridiculous. It wasn't. Instead it seemed somehow sinister—these utterly inexplicable, meticulously constructed stick lattices spread through a wilderness where only a tree-grown embankment or a forgotten stone wall gave evidence that man had ever passed through. Leverett forgot about trout and frog-legs, instead dug into his pockets for a notebook and stub of pencil. Busily he began to sketch the more intricate structures. Perhaps someone could explain them; perhaps there was something to their insane complexity that warranted closer study for his own work.

Leverett was roughly two miles from the bridge when he came upon the ruins of a house. It was an unlovely colonial farmhouse, box-shaped and gambrel-roofed, fast falling into the ground. Windows were dark and empty; the chimneys on either end looked ready to topple. Rafters showed through open spaces in the room, and the weathered boards of the walls had in places rotted away to reveal hewn timber beams. The foundation was stone and disproportionately massive. From the size of the unmortared stone blocks, its builder had intended the foundation to stand forever.

The house was nearly swallowed up by undergrowth and rampant lilac bushes, but Leverett could distinguish what had been a lawn with imposing shade trees. Farther back were gnarled and sickly apple trees and an overgrown garden where a few lost flowers still bloomed—wan and serpentine from years in the wild. The stick lattices were everywhere—the lawn, the trees, even the house were covered with the uncanny structures. They reminded Leverett of a hundred misshapen spider webs—grouped so closely together as to almost ensnare the entire house and clearing. Wondering, he sketched page on page of them, as he cautiously approached the abandoned house.

He wasn't certain just what he expected to find inside. The aspect of the farmhouse was frankly menacing, standing as it did in gloomy desolation where the forest had devoured the works of man—where the only sign that man had been here in this century were these insanely wrought latticeworks of sticks and board. Some might have turned back at this point. Leverett, whose fascination for the macabre was evident in his art, instead was intrigued. He drew a rough sketch of the farmhouse and the grounds, overrun with the enigmatic devices, with thickets of hedges and distorted flowers. He regretted that it might be years before he could capture the eeriness of this place on scratchboard or canvas.

The door was off its hinges, and Leverett gingerly stepped within, hoping that the flooring remained sound enough to bear even his sparse frame. The afternoon sun pierced the empty windows, mottling the decaying floorboards with great blotches of light. Dust drifted in the sunlight. The house was empty—stripped of furnishings other than indistinct tangles of rubble mounded over with decay and the drifted leaves of many seasons.

Someone had been here, and recently. Someone who had literally covered the mildewed walls with diagrams of the mysterious lattice structures. The drawings were applied directly to the walls, crisscrossing the rotting wallpaper and crumbling plaster in bold black lines. Some of vertiginous complexity covered an entire wall like a mad mural. Others were small, only a few crossed lines, and reminded Leverett of cuneiform glyphics.

His pencil hurried over the pages of his notebook. Leverett noted with fascination that a number of the drawings were recognizable as schematics of lattices he had earlier sketched. Was this then the planning room for the madman or educated idiot who had built these structures? The gouges etched by the charcoal into the soft plaster appeared fresh—done days or months ago, perhaps.

A darkened doorway opened into the cellar. Were there drawings there as well? And what else? Leverett wondered if he should dare it. Except for streamers of light that crept thorough cracks in the flooring, the cellar was in darkness.

"Hello?" he called. "Anyone here?" It didn't seem silly just then.

These stick lattices hardly seemed the work of a rational mind. Leverett wasn't enthusiastic with the prospect of encountering such a person in this dark cellar. It occurred to him that virtually anything might transpire here, and no one in the world of 1942 would ever know.

And that in itself was too great a fascination for one of Leverett's temperament. Carefully he started down the cellar stairs. They were stone and thus solid, but treacherous with moss and debris.

The cellar was enormous—even more so in the darkness. Leverett reached the foot of the steps and paused for his eyes to adjust to the damp gloom. An earlier impression recurred to him. The cellar was too big for the house. Had another dwelling stood here originally—perhaps destroyed and rebuilt by one of lesser fortune? He examined the stonework. Here were great blocks of gneiss that might support a castle. On closer look they reminded him of a fortress—for the dry-wall technique was startlingly Mycenaean.

Like the house above, the cellar appeared to be empty, although without light Leverett could not be certain what the shadows hid. There seemed to be darker areas of shadow along sections of the foundation wall, suggesting openings to chambers beyond. Leverett began to feel uneasy in spite of himself.

There was something here—a large tablelike bulk in the center of the cellar. Where a few ghosts of sunlight drifted down to touch its edges, it seemed to be of stone. Cautiously he crossed the stone paving to where it loomed—waist-high, maybe eight feet long and less wide. A roughly shaped slab of gneiss, he judged, and supported by pillars of unmortared stone. In the darkness he could only get a vague conception of the object. He ran his hand along the slab. It seemed to have a groove along its edge.

His groping fingers encountered fabric, something cold and leathery and yielding. Mildewed harness, he guessed in distaste.

Something closed on his wrist, set icy nails into his flesh.

Leverett screamed and lunged away with frantic strength. He was held fast, but the object on the stone slab pulled upward.

A sickly beam of sunlight came down to touch one end of the slab. It was enough As Leverett struggled backward and the thing that held him heaved up from the stone table, its face passed through the beam of light.

It was a lich's face—desiccated flesh tight over its skull. Filthy strands of hair were matted over its scalp, tattered lips were drawn away from broken yellowed teeth, and, sunken in their sockets, eyes that should be dead were bright with hideous life.

Leverett screamed again, desperate with fear. His free hand clawed the iron skillet tied to his belt. Ripping it loose, he smashed at the nightmarish face with all his strength.

For one frozen instant of horror the sunlight let him see the skillet crush through the mould-eaten forehead like an axe—cleaving the dry flesh and brittle bone. The grip on his wrist failed. The cadaverous face fell away, and the sight of its caved-in forehead and unblinking eyes from between which thick blood had begun to ooze would awaken Leverett from nightmare on countless nights.

But now Leverett tore free and fled. And when his aching legs faltered as he plunged headlong through the scrub-growth, he was spurred to desperate energy by the memory of the footsteps that had stumbled up the cellar stairs behind him.

2

When Colin Leverett returned from the war, his friends marked him a changed man. He had aged. There were streaks of gray in his hair; his springy step had slowed. The athletic leanness of his body had withered to an unhealthy gauntness. There were indelible lines to his face, and his eyes were haunted.

More disturbing was an alteration of temperament. A mordant cynicism had eroded his earlier air of whimsical asceticism. His fascination with the macabre had assumed a darker mood, a morbid obsession that his old acquaintances found disquieting. But it had been that kind of a war, especially for those who had fought through the Apennines.

Leverett might have told them otherwise, had he cared to discuss his nightmarish experience on Mann Brook. But Leverett kept his own counsel, and when he grimly recalled that creature he had struggled with in the abandoned cellar, he usually convinced himself it had only been a derelict—a crazy hermit whose appearance had been distorted by the poor light and his own imagination. Nor had his blow more than glanced off the man's forehead, he reasoned, since the other had recovered quickly enough to give chase. It was best not to dwell upon such matters, and this rational explanation helped restore sanity when he awoke from nightmares of that face.

Thus Colin Leverett returned to his studio, and once more plied his pens and brushes and carving knives. The pulp magazines, where fans had acclaimed his work before the war, welcomed him back with long lists of assignments. There were commissions from galleries and collectors, unfinished sculptures and wooden models. Leverett busied himself.

There were problems now. *Short Stories* returned a cover painting as "too grotesque." The publishers of a new anthology of horror stories sent back a pair of his interior drawings—"too gruesome, especially the rotted, bloated faces of those hanged men." A customer returned a silver figurine, complaining that the martyred saint was too thoroughly martyred. Even *Weird Tales*, after heralding his return to its ghoul-haunted pages, began returning illustrations they considered "too strong, even for our readers."

Leverett tried half-heartedly to tone things down, found the results vapid and uninspired. Eventually the assignments stopped trickling in. Leverett, becoming more the recluse as years went by, dismissed the pulp days from his mind. Working quietly in his isolated studio, he found a living doing occasional commissioned pieces and gallery work, from time to time selling a painting or sculpture to major museums. Critics had much praise for his bizarre abstract sculptures.

3

The war was twenty-five years history when Colin Leverett received a letter from a good friend of the pulp days—Prescott Brandon, now editor-publisher of Gothic House, a small press that specialized in books of the weird-fantasy genre. Despite a lapse in correspondence of many years, Brandon's letter began in his typically direct style:

The Eyrie/Salem, Mass./Aug. 2

To the Macabre Hermit of the Midlands:

Colin, I'm putting together a deluxe three-volume collection of H. Kenneth Allard's horror stories. I well recall that Kent's stories were personal favorites of yours. How about shambling forth from retirement and illustrating these for me? Will need two-color jackets and a dozen line interiors each. Would hope that you can startle fandom with some especially ghastly drawings for these—something different from the hackneyed skulls and bats and werewolves carting off half-dressed ladies.

Interested? I'll send you the materials and details, and you can have a free hand. Let us hear—Scotty.

Leverett was delighted. He felt some nostalgia for the pulp days, and he had always admired Allard's genius in transforming visions of cosmic horror into convincing prose. He wrote Brandon an enthusiastic reply.

He spent hours rereading the stories for inclusion, making notes and preliminary sketches. No squeamish subeditors to offend here; Scotty meant what he said. Leverett bent to his task with maniacal relish.

Something different, Scotty had asked. A free hand. Leverett studied his pencil sketches critically. The figures seemed headed in the right direction, but the drawings needed something more—something that would inject the mood of sinister evil that pervaded Allard's work. Grinning skulls and leathery bats? Trite. Allard demanded more.

The idea had inexorably taken hold of him. Perhaps because Allard's tales evoked that same sense of horror; perhaps because Allard's visions of crumbling Yankee farmhouses and their depraved secrets so reminded him of that spring afternoon at Mann Brook . . .

Although he had refused to look at it since the day he had staggered in, half-dead from terror and exhaustion, Leverett perfectly recalled where he had flung his notebook. He retrieved it from the back of a seldom used file, thumbed through the wrinkled pages thoughtfully. These hasty sketches reawakened the sense of foreboding evil, the charnel horror of that day. Studying the bizarre lattice patterns, it seemed impossible to Leverett that others would not share his feeling of horror that the stick structures evoked in him.

He began to sketch bits of stick latticework into his pencil roughs The sneering faces of Allard's degenerate creatures took on an added shadow of menace. Leverett nodded, pleased with the effect.

4

Some months afterward a letter from Brandon informed Leverett he had received the last of the Allard drawings and was enormously pleased with the work. Brandon added a postcript:

For God's sake Colin—What is it with these insane sticks you've got poking up everywhere in the illos! The damn things get really creepy after awhile. How on earth did you get onto this?

Leverett supposed he owed Brandon some explanation. Dutifully he wrote a lengthy letter, setting down the circumstances of his experience at Mann Brook—omitting only the horror that had seized his wrist in the cellar. Let Brandon think him eccentric, but not madman and murderer.

Brandon's reply was immediate:

Colin—Your account of the Mann Brook episode is fascinating—and incredible! It reads like the start of one of Allard's stories! I have taken the liberty of forwarding your letter to Alexander Stefroi in Pelham. Dr. Stefroi is an earnest scholar of this region's history—as you may already know. I'm certain your account will interest him, and he may have some light to shed on the uncanny affair.

Expect 1st volume, Voices from the Shadow, *to be ready from the binder next month. The proofs looked great. Best—Scotty.*

The following week brought a letter postmarked Pelham, Massachusetts:

A mutual friend, Prescott Brandon, forwarded your fascinating account of discovering curious sticks and stone artifacts on an abandoned farm in up-state New York. I found this most intriguing, and wonder if you recall further details? Can you relocate the exact site after thirty years? If possible, I'd like to examine the foundations this spring, as they call to mind similar megalithic sites of this region. Several of us are interested in locating what we believe are remains of megalithic constructions dating back to the Bronze Age, and to determine their possible use in rituals of black magic in colonial days.

Present archaeological evidence indicates that ca. 1700-2000 B.C. there was an influx of Bronze Age peoples into the Northeast from Europe. We know that the Bronze Age saw the rise of an extremely advanced culture, and that as seafarers they were to have no peers until the Vikings. Remains of a megalithic culture originating in the Mediterranean can be seen in the Lion Gate in Mycenae, in the Stonehenge, and in dolmens, passage graves and barrow mounds throughout Europe. Moreover, this seems to have represented far more than a style of architecture peculiar to the era. Rather, it appears to have been a religious cult whose adherents worshipped a sort of Earth-mother, served her with fertility rituals and sacrifices, and believed that immortality of the soul could be secured through interment in megalithic tombs.

That this culture came to America cannot be doubted from the hundreds of megalithic remnants found—and now recognized—in our region. The most important site to date is Mystery Hill in N.H., comprising a great many walls and dolmens of megalithic construction—most notably the Y Cavern barrow mound and the Sacrificial Table (see postcard). Less spectacular megalithic sites include the group of cairns and carved stones at Mineral Mt., subterranean chambers with stone passageways such as at Petersham and Shutesbury, and uncounted shaped megaliths and buried "monks' cells" throughout this region.

Of further interest, these sites seem to have retained their mystic aura for the early colonials, and numerous megalithic sites show evidence of having been used for sinister purposes by colonial sorcerers and alchemists. This became particularly true after the witchcraft persecutions drove many practitioners into the western wilderness—explaining why upstate New York and western Mass. have seen the emergence of so many cultist groups in later years.

Of particular interest here is Shadrach Ireland's "Brethren of the New Light," who believed that the world was soon to be destroyed by sinister "Powers from Outside" and that they, the elect, would then attain physical immortality. The elect who died beforehand were to have their bodies preserved on tables of stone until the "Old Ones" came forth to return them to life. We have definitely linked the megalithic sites at Shutesbury to later unwholesome practices of the New Light cult. They were absorbed in 1781 by Mother Ann Lee's Shakers, and Ireland's putrescent corpse was hauled from the stone table in his cellar and buried.

Thus I think it probable that your farmhouse may have figured in similar hidden practices. At Mystery Hill a farmhouse was built in 1826 that incorporated one dolmen in its foundations. The house burned down ca. 1848–55, and there were some unsavory local stories as to what took place there. My guess is that your farmhouse had been built over or incorporated a similar megalithic site—and that your "sticks" indicate some unknown cult still survived there. I can recall certain vague references to lattice devices figuring in secret ceremonies, but can pinpoint nothing definite. Possibly they represent a development of occult symbols to be used in certain conjurations, but this is just a guess. I suggest you consult Waite's *Ceremonial Magic* or such to see if you can recognize similar magical symbols.

Hope this is of some use to you. Please let me hear back.

Sincerely, Alexander Stefroi.

There was a postcard enclosed—a photograph of a four-and-a-half-ton slab, ringed by a deep groove with a spout, identified as the Sacrificial Table at Mystery Hill. On the back Stefroi had written:

You must have found something similar to this. They are not rare—we have one in Pelham removed from a site now beneath Quabbin Reservoir. They were used for sacrifice—animal and human—and the groove is to channel blood into a bowl, presumably.

Leverett dropped the card and shuddered. Stefroi's letter reawakened the old horror, and he wished now he had let the matter lie forgotten in his files. Of course, it couldn't be forgotten—even after thirty years.

He wrote Stefroi a careful letter, thanking him for his information and adding a few minor details to his account. This spring, he promised, wondering if he would keep that promise, he would try to relocate the farmhouse on Mann Brook.

5

Spring was late that year, and it was not until early June that Colin Leverett found time to return to Mann Brook. On the surface, very little had changed in three decades. The ancient stone bridge yet stood, nor had the country lane been paved. Leverett wondered whether anyone had driven past since his terror-sped flight.

He found the old railroad grade easily as he started downstream. Thirty years, he told himself—but the chill inside him only tightened. The going was far more difficult than before. The day was unbearably hot and humid. Wading through the rank underbrush raised clouds of black flies that savagely bit him.

Evidently the stream had seen severe flooding in the past years, judging from piled logs and debris that blocked his path. Stretches were scooped out to barren rocks and gravel. Elsewhere gigantic barriers of uprooted trees and debris looked like ancient and mouldering fortifications. As he worked his way down the valley, he realized that his search would yield nothing. So intense had been the force of the long-ago flood that even the course of the stream had changed. Many of the dry-wall culverts no longer spanned the brook, but sat lost and alone far back from its present banks. Others had been knocked flat and swept away, or were buried beneath tons of rotting logs.

At one point Leverett found remnants of an apple orchard groping through weeds and bushes. He thought that the house must be close by, but here the flooding had been particularly severe, and evidently even those ponderous stone foundations had been toppled over and buried beneath debris.

Leverett finally turned back to his car. His step was lighter.

A few weeks later he received a response from Stefroi to his reported failure:

Forgive my tardy reply to your letter of 13 June. I have reently been pursuing inquiries which may, I hope, lead to the discovery of a previously unreported megalithic site of major significance. Naturally I am disappoint-ed that no traces remained of the Mann Brook site. While I tried not to get my hopes up, it did seem likely that the foundations would have survived. In searching through regional data, I note that there were particularly severe flashfloods in the Otselic area in July 1942 and again in May 1946. Very probably your old farmhouse with its enigmatic devices was utterly destroyed not very long after your discovery of the site. This is weird and wild country, and doubtless there is much we shall never know.

I write this with a profound sense of personal loss over the death two nights ago of Prescott Brandon. This was a severe blow to me—as I am sure it was to you and to all who knew him. I only hope the police will catch the vicious killers who did this senseless act—evidently thieves surprised while ransacking his office. Police believe the killers were high on drugs from the mindless brutality of their crime.

I had just received a copy of the third Allard volume, Unhallowed Places. *A superbly designed book, and this tragedy becomes all the more insuperable with the realization that Scotty will give the world no more such treasures. In Sorrow, Alexander Stefroi.*

Leverett stared at the letter in shock. He had not received news of Brandon's death—had only a few days before opened a parcel from the publisher containing a first copy of *Unhallowed Places*. A line in Brandon's last letter recurred to him—a line that seemed amusing to him at the time:

Your sticks have bewildered a good many fans, Colin, and I've worn out a ribbon answering inquiries. One fellow in particular—a Major George Leonard—has pressed me for details, and I'm afraid that I told him too much. He has written several times for your address, but knowing how you value your privacy I told him simply to permit me to forward any correspondence.

He wants to see your original sketches, I gather, but these overbearing occult types give me a pain. Frankly, I wouldn't care to meet the man myself.

6

"Mr. Colin Leverett?"

Leverett studied the tall lean man who stood smiling at the doorway of his studio. The sports car he had driven up in was black and looked expensive. The same held for the turtleneck and leather slacks he wore, and the sleek briefcase he carried. The blackness made his thin face deathly pale. Leverett guessed his age to be late forty by the thinning of his hair. Dark glasses hid his eyes, black driving gloves his hands.

"Scotty Brandon told me where to find you," the stranger said.

"Scotty?" Leverett's voice was wary.

"Yes, we lost a mutual friend, I regret to say. I'd been talking with him just before. . . . But I see by your expression that Scotty never had time to write."

He fumbled awkwardly. "I'm Dana Allard."

"Allard?"

His visitor seemed embarrassed. "Yes—H. Kenneth Allard was my uncle."

"I hadn't realized Allard left a family," mused Leverett, shaking the extended hand. He had never met the writer personally, but there was a strong resemblance to the few photographs he had seen. And Scotty had been paying royalty checks to an estate of some sort, he recalled.

"My father was Kent's half-brother. He later took his father's name, but there was no marriage, if you follow."

"Of course." Leverett was abashed. "Please find a place to sit down. And what brings you here?"

Dana Allard tapped his briefcase. "Something I'd been discussing with Scotty. Just recently I turned up a stack of my uncle's unpublished manuscripts." He unlatched the briefcase and handed Leverett a sheaf of yellowed paper. "Father collected Kent's personal effects from the state hospital as next-of-kin. He never thought much of my uncle, or his writing. He stuffed this away in our attic and forgot about it. Scotty was quite excited when I told him of my discovery."

Leverett was glancing through the manuscipt—page on page of cramped handwriting, with revisions pieced throughout like an indecipherable puzzle. He had seen photographs of Allard manuscripts. There was no mistaking this.

Or the prose. Leverett read a few passages with rapt absorption. It was authentic—and brilliant.

"Uncle's mind seems to have taken an especially morbid turn as his illness drew on," Dana hazarded. "I admire his work very greatly but I find these last few pieces . . . well, a bit *too* horrible. Especially his translation of his mythical *Book of Elders*."

It appealed to Leverett perfectly. He barely noticed his guest as he pored over the brittle pages. Allard was describing a megalithic structure his doomed narrator had encountered in the crypts beneath an ancient churchyard. There were references to "elder glyphics" that resembled his lattice devices.

"Look here," pointed Dana. "These incantations he records here from Alorri-Zrokros's forbidden tome: 'Yogth-Yugth-Sut-Hyrath-Yogng'—hell, I can't pronounce them. And he has pages of them."

"This is incredible!" Leverett protested. He tried to mouth the alien syllables. It could be done. He even detected a rhythm.

"Well, I'm relieved that you approve. I'd feared these last few stories and fragments might prove a little too much for Kent's fans."

"Then you're going to have them published?"

Dana nodded. "Scotty was going to. I just hope those thieves weren't searching for this—a collector would pay a fortune. But Scotty said he was going to keep this secret until he was ready for announcement." His thin face was sad.

"So now I'm going to publish it myself—in a deluxe edition. And I want you to illustrate it."

"I'd feel honored!" vowed Leverett, unable to believe it.

"I really liked those drawings you did for the trilogy. I'd like to see more like those—as many as you feel like doing. I mean to spare no expense in publishing this. And those stick things . . ."

"Yes?"

"Scotty told me the story on those. Fascinating! And you have a whole notebook of them? May I see it?"

Leverett hurriedly dug the notebook from his file, returned to the manuscript.

Dana paged through the book in awe. "These things are totally bizarre—and there are references to such things in the manuscript, to make it even more fantastic. Can you reproduce them all for the book?"

"All I can remember," Leverett assured him. "And I have a good memory. But won't that be overdoing it?"

"Not at all! They fit into the book. And they're utterly unique. No, put everything you've got into this book. I'm going to entitle it *Dwellers in the Earth*, after the longest piece. I've already arranged for its printing, so we begin as soon as you can have the art ready. And I know you'll give it your all."

7

He was floating in space. Objects drifted past him. Stars, he first thought. The objects drifted closer.

Sticks. Stick lattices of all configurations. And then he was drifting among them, and he saw that they were not sticks—not of wood. The lattice designs were of dead-pale substance, like streaks of frozen starlight. They reminded him of glyphics of some unearthly alphabet—complex, enigmatic symbols arranged to spell . . . what? And there *was* an arrangment—a three-dimensional pattern. A maze of utterly baffling intricacy . . .

Then somehow he was in a tunnel. A cramped, stone-lined tunnel through which he must crawl on his belly. The dank, moss-slimed stones pressed close about his wriggling form, evoking shrill whispers of claustrophic dread.

And after an indefinite space of crawling through this and other stone-lined burrows, and sometimes through passages whose angles hurt his eyes, he would creep forth into a subterranean chamber. Great slabs of granite a dozen feet across formed the walls and ceiling of this buried chamber, and between the slabs other burrows pierced the earth. Altarlike, a gigantic slab of gneiss waited in the center of the chamber. A spring welled darkly between the stone pillars that supported the table. Its outer edge was encircled by a groove, sickeningly stained by the substance that clotted in the stone bowl beneath its collecting spout.

Others were emerging from the darkened burrows that ringed the chamber—slouched figures only dimly glimpsed and vaguely human. And a figure in a tattered cloak came toward him from the shadow—stretched out a clawlike hand to seize his wrist and draw him toward the sacrificial table. He followed unresistingly, knowing that something was expected of him.

They reached the altar and in the glow from the cuneiform lattices chiseled into the gneiss slab he could see the guide's face. A mouldering corpse-face, the rotten bone of its forehead smashed inward upon the foulness that oozed forth . . .

And Leverett would awaken to the echo of his screams . . .

He'd been working too hard, he told himself, stumbling about in the darkness, getting dressed because he was too shaken to return to sleep. The nightmares had been coming every night. No wonder he was exhausted.

But in his studio his work awaited him. Almost fifty drawings finished now, and he planned another score. No wonder the nightmares.

It was a grueling pace, but Dana Allard was ecstatic with the work he had done. And *Dwellers in the Earth* was waiting. Despite problems with typesetting, with getting the special paper Dana wanted—the book only waited on him.

Though his bones ached with fatigue, Leverett determinedly trudged through the graying night. Certain features of the nightmare would be interesting to portray.

8

The last of the drawings had gone off to Dana Allard in Petersham, and Leverett, fifteen pounds lighter and gut-weary, converted part of the bonus check into a case of good whiskey. Dana had the offset presses rolling as soon as the plates were shot from the drawings. Despite his precise planning, presses had broken down, one printer quit for reasons not stated, there had been a bad accident at the new printer—seemingly innumerable problems, and Dana had been furious at each delay. But the production pushed along quickly for all that. Leverett wrote that the book was cursed, but Dana responded that a week would see it ready.

Leverett amused himself in his studio constructing stick lattices and trying to catch up on his sleep. He was expecting a copy of the book when he received a letter from Stefroi:

Have tried to reach you by phone last few days, but no answer at your house. I'm pushed for time just now, so must be brief. I have indeed uncovered an unsuspected megalithic site of enormous importance. It's located on the estate of a long-prominent Mass. family—and as I cannot receive authorization to visit it, I will not say where. Have investigated secretly (and quite illegally) for a short time one night and was nearly caught. Came across reference to the place in collection of seventeenth century letters and papers in a divinity school library. Writer denouncing the family as a brood of sorcerers and witches, references to alchemical activities and other less savory rumors—and describes underground stone chambers, megalithic artifacts, etc. which are put to "foul usage and diabolic praktise." Just got a quick glimpse but his description was not exaggerated. And Colin—in creeping through the woods to get to the site, I came across dozens of your mysterious "sticks!" Brought a small one back and have it here to show you. Recently constructed and exactly like your drawings. With luck, I'll gain admittance and find out their significance—undoubtedly they have significance—though these cultists can be stubborn about sharing their secrets. Will explain my interest is scientific, no exposure to ridicule—and see what they say. Will get a closer look one way or another. And so—I'm off! Sincerely, Alexander Stefroi.

Leverett's bushy brows rose. Allard had intimated certain dark rituals in which the stick lattices figured. But Allard had written over thirty years ago, and Leverett assumed the writer had stumbled onto something similar to the Mann Brook site. Stefroi was writing about something current.

He rather hoped Stefroi would discover nothing more than an inane hoax.

The nightmares haunted him still—familiar now, for all that its scenes and phantasms were visited by him only in dream. Familiar. The terror that they evoked was undiminished.

Now he was walking through forest—a section of hills that seemed to be close by. A huge slab of granite had been dragged aside, and a pit yawned where it had lain. He entered the pit without hesitation, and the rounded steps that led downward were known to his tread. A buried stone chamber, and leading from it stone-lined burrows. He knew which one to crawl into.

And again the underground room with its sacrificial altar and its dark spring beneath, and the gathering circle of poorly glimpsed figures. A knot of them clustered about the stone table, and as he stepped toward them he saw they pinned a frantically writhing man.

It was a stoutly built man, white hair disheveled, flesh gouged and filthy. Recognition seemed to burst over the contorted features, and he wondered if he should know the man. But now the lich with the caved-in skull was whispering in his ear, and he tried not to think of the unclean things that peered from that cloven brow, and instead took the bronze knife from the skeletal hand, and raised the knife high, and because he could not scream and awaken, did with the knife as the tattered priest had whispered . . .

And when after an interval of unholy madness, he at last did awaken, the stickiness that covered him was not cold sweat, nor was it nightmare the half-devoured heart he clutched in one fist.

9

Leverett somehow found sanity enough to dispose of the shredded lump of flesh. He stood under the shower all morning, scrubbing his skin raw. He wished he could vomit.

There was a news item on the radio. The crushed body of noted archaeologist, Dr. Alexander Stefroi, had been discovered beneath a fallen granite slab near Whately. Police speculated the gigantic slab had shifted with the scientist's excavations at its base. Identification was made through personal effects.

When his hands stopped shaking enough to drive, Leverett fled to Petersham—reaching Dana Allard's old stone house about dark. Allard was slow to answer his frantic knock.

"Why, good evening, Colin! What a coincidence your coming here just now! The books are ready. The bindery just delivered them."

Leverett brushed past him. "We've got to destroy them!" he blurted. He'd thought a lot since morning.

"Destroy them?"

"There's something none of us figured on. Those stick lattices—there's a cult, some damnable cult. The lattices have some significance in their rituals. Stefroi hinted once they might be glyphics of some sort, I don't know. But the cult is still alive. They killed Scotty

. . . they killed Stefroi. They're onto me—I don't know what they intend. They'll kill you to stop you from releasing this book!"

Dana's frown was worried, but Leverett knew he hadn't impressed him the right way. "Colin, this sounds insane. You really have been overextending yourself, you know. Look, I'll show you the books. They're in the cellar."

Leverett let his host lead him downstairs. The cellar was quite large, flagstoned and dry. A mountain of brown-wrapped bundles awaited them.

"Put them down here where they wouldn't knock the floor out," Dana explained. "They start going out to distributors tomorrow. Here, I'll sign your copy."

Distractedly Leverett opened a copy of *Dwellers in the Earth*. He gazed at his lovingly rendered drawings of rotting creatures and buried stone chambers and stained altars—and everywhere the enigmatic latticework structures. He shuddered.

"Here." Dana Allard handed Leverett the book he had signed. "And to answer your question, they *are* elder glyphics."

But Leverett was staring at the inscription in its unmistakable handwriting: "For Colin Leverett, Without whom this work could not have seen completion—H. Kenneth Allard."

Allard was speaking. Leverett saw places where the hastily applied flesh-toned make-up didn't quite conceal what lay beneath. "Glyphics symbolic of alien dimensions—inexplicable to the human mind, but essential fragments of an evocation so unthinkably vast that the 'pentagram' (if you will) is miles across. Once before we tried—but your iron weapon destroyed part of Althol's brain. He erred at the last instant—almost annihilating us all. Althol had been formulating the evocation since he fled the advance of iron four millennia past.

"Then you reappeared, Colin Leverett—you with your artist's knowledge and diagrams of Althol's symbols. And now a thousand new minds will read the evocation you have returned to us, unite with our minds as we stand in the Hidden Places. And the Great Old Ones will come forth from the earth, and we, the dead who have steadfastly served them, shall be masters of the living."

Leverett turned to run, but now they were creeping forth from the shadows of the cellar, as massive flagstones slid back to reveal the tunnels beyond. He began to scream as Althol came to lead him away, but he could not awaken, could only follow.

Sardonicus

RAY RUSSELL

Ray Russell is an important figure in modern horror/fantasy/science fiction as both a writer and an editor. He was heavily responsible for making the early Playboy *a center (and a high-paying one) for the publication of quality speculative fiction, and he is the uncredited editor of most or all of the Playboy Press paperbacks in these fields. As a writer, he has published dozens of outstanding stories in a variety of markets, and his sadly neglected* The Case Against Satan *(1962) anticipated and prefigured* The Exorcist. *Other notable books include* Incubus *(1976, optioned for the movies), and a 1961 collection which bears the title of the present selection (filmed as* Mr. Sardonicus *the same year).*

In the late summer of the year 18—, a gratifying series of professional successes had brought me to a state of such fatigue that I had begun seriously to contemplate a long rest on the Continent. I had not enjoyed a proper holiday in nearly three years, for, in addition to my regular practice, I had been deeply involved in a program of research, and so rewarding had been my progress in this special work (it concerned the ligaments and muscles, and could, it was my hope, be beneficially applied to certain varieties of paralysis) that I was loath to leave the city for more than a week at a time. Being unmarried, I lacked a solicitous wife who might have expressed concern over my health; thus it was that I had overworked myself to a point that a holiday had become absolutely essential to my well-being; hence, the letter which was put in my hand one morning near the end of that summer was most welcome.

When it was first presented to me by my valet, at breakfast, I turned it over and over, feeling the weight of its fine paper which was almost of the heaviness and stiffness of parchment; pondering the large seal of scarlet wax upon which was imprinted a device of such complexity that it was difficult to decipher; examining finally the hand in which the address had been written: *Sir Robert Cargrave, Harley Street, London.* It was a feminine hand, that much was certain, and there was

347

a curious touch of familiarity to its delicacy as well as to its clearness (this last an admirable quality far too uncommon in the handwriting of ladies). The fresh clarity of that hand—and where had I seen it before?—bespoke a directness that seemed contrary to the well-nigh unfathomable ornamentation of the seal, which, upon closer and more concentrated perusal, I at length concluded to be no more than a single "S," but an "S" whose writhing curls seemed almost to grin presumptuously at one, an "S" which seemed to be constructed of little else than these grins, an "S" of such vulgar pretension that I admit to having felt vexed for an instant, and then, in the next instant, foolish at my own vexation—for surely, I admonished myself, there are things a deal more vexing than a seal which you have encountered without distemper?

Smiling at my foible, I continued to weigh the letter in my hand, searching my mind for a friend or acquaintance whose name began with "S." There was old Shipley of the College of Surgeons; there was Lord Henry Stanton, my waggish and witty friend; and that was the extent of it. Was it Harry? He was seldom in one place for very long and was a faithful and gifted letterwriter. Yet Harry's bold hand was far from effeminate, and, moreover, he would not use such a seal—unless it were as a lark, as an antic jest between friends. My valet had told me, when he put the letter in my hand, that it had come not by the post but by special messenger, and although this intelligence had not struck me as remarkable at the time, it now fed my curiosity and I broke that vexing seal and unfolded the stiff, crackling paper.

The message within was written in that same clear, faintly familiar hand. My eye first traveled to the end to find the signature, but that signature—*Madam S.*—told me nothing, for I knew of no Madam S. among my circle.

I read the letter. It is before me now as I set down this account, and I shall copy it out verbatim:

My dear Sir Robert,

It has been close to seven years since last we met—indeed, at that time you were not yet Sir Robert at all, but plain Robert Cargrave (although some talk of imminent knighthood was in the air), and so I wonder if you will remember Maude Randall?

Remember Maude Randall! Dear Maude of the bell-like voice, of the chestnut hair and large brown eyes, of a temperament of such sweetness and vivacity that the young men of London had eyes for no one else. She was of good family, but during a stay in Paris there had been something about injudicious speculation by her father that had diminished the family fortunes to such an extent that the wretched man had taken his own life and the Randalls had vanished from London society altogether. Maude, or so I had heard, had married a foreign gentleman and had remained in Europe. It had been sad news, for no young man of London had ever had more doting eyes for Maude than had I, and it had pleased my fancy to think that my feelings were, at least in part, reciprocated. Remember Maude Randall? Yes, yes, I almost said aloud. And now, seven years later, she was "Madam S.," writing in that same hand I had seen countless times on invitations. I continued to read.

I often think of you, for—although it may not be seemly to say it—the company of few gentlemen used to please me so much as yours, and the London soirees given by my dear mother, at which you were present, are among my most cherished recollections now. But there! Frankness was always my failing, as mother used to remind me. She, dear kind lady, survived less than a year after my poor father died, but I suppose you know this.

I am quite well, and we live in great comfort here, although we receive but rarely and are content with our own company most of the time. Mr. S. is a gracious gentleman, but of quiet and retiring disposition, and throngs of people, parties, balls, etc., are retrograde to his temperament; thus it is a special joy to me that he has expressly asked me to invite you here to the castle for a fortnight—or, if I may give you his exact words: "For a fortnight at least, but howsoever long as it please Sir Robert to stay among such drab folk as he will think us." (You see, I told you he was gracious!)

I must have frowned while reading, for the words of Mr. S. were not so much gracious, I thought, as egregious, and as vulgar as his absurd seal. Still, I held these feelings in check, for I knew that my emotions toward this man were not a little colored by jealousy. He, after all, had wooed and won Maude Randall, a young lady of discernment and fine sensibilities: could she have been capable of wedding an obsequious boor? I thought it not likely. And a castle! Such romantic grandeur! ". . . Invite you here to the castle . . ." she had written, but where was "here"? The letter's cover, since it had not come by the post, offered no clue; therefore I read on:

It was, indeed, only yesterday, in the course of conversation, that I was recalling my old life in London, and mentioned your name. Mr. S., I thought, was, of a sudden, interested. "Robert Cargrave?" he said. "There is a well-known physician of that name, but I do not imagine it is the same gentleman." I laughed and told him it *was* the same gentleman, and that I had known you before you had become so illustrious. "Did you know him well?" Mr. S. then asked me, and you will think me silly, but I must tell you that for a moment I assumed him to be jealous! Such was not the case, however, as further conversation proved. I told him you had been a friend of my family's and a frequent guest at our house. "This is a most happy coincidence," he said. "I have long desired to meet Sir Robert Cargrave, and your past friendship with him furnishes you with an excellent opportunity to invite him here for a holiday."

And so, Sir Robert, I am complying with his request—and at the same time obeying the dictates of my own inclination—by most cordially inviting you to visit us for as long as you choose. I entreat you to come, for we see so few people here and it would be a great pleasure to talk with someone from the old days and to hear the latest London gossip. Suffer me, then, to receive a letter from you at once. Mr. S. does not trust the post, hence I have sent this by a servant of ours who was to be in London on special business; please relay your answer by way of him—

I rang for my man. "Is the messenger who delivered this letter waiting for a reply?" I asked.

"He is sitting in the vestibule, Sir Robert," he said.

"You should have told me."

"Yes, sir."

"At any rate, send him in now. I wish to see him."

My man left, and it took me but a minute to dash off a quick note of acceptance. It was ready for the messenger when he was ushered into the room. I addressed him: "You are in the employ of Madam—" I realized for the first time that I did not know her husband's name.

The servant—a taciturn fellow with Slavic features—spoke in a thick accent: "I am in the employ of Mr. Sardonicus, sir."

Sardonicus! A name as flamboyant as the seal, I thought to myself. "Then deliver this note, if you please, to Madam Sardonicus, immediately you return."

He bowed slightly and took the note from my hand. "I shall deliver it to my master straightway, sir," he said.

His manner nettled me. I corrected him. "To your mistress," I said coldly.

"Madam Sardonicus will receive your message, sir," he said.

I dismissed him, and only then did it strike me that I had not the faintest idea where the castle of Mr. Sardonicus was located. I referred once again to Maude's letter:

... Please relay your answer by way of him and pray make it affirmative, for I do hope to make your stay in ——— a pleasant one.

I consulted an atlas. The locality she mentioned, I discovered, was a district in a remote and mountainous region of Bohemia.

Filled with anticipation, I finished my breakfast with renewed appetite, and that very afternoon began to make arrangements for my journey.

I am not—as my friend Harry Stanton is—fond of travel for its own sake. Harry has often chided me on this account, calling me a dry-as-dust academician and "an incorrigible Londoner"—which I suppose I am. For, in point of fact, few things are more tiresome to me than ships and trains and carriages; and although I have found deep enjoyment and spiritual profit in foreign cities, having arrived, the tedium of travel itself has often made me think twice before starting out on a long voyage.

Still, in less than a month after I had answered Maude's invitation, I found myself in her adopted homeland. Sojourning from London to Paris, thence to Berlin, finally to Bohemia, I was met at ——— by a coachman who spoke imperfect English but who managed, in his solemn fashion, to make known to me that he was a member of the staff at Castle Sardonicus. He placed at my disposal a coach drawn by two horses, and, after taking my bags, proceeded to drive me on the last leg of my journey.

Alone in the coach, I shivered, for the air was brisk and I was very tired. The road was full of ruts and stones, and the trip was far from smooth. Neither did I derive much pleasure by bending my glance to the view afforded by the windows, for the night was dark, and the country was, at any rate, wild and raw, not made for serene contemplation. The only sounds were the clatter of hooves and wheels, the creak of the coach, and the harsh, unmusical cries of unseen birds.

"We receive but rarely," Maude had written, and now I told myself—Little wonder! In this ragged and, one might say, uninhabitable place, far from the graces of civilized society, who indeed is there to *be* received, or, for the matter of that, to receive one? I sighed, for the desolate landscape and the thought of what might prove a holiday devoid of refreshing incident, had combined to cloak my already wearied spirit in a melancholic humor.

It was when I was in this condition that Castle Sardonicus met my

eye—a dense, hunched outline at first, then, with an instantaneous
flicker of moonlight, a great gaping death's head, the sight of which
made me inhale sharply. With the exhalation, I chuckled at myself.
"Come, come, Sir Robert," I inwardly chided, "it is, after all, but a
castle, and you are not a green girl who starts at shadows and quails at
midnight stories!"

The castle is situated at the terminus of a long and upward winding
mountain road. It presents a somewhat forbidding aspect to the world,
for there is little about it to suggest gaiety or warmth or any of those
qualities that might assure the wayfarer of welcome. Rather, this vast
edifice of stone exudes an austerity, cold and repellent, a hint of
ancient mysteries long buried, an effluvium of medieval dankness and
decay. At night, and most particularly on nights when the moon is slim
or cloud-enshrouded, it is a heavy blot upon the horizon, a shadow
only, without feature save for its many-turreted outline; and should
the moon be temporarily released from her cloudy confinement, her
fugitive rays lend scant comfort, for they but serve to throw the castle
into sudden, startling chiaroscuro, its windows fleetingly assuming
the appearance of sightless though all-seeing orbs, its portcullis
becoming for an instant a gaping mouth, its entire form striking the
physical and the mental eye as would the sight of a giant skull.

But, though the castle had revealed itself to my sight, it was a full
quarter of an hour before the coach had creaked its way up the steep
and tortuous road to the great gate that barred the castle grounds from
intruders. Of iron the gate was wrought—black it seemed in the scant
illumination—and composed of intricate twists that led, every one of
them, to a central, huge device, of many curves, which in the infrequent glints of moonglow appeared to smile metallically down, but
which, upon gathering my reason about me, I made out to be no more
than an enlarged edition of that presumptuous seal: a massive single
"S." Behind it, at the end of the rutted road, stood the castle
itself—dark, save for lights in two of its many windows.

Some words in a foreign tongue passed between my coachman and a
person behind the gate. The gate was unlocked from within and swung
open slowly, with a long rising shriek of rusted hinges; and the coach
passed through.

As we drew near, the door of the castle was flung open and cheery
light spilled out upon the road. The portcullis, which I had previously
marked, was evidently a remnant from older days and now inactive.

The coach drew to a halt, and I was greeted with great gravity by a butler whom I saw to be he who had carried Maude's invitation to London. I proffered him a nod of recognition. He acknowledged this and said, "Sir Robert, Madam Sardonicus awaits you, and if you wil' be good enough to follow me, I will take you to her presence." The coachman took charge of my bags, and I followed the butler into the castle.

It dated, I thought, to the twelfth or thirteenth century. Suits of armor—priceless relics, I ascertained them to be—stood about the vast halls; tapestries were in evidence throughout; strong, heavy, richly carved furniture was everywhere. The walls were of time-defying stone, great gray blocks of it. I was led into a kind of *salon*, with comfortable chairs, a tea table, and a spinet. Maude rose to greet me.

"Sir Robert," she said softly, without smiling. "How good to see you at last."

I took her hand. "Dear lady," said I, "we meet again."

"You are looking well and prosperous," she said.

"I am in good health, but just now rather tired from the journey."

She gave me leave to sit, and did so herself, venturing the opinion that a meal and some wine would soon restore me. "Mr. Sardonicus will join us soon," she added.

I spoke of her appearance, saying that she looked not a day older than when I last saw her in London. This was true, in regard to her physical self, for her face bore not a line, her skin was of the same freshness, and her glorious chestnut hair was still rich in color and gleaming with health. But what I did not speak of was the change in her spirit. She who had been so gay and vivacious, the delight of soirees, was now distant and aloof, of serious mien, unsmiling. I was sorry to see this, but attributed it to the seven years that had passed since her carefree girlhood, to the loss of her loved parents, and even to the secluded life she now spent in this place.

"I am eager to meet your husband," I said.

"And he, Sir Robert, is quite eager to meet you," Maude assured me. "He will be down presently. Meanwhile, do tell me how you have fared in the world."

I spoke, with some modesty, I hope, of my successes in my chosen field, of the knighthood I had received from the Crown; I described my London apartment, laboratory and office; I made mention of certain mutual friends, and generally gave her news of London life, speaking particularly of the theater (for I knew Maude had loved it) and describing Mr. Macready's farewell appearance as Macbeth at the Haymarket. When Maude had last been in London, there had been rumors of making an opera house out of Covent Garden theater, and I told her that those plans had been carried through. I spoke of the London premiere of Mr. Verdi's latest piece at Her Majesty's. At my mention of these theaters and performances, her eyes lit up, but she was not moved to comment until I spoke of the opera.

"The opera!" she sighed. "Oh, Sir Robert, if you could but know how I miss it. The excitement of a premiere, the ladies and gentlemen in their finery, the thrilling sounds of the overture, and then the curtain rising—" She broke off, as if ashamed of her momentary transport. "But I receive all the latest scores, and derive great satisfaction from playing and singing them to myself. I must order the new Verdi from Rome. It is called *Ernani*, you say?"

I nodded, adding, "With your permission, I will attempt to play some of the more distinctive airs."

"Oh, pray do, Sir Robert!" she said.

"You will find them, perhaps, excessively modern and dissonant." I sat down at the spinet and played—just passably, I fear, and with some improvisation when I could not remember the exact notes—a potpourri of melodies from the opera.

She applauded my playing. I urged her to play also, for she was an accomplished keyboard artist and possessed an agreeable voice, as well. She complied by playing the minuet from *Don Giovanni* and then singing the *Voi che sapete* from *Le Nozze di Figaro*. As I stood over her, watching her delicate hands move over the keys, hearing the pure, clear tones of her voice, all my old feelings washed over me in a rush, and my eyes smarted at the unalloyed sweetness and goodness of this lady. When she asked me to join her in the duet, *Là ci darem la mano*, I agreed to do it, although my voice is less than ordinary. On the second singing of the word *mano—hand—*I was seized by a vagrant impulse and took her left hand in my own. Her playing was hampered, of course, and the music limped for a few measures; and then, my face burning, I released her hand and we finished the duet. Wisely, she neither rebuked me for my action nor gave me encouragement; rather, she acted as if the rash gesture had never been committed.

To mask my embarrassment, I now embarked upon some light

chatter, designed to ease whatever tension existed between us; I spoke of many things, foolish things, for the most part, and even asked if Mr. Sardonicus had later demonstrated any of the jealousy she had said, in her letter, that she had erroneously thought him to have exhibited. She laughed at this—and it brightened the room, for it was the first time her face had abandoned its grave expression; indeed, I was taken by the thought that this was the first display of human merriment I had marked since stepping into the coach—and she said, "Oh, no! To the contrary, Mr. Sardonicus said that the closer we had been in the old days, the more he would be pleased."

This seemed an odd and even coarse thing for a man to say to his wife, and I jovially replied: "I hope Mr. Sardonicus was smiling when he said that."

At once, Maude's own smile vanished from her face. She looked away from me and began to talk of other things. I was dumbfounded. Had my innocent remark given offense? It seemed not possible. A moment later, however, I knew the reason for her strange action, for a tall gentleman entered the room with a gliding step, and one look at him explained many things.

"Sir Robert Cargrave?" he asked, but he spoke with difficulty, certain sounds—such as the *b* in Robert and the *v* in Cargrave—being almost impossible for him to utter. To shape these sounds, the lips must be used, and the gentleman before me was the victim of some terrible affliction that had caused his lips to be pulled perpetually apart from each other, baring his teeth in a continuous ghastly smile. It was the same humorless grin I had seen once before: on the face of a person in the last throes of lockjaw. We physicians have a name for that chilling grimace, a Latin name, and as it entered my mind, it seemed to dispel yet another mystery, for the term we use to describe the lockjaw smile is: *Risus sardonicus*. A pallor approaching phosphorescence completed his astonishing appearance.

"Yes," I replied, covering my shock at the sight of his face. "Do I have the pleasure of addressing Mr. Sardonicus?"

We shook hands. After an exchange of courtesies, he said, "I have ordered dinner to be served in the large dining hall one hour hence. In the meantime, my valet will show you to your rooms, for I am sure you will wish to refresh yourself after your journey."

"You are most kind." The valet appeared—a man of grave countenance, like the butler and the coachman—and I followed him up a
long flight of stone stairs. As I walked behind him, I reflected on the
unsmiling faces in this castle, and no longer were they things of
wonder. For who would be disposed to smile under the same roof with
him who must smile forever? The most spontaneous of smiles would
seem a mockery in the presence of that afflicted face. I was filled with
pity for Maude's husband: of all God's creatures, man alone is blest
with the ability to smile; but for the master of Castle Sardonicus,
God's great blessing had become a terrible curse. As a physician, my
pity was tempered with professional curiosity. His smile resembled the
risus of lockjaw, but lockjaw is a mortal disease, and Mr. Sardonicus,
his skullish grin notwithstanding, was very much alive. I felt shame for
some of my earlier uncharitable thoughts toward this gentleman, for
surely such an unfortunate could be forgiven much. What bitterness
must fester in his breast; what sharp despair gnaw at his inwards!

My rooms were spacious and certainly as comfortable as this dark
stone housing could afford. A hot tub was prepared, for which my tired
and dustry frame was most grateful. As I lay in it, I began to experience
the pleasant pangs of appetite. I looked forward to dinner. After my
bath, I put on fresh linen and a suit of evening clothes. Then, taking
from my bag two small gifts for my host and hostess—a bottle of scent
for Maude, a box of cigars for her husband—I left my rooms.

I was not so foolish as to expect to find my way, unaided, to the
main dining hall; but since I was early, I intended to wander a bit and
let the ancient magnificence of the castle impress itself upon me.

Tapestries bearing my host's "S" were frequently displayed. They
were remarkably new, their colors fresh, unlike the faded grandeur of
their fellow tapestries. From this—and from Mr. Sardonicus's lack of
title—I deduced that the castle had not been inherited through a
family line, but merely purchased by him, probably from an impov-
erished nobleman. Though not titled, Mr. Sardonicus evidently possessed enormous wealth. I pondered its source. My ponderings were
interrupted by the sound of Maude's voice.

I looked up. The acoustical effects in old castles are often strange—I
had marked them in our own English castles—and though I stood near
neither room nor door of any kind, I could hear Maude speaking in a
distressed tone. I was standing at an open window which overlooked a
kind of courtyard. Across this court, a window was likewise open. I

took this to be the window of Maude's room; her voice was in some way being amplified and transported by the circumstantial shape of the courtyard and the positions of the two windows. By listening very attentively, I could make out most of her words.

She was saying, "I shan't. You must not ask me. It is unseemly." And then the voice of her husband replied: "You shall and will, madam. In my castle, it is I who decide what is seemly or unseemly. Not you." I was embarrassed at overhearing this private discussion on what was obviously a painful subject, so I made to draw away from the window that I might hear no more, but was restrained by the sound of my own name on Maude's lips. "I have treated Sir Robert with courtesy," she said. "You must treat him with more than courtesy," Mr. Sardonicus responded. "You must treat him with warmth. You must rekindle in his breast those affections he felt for you in other days . . ."

I could listen no longer. The exchange was vile. I drew away from the window. What manner of creature was this Sardonicus who threw his wife into the arms of other men? As a practitioner of medicine, a man dedicated to healing the ills of humankind, I had brought myself to learn many things about the minds of men, as well as about their bodies. I fully believed that, in some future time, physicians would heal the body by way of the mind, for it is in that *terra incognita* that all secrets lie hidden. I knew that love has many masks; masks of submission and of oppression; and even more terrible masks that make Nature a stranger to herself and "turn the truth of God into a lie," as St. Paul wrote. There is even a kind of love, if it can be elevated by that name, that derives its keenest pleasure from the sight of the beloved in the arms of another. These are unpleasant observations, which may one day be codified and studied by healers, but which, until then, may not be thought on for too long, lest the mind grow morbid and stagger under its load of repugnance.

With a heavy heart, I sought out a servant and asked to be taken to the dining hall. It was some distance away, and by the time I arrived there, Sardonicus and his lady were already at table, awaiting me. He arose, and with that revolting smile, indicated a chair; she also arose, and took my arm, addressing me as "dear Sir Robert" and leading me to my place. Her touch, which at any previous time would have gladdened me, I now found distinctly not to my liking.

A hollow joviality hung over the dinner table throughout the meal. Maude's laughter struck me as giddy and false; Sardonicus drank too much wine and his speech became even more indistinct. I contrived to talk on trivial subjects, repeating some anecdotes about the London theater which I had hitherto related to Maude, and describing Mr. Macready's interpretation of Macbeth.

"Some actors," said Sardonicus, "interpret the Scottish chieftain as a creature compounded of pure evil, unmingled with good qualities of any kind. Such interpretations are often criticized by those who feel no human being can be so unremittingly evil. Do you agree, Sir Robert?"

"No," I said, evenly; then, looking Sardonicus full in the face, I added, "I believe it is entirely possible for a man to possess not a single one of the virtues, to be a demon in human flesh." Quickly, I embarked upon a discussion of the character of Iago, who took ghoulish delight in tormenting his fellow man.

The dinner was, I suppose, first-rate, and the wine an honorable vintage, but I confess to tasting little of what was placed before me. At the end of the meal, Maude left us for a time and Sardonicus escorted me into the library, whither he ordered brandy to be brought. He opened the box of cigars, expressed his admiration of them and gratitude for them, and offered them to me. I took one and we both smoked. The smoking of the cigar made Sardonicus look even more grotesque: being unable to hold it in his lips, he clenched it in his constantly visible teeth, creating a unique spectacle. Brandy was served; I partook of it freely, though I am not customarily given to heavy drinking, for I now deemed it to be beneficial to my dampened spirits.

"You used the word *ghoulish* a few moments ago, Sir Robert," said Sardonicus. "It is one of those words one uses so easily in conversation—one utters it without stopping to think of its meaning. But, in my opinion, it is not a word to be used lightly. When one uses it, one should have in one's mind a firm, unwavering picture of a ghoul."

"Perhaps I did," I said.

"Perhaps," he admitted. "And perhaps not. Let us obtain a precise definition of the word." He arose and walked to one of the bookcases that lined the room's walls. He reached for a large two-volume dictionary. "Let me see," he murmured. "We desire Volume One, from A to M, do we not? Now then: 'ghee' . . . 'gherkin' . . . 'ghetto' . . . 'ghoom' (an odd word, eh, Sir Robert? 'To search for game in the dark') ... 'ghost' ... ah, 'ghoul!' 'Among Eastern nations, an imaginary evil being who robs graves and feeds upon corpses.' One might say, then, that he ghooms?" Sardonicus chuckled. He returned to his chair and helped himself to more brandy. "When you described Iago's actions as 'ghoulish,' " he continued, "did you think of him as the inhabitant of an Eastern nation? Or an imaginary being as against the reality of Othello and Desdemona? And did you mean seriously to suggest that it was his custom to rob graves and then to feed upon the disgusting nourishment he found therein?"

"I used the word in a figurative sense," I replied.

"Ah," said Sardonicus. "That is because you are English and do not believe in ghouls. Were you a Middle European, as am I, you would believe in their existence, and would not be tempted to use the word other than literally. In my country—I was born in Poland—we understood such things. I, in point of fact, have known a ghoul." He paused for a moment and looked at me, then said, "You English are so blasé. Nothing shocks you. I sit here and tell you a thing of dreadful import and you do not even blink your eyes. Can it be because you do not believe me?"

"It would be churlish to doubt the word of my host," I replied.

"And an Englishman may be many things, but never a churl, eh, Sir Robert? Let me refill your glass, my friend, and then let me tell you about ghouls—which, by the way, are by no means imaginary, as that stupid lexicon would have us to think, and which are not restricted to Eastern nations. Neither do they—necessarily—feed upon carrion flesh, although they are interested, *most* interested, in the repellent contents of graves. Let me tell you a story from my own country, Sir Robert, a story that—if I have any gift at all as a spinner of tales—will create in you a profound belief in ghouls. You will be entertained, I hope, but I also hope you will add to your learning. You will learn, for example, how low a human being can sink, how truly *monstrous* a man can become."

"You must transport your mind," said Sardonicus, "back a few years and to a rural region of my homeland. You must become acquainted with a family of country folk—hard-working, law-abiding, God-fearing, of moderate means—the head of which was a simple, good man named Tadeusz Boleslawski. He was an even-tempered personage, kindly disposed to all men, the loving husband of a devoted wife and father of five strong boys. He was also a firm churchman, seldom even taking the Lord's name in vain. The painted women who plied their trade in certain elaborate houses of the nearest large city, Warsaw, held no attraction for him, though several of his masculine neighbors, on their visits to the metropolis, succumbed to such blandishments with tidal regularity. Neither did he drink in excess: a glass of beer with his evening meal, a toast or two in wine on special occasions. No: hard liquor, strong language, fast women—these were not the weaknesses of Tadeusz Boleslawski. His weakness was gambling.

"Every month he would make the trip to Warsaw, to sell his produce at the markets and to buy certain necessaries for his home. While his comrades visited the drinking and wenching houses, Tadeusz would attend strictly to business affairs—except for one minor deviation. He would purchase a lottery ticket, place it securely in a small, tight pocket of his best waistcoat—which he wore only on Sundays and on his trips to the city—then put it completely out of his mind until the following month, when, on reaching the city, he would remove it from his pocket and closely scan the posted list of winners. Then, after methodically tearing the ticket to shreds (for Tadeusz never lived to win a lottery), he would purchase another. This was a ritual with him; he performed it every month for twenty-three years, and the fact that he never won did not discourage him. His wife knew of this habit, but since it was the good man's only flaw, she never remarked upon it."

Outside, I could hear the wind howling dismally. I took more brandy as Sardonicus continued:

"Years passed; three of the five sons married; two (Henryk and Marek, the youngest) were still living with their parents, when Tadeusz—who had been of sturdy health—collapsed one day in the fields and died. I will spare you an account of the family's grief; how the married sons returned with their wives to attend the obsequies; of the burial in the small graveyard of that community. The good man had left few possessions, but these few were divided, according to his written wish, among his survivors, with the largest share going, of course, to the eldest son. Though this was custom, the other sons could not help feeling a trifle disgruntled, but they held their peace for the most part—especially the youngest, Marek, who was perhaps the most amiable of them and a lad who was by nature quiet and interested in improving his lot through the learning he found in books.

"Imagine, sir, the amazement of the widow when, a full three weeks after the interment of her husband, she received word by men returning from Warsaw that the lottery ticket Tadeusz had purchased had now been selected as the winner. It was a remarkable irony, of course, but conditions had grown hard for the poor woman, and would grow harder with her husband dead, so she had no time to reflect upon that irony. She set about looking through her husband's possessions for the lottery ticket. Drawers were emptied upon the floor; boxes and cupboards were ransacked; the family Bible was shaken out; years before, Tadeusz had been in the habit of temporarily hiding money under a loose floorboard in the bedroom—this cavity was thoroughly but vainly plumbed. The sons were sent for: among the few personal effects they had been bequeathed, did the ticket languish there? In the snuff box? In any article of clothing?

"And at that, Sir Robert, the eldest son leapt up. 'An article of clothing!' he cried. 'Father always wore his Sunday waistcoat to the city when he purchased the lottery tickets—the very waistcoat in which he was buried!'

" 'Yes, yes!' the other sons chorused, saving Marek, and plans began to be laid for the exhuming of the dead man. But the widow spoke firmly: 'Your father rests peacefully,' she said. 'He must not be disturbed. No amount of gold would soothe our hearts if we disturbed him.' The sons protested with vehemence, but the widow stood her ground. 'No son of mine will profane his father's grave—unless he first kills his mother!' Grumbling, the sons withdrew their plans. But that night, Marek awoke to find his mother gone from the house. He was frightened, for this was not like her. Intuition sent him to the graveyard, where he found her, keeping a lonely vigil over the grave of her husband, protecting him from the greed of grave robbers. Marek implored her to come out of the cold, to return home; she at first refused; only when Marek offered to keep vigil all night himself did she relent and return home, leaving her youngest son to guard the grave from profanation.

"Marek waited a full hour. Then he produced from under his shirt a small shovel. He was a strong boy, and the greed of a youngest son who has been deprived of inheritance lent added strength to his arms. He dug relentlessly, stopping seldom for rest, until finally the coffin was uncovered. He raised the creaking lid. An overpowering fetor filled his nostrils and nearly made him faint. Gathering courage, he searched the pockets of the mouldering waistcoat.

"The moon proved to be his undoing, Sir Robert. For suddenly its rays, hitherto hidden, struck the face of his father, and at the sight of that face, the boy recoiled and went reeling against the wall of the grave, the breath forced from his body. Now, you must know that the mere sight of his father—even in an advanced state of decomposition—he had steeled himself to withstand; but what he had *not* foreseen—"

Here, Sardonicus leaned close to me and his pallid, grinning head filled my vision. "What he had not foreseen, my dear sir, was that the face of his father, in the rigor of death, would look directly and hideously upon him." Sardonicus's voice became an ophidian hiss. "And, Sir Robert," he added, "most terrible and most unforeseen of all, the dead lips were drawn back from the teeth *in a constant and soul-shattering smile!*"

I know not whether it was the ghastliness of his story, or the sight of his hideous face so close to mine, or the cheerless keening of the wind outside, or the brandy I had consumed, or all of these in combination; but when Sardonicus uttered those last words, my heart was clutched by a cold hand, and for a moment—a long moment ripped from the texture of time—I was convinced beyond doubt and beyond logic that the face I looked into was the face of that cadaver, reanimated by obscure arts, to walk among the living, dead though not dead.

The moment of horror passed, at length, and reason triumphed. Sardonicus, considerably affected by his own tale, sat back in his chair, trembling. Before too long, he spoke again:

"The remembrance of that night, Sir Robert, though it is now many years past, fills me still with dread. You will appreciate this when I tell you what you have perhaps already guessed—that *I* am that ghoulish son, Marek."

I had not guessed it; but since I had no wish to tell him that I had for an instant thought he was the dead father, I said nothing.

"When my senses returned," said Sardonicus, "I scrambled out of the grave and ran as swiftly as my limbs would carry me. I had reached the gate of the graveyard when I was smitten by the fact that I had not accomplished the purpose of my mission—the lottery ticket remained in my father's pocket!"

"But surely—" I started to say.

"Surely I ignored the fact and continued to run? No, Sir Robert. My terror notwithstanding, I halted, and forced myself to retrace those hasty steps. My fear notwithstanding, I descended once more into that noisome grave. My disgust notwithstanding, I reached into the pocket of my decaying father's waistcoat and extracted the ticket! I need hardly add that, this time, I averted my eyes from his face.

"But the horror was not behind me. Indeed, it had only begun. I reached my home at a late hour, and my family was asleep. For this I was grateful, since my clothes were covered with soil and I still trembled from my fearful experience. I quietly poured water into a basin and prepared to wash some of the graveyard dirt from my face and hands. In performing my ablutions, I looked up into a mirror—*and screamed so loudly as to wake the entire house*!

"My face was as you see it now, a replica of my dead father's: the lips drawn back in a perpetual, mocking grin. I tried to close my mouth. I could not. The muscles were immovable, as if held in the gelid rigor of death. I could hear my family stirring at my scream, and since I did not wish them to look upon me, I ran from the house—never, Sir Robert, to return.

"As I wandered the rural roads, my mind sought the cause of the affliction that had been visited upon me. Though but a country lad, I had read much and I had a blunt, rational mind that was not susceptible to the easy explanations of the supernatural. I would not believe that God had placed a malediction upon me to punish me for my act. I would not believe that some black force from beyond the grave had reached out to stamp my face. At length, I began to believe it was the massive shock that had forced my face to its present state, and that my great guilt had helped to shape it even as my father's dead face was shaped. Shock and guilt: strong powers not from God above or the Fiend below, but from within my own breast, my own brain, my own soul.

"Let me bring this history to a hasty close, Sir Robert. You need only know that, despite my blighted face, I redeemed the lottery ticket and thus gained an amount of money that will not seem large to you, but which was more than I had ever seen before that time. It was the fulcrum from which I plied the lever that was to make me, by dint of shrewd speculation, one of the richest men in Central Europe. Naturally, I sought out physicians and begged them to restore my face to its previous state. None succeeded, though I offered them vast sums. My face remained fixed in this damnable unceasing smile, and my heart knew the most profound despair imaginable. I could not even pronounce my own name! By a dreadful irony, the initial letters of my first and last names were impossible for my frozen lips to form. This seemed the final indignity. I will admit to you that, at this period, I was perilously near the brink of self-destruction. But the spirit of preservation prevailed, and I was saved from that course. I changed my name. I had read of the *Risus sardonicus*, and its horrible aptness appealed to my bitter mind, so I became Sardonicus—a name I can pronounce with no difficulty."

Sardonicus paused and sipped his brandy. "You are wondering," he then said, "in what way my story concerns you."

I could guess, but I said: "I am."

"Sir Robert," he said, "you are known throughout the medical world. Most laymen, perhaps, have not heard of you; but a layman such as I, a layman who avidly follows the medical journals for tidings of any recent discoveries in the curing of paralyzed muscles, has heard of you again and again. Your researches into these problems have earned you high professional regard; indeed, they have earned you a knighthood. For some time, it has been in my mind to visit London and seek you out. I have consulted many physicians, renowned men—Keller in Berlin, Morignac in Paris, Buonagente in Milan—and none have been able to help me. My despair has been utter. It prevented me from making the long journey to England. But when I heard—sublime coincidence!—that my own wife had been acquainted with you, I took heart. Sir Robert, I entreat you to heal me, to lift from me this curse, to make me look once more like a man, that I may walk in the sun again, among my fellow human beings, as one of them, rather than as a fearsome gargoyle to be shunned and feared and ridiculed. Surely you cannot, *will* not deny me?"

My feelings for Sardonicus, pendulumlike, again swung toward his favor. His story, his plight, had rent my heart, and I reverted to my earlier opinion that such a man should be forgiven much. The strange overheard conversation between Maude and him was momentarily forgotten. I said, "I will examine you, Mr. Sardonicus. You were right to ask me. We must never abandon hope."

He clasped his hands together. "Ah, sir! May you be blest forever!"

I performed the examination then and there. Although I did not tell him this, never had I encountered muscles as rigid as those of his face. They could only be compared to stone, so inflexible were they. Still, I said, "Tomorrow we will begin treatment. Heat and massage."

"These have been tried," he said, hopelessly.

"Massage differs from one pair of hands to another," I replied. "I have had success with my own techniques, and therefore place faith in them. Be comforted then, sir, and share my faith."

He seized my hand in his. "I do," he said. "I must. For if you—if even *you*, Sir Robert Cargrave, fail me . . ." He did not complete the sentence, but his eyes assumed an aspect so bitter, so full of hate, so strangely cold yet flaming, that they floated in my dreams that night.

I slept not well, awakening many times in a fever compounded of drink and turbulent emotions. When the first rays of morning crept onto my pillow, I arose, little refreshed. After a cold tub and a light breakfast in my room, I went below to the *salon* whence music issued. Maude was already there, playing a pretty little piece upon the spinet. She looked up and greeted me. "Good morning, Sir Robert. Do you know the music of Mr. Gottschalk? He is an American pianist: this is his *Maiden's Blush*. Amiable, is it not?"

"Most amiable," I replied, dutifully, although I was in no mood for the embroideries of *politesse*.

Maude soon finished the piece and closed the album. She turned to me and said, in a serious tone, "I have been told what you are going to do for my poor husband, Sir Robert. I can scarce express my gratitude."

"There is no need to express it," I assured her. "As a physician—as well as your old friend—I could not do less. I hope you understand, however, that a cure is not a certainty. I will try, and I will try to the limit of my powers, but beyond that I can promise nothing."

Her eyes shone with supplication: "Oh, cure him, Sir Robert! That I beg of you!"

"I understand your feelings, madam," I said. "It is fitting that you should hope so fervently for his recovery; a devoted wife could feel no other way."

"Oh, sir," she said, and into her voice crept now a harshness, "you misunderstand. My fervent hope springs from unalloyed selfishness."

"How may that be?" I asked.

"If you do not succeed in curing him," she told me, "I will suffer."

"I understand that, but—"

"No, you do not understand," she said. "But I can tell you little more without offending. Some things are better left unspoken. Suffice it to be said that, in order to urge you toward an ultimate effort, to the 'limit of your powers' as you have just said, my husband intends to hold over your head the threat of my punishment."

"This is monstrous!" I cried. "It cannot be tolerated. But in what manner, pray, would he dare punish you? Surely he would not beat you?"

"I wish he would be content with a mere beating," she groaned, "But his cleverness knows a keener torture. No, he holds over me—and over you, through me—a punishment far greater; a punishment (believe me!) so loathsome to the sensibilities, so unequivocably vile and degraded, that my mind shrinks from contemplating it. Spare me your further questions, sir, I implore you; for to describe it would plunge me into an abyss of humiliation and shame!"

She broke into sobbing, and tears coursed down her cheeks. No longer able to restrain my tender feelings for her, I flew to her side and took her hands in mine. "Maude," I said, "may I call you that? In the past I addressed you only as Miss Randall; at present I may only call you Madam Sardonicus; but in my heart—then as now—you are, you always have been, you always will be, simply Maude, my own dear Maude!"

"Robert," she sighed; "dearest Robert. I have yearned to hear my Christian name from your lips all these long years."

"The warmth we feel," I said, "may never, with honor, reach fulfillment. But—trust me, dearest Maude!—I will in some wise deliver you from the tyranny of that creature: this I vow!"

"I have no hope," she said, "save in you. Whether I go on as I am, or am subjected to an unspeakable horror, rests with you. My fate is in your hands—these strong, healing hands, Robert." Her voice dropped to a whisper: "Fail me not! Oh fail me not!"

"Govern your fears," I said. "Return to your music. Be of good spirits; or, if you cannot, make a show of it. I go now to treat your husband, and also to confront him with what you have told me."

"Do not!" she cried. "Do not, I beseech you, Robert; lest, in the event of your failure, he devise foul embellishments upon the agonies into which he will cast me!"

"Very well," I said. "I will not speak of this to him. But my heart aches to learn the nature of the torments you fear."

"Ask no more, Robert," she said, turning away. "Go to my husband. Cure him. Then I will no longer fear those torments."

I pressed her dear hand and left the *salon*.

Sardonicus awaited me in his chambers. Thither, quantities of hot water and stacks of towels had been brought by the servants, upon my orders. Sardonicus was stripped to the waist, displaying a trunk strong and of good musculature, but with the same near-phosphorescent pallor of his face. It was, I now understood, the pallor of one who has avoided daylight for years. "As you see, sir," he greeted me, "I am ready for your ministrations."

I bade him recline upon his couch, and began the treatment.

Never have I worked so long with so little reward. After alternating applications of heat and of massage, over a period of three and a quarter hours, I had made no progress. The muscles of his face were still as stiff as marble; they had not relaxed for an instant. I was mortally tired. He ordered our luncheon brought to us in his chambers, and after a short respite, I began again. The clock tolled six when I at last sank into a chair, shaking with exhaustion and strain. His face was exactly as before.

"What remains to be done, sir?" he asked me.

"I will not deceive you," I said. "It is beyond my skill to alleviate your condition. I can do no more."

He rose swiftly from the couch. "You *must* do more!" he shrieked. "You are my last hope!"

"Sir," I said, "new medical discoveries are ever being made. Place your trust in Him who created you—"

"Cease that detestable gibberish at once!" he snapped. "Your puling sentiments sicken me! Resume the treatment."

I refused. "I have applied all my knowledge, all my art, to your affliction," I assured him. "To resume the treatment would be idle and foolish, for—as you have divined—the condition is a product of your own mind."

"At dinner last night," countered Sardonicus, "we spoke of the character of Macbeth. Do you not remember the words he addressed to *his* doctor?—

> *Canst thou not minister to a mind diseas'd;*
> *Pluck from the memory a rooted sorrow;*
> *Raze out the written troubles of the brain;*
> *And with some sweet oblivious antidote*
> *Cleanse the stuff'd bosom of that perilous stuff*
> *Which weighs upon the heart?*

"I remember them," I said; "and I remember, as well, the doctor's reply: '*Therein the patient must minister to himself.*'" I arose and started for the door.

"One moment, Sir Robert," he said. I turned. "Forgive my precipitate outburst a moment ago. However, the mental nature of my affliction notwithstanding, and even though this mode of treatment has failed, surely there are other treatments?"

"None," I said, "that have been sufficiently tested. None I would venture to use upon a human body."

"Ah!" he cried. "Then other treatments *do* exist!"

I shrugged. "Think not of them, sir. They are at present unavailable to you." I pitied him, and added: "I am sorry."

"Doctor!" he said; "I implore you to use whatever treatments exist, be they ever so untried!"

"They are fraught with danger," I said.

"Danger?" He laughed. "Danger of what? Of disfigurement? Surely no man has ever been more disfigured than I! Of death? I am willing to gamble my life!"

"*I* am not willing to gamble your life," I said. "All lives are precious. Even yours."

"Sir Robert, I will pay you a thousand pounds."

"This is not a question of money."

"Five thousand pounds, Sir Robert, *ten* thousand!"

"No."

He sank onto the couch. "Very well," he said. "Then I will offer you the ultimate inducement."

"Were it a million pounds," I said, "you could not sway me."

"The inducement I speak of," he said, "is not money. Will you hear?"

I sat down. "Speak, sir," I said, "since that is your wish. But nothing will persuade me to use a treatment that might cost you your life."

"Sir Robert," he said, after a pause, "yestereve, when I came down to meet you for the first time, I heard happy sounds in the *salon*. You were singing a charming melody with my wife. Later, I could not help but notice the character of your glances toward her . . ."

"They were not reciprocated, sir," I told him, "and herewith I offer you a most abject apology for my unbecoming conduct."

"You obscure my point," he said. "You are a friend of hers, from the old days in London; at that period, you felt an ardent affection for her, I would guess. This is not surprising: for she is a lady whose face and form promise voluptuous delights and yet a lady whose manner is most decorous and correct. I would guess further: that your ardor has not diminished over the years; that, at the sight of her, the embers have burst into a flame. No, sir, hear me out. What would you say, Sir Robert, were I to tell you—that you may quench that flame?"

I frowned. "Your meaning, sir?—"

"Must I speak even more plainly? I am offering you a golden opportunity to requite the love that burns in your heart. To requite it in a single night, if that will suffice you, or over an extended period of weeks, months; a year, if you will; as long as you need—"

"Scoundrel!" I roared, leaping up.

He heeded me not, but went on speaking: ". . . As my guest, Sir Robert! I offer you a veritable Oriental paradise of unlimited raptures!" He laughed, then entered into a catalogue of his wife's excellences. "Consider, sir," he said, "that matchless bosom, like alabaster which has been imbued with the pink of the rose, those creamy limbs—"

"Enough!" I cried. "I will hear no more of your foulness." I strode to the door.

"Yes, you will, Sir Robert," he said immediately. "You will hear a good deal more of my foulness. You will hear what I plan to do to your beloved Maude, should you fail to relieve me of this deformity."

Again, I stopped and turned. I said nothing, but waited for him to speak further.

"I perceive that I have caught your interest," he said. "Hear me: for if you think I spoke foully before, you will soon be forced to agree that my earlier words were, by comparison, as blameless as *The Book of Common Prayer*. If rewards do not tempt you, then threats may coerce you. In fine, Maude will be punished if you fail, Sir Robert."

"She is an innocent."

"Just so. Hence, the more exquisite and insupportable to you should be the thought of her punishment."

My mind reeled. I could not believe such words were being uttered.

"Deep in the bowels of this old castle," said Sardonicus, "are dungeons. Suppose I were to tell you that my intention is to drag my wife thither and stretch her smooth body to unendurable length upon the rack—"

"You would not dare!" I cried.

"My daring or lack of it is not the issue here. I speak of the rack only that I may go on to assure you that Maude would *infinitely prefer* that dreadful machine to the punishment I have in truth designed for her. I will describe it to you. You will wish to be seated, I think."

"I will stand," I said.

"As you please." Sardonicus himself sat down. "Perhaps you have marveled at the very fact of Maude's marriage to me. When the world was so full of personable men—men like yourself, who adored her—why did she choose to wed a monster, a creature abhorrent to the eyes and who did not, moreover, have any redeeming grace of spiritual beauty, or kindness, or charm?

"I first met Maude Randall in Paris. I say 'met,' but it would be truer to simply say I saw her—from my hotel window, in fact. Even in Paris society, which abounds in ladies of remarkable pulchritude, she was to be remarked upon. You perhaps would say I fell in love with her, but I dislike that word *love*, and will merely say that the sight of her smote my senses with most agreeable emphasis. I decided to make her mine. But how? By presenting my irresistibly handsome face to her view? Hardly. I began methodically: I hired secret operatives to find out everything about her and about her mother and father—both of whom were then alive. I discovered that her father was in the habit of speculating, so I saw to it that he received some supposedly trustworthy but very bad advice. He speculated heavily and was instantly ruined. I must admit I had not planned his consequent suicide, but when that melancholy event occurred, I rejoiced, for it worked to my advantage. I presented myself to the bereaved widow and daughter, telling them the excellent qualities of Mr. Randall were widely known in the world of affairs and that I considered myself almost a close friend. I offered to help them in any possible way. By dint of excessive humility and persuasiveness, I won their trust and succeeded in diminishing their aversion to my face. This, you must understand, from first to last, occupied a period of many months. I spoke nothing of marriage, made no sign of affection toward the daughter for at least six of these months; when I did—again, with great respect and restraint—she gently refused me. I retreated gracefully, saying only that I hoped I might remain her and her mother's friend. She replied that she sincerely shared that hope, for, although she could never look upon me as an object of love, she indeed considered me a true friend. The mother, who pined excessively after the death of the father, soon expired: another incident unplanned but welcomed by me. Now the lovely child was alone in the world in a foreign city, with no money, no one to guide her, no one to fall back upon—save kindly Mr. Sardonicus. I waited many weeks, then I proposed marriage again. For several days, she continued to decline the offer, but her declinations grew weaker and weaker until, at length, on one day, she said this to me:

" 'Sir, I esteem you highly as a friend and benefactor, but my other feelings toward you have not changed. If you could be satisfied with such a singular condition; if you could agree to enter into marriage with a lady and yet look upon her as no more than a companion of kindred spirit; if the prospect of a dispassionate and childless marriage does not repulse you—as well it might—then, sir, my unhappy circumstances would compel me to accept your kind offer.'

"Instantly, I told her my regard for her was of the purest and most elevated variety; that the urgings of the flesh were unknown to me; that I lived on a spiritual plane and desired only her sweet and stimulating companionship through the years. All this, of course, was a lie. The diametric opposite was true. But I hoped, by this falsehood, to lure her into marriage; after which, by slow and strategic process, I could bring about her submission and my rapture. She still was hesitant; for, as she frankly told me, she believed that love was a noble and integral part of marriage; and that marriage without it could be only a hollow thing; and that though I knew not the urgings of the flesh, she could not with honesty say the same of herself. Yet she reiterated that, so far as my own person was concerned, a platonic relationship was all that could ever exist between us. I calmed her misgivings. We were married not long after.

"And now, Sir Robert, I will tell you a surprising thing. I have confessed myself partial to earthly pleasures; as a physician and as a man of the world, you are aware that a gentleman of strong appetites may not curb them for very long without fomenting turmoil and distress in his bosom. And yet, sir, not once in the years of our marriage—not *once*, I say—have I been able to persuade or cajole my wife into relenting and breaking the stringent terms of our marriage agreement. Each time I have attempted, she has recoiled from me with horror and disgust. This is not because of an abhorrence of all fleshly things—by her own admission—but because of my monstrous face.

"Perhaps now you will better understand the vital necessity for this cure. And perhaps also you will understand the full extent of Maude's suffering should you fail to effect that cure. For, mark me well: if you fail, my wife will be made to become a true wife to me—by main force, and not for one fleeting hour, but every day and every night of her life, whensoever I say, in whatsoever manner I choose to express my conjugal privilege!" As an afterthought, he added, "I am by nature imaginative."

I had been shocked into silence. I could only look upon him with disbelief. He spoke again:

"If you deem it a light punishment, Sir Robert, then you do not know the depth of her loathing for my person, you do not know the revulsion that wells up inside her when I but place my fingers upon her arm, you do not know what mastery of her very gorge is required of her when I kiss her hand. Think, then; think of the abomination she would feel were my attentions to grow more ardent, more demanding! It would unseat her mind, sir; of that I am sure, for she would as soon embrace a reptile."

Sardonicus arose and put on his shirt. "I suggest we both begin dressing for dinner," he said. "Whilst you are dressing, reflect. Ask yourself, Sir Robert: could you ever again look upon yourself with other than shame and loathing if you were to sacrifice the beautiful and blameless Maude Randall on an altar of the grossest depravity? Consider how ill you would sleep in your London bed, night after night, knowing what she was suffering at that very moment; suffering because *you* abandoned her, because *you* allowed her to become an entertainment for a monster."

The days that passed after that time were, in the main, tedious yet filled with anxiety. During them, certain supplies were being brought from London and other places; Sardonicus spared no expense in procuring for me everything I said was necessary to the treatment. I avoided his society as much as I could, shunning even his table, and instructing the servants to bring my meals to my rooms. On the other hand, I sought out the company of Maude, endeavoring to comfort her and allay her fears. In those hours when her husband was occupied with business affairs, we talked together in the *salon*, and played music. Thus, they were days spotted with small pleasures that seemed the greater for having been snatched in the shadow of wretchedness.

I grew to know Maude, in that time, better than I had ever known her in London. Adversity stripped the layers of ceremony from our congress, and we spoke directly. I came to know her warmth, but I came to know her strength, too. I spoke outright of my love, though in the next breath I assured her I was aware of the hopelessness of that love. I did not tell her of the "reward" her husband had offered me—and which I had refused—and I was gladdened to learn (as I did by indirection) that Sardonicus, though he had abjured her to be excessively cordial to me, had not revealed the ultimate and ignoble purpose of that cordiality.

"Robert," she said once, "is it likely that he will be cured?"

I did not tell her how unlikely it was. "For your sake, Maude," I said, "I will persevere more than I have ever done in my life."

At length, a day arrived when all the necessaries had been gathered: some plants from the New World, certain equipment from London, and a vital instrument from Scotland. I worked long and late, in complete solitude, distilling a needed liquor from the plants. The next day, dogs were brought to me alive, and carried out dead. Three days after that, a dog left my laboratory alive and my distilling labors came to an end.

I informed Sardonicus that I was ready to administer the treatment. He came to my laboratory, and I imagined there was almost a gloating triumph in his immobile smile. "Such are the fruits of concentrated effort," he said. "Man is an indolent creature, but light the fire of fear under him, and of what miracles is he not capable!"

"Speak not of miracles," I said, "though prayers would do you no harm now, for you will soon be in peril of your life." I motioned him toward a table and bade him lie upon it. He did so, and I commenced explaining the treatment to him. "The explorer Magellan," I said, "wrote of a substance used on darts by the savage inhabitants of the South American continent. It killed instantly, dropping large animals in their tracks. The substance was derived from certain plants, and is, in essence, the same substance I have been occupied in extracting these past days."

"A poison, Sir Robert?" he asked, wryly.

"When used full strength," I said, "it kills by bringing about a *total* relaxation of the muscles—particularly the muscles of the lungs and heart. I have long thought that a dilution of that poison might beneficially slacken the rigidly tensed muscles of paralyzed patients."

"Most ingenious, sir," he said.

"I must warn you," I went on, "that this distillment has never been used on a human subject. It may kill you. I must, perforce, urge you again not to insist upon its use; to accept your lot; and to remove the threat of punishment you now hold over your wife's head."

"You seek to frighten me, doctor," chuckled Sardonicus; "to plant distrust in my bosom. But I fear you not—an English knight and a respected physician would never do a deed so dishonorable as to wittingly kill a patient under his care. You would be hamstrung by your gentleman's code as well as by your professional oath. Your virtues are, in short, my vices' best ally."

I bristled. "I am no murderer such as you," I said. "If you force me to use this treatment, I will do everything in my power to insure its success. But I cannot conceal from you the possibility of your death."

"See to it that I live," he said flatly, "for if I die, my men will kill both you and my wife. They will not kill you quickly. See to it, also, that I am cured—lest Maude be subjected to a fate she fears more than the slowest of tortures." I said nothing. "Then bring me this elixir straightway," he said, "and let me drink it off and make an end of this!"

"It is not to be drunk," I told him.

He laughed. "Is it your plan to smear it on darts, like the savages?"

"Your jest is most apposite," I said. "I indeed plan to introduce it into your body by means of a sharp instrument—a new instrument not yet widely known, that was sent me from Scotland. The original suggestion was put forth in the University of Oxford some two hundred years ago by Dr. Christopher Wren, but only recently, through development by my friend, Dr. Wood of Edinburgh, has it seemed practical. It is no more than a syringe"—I showed him the instrument—"attached to a needle; but the needle is hollow, so that, when it punctures the skin, it may carry healing drugs directly into the bloodstream."

"The medical arts will never cease earning my admiration," said Sardonicus.

I filled the syringe. My patient said, "Wait."

"Are you afraid?" I asked.

"Since that memorable night in my father's grave," he replied, "I have not known fear. I had a surfeit of it then; it will last out my lifetime. No: I simply wish to give instructions to one of my men." He arose from the table, and, going to the door, told one of his helots to bring Madam Sardonicus to the laboratory.

"Why must she be here?" I asked.

"The sight of her," he said, "may serve you as a remembrancer of what awaits her in the event of my death, or of that other punishment she may expect should your treatment prove ineffectual."

Maude was brought into our presence. She looked upon my equipment—the bubbling retorts and tubes, the pointed syringe—with amazement and fright. I began to explain the principle of the treatment to her, but Sardonicus interrupted: "Madam is not one of your students, Sir Robert; it is not necessary she know these details. Delay no longer; begin at once!"

He stretched out upon the table again, fixing his eyes upon me. I proffered Maude a comforting look, and walked over to my patient. He did not wince as I drove the needle of the syringe into the left, and then the right, side of his face. "Now, sir," I said—and the tremor in my voice surprised me—"we must wait a period of ten minutes." I joined Maude, and talked to her in low tones, keeping my eyes always upon my patient. He stared at the ceiling; his face remained solidified in that unholy grin. Precisely ten minutes later, a short gasp escaped him; I rushed to his side, and Maude followed close behind me.

We watched with consuming fascination as that clenched face slowly softened, relaxed, changed; the lips drawing closer and closer to each other, gradually covering those naked teeth and gums, the graven creases unfolding and becoming smooth. Before a minute had passed, we were looking down upon the face of a serenely handsome man. His eyes flashed with pleasure, and he made as if to speak.

"No," I said, "do not attempt speech yet. The muscles of your face are so slackened that it is beyond your power, at present, to move your lips. This condition will pass." My voice rang with exultation, and for the moment our enmity was forgotten. He nodded, then leapt from the table and dashed to a mirror which hung on a wall nearby. Though his face could not yet express his joy, his whole body seemed to uifurl in a great gesture of triumph and a muffled cry of happiness burst in his throat.

He turned and seized my hand; then he looked full into Maude's face. After a moment, she said, "I am happy for you, sir," and looked away. A rasping laugh sounded in his throat, and he walked to my work bench, tore a leaf from one of my notebooks, and scribbled upon it.

This he handed to Maude, who read it and passed it over to me. The writing said:

Fear not, lady. You will not be obliged to endure my embraces. I know full well that the restored beauty of my face will weigh not a jot in the balance of your attraction and repugnance. By this document, I dissolve our pristine marriage. You who have been a wife only in name are no longer even that. I give you your freedom.

I looked up from my reading. Sardonicus had been writing again. He ripped another leaf from the notebook and handed it directly to me. It read:

This paper is your safe conduct out of the castle and into the village. Gold is yours for the asking, but I doubt if your English scruples will countenance the accepting of my money. I will expect you to have quit these premises before morning, taking her with you.

"We will be gone within the hour," I told him, and guided Maude toward the door. Before we left the room, I turned for the last time to Sardonicus.

"For your unclean threats," I said; "for the indirect but no less vicious murder of this lady's parents; for the defiling of your own father's grave; for the greed and inhumanity that moved you even before your blighted face provided you with an excuse for your conduct; for these and for what crimes unknown to me blacken your ledger—accept this token of my censure and detestation." I struck him forcibly on the face. He did not respond. He was standing there in the laboratory when I left the room with Maude.

This strange account should probably end here. No more can be said of its central character, for neither Maude nor I saw him or heard of him after that night. And of us two, nothing need be imparted other than the happy knowledge that we have been most contentedly married for the past twelve years and are the parents of a sturdy boy and two girls who are the lovely images of their mother.

However, I have mentioned my friend Lord Henry Stanton, the inveterate traveler and faithful letterwriter, and I must copy out now a portion of a missive I received from him only a week since, and which, in point of fact, has been the agent that has prompted me to unfold this whole history of Mr. Sardonicus:

. . . But, my dear Bobbie [wrote Stanton], in truth there is small pleasure to be found in this part of the world, and I shall be glad to see London again. The excitements and the drama have all departed (if, indeed, they ever existed) and one must content one's self with the stories told at the hearthstones of inns, with the flames crackling and the mulled wine agreeably stinging one's throat. The natives here are most fond of harrowing stories, tales of gore and grue, of ghosts and ghouls and ghastly events, and I must confess a partiality to such entertainments myself. They will show you a stain on a wall and tell you it is the blood of a murdered innocent who met her death there fifty years before: no amount of washing will ever remove that stain, they tell you in sepulchral tones, and indeed it deepens and darkens on a certain day of the year, the anniversary of her violent passing. One is expected to nod gravely, of course, and one does, if one wishes to encourage the telling of more stories. Back in the eleventh century, you will be apprised, a battalion of foreign invaders were vanquished by the skeletons of long-dead patriots who arose from their tombs to defend their homeland and then returned to the earth when the enemy had been driven from their borders. (And since they are able to show you the very graves of these lively bones, how can one disbelieve them, Bobbie?) Or they will point to a desolate skull of a castle (the country here abounds in such depressing piles) and tell you of the spectral tyrant who, a scant dozen years before, despaired and died alone there. Deserted by the minions who had always hated him, the frightening creature roamed the village, livid and emaciated, his mind shattered, mutely imploring the succour of even the lowliest beggars. I say *mutely*, and that is the best part of this tall tale: for, as they tell it around the fire, these inventive folk, this poor unfortunate could not speak, could not eat, and could not drink. You ask why? For the simple reason that, though he clawed most horribly at his own face, and though he enlisted the aid of strong men—he was absolutely unable to open his mouth. Cursed by Lucifer, they say, he thirsted and starved in the midst of plenty, surrounded by kegs of drink and tables full of the choicest viands, suffering the tortures of Tantalus, until he finally died. Ah, Bobbie! The efforts of our novelists are pale stuff compared to this! English *literateurs* have not the shameless wild imaginations of these people! I will never again read Mrs. Radcliffe with pleasure, I assure you, and the ghost of King Hamlet will, from this day hence, strike no terror to my soul, and will fill my heart with but paltry pity. Still, I have journeyed in foreign climes quite enough for one trip, and

I long for England and that good English dullness which is relieved
only by you and your dear lady (to whom you must commend me most
warmly). Until next month, I remain, Your wayward friend, *Harry
Stanton* (Bohemia, March, 18–).

Now, it would not be a difficult feat for the mind to instantly
assume that the unfortunate man in that last tale was
Sardonicus—indeed, it is for that reason that I have not yet shown
Stanton's letter to Maude: for she, albeit she deeply loathed Sardonicus, is of such a compassionate and susceptible nature that she would
grieve to hear of him suffering a death so horrible. But I am a man of
science, and I do not form conclusions on such gossamer evidence.
Harry did not mention the province of Bohemia that is supposed to
have been the stage of that terrible drama; and his letter, though
written in Bohemia, was not mailed by Harry until he reached Berlin,
so the postmark tells me nothing. Castles like that of Sardonicus are
not singular in Bohemia—Harry himself says the country "abounds in
such depressing piles"—so I plan to suspend conclusive thoughts on
the matter until I welcome Harry home and can elicit from him details
of the precise locality.

For if that "desolate skull of a castle" *is* Castle Sardonicus, and if
the story of the starving man is to be believed, then I will be struck by
an awesome and curious thing:

Five days I occupied myself in extracting a liquor from the South
American plants. During those days, dogs were carried dead from my
laboratory. I had deliberately killed the poor creatures with the un-
diluted poison, in order to impress Sardonicus with its deadliness. I
never intended to—and, in fact, never did—prepare a safe dilution of
that lethal drug, for its properties were too unknown, its potentiality
too dangerous. The liquid I injected into Sardonicus was pure, distilled water—nothing more. This had always been my plan. The or-
dering of *materia medica* from far-flung lands was but an elaborate
façade designed to work not upon the physical part of Sardonicus, but
upon his mind; for after Keller, Morignac, Buonagente and my own
massaging techniques had failed, I was convinced that it was only
through his mind that his body could be cured. It was necessary to
persuade him, however, that he was receiving a powerful medicament.
His mind, I had hoped, would provide the rest—as, in truth, it did.

If the tale of the "spectral tyrant" prove true, then we must look upon the human mind with wonderment and terror. For, in that case, there was nothing—nothing corporeal—to prevent the wretched creature from opening his mouth and eating his fill. Alone in that castle, food aplenty at his fingertips, he had suffered a dire punishment which came upon him—to paraphrase Sardonicus's very words—*not from God above or the Fiend below, but from within his own breast, his own brain, his own soul.*

A Teacher's Rewards

ROBERT PHILLIPS

Life is replication—the great lesson of mortality and middle age—but replication is the second step; the first is understanding. ("The first forty years is text, the remainder commentary," is the way someone else put it.) Phillips, an award-winning poet, prolific writer of short stories, anthologist (Aspects of Alice, 1972) and biographer (Denton Welch: The Lost Poetry of Delmore Schwartz), makes his case for the first stage with quiet and awful elegance.

"What'd you say your name was?" the old lady asked through the screen door. He stood on the dark porch.

"Raybe. Raybe Simpson. You taught me in the third grade, remember?"

"Simpson . . . Simpson. Yes, I suppose so," she said. Her hand remained on the latch.

"Of course you do. I was the boy with white hair. 'Old Whitehead,' my grandfather used to call me, though you wouldn't know that. I sat in the front row. You used to rap my knuckles with your ruler, remember?"

"Oh, I rapped a lot of knuckles in my time. Boys will be boys. Still, the white hair, the front row . . ." Her voice trailed off as she made an almost audible effort to engage the ancient machinery of her memory.

"Sure you remember," he said. " 'Miss Scofield never forgets a name.' That's what all the older kids told us. That's what all the other teachers said. 'Miss Scofield never forgets a name.' "

"Of course she doesn't. I never forgot a pupil's name in forty-eight years of teaching. Come right in." She unlatched the screen door and swung it wide. The spring creaked.

"I can't stay long. I was in town for the day and thought I'd look you up. You were such a good teacher. I've never forgotten what you did for me."

"Well, now, I consider that right kindly of you." She looked him up and down through wire-rimmed spectacles. "Just when was it I taught you?"

"Nineteen thirty-eight. Out to the old school."

"Ah, yes. The old school. A pity about that fire."

"I heard something about it burning down. But I've been away. When was that fire?"

"Oh, years ago. A year or two before I retired. After that I couldn't teach in the new brick schoolhouse they built. Something about the place. Too cold, too bright. And the classroom was so long. A body couldn't hardly see from the one end of it to the other . . ." She made a helpless gesture with her hand. He watched the hand in its motion: tiny, fragile, transparent, a network of blue veins running clearly beneath the surface; the skin hung in wrinkles like wet crepe paper. Denison paper, it had been called, when he was in school.

"That's rough. But you must have been about ready to retire anyhow, weren't you?"

Her watery blue eyes snapped. "I should say not! All my life I've had a real calling for teaching. A real calling. I always said I would teach until I dropped in my tracks. It's such a rewarding field. A teacher gets her reward in something other than money . . . It was just that new red-brick schoolhouse! The lights were too bright, new-fangled fluorescent lights, bright yellow. And the room was too long . . ." Her gaze dared him to contradict her.

"I don't think much of these modern buildings, either."

"Boxes," she said firmly.

"Come again?"

"Boxes, boxes, nothing but boxes, that's all they are. I don't know what we're coming to, I declare. Well, now, Mr.—"

"Simpson. Mr. Simpson. But you can call me Raybe, like you always did."

"Yes. Raybe. That's a nice name. Somehow it has an *honest* sound. Really, the things people name their children *these* days! There's one family named their children Cindy, Heidi and Dawn. They sound like creatures out of Walt Disney. The last year I taught, I had a student named Crystal. A little girl named Crystal! Why not name her Silverware, or China? And a boy named Jet. That was his first name, Jet. Or was it Astronaut? I don't know. Whatever it was, it was terrible."

"You once called me Baby-Raybe, and it caught on. That's what all the kids called me after that."

"Did I? Oh, dear. Well, you must have done something babyish at the time."

A shaft of silence fell between them. At last she smiled, as if to herself, and said cheerily, "I was just fixing to have some tea before you happened by. Would you like some nice hot tea?"

"Well, I wasn't fixing to stay long, like I said." He shuffled his feet.

"It'll only take a second. The kettle's been on all this time." She seemed to have her heart set, and he was not one to disappoint. "Okay, if you're having some."

"Good. Do you take lemon or cream?"

"Neither. Actually I don't drink much tea. I'll just try it plain. With sugar. I've got a sweet tooth."

"A sweet tooth! Let me see. Is that one of the things I remember about you? Raybe Simpson, a sweet tooth? No, I don't think so. One of the boys always used to eat Baby Ruth candy bars right in class. The minute my back was turned he'd sneak another Baby Ruth out of his desk. But that wasn't you, was it?"

"No."

"I didn't think it was you," she said quickly. "I called it the black-board. Did you know, in that new school building, it was green?"

"What was green?"

"The blackboard was *green*. And the chalk was *yellow*. Something about it being easier on the children's eyes. And they had the nerve to call them blackboards, too, mind you. How do you expect children to learn if you call what's green, black?"

"Hmmm."

She was getting down two dainty cups with pink roses painted on them. She put them on a tin tray and placed a sugar bowl between them. The bowl was cracked down the middle and had been taped with Scotch tape, which had yellowed. When the tea finally was ready, they adjourned to the living room. The parlor, she called it.

"Well, how've you been, Miss Scofield?" he asked.

"Can't complain, except for a little arthritis in my hands. Can't complain."

"Good." He studied her hands, then glanced around. "Nice little place you got here." He took a sip of the tea, found it strong and bitter, added two more heaping spoons of sugar.

"Well, it's small, of course, but it serves me. It serves me." She settled back in her rocker.

"You still Miss Scofield?"

"How's that?" She leaned forward on her chair, as if to position her ear closer to the source.

"I asked you, your name is still Miss Scofield? You never got married?

"Mercy no. I've always been an unclaimed blessing. That's what I've always called myself. 'An unclaimed blessing.' " She smiled sweetly.

"You still live alone, I take it."

"Yes indeed. I did once have a cat. A greedy old alley cat named Tom. But he died. Overeating did it, I think. Ate me out of house and home, pretty near."

"You don't say."

"Oh, yes indeed. He'd eat anything. Belly got big as a basketball, nearabout. He was good company, though. Sometimes I miss that old Tom."

"I should think so."

An old-fashioned clock chimed overhead.

"What business did you say you were in, Mr. Simp . . . Raybe?"

"Didn't say."

"That's right, you didn't say. Well, just what is it?"

"Right now I'm unemployed."

She set her teacup upon a lace doily on the tabletop and made a little face of disapproval. "Unemployed. I see. Then how do you get along?"

"Oh, I manage, one way or the other. I've been pretty well taken care of these last ten years. I been away."

"You're living with your folks? Is that it?" Encouragement bloomed on her cheeks.

"My folks are dead. They were dead when I was your student, if you'll remember. Grandfather died too. I lived with an aunt. She's dead now."

"Oh, I'm sorry. I don't think I realized at the time—"

"No, I don't think you did . . . That's all right, Miss Scofield. You had a lot of students to look after."

"Yes, but still and all, it's unlike me not to have remembered or known that one of my boys was an *orphan*. You don't mind if I use that word, do you, Mr. . . . Raybe? Lots of people are sensitive about words."

"I don't mind. I'm not sensitive."

"No, I should think not. You're certainly a big boy, now. And what happened to all that hair? Why, you're bald as a baby." Looking at his head, she laughed a laugh as scattered as buckshot. "My, you must be hot in that jacket. Why don't you take it off? It looks very heavy."

"I'll keep it on, if you don't mind."

"Don't mind a bit, so long's you're comfortable." What did he have in that jacket, she wondered. He was carrying something in there.

"I'm just fine," he said, patting the jacket.

She began to rock in her chair and looked around the meager room to check its presentability to unexpected company. Maybe he had his dinner in there, in a paper poke, and was too embarrassed to show it.

"Well, now, what do you remember about our year together that I may have forgotten? Were you in Jay McMaster's class? Jay was a *lovely* boy. So polite. You can always tell good breeding—"

"He was a year or two ahead of me. You're getting close, though."

"Well, of course I am. How about Nathan Pillsbury? The dentist's son. He was in your class, wasn't he?"

"That's right."

"See!" She exclaimed triumphantly. "Another lovely boy. His parents had a swimming pool. One Christmas Nathan brought me an enormous poinsettia plant. It filled the room, nearly."

"He was in my class, all right. He was the teacher's pet, you might say." Raybe observed her over the rim of his bitter cup. He looked at her knuckles.

"Nathan, my pet? Nathan Pillsbury? I don't remember any such thing. Besides, I never played favorites. That's a bad practice." She worked her lips to and fro.

"So's rapping people's knuckles," he laughed, putting his half-full cup on the floor.

She laughed her scattered little laugh again. "Oh, come now, Raybe. Surely it was deserved, if indeed I ever *did* rap your knuckles."

"You rapped them, all right," he said soberly.

"Did I? Did I really? Yes, I suppose I did. What was it for, do you remember? Passing notes? Gawking out the window?"

"Wasn't for any one thing. You did it lots of times. *Dozens* of times." He cleared his throat.

"Did I? Mercy me. It doesn't seem to me that I did. I only rapped knuckles upon extreme provocation, you know. *Extreme* provocation." She took a healthy swallow of tea. What was it she especially remembered about this boy? Something. It nagged at her. She couldn't remember what it was. Some trait of personality.

"You did it lots of times," he continued. "In front of the whole class. They laughed at me."

"I did? Goodness, what a memory! Well, it doesn't seem to have done you any harm. A little discipline never hurt anybody . . . What was it you said you've been doing professionally?"

"I been in prison," he said with a pale smile. He watched her mouth draw downward.

"Prison? You've been in *prison*? Oh, I see, it's a joke." She tried to laugh again, but this time the little outburst wouldn't scatter.

"*You* try staying behind those walls for ten years and see if you think it's a joke." He fumbled in his pocket for a pack of cigarettes, withdrew a smoke and slowly lit it. He blew a smoke ring across the table.

"Well, I must say! You're certainly the only boy I ever had that . . . that ended up in prison! But I'm sure there were . . . *circumstances* . . . leading up to that. I'm sure you're a fine lad, through it all." She worked her lips faster now. Her gaze traveled to the window that looked out upon the night.

"Yeah, there were *circumstances*, as you call it. Very special circumstances." He blew an enormous smoke ring her way. The old woman began to cough. "It's the smoke. I'm not used to people smoking around me. Do you mind refraining?"

"Yeah, I do mind," he said roughly. "I'm going to finish this cigarette, no matter what."

"Well, if you must, you must," she said nervously, half-rising. "But let me just open that window a little—"

"SIT BACK DOWN IN THAT CHAIR!"

She fell back into the rocker.

"Now, you listen to me, you old bitch," he began.

"Don't call me names. Don't you dare! How *dare* you? No wonder you were behind bars. A common jailbird. A degenerate. No respect for your elders."

"Shut up, grandma." He tossed the cigarette butt to the floor and ground it out on what looked like an Oriental rug. Her eyes bulged.

"I remember you very clearly, now," she exclaimed, her hands to her brow. "I remember you! You were no good to start with. No motivation. No follow-through. I knew just where you'd end up. You've run true to form." Her gaze was defiant.

"Shut your mouth, bitch," he said quietly, beginning at last to unzip his leather jacket.

"I will *not*, I'll have my say. You were a troublemaker, too. I remember the day you wrote nasty, nasty words on the wall in the supply closet. Horrible words. And then when I went back to get papers to distribute, I saw those words. I had to read them, and I knew who wrote them, all right."

"I didn't write them."

"Oh, you wrote them, all right. And I whacked your knuckles good with a ruler, if I remember right."

"You whacked my knuckles good, but I didn't write those words."

"*Did!*"

"*Didn't.*" They sounded like a pair of school children. He squirmed out of the jacket.

"I never made mistakes of that kind," she said softly, watching him shed the jacket. "I knew just who needed strict discipline in my class."

He stood before her now, holding the heavy jacket in his hand. Underneath he wore only a tee shirt of some rough gray linsey-woolsey material. She saw that his arms were heavily muscled, and he saw that she saw. She was positive she could smell the odor of the prison upon him, though the closest she had come to a prison was reading Dickens.

"I never made mistakes," she repeated feebly. "And now, you'd better put that coat right back on and leave. Go back to wherever you came from."

"Can't do that just yet, bitch. I got a score to settle."

"Score? To settle?" She placed her hands upon the rocker arms for support.

"Yeah. I had a long time to figure it all out. Ten years to figure it out. Lots of nights I'd lie there on that board of a bed in that puke-hole and I'd try to piece it all together. How I come to be *there*. Was it my aunt? Naw, she did the best she could without any money. Was it the fellas I took up with in high school? Naw, something happened before that, or I'd never have taken up with the likes of them in the first place, that rocky crowd. And then one night it came to me. *You* were the one."

"Me? The one? The one for what?" Her lips worked furiously now, in and out like a bellows. Her hands tightly gripped the rocker's spindle arms.

"The one who sent me there. Because you *picked* on me all the time. Made me out worse than I was. You never gave me the chance the others had. The other kids left me out of things, because you were always saying I was bad. And you always told me I was dirty. Just because my aunt couldn't keep me in clean shirts like some of the others. You punished me for everything that happened. But the worst was the day of the words on the wall. You hit me so hard my knuckles bled. My hands were sore as boils for weeks."

"*That's* an exaggeration."

"No it isn't. They're *my* hands, I ought to know. And do you know who wrote those words on the closet wall? *Do you know?*" he screamed, putting his face right down next to hers.

"No, who?" she whispered, breathless with fright.

"*Nathan Pillsbury*, that's who!" he shouted, clenching his teeth and shaking her frail body within his grasp. "*Nathan Pillsbury, Nathan Pillsbury!*"

"Let me go," she whimpered. "Let me go."

"I'll let you go after my score is settled."

The old woman's eyes rolled toward the black, unseeing windows. "What are you going to do to me?" she rasped.

"Just settle, lady," he said, taking the hammer from his jacket. "Now, put you hands on the tabletop."

"My hands? On the tabletop?" she whispered.

"On the tabletop," he repeated pedantically, a teacher. "Like this." He made two fists and placed them squarely on the surface.

She refused.

"*Like this!*" he yelled, wrenching her quivering hands and forcing them to the tabletop. Then with his free hand he raised the hammer.

For once, he finished something.

The Roaches

THOMAS M. DISCH

Thomas Disch, the author of Camp Concentration *(1968), 334 (1974) and* The Genocides *(1965) is one of the finest American writers to emerge from the science fiction genre in its fifty-year history. In this elegantly crafted early piece the young writer, at the top of his form, revels in a classical format with ease and elegance, in a story which not only prefigures the horrific visions of the 1970's but also pays homage to the more contained and visible horror with which America in the 1950's faced the edges of the night.*

Miss Marcia Kenwell had a perfect horror of cockroaches. It was an altogether different horror than the one which she felt, for instance, toward the color puce. Marcia Kenwell loathed the little things. She couldn't see one without wanting to scream. Her revulsion was so extreme that she could not bear to crush them under the soles of her shoes. No, that would be too awful. She would run, instead, for the spray can of Black Flag and inundate the little beast with poison until it ceased to move or got out of reach into one of the cracks where they all seemed to live. It was horrible, unspeakably horrible, to think of them nestling in the walls, under the linoleum, only waiting for the lights to be turned off, and then . . . No, it was best not to think about it.

Every week she looked through the *Times* hoping to find another apartment, but either the rents were prohibitive (this *was* Manhattan, and Marcia's wage was a mere $62.50 a week, gross) or the building was obviously infested. She could always tell: there would be husks of dead roaches scattered about in the dust beneath the sink, stuck to the greasy backside of the stove, lining the out-of-reach cupboard shelves like the rice on the church steps after a wedding. She left such rooms in a passion of disgust, unable even to think till she reached her own apartment, where the air would be thick with the wholesome odors of Black Flag, Roach-It, and the toxic pastes that were spread on slices of potato and hidden in a hundred cracks which only she and the roaches knew about.

388

At least, she thought, *I keep my apartment clean*. And truly, the linoleum under the sink, the backside and underside of the stove, and the white contact paper lining her cupboards were immaculate. She could not understand how other people could let these matters get so entirely out-of-hand. *They must be Puerto Ricans*, she decided—and shivered again with horror, remembering that litter of empty husks, the filth and the disease.

Such extreme antipathy toward insects—toward one particular insect—may seem excessive, but Marcia Kenwell was not really exceptional in this. There are many women, bachelor women like Marcia chiefly, who share this feeling, though one may hope, for sweet charity's sake, that they escape Marcia's peculiar fate.

Marcia's phobia was, as in most such cases, hereditary in origin. That is to say, she inherited it from her mother, who had a morbid fear of anything that crawled or skittered or lived in tiny holes. Mice, frogs, snakes, worms, bugs—all could send Mrs. Kenwell into hysterics, and it would indeed have been a wonder, if little Marcia had not taken after her. It was rather strange, though, that her fear had become so particular, and stranger still that it should particularly be cockroaches that captured her fancy, for Marcia had never seen a single cockroach, didn't know what they were. (The Kenwells were a Minnesota family, and Minnesota families simply don't have cockroaches.) In fact, the subject did not arise until Marcia was nineteen and setting out (armed with nothing but a high school diploma and pluck, for she was not, you see, a very attractive girl) to conquer New York.

On the day of her departure, her favorite and only surviving aunt came with her to the Greyhound Terminal (her parents being deceased) and gave her this parting advice: "Watch out for the roaches, Marcia darling. New York City is full of cockroaches." At that time (at almost any time really) Marcia hardly paid attention to her aunt, who had opposed the trip from the start and given a hundred or more reasons why Marcia had better not go, not till she was older at least.

Her aunt had been proven right on all counts: Marcia after five years and fifteen employment agency fees could find nothing in New York but dull jobs at mediocre wages; she had no more friends than when she lived on West Sixteenth and, except for its view (the Chock Full O'Nuts warehouse and a patch of sky), her present apartment on lower Thompson Street was not a great improvement on its predecessor.

The city was full of promises, but they had all been pledged to other people. The city Marcia knew was sinful, indifferent, dirty and dangerous. Every day she read accounts of women attacked in subway stations, raped in the streets, knifed in their own beds. A hundred people looked on curiously all the while and offered no assistance. And on top of everything else there were the roaches!

There were roaches everywhere, but Marcia didn't see them until she'd been in New York a month. They came to her—or she to them—at Silversmith's on Nassau Street, a stationery shop where she had been working for three days. It was the first job she'd been able to find. Alone or helped by a pimply stockboy (in all fairness it must be noted that Marcia was not without an acne problem of her own), she wandered down rows of rasp-edged metal shelves in the musty basement, making an inventory of the sheaves and piles and boxes of bond paper, leatherette-bound diaries, pins and clips, and carbon paper. The basement was dirty and so dim that she needed a flashlight for the lowest shelves. In the obscurest corner, a faucet leaked perpetually into a gray sink: she had been resting near this sink, sipping a cup of tepid coffee (saturated, in the New York manner, with sugar and drowned in milk), thinking, probably, of how she could afford several things she simply couldn't afford, when she noticed the dark spots moving on the side of the sink. At first she thought they might be no more than motes floating in the jelly of her eyes, or the giddy dots that one sees after overexertion on a hot day. But they persisted too long to be illusory, and Marcia drew nearer, feeling compelled to bear witness. *How do I know they are insects?* she thought.

How are we to explain the fact that what repels us most can be at times—at the same time—inordinately attractive? Why is the cobra poised to strike so beautiful? The fascination of the abomination is something that . . . Something which we would rather not account for. The subject borders on the obscene, and there is no need to deal with it here, except to note the breathless wonder with which Marcia observed these first roaches of hers. Her chair was drawn so close to the sink that she could see the mottling of their oval, unsegmented bodies, the quick scuttering of their thin legs, and the quicker flutter of their antennae. They moved randomly, proceeding nowhere, centered nowhere. They seemed greatly disturbed over nothing. *Perhaps*, Marcia thought, *my presence has a morbid effect on them?*

Only then did she become aware, aware fully, that these were the cockroaches of which she had been warned. Repulsion took hold; her flesh curdled on her bones. She screamed and fell back in her chair, almost upsetting a shelf of odd-lots. Simultaneously the roaches disappeared over the edge of the sink and into the drain.

Mr. Silversmith, coming downstairs to inquire the source of Marcia's alarm, found her supine and unconscious. He sprinkled her face with tapwater, and she awoke with a shudder of nausea. She refused to explain why she had screamed and insisted that she must leave Mr. Silversmith's employ immediately. He, supposing that the pimply stockboy (who was his son) had made a pass at Marcia, paid her for the three days she had worked and let her go without regrets. From that moment on, cockroaches were to be a regular feature of Marcia's existence.

On Thompson Street Marcia was able to reach a sort of stalemate with the cockroaches. She settled into a comfortable routine of pastes and powders, scrubbing and waxing, prevention(she never had even a cup of coffee without washing and drying cup and coffeepot immediately afterward) and ruthless extermination. The only roaches who trespassed upon her two cozy rooms came up from the apartment below, and they did not stay long, you may be sure. Marcia would have complained to the landlady, except that it was the landlady's apartment and her roaches. She had been inside, for a glass of wine on Christmas Eve, and she had to admit that it wasn't exceptionally dirty. It was, in fact, more than commonly clean—but *that* was not enough in New York. If *everyone*, Marcia thought, *took as much care as I, there would be soon be no cockroaches in New York City.*

Then (it was March and Marcia was halfway through her sixth year in the city) the Shchapalovs moved in next door. There were three of them—two men and a woman—and they were old, though exactly how old it was hard to say: they had been aged by more than time. Perhaps they weren't more than forty. The woman, for instance, though she still had brown hair, had a face wrinkly as a prune and was missing several teeth. She would stop Marcia in the hallway or on the street, grabbing hold of her coat sleeve, and talk to her—always a simple lament about the weather, which was too hot or too cold or too wet or too dry. Marcia never knew half of what the old woman was saying, she mumbled so. Then she'd totter off to the grocery with her bagful of empties.

The Shchapalovs, you see, drank. Marcia, who had a rather exaggerated idea of the cost of alcohol (the cheapest thing she could imagine was vodka), wondered where they got the money for all the drinking they did. She knew they didn't work, for on days when Marcia was home with the flu she could hear the three Shchapalovs through the thin wall between their kitchen and hers screaming at each other to exercise their adrenal glands. *They're on welfare*, Marcia decided. Or perhaps the man with only one eye was a veteran on pension.

She didn't so much mind the noise of their arguments (she was seldom home in the afternoon), but she couldn't stand their singing. Early in the evening they'd start in, singing along with the radio stations. Everything they listened to sounded like Guy Lombardo. Later, about eight o'clock they sang *a cappella*. Strange, soulless noises rose and fell like Civil Defense sirens; there were bellowings, bayings and cries. Marcia had heard something like it once on a Folkways record of Czechoslovakian wedding chants. She was quite beside herself whenever the awful noise started up and had to leave the house until they were done. A complaint would do no good: the Shchapalovs had a right to sing at that hour.

Besides, one of the men was said to be related by marriage to the landlady. That's how they got the apartment, which had been used as a storage space until they moved in. Marcia couldn't understand how the three of them could fit into such a little space—just a room-and-a-half with a narrow window opening onto the air shaft. (Marcia had discovered that she could see their entire living space through a hole that had been broken through the wall when the plumbers had installed a sink for the Shchapalovs.)

But if their singing distressed her, *what* was she to do about the roaches? The Shchapalov woman, who was the sister of one man and married to the other—or else the men were brothers and she was the wife of one of them (sometimes, it seemed to Marcia, from the words that came through the walls, that she was married to neither of them—or to both), was a bad housekeeper, and the Shchapalov apartment was soon swarming with roaches. Since Marcia's sink and the Shchapalovs' were fed by the same pipes and emptied into a common drain, a steady overflow of roaches was disgorged into Marcia's immaculate kitchen. She could spray and lay out more poisoned pota-toes; she could scrub and dust and stuff Kleenex tissues into holes where pipes passed through the wall: it was all to no avail. The Shchapalov roaches could always lay another million eggs in the gar-bage bags rotting beneath the Shchapalov sink. In a few days they would be swarming through the pipes and cracks and into Marcia's cupboards. She would lay in bed and watch them (this was possible because Marcia kept a nightlight burning in each room) advancing across the floor and up the walls, trailing the Shchapalovs' filth and disease everywhere they went.

One such evening the roaches were especially bad, and Marcia was trying to muster the resolution to get out of her warm bed and attack them with Roach-It. She had left the windows open from the convic-tion that cockroaches do not like the cold, but she found she liked it much less. When she swallowed, it hurt, and she knew she was coming down with a cold. And all because of *them!*

"*Oh go away!*" she begged. "*Go away! Go away! Get out of my apartment.*"

She addressed the roaches with the same desperate intensity with which she sometimes (though not often in recent years) addressed prayers to the Almighty. Once she had prayed all night long to get rid of her acne, but in the morning it was worse than ever. People in intolerable circumstances will pray to anything. Truly, there are no atheists in foxholes: the men there pray to the bombs that they may land somewhere else.

The only strange thing in Marcia's case is that her prayers were answered. The cockroaches fled from her apartment as quickly as their little legs could carry them—and in straight lines, too. Had they heard her? Had they understood?

Marcia could still see one cockroach coming down from the cupboard. "*Stop!*" she commanded. And it stopped.

At Marcia's spoken command, the cockroach would march up and down, to the left and to the right. Suspecting that her phobia had matured into madness, Marcia left her warm bed, turned on the light, and cautiously approached the roach, which remained motionless, as she had bidden it. "*Wiggle your antennas,*" she commanded. The cockroach wiggled its antennae.

She wondered if they would all obey her and found, within the next few days, that they all would. They would do anything she told them to. They would eat poison out of her hand. Well, not exactly out of her hand, but it amounted to the same thing. They were devoted to her. Slavishly.

It is the end, she thought, *of my roach problem.* But of course it was only the beginning.

Marcia did not question too closesly the reason the roaches obeyed her. She had never much troubled herself with abstract problems. After expending so much time and attention on them, it seemed only natural that she should exercise a certain power over them. However she was wise enough never to speak of this power to anyone else—even to Miss Bismuth at the insurance office. Miss Bismuth read the horoscope magazines and claimed to be able to communicate with her mother, aged sixth-eight, telepathically. Her mother lived in Ohio. But what would Marcia have said: that *she* could communicate telepathically with cockroaches? Impossible.

Nor did Marcia use her power for any other purpose than keeping the cockroaches out of her apartment. Whenever she saw one, she simply commanded it to go to the Shchapalov apartment and stay there. It was surprising then that there were always more roaches coming back through the pipes. Marcia assumed that they were younger generations. Cockroaches are known to breed fast. But it was easy enough to send them back to the Shchapalovs.

"Into their beds," she added as an afterthought. *"Go into their beds."* Disgusting as it was, the idea gave her a queer thrill of pleasure.

The next morning, the Shchapalov woman, smelling a little worse than usual (Whatever was it, Marcia wondered, that they drank?), was waiting at the open door of her apartment. She wanted to speak to Marcia before she left for work. Her housedress was mired from an attempt at scrubbing the floor, and while she sat there talking, she tried to wring out the scrubwater.

"No idea!" she exclaimed. "You ain't got no idea how bad! 'S terrible!"

"What?" Marcia asked, knowing perfectly well what.

"The boogs! Oh, the boogs are just everywhere. Don't you have 'em, sweetheart? I don't know what to do. I try to keep a decent house, God knows—" She lifted her rheumy eyes to heaven, testifying. "—but I don't know what to do." She leaned forward, confidingly. "You won't believe this, sweetheart, but last night . . ." A cockroach began to climb out of the limp strands of hair straggling down into the woman's eyes. ". . . they got into bed with us! Would you believe it? There must have been a hundred of 'em. I said to Osip, I said—what's wrong, sweetheart?"

Marcia, speechless with horror, pointed at the roach, which had almost reached the bridge of the woman's nose. "Yech!" the woman agreed, smashing it and wiping her dirtied thumb on her dirtied dress. "Goddam, boogs! I hate 'em, I swear to God. But what's a person gonna do? Now, what I wanted to ask, sweetheart, is do you have a problem with the boogs! Being as how you're right next door, I thought—" She smiled a confidential smile, as though to say this is just between us ladies. Marcia almost expected a roach to skitter out between her gapped teeth.

"No," she said. "No, I use Black Flag." She backed away from the doorway toward the safety of the stairwell. "Black Flag," she shouted from the foot of the stairs. Her knees trembled so, that she had to hold onto the metal banister for support.

At the insurance office that day, Marcia couldn't keep her mind on her work five minutes at a time. (Her work in the actuarial dividends department consisted of adding up long rows of two-digit numbers on a Burroughs adding machine and checking the similar additions of her co-workers for errors.) She kept thinking of the cockroaches in the tangled hair of the Shchapalov woman, of her bed teeming with roaches, and of other, less concrete horrors on the periphery of consciousness. The numbers swam and swarmed before her eyes, and twice she had to go to the ladies' room, but each time it was a false alarm. Nevertheless, lunchtime found her with no appetite. Instead of going down to the employee cafeteria she went out into the fresh April air and strolled along Twenty-Third Street. Despite the spring, it all seemed to bespeak a sordidness, a festering corruption. The stones of the Flatiron Building oozed damp blackness; the gutters were heaped with soft decay; the smell of burning grease hung in the air outside the cheap restaurants like cigarette smoke in a close room.

The afternoon was worse. Her fingers would not touch the correct numbers on the machine unless she looked at them. One silly phrase kept running through her head: "Something must be done." She had quite forgotten that she had sent the roaches into the Shchapalovs' bed in the first place.

That night, instead of going home immediately, she went to a double feature on Forty-Second Street. She couldn't afford the better movies. Susan Hayward's little boy almost drowned in quicksand. That was the only thing she remembered afterward.

She did something then that she had never done before. She had a drink in a bar. She had two drinks. Nobody bothered her; nobody even looked in her direction. She took a taxi to Thompson Street (the subways weren't safe at that hour) and arrived at her door by eleven o'clock. She didn't have anything left for a tip. The taxi driver said he understood.

There was a light on under the Shchapalovs' door, and they were singing. It was eleven o'clock. "Something must be done," Marcia whispered to herself earnestly. "Something must be *done*."

Without turning on her own light, without even taking off her new spring jacket from Ohrbach's, Marcia got down on her knees and crawled under the sink. She tore out the Kleenexes she had stuffed into the cracks around the pipes.

There they were, the three of them, the Shchapalovs, drinking, the woman plumped on the lap of the one-eyed man, and the other man, in a dirty undershirt, stamping his foot on the floor to accompany the loud discords of their song. Horrible. They were drinking of course, she might have known it, and now the woman pressed her roachy mouth against the mouth of the one-eyed man—kiss, kiss. Horrible, horrible. Marcia's hands knotted into her mouse-colored hair, and she thought: *the filth, the disease!* Why, they hadn't learned a thing from last night!

Some time later (Marcia had lost track of time) the overhead light in the Shchapalovs' apartment was turned off. Marcia waited till they made no more noise. "Now," Marcia said, "all of you.

"All of you in this building, all of you that can hear me, gather round the bed, but wait a little while yet. Patience. All of you . . ." The words of her command fell apart into little fragments, which she told like the beads of a rosary—like brown ovoid wooden beads. ". . . gather round . . . wait a little while yet . . . all of you . . . patience . . . gather round . . . " Her hand stroked the cold water pipes rhythmically, and it seemed that she could hear them—gathering, scuttering up through the walls, coming out of the cupboards, the garbage bags—a host, an army, and she was their absolute queen.

"Now!" she said. "Mount them! Cover them! Devour them!"

There was no doubt that she could hear them now. She heard them quite palpably. Their sound was like grass in the wind, like the first stirrings of gravel dumped from a truck. Then there was the

Shchapalov woman's scream, and curses from the men, such terrible curses that Marcia could hardly bear to listen.

A light went on, and Marcia could see them, the roaches, everywhere. Every surface, the walls, the floors, the shabby sticks of furniture, was mottly thick with *Blattelae germanicae.* There was more than a single thickness.

The Shchapalov woman, standing up in her bed, screamed monotonously. Her pink rayon nightgown was speckled with brown-black dots. Her knobby fingers tried to brush bugs out of her hair, off her face. The man in the undershirt who a few minutes before had been stomping his feet to the music stomped now more urgently, one hand still holding onto the lightcord. Soon the floor was slimy with crushed roaches, and he slipped. The light went out. The women's scream took on a rather choked quality, as though . . .

But Marcia wouldn't think of that. "Enough,"she whispered. "No more. Stop."

She crawled away from the sink, across the room on to her bed, which tried, with a few tawdry cushions, to dissemble itself as a couch for the daytime. Her breathing came hard, and there was a curious constriction in her throat. She was sweating incontinently.

From the Shchapalovs' room came scuffling sounds, a door banged, running feet, and then a louder, muffled noise, perhaps a body falling downstairs. The landlady's voice: "What the hell do you think you're—" Other voices overriding hers. Incoherences, and footsteps returning up the stairs. Once more the landlady: "There ain't no *boogs* here, for heaven's sake. The boogs is in your heads. You've got the d.t.'s, that's what. And it wouldn't be any wonder, if there were boogs. The place is filthy. Look at that crap on the floor. Filth! I've stood just about enough from you. Tomorrow you move out, hear? This *used* to be a decent building."

The Shchapalovs did not protest their eviction. Indeed they did not wait for the morrow to leave. They quitted their apartment with only a suitcase, a laundry bag, and an electric toaster. Marcia watched them go down the steps through her half-opened door. *It's done,* she thought. It's all *over.*

With a sigh of almost sensual pleasure, she turned on the lamp beside the bed, then the other lamps. The room gleamed immaculately. Deciding to celebrate her victory, she went to the cupboard, where she kept a bottle of crème de menthe.

The cupboard was full of roaches.

She had not told them where to go, where *not* to go, when they left the Shchapalov apartment. It was her own fault.

The great silent mass of roaches regarded Marcia calmly, and it seemed to the distracted girl that she could read *their* thoughts, their thought rather, for they had but a single thought. She could read it as clearly as she could read the illuminated billboard for Chock Full O'Nuts outside her window. It was delicate as music issuing from a thousand tiny pipes. It was an ancient music box open after centuries of silence: "We love you we love you we love you we love you."

Something strange happened inside Marcia then, something unprecedented: she responded.

"I love you too," she replied. "Oh, I love you. Come to me, all of you. Come to me. I love you. Come to me. I love you. Come to me."

From every corner of Manhattan, from the crumbling walls of Harlem, from restaurants on Fifty-Sixth Street, from warehouses along the river, from sewers and from orange peels moldering in garbage cans, the loving roaches came forth and began to crawl toward their mistress.

The Jam

HENRY SLESAR

A small gem by yet another underappreciated talent, this story should haunt you every time you find yourself caught in heavy traffic.

They left Stukey's pad around eight in the morning; that was the kind of weekend it had been. Early to bed, early to rise. Stukey laughed, squinting through the dirt-stained windshield of the battered Ford, pushing the pedal until the needle swung twenty, thirty miles over the speed limit. It was all Mitch's fault, but Mitch, curled up on the seat beside him like an embryo in a black leather womb, didn't seem to care. He was hurting too much, needing the quick jab of the sharp sweet point and the hot flow of the stuff in his veins. Man, what a weekend, Stukey thought, and it wasn't over yet. The fix was out there, someplace in the wilds of New Jersey, and Stukey, who never touched the filthy stuff himself, was playing good Samaritan. He hunched over the wheel like Indianapolis, pounding the horn with the heel of his right hand, shouting at the passing cars to *move over, move over you sonofabitch, watch where you're going, stupid, pull over, pull over, you lousy . . .*

"You tell 'em, man," Mitch said softly, "you tell 'em what to do."

Stukey didn't tell them, he showed them. He skinned the paint off a Buick as he snaked in and out of the line, and crowded so close to the tail of an MG that he could have run right over the little red wagon. Mitch began to giggle, urging him on, forgetting for the moment his destination and his need, delighting in the way Stukey used the car like a buzz saw, slicing a path through the squares in their Sunday driving stupor. "Look out, man," Mitch cackled, "here comes old Stukey, here comes nothin'."

The traffic artery was starting to clot at the entrance to the tunnel, and Stukey poured it on, jockeying the car first left and then right, grinning at the competitive game. Nobody had a chance to win with Stukey at the controls; Stukey could just shut his eyes and gun her; nobody else could do that. They made the tunnel entrance after sideswiping a big yellow Caddy, an episode that made Mitch laugh aloud with glee. They both felt better after that, and the tunnel was cool after the hot morning sun. Stukey relaxed a little, and Mitch stopped his low-pitched giggling, content to stare hypnotically at the blur of white tiles.

"I hope we find that fix, man," Mitch said dreamily. "My cousin, he says that's the place to go. How long you think, Stukey? How long?"

Whish! A Chevy blasted by him on the other lane, and Stukey swore. *Whish!* went an old Oldsmobile, and Stukey bore down on the accelerator, wanting his revenge on the open road outside the tunnel. But the tunnel wound on, endlessly, longer than it ever had before. It was getting hot and hard to breathe; little pimples of sweat covered his face and trickled down into his leather collar; under the brass-studded coat, the sport shirt clung damply to his back and underarms. Mitch started to whine, and got that wide-eyed fishmouth look of his, and he gasped: "Man, I'm suffocating. I'm passing out . . ."

"What do you want me to do?" Stukey yelled. Still the tunnel wound on. *Whish!* went the cars in the parallel lane, and Stukey cursed his bad choice, cursed the heat, cursed Mitch, cursed all the Sundays that ever were. He shot a look at the balcony where the cops patrolled the traffic, and decided to take a chance. He slowed the car down to thirty-five, and yanked the wheel sharply to the right to slip the car into a faster lane, right in front of a big, children-filled station wagon. Even in the tunnel roar they could hear its driver's angry shout, and Stukey told him what he could do with his station wagon and his children. Still the tunnel wound on.

They saw the hot glare of daylight at the exit. Mitch moaned in relief, but nothing could soften Stukey's ire. They came out of the tunnel and turned onto the highway, only to jerk to a halt behind a station wagon with a smelly exhaust. "Come on, come on!" Stukey muttered, and blew his horn. But the horn didn't start the cars moving, and Stukey, swearing, opened the door and had himself a look.

"Oh, man, man, they're stacked up for miles!" he groaned. "You wouldn't believe it, you wouldn't think it possible . . ."

"What is it?" Mitch said, stirring in his seat. "What is it? An accident?"

"I dunno, I can't see a thing. But they just ain't movin', not a foot—"

"I'm sick," Mitch groaned. "I'm sick, Stukey."

"Shut up! Shut up!" Stukey said, hopping out of the car to stare at the sight again, at the ribbon of automobiles vanishing into a horizon ten, fifteen miles away. Like one enormous reptile it curled over the highway, a snake with multicolored skin, lying asleep under the hot sun. He climbed back in again, and the station wagon moved an inch, a foot, and greedily, he stomped the gas pedal to gobble up the gap. A trooper on a motorcycle bounced between the lanes, and Stukey leaned out of the window to shout at him, inquiring; he rumbled on implacably. The heat got worse, furnacelike and scorching, making him yelp when his hands touched metal. Savagely, Stukey hit the horn again, and heard a dim chorus ahead. Every few minutes, the station wagon jumped, and every few minutes, Stukey closed the gap. But an hour accumulated, and more, and they could still see the tunnel exit behind them. Mitch was whimpering now, and Stukey climbed in and out of the car like a madman, his clothes sopping with sweat, his eyes wild, cursing whenever he hit the gas pedal and crawled another inch, another foot forward . . .

"A cop! A cop!" he heard Mitch scream as a trooper, on foot, marched past the window. Stukey opened the car door and caught the uniformed arm. "Help us, will ya?" he pleaded. "What the hell's going on here? How do we get outa this?"

"You don't," the trooper said curtly. "You can't get off anyplace. Just stick it out, mac."

"We'll even leave the goddamn *car*. We'll *walk*, for God's sake. I don't care about the goddamn *car* . . ."

"Sorry, mister. Nobody's allowed off the highway, even on foot. You can't leave this heap here, don't you know that?" He studied Stukey's sweaty face, and grinned suddenly. "Oh, I get it. You're new here, ain't you?"

"What do you mean, new?"

"I thought I never saw you in the Jam before, pal. Well, take it easy, fella."

"How long?" Stukey said hoarsely. "How long you think?"

"That's a stupid question," the trooper sneered. "Forever, of course. Eternity. Eternity. Where the hell do you think you are?" He jabbed a finger into Stukey's chest. "But don't give *me* a hard time, buster. That was your *own* wreck back there."

"Wreck?" Mitch rasped from inside the car. "What wreck? What's he talking about, man?"

"The wreck you had in the tunnel." He waved his gloved hand

toward the horizon. "That's where *all* these jokers come from, the tunnel wrecks. If you think this is bad, you ought to see the Jam on the turnpike."

"Wreck? Wreck?" Mitch screamed, as Stukey climbed behind the wheel. "What's he talking about wrecks for, Stukey?"

"Shut up, shut up!" Stukey sobbed, pounding his foot on the gas pedal to gain yet another inch of road. "We gotta get outa here, we gotta get out!" But even when the station wagon jerked forward once more, he knew he was asking for too much, too late.

Black Wind

BILL PRONZINI

One of the last places you might expect to find horror is in the marital relationship. But consider. Men and women may marry for love, but love can turn to hate, and hate is a breeding ground for the seeds of horror. Especially if those seeds have been carried long and far on a "Black Wind" . . .

It was one of those freezing late-November nights, just before the winter snows, when a funny east wind comes howling down out of the mountains and across Woodbine Lake a quarter-mile from the village. The sound that wind makes is something hellish, full of screams and wailings that can raise the hackles on your neck if you're not used to it. In the old days the Indians who used to live around here called it a "black wind"; they believed that it carried the voices of evil spirits, and that if you listened to it long enough it could drive you mad.

Well, there are a lot of superstitions in our part of upstate New York; nobody pays much mind to them in this modern age. Or if they do, they won't admit it even to themselves. The fact is, though, that when the black wind blows the local folks stay pretty close to home and the village, like as not, is deserted after dusk.

That was the way it was on this night. I hadn't had a customer in my diner in more than an hour, since just before seven o'clock, and I had about decided to close up early and go on home. To a glass of brandy and a good hot fire.

I was pouring myself a last cup of coffee when the headlights swung into the diner's parking lot.

They whipped in fast, off the county highway, and I heard the squeal of brakes on the gravel just out front. Kids, I thought, because that was the way a lot of them drove, even around here—fast and a little reckless. But it wasn't kids. It turned out instead to be a man and a woman in their late thirties, strangers, both of them bundled up in winter coats and mufflers, the woman carrying a big fancy alligator purse.

The wind came in with them, shrieking and swirling. I could feel the

403

numbing chill of it even in the few seconds the door was open; it cuts through you like the blade of a knife, that wind, right straight to the bone.

The man clumped immediately to where I was behind the counter, letting the woman close the door. He was handsome in a suave, barbered city way; but his face was closed up into a mask of controlled rage.

"Coffee," he said. The word came out in a voice that matched his expression—hard and angry, like a threat.

"Sure thing. Two coffees."

"One coffee," he said. "Let her order her own."

The woman had come up on his left, but not close to him—one stool between them. She was nice-looking in the same kind of made-up, city way. Or she would have been if her face wasn't pinched up worse than his; the skin across her cheekbones was stretched so tight it seemed ready to split. Her eyes glistened like a pair of wet stones and didn't blink at all.

"Black coffee," she said to me.

I looked at her, at him, and I started to feel a little uneasy. There was a kind of savage tension between them, thick and crackling; I could feel it like static electricity. I wet my lips, not saying anything, and reached behind me for the coffee pot and two mugs.

The man said, "I'll have a ham-and-cheese sandwich on rye bread. No mustard, no mayonnaise; just butter. Make it to go."

"Yes, sir. How about you, ma'am?"

"Tuna fish on white," she said thinly. She had close-cropped blonde hair, wind-tangled under a loose scarf; she kept brushing at it with an agitated hand. "I'll eat here."

"No, she won't," the man said to me. "Make it to go, just like mine."

She threw him an ugly look. "I want to eat here."

"Fine," he said—to me again; it was as if she wasn't there. "But I'm leaving in five minutes, as soon as I drink my coffee. I want that ham-and-cheese ready by then."

"Yes, sir."

I finished pouring out the coffee and set the two mugs on the counter. The man took his, swung around, and stomped over to one of the tables. He sat down and stared at the door, blowing into the mug, using it to warm his hands.

"All right," the woman said, "all right, all right. All right." Four times like that, all to herself. Her eyes had cold little lights in them now, like spots of foxfire.

I said hesitantly, "Ma'am? Do you still want the tuna sandwich to eat here?"

She blinked then, for the first time, and focused on me. "No. To hell with it. I don't want anything to eat." She caught up her mug and took it to another of the tables, two away from the one he was sitting at.

I went down to the sandwich board and got out two pieces of rye bread and spread them with butter. The stillness in there had a strained feel, made almost eerie by the constant wailing outside. I could feel myself getting more jittery as the seconds passed.

While I sliced ham I watched the two of them at the tables—him still staring at the door, drinking his coffee in quick angry sips; her facing the other way, her hands fisted in her lap, the steam from her cup spiraling up around her face. Well-off married couple from New York City, I thought: they were both wearing the same type of expensive wedding ring. On their way to a weekend in the mountains, maybe, or up to Canada for a few days. And they'd had a hell of a fight over something, the way married people do on long tiring drives; that was all there was to it.

Except that that *wasn't* all there was to it.

I've owned this diner thirty years and I've seen a lot of folks come and go in that time; a lot of tourists from the city, with all sorts of marital problems. But I'd never seen any like these two. That tension between them wasn't anything fresh-born, wasn't just the brief and meaningless aftermath of a squabble. No, there was real hatred on both sides—the kind that builds and builds, seething, over long bitter weeks or months or even years. The kind that's liable to explode some day.

Well, it wasn't really any of my business. Not unless the blowup happened in here, it wasn't, and that wasn't likely. Or so I kept telling myself. But I was a little worried just the same. On a night like this, with the damned black wind blowing and playing hell with people's nerves, anything could happen. Anything at all.

I finished making the sandwich, cut it in half, and plastic-bagged it. Just as I slid it into a paper sack, there was a loud banging noise from across the room that made me jump half a foot; it sounded like a pistol shot. But it had only been the man slamming his empty mug down on the table.

I took a breath, let it out silently. He scraped back his chair as I did that, stood up, and jammed his hands into his coat pockets. Without looking at her, he said to the woman, "You pay for the food," and started past her table toward the restrooms in the rear.

She said, "Why the hell should I pay for it?"

He paused and glared back at her. "You've got all the money."

"I've got all the money? Oh, that's a laugh. *I've* got all the money!"

"Go on, keep it up." Then in a louder voice, as if he wanted to make sure I heard, he said, "Bitch." And stalked away from her.

She watched him until he was gone inside the corridor leading to the restrooms; she was as rigid as a chunk of wood. She sat that way for another five or six seconds, until the wind gusted outside, thudded against the door and the window like something trying to break in. Jerkily she got to her feet and came over to where I was at the sandwich board. Those cold lights still glowed in her eyes.

"Is his sandwich ready?"

I nodded and made myself smile. "Will that be all, ma'am?"

"No. I've changed my mind. I want something to eat too." She leaned forward and stared at the glass pastry container on the back counter. "What kind of pie is that?"

"Cinnamon apple."

"I'll have a piece of it."

"Okay—sure. Just one?"

"Yes. Just one."

I turned back there, got the pie out, cut a slice, and wrapped it in waxed paper. When I came around with it she was rummaging in her purse, getting her wallet out. Back in the restroom area, I heard the man's hard, heavy steps; in the next second he appeared. And headed straight for the door.

The woman said, "How much do I owe you?"

I put the pie into the paper sack with the sandwich, and the sack on the counter. "That'll be three eighty."

The man opened the door; the wind came shrieking in, eddying drafts of icy air. He went right on out, not even glancing at the woman or me, and slammed the door shut behind him.

She laid a five-dollar bill on the counter. Caught up the sack, pivoted, and started for the door.

"Ma'am?" I said. "You've got change coming."

She must have heard me, but she didn't look back and she didn't slow up. The pair of headlights came on out front, slicing pale wedges from the darkness; through the front window I could see the evergreens at the far edge of the lot, thick swaying shadows bent almost double by the wind. The shrieking rose again for two or three seconds, then fell back to a muted whine; she was gone.

I had never been gladder or more relieved to see customers go. I let out another breath, picked up the fiver, and moved over to the cash register. Outside, above the thrumming and wailing, the car engine revved up to a roar and there was the ratcheting noise of tires spinning on gravel. The headlights shot around and probed out toward the county highway.

Time now to close up and go home, all right; I wanted a glass of brandy and a good hot fire more than ever. I went around to the tables they'd used, to gather up the coffee cups. But as much as I wanted to forget the two of them, I couldn't seem to get them out of my mind. Especially the woman.

I kept seeing those eyes of hers, cold and hateful like the wind, as if there was a black wind blowing inside her, too, and she'd been listening to it too long. I kept seeing her lean forward across the counter and stare at the pastry container. And I kept seeing her rummage in that big alligator purse when I turned around with the slice of pie. Something funny about the way she'd been doing that. As if she hadn't just been getting her wallet out to pay me. As if she'd been—

Oh my God, I thought.

I ran back behind the counter. Then I ran out again to the door, threw it open, and stumbled onto the gravel lot. But they were long gone; the night was a solid ebony wall.

I didn't know what to do. What could I do? Maybe she'd done what I suspicioned, and maybe she hadn't; I couldn't be sure because I don't keep an inventory on the slots of utensils behind the sandwich board. And I didn't know who they were or where they were going. I didn't even know what kind of car they were riding in.

I kept on standing there, chills racing up and down my back, listening to that black wind scream and scream around me. Feeling the cold sharp edge of it cut into my bare flesh, cut straight to the bone.

Just like the blade of a knife . . .

The Road to Mictlantecutli

ADOBE JAMES

In the realm of the horror story, as in other realms, there are unsung heroes—writers whose work is consistently fresh, evocative and certain to raise a goosebump or two, but who have consistently (and inexplicably) been overlooked by anthologists and aficionados. Adobe James (the pseudonym of a California teacher, novelist and story-teller) is such a writer. Most of his work appeared in the men's magazines of the 1960's, and only a handful of his stories has had book publication over the years. The appearance in these pages of "The Road to Mictlantecutli," it is hoped, will change all of that. This hellish excursion into the supernatural may be the best of his tales, and anyone who reads it is not likely to forget it. Or the name of Adobe James.

The ribbon of asphalt—once black, now gray from the years of unrelenting sun—stretched out like a never-ending arrow shaft; in the distance, mirages—like dreams—sprang into life, shimmered and silently dissolved at the approach of the speeding automobile.

Rivulets of sweat poured down the face of Hernandez, the driver. Earlier in the day—when they had been in the good land—he had been congenial, expansive, even sympathetic. Now he drove quickly, apprehensively, almost angrily, not wanting to be caught in the bad land after sunset.

"Semejante los buitres no tienen gordo en este distrito execrable," he muttered, squinting his eyes against the glare of the late afternoon sun.

Seated next to him, the man called Morgan smiled at the remark. "Even the vultures are skinny in this lousy land." Hernandez had a sense of humor; for that reason—and that reason, alone—Morgan was sorry that it was necessary to kill him. But Hernandez was a policeman—a Mexican federal cop—who was taking him back to the United States border where Morgan would be handed over to the criminal courts to hang, twitching, at the end of a long Texan rope.

No, Morgan thought, and knew the thought to be true, they won't hang me this time; next time, maybe, but not now. Hernandez was stupid, and it would be only a matter of time before he made a mistake. Completely relaxed, Morgan dozed, his manacled hands lying docilely in his lap . . . waiting . . . waiting . . . waiting.

It was almost five o'clock before Morgan, with all the keen instincts of the hunted, sensed his moment of freedom might be approaching. Hernandez was becoming uncomfortable—the result of two bottles of beer after lunch. The policeman would be stopping soon. Morgan would make his move then.

On their right, a range of gently sloping foothills gradually had been rising from the flat surface of the desert.

Morgan asked, pretending boredom, "Anything over there?"

Hernandez sighed. "*Quien sabe?* Who knows? The plateau on the other side of the mountain range is supposed to be worse than this side. *Es imposible!* No one can exist there except a few wild Indians who speak a language that was old long before the Aztecs came. It's uncharted, untamed, uncivilized . . . ruled by Mictlantecutli."

Now, slowly, as shadows lengthened, the land was changing all around them. For the first time since leaving Agua Lodoso, they could see some signs of vegetation—mesquite bushes, cactus, shrub brush. Ahead, standing like a lonely outpost sentinel, was a giant Saguaro cactus almost fifty feet high. Hernandez slowed the car and stopped in the shade of the plant. "Stretch your legs if you want, *amigo*, this is the last stop before Santa Maria."

Hernandez got out, walked around the car, and opened the door for his prisoner. Morgan slipped out and stood, stretching like a cat. While the Mexican was relieving himself against the cactus, Morgan walked over to what had first appeared to be a crude cross stuck in the sand. He peered at it; the cross was an old sign, weather-beaten and pock-marked by the talons of vultures who had used it as a roosting place.

Hernandez strolled over and joined him. He, too, stared at the sign, his lips pursed in puzzlement under his black moustaches. "Linaculan—one hundred twenty kilometers! I did not know there was a road . . ." Then he brightened, "Ah, *si!* I remember now. This must be the old *Real Militar* leading from the interior to the east coast."

That was all Morgan needed to know. If Linaculan was on the road to the east coast, then Linaculan meant freedom. He yawned again, his impassive face a portrait of indifference.

"Ready, *amigo!*"

Morgan nodded. "As ready as any man is to be hung."

The Mexican laughed, coughed and spat in the dust. "Come on then." He led the way towards the car and stood by its open door waiting for his prisoner. Morgan shambled towards him, his shoulders slumped forward as if protecting him from the oppressive heat of the late afternoon. When he did move, it was as a snake strikes an unsuspecting victim. His manacled hands came down, viciously, on top of Hernandez's head. The policeman moaned and toppled to the ground. Morgan was on him immediately; his hands seeking, and finding, the gun he knew was in the Mexican's waistband. Then he stood upright—about four paces away from the figure on the ground.

Hernandez shook his head groggily, blinked his eyes and started to rise. He had struggled to his knees when Morgan's cold voice froze him into immobility.

Morgan said, "Good-by, Hernandez. No hard feelings."

The Mexican looked up; he saw death. "*Dios . . . Dios.* No!" That was as far as he got; the .44 slug caught him above the ridge of the left eye and he was thrown ten feet backward by the force of the bullet. He shuddered once, his legs beat a small tattoo in the dust and then he was still.

Morgan walked over, shaking his head mournfully, "I sure had you pegged wrong, pal. You didn't look like the kind of a coward who would beg for his life." He sighed at the dead man's lack of dignity—feeling almost as if he had been betrayed by a weak-willed friend.

He squatted and began searching the body. There was a wallet containing a badge, five hundred pesos and a color photograph of an overweight Mexican woman surrounded by three laughing small girls and two self-consciously grinning young boys. Morgan grunted non-committally and continued his search.

He found the handcuff keys taped to the calloused white soles of the dead man's foot.

Twilight was beginning to turn the Mexican hills to a red bronze when Morgan loaded Hernandez in the trunk of the car. He strolled back over to the road sign. After the mileage there were the words, "*Cuidado—Peligroso,*" "Take Heed—Dangerous." What a joke, he thought. Could anything be more dangerous than being hung? Or playing the part of a fox hounded by international police? He had been trapped and sentenced to die four different times in his life; and yet he was still a free man. And . . . there could be nothing, absolutely nothing, ahead of him on this insignificant dirt road that could match Morgan's wits, Morgan's reactions or Morgan's gun!

He got behind the wheel of the car and turned on to the road. It was rougher than it had appeared at first, but nonetheless, he made good time for the first thirty miles, and was able to drive fast enough that the dust remained spread out behind him like the brown tail of a comet hanging luminously in the fading light.

The sun dropped below the horizon line, but then, as Morgan began climbing the range of hills, it came back into sight once more—looking like the malevolent inflamed eye of a god angry at being awakened again.

Morgan crested the hill and began a downward ascent into a valley. Here darkness was embracing the land. He stopped once, where a *barranca* sloped down from the road, and threw over Hernandez's body. He watched it, rolling and tumbling, until it finally disappeared from sight in the black shadows beneath a stand of mesquite bushes some hundred feet below the road.

Morgan drove on. He turned on the car lights as night closed in swiftly around him.

Abruptly, as he reached the valley floor, he began cursing, for the road was really no longer a road—just a scarred and broken path leading across the wilderness.

The next five kilometers took at least fifteen thousand miles out of the automobile Morgan was forced to shift down to first gear as potholes—deep as wading pools—wrecked the front-end alignment and suspension system. Jagged hidden boulders in the middle of the road scraped at the undercarriage with a thousand steel fingers.

And dust! Dust was everywhere . . . it hung like a dark ominous cloud all about him; it coated the inside of the car as though it had been sprayed with beige velvet. It crept into Morgan's nostrils and throat until it became painful to breathe or swallow.

Minutes later, over the smell of dust, came the odor of hot water—steam—and he knew the cooling system had ruptured somewhere. It was then Morgan realized the car would never make it to Linaculan. By the last barely perceptible horizon glow, he searched the landscape for some evidence of life . . . and saw only the grotesque silhouettes of cactus and stunted desert brush.

The speedometer indicated that he had traveled forty-four miles when his bouncing-weaving headlights picked up the solitary figure of a priest walking slowly alongside the road. Morgan's eyes narrowed as he weighed the value of offering a ride to the padre. But that would be stupid, he thought; the man could be a *bandido* who would produce, and skillfully use, a knife while Morgan was concentrating on the road.

The padre loomed up larger in the headlights. He did not turn towards the car; it seemed as though he were totally unaware of the car's approach.

Morgan passed without slowing. The figure was lost immediately in the dust and blackness of the Mexican night.

Suddenly, just as though several automatic relays had clicked open somewhere in his brain, all of Morgan's instincts were screaming at him. Something was wrong—terribly wrong. A trap of some sort had been entered. The feeling was familiar; there had been other traps before. Unafraid, he grinned wryly, pulled the gun from his pocket and laid it on the seat beside him in preparation.

The next three miles seemed endless as he waited, almost eagerly, for the trap to swing shut. When nothing happened, he grew irritable and began cursing his imagination. The smell of hot oil and steam had grown humidly overpowering, and the engine was beginning to labor. Morgan glanced down at the temperature gauge and the needle had long since climbed into the red danger zone.

And, it was at this moment, while his attention was distracted, that the left front wheel slammed into a jagged rock which ripped through the tire's sidewall. The vehicle began bucking and weaving from side to side like a wild enraged animal. Morgan hit his brakes, knowing it was too late. The car skidded sideways on the gravel, swerved to the right, teetered for a second on an embankment and then—almost as if it were a movie being projected in slow motion—rolled end over end down the incline.

The last thing Morgan saw was a monstrous boulder looming up in the night like some huge basalt fist of God.

For a long time after he regained consciousness, Morgan lay still with his eyes closed. Someone had wiped his forehead and spoken to him. A man! Possibly . . . the priest? He listened to the man's coarse breathing; there was no other sound. They were alone.

Morgan opened his eyes. It was dark, but not as dark as before. A little moonlight was seeping through the high thin clouds. The priest—black of clothes and dark of face—was beside him.

"*Señor*, you are all right?"

Morgan flexed his leg muscles, moved his ankles, moved his shoulders and turned his head from side to side. There were no aches, no pains; he felt surprisingly good. Well, no sense in letting the other man know; let the priest believe Morgan had injured his back and was incapable of rapid movement . . . then, when he had to move fast, the other would be unprepared.

"I hurt my back," he said.

"Can you stand?"

"I think so. Help me."

The priest reached out; Morgan took the proffered hand, and, groaning audibly, stood erect.

"You are fortunate that I came along."

"Yes I am grateful." Morgan felt in his pocket. The wallet was still there; the gun was gone, or had it been in his pocket? Then he remembered, it had been on the seat beside him. Well, no chance of finding it in the darkness . . . and there would always be other weapons.

"Where were you going?" the priest asked.

"To Linaculan."

"Oh yes . . . a fine old city." The priest was standing quite close to Morgan, staring at the American. The moon slipped in and out of the clouds. There was a moment of light, only a moment, but enough. Suddenly, for the first time in many years, Morgan was afraid . . . frightened by the padre's eyes; they were too black, too piercing, too fierce for a clergyman.

Morgan stepped back three paces—far enough away from the priest that the other man's eyes were lost in the darkness.

"You need not fear," the priest said quietly, "I cannot harm you. I can only help you."

It sounded sincere. Some of Morgan's nervousness began to abate. Mentally, he sniffed the wind; the odor of the trap was there, but not as strong as before. After a few moments, some of the old cockiness returned. Where do we go from here? he thought. He was at least halfway towards Linaculan, so it would seem prudent to continue on, unless . . . there would be other transportation before then.

Morgan asked, "Is Linaculan the nearest town?"

"Yes."

"Is that where you were going?"

"No."

Hopefully then, "Do you have a church nearby?"

"No. But I frequently trod this road."

"For Christ's sake," Morgan exclaimed, "why walk this miserable road?"

"For the very reason you mentioned—for Christ's sake."

Now Morgan was completely at ease. The padre was harmless. A bit of a nut, perhaps, but harmless. "Well," he said almost jauntily, "I've got a long walk ahead of me. See you."

Morgan thought he saw the priest's expression soften with the remark. "I will walk part way with you," the churchman said.

"Suit yourself, padre. My name's . . . Dan Morgan. I'm an American."

"Yes . . . I know."

The answer surprised Morgan for a moment; then he felt his guard rising again. Obviously the priest had gone through his belongings while he was unconscious . . . and perhaps that was where the gun had wound up.

They began walking in silence. The moon—that glob of cold white light—won its battle with the clouds and now shone brightly behind them. Long slender shadows raced along the road in front of the two men. The folds of the padre's cassock made whispering noises with each stride he took; his sandals went slap-slap-slap in the thick dust of the road.

In an effort to make conversation, Morgan asked, "How far is Linaculan from here?"

"A great distance."

"But," Morgan exploded, "I thought it was only about another fifty kilometers."

"The candlelights of Linaculan are fifty-four kilometers from the point of your crash."

Well, that was nice to know anyway. With luck, Morgan could make the thirty miles by tomorrow afternoon . . . and then it would be a simple matter to arrange other transportation. He began taking longer strides; the priest kept pace beside him.

In time, the moon was cut off by a range of hills. Their shadows disappeared. The darkness that came in around them now was a tangible thing, warm, disquieting, fearful as the interior of a locked coffin. Morgan glanced at his watch. The luminous hands had stopped at eight eighteen; apparently something snapped when the crash occurred. He didn't know how long he had been unconscious, but they had been walking for at least two hours . . . so, perhaps, it was around midnight.

They plodded on, two dark figures—shadows almost—walking a desolate road. They climbed a short hill and were bathed in moonlight again. Morgan liked that. The darkness had been too dark; it seemed to him that there were things—unseen, unheard, unreal—out there beyond the moonlight.

They started down the other side of the hill, and night crept back . . .

"Don't you have any lights at all in this godforsaken place?" Morgan asked irritably.

The padre did not answer. Morgan repeated the question, and his voice was full of frustrated threat.

Still there was no reply. Morgan shrugged and mentally said, "To hell with you, my sullen Catholic friend. I'll take care of you later."

The road led down the far side of the hill. Now the horribly oppressive darkness of the claustrophobic closed in menacingly . . . it seemed to billow like impenetrable black smoke. For the moment, Morgan was glad the priest—or whatever the other man was, *bandido*, lunatic, killer—was beside him.

They were in the fearful gully for a long time before reaching another hill—this time, no moonlight greeted them; the only illumination was the hollow glow from behind the horizon clouds. It was enough to show a fork in the road.

The priest stopped. The fierce black pupils of his eyes had grown large; so large, in fact, there seemed to be no longer any white to his eyes at all. He stretched out his arms to adjust his cassock, and at that moment looked like some evil black praying mantis about to devour a victim. Even in the semi-darkness, he cast a shadow . . . a black elongated shadow of the cross.

And now, the cornered killer instinct took hold of Morgan. "Answer my question," he snarled. "Which way to Linaculan?"

"Have you so little faith?"

Morgan's voice was shaking in fury, "Listen, you surly bastard! You've refused to answer my questions . . . or even make conversation. What does faith have to do with it? Just tell me how much further I have to go to get to Linaculan; that's all I want from you. No psalm singing, no preaching. Nothing! Understand?"

"You still have a great distance to go . . . " his voice trailed off, and Morgan sensed a change in the padre's attitude. A moment later, Morgan heard it too . . . the far-off drumbeat of a horse's hooves.

The moon, as if curious, parted the clouds for the last time. There was only a shadow moving across the landscape at first, but as the horse came nearer, Morgan could see the animal, its mane and tail rippling like black flags straining at their halyards. It was a magnificent beast, quite the largest he had ever seen—coal black as the midnight and spirited as a thunderhead.

What really took Morgan's breath away, however, was the girl. She rode the animal as though she were an integral part of it. The moonlight played with her, for she was dressed completely in white, from boots and jodhpurs to the form-fitting long-sleeved blouse and Spanish *grandee* hat. Her hair, though, was black—black as a raven's wing and it hung like a soft ebony cloud from her shoulders.

Savagely, she reined the stallion to a halt in front of the two men. The horse reared; Morgan jumped back nervously, but the priest stood his ground.

"Well, padre," she said, smiling and—at the same time—slapping her jodhpurs with a riding whip, "I see you have taken another unfortunate under your wing." She put an odd emphasis on the word **unfortunate**; Morgan didn't know whether to be angry or puzzled. He waited, silently watching the dramatic by-play going on between the two people. Perhaps the entire thing was elaborately staged—all part of the trap. It was of no matter—there was no immediate danger to him. So, for the moment, he was content to merely stand and enjoy the woman's proud body.

In time, the girl became aware of Morgan's stare; her own eyes, answering, were as bold and insolent as the man's. She threw back her head and laughed throatily, "You are in bad hands, my American friend. This *hombre* here," she nodded contemptuously towards the priest, "is called 'old bad luck' by my people. Each time he is on the road, there is an accident. You have had trouble . . . no?"

Morgan nodded once, then glanced sideways at the priest.

The padre, however, was watching the girl. She laughed under his scrutiny, "Don't look so angry, old man. You can't frighten me. Why don't you run along now; I'll see that our American friend reaches his destination."

The priest held out his hand to Morgan. "You must not go with her. She is evil. Evil personified." He made three crosses in the air.

There was no doubt in Morgan's mind about his decision. The padre had said she was "evil"; coming from a priest, that was a real recommendation. Besides, only an idiot would continue to walk the dark road when there was a chance to ride, a chance for pleasant conversation, a chance—really, a promise if he had correctly interpreted her look—for even more! He hesitated, though, still a wild hunted animal wary of the trap.

The girl gently patted the sweating neck of her horse. "Where are you going?"

"Linaculan," Morgan answered.

"That isn't too far away. Come on, I'll give you a ride to Mictlantecutli's ranch . . . you can call for help from there." Her lips were half-parted; she seemed almost breathless as she awaited his answer.

Morgan turned to the priest, "Well, thanks for the company, padre. See you around sometime."

The priest took two quick steps towards Morgan, and put out his hands, beseeching, "Stay at my side. She is evil, I say."

The girl laughed delightedly. "It's two against one, churchman. You've lost another victim."

"Victim?" Morgan's eyes narrowed. He'd been right about the old devil after all—a *bandido*.

The priest gazed back over his shoulder towards the setting moon; it would be dark within seconds now. He reached inside his cassock and withdrew an ivory cross about eight or ten inches high. "The night is coming. Hold on to the cross. Believe me. Do not go to Mictlantecutli. I am your last chance."

"Go on, get away from him, you old fool," the girl shouted. "The authorities should take care of you idiots who molest and frighten travelers on this road . . . and prevent them from reaching their destinations."

The priest paid no heed to the girl; he implored Morgan once again, and this time his voice was strong as he watched the last red lip of the moon disappear below the hill. "There still is time . . ."

The girl viciously pulled back on the reins and dug her spurs into the horse's flanks; it screamed in rage and reared, its front hooves blotting out the stars. When back on all fours, the stallion was between Morgan and the priest. Her face was a soft glow as she smiled and withdrew a boot from her stirrups, "Come, my friend. Place your foot here. Vault up behind me." She held out a helping hand, and as she bent over, her blouse gaped open slightly. Morgan grinned and took her hand. He pulled himself astride the horse. "Put your arms around me and hold on," she ordered. Morgan did so, happily. Her body was supple, delightful to hold and the faint scent of some exotic perfume wafted back to him from her hair.

He gazed down at the priest; the old man's face was once more unfathomable. "So long, padre. Don't take any wooden *pesos*."

The girl did not wait for an answer. She raked the flank of the horse with her spurs and the beast tore out into the night. "Hold tight," she shouted. "Hold tight!"

They rode at breakneck speed for almost ten minutes before she reined the stallion to a walk. With their pace slowed, Morgan became aware of the girl's body again, and desire built up rapidly inside him. It had been a long time; there was no one around to stop him . . . and the girl had shown a spirited wantonness that led him to believe she would welcome his advances. They rode with only the hoarse breathing and clip-clop of the horse, and the creak of their saddle breaking the silence. Surreptitiously, his hand began to ride higher and higher on her rib cage. She made no protest, so he became bolder. Finally, he could feel the soft full roundness of her breasts.

It was easier than Morgan had ever believed possible. She simply reined in the horse and turned partially around, "We can stop here . . . . if you want."

Morgan's voice was guttural, his body pounding in desire, as he said, "Yeh, I want."

She slid from the horse, and Morgan was beside her immediately. Her arms went around his neck. Their lips met in a brutal bruising parody of love. Her fingernails dug into his shoulders as his hands sought immediate demanding familiarity with her body. She moaned deep in her throat as Morgan fumbled with her clothes. And then, with only the disinterested horse grazing nearby and the brittle eyes of the stars glittering as they watched, their bodies joined in a violent collision of hot implacable lust . . .

Morgan could feel the lassitude of his body when he awakened. That was the his first impression. His second was that he was still embracing the girl. The third—an overpowering horrible odor of putrefaction.

He opened his eyes.

And screamed.

It was a scream wrenched involuntarily from his soul, for there, in the faint light of an approaching dawn, he could see that he was holding in his arms the rotting cadaver of a woman—a body from which the flesh was peeling in great huge strips like rotten liver, from which the death grimace revealed crooked brown teeth, and eyeless sockets.

Morgan whimpered and jumped to his feet. His heart was hammering as though it were an overtaxed runaway machine about to explode into pieces. His breath came in deep animal-like pants of fright. His eyes darted frantically around like those of a madman tormented by phantoms.

"I . . . I . . . I . . ." he croaked. It was all he could say. Naked, he began running down the road. He fell twice, painfully ripping open his legs and hands on the rocky surface of the land. "I . . . I . . . I . . ." and then, the words he wanted most to say came spewing out, "Help me . . . someone! Help me!"

He heard the horse's hooves behind him. It was the girl; she was alive . . . and whole! She smiled, reassuringly. "Where did you go?" she asked. And then she grinned, impishly. "Where are your clothes?"

"I . . . I . . . I . . ." Morgan could not speak.

"Come," she said.

Morgan shook his head. He could not marshal his thoughts, but this much was certain; he knew he was not going with the girl.

"Come!" This time it was an imperative command. The girl was no longer amused at his nudity, his frightened inarticulateness.

Morgan willed himself to turn and run away, but his body did not respond to his mental orders. Instead, like a mindless zombie, he mounted the horse.

"That's better," the girl said soothingly. "Of course, you should have put on your clothes . . . but it doesn't matter." She glanced towards the east, "Night is almost gone. We must hurry. There is something I want you to see before we get to Mictlantecutli's ranch."

She slapped the stallion with her whip, and the animal began chasing the blackness of the night.

Now, behind them, the sky definitely was beginning to lighten as dawn came to the Mexican desert. In the near-light of the new day, Morgan could see a landmark that looked familiar. And then, off the road, at the bottom of the ravine, he saw his car. Gingerly, the horse picked its way down the slope until they were beside the wrecked vehicle.

Ugly, red-necked vultures screamed and flapped their wings as the horse approached. Several were fighting over what appeared to be elongated white ropes hanging out of the car windows. A few of the birds took to the air . . . the rest, arrogant and unafraid, moved only a few reluctant steps away. "But . . . but . . . what are they doing here?" Morgan asked. "There was no one in the car but me?"

He could feel the girl's body shaking in silent laughter. She pointed. By squinting his eyes, Morgan could make out a figure impaled on the steering-wheel post. The cold undulating horror he had felt earlier closed in around him. The body was familiar—too familiar! Morgan whimpered as the girl urged the stallion closer. The vultures had gone for the eyes first—as they usually do—the entrails of the dead man hung out the open window, and these had been the reason for the fighting among the birds.

Morgan saw the clothes. The dead man was dressed the same as he had been. He wore the same shape wristwatch. What terrifying nightmare was this? Awaken . . . wake up . . . wake up he mentally shouted. But the nightmare, more real than life itself, remained. The dead man was Morgan, there could be no doubt about it.

Morgan's mind was forced in a corner by the realization, his sanity backed away from the fact. He began to lose all control. He screamed; it was the maddened howl of a lunatic.

At his cry, the girl shouted and whipped the stallion. The horse scrambled up the side of the ravine.

There, in the roadway, stood the priest.

"Help me, father. Help me. God help . . . " Morgan mumbled, the saliva trickling slowly from both sides of his lax mouth.

"You made your choice," the padre said. "I am sorry."

"But I did not know . . . . "

"Mictlantecutli is known by many names: Diablo, Satan, Devil, Lucifer, Mephistopheles. The particular name of evil is never important, for the precepts are the same in every country. You have embraced evil; you have made your last earthly choice. I am powerless now to aid you. Good-by . . ."

He felt, then heard, the girl's laughter—shrill, maniacal, satisfied. Her whip bit into the horse's neck and her spurs drew blood. They tore down the road, galloping, galloping, galloping towards the night. The stench was back again, and shreds of the girl's flesh began sloughing off in the wind.

She turned . . . slowly this time . . . and Morgan saw the horrible grinning expression of a skeleton.

He twisted around, refusing to look at the apparition, and cried out once more for the priest. Far back in the distance—as if he were viewing something in another world—Morgan could see the padre's solitary figure at the top of a hill, plodding towards the east, the rising sun and a new day.

When Morgan turned back again, weeping and knowing now the desperate futility of hope, they had already reached the edge of night . . . and the everlasting darkness of the dead and the damned reached out to embrace them.

Passengers

ROBERT SILVERBERG

Voted the best short story published as science fiction in 1969, by the Science Fiction Writers of America, "Passengers" is a paradigm of entrapment—cool and brisk and terrible, and not, upon close inspection, really science fiction at all (a statement erroneously made about most great science fiction, which in this instance is true). Robert Silverberg, perhaps the finest science fiction writer of our time, is the author of many novels of the first rank and hundreds of short stories, and he, no less than Joyce Carol Oates or Truman Capote, may have missed his truest vocation—to terrify and to quicken.

There are only fragments of me left now. Chunks of memory have broken free and drifted away like calved glaciers. It is always like that when a Passenger leaves us. We can never be sure of all the things our borrowed bodies did. We have only the lingering traces, the imprints.

Like sand clinging to an ocean-tossed bottle. Like the throbbings of amputated legs.

I rise. I collect myself. My hair is rumpled; I comb it. My face is creased from too little sleep. There is sourness in my mouth. Has my Passenger been eating dung with my mouth? They do that. They do anything.

It is morning.

A gray, uncertain morning. I stare at it a while, and then, shuddering, I opaque the window and confront instead the gray, uncertain surface of the inner panel. My room looks untidy. Did I have a woman here? There are ashes in the trays. Searching for butts, I find several with lipstick stains. Yes, a woman was here.

I touch the bedsheets. Still warm with shared warmth. Both pillows tousled. She has gone, though, and the Passenger is gone, and I am alone.

How long did it last, this time?

I pick up the phone and ring Central. "What is the date?"

The computer's bland feminine voice replies, "Friday, December 4th, 1987."

"The time?"

"Nine fifty-one, Eastern Standard Time."

"The weather forecast?"

"Predicted temperature range for today thirty to thirty-eight. Current temperature, thirty-one. Wind from the north, sixteen miles an hour. Chances of precipitation slight."

"What do you recommend for a hangover?"

"Food or medication?"

"Anything you like," I say.

The computer mulls that one over for a while. Then it decides on both, and activates my kitchen. The spigot yields cold tomato juice. Eggs begin to fry. From the medicine slot comes a purplish liquid. The Central Computer is always so thoughtful. Do the Passengers ever ride it, I wonder? What thrills could that hold for them? Surely it must be more exciting to borrow the million minds of Central than to live a while in the faulty, short-circuited soul of a corroding human being!

December 4th, Central said. Friday. So the Passenger had me for three nights.

I drink the purplish stuff and probe my memories in a gingerly way, as one might probe a festering sore.

I remember Tuesday morning. A bad time at work. None of the charts will come out right. The section manager irritable; he has been taken by Passengers three times in five weeks, and his section is in disarray as a result, and his Christmas bonus is jeopardized. Even though it is customary not to penalize a person for lapses due to Passengers, according to the system, the section manager seems to feel he will be treated unfairly. We have a hard time. Revise the charts, fiddle with the program, check the fundamentals ten times over. Out they come: the detailed forecasts for price variations of public utility securities, February–April, 1988. That afternoon we are to meet and discuss the charts and what they tell us.

I do not remember Tuesday afternoon.

That must have been when the Passenger took me. Perhaps at work; perhaps in the mahogany-paneled boardroom itself, during the conference. Pink concerned faces all about me; I cough, I lurch, I stumble from my seat. They shake their heads sadly. No one reaches for me. No one stops me. It is too dangerous to interfere with one who has a Passenger. The chances are great that a second Passenger lurks nearby in the discorporate state, looking for a mount. So I am avoided. I leave the building.

After that, what?

Sitting in my room on bleak Friday morning, I eat my scrambled eggs and try to reconstruct the three lost nights.

Of course it is impossible. The conscious mind functions during the period of captivity, but upon withdrawal of the Passenger nearly every recollection goes too. There is only a slight residue, a gritty film of faint and ghostly memories. The mount is never precisely the same person afterwards; though he cannot recall the details of his experience, he is subtly changed by it.

I try to recall.

A girl? Yes: lipstick on the butts. Sex, then, here in my room. Young? Old? Blonde? Dark? Everything is hazy. How did my borrowed body behave? Was I a good lover? I try to be, when I am myself. I keep in shape. At thirty-eight, I can handle three sets of tennis on a summer afternoon without collapsing. I can make a woman glow as a woman is meant to glow. Not boasting; just categorizing. We have our skills. These are mine.

But Passengers, I am told, take wry amusement in controverting our skills. So would it have given my rider a kind of delight to find me a woman and force me to fail repeatedly with her?

I dislike that thought.

The fog is going from my mind now. The medicine prescribed by Central works rapidly. I eat, I shave, I stand under the vibrator until my skin is clean. I do my exercises. Did the Passenger exercise my body Wednesday and Thursday mornings? Probably not. I must make up for that. I am close to middle age, now; tonus lost is not easily regained.

I touch my toes twenty times, knees stiff.

I kick my legs in the air.

I lie flat and lift myself on pumping elbows.

The body responds, maltreated though it has been. It is the first bright moment of my awakening: to feel the inner tingling, to know that I still have vigor.

Fresh air is what I want next. Quickly I slip into my clothes and leave. There is no need for me to report to work today. They are aware that since Tuesday afternoon I have had a Passenger; they need not be aware that before dawn on Friday the Passenger departed. I will have a free day. I will walk the city's streets, stretching my limbs, repaying my body for the abuse it has suffered.

I enter the elevator. I drop fifty stories to the ground. I step out into the December dreariness.

The towers of New York rise about me.

In the street the cars stream forward. Drivers sit edgily at their wheels. One never knows when the driver of a nearby car will be borrowed, and there is always a moment of lapsed coordination as the Passenger takes over. Many lives are lost that way on our streets and highways; but never the life of a Passenger.

I began to walk without purpose. I cross Fourteenth Street, heading north, listening to the soft violent purr of the electric engines. I see a boy jigging in the street and know he is being ridden. At Fifth and Twenty-Second a prosperous-looking paunchy man approaches, his necktie askew, this morning's *Wall Street Journal* jutting from an overcoat pocket. He giggles. He thrusts out his tongue. Ridden. Ridden. I avoid him. Moving briskly, I come to the underpass that carries traffic below Thirty-Fourth Street toward Queens, and pause for a moment to watch two adolescent girls quarreling at the rim of the pedestrian walk. One is a Negro. Her eyes are rolling in terror. The other pushes her closer to the railing. Ridden. But the Passenger does not have murder on its mind, merely pleasure. The Negro girl is released and falls in a huddled heap, trembling. Then she rises and runs. The other girl draws a long strand of gleaming hair into her mouth, chews on it, seems to awaken. She looks dazed.

I avert my eyes. One does not watch while a fellow sufferer is awakening. There is a morality of the ridden; we have so many new tribal mores in these dark days.

I hurry on.

Where am I going so hurriedly? Already I have walked more than a mile. I seem to be moving toward some goal, as though my Passenger still hunches in my skull, urging me about. But I know that is not so. For the moment, at least, I am free.

Can I be sure of that?

Cogito ergo sum no longer applies. We go on thinking even while we are ridden, and we live in quiet desperation, unable to halt our courses no matter how ghastly, no matter how self-destructive. I am certain that I can distinguish between the condition of bearing a Passenger and the condition of being free. But perhaps not. Perhaps I bear a particularly devilish Passenger which has not quitted me at all, but which merely has receded to the cerebellum, leaving me the illusion of freedom while all the time surreptitiously driving me onward to some purpose of its own.

Did we ever have more than that: the illusion of freedom?

But this is disturbing, the thought that I may be ridden without realizing it. I burst out in heavy perspiration, not merely from the exertion of walking. Stop. Stop here. Why must you walk? You are at Forty-Second Street. There is the library. Nothing forces you onward. Stop a while, I tell myself. Rest on the library steps.

I sit on the cold stone and tell myself that I have made this decision for myself.

Have I? It is the old problem, free will versus determinism, translated into the foulest of forms. Determinism is no longer a philosopher's abstraction; it is cold alien tendrils sliding between the cranial sutures. The Passengers arrived three years ago. I have been ridden five times since then. Our world is quite different now. But we have adjusted even to this. We have adjusted. We have our mores. Life goes on. Our governments rule, our legislatures meet, our stock exchanges transact business as usual, and we have methods for compensating for the random havoc. It is the only way. What else can we do? Shrivel in defeat? We have an enemy we cannot fight; at best we can resist through endurance. So we endure.

The stone steps are cold against my body. In December few people sit here.

I tell myself that I made this long walk of my own free will, that I halted of my own free will, that no Passenger rides my brain now. Perhaps. Perhaps. I cannot let myself believe that I am not free.

Can it be, I wonder, that the Passenger left some lingering command in me? Walk to this place, halt at this place? That is possible too.

I look about me at the others on the library steps.

An old man, eyes vacant, sitting on newspaper. A boy of thirteen or so with flaring nostrils. A plump woman. Are all of them ridden? Passengers seem to cluster about me today. The more I study the ridden ones the more convinced I become that I am, for the moment, free. The last time, I had three months of freedom between rides. Some people, they say, are scarcely ever free. Their bodies are in great demand, and they know only scattered bursts of freedom, a day here, a week there, an hour. We have never been able to determine how many Passengers infest our world. Millions, maybe. Or maybe five. Who can tell?

A wisp of snow curls down out of the gray sky. Central had said the chance of precipitation was slight. Are they riding Central this morning too?

I see the girl.

She sits diagonally across from me, five steps up and a hundred feet away, her black skirt pulled up on her knees to reveal handsome legs. She is young. Her hair is deep, rich auburn. Her eyes are pale; at this distance, I cannot make out the precise color. She is dressed simply. She is younger than thirty. She wears a dark green coat and her lipstick has a purplish tinge. Her lips are full, her nose slender, high-bridged, her eyebrows carefully plucked.

I know her.

I have spent the past three nights with her in my room. She is the one. Ridden, she came to me, and ridden, I slept with her. I am certain of this. The veil of memory opens; I see her slim body naked on my bed.

How can it be that I remember this?

It is too strong to be an illusion. Clearly this is something that I have been *permitted* to remember for reasons I cannot comprehend. And I remember more. I remember her soft gasping sounds of pleasure. I know that my own body did not betray me those three nights, nor did I fail her need.

And there is more. A memory of sinuous music; a scent of youth in her hair; the rustle of winter trees. Somehow she brings back to me a time of innocence, a time when I am young and girls are mysterious, a time of parties and dances and warmth and secrets.

I am drawn to her now.

There is an etiquette about such things, too. It is in poor taste to approach someone you have met while being ridden. Such an encounter gives you no privilege; a stranger remains a stranger, no matter what you and she may have done and said during your involuntary time together.

Yet I am drawn to her.

Why this violation of taboo? Why this raw breach of etiquette? I have never done this before. I have been scrupulous.

But I get to my feet and walk along the step on which I have been sitting until I am below her, and I look up, and automatically she folds her ankles together and angles her knees as if in awareness that her position is not a modest one. I know from that gesture that she is not ridden now. My eyes meet hers. Her eyes are hazy green. She is beautiful, and I rack my memory for more details of our passion.

I climb step by step until I stand before her.

"Hello," I say.

She gives me a neutral look. She does not seem to recognize me. Her eyes are veiled, as one's eyes often are, just after the Passenger has gone. She purses her lips and appraises me in a distant way.

"Hello," she replies coolly. "I don't think I know you."

"No. You don't. But I have the feeling you don't want to be alone just now. And I know I don't." I try to persuade her with my eyes that my motives are decent. "There's snow in the air," I say. "We can find a warmer place. I'd like to talk to you."

"About what?"

"Let's go elsewhere, and I'll tell you. I'm Charles Roth."

"Helen Martin."

She gets to her feet. She still has not cast aside her cool neutrality; she is suspicious, ill at ease. But at least she is willing to go with me. A good sign.

"Is it too early in the day for a drink?" I ask.

"I'm not sure. I hardly know what time it is."

"Before noon."

"Let's have a drink anyway," she says, and we both smile.

We go to a cocktail lounge across the street. Sitting face to face in the darkness, we sip drinks, daiquiri for her, bloody mary for me. She relaxes a little. I ask myself what I want from her. The pleasure of her company, yes. Her company in bed? But I have already had that pleasure, three nights of it, though she does not know that. I want something more. Something more. What?

Her eyes are bloodshot. She has had little sleep these past three nights.

I say, "Was it very unpleasant for you?"

"What?"

"The Passenger."

A whiplash of reaction crosses her face. "How did you know I've had a Passenger?"

"I know."

"We aren't supposed to talk about it."

"I'm broadminded," I tell her. "My Passenger left me some time during the night. I was ridden since Tuesday afternoon."

"Mine left me about two hours ago, I think." Her cheeks color. She is doing something daring, talking like this. "I was ridden since Monday night. This was my fifth time."

"Mine also."

We toy with our drinks. Rapport is growing, almost without the need of words. Our recent experiences with Passengers give us something in common, although Helen does not realize how intimately we shared those experiences.

We talk. She is a designer of display windows. She has a small apartment several blocks from here. She lives alone. She asks me what I do. "Securities analyst," I tell her. She smiles. Her teeth are flawless. We have a second round of drinks. I am positive, now, that this is the girl who was in my room while I was ridden.

A seed of hope grows in me. It was a happy chance that brought us together again so soon after we parted as dreamers. A happy chance, too, that some vestige of the dream lingered in my mind.

We have shared something, who knows what, and it must have been good to leave such a vivid imprint on me, and now I want to come to her conscious, aware, my own master, and renew that relationship, making it a real one this time. It is not proper, for I am trespassing on a privilege that is not mine except by virture of our Passengers' brief presence in us. Yet I need her. I want her.

She seems to need me, too, without realizing who I am. But fear holds her back.

I am frightened of frightening her, and I do not try to press my advantage too quickly. Perhaps she would take me to her apartment with her now, perhaps not, but I do not ask. We finish our drinks. We arrange to meet by the library steps again tomorrow. My hand momentarily brushes hers. Then she is gone.

I fill three ashtrays that night. Over and over I debate the wisdom of what I am doing. But why not leave her alone? I have no right to follow her. In the place our world has become, we are wisest to remain apart.

And yet—there is that stab of half-memory when I think of her. The blurred lights of lost chances behind the stairs, of girlish laughter in second-floor corridors, of stolen kisses, of tea and cake. I remember the girl with the orchid in her hair, and the one in the spangled dress, and the one with the child's face and the woman's eyes, all so long ago, all lost, all gone, and I tell myself that this one I will not lose, I will not permit her to be taken from me.

Morning comes, a quiet Saturday. I return to the library, hardly expecting to find her there, but she is there, on the steps, and the sight of her is like a reprieve. She looks wary, troubled; obviously she has done much thinking, little sleeping. Together we walk along Fifth Avenue. She is quite close to me, but she does not take my arm. Her steps are brisk, short, nervous.

I want to suggest that we go to her apartment instead of to the cocktail lounge. In these days we must move swiftly while we are free. But I know it would be a mistake to think of this as a matter of tactics. Coarse haste would be fatal, bringing me perhaps an ordinary victory, a numbing defeat within it. In any event her mood hardly seems promising. I look at her, thinking of string music and new snowfalls, and she looks toward the gray sky.

She says, "I can feel them watching me all the time. Like vultures swooping overhead, waiting, waiting. Ready to pounce."

"But there's a way of beating them. We can grab little scraps of life when they're not looking."

"They're *always* looking."

"No," I tell her. "There can't be enough of them for that. Sometimes they're looking the other way. And while they are, two people can come together and try to share warmth."

"But what's the use?"

"You're too pessimistic, Helen. They ignore us for months at a time. We have a chance. We have a chance."

But I cannot break through her shell of fear. She is paralyzed by the nearness of the Passengers, unwilling to begin anything for fear it will be snatched away by our tormentors. We reach the building where she lives, and I hope she will relent and invite me in. For an instant she wavers, but only for an instant: she takes my hand in both of hers, and smiles, and the smile fades, and she is gone, leaving me only with the words, "Let's meet at the library again tomorrow. Noon."

I make the long chilling walk home alone.

Some of her pessimism seeps into me that night. It seems futile for us to try to salvage anything. More than that: wicked for me to seek her out, shameful to offer a hesitant love when I am not free. In this world, I tell myself, we should keep well clear of others, so that we do not harm anyone when we are seized and ridden.

I do not go to meet her in the morning.

It is best this way, I insist. I have no business trifling with her. I imagine her at the library, wondering why I am late, growing tense, impatient, then annoyed. She will be angry with me for breaking our date, but her anger will ebb, and she will forget me quickly enough.

Monday comes. I return to work.

Naturally, no one discusses my absence. It is as though I have never been away. The market is strong that morning. The work is challenging; it is mid-morning before I think of Helen at all. But once I think of her, I can think of nothing else. My cowardice in standing her up. The childishness of Saturday night's dark thoughts. Why accept fate so passively? Why give in? I want to fight, now, to carve out a pocket of security despite the odds. I feel a deep conviction that it can be done. The Passengers may never bother the two of us again, after all. And that flickering smile of hers outside her building Saturday, that momentary glow—it should have told me that behind her wall of fear she felt the same hopes. She was waiting for me to lead the way. And I stayed home instead.

At lunchtime I go to the library, convinced it is futile.

But she is there. She paces along the steps; the wind slices at her slender figure. I go to her.

She is silent a moment. "Hello," she says finally.

"I am sorry about yesterday."

"I waited a long time for you."

I shrug. "I made up my mind that it was no use to come. But then I changed my mind again."

She tries to look angry. But I know she is pleased to see me again—else why did she come here today? She cannot hide her inner pleasure. Nor can I. I point across the street to the cocktail lounge.

"A daiquiri?" I say. "As a peace offering?

"All right."

Today the lounge is crowded, but we find a booth somehow. There is a brightness in her eyes that I have not seen before. I sense that a barrier is crumbling within her.

"You're less afraid of me, Helen," I say.

"I've never been afraid of you. I'm afraid of what could happen if we take the risks."

"Don't be. Don't be."

"I'm trying not to be afraid. But sometimes it seems so hopeless. Since *they* came here—"

"We can still try to live our own lives."

"Maybe."

"We have to. Let's make a pact, Helen. No more gloom. No more worrying about the terrible things that might just happen. All right?"

A pause. Then a cool hand against mine.

"All right."

We finish our drinks, and I present my Credit Central to pay for them, and we go outside. I want her to tell me to forget about this afternoon's work and come home with her. It is inevitable, now, that she will ask me, and better sooner than later.

We walk a block. She does not offer the invitation. I sense the struggle inside her, and I wait, letting that struggle reach its own resolution without interference from me. We walk a second block. Her arm is through mine, but she talks only of her work, of the weather, and it is a remote, arm's-length conversation. At the next corner she swings around, away from her apartment, back toward the cocktail lounge. I try to be patient with her.

I have no need to rush things now, I tell myself. Her body is not a secret to me. We have begun our relationship topsy-turvy, with the physical part first; now it will take time to work backward to the more difficult part that some people call love.

But of course she is not aware that we have known each other that way. The wind blows swirling snowflakes in our faces, and somehow the cold sting awakens honesty in me. I know what I must say. I must relinquish my unfair advantage.

I tell her, "While I was ridden last week, Helen, I had a girl in my room."

"Why talk of such things now?"

"I have to Helen. You were the girl."

She halts. She turns to me. People hurry past us in the street. Her face is very pale, with dark red spots growing in her cheeks.

"That's not funny, Charles."

"It wasn't meant to be. You were with me from Tuesday night to early Friday morning."

"How can you possibly know that?"

"I do. I do. The memory is clear. Somehow it remains, Helen. I see your whole body."

"Stop it, Charles."

"We were very good together," I say. "We must have pleased our Passengers because we were so good. To see you again—it was like waking from a dream, and finding that the dream was real, the girl right there—"

"No!"

"Let's go to your apartment and begin again."

She says, "You're being deliberately filthy, and I don't know why, but there wasn't any reason for you to spoil things. Maybe I was with you and maybe I wasn't, but you wouldn't know it, and if you did know it you should keep your mouth shut about it, and—"

"You have a birthmark the size of a dime," I say, "about three inches below your left breast."

She sobs and hurls herself at me, there in the street. Her long silvery nails rake my cheeks. She pummels me. I seize her. Her knees assail me. No one pays attention; those who pass by assume we are ridden, and turn their heads. She is all fury, but I have my arms around hers like metal bands, so that she can only stamp and snort, and her body is close against mine. She is rigid, anguished.

In a low, urgent voice I say, "We'll defeat them, Helen. We'll finish what they started. Don't fight me. There's no reason to fight me. I know, it's a fluke that I remember you, but let me go with you and I'll prove that we belong together."

"Let—go—"

"Please. Please. Why should we be enemies? I don't mean you any harm. I love you Helen. Do you remember, when we were kids, we could play at being in love? I did; you must have done it too. Sixteen, seventeen years old. The whispers, the conspiracies—all a big game, and we knew it. But the game's over. We can't afford to tease and run. We have so little time, when we're free—we have to trust, to open ourselves—"

"It's wrong."

"No. Just because it's the stupid custom for two people brought together by Passengers to avoid one another, that doesn't mean we have to follow it. Helen—Helen—"

Something in my tone registers with her. She ceases to struggle. Her rigid body softens. She looks up at me, her tear-streaked face thawing, her eyes blurred.

"Trust me," I say. "Trust me, Helen!"

She hesitates. Then she smiles.

In that moment I feel the chill at the back of my skull, the sensation as of a steel needle driven deep through the bone. I stiffen. My arms drop away from her. For an instant I lose touch, and when the mists clear all is different.

"Charles?" she says. "*Charles?*"

Her knuckles are against her teeth. I turn, ignoring her, and go back into the cocktail lounge. A young man sits in one of the front booths. His dark hair gleams with pomade; his cheecks are smooth. His eyes meet mine.

I sit down. He orders drinks. We do not talk.

My hand falls on his wrist, and remains there. The bartender, serving the drinks, scowls but says nothing. We sip our cocktails and put the drained glasses down.

"Let's go," the young man says.

I follow him out.

The Explosives Expert

JOHN LUTZ

And sometimes the horror comes by indirection—a sound heard outside the door or across the street, a bare flicker from another part of the city. Sometimes the horror by indirection is the quietest and most deeply set horror of all. In this masterful story, John Lutz—the author of several hundred short stories and several novels, most recently Jericho Man *and* Lazarus Man—*makes the case.*

Billy Edgemore, the afternoon bartender, stood behind the long bar of the Last Stop Lounge and squinted through the dimness at the sunlight beyond the front window. He was a wiry man, taller than he appeared at first, and he looked like he should be a bartender, with his bald head, cheerfully seamed face and his brilliant red vest that was the bartender's uniform at the Last Stop. Behind him long rows of glistening bottles picked up the light on the mirrored backbar, the glinting clear gins and vodkas, the beautiful amber bourbons and lighter Scotches, the various hues of the assorted wines, brandies and liqueurs. The Last Stop's bar was well stocked.

Beyond the ferns that blocked the view out (and in) the front window, Billy saw a figure cross the small patch of light and turn to enter the stained-glass front door, the first customer he was to serve that day.

It was Sam Daniels. Sam was an employee of the Hulton Plant up the street, as were most of the customers of the Last Stop.

"Afternoon, Sam," Billy said, turning on his professional smile. "Kind of early today, aren't you?"

"Off work," Sam said, mounting a bar stool as if it were a horse. "Beer."

Billy drew a beer and set the wet schooner in front of Sam on the mahogany bar. "Didn't expect a customer for another two hours, when the plant lets out," Billy said.

"Guess not," Sam said, sipping his beer. He was a short man with a swarthy face, a head of curly hair, and a stomach paunch too big for a man in his early thirties—a man who liked his drinking.

435

"Figured you didn't go to work when I saw you weren't wearing your badge," Billy said. The Hulton Plant manufactured some secret government thing, a component for the hydrogen bomb, and each employee had to wear his small plastic badge with his name, number and photograph on it in order to enter or leave the plant.

"Regular Sherlock," Sam said, and jiggled the beer in his glass.

"You notice lots of things when you're a bartender," Billy said, wiping down the bar with a clean white towel. *You notice things,* Billy repeated to himself, *and you get to know people, and when you get to know them, really get to know them, you've got to dislike them.* "I guess I tended bar in the wrong places."

"What's that?" Sam Daniels asked.

"Just thinking out loud," Billy said, and hung the towel on its chrome rack. When Billy looked at his past he seemed to be peering down a long tunnel of empty bottles, drunks and hollow laughter; of curt orders, see-through stares and dreary conversations. He'd never liked his job, but it was all he'd known for the past thirty years.

"Wife's supposed to meet me here pretty soon," Sam said. "She's getting off work early." He winked at Billy. "Toothache."

Billy smiled his automatic smile and nodded. He never had liked Sam, who had a tendency to get loud and violent when he got drunk.

Within a few minutes Rita Daniels entered. She was a tall, pretty woman, somewhat younger than her husband. She had a good figure, dark eyes, and expensively bleached blonde hair that looked a bit stringy now from the heat outside.

"Coke and bourbon," she ordered, without looking at Billy. He served her the highball where she sat next to her husband at the bar.

No one spoke for a while as Rita sipped her drink. The faint sound of traffic, muffled through the thick door of the Last Stop, filled the silence. When a muted horn sounded, Rita said, "It's dead in here. Put a quarter in the jukebox."

Sam did as his wife said, and soft jazz immediately displaced the traffic sounds.

"You know I don't like jazz, Sam." Rita downed her drink quicker than she should have, then got down off the stool to go to the powder room.

"Saw Doug Baker last night," Billy said, picking up the empty glass. Doug Baker was a restaurant owner who lived on the other side of town, and it was no secret that he came to the Last Stop only to see Rita Daniels, though Rita was almost always with her husband.

"How 'bout that," Sam said. "Two more of the same."

Rita returned to her stool, and Billy put two highballs before her and her husband.

"I was drinking beer," Sam said in a loud voice.

"So you were," Billy answered, smiling his My Mistake smile. He shrugged and motioned toward the highballs. "On the house. Unless you'd rather have beer."

"No," Sam said, "think nothing of it."

That was how Billy thought Sam would answer. His cheapness was one of the things Billy disliked most about the man. It was one of the things he knew Rita disliked most in Sam Daniels, too.

"How'd it go with the hydrogen bombs today?" Rita asked her husband. "Didn't go in at all, huh?"

Billy could see she was aggravated and was trying to nag him.

"No," Sam said, "and I don't make hydrogen bombs."

"Ha!" Rita laughed. "You oughta think about it. That's about all you can make." She turned away before Sam could answer. "Hey, Billy, you know anything about hydrogen bombs?"

"Naw," Billy said. "Your husband knows more about that than me."

"Yeah," Rita said, "the union rates him an expert. Some expert! Splices a few wires together."

"Five dollars an hour," Sam said, "and double time for overtime."

Rita whirled a braceleted arm above her head. "Wheee . . ."

Like many married couples, Sam and Rita never failed to bicker when they came into the Last Stop. Billy laughed. "The Friendly Daniels." Sam didn't laugh.

"Don't bug me today," Sam said to Rita. "I'm in a bad mood."

"Cheer up, Sam," Billy said. "It's a sign she loves you, or loves somebody, anyway."

Sam ignored Billy and finished his drink. "Where'd you go last night?" he asked his wife.

"You know I was at my sister's. I even stopped in here for about a half-hour on the way. Billy can verify it."

"Right," Billy said.

"I thought you said Doug Baker was in here last night," Sam said to him, his eyes narrow.

"He was," Billy said. "He, uh, came in late." He turned to make more drinks, placing the glasses lip to lip and pouring bourbon into each in one deft stream without spilling a drop. He made them a little stronger this time, shooting in the soda expertly, jabbing swizzle sticks between the ice cubes and placing the glasses on the bar.

"You wouldn't be covering up or anything, would you, Billy?" Sam's voice had acquired a mean edge.

"Now *wait a minute?*" Rita said. "If you think I came in here last night to see Doug Baker, you're crazy!"

"Well," Sam stirred his drink viciously and took a sip, "Billy mentioned Baker was in here . . ."

"I said he came in late," Billy said quickly.

"And he acted like he was covering up or something," Sam said, looking accusingly at Billy.

"*Covering up?*" Rita turned to Billy, her penciled eyebrows knitted in a frown. "Have you ever seen me with another man?"

"Naw," Billy said blandly, "of course not. You folks shouldn't fight."

Still indignant, Rita swiveled on her stool to face her husband. "Have I ever been unfaithful?"

"How the hell should I know?"

"Good point," Billy said with a forced laugh.

"It's not funny!" Rita snapped.

"Keep it light, folks," Billy said seriously. "You know we don't like trouble in here."

"Sorry," Rita said, but her voice was hurt. She swiveled back to face the bar and gulped angrily on her drink. Billy could see that the liquor was getting to her, was getting to them both.

There was silence for a while, then Rita said morosely "I *oughta* go out on you Mr. Five-dollar-hydrogen-bomb-expert! You think I do anyway, and at least Doug Baker's got money."

Sam grabbed her wrist, making the bracelets jingle. She tried to jerk away but he held her arm so tightly that his knuckles were white. "You ever see Baker behind my back and I'll kill you both!" He almost spit the words out.

"Hey, now," Billy said gently, "don't talk like that, folks!" He placed his hands on Sam Daniels's arm and felt the muscles relax as Sam released his wife. She bent over silently on her stool and held the wrist as if it were broken. "Have one on the house," Billy said, taking up their almost empty glasses. "One to make up by."

"Make mine straight," Sam said. He was breathing hard and his face was red.

"*Damn you!*" Rita moaned. She half-fell off the stool and walked quickly but staggeringly to the powder room again.

Billy began to mix the drinks deftly, speedily, as if there were a dozen people at the bar and they all demanded service. In the faint red glow from the beer-ad electric clock he looked like an ancient alchemist before his rows of multicolored bottles. "You shouldn't be so hard on her," he said absently as he mixed. "Can't believe all the rumors you hear about a woman as pretty as Rita, and a harmless kiss in fun never hurt nobody."

"Rumors?" Sam leaned over the bar. "Kiss? What kiss? Did she kiss Baker last night?"

"Take it easy," Billy said. "I told you Baker came in late." The phone rang, as it always did during the fifteen minutes before the Hulton Plant let out, with wives leaving messages and asking for errant husbands. When Billy returned, Rita was back at the bar.

"Let's get out of here," she said. There were tear streaks in her make-up.

"Finish your drinks and go home happy, folks." Billy shot a glance at the door and set the glasses on the bar.

Rita drank hers slowly, but Sam tossed his drink down and stared straight ahead. Quietly, Billy put another full glass in front of him.

"I hear you *were* in here with Baker last night," Sam said in a low voice. "Somebody even saw you kissing him."

"You're *crazy!*" Rita's thickened voice was outraged.

Billy moved quickly toward them. "I didn't say that."

"I know you were covering up!" Sam glared pure hate at him. "We'll see what Baker says, because I'm going to drive over to his place right now and bash his brains out!"

"*But I didn't even see Baker last night!*" Rita took a pull on her drink, trying to calm herself. Sam swung sharply around with his forearm, hitting Rita's chin and the highball glass at the same time. There was a clink as the glass hit her teeth and she fell backward off the stool.

Billy reached under the bar and his hand came up with a glinting chrome automatic that seemed to catch every ray of light in the place. It was a gentleman's gun, and standing there in his white shirt and red vest Billy looked like a gentleman holding it.

"Now, don't move, folks." He aimed the gun directly at Sam's stomach. "You know we don't go for that kind of trouble in here." He looked down and saw blood seeping between Rita's fingers as she held her hand over her mouth. Billy wet a clean towel and tossed it to her, and she held it to her face and scooted backward to sit sobbing in the farthest booth.

Billy leaned close to Sam. "Listen," he said, his voice a sincere whisper, "I don't want to bring trouble on Baker, or on you for that matter, so I can't stand by and let you go over there and kill him and throw your own life away. It wasn't him she was in here with. He came in later."

"Wasn't him?" Sam asked in bewildered fury. "Who was it then?"

"I don't know," Billy said, still in a whisper so Rita couldn't hear. "He had a badge on, so he worked at the plant, but I don't know who he is and that's the truth."

"*Oh, no!*"

"Take it easy, Sam. She only kissed him in that booth there. And I'm not even sure I saw that. The booth was dark."

Sam tossed down the drink that was on the bar and moaned. He was staring at the automatic and Billy could see he wanted desperately to move.

A warm silence filled the bar, and then the phone rang shrilly, turning the silence to icicles.

"Now take it easy," Billy said, backing slowly down the bar toward where the phone hung on the wall. "A kiss isn't anything." As the phone rang again he could almost see the shrill sound grate through Sam's tense body. Billy placed the automatic on the bar and took the last five steps to the phone. He let it ring once more before answering it.

"Naw," Billy said into the receiver, standing with his back to Sam and Rita, "he's not here." He stood for a long moment instead of hanging up, as if someone were still on the other end of the line.

The shot was a sudden, angry bark.

Billy put the receiver on the hook and turned. Sam was standing slumped with a supporting hand on a bar stool. Rita was crumpled on the floor beneath the table of the booth she'd been sitting in, her eyes open, her blonde hair bright with blood.

His head still bowed, Sam began to shake.

Within minutes the police were there, led by a young plainclothes detective named Parks.

"You say they were arguing and he just up and shot her?" Parks was asking as his men led Sam outside.

"He accused her of running around," Billy said. "They were arguing, he hit her, and I was going to throw them out when the phone rang. I set the gun down for a moment when I went to answer the phone, and he grabbed it and shot."

"Uh-hm," Parks said efficiently, flashing a look toward where Rita's body had lain before they'd photographed it and taken it away. "Pretty simple, I guess. Daniels confessed as soon as we got here. In fact, we couldn't shut him up. Pretty broken."

"Who wouldn't be?" Billy said.

"Save some sympathy for the girl." Parks looked around. "Seems like a nice place. I don't know why there's so much trouble in here."

Billy shrugged. "In a dive, a class joint or a place like this, people are mostly the same."

Parks grinned. "You're probably right," he said, and started toward the door. Before pushing it open, he paused and turned. "If you see anything like this developing again, give us a call, huh?"

"Sure," Billy said, polishing a glass and holding it up to the fading afternoon light. "You know we don't like trouble in here."

Call First

RAMSEY CAMPBELL

Here is a powerful story about cruelty by one of the field's youngest yet most experienced masters. For although Ramsey Campbell is only in his mid-thirties, he is already a veteran of eighteen years as a published writer in the genre. One of his great virtues (apparent in such books as Demons by Daylight, *1973;* The Height of the Scream, *1976; and* The Doll Who Ate His Mother, *1978) is his unequaled ability to make the everyday truly frightening.*

It was the other porters who made Ned determined to find out who answered the phone in the old man's house.

Not that he hadn't wanted to know before. He'd felt it was his right almost as soon as the whole thing had begun, months ago. He'd been sitting behind his desk in the library entrance, waiting for someone to try to take a bag into the library so he could shout after them that they couldn't, when the reference librarian ushered the old man to Ned's desk and said, "Let this gentleman use your phone." Maybe he hadn't meant every time the old man came to the library, but then he should have said so. The old man used to talk to the librarian and tell him things about books even he didn't know, which was why he let him phone. All Ned could do was feel resentful. People weren't supposed to use his phone, and even he wasn't allowed to phone outside the building. And it wasn't as if the old man's calls were interesting. Ned wouldn't have minded if they'd been worth hearing.

"I'm coming home now." That was all he ever said; then he'd put down the receiver and hurry away. It was the way he said it that made Ned wonder. There was no feeling behind the words, they sounded as if he were saying them only because he had to, perhaps wishing he needn't. Ned knew people talked like that: his parents did in church, and most of the time at home. He wondered if the old man were calling his wife, because he wore a ring on his wedding finger, although in the claw where a stone should be was what looked like a piece of yellow finger nail. But Ned didn't think it could be his wife. Each day the old man left the library at the same time, so why would he bother to phone?

Then there was the way the old man looked at Ned when he phoned: as if he didn't matter and couldn't understand the way most of the porters looked at him. That was the look that swelled up inside Ned one day and made him persuade one of the other porters to take charge of his desk while Ned waited to listen in on the old man's call. The girl who always smiled at Ned was on the switchboard, and they listened together. They heard the phone in the house ringing then lifted, and the old man's call and his receiver going down: nothing else, not even breathing apart from the old man's. "Who do you think it is?" the girl said, but Ned thought she'd laugh if he said he didn't know. He shrugged extravagantly and left.

Now he was determined. The next time the old man came to the library Ned phoned his house, having read what the old man dialed. When the ringing began, its pulse sounded deliberately slow, and Ned felt the pumping of his blood rushing ahead. Seven trills and the phone in the house opened with a violent click. Ned held his breath, but all he could hear was his blood thumping his ears. "Hello," he said and after a silence, clearing his throat, "Hello!" Perhaps it was one of those answering machines people in films used in their offices. He felt foolish and uneasy greeting the wide silent metal ear, and put down the receiver. He was in bed and falling asleep before he wondered why the old man should tell an answering machine that he was coming home.

The following day, in the bar where all the porters went at lunchtime, Ned told them about the silently listening phone. "He's weird, that old man," he said, but now the others had finished joking with him they didn't seem interested, and he had to make a grab for the conversation. "He reads weird books," he said. "All about witches and magic. Real ones, not stories."

"Now tell us something we didn't know," someone said and the conversation turned its back on Ned. His attention began to wander, he lost his hold on what was being said, he had to smile and nod as usual when they looked at him, and he was thinking: they're looking at me like the old man does. I'll show them. I'll go in his house and see who's there. Maybe I'll take something that'll show I've been there. Then they'll have to listen.

But next day at lunchtime, when he arrived at the address he'd seen on the old man's library card, Ned felt more like knocking at the front door and running away. The house was menacingly big, the end house of a street whose other windows were brightly bricked up. Exposed foundations like broken teeth protruded from the mud that surrounded the street, while hundreds of yards away stood a five-story crescent of flats that looked as if it had been designed in sections to be fitted together by a two-year-old. Ned tried to keep the house between him and the flats as he peered in the windows.

All he could see through the grimy front window was bare floorboards; when he coaxed himself to look through the side window, the same. He dreaded being caught by the old man, even though he'd seen him sitting behind a pile of books ten minutes ago. It had taken Ned that long to walk here; the old man couldn't walk so fast, and there wasn't a bus he could catch. At last Ned dodged round the back and peered into the kitchen: a few plates in the sink, some tins of food, an old cooker. Nobody to be seen. He returned to the front, wondering what to do. Maybe he'd knock after all. He took hold of the bar of the knocker, trying to think what he'd say, and the door opened.

The hall leading back to the kitchen was long and dim. Ned stood shuffling indecisively on the step. He would have to decide soon, for his lunch hour was dwindling. It was like one of the empty houses he'd used to play in with the other children, daring each other to go up the tottering stairs. Even the things in the kitchen didn't make it seem lived in. He'd show them all. He went in. Acknowledging a vague idea that the old man's companion was out, he closed the door to hear if they returned.

On his right was the front room; on his left, past the stairs and the phone, another of the bare rooms he'd seen. He tiptoed upstairs. The stairs creaked and swayed a little, perhaps unused to anyone of Ned's weight. He reached the landing, breathing heavily, feeling dust chafe his throat. Stairs led up to a closed attic door, but he looked in the rooms off the landing.

Two of the doors which he opened stealthily showed him nothing but boards and flurries of floating dust. The landing in front of the third looked cleaner, as if the door were often opened. He pulled it toward him, holding it up all the way so it didn't scrape the floor, and entered.

Most of it didn't seem to make sense. There was a single bed with faded sheets. Against the walls were tables and piles of old books. Even some of the books looked disused. There were black candles and racks of small cardboard boxes. On one of the tables lay a single book. Ned padded across the fragments of carpet and opened the book in a thin path of sunlight through the shutters.

Inside the sagging covers was a page which Ned slowly realized had been ripped from the Bible. It was the story of Lazarus. Scribbles that might be letters filled the margin, and at the bottom of the page: "p. 491." Suddenly inspired, Ned turned to that page in the book. It showed a drawing of a corpse sitting up in his coffin, but the book was all in the language they sometimes used in church: Latin. He thought of asking one of the librarians what it meant. Then he remembered that he needed proof he'd been in the house. He stuffed the page from the Bible into his pocket.

As he crept swiftly downstairs, something was troubling him. He reached the hall and thought he knew what it was. He still didn't know who lived in the house with the old man. If they lived in the back perhaps there'd be signs in the kitchen. Though if it were his wife, Ned thought as he hurried down the hall, she couldn't be like Ned's mother, who would never have left torn strips of wallpaper hanging at shoulder height from both walls. He'd reached the kitchen door when he realized what had been bothering him. When he'd emerged from the bedroom the attic door had been open.

He looked back involuntarily, and saw a woman walking away from him down the hall.

He was behind the closed kitchen door before he had time to feel fear. That came only when he saw that the back door was nailed rustily shut. Then he controlled himself. She was only a woman; she couldn't do much if she found him. He opened the door minutely. The hall was empty.

Halfway down the hall he had to slip into the side room, heart punching his chest, for she'd appeared again from between the stairs and the front door. He felt the beginnings of anger and recklessness, and they grew faster when he opened the door and had to flinch back as he saw her hand passing. The fingers looked famished, the color of old lard, with long yellow cracked nails. There was no nail on her wedding finger, which wore a plain ring. She was returning from the direction of the kitchen, which was why Ned hadn't expected her.

Through the opening of the door he heard her padding upstairs. She sounded barefoot. He waited until he couldn't hear her, then edged out into the hall. The door began to fall open with a faint creak, and he drew it stealthily closed. He paced toward the front door. If he hadn't seen her shadow creeping down the stairs he would have come face to face with her.

He was listening behind the kitchen door, and near to panic, when he realized she knew he was in the house. She was playing a game with him. At once he was furious. She was only an old woman, her body beneath the long white dress was sure to be as thin as her hands, she could only shout when she saw him, she couldn't stop him leaving. In a minute he'd be late for work. He threw open the kitchen door and swaggered down the hall.

The sight of her lifting the phone receiver broke his stride for a moment. Perhaps she was phoning the police. He hadn't done anything; she could have her Bible page back. But she had laid the receiver beside the phone. Why? Was she making sure the old man couldn't ring?

As she unbent from stooping to the phone she grasped two uprights of the banisters to support herself. They gave a loud splintering creak and bent together. Ned halted, confused. He was still struggling to react when she turned toward him, and he saw her face. Part of it was still on the bone.

He didn't back away until she began to advance on him, her nails tearing new strips from both walls. All he could see was her protruding eyes, unsupported by flesh. His mind was backing away faster than he was, but it had come up against a terrible insight. He even knew why she'd made sure the old man couldn't interrupt until she'd finished. His calls weren't like speaking to an answering machine at all. They were exactly like switching off a burglar alarm.

The Fly

ARTHUR PORGES

Speculative fiction has had many unsung stars and Arthur Porges is one of the most shamefully neglected. Here is a man who has done consistently interesting and frequently brilliant work in science fiction, fantasy and horror, and yet his work has never been collected. A mathematician, he taught at several universities until his retirement in 1975. His work was published steadily throughout the 1950's and 1960's—the best of it appeared in The Magazine of Fantasy & Science Fiction. *Although he also wrote mystery stories, his greatest talent was in fantasy and horror, as testified to by "The Fly," a story you will always remember whenever you hear a buzz in your ear.*

Shortly after noon the man unslung his Geiger counter and placed it carefully upon a flat rock by a thick, inviting patch of grass. He listened to the faint, erratic background ticking for a moment, then snapped off the current. No point in running the battery down just to hear stray cosmic rays and residual radioactivity. So far he'd found nothing potent, not a single trace of workable ore.

Squatting, he unpacked an ample lunch of hard-boiled eggs, bread, fruit, and a thermos of black coffee. He ate hungrily, but with the neat, crumbless manners of an outdoorsman; and when the last bite was gone, he stretched out, braced on his elbows, to sip the remaining drops of coffee. It felt mighty good, he thought, to get off your feet after a six-hour hike through rough country.

As he lay there, savoring the strong brew, his gaze suddenly narrowed and became fixed. Right before his eyes, artfully spun between two twigs and a small, mossy boulder, a cunning snare for the unwary spread its threads of wet silver in the network of death. It was the instinctive creation of a master engineer, a nearly perfect logarithmic spiral, stirring gently in a slight updraft.

He studied it curiously, tracing with growing interest the special cable, attached only at the ends, that led from a silk cushion at the web's center up to a crevice in the boulder. He knew that the mistress of this snare must be hidden there, crouching with one hind foot on

447

her primitive telegraph wire and awaiting those welcome vibrations which meant a victim thrashing hopelessly among the sticky threads.

He turned his head and soon found her. Deep in the dark crevice the spider's eyes formed a sinsister, jeweled pattern. Yes, she was at home, patiently watchful. It was all very efficient and, in a reflective mood, drowsy from his exertions and a full stomach, he pondered the small miracle before him: how a speck of protoplasm, a mere dot of white nerve tissue which was a spider's brain, had antedated the mind of Euclid by countless centuries. Spiders are an ancient race; ages before man wrought wonders through his subtle abstractions of points and lines, a spiral not to be distinguished from this one winnowed the breezes of some prehistoric summer.

Then he blinked, his attention once more sharpened. A glowing gem, glistening metallic blue, had planted itself squarely upon the web. As if manipulated by a conjurer, the bluebottle fly had appeared from nowhere. It was an exceptionally fine specimen, he decided, large, perfectly formed, and brilliantly rich in hue.

He eyed the insect wonderingly. Where was the usual panic, the frantic struggling, the shrill, terrified, buzzing? It rested there with an odd indifference to restraint that puzzled him.

There was at least one reasonable explanation. The fly might be sick or dying, the prey of parasites. Fungi and the ubiquitous roundworms shattered the ranks of even the most fertile. So unnaturally still was this fly that the spider, wholly unaware of its feathery landing, dreamed on in her shaded lair.

Then, as he watched, the bluebottle, stupidly perverse, gave a single sharp tug; its powerful wings blurred momentarily and a high-pitched buzz sounded. The man sighed, almost tempted to interfere. Not that it mattered how soon the fly betrayed itself. Eventually the spider would have made a routine inspection; and unlike most people, he knew her for a staunch friend of man, a tireless killer of insect pests. It was not for him to steal her dinner and tear her web.

But now, silent and swift, a pea on eight hairy, agile legs, she glided over her swaying net. An age-old tragedy was about to be enacted, and the man waited with pitying interest for the inevitable denouement.

About an inch from her prey, the spider paused briefly, estimating the situation with diamond-bright, soulless eyes. The man knew what would follow. Utterly contemptuous of a mere fly, however large, lacking either sting or fangs, the spider would unhesitatingly close in, swathe the insect with silk, and drag it to her nest in the rock, there to be drained at leisure.

But instead of a fearless attack, the spider edged cautiously nearer. She seemed doubtful, even uneasy. The fly's strange passivity apparently worried her. He saw the needle-pointed mandibles working, ludicrously suggestive of a woman wringing her hands in agonized indecision.

Reluctantly she crept forward. In a moment she would turn about, squirt a preliminary jet of silk over the bluebottle, and by dexterously rotating the fly with her hind legs, wrap it in a gleaming shroud.

And so it appeared, for satisfied with a closer inspection, she forgot her fears and whirled, thrusting her spinnerets towards the motionless insect.

Then the man saw a startling, an incredible thing. There was a metallic flash as a jointed, shining rod stabbed from the fly's head like some fantastic rapier. It licked out with lightning precision, pierced the spider's plump abdomen, and remained extended, forming a ter- rible link between them.

He gulped, tense with disbelief. A bluebottle fly, a mere lapper of carrion, with an extensible, sucking proboscis! It was impossible. Its tongue is only an absorbing cushion, designed for sponging up liquids. But then was this really a fly after all? Insects often mimic each other and he was no longer familiar with such points. No, a bluebottle is unmistakable; besides, this was a true fly, two wings and everything. Rusty or not, he knew that much.

The spider had stiffened as the queer lance struck home. Now she was rigid, obviously paralyzed. And her swollen abdomen was contracting like a tiny fist as the fly sucked its juices through that slender, pulsating tube.

He peered more closely, raising himself to his knees and longing for a lens. It seemed to his straining gaze as if that gruesome beak came not from the mouth region at all, but through a minute, hatchlike opening between the faceted eyes, with a nearly invisible square door ajar. But that was absurd; it must be the glare, and—ah! Flickering, the rod retracted; there was definitely no such opening now. Apparently the bright sun was playing tricks. The spider stood shriveled, a pitiful husk, still upright on her thin legs.

One thing was certain, he must have this remarkable fly. If not a new species, it was surely very rare. Fortunately it was stuck fast in the web. Killing the spider could not help it. He knew the steely toughness of those elastic strands, each a tight helix filled with superbly tenacious gum. Very few insects, and those only among the stongest, ever tear free. He gingerly extended his thumb and forefinger. Easy now; he had to pull the fly loose without crushing it.

Then he stopped, almost touching the insect, and staring hard. He was uneasy, a little frightened. A brightly glowing spot, brilliant even in the glaring sunlight, was throbbing on the very tip of the blue abdomen. A reedy, barely audible whine was coming from the trapped insect. He though momentarily of fireflies, only to dismiss the notion with scorn for his own stupidity. Of course, a firefly is actually a beetle, and this thing was—not that, anyway.

Excited, he reached forward again, but as his plucking fingers approached, the fly rose smoothly in a vertical ascent, lifting a pyramid of taut strands and tearing a gap in the web as easily as a falling stone. The man was alert, however. His cupped hand, nervously swift, snapped over the insect, and he gave a satisfied grunt.

But the captive buzzed in his eager grasp with a furious vitality that appalled him, and he yelped as a searing, slashing pain scalded the sensitive palm. Involuntarily he relaxed his grip. There was a streak of electric blue as his prize soared, glinting in the sun. For an instant he saw that odd glowworm taillight, a dazzling spark against the darker sky, then nothing.

He examined the wound, swearing bitterly. It was purple, and already little blisters were forming. There was no sign of a puncture. Evidently the creature had not used its lancet, but merely spurted venom—acid, perhaps—on the skin. Certainly the injury felt very much like a bad burn. Damn and blast! He'd kicked away a real find, an insect probably new to science. With a little more care he might have caught it.

Stiff and vexed, he got sullenly to his feet and repacked the lunch kit. He reached for the Geiger counter, snapped on the current, took one step towards a distant rocky outcrop—and froze. The slight background noise had given way to a veritable roar, an electronic avalanche that could mean only one thing. He stood there, scrutinizing the grassy knoll and shaking his head in profound mystification. Frowning, he put down the counter. As he withdrew his hand, the frantic chatter quickly faded out. He waited, half-stooped, a blank look in his eyes. Suddenly they lit with doubting, half-fearful comprehension. Catlike, he stalked the clicking instrument, holding one arm outstretched, gradually advancing the blistered palm.

And the Geiger counter raved anew.

Namesake

ELIZABETH MORTON

In the beginning was the Word—

Tasard squeezed into the upper cubicle through the thin wire, telling himself that the anxiety was normal. The anxiety was nothing to worry about; everyone felt that on being Called. Even as he wound himself to the smooth, familiar surface (so much like the cubicle below) and settled into Meditation, the anxiety began to drain. Remember the inexplicable joy of the Chosen had been their advice as they had sent him to the upper level. "The inexplicable joy of the Chosen," Tasard said, "their loneliness and their obligation." Mantra. The Surveyors were right, weren't they? And if not, how would he know? Tasard felt the nervousness again. Not acceptable. He sighed and crouched, sinking into Meditation through force of will.

The dreams of transcendence had become more intense recently (they had been readying him for the Call) and he gave himself to them, allowing their sensuousness. The dreams were of warmth and penetration, liquid and fire, rising and falling and as they seized him now it was as if it were no longer Meditation but the fire itself, the liquefying fire—

He heard the roar and knew then that it was no longer Meditation. They had, in the end, lied to him; this was happening now.

He was lifted.

Force flung him toward the opposite end of the cubicle; flickers of light strobed his vision. He smelled incense and was flung hopelessly into the world.

And bellowed with the inexplicable joy of the Chosen.

Leon Tasard picked up the revolver and pointed it at his head, his finger on the trigger. For just a moment he hesitated, the terrible, weakening reluctance stayed his finger and he looked out the window at the light he would never see again, the buildings, the aspect of the city . . . but no, it was too late for that, he was beyond remorse, beyond

452

delusion. *It will always be the same,* Tasard thought, *and so it must end*. Suicide is an affirmation.

Weeping, he pulled the trigger.

The bullet with his name on it tore through his temple.

Camps

JACK DANN

The real horrors, of course, move in flesh and blood, and are those
for which the more familiar ghosts and ghouls are merely metaphors.
In this most modern and fully realized of horror stories, Jack Dann
shows us the forms which will stalk the posttechnological night. Like
all masterpieces, it is about what it is about at the same time that it is
about many other things as well. Dann, still a young writer whose
second novel, *Junction,* will appear shortly before this anthology, is
one of the most significant literary voices to emerge in the specter-
laden seventies.

As Stephen lies in bed, he can think only of pain.

He imagines it as sharp and blue. After receiving an injection of
Demerol, he enters pain's cold regions as an explorer, an objective
visitor. It is a country of ice and glass, monochromatic plains and
valleys filled with wash blue shards of ice, crystal pyramids and pinna-
cles, squares, oblongs, and all manner of polyhedron—block upon
block of painted blue pain.

Although it is mid-afternoon, Stephen pretends it is dark. His eyes
are tightly closed, but the daylight pouring into the room from two
large windows intrudes as a dull red field extending infinitely behind
his eyelids.

"Josie," he asks through cotton mouth, "aren't I due for another
shot?" Josie is crisp and fresh and large in her starched white uniform.
Her peaked nurse's cap is pinned to her mouse brown hair.

"I've just given you an injection, it will take effect soon." Josie
strokes his hand, and he dreams of ice.

"Bring me some ice," he whispers.

"If I bring you a bowl of ice, you'll only spill it again."

"Bring me some ice. . . ." By touching the ice cubes, by turning them
in his hand like a gambler favoring his dice, he can transport himself
into the beautiful blue country. Later, the ice will melt, and he will
spill the bowl. The shock of cold and pain will awaken him.

Stephen believes that he is dying, and he has resolved to die properly. Each visit to the cold country brings him closer to death; and death, he has learned, is only a slow walk through icefields. He has come to appreciate the complete lack of warmth and the beautifully etched face of his magical country.

But he is connected to the bright, flat world of the hospital by plastic tubes—one breathes cold oxygen into his left nostril; another passes into his right nostril and down his throat to his stomach; one feeds him intravenously, another draws his urine.

"Here's your ice," Josie says. "But mind you, don't spill it." She places the small bowl on his tray table and wheels the table close to him. She has a musky odor of perspiration and perfume; Stephen is reminded of old women and college girls.

"Sleep now, sweet boy."

Without opening his eyes, Stephen reaches out and places his hand on the ice.

"Come now, Stephen, wake up. Dr. Volk is here to see you."

Stephen feels the cool touch of Josie's hand, and he opens his eyes to see the doctor standing beside him. The doctor has a gaunt long face and thinning brown hair; he is dressed in a wrinkled green suit.

"Now we'll check the dressing, Stephen," he says as he tears away a gauze bandage on Stephen's abdomen.

Stephen feels the pain, but he is removed from it. His only wish is to return to the blue dreamlands. He watches the doctor peel off the neat crosshatchings of gauze. A terrible stink fills the room.

Josie stands well away from the bed.

"Now we'll check your drains." The doctor pulls a long drainage tube out of Sephen's abdomen, irrigates and disinfects the wound, inserts a new drain, and repeats the process by pulling out another tube just below the rib cage.

Stephen imagines that he is swimming out of the room. He tries to cross the hazy border into cooler regions, but it is difficult to concentrate. He has only a half-hour at most before the Demerol will wear off. Already, the pain is coming closer, and he will not be due for another injection until the night nurse comes on duty. But the night nurse will not give him an injection without an argument. She will tell him to fight the pain.

But he cannot fight without a shot.

"Tomorrow we'll take that oxygen tube out of your nose," the doctor says, but his voice seems far away, and Stephen wonders what he is talking about.

He reaches for the bowl of ice, but cannot find it.

"Josie, you've taken my ice."

"I took the ice away when the doctor came. Why don't you try to watch a bit of television with me; Soupy Sales is on."

"Just bring me some ice," Stephen says. "I want to rest a bit." He can feel the sharp edges of pain breaking through the gauzy wraps of Demerol.

"I love you, Josie," he says sleepily as she places a fresh bowl of ice on his tray.

As Stephen wanders through his ice blue dreamworld, he sees a rectangle of blinding white light. It looks like a doorway into an adjoining world of brightness. He has glimpsed it before on previous Demerol highs. A coal-dark doorway stands beside the bright one.

He walks toward the portals, passes through white-blue cornfields.

Time is growing short. The drug cannot stretch it much longer. Stephen knows that he has to choose either the bright doorway or the dark, one or the other. He does not even consider turning around, for he has dreamed that the ice and glass and cold blue gem-stones have melted behind him.

It makes no difference to Stephen which doorway he chooses. On impulse he steps into blazing, searing whiteness.

Suddenly he is in a cramped world of people and sound.

The boxcar's doors were flung open. Stephen was being pushed out of the cramped boxcar that stank of sweat, feces and urine. Several people had died in the car, and added their stink of death to the already fetid air.

"Carla, stay close to me," shouted a man beside Stephen. He had been separated from his wife by a young woman who pushed between them, as she tried to return to the dark safety of the boxcar.

SS men in black, dirty uniforms were everywhere. They kicked and pummeled everyone within reach. Alsatian guard dogs snapped and barked. Stephen was bitten by one of the snarling dogs. A woman beside him was being kicked by soldiers. And they were all being methodically herded past a high barbed-wire fence. Beside the fence was a wall.

Stephen looked around for an escape route, but he was surrounded by other prisoners, who were pressing against him. Soldiers were shooting indiscriminately into the crowd, shooting women and children alike.

The man who had shouted to his wife was shot.

"Sholom, help me, help me," screamed a scrawny young woman whose skin was as yellow and pimpled as chicken flesh.

And Stephen understood that *he* was Sholom. He was a Jew in this burning, stinking world, and this woman, somehow, meant something to him. He felt the yellow star sewn on the breast of his filthy jacket. He grimaced uncontrollably. The strangest thoughts were passing through his mind, remembrances of another childhood: morning prayers with his father and rich uncle, large breakfasts on Saturdays, the sounds of his mother and father quietly making love in the next room, *yortzeit* candles burning in the living room, his brother reciting the "four questions" at the Passover table.

He touched the star again and remembered the Nazi's facetious euphemism for it: *Pour le Semite*.

He wanted to strike out, to kill the Nazis, to fight and die. But he found himself marching with the others, as if he had no will of his own. He felt that he was cut in half. He had two selves now; one watched the other. One self wanted to fight. The other was numbed; it cared only for itself. It was determined to survive.

Stephen looked around for the woman who had called out to him. She was nowhere to be seen.

Behind him were railroad tracks, electrified wire, and the conical tower and main gate of the camp. Ahead was a pitted road littered with corpses and their belongings. Rifles were being fired and a heavy, sickly sweet odor was everywhere. Stephen gagged, others vomited. It was the overwhelming stench of death, of rotting and burning flesh. Black clouds hung above the camp, and flames spurted from the tall chimneys of ugly buildings, as if from infernal machines.

Stephen walked onward; he was numb, unable to fight or even talk. Everything that happened around him was impossible, the stuff of dreams.

The prisoners were ordered to halt, and the soldiers began to separate those who would be burned from those who would be worked to death. Old men and women and young children were pulled out of the crowd. Some were beaten and killed immediately while the others looked on in disbelief. Stephen looked on, as if it was of no concern to him. Everything was unreal, dreamlike. He did not belong here.

The new prisoners looked like *Musselmänner*, the walking dead. Those who became ill, or were beaten or starved before they could "wake up" to the reality of the camps became *Musselmänner*. *Musselmänner* could not think or feel. They shuffled around, already dead in spirit, until a guard or disease or cold or starvation killed them.

"Keep marching," shouted a guard, as Stephen stopped before an emaciated old man crawling on the ground. "You'll look like him soon enough."

Suddenly, as if waking from one dream and finding himself in another, Stephen remembered that the chicken-skinned girl was his wife. He remembered their life together, their children and crowded flat. He remembered the birthmark on her leg, her scent, her hungry love-making. He had once fought another boy over her.

His glands opened up with fear and shame; he had ignored her screams for help.

He stopped and turned, faced the other group. "Fruma," he shouted, then started to run.

A guard struck him in the chest with the butt of his rifle, and Stephen fell into darkness.

He spills the icewater again and awakens with a scream.

"It's my fault," Josie says, as she peels back the sheets. "I should have taken the bowl away from you. But you fight me."

Stephen lives with the pain again. He imagines that a tiny fire is burning in his abdomen, slowly consuming him. He stares at the television high on the wall and watches Soupy Sales.

As Josie changes the plastic sac containing his intravenous saline solution, an orderly pushes a cart into the room and asks Stephen if he wants a print for his wall.

"Would you like me to choose something for you?" Josie asks.

Stephen shakes his head and asks the orderly to show him all the prints. Most of them are familiar still-lifes and pastorals, but one catches his attention. It is a painting of a wheat field. Although the sky looks ominously dark, the wheat is brightly rendered in great broad strokes. A path cuts through the field and crows fly overhead.

"That one," Stephen says. "Put that one up."

After the orderly hangs the print and leaves, Josie asks Stephen why he chose that particular painting.

"I like Van Gogh," he says dreamily, as he tries to detect a rhythm in the surges of abdominal pain. But he is not nauseated, just gaseous.

"Any particular reason why you like Van Gogh?" asks Josie. "He's my favorite artist, too."

"I didn't say he was my favorite," Stephen says, and Josie pouts, an expression which does not fit her prematurely lined face. Stephen closes his eyes, glimpses the cold country, and says, "I like the painting because it's so bright that it's almost frightening. And the road going through the field"—he opens his eyes—"doesn't go anywhere. It just ends in the field. And the crows are flying around like vultures."

"Most people see it as just a pretty picture," Josie says.

"What's it called?"

" 'Wheatfields with Blackbirds.' "

"Sensible. My stomach hurts, Josie. Help me turn over on my side." Josie helps him onto his left side, plumps up his pillows, and inserts a short tube into his rectum to relieve the gas. "I also like the painting with the large stars that all look out of focus," Stephen says. "What's it called?"

" 'Starry Night.' "

"That's scary, too," Stephen says. Josie takes his blood pressure, makes a notation on his chart, then sits down beside him and holds his hand. "I remember something," he says. "Something just—" He jumps as he remembers, and pain shoots through his distended stomach. Josie shushes him, checks the intravenous needle, and asks him what he remembers.

But the memory of the dream recedes as the pain grows sharper. "I hurt all the fucking time, Josie," he says, changing position. Josie removes the rectal tube before he is on his back.

"Don't use such language, I don't like to hear it. I know you have a lot of pain," she says, her voice softening.

"Time for a shot."

"No, honey, not for some time. You'll just have to bear with it."

Stephen remembers his dream again. He is afraid of it. His breath is short and his heart feels as if it is beating in his throat, but he recounts the entire dream to Josie.

He does not notice that her face has lost its color.

"It's only a dream, Stephen. Probably something you studied in history."

"But it was so real, not like a dream at all."

"That's enough!" Josie says.

"I'm sorry I upset you. Don't be angry."

"I'm *not* angry."

"I'm sorry," he says, fighting the pain, squeezing Josie's hand tightly. "Didn't you tell me that you were in the Second World War?"

Josie is composed once again. "Yes, I did, but I'm surprised you remembered. You were very sick. I was a nurse overseas, spent most of the war in England. But I was one of the first servicewomen to go into any of the concentration camps."

Stephen drifts with the pain; he appears to be asleep.

"You must have studied very hard," Josie whispers to him. Her hand is shaking just a bit.

It is twelve o'clock and his room is death quiet. The sharp shadows seem to be the hardest objects in the room. The fluorescents burn steadily in the hall outside.

Stephen looks out into the hallway, but he can see only the far white wall. He waits for his night nurse to appear: it is time for his injection. A young nurse passes by his doorway. Stephen imagines that she is a cardboard ship sailing through the corridors.

He presses the buzzer, which is attached by a clip to his pillow. The night nurse will take her time, he tells himself. He remembers arguing with her. Angrily, he presses the buzzer again.

Across the hall, a man begins to scream, and there is a shuffle of nurses into his room. The screaming turns into begging and whining. Although Stephen has never seen the man in the opposite room, he has come to hate him. Like Stephen, he has something wrong with his stomach, but he cannot suffer well. He can only beg and cry, try to make deals with the nurses, doctors, God and angels. Stephen cannot muster any pity for this man.

The night nurse finally comes into the room, says, "You have to try to get along without this," and gives him an injection of Demerol.

"Why does the man across the hall scream so?" Stephen asks, but the nurse is already edging out of the room.

"Because he's in pain."

"So am I," Stephen says in a loud voice. "But I can keep it to myself."

"Then stop buzzing me constantly for an injection. That man across the hall has had half of his stomach removed. He's got something to scream about."

So have I, Stephen thinks; but the nurse disappears before he can tell her. He tries to imagine what the man across the hall looks like. He thinks of him as being bald and small, an ancient baby. Stephen tries to feel sorry for the man, but his incessant whining disgusts him.

The drug takes effect; the screams recede as he hurtles through the dark corridors of a dream. The cold country is dark, for Stephen cannot persuade his night nurse to bring him some ice. Once again, he sees two entrances. As the world melts behind him, he steps into the coal-black doorway.

In the darkness he hears an alarm, a bone-jarring clangor.

He could smell the combined stink of men pressed closely together. They were all lying upon two badly constructed wooden shelves. The floor was dirt; the smell of urine never left the barracks.

"Wake up," said a man Stephen knew as Viktor. "If the guard finds you in bed, you'll be beaten again."

Stephen moaned, still wrapped in dreams. "Wake up, wake up," he mumbled to himself. He would have a few more minutes before the guard arrived with the dogs. At the very thought of dogs, Stephen felt revulsion. He had once been bitten in the face by a large dog.

He opened his eyes, yet he was still half-asleep, exhausted. You are in a death camp, he said to himself. You must wake up. You must fight by waking up. Or you will die in your sleep. Shaking uncontrollably, he said, "Do you want to end up in the oven; perhaps you will be lucky today and live."

As he lowered his legs to the floor; he felt the sores open on the soles of his feet. He wondered who would die today and shrugged. It was his third week in the camp. Impossibly, against all odds, he had survived. Most of those he had known in the train had either died or become *Musselmänner*. If it was not for Viktor, he, too, would have become a *Musselmänner*. He had a breakdown and wanted to die. He babbled in English. But Viktor talked him out of death, shared his portion of food with him, and taught him the new rules of life.

"Like everyone else who survives, I count myself first, second and third—then I try to do what I can for someone else," Viktor had said.

"I will survive," Stephen repeated to himself, as the guards opened the door, stepped into the room, and began to shout. Their dogs growled and snapped but heeled beside them. The guards looked sleepy; one did not wear a cap, and his red hair was tousled.

Perhaps he spent the night with one of the whores, Stephen thought. Perhaps today would not be so bad. . . .

And so begins the morning ritual: Josie enters Stephen's room at quarter to eight, fusses with the chart attached to the footboard of his bed, pads about aimlessly, and finally goes to the bathroom. She returns, her stiff uniform making swishing sounds. Stephen can feel her standing over the bed and staring at him. But he does not open his eyes. He waits a beat.

She turns away, then drops the bedpan. Yesterday it was the metal ashtray; day before that, she bumped into the bedstand.

"Good morning, darling, it's a beautiful day," she says, then walks across the room to the windows. She parts the faded orange drapes and opens the blinds.

"How do you feel today?"

"Okay, I guess."

Josie takes his pulse and asks, "Did Mr. Gregory stop in to say hello last night?"

"Yes," Stephen says. "He's teaching me how to play gin rummy. What's wrong with him?"

"He's very sick."

"I can see that; has he got cancer?"

"I don't know," says Josie, as she tidies up his night table.

"You're lying again," Stephen says, but she ignores him. After a time, he says, "His girl friend was in to see me last night. I bet his wife will be in today."

"Shut your mouth about that," Josie says. "Let's get you out of that bed so I can change the sheets."

Stephen sits in the chair all morning. He is getting well but is still very weak. Just before lunchtime, the orderly wheels his cart into the room and asks Stephen if he would like to replace the print hanging on the wall.

"I've seen them all," Stephen says. "I'll keep the one I have." Stephen does not grow tired of the Van Gogh painting; sometimes, the crows seem to have changed position.

"Maybe you'll like this one," the orderly says as he pulls out a cardboard print of Van Gogh's "Starry Night." It is a study of a village nestled in the hills, dressed in shadows. But everything seems to be boiling and writhing as in a fever dream. A cypress tree in the foreground looks like a black flame, and the vertiginous sky is filled with great blurry stars. It is a drunkard's dream. The orderly smiles.

"So you did have it," Stephen says.

"No, I traded some other pictures for it. They had a copy in the West Wing."

Stephen watches him hang it, thanks him, and waits for him to leave. Then he gets up and examines the painting carefully. He touches the raised facsimile brushstrokes and turns toward Josie, feeling an odd sensation in his groin. He looks at her, as if seeing her for the first time. She has an overly full mouth which curves downward at the corners when she smiles. She is not a pretty woman—too fat, he thinks.

"Dance with me," he says, as he waves his arms and takes a step forward, conscious of the pain in his stomach.

"You're too sick to be dancing just yet," but she laughs at him and bends her knees in a mock plié.

She has small breasts for such a large woman, Stephen thinks. Feeling suddenly dizzy, he takes a step toward the bed. He feels himself slip to the floor, feels Josie's hair brushing against his face, dreams that he's all wet from her tongue, feels her arms around him, squeezing, then feels the weight of her body pressing down on him, crushing him. . . .

He wakes up in bed, catheterized. He has an intravenous needle in his left wrist, and it is difficult to swallow, for he has a tube down his throat.

He groans, tries to move.

"Quiet, Stephen," Josie says, stroking his hand.

"What happened?" he mumbles. He can only remember being dizzy.

"You've had a slight setback, so just rest. The doctor had to collapse your lung; you must lie very still."

"Josie, I love you," he whispers, but he is too far away to be heard. He wonders how many hours or days have passed. He looks toward the window. It is dark, and there is no one in the room.

He presses the buzzer attached to his pillow and remembers a dream. . . .

"You must fight," Viktor said.

It was dark, all the other men were asleep, and the barracks was filled with snoring and snorting. Stephen wished they could all die, choke on their own breath. It would be an act of mercy.

"Why fight?" Stephen asked, and he pointed toward the greasy window, beyond which were the ovens that smoked day and night. He made a fluttering gesture with his hand—smoke rising.

"You must fight, you must live, living is everything. It is the only thing that makes sense here."

"We're all going to die, anyway," Stephen whispered. "Just like your sister . . . and my wife."

"No, Sholom, we're going to live. The others may die, but we're going to live. You must believe that."

Stephen understood that Viktor was desperately trying to convince himself to live. He felt sorry for Viktor; there could be no sensible rationale for living in a place like this.

Stephen grinned, tasted blood from the corner of his mouth, and said, "So we'll live through the night, maybe."

And maybe tomorrow, he thought. He would play the game of survival a little longer.

He wondered if Viktor would be alive tomorrow. He smiled and thought: If Viktor dies, then I will have to take his place and convince others to live. For an instant, he hoped Viktor would die so that he could take his place.

The alarm sounded. It was three o'clock in the morning, time to begin the day.

This morning Stephen was on his feet before the guards could unlock the door.

"Wake up," Josie says, gently tapping his arm. "Come on, wake up."

Stephen hears her voice as an echo. He imagines that he has been flung into a long tunnel; he hears air whistling in his ears but cannot see anything.

"Whassimatter?" he asks. His mouth feels as if it is stuffed with cotton; his lips are dry and cracked. He is suddenly angry at Josie and the plastic tubes that hold him in his bed as if he was a latter-day Gulliver. He wants to pull out the tubes, smash the bags filled with saline, tear away his bandages.

"You were speaking German," Josie says. "Did you know that?"

"Can I have some ice?"

"No," Josie says impatiently. "You spilled again, you're all wet."

". . . for my mouth, dry . . ."

"Do you remember speaking German, honey. I have to know."

"Don't remember, bring ice, I'll try to think about it."

As Josie leaves to get him some ice, he tries to remember his dream.

"Here, now, just suck on the ice." She gives him a little hill of crushed ice on the end of a spoon.

"Why did you wake me up, Josie?" The layers of dream are beginning to slough off. As the Demerol works out of his system, he has to concentrate on fighting the burning ache in his stomach.

"You were speaking German. Where did you learn to speak like that?"

Stephen tries to remember what he said. He cannot speak any German, only a bit of classroom French. He looks down at his legs (he has thrown off the sheet) and notices, for the first time, that his legs are as thin as his arms. "My God, Josie, how could I have lost so much weight?"

"You lost about forty pounds, but don't worry, you'll gain it all back. You're on the road to recovery now. Please, try to remember your dream."

"I can't, Josie! I just can't seem to get ahold of it."

"Try."

"Why is it so important to you?"

"You weren't speaking college German, darling. You were speaking slang. You spoke in a patois that I haven't heard since the forties."

Stephen feels a chill slowly creep up his spine. "What did I say?"

Josie waits a beat, then says, "You talked about dying."

"Josie?"

"Yes," she says, pulling at her fingernail.

"When is the pain going to stop?"

"It will be over soon." She gives him another spoonful of ice. "You kept repeating the name Viktor in your sleep. Can you remember anything about him?"

Viktor, Viktor, deep-set blue eyes, balding head and broken nose, called himself a Galitzianer. Saved my life. "I remember," Stephen says. "His name is Viktor Shmone. He is in all my dreams now."

Josie exhales sharply.

"Does that mean anything to you?" Stephen asks anxiously.

"I once knew a man from one of the camps." She speaks very slowly and precisely. "His name was Viktor Shmone. I took care of him. He was one of the few people left alive in the camp after the Germans fled." She reaches for her purse, which she keeps on Stephen's night table, and fumbles an old, torn photograph out of a plastic slipcase.

As Stephen examines the photograph, he begins to sob. A thinner and much younger Josie is standing beside Viktor and two other emaciated-looking men. "Then I'm not dreaming," he says, "and I'm going to die. That's what it means." He begins to shake, just as he did in his dream, and, without thinking, he makes the gesture of rising smoke to Josie. He begins to laugh.

"Stop that," Josie says, raising her hand to slap him. Then she embraces him and says, "Don't cry, darling, it's only a dream. Somehow, you're dreaming the past."

"Why?" Stephen asks, still shaking.

"Maybe you're dreaming because of me, because we're so close. In some ways, I think you know me better than anyone else, better than any man, no doubt. You might be dreaming for a reason; maybe I can help you."

"I'm afraid, Josie."

She comforts him and says, "Now tell me everything you can remember about the dreams."

He is exhausted. As he recounts his dreams to her, he sees the bright doorway again. He feels himself being sucked into it. "Josie," he says, "I must stay awake, don't want to sleep, dream. . . ."

Josie's face is pulled tight as a mask; she is crying.

Stephen reaches out to her, slips into the bright doorway, into another dream.

It was a cold cloudless morning. Hundreds of prisoners were working in the quarries; each work gang came from a different barracks. Most of the gangs were made up of *Musselmänner,* the faceless majority of the camp. They moved like automatons, lifting and carrying the great stones to the numbered carts, which would have to be pushed down the tracks.

Stephen was drenched with sweat. He had a fever and was afraid that he had contracted typhus. An epidemic had broken out in the camp last week. Every morning several doctors arrived with the guards. Those who were too sick to stand up were taken away to be gassed or experimented upon in the hospital.

Although Stephen could barely stand, he forced himself to keep moving. He tried to focus all his attention on what he was doing. He made a ritual of bending over, choosing a stone of certain size, lifting it, carrying it to the nearest cart, and then taking the same number of steps back to his dig.

A *Musselmänn* fell to the ground, but Stephen made no effort to help him. When he could help someone in a little way, he would, but he would not stick his neck out for a *Musselmänn*. Yet something niggled at Stephen. He remembered a photograph in which Viktor and this *Musselmänn* were standing with a man and a woman he did not recognize. But Stephen could not remember where he had ever seen such a photograph.

"Hey, you," shouted a guard. "Take the one on the ground to the cart."

Stephen nodded to the guard and began to drag the *Musselmänn* away.

"Who's the new patient down the hall?" Stephen asks as he eats a bit of cereal from the breakfast tray Josie has placed before him. He is feeling much better now; his fever is down, and the tubes, catheter and intravenous needle have been removed. He can even walk around a bit.

"How did you find out about that?" Josie asks.

"You were talking to Mr. Gregory's nurse. Do you think I'm dead already? I can still hear."

Josie laughs and takes a sip of Stephen's tea. "You're far from dead! In fact, today is a red-letter day; you're going to take your first shower. What do you think about that?"

"I'm not well enough yet," he says, worried that he will have to leave the hospital before he is ready.

"Well, Dr. Volk thinks differently, and his word is law."

"Tell me about the new patient."

"They brought in a man last night who drank two quarts of motor oil; he's on the dialysis machine."

"Will he make it?"

"No, I don't think so; there's too much poison in his system."

We should all die, Stephen thinks. It would be an act of mercy. He glimpses the camp.

"Stephen!"

He jumps, then awakens.

"You've had a good night's sleep; you don't need to nap. Let's get you into that shower and have it done with." Josie pushes the tray table away from the bed. "Come on, I have your bathrobe right here."

Stephen puts on his bathrobe, and they walk down the hall to the showers. There are three empty shower stalls, a bench and a whirlpool bath. As Stephen takes off his bathrobe, Josie adjusts the water pressure and temperature in the corner stall.

"What's the matter?" Stephen asks, after stepping into the shower. Josie stands in front of the shower stall and holds his towel, but she will not look at him. "Come on," he says, "you've seen me naked before."

"That was different."

"How?" He touches a hard, ugly scab that has formed over one of the wounds on his abdomen.

"When you were very sick, I washed you in bed, as if you were a baby. Now it's different." She looks down at the wet tile floor, as if she is lost in thought.

"Well, I think it's silly," he says. "Come on, it's hard to talk to someone who's looking the other way. I could break my neck in here and you'd be staring down at the fucking floor."

"I've asked you not to use that word," she says in a very low voice.

"Do my eyes still look yellowish?"

She looks directly at his face and says, "No, they look fine."

Stephen suddenly feels faint, then nauseated; he has been standing too long. As he leans against the cold shower wall, he remembers his last dream. He is back in the quarry. He can smell the perspiration of the men around him, feel the sun baking him, draining his strength. It is so bright. . . .

He finds himself sitting on the bench and staring at the light on the opposite wall. I've got typhus, he thinks, then realizes that he is in the hospital. Josie is beside him.

"I'm sorry," he says.

"I shouldn't have let you stand so long; it was my fault."

"I remembered another dream." He begins to shake, and Josie puts her arms around him.

"It's all right now, tell Josie about your dream."

She's an old, fat woman, Stephen thinks. As he describes the dream, his shaking subsides.

"Do you know the man's name?" Josie asks. "The one the guard ordered you to drag away."

"No," Stephen says. "He was a *Musselmänn*, yet I thought there was something familiar about him. In my dream I remembered the photograph you showed me. He was in it."

"What will happen to him?"

"The guards will give him to the doctors for experimentation. If they don't want him, he'll be gassed."

"You must not let that happen," Josie says, holding him tightly.

"Why?" asks Stephen, afraid that he will fall into the dreams again.

"If he was one of the men you saw in the photograph, you must not let him die. Your dreams must fit the past."

"I'm afraid."

"It will be all right, baby," Josie says, clinging to him. She is shaking and breathing heavily.

Stephen feels himself getting an erection. He calms her, presses his face against hers, and touches her breasts. She tells him to stop, but does not push him away.

"I love you," he says as he slips his hand under her starched skirt. He feels awkward and foolish and warm.

"This is wrong," she whispers.

As Stephen kisses her and feels her thick tongue in his mouth, he begins to dream. . . .

Stephen stopped to rest for a few seconds. The *Musselmänn* was dead weight. I cannot go on, Stephen thought; but he bent down, grabbed the *Musselmänn* by his coat, and dragged him toward the cart. He glimpsed the cart, which was filled with the sick and dead and exhausted; it looked no different than a carload of corpses marked for a mass grave.

A long, gray cloud covered the sun, then passed, drawing shadows across gutted hills.

On impulse, Stephen dragged the *Musselmänn* into a gully behind several chalky rocks. Why am I doing this? he asked himself. If I'm caught, I'll be ash in the ovens, too. He remembered what Viktor had told him: "You must think of yourself all the time, or you'll be no help to anyone else."

The *Musselmänn* groaned, then raised his arm. His face was gray with dust and his eyes were glazed.

"You must lie still," Stephen whispered. "Do not make a sound. I've hidden you from the guards, but if they hear you, we'll all be punished. One sound from you and you're dead. You must fight to live, you're in a death camp, you must fight so you can tell of this later."

"I have no family, they're all—"

Stephen clapped his hand over the man's mouth and whispered, "Fight, don't talk. Wake up, you cannot survive the death camp by sleeping."

The man nodded, and Stephen climbed out of the gully. He helped two men carry a large stone to a nearby cart.

"What are you doing?" shouted a guard.

"I left my place to help these men with this stone; now I'll go back where I was."

"What the hell are you trying to do?" Viktor asked.

Stephen felt as if he was burning up with fever. He wiped the sweat from his eyes, but everything was still blurry.

"You're sick, too. You'll be lucky if you last the day."

"I'll last," Stephen said, "But I want you to help me get him back to the camp."

"I won't risk it, not for a *Musselmänn*. He's already dead, leave him."

"Like you left me?"

Before the guards could take notice, they began to work. Although Viktor was older than Stephen, he was stronger, He worked hard every day and never caught the diseases that daily reduced the barracks' numbers. Stephen had a touch of death, as Viktor called it, and was often sick.

They worked until dusk, when the sun's oblique rays caught the dust from the quarries and turned it into veils and scrims. Even the guards sensed that this was a quiet time, for they would congregate together and talk in hushed voices.

"Come, now, help me," Stephen whispered to Viktor. "I've been doing that all day," Viktor said. "I'll have enough trouble getting you back to the camp, much less carry this *Musselmänn*."

"We can't leave him."

"Why are you so preoccupied with this *Musselmänn*? Even if we can get him back to the camp, his chances are nothing. I know, I've seen enough, I know who has a chance to survive."

"You're wrong this time," Stephen said. He was dizzy and it was difficult to stand. The odds are I won't last the night, and Viktor knows it, he told himself. "I had a dream that if this man dies, I'll die, too. I just feel it."

"Here we learn to trust our dreams," Viktor said. "They make as much sense as this. . . ." He made the gesture of rising smoke and gazed toward the ovens, which were spewing fire and black ash.

The western portion of the sky was yellow, but over the ovens it was red and purple and dark blue. Although it horrified Stephen to consider it, there was a macabre beauty here. If he survived, he would never forget these sense impressions, which were stronger than anything he had ever experienced before. Being so close to death, he was, perhaps for the first time, really living. In the camp, one did not even consider suicide. One grasped for every moment, sucked at life like an infant, lived as if there was no future.

The guards shouted at the prisoners to form a column; it was time to march back to the barracks.

While the others milled about, Stephen and Viktor lifted the *Musselmänn* out of the gully. Everyone nearby tried to distract the guards. When the march began, Stephen and Viktor held the *Musselmänn* between them, for he could barely stand.

"Come on, dead one, carry your weight," Viktor said. "Are you so dead that you cannot hear me? Are you as dead as the rest of your family?" The *Musselmänn* groaned and dragged his legs. Viktor kicked him. "You'll walk or we'll leave you here for the guards to find."

"Let him be," Stephen said.

"Are you dead or do you have a name?" Viktor continued.

"Berek," croaked the *Musselmänn*. "I am not dead."

"Then we have a fine bunk for you," Viktor said. "You can smell the stink of the sick for another night before the guards make a selection." Viktor made the gesture of smoke rising.

Stephen stared at the barracks ahead. They seemed to waver as the heat rose from the ground. He counted every step. He would drop soon, he could not go on, could not carry the _Musselmänn_.

He began to mumble in English.

"So you're speaking American again," Viktor said.

Stephen shook himself awake, placed one foot before the other.

"Dreaming of an American lover?"

"I don't know English and I have no American lover."

"Then who is this Josie you keep taking about in your sleep . . .?"

"Why were you screaming?" Josie asks, as she washes his face with a cold washcloth.

"I don't remember screaming," Stephen says. He discovers a fever blister on his lip. Expecting to find an intravenous needle in his wrist, he raises his arm.

"You don't need an IV," Josie says. "You just have a bit of a fever. Dr. Volk has prescribed some new medication for it."

"What time is it?" Stephen stares at the whorls in the ceiling.

"Almost three P.M. I'll be going off soon."

"Then I've slept most of the day away," Stephen says, feeling something crawling inside him. He worries that his dreams still have a hold on him. "Am I having another relapse?"

"You'll do fine," Josie says.

"I should be fine now. I don't want to dream anymore."

"Did you dream again, do you remember anything?"

"I dreamed that I saved the _Musselmänn_," Stephen says.

"What was his name?" asks Josie.

"Berek, I think. Is that the man you knew?"

Josie nods and Stephen smiles at her. "Maybe that's the end of the dreams," he says, but she does not respond. He asks to see the photograph again.

"Not just now," Josie says.

"But I have to see it. I want to see if I can recognize myself . . . .

Stephen dreamed he was dead, but it was only the fever. Viktor sat beside him on the floor and watched the others. The sick were moaning and crying; they slept on the cramped platform, as if proximity to one another could insure a few more hours of life. Wan moonlight seemed to fill the barracks.

Stephen awakened, feverish. "I'm burning up," he whispered to Viktor.

"Well," Viktor said, "you've got your *Musselmänn*. If he lives, you live. That's what you said, isn't it?"

"I don't remember, I just knew that I couldn't let him die."

"You'd better go back to sleep, you'll need your strength. Or we may have to carry *you*, tomorrow."

Stephen tried to sleep, but the fever was making lights and spots before his eyes. When he finally fell asleep, he dreamed of a dark country filled with gem-stones and great quarries of ice and glass.

"What?" Stephen asked, as he sat up suddenly, awakened from damp black dreams. He looked around and saw that everyone was watching Berek, who was sitting under the window at the far end of the room.

Berek was singing the *Kol Nidre* very softly. It was the Yom Kippur prayer, which was sung on the most holy of days. He repeated the prayer three times, and then once again in a louder voice. The others responded, intoned the prayer as a recitative. Viktor was crying quietly, and Stephen imagined that the holy spirit animated Berek. Surely, he told himself, that face and those pale unseeing eyes were those of a dead man. He remembered the story of the golem, shuddered, found himself singing and pulsing with fever.

When the prayer was over, Berek fell back into his fever trance. The others became silent, then slept. But there was something new in the barracks with them tonight, a palpable exultation. Stephen looked around at the sleepers and thought: We're surviving, more dead than alive, but surviving . . . .

"You were right about that *Musslemänn*," Viktor whispered. "It's good that we saved him."

"Perhaps we should sit with him," Stephen said. "He's alone." But Viktor was already asleep; and Stephen was suddenly afraid that if he sat beside Berek, he would be consumed by his holy fire.

As Stephen fell through sleep and dreams, his face burned with fever.

Again he wakes up screaming.

"Josie," he says, "I can remember the dream, but there's something else, something I can't see, something terrible . . . ."

"Not to worry," Josie says, "it's the fever." But she looks worried, and Stephen is sure that she knows something he does not.

"Tell me what happened to Viktor and Berek," Stephen says. He presses his hands together to stop them from shaking.

"They lived, just as you are going to live and have a good life."

Stephen calms down and tells her his dream.

"So you see," she says, "you're even dreaming about surviving."

"I'm burning up."

"Dr. Volk says you're doing very well." Josie sits beside him, and he watches the fever patterns shift behind his closed eyelids.

"Tell me what happens next, Josie."

"You're going to get well."

"There's something else . . . ."

"Shush, now, there's nothing else." She pauses, then says, "Mr. Gregory is supposed to visit you tonight. He's getting around a bit; he's been back and forth all day in his wheelchair. He tells me that you two have made some sort of a deal about dividing up all the nurses."

Stephen smiles, opens his eyes, and says, "It was Gregory's idea. Tell me what's wrong with him."

"All right, he has cancer, but he doesn't know it, and you must keep it a secret. They cut the nerve in his leg because the pain was so bad. He's quite comfortable now, but, remember, you can't repeat what I've told you."

"Is he going to live?" Stephen asks. "He's told me about all the new projects he's planning. So I guess he's expecting to get out of here."

"He's not going to live very long, and the doctor didn't want to break his spirit."

"I think he should be told."

"That's not your decision to make, nor mine."

"Am I going to die, Josie?"

"No!" she says, touching his arm to reassure him.

"How do I know that's the truth?"

"Because I say so, and I couldn't look you straight in the eye and tell you if it wasn't true. I should have known it would be a mistake to tell you about Mr. Gregory."

"You did right," Stephen says. "I won't mention it again. Now that I know, I feel better." He feels drowsy again.

"Do you think you're up to seeing him tonight?"

Stephen nods, although he is bone-tired. As he falls asleep, the fever patterns begin to dissolve, leaving a bright field. With a start, he opens his eyes: he has touched the edge of another dream.

"What happened to the man across the hall, the one who was always screaming?"

"He's left the ward," Josie says. "Mr. Gregory had better hurry, if he wants to play cards with you before dinner. They're going to bring the trays up soon."

"You mean he died, don't you."

"Yes, if you must know, he died. But *you're* going to live."

There is a crashing noise in the hallway. Someone shouts, and Josie runs to the door.

Stephen tries to stay awake, but he is being pulled back into the cold country.

"Mr. Gregory fell trying to get into his wheelchair by himself," Josie says. "He should have waited for his nurse, but she was out of the room and he wanted to visit you."

But Stephen does not hear a word she says.

There were rumors that the camp was going to be liberated. It was late, but no one was asleep. The shadows in the barracks seemed larger tonight.

"It's better for us if the Allies don't come," Viktor said to Stephen.

"Why do you say that?"

"Haven't you noticed that the ovens are going day and night? The Nazis are in a hurry."

"I'm going to try to sleep," Stephen said.

"Look around you, even the *Musslemänner* are agitated," Viktor said. "Animals become nervous before the slaughter. I've worked with animals. People are not so different."

"Shut up and let me sleep," Stephen said, and he dreamed that he could hear the crackling of distant gunfire.

"Attention," shouted the guards as they stepped into the barracks. There were more guards than usual, and each one had two Alsatian dogs. "Come on, form a line. Hurry."

"They're going to kill us," Viktor said, "then they'll evacuate the camp and save themselves."

The guards marched the prisoners toward the north section of the camp. Although it was still dark, it was hot and humid, without a trace of the usual morning chill. The ovens belched fire and turned the sky aglow. Everyone was quiet, for there was nothing to be done. The guards were nervous and would cut down anyone who uttered a sound, as an example for the rest.

The booming of big guns could be heard in the distance. If I'm going to die, Stephen thought, I might as well go now and take a Nazi with me. Suddenly, all of his buried fear, aggression and revulsion surfaced; his face became hot and his heart felt as if it was pumping in his throat. But Stephen argued with himself. There was always a chance. He had once heard of some women who were waiting in line for the ovens; for no apparent reason the guards sent them back to their barracks. Anything could happen. There was always a chance. But to attack a guard would mean certain death.

The guns became louder. Stephen could not be sure, but he thought the noise was coming from the west. The thought passed through his mind that everyone would be better off dead. That would stop all the guns and screaming voices, the clenched fists and wildly beating hearts. The Nazis should kill everyone, and then themselves, as a favor to humanity.

The guards stopped the prisoners in an open field surrounded on three sides by forestland. Sunrise was moments away; purple black clouds drifted across the sky, touched by gray in the east. It promised to be a hot, gritty day.

Half-Step Walter, a Judenrat sympathizer who worked for the guards, handed out shovel heads to everyone.

"He's worse than the Nazis," Viktor said to Stephen.

"The Judenrat thinks he will live," said Berek, "but he will die like a Jew with the rest of us."

"Now, when it's too late, the *Musselmïnann* regains consciousness," Viktor said.

"Hurry," shouted the guards, "or you'll die now. As long as you dig, you'll live."

Stephen hunkered down on his knees and began to dig with the shovel head.

"Do you think we might escape?" Berek whined.

"Shut up and dig," Stephen said. "There is no escape, just stay alive as long as you can. Stop whining, are you becoming a *Musselmänn* again?" Stephen noticed that other prisoners were gathering up twigs and branches. So the Nazis plan to cover us up, he thought.

"That's enough," shouted a guard. "Put your shovels down in front of you and stand a line."

The prisoners stood shoulder to shoulder along the edge of the mass grave. Stephen stood between Viktor and Berek. Someone screamed and ran and was shot immediately.

I don't want to see trees or guards or my friends, Stephen thought as he stared into the sun. I only want to see the sun, let it burn out my eyes, fill up my head with light. He was shaking uncontrollably, quaking with fear.

Guns were booming in the background.

Maybe the guards won't kill us, Stephen thought, even as he heard the crack-crack of their rifles. Men were screaming and begging for life. Stephen turned his head, only to see someone's face blown away.

Screaming, tasting vomit in his mouth, Stephen fell backward, pulling Viktor and Berek into the grave with him.

Darkness, Stephen thought. His eyes were open, yet it was dark, I must be dead, this must be death . . . .

He could barely move. Corpses can't move, he thought. Something brushed against his face; he stuck out his tongue, felt something spongy. It tasted bitter. Lifting first one arm and then the other, Stephen moved some branches away. Above, he could see a few dim stars; the clouds were lit like lanterns by a quarter moon.

He touched the body beside him; it moved. That must be Viktor, he thought. "Viktor, are you alive, say something if you're alive." Stephen whispered, as if in fear of disturbing the dead.

Viktor groaned and said, "Yes, I'm alive, and so is Berek."

"And the others?"

"All dead. Can't you smell the stink? You, at least, were unconscious all day."

"They can't *all* be dead," Stephen said, then he began to cry

"Shut up," Viktor said, touching Stephen's face to comfort him. "We're alive, that's something. They could have fired a volley into the pit."

"I though I was dead," Berek said. He was a shadow among shadows.

"Why are we still here?" Stephen asked.

"We stayed in here because it is safe," Viktor said.

"But they're all dead," Stephen whispered, amazed that there could be speech and reason inside a grave.

"Do you think it's safe to leave now?" Berek asked Viktor.

"Perhaps. I think the killing has stopped. By now the Americans or English or whoever they are have taken over the camp. I heard gunfire and screaming. I think it's best to wait a while longer."

"Here?" asked Stephen. "Among the dead?"

"It's best to be safe."

It was late afternoon when they climbed out of the grave. The air was thick with flies. Stephen could see bodies sprawled in awkward positions beneath the covering of twigs and branches. "How can I live when all the others are dead?" he asked himself aloud.

"You live, that's all," answered Viktor.

They kept close to the forest and worked their way back toward the camp.

"Look there," Viktor said, motioning Stephen and Berek to take cover. Stephen could see trucks moving toward the camp compound.

"Americans," whispered Berek.

"No need to whisper now," Stephen said. "We're safe."

"Guards could be hiding anywhere," Viktor said. "I haven't slept in the grave to be shot now."

They walked into the camp through a large break in the barbed-wire fence, which had been hit by an artillery shell. When they reached the compound, they found nurses, doctors, and army personnel bustling about.

"You speak English," Viktor said to Stephen, as they walked past several quonsets. "Maybe you can speak for us."

"I told you, I can't speak English."

"But I've heard you!"

"Wait," shouted an American army nurse. "You fellows are going the wrong way." She was stocky and spoke perfect German. "You must check in at the hospital; it's back that way."

"No," said Berek, shaking his head. "I won't go in there."

"There's no need to be afraid now," she said. "You're free. Come along, I'll take you to the hospital."

Something familiar about her, Stephen thought. He felt dizzy and everything turned gray.

"Josie," he murmured, as he fell to the ground.

"What is it?" Josie asks. "Everything is all right, Josie is here."

"Josie," Stephen mumbles.

"You're all right."

"How can I live when they're all dead?" he asks.

"It was a dream," she says as she wipes the sweat from his forehead. "You see, your fever has broken, you're getting well."

"Did you know about the grave?"

"It's all over now, forget the dream."

"Did you know?"

"Yes," Josie says. "Viktor told me how he survived the grave, but that was so long ago, before you were even born. Dr. Volk tells me you'll be going home soon."

"I don't want to leave, I want to stay with you."

"Stop that talk, you've got a whole life ahead of you. Soon, you'll forget all about this, and you'll forget me, too."

"Josie," Stephen asks, "let me see that old photograph again. Just one last time."

"Remember, this is the last time," she says as she hands him the faded photograph.

He recognizes Viktor and Berek, but the young man standing between them is not Stephen. "That's not me," he says, certain that he will never return to the camp.

Yet the shots still echo in his mind.

You Know Willie

THEODORE R. COGSWELL

Theodore Cogswell, always an underrated science fiction writer, produced an uneven but intermittently astonishing body of work through the 1950's, work which moved closer against the buried veins of his time than most. "You Know Willie" is a perfect and stark nightmare with an ending, resonant by its understatement, which goes on and on and on...

In the old days there wouldn't have been any fuss about Willie McCracken shooting a Negro, but these weren't the old days. The judge sat sweating, listening to the voice from the state capital that roared through the telephone receiver.

"But you can't hang no white man for shooting no nigger!"

"Who said anything about hanging?" said the voice impatiently. "I want it to look good, that's all. So don't make it any half-hour job—take two weeks if you have to."

The judge obediently took two weeks. There was a long parade of witnesses for the defense and an equally long one for the prosecution, and through it all the jury, having been duly instructed beforehand, sat gravely, happy for a respite from the hot sun and fields—and the cash money that was accruing to each of them at the rate of three dollars a day. A bright young man was down from the capital to oversee all major matters, and as a result, the trial of Willie McCracken was model of juridical propriety.

The prosecution made as strong a case against Willie as it could without bringing in such prejudicial evidence as that the little garage the dead man had opened after he came back from Korea had been taking business away from the one Willie ran at an alarming rate, or that it was common knowledge that Willie was the Thrice High Warlock of the local chapter of The Knights of the Flaming Sword and in his official capacity had given the deceased one week to get out of town or else.

There were two important witnesses. One was very old and very black, the other wasn't quite as young as she used to be but she was white. The first could technically be classed as a witch—though there was another and more sonorous name for what she was in the forgotten tribal language she used on ritual occasions—but contrary to the ancient injunction, she had not only been permitted to live, but to flourish in a modest fashion. There were few in the courtroom who had not at one time or another made secret use of Aunt Hattie's services. And although most of the calls had been for relatively harmless love potions or protective amulets, there were enough who had called with darker things in mind to cause her to be treated with unusual respect.

Aunt Hattie was the town's oldest inhabitant—legend had it that she was already a grown woman when Lincoln larcenously freed the slaves—and the deceased had been her only living blood relative.

Having been duly sworn, she testified that the defendant, Willie McCracken, had come to her cabin just as she was getting supper, asked for the deceased, and then shot him between the eyes when he came to the door.

She was followed by Willie's wife, a plumpish little blonde in an over-tight dress who was obviously enjoying all the attention she was getting. She in turn swore that Willie had been home in bed with her where he belonged at the time in question. From the expressions on the jurymen's faces, it was obvious that they were thinking that if he hadn't been, he was a darned fool.

There were eight Knights of the Flaming Sword sitting around the table in Willie's kitchen. Willie pulled a jug from the floor beside him, took a long swallow, and wiped his mouth nervously with the hairy back of his hand. He looked up at the battered alarm clock on the shelf over the sink and then lifted the jug again. When he set it down Pete Martin reached over and grabbed it.

"Buck up, Willie boy," he said as he shook the countainer to see how much was left in it. "Ain't nobody going to get at you with us here."

Willie shivered. "You ain't seen her squatting out under that cottonwood every night like I have." He reached out for the jug but Martin laughed and pulled it out of reach.

"You lay off that corn and you won't be seeing Aunt Hattie every time you turn around. The way you've been hitting the stuff since the trial it's a wonder you ain't picking snakes up off the table by now."

"I seen her, I tell you," said Willie sullenly. "Six nights running now I seen her plain as day just sitting out under that tree waiting for the moon to get full." He reached for the jug again but Martin pushed his hand away.

"You've had enough. Now you just sit there quiet like while I talk some sense. Aunt Hattie's dead and Jackson's dead and they're both safe six foot under. I don't blame you for getting your wind up after what she yelled in the courtroom afore she keeled over, but just remember that there ain't no nigger the knights can't take of, dead or alive. Now you go upstairs and get yourself a little shuteye. You're plumb beat. I don't think you've had six hours good sleep since the finish of the trial. You don't notice Winnie Mae losing any rest, do you?"

Willie kneaded his bald scalp with thick fingers. "Couldn't sleep," he said hoarsely. "Not with her out there. She said he'd come back first full moon rise and every night it's been getting rounder and rounder."

"He comes back, we'll fix him for you, Willie," said Martin in a soothing voice. "Now you do like I said. Moon won't be up for a good two hours yet. You go get a little sleep and we'll call you in plenty of time."

Willie hesitated and then got to his feet and lumbered up the stairs. He was so tired he staggered as he walked. When he got into the dark bedroom he pulled off his clothes and threw himself down on the brass bed beside Winnie Mae. He tried to keep awake but he couldn't. In a moment his heavy snores were blending with her delicate ones.

The moonlight was strong and bright in the room when Willie woke. They hadn't called him! From the kitchen below he heard a rumble of voices and then drunken laughter. Slowly, as if hypnotized, he swung his fat legs over the side of the bed and stumbled to the window. He tried to keep from looking but he couldn't. She would be there, squatting beneath the old cottonwood, a shriveled little black mummy that waited . . . waited . . . waited . . .

Willie dug his knuckles suddenly into his eyes, rubbed hard, and then looked again. There was nothing! Nothing where the thick old trunk met the ground but a dusty clump of crabgrass. He stood trembling, staring down at the refuse littered yard as if it was the most beautiful thing he had ever seen. There was something healing in the calm flood of moonlight. The hard knot he had been carrying inside his head dissolved and he felt strong and young again. He wanted to shout, to caper around the room.

Winnie Mae mumbled in her sleep and he turned to look at her. Her thin cotton nightgown was bunched up under her arms and she lay, legs astraddle, her plump body gleaming whitely in the moonlight. She whimpered as she pulled herself up out of her slumber and then closed her arms around the heavy body that was pressing down on her. "Remember me," he whispered, "I'm Willie. You know Willie."

She giggled and pulled him tighter against her. Her breath began to come faster and her fingers made little cat clawings on his back. As she squirmed under him her hand crept higher, over his shoulders, up his neck . . .

There was a sudden explosion under him and a caterwauling scream of sheer horror. Willie jerked back as her nails raked across his face, and then he felt a sudden stabbing agony as she jabbed up with her knee. He staggered away from the bed, his hands cupped over his bleeding face.

His hands! Time slid to a nightmarish stop as his fingertips sent a message pulsing down through nerve endings that his bald scalp had somehow sprouted a thick mop of kinky hair. He jerked his hands down and held them cupped before him. The fresh blood was black in the moonlight, and not only the blood. He spun toward the cracked mirror and saw himself for the first time. The flabby body with its sagging belly was gone. In its place was that of a dark-skinned stranger . . . but not a stranger.

His fingers crept across his forehead looking for a small red bullet hole that was no longer there.

And then time started to rush forward again. Winnie Mae's screaming went on and on and there was a rushing of heavy feet up the stairs from the kitchen.

He tried to explain but there was a new softness to his speech that put the lie to his stumbling words. When the door burst open he stood for a moment, hands stretched out in supplication.

"No," he whimpered. "I'm Willie. You know Willie."

As they came slowly out of the shadows he broke. He took one slow step backwards, and then two, and then when he felt the low sill press against his calves, turned and dove out the window onto the sloping roof. When he got to the ground he tried again to explain but somebody remembered his gun.

Willie as he had been would have been run to ground within the mile, but his new lithe body carried him effortlessly through the night. If it hadn't been for the dogs he might have got away.

Somebody had a deck of cards and they all drew. Pete Martin was low man so he had to go back after the gasoline.

The Mindworm

C. M. KORNBLUTH

The late (1923-1958) and deeply lamented Cyril M. Kornbluth produced many notable stories in his too-short life. Some were bittersweet, some quite serious and ambitious, some satirical, and some, like the present selection, were terrifying. None were funny, however—Kornbluth was never funny on paper.

The vampire is among the most honored of the creatures of horror, but in all the literature there has never been one quite like "The Mindworm."

The handsome j.g. and the pretty nurse held out against it as long as they reasonably could, but blue Pacific water, languid tropical nights, the low atoll dreaming on the horizon—and the complete absence of any other nice young people for company on the small, uncomfortable parts boat—did their work. On June 30th they watched through dark glasses as the dazzling thing burst over the fleet and the atoll. Her manicured hand gripped his arm in excitement and terror. Unfelt radiation sleeted through their loins.

A storekeeper-third-class named Bielaski watched the young couple with more interest than he showed in Test Able. After all, he had twenty-five dollars riding on the nurse. That night he lost it to a chief bosun's mate who had backed the j.g.

In the course of time, the careless nurse was discharged under conditions other than honorable. The j.g., who didn't like to put things in writing, phoned her all the way from Manila to say it was a damned shame. When her gratitude gave way to specific inquiry, their overseas connection went bad and he had to hang up.

She had a child, a boy, turned it over to the foundling home, and vanished from his life into a series of good jobs and finally marriage.

The boy grew up stupid, puny and stubborn, greedy and miserable. To the home's hilarious young athletics directer he suddenly said: "You hate me. You think I make the rest of the boys look bad."

The athletics director blustered and laughed, and later told the doc-

485

tor over coffee: "I watch myself around the kids. They're sharp—they catch a look or a gesture and it's like a blow in the face to them, I know that, so I watch myself. So how did he know?"

The doctor told the boy: "Three pounds more this month isn't bad, but how about you pitch in and clean up your plate *every* day? Can't live on meat and water; those vegetables make you big and strong."

The boy said: "What's 'neurasthenic' mean?"

The doctor later said to the director: "It made my flesh creep. I was looking at his little spindling body and dishing out the old pep talk about growing big and strong, and inside my head I was thinking 'we'd call him neurasthenic in the old days' and then out he popped with it. What should we do? Should we do anything? Maybe it'll go away. I don't know anything about these things. I don't know whether anybody does."

"Reads minds, does he?" asked the director. *Be damned if he's going to read my mind about Schultz Meat Market's ten percent.* "Doctor, I think I'm going to take my vacation a little early this year. Has anybody shown any interest in adopting the child?"

"Not him. He wasn't a baby doll when we got him, and at present he's an exceptionally unattractive-looking kid. You know how people don't give a damn about anything but their looks."

"*Some* couples would take anything, or so they tell me."

"Unapproved for foster-parenthood, you mean?"

"Red tape and arbitrary classifications sometimes limit us too severely in our adoptions."

"If you're going to wish him on some screwball couple that the courts turned down as unfit, I want no part of it."

"You don't have to have any part of it, doctor. By the way, which dorm does he sleep in?"

"West," grunted the doctor, leaving the office.

The director called a few friends—a judge, a couple the judge referred him to, a court clerk. Then he left by way of the east wing of the building.

The boy survived three months with the Berrymans. Hard-drinking Mimi alternately caressed and shrieked at him; Edward W. tried to be a good scout and just gradually lost interest, looking clean through him. He hit the road in June and got by with it for a while. He wore a Boy Scout uniform, and Boy Scouts can turn up anywhere, any time. The money he had taken with him lasted a month. When the last penny of the last dollar was three days spent, he was adrift on a

Nebraska prairie. He had walked out of the last small town because the constable was beginning to wonder what on earth he was hanging around for and who he belonged to. The town was miles behind on the two-lane highway; the infrequent cars did not stop.

One of Nebraska's "rivers," a dry bed at this time of year, lay ahead, spanned by a railroad culvert. There were some men in its shade, and he was hungry.

They were ugly, dirty men, and their thoughts were muddled and stupid. They called him "Shorty" and gave him a little dirty bread and some stinking sardines from a can. The thoughts of one of them became less muddled and uglier. He talked to the rest out of the boy's hearing, and they whooped with laughter. The boy got ready to run, but his legs wouldn't hold him up.

He could read the thoughts of the men quite clearly as they headed for him. Outrage, fear and disgust blended in him and somehow turned inside-out and one of the men was dead on the dry ground, grasshoppers vaulting onto his flannel shirt, the others backing away, frightened now, not frightening.

He wasn't hungry any more; he felt quite comfortable and satisfied. He got up and headed for the other men, who ran. The rearmost of them was thinking *Jeez he folded up the evil eye we was only gonna*—

Again the boy let the thoughts flow into his head and again he flipped his own thoughts around them; it was quite easy to do. It was different—this man's terror from the other's lustful anticipation. But both had their points . . .

At his leisure, he robbed the bodies of three dollars and twenty-four cents.

Thereafter his fame preceded him like a death wind. Two years on the road and he had his growth and his fill of the dull and stupid minds he met there. He moved to northern cities, a year here, a year there, quiet, unobtrusive, prudent, an epicure.

Sebastian Long woke suddenly, with something on his mind. As night fog cleared away he remembered, happily. Today he started the Demeter Bowl! At last there was time, at last there was money—six hundred and twenty-three dollars in the bank. He had packed and shipped the three dozen cocktail glasses last night, engraved with Mrs. Klausman's initials—his last commercial order for as many months as the bowl would take.

He shifted from nightshirt to denims, gulped coffee, boiled an egg but was too excited to eat it. He went to the front of his shop-work-room-apartment, checked the lock, waved at neighbors' children on their way to school, and ceremoniously set a sign in the cluttered window.

It said: NO COMMERCIAL ORDERS TAKEN UNTIL FURTHER NOTICE.

From a closet he tenderly carried a shrouded object that made a double armful and laid it on his workbench. Unshrouded, it was a glass bowl—*what* a glass bowl! The clearest Swedish lead glass, the purest lines he had ever seen, his secret treasure since the crazy day he had bought it, long ago, for six months' earnings. His wife had given him hell for that until the day she died. From the closet he brought a portfolio filled with sketches and designs dating back to the day he had bought the bowl. He smiled over the first, excitedly scrawled—a florid, rococo conception, unsuited to the classicism of the lines and the serenity of the perfect glass.

Through many years and hundreds of sketches he had refined his conception to the point where it was, he humbly felt, not unsuited to the medium. A strongly molded Demeter was to dominate the piece, a matron as serene as the glass, and all the fruits of the earth would flow from her gravely ourstretched arms.

Suddenly and surely, he began to work. With a candle he thinly smoked an oval area on the outside of the bowl. Two steady fingers clipped the Demeter drawing against the carbon black; a hair-fine needle in his other hand traced her lines. When the transfer of the design was done, Sebastian Long readied his lathe. He fitted a small copper wheel, slightly worn as he liked them, into the chuck and with his fingers charged it with the finest rouge from Rouen. He took an ashtray cracked in delivery and held it against the spinning disc. It bit in smoothly, with the *wiping* feel to it that was exactly right.

Holding out his hands, seeing that the fingers did not tremble with excitement, he eased the great bowl to the lathe and was about to make the first tiny cut of the millions that would go into the masterpiece.

Somebody knocked on his door and rattled the doorknob.

Sebastian Long did not move or look toward the door. Soon the busybody would read the sign and go away. But the pounding and the rattling of the knob went on. He eased down the bowl and angrily went to the window, picked up the sign, and shook it at whoever it was—he couldn't make out the face very well. But the idiot wouldn't go away.

The engraver unlocked the door, opened it a bit, and snapped: "The shop is closed. I shall not be taking any orders for several months. Please don't bother me now."

"It's about the Demeter Bowl," said the intruder.

Sebastian Long stared at him. "What the devil do you know about my Demeter Bowl?" He saw the man was a stranger, undersized by a little, middle-aged . . .

"Just let me in please," urged the man. "It's important. Please!"

"I don't know what you're talking about," said the engraver. "But what do you know about my Demeter Bowl?" He hooked his thumbs pugnaciously over the waistband of his denims and glowered at the stranger. The stranger promptly took advantage of his hand being removed from the door and glided in.

Sebastian Long thought briefly that it might be a nightmare as the man darted quickly about his shop, picking up a graver and throwing it down, picking up a wire scratch-wheel and throwing it down. "Here, you!" he roared, as the stranger picked up a crescent wrench which he did not throw down.

As Long started for him, the stranger darted to the workbench and brought the crescent wrench down shatteringly on the bowl.

Sebastian Long's heart was bursting with sorrow and rage; such a storm of emotions as he never had known thundered through him. Paralyzed, he saw the stranger smile with anticipation.

The engraver's legs folded under him and he fell to the floor, drained and dead.

The Mindworm, locked in the bedroom of his brownstone front, smiled again, reminiscently.

Smiling, he checked the day on a wall calendar.

"Dolores!" yelled her mother in Spanish. "Are you going to pass the whole day in there?"

She had been practicing low-lidded, sexy half-smiles like Lauren Bacall in the bathroom mirror. She stormed out and yelled in English: "I don't know how many times I tell you not to call me that spick name no more!"

"Dolly!" sneered her mother. "Dah-lee! When was there a St. Dah-lee that you call yourself after, eh?"

The girl snarled a Spanish obscenity at her mother and ran down the tenement stairs. Jeez, she was gonna be late for sure!

Held up by a stream of traffic between her and her streetcar, she danced with impatience. Then the miracle happened. Just like in the movies, a big convertible pulled up before her and its lounging driver said, opening the door: "You seem to be in a hurry. Could I drop you somewhere?"

Dazed at the sudden realization of a hundred daydreams, she did not fail to give the driver a low-lidded, sexy smile as she said: "Why, *thanks!*" and climbed in. He wasn't no Cary Grant, but he had all his hair . . . kind of small, but so was she . . . and jeez, the convertible had *leopard-skin seat covers!*

The car was in the stream of traffic, purring down the avenue. "It's a lovely day," she said. "Really too nice to work."

The driver smiled shyly, kind of like Jimmy Stewart but of course not so tall, and said: "I feel like playing hooky myself. How would you like a spin down Long Island?"

"Be wonderful!" The convertible cut left on an odd-numbered street.

"Play hooky, you said. What do you do?"

"Advertising."

"*Advertising!*" Dolly wanted to kick herself for ever having doubted, for ever having thought in low, self-loathing monents that it wouldn't work out, that she'd marry a grocer or a mechanic and live forever after in a smelly tenement and grow old and sick and stooped. She felt vaguely in her happy daze that it might have been cuter, she might have accidentally pushed him into a pond or something, but this was cute enough. An advertising man, leopard-skin seat covers . . . what more could a girl with a sexy smile and a nice little figure want?

Speeding down the South Shore she learned that his name was Michael Brent, exactly as it ought to be. She wished she could tell him she was Jennifer Brown or one of those real cute names they had nowadays, but was reassured when he told her he thought Dolly Gonzalez was a beautiful name. He didn't, and she noticed the omission, add: "It's the most beautiful name I ever heard!" That, she comfortably thought as she settled herself against the cushions, would come later.

They stopped at Medford for lunch, a wonderful lunch in a little restaurant where you went down some steps and there were candles on the table. She called him "Michael" and he called her "Dolly." She learned that he liked dark girls and thought the stories in *True Story* really were true, and that he thought she was just tall enough, and that Greer Garson was wonderful, but not the way she was, and that he thought her dress was just wonderful.

They drove slowly after Medford, and Michael Brent did most of the talking. He had traveled all over the world. He had been in the war and wounded—just a flesh wound. He was thirty-eight, and had been married once, but she died. There were no children. He was alone in the world. He had nobody to share his townhouse in the fifties, his country place in Westchester, his lodge in the Maine woods. Every word sent the girl floating higher and higher on a tide of happiness; the signs were unmistakable.

When they reached Montauk Point, the last sandy bit of the continent before blue water and Europe, it was sunset, with a great wrinkled sheet of purple and rose stretching half across the sky and the first stars appearing above the dark horizon of the water.

The two of them walked from the parked car out onto the sand, alone, bathed in glorious Technicolor. Her heart was nearly bursting with joy as she heard Michael Brent say, his arms tightening around her: "Darling, will you marry me?"

"Oh, *yes*, Michael!" she breathed, dying.

The Mindworm, drowsing, suddenly felt the sharp sting of danger. He cast out through the great city, dragging tentacles of thought:

". . . die if she don't let me . . ."

". . . six an' six is twelve an' carry one an' three is four . . ."

". . . gobblegobble madre de dios pero soy gobblegobble . . ."

". . . parlay Domino an' Missab and shoot the roll on Duchess Peg in the feature . . ."

". . . melt resin add the silver chloride and dissolve in oil of lavender stand and decant and fire to cone zero twelve give you shimmering streaks of luster down the walls . . ."

". . . moiderin' square-headed gobblegobble tried ta poke his eye out wassamatta witta ref . . ."

". . . O God I am most heartily sorry I have offended thee in . . ."

". . . talk like a commie . . ."

". . . gobblegobblegobble two dolla twenny'fi" sense gobble. . ."

". . . just a nip and fill it up with water and brush my teeth . . ."

"... really know I'm God but fear to confess their sins ..."

"... dirty lousy rock-headed claw-handed paddle-footed goggle-eyed snot-nosed hunch-backed feeble-minded pot-bellied son of ..."

"... write on the wall alfie is a stunkur and then..."

"... thinks I believe it's a television set but I know he's got a bomb in there but who can I tell who can help so alone ..."

"... gabble was ich weiss nicht gabble geh bei Broadvay gabble ..."

"... habt mein daughter Rosie such a fella gobblegobble ..."

"... wonder if that's one didn't look back ..."

"... seen with her in the Medford restaurant ..."

The Mindworm struck into that thought.

"... not a mark on her but the M. E.'s have been wrong before and heart failure don't mean a thing anyway try to talk to her old lady authorize an autopsy get Pancho little guy talks Spanish be best ..."

The Mindworm knew he would have to be moving again—soon. He was sorry; some of the thoughts he had tapped indicated good ... hunting?

Regretfully, he again dragged his net:

"... with chartreuse drinks I mean drapes could use a drink come to think of it..."

"... reep-beep-reep-beep reepiddy-beepiddy-beep bop man wadda beat ..."

"$(\Delta^2\Psi_n + 8x\pi^2 M/H^2 E_n + \frac{E^2 Z}{r})\Psi_n = 0$ *What the Hell was that?*"

The Mindworm withdrew, in frantic haste. The intelligence was massive, its overtones those of a vigorous adult. He had learned from certain dangerous children that there was peril of a leveling flow. Shaken and scared, he contemplated traveling. He would need more than that wretched girl had supplied, and it would not be epicurean. There would be no time to find individuals at a ripe emotional crisis, or goad them to one. It would be plain—munching. The Mindworm drank a glass of water, also necessary to his metabolism.

EIGHT FOUND DEAD
IN UPTOWN MOVIE:
"MOLESTER" SOUGHT

Eight persons, including three women, were found dead Wednesday night of unknown causes in widely separated seats in the balcony of the Odeon Theater at 117th St. and Broadway. Police are seeking a man described by the balcony usher, Michael Fenelly, 18, as "acting like a woman-molester."

Fenelly discovered the first of the fatalities after seeing the man "moving from one empty seat to another several times." He went to ask a woman in a seat next to one the man had just vacated whether he had annoyed her. She was dead.

Almost at once, a scream rang out. In another part of the balcony Mrs. Sadie Rabinowitz, 40, uttered the cry when another victim toppled from his seat next to her.

Theater manager I. J. Marcusohn stopped the show and turned on the house lights. He tried to instruct his staff to keep the audience from leaving before the police arrived. He failed to get word to them in time, however, and most of the audience was gone when a detail from the 24th Pct. and an ambulance from Harlem hospital took over at the scene of the tragedy.

The Medical Examiner's office has not yet made a report as to the causes of death. A spokesman said the victims showed no signs of poisoning or violence. He added that it "was inconceivable that it could be a coincidence."

Lt. John Braidwood of the 24th Pct. said of the alleged molester: "We got a fair description of him and naturally we will try to bring him in for questioning."

Clickety-click, clickety-click sang the rails as the Mindworm drowsed in his coach seat.

Some people were walking forward from the diner. One was thinking: "Different-looking fellow. (a) he's aberrant. (b) he's nonaberrant and ill. Cancel (b)—respiration normal, skin smooth and healthy, no tremor of limbs, well-groomed. Is aberrant (1) trivially. (2) significantly. Cancel (1)—displayed no involuntary interest when . . . odd! *Running* for the washroom! Unexpected because (a) neat grooming indicates amour propre inconsistent with amusing others; (b) evident health inconsistent with . . . " It had taken one second, was fully detailed.

The Mindworm, locked in the toilet of the coach, wondered what the next stop was. He was getting off at it—not frightened, just careful. Dodge them, keep dodging them and everything would be all right. Send out no mental taps until the train was far away and everything would be all right.

He got off at a West Virginia coal and iron town surrounded by ruined mountains and filled with the offscourings of Eastern Europe. Serbs, Albanians, Croats, Hungarians, Slovenes, Bulgarians, and all possible combinations and permutations thereof. He walked slowly from the smoke-stained, brownstone passenger station. The train had roared on its way.

"...ain' no gemmum that's fo sho', fi-cen' tip fo' a good shine lak ah give um ..."

"...dumb bassar don't know how to make out a billa lading yet he ain't never gonna know so fire him get it over with ... "

"...gabblegabblegabble ..." Not a word he recognized in it.

"...gobblegobble dat tam vooman I brek she nack ..."

"...gobble trink visky chin glassabeer gobblegobblegobble ..."

"...gabblegabblegabble ..."

"...makes me so gobblegobble mad little no-good tramp no she ain' but I don' like no standup from no dame ..."

A blonde, square-headed boy fuming under a streetlight.

"...out wit' Casey Oswiak I could kill that dumb bohunk alla time trine ta paw her ..."

It was a possibility. The Mindworm drew near.

"...stand me up for that gobblegobble bohunk I oughtta slap her inna mush like my ole man says ..."

"Hello," said the Mindworm.

"Waddaya wan'?"

"Casey Oswiak told me to tell you not to wait up for your girl. He's taking her out tonight."

The blonde boy's rage boiled into his face and shot from his eyes. He was about to swing when the Mindworm began to feed. It was like pheasant after chicken, venison after beef. The coarseness of the environment, or the ancient strain? The Mindworm wondered as he strolled down the street. A girl passed him:

"...oh but he's gonna be mad like last time wish I came right away so jealous kinda nice but he might bust me one someday be nice to him tonight there he is lam'post leaning on it looks kinda funny gawd I hope he ain't drunk looks kinda funny sleeping sick or bozhe moi gabblegabblegabble ..."

Her thoughts trailed into a foreign language of which the Mindworm knew not a word. After hysteria had gone she recalled, in the foreign language, that she had passed him.

The Mindworm, stimulated by the unfamiliar quality of the last feeding, determined to stay for some days. He checked in at a Main Street hotel.

Musing, he dragged his net:

"...gobblegobblewhompyeargobblecheskygobblegabblechyesh ..."

"...take him down cellar beat the can off the damn chesky thief put the fear of god into him teach him can't bust into no boxcars in mah parta the caounty . . ."

". . . gabblegabble . . ."

". . . phone ole Mister Ryan in She-cawgo and he'll tell them three-card monte grifters who got the horse-room rights in this necka the woods by damn don't pay protection money for no protection . . ."

The Mindworm followed that one further; it sounded as though it could lead to some money if he wanted to stay in the town long enough.

The Eastern Europeans of the town, he mistakenly thought, were like the tramps and bums he had known and fed on during his years on the road—stupid and safe, safe and stupid, quite the same thing.

In the morning he found no mention of the square-headed boy's death in the town's paper and thought it had gone practically unnoticed. It had—by the paper, which was of, by, and for the coal and iron company and its native-American bosses and straw bosses. The other town, the one without a charter or police force, with only an imported weekly newspaper or two from the nearest city, noticed it. The other town had roots more than two thousand years deep, which are hard to pull up. But the Mindworm didn't know it was there.

He fed again that night, on a giddy young streetwalker in her room. He had astounded and delighted her with a fistful of ten-dollar bills before he began to gorge. Again the delightful difference from city-bred folk was there . . .

Again in the morning he had been unnoticed, he thought. The chartered town, unwilling to admit that there were streetwalkers or that they were found dead, wiped the slate clean; its only member who really cared was the native-American cop on the beat who had collected weekly from the dead girl.

The other town, unknown to the Mindworm, buzzed with it. A delegation went to the other town's only public officer. Unfortunately he was young, American-trained, perhaps even ignorant about some important things. For what he told them was: "My children, that is foolish superstition. Go home."

The Mindworm, through the day, roiled the surface of the town proper by allowing himself to be roped into a poker game in a parlor of the hotel. He wasn't good at it, he didn't like it, and he quit with relief when he had cleaned six shifty-eyed, hard-drinking loafers out of about three hundred dollars. One of them went straight to the police station and accused the unknown of being a sharper. A humorous sergeant, the Mindworm was pleased to note, joshed the loafer out of his temper.

Nightfall again, hunger again . . .

He walked the streets of the town and found them empty. It was strange. The native-American citizens were out, tending bar, walking their beats, locking up their newspaper on the stones, collecting their rents, managing their movies—but where were the others? He cast his net:

". . . gobblegobblegobble whomp year gobble . . ."

". . . crazy old pollack mama of mine try to lock me in with Errol Flynn at the Majestic never know the difference if I sneak out the back. . ."

That was near. He crossed the street and it was nearer. He homed on the thought:

". . . jeez he's a hunka man like Stanley but he never looks at me that Vera Kowalik I'd like to kick her just once in the gobblegobblegobble crazy old mama won't be American so ashamed . . ."

It was half a block, no more, down a sidestreet. Brick houses, two stories, with backyards on an alley. She was going out the back way.

How strangely quiet it was in the alley.

". . . ea-sy down them steps fix that damn board that's how she caught me last time what the hell are they all so scared of went to see Father Drugas won't talk bet somebody got it again that Vera Kowalik and her big . . ."

". . . gobble bozhe gobble whomp year gobble . . ."

She was closer; she was closer.

"All think I'm a kid show them who's a kid bet if Stanley caught me all alone out here in the alley dark and all he wouldn't think I was a kid that damn Vera Kowalik her folks don't think she's a kid . . ."

For all her bravado she was stark terrified when he said: "Hello."

"Who—who—who—?" she stammered.

Quick, before she screamed. Her terror was delightful.

Not too replete to be alert, he cast about, questing.

". . . gobblegobblegobble whomp year."

The countless eyes of the other town, with more than two thousand years of experience in such things, had been following him. What he had sensed as a meaningless hash of noise was actually an impassioned outburst in a nearby darkened house.

"Fools! fools! Now he has taken a virgin! I said not to wait. What will we say to her mother?"

An old man with handlebar moustache and, in spite of the heat, his shirtsleeves decently rolled down and buttoned at the cuffs, evenly replied: "My heart in me died with hers, Casimir, but one must be sure. It would be a terrible thing to make a mistake in such an affair."

The weight of conservative elder opinion was with him. Other old men with moustaches, some perhaps remembering mistakes long ago, nodded and said: "A terrible thing. A terrible thing."

The Mindworm strolled back to his hotel and napped on the made bed briefly. A tingle of danger awakened him. Instantly he cast out:

". . . gobblegobble whompyear."

". . . whampyir."

"WAMPYIR!"

Close! Close and deadly!

The door of his room burst open, and moustached old men with their shirtsleeves rolled down and decently buttoned at the cuffs unhesitatingly marched in, their thoughts a turmoil of alien noises, foreign gibberish that he could not wrap his mind around, disconcerting, from every direction.

The sharpened stake was through his heart and the scythe blade through his throat before he could realize that he had not been the first of his kind; and that what clever people have not yet learned, some quite ordinary people have not yet entirely forgotten.

Warm

ROBERT SHECKLEY

Robert Sheckley in the early years of his career, from 1952 to 1956, was able to place in the science fiction magazines (primarily Galaxy) *a series of beautifully contrived, almost perfectly solipsistic nightmares which, for evasive and miraculous reasons, fit almost indistinguishably into the format of those publications at the time. Of them, "Warm" (*Galaxy, *June 1953), is among the earliest and almost certainly the best. Sheckley went on to one of the most distinguished careers in science fiction, peaking perhaps with his unknown masterpiece* Dimension of Miracles *(1968; recently reissued), but "Warm" somehow compresses the sense of his work into thirty-five hundred deadly, discomfiting words.*

Anders lay on his bed, fully dressed except for his shoes and black bowtie, contemplating, with a certain uneasiness, the evening before him. In twenty minutes he would pick up Judy at her apartment, and that was the uneasy part of it.

He had realized, only seconds ago, that he was in love with her.

Well, he'd tell her. The evening would be memorable. He would propose, there would be kisses, and the seal of acceptance would, figuratively speaking, be stamped across his forehead.

Not too pleasant an outlook, he decided. It really would be much more comfortable not to be in love. What had done it? A look, a touch, a thought? It didn't take much, he knew, and stretched his arms for a thorough yawn.

"Help me!" a voice said.

His muscles spasmed, cutting off the yawn in mid-moment. He sat upright on the bed, then grinned and lay back again.

"You must help me!" the voice insisted.

Anders sat up, reached for a polished shoe and fitted it on, giving his full attention to the tying of the laces.

"Can you hear me?" the voice asked. "You can, can't you?"

That did it. "Yes, I can hear you," Anders said, still in a high good humor. "Don't tell me you're my guilty subconscious, attacking me for a childhood trauma I never bothered to resolve. I suppose you want me to join a monastery."

"I don't know what you're talking about," the voice said. "I'm no one's subconscious. I'm *me*. Will you help me?"

Anders believed in voices as much as anyone; that is, he didn't believe in them at all, until he heard them. Swiftly he catalogued the possibilities. Schizophrenia was the best answer, of course, and one in which his colleagues would concur. But Anders had a lamentable confidence in his own sanity. In which case—

"Who are you?" he asked.

"I don't know," the voice answered.

Anders realized that the voice was speaking within his own mind. Very suspicious.

"You don't know who you are," Anders stated. "Very well. *Where* are you?"

"I don't know that, either." The voice paused, and went on. "Look, I know how ridiculous this must sound. Believe me, I'm in some sort of limbo. I don't know how I got here or who I am, but I want desperately to get out. Will you help me?"

Still fighting the idea of a voice speaking within his head, Anders knew that his next decision was vital. He had to accept—or reject—his own sanity.

He accepted it.

"All right," Anders said, lacing the other shoe. "I'll grant that you're a person in trouble, and that you're in some sort of telepathic contact with me. Is there anything else you can tell me?"

"I'm afraid not," the voice said, with infinite sadness. "You'll have to find out for yourself."

"Can you contact anyone else?"

"No."

"Then how can you talk with me?"

"I don't know."

Anders walked to his bureau mirror and adjusted his black bowtie, whistling softly under his breath. Having just discovered that he was in love, he wasn't going to let a little thing like a voice in his mind disturb him.

"I really don't see how I can be of any help," Anders said, brushing a bit of lint from his jacket. "You don't know where you are, and there don't seem to be any distinguishing landmarks. How am I to find you?" He turned and looked around the room to see if he had forgotten anything.

"I'll know when you're close," the voice said. "You were warm just then."

"Just then?" All he had done was look around the room. He did so again, turning his head slowly. Then it happened.

The room, from one angle, looked different. It was suddenly a mixture of muddled colors, instead of the carefully blended pastel shades he had selected. The lines of wall, floor and ceiling were strangely off proportion, zigzag, unrelated.

Then everything went back to normal.

"You were *very* warm," the voice said.

Anders resisted the urge to scratch his head, for fear of disarranging his carefully combed hair. What he had seen wasn't so strange. Everyone sees one or two things in his life that make him doubt his normality, doubt sanity, doubt his very existence. For a moment the orderly universe is disarranged and the fabric of belief is ripped.

But the moment passes.

Anders remembered once, as a boy, awakening in his room in the middle of the night. How strange everything had looked! Chairs, table, all out of proportion, swollen in the dark. The ceiling pressing down, as in a dream.

But that also had passed.

"Well, old man," he said, "if I get warm again, tell me."

"I will," the voice in his head whispered. "I'm sure you'll find me."

"I'm glad you're so sure," Anders said gaily, switched off the lights and left.

Lovely and smiling, Judy greeted him at the door. Looking at her, Anders sensed her knowledge of the moment. Had she felt the change in him, or predicted it? Or was love making him grin like an idiot?

"Would you like a before-party drink?" she asked.

He nodded, and she led him across the room, to the improbable green-and-yellow couch. Sitting down, Anders decided he would tell her when she came back with the drink. No use in putting off the fatal moment. A lemming in love, he told himself.

"You're getting warm again," the voice said.

He had almost forgotten his invisible friend. Or fiend, as the case could well be. What would Judy say if she knew he was hearing voices?

Little things like that, he reminded himself, often break up the best of romances.

"Here," she said, handing him a drink.

Still smiling, he noticed. The number two smile—to a prospective suitor, provocative and understanding. It had been preceded, in their relationship, by the number one nice-girl smile, the don't-misunderstand-me smile, to be worn on all occasions, until the correct words have been mumbled.

"That's right," the voice said. "It's in how you look at things."

Look at what? Anders glanced at Judy, annoyed at his thoughts. If he was going to play the lover, let him play it. Even through the astigmatic haze of love, he was able to appreciate her blue gray eyes, her fine skin (if one overlooked a tiny blemish on the left temple), her lips, slightly reshaped by lipstick.

"How did your classes go today?" she asked.

Well, of course she'd ask that, Anders thought. Love is marking time.

"All right," he said. "Teaching psychology to young apes—"

"Oh, come now!"

"Warmer," the voice said.

What's the matter with me, Anders wondered. She really is a lovely girl. The *gestalt* that is Judy, a pattern of thoughts, expressions, movements, making up the girl I—

I what?

Love?

Anders shifted his long body uncertainly on the couch. He didn't quite understand how this train of thought had begun. It annoyed him. The analytical young instructor was better off in the classroom. Couldn't science wait until nine ten in the morning?

"I was thinking about you today," Judy said, and Anders knew that she had sensed the change in his mood.

"Do you see?" the voice asked him. "You're getting much better at it."

"I don't see anything," Anders thought, but the voice was right. It was as though he had a clear line of inspection into Judy's mind. Her feelings were nakedly apparent to him, as meaningless as his room had been in the flash of undistorted thought.

"I really was thinking about you," she repeated.

"Now look," the voice said.

Anders, watching the expressions on Judy's face, felt the strangeness descend on him. He was back in the nightmare perception of that moment in his room. This time it was as though he were watching a machine in a laboratory. The object of this operation was the evocation and preservation of a particular mood. The machine goes through a searching process, invoking trains of ideas to achieve the desired end.

"Oh, were you?" he asked, amazed at his new perspective.

"Yes . . . I wondered what you were doing at noon," the reactive machine opposite him on the couch said, expanding its shapely chest slightly.

"Good," the voice said, commending him for his perception.

"Dreaming of you, of course," he said to the flesh-clad skeleton behind the total *gestalt* Judy. The flesh machine rearranged its limbs, widened its mouth to denote pleasure. The mechanism searched through a complex of fears, hopes, worries, through half-remembrances of analogous situations, analogous solutions.

And this was what he loved. Anders saw too clearly and hated himself for seeing. Through his new nightmare perception, the absurdity of the entire room struck him.

"Were you really?" the articulating skeleton asked him.

"You're coming closer," the voice whispered.

To what? The personality? There was no such thing. There was no true cohesion, no depth, nothing except a web of surface reactions, stretched across automatic visceral movements.

He was coming closer to the truth.

"Sure," he said sourly.

The machine stirred, searching for a response.

Anders felt a quick tremor of fear at the sheer alien quality of his viewpoint. His sense of formalism had been sloughed off, his agreed-upon reactions bypassed. What would be revealed next?

He was seeing clearly, he realized, as perhaps no man had ever seen before. It was an oddly exhilarating thought.

But could he still return to normality?

"Can I get you a drink?" the reaction machine asked.

At that moment Anders was as thoroughly out of love as a man could be. Viewing one's intended as a depersonalized, sexless piece of machinery is not especially conducive to love. But it is quite stimulating, intellectually.

Anders didn't want normality. A curtain was being raised and he wanted to see behind it. What was it some Russian scientist—Ouspensky, wasn't it—had said?

"Think in other categories."

That was what he was doing, and would continue to do.

"Good-by," he said suddenly.

The machine watched him, open-mouthed, as he walked out the door. Delayed circuit reactions kept it silent until it heard the elevator door close.

"You were very warm in there," the voice within his head whispered, once he was on the street. "But you still don't understand everything."

"Tell me, then," Anders said, marveling a little at his equanimity. In an hour he had bridged the gap to a completely different viewpoint, yet it seemed perfectly natural.

"I can't," the voice said. "You must find it yourself."

"Well, let's see now," Anders began. He looked around at the masses of masonry, the convention of streets cutting through the architectural piles. "Human life," he said, "is a series of conventions. When you look at a girl, you're supposed to see—a pattern, not the underlying formlessness."

"That's true," the voice agreed, but with a shade of doubt.

"Basically, there is no form. Man produces *gestalts*, and cuts form out of the plethora of nothingness. It's like looking at a set of lines and saying that they represent a figure. We look at a mass of material, extract it from the background and say it's a man. But in truth, there is no such thing. There are only the humanizing features that we—myopically—attach to it. Matter is conjoined, a matter of viewpoint."

"You're not seeing it now," said the voice.

"Damn it," Anders said. He was certain that he was on the track of something big, perhaps something ultimate. "Everyone's had the experience. At some time in his life, everyone looks at a familiar object and can't make any sense out of it. Momentarily, the *gestalt* fails, but the true moment of sight passes. The mind reverts to the superimposed pattern. Normalcy continues."

The voice was silent. Anders walked on, through the *gestalt* city.

"There's something else, isn't there?" Anders asked.

"Yes."

What could that be, he asked himself. Through clearing eyes, Anders looked at the formality he had called his world.

He wondered momentarily if he would have come to this if the voice hadn't guided him. Yes, he decided after a few moments, it was inevitable.

But who was the voice? And what had he left out?

"Let's see what a party looks like now," he said to the voice.

The party was a masquerade; the guests were all wearing their faces. To Anders, their motives, individually and collectively, were painfully apparent. Then his vision began to clear further.

He saw that the people weren't truly individual. They were discontinuous lumps of flesh sharing a common vocabulary, yet not even truly discontinuous.

The lumps of flesh were a part of the decoration of the room and almost indistinguishable from it. They were one with the lights, which lent their tiny vision. They were joined to the sounds they made, a few feeble tones out of the great possibility of sound. They blended into the walls.

The kaleidoscopic view came so fast that Anders had trouble sorting his new impressions. He knew now that these people existed only as patterns, on the same basis as the sounds they made and the things they thought they saw.

Gestalts, sifted out of the vast, unbearable real world.

"Where's Judy?" a discontinuous lump of flesh asked him. This particular lump possessed enough nervous mannerisms to convince the other lumps of his reality. He wore a loud tie as further evidence.

"She's sick," Anders said. The flesh quivered into an instant sympathy. Lines of formal mirth shifted to formal woe.

"Hope it isn't anything serious," the vocal flesh remarked.

"You're warmer," the voice said to Anders.

Anders looked at the object in front of him.

"She hasn't long to live," he stated.

The flesh quivered. Stomach and intestines contracted in sympathetic fear. Eyes distended, mouth quivered.

The loud tie remained the same.

"My God! You don't mean it!"

"What are you?" Anders asked quietly.

"What do you mean?" the indignant flesh attached to the tie

demanded. Serene within its reality, it gaped at Anders. Its mouth twitched, undeniable proof that it was real and sufficient. "You're drunk," it sneered.

Anders laughed and left the party.

"There is still something you don't know," the voice said. "But you were hot! I could feel you near me."

"What are you?" Anders asked again.

"I don't know," the voice admitted. "I am a person. I am I. I am trapped."

"So are we all," Anders said. He walked on asphalt, surrounded by heaps of concrete, silicates, aluminum and iron alloys. Shapeless, meaningless heaps that made up the *gestalt* city.

And then there were the imaginary lines of demarcation dividing city from city, the artificial boundaries of water and land.

All ridiculous.

"Give me a dime for some coffee, mister?" something asked, a thing indistinguishable from any other thing.

"Old Bishop Berkeley would give a nonexistent dime to your non-existent presence," Anders said gaily.

"I'm really in a bad way," the voice whined, and Anders perceived that it was no more than a series of modulated vibrations.

"Yes! Go on!" the voice commanded.

"If you could spare me a quarter—" the vibrations said, with a deep pretense at meaning.

No, what was there behind the senseless patterns? Flesh, mass. What was that? All made up of atoms.

"I'm really hungry," the intricately arranged atoms muttered.

All atoms. Conjoined. There were no true separations between atom and atom. Flesh was stone, stone was light. Anders looked at the masses of atoms that were pretending to solidity, meaning and reason.

"Can't you help me?" a clump of atoms asked. But the clump was identical with all the other atoms. Once you ignored the superimposed patterns, you could see the atoms were random, scattered.

"I don't believe in you," Anders said.

The pile of atoms was gone.

"Yes!" the voice cried. "Yes!"

"I don't believe in any of it," Anders said. After all, what was an atom?

"Go on!" the voice shouted. "You're hot! Go on!"

What was an atom? An empty space surrounded by an empty space. Absurd!

"Then it's all false!" Anders said. And he was alone under the stars.

"That's right!" the voice within his head screamed. "Nothing!"

But stars, Anders thought. How can one believe—

The stars disappeared. Anders was in a gray nothingness, a void. There was nothing around him except shapeless gray.

Where was the voice?

Gone.

Anders perceived the delusion behind the grayness, and then there was nothing at all.

Complete nothingness, and himself within it.

Where was he? What did it mean? Anders' mind tried to add it up. Impossible. *That* couldn't be true.

Again the score was tabulated, but Anders's mind couldn't accept the total. In desparation, the overloaded mind erased the figures, eradicated the knowledge, erased itself.

"Where am I?"

In nothingness. Alone.

Trapped.

"Who am I?"

A voice.

The voice of Anders searched the nothingness, shouted, "Is there anyone here?"

No answer.

But there was someone. All directions were the same, yet moving along one he could make contact . . . with someone. The voice of Anders reached back to someone who could save him, perhaps.

"Save me," the voice said to Anders, lying fully dressed on his bed, except for his shoes and black bowtie.

Transfer

BARRY N. MALZBERG

The theme of the changeling is one of the oldest in literature. Appearing long before Shakespeare (whose King Lear is a distinct use of it) or even Greek tragedy (consider Medusa or for that matter Medea), it may be found in its earliest example in the opening chapter, no less, of the Book of Genesis. Any modern realistic handling of the theme would have to take account of not only mythic but psychological literature on the subject, and "Transfer" is a modern utilization of the theme whose New York, while no Garden of Eden, may resemble those premises just after (or during) the Fall.

I have met the enemy and he is me. Or me is he. Or me and he are we; I really find it impossible to phrase this or to reach any particular facility of description. The peculiar and embarrassing situation in which I now find myself has lurched quite out of control, ravaging its way toward what I am sure will be a calamitous destiny and, yet, I have always been a man who believed in order, who believed that events no matter how chaotic would remit, would relent, would suffer containment in the pure limpidity of The Word engraved patiently as if upon stone. I must stop this and get hold of myself.

I have met the enemy and he is me.

Staring into the mirror, watching the waves and the ripples of The Change, seeing in the mirror that beast take shape (it is always in the middle of the night; I am waiting for the transference to occur during the morning or worse yet at lunch hour in the middle of a cafeteria, waves may overtake me and I will become something so slimy and horrible even by the standards of midtown Manhattan that I will cause most of the congregants to lose their lunch), I feel a sense of rightness. It must always have been meant to be this way. Did I not feel myself strange as a child, as a youth, as an adolescent? Even as an adult I felt the strangeness within me; on the streets they stared with knowledge which could not have possibly been my own. Women turned away from me with little smiles when I attempted to connect with them, my fellow employees here at the Bureau treated me with that offhandedness and solemnity which always bespeaks private laughter. I know what they think of me.

I know what they think of me.

I have spent a lifetime in solitude gauging these reactions to some purpose, and I know that I am separate from the run of ordinary men as these men are separate from the strange heavings and commotion, ruins and darkness which created them. Staring in the mirror. Staring in the mirror I see.

Staring in the mirror I see the beast I have become, a thing with tentacles and spikes, strange loathsome protuberances down those appendages which my arms have become, limbs sleek and horrible despite all this devastation, limbs to carry me with surging power and constancy through the sleeping city, and now that I accept what I have become, what the night will strike me, I am no longer horrified but accepting. One might even say exalted at this moment because I always knew that it would have to be this way, that in the last of all the nights a mirror would be held up to my face and I would see then what I was and why the mass of men avoided me. I know what I am, those calm, cold eyes staring back at me in the mirror from the center of the monster know too well what I am also and turning them from the mirror, confronting the rubbled but still comfortable spaces of my furnished room, I feel the energy coursing through me in small flashes and ripples of light, an energy which I know, given but that one chance it needs, could redeem the world. The beast does not sleep. In my transmogrification I have cast sleep from me like the cloak of all reason and I spring from these rooms, scuttle the three flights of the brownstone to the street and coming upon it in the dense and sleeping spaces of the city, see no one, confront no one (but I would not, I never have) as I move downtown to enact my dreadful but necessary tasks.

The beast does not sleep, therefore I do not sleep. At first the change came upon me once a week and then twice . . . but in recent months it has been coming faster and faster, now six or seven times a week, and furthermore I can *will* the change. Involuntary at first, overtaking me like a stray bullet, it now seems to be within my control as my power and facility increase. A *latent* characteristic then, some recessive gene which peeked its way out shyly at the age of twenty-five, first with humility and then with growing power and finally as I became accustomed to the power, it fell within my control.

I can now become the beast whenever I wish.

Now it is not the beast but I who pokes his way from the covers during the hours of despair and lurches his way to the bathroom; standing before that one mirror, I call the change upon myself, ring the changes, and the beast, then, confronts me, a tentacle raised as if in greeting or repudiation. Shrugging, I sprint down the stairs and into the city. At dawn I return. In between that time—

—I make my travels.

My travels, my errands! Over manhole covers, sprinting as if filled with helium (the beast is powerful; the beast has endless stamina) in and out of the blocks of the West Side, vaulting to heights on abandoned stoops, then into the gutter again, cutting a swath through the city, ducking the occasional prowl cars which come through indolently, swinging out of sight behind gates to avoid garbage trucks, no discovery ever having been made of the beast in all the months that this has been going on . . . and between the evasions I do my business.

Pardon. Pardon if you will. I do not do *my* business. The beast does *his* business.

I must separate the beast and myself because the one is not the other and I have very little to *do* with the beast although, of course, I am he. And he is me.

And attack them in the darkness.

Seize hapless pedestrians or dawn drunks by the throat, coming up from their rear flank, diving upon them then with facility and ease, sweeping upon them to clap a hand upon throat or groin with a touch as sure and cunning as any I have ever known and then, bringing them to their knees, straddling them in the gutter, I—

Well, I—

—Well, now, is it necessary for me to say what I do? Yes, it is necessary for me to say, I suppose; these recollections are not careless nor are they calculated but merely an attempt, as it were, to set the record straight. The rumors, reports and evasions about the conduct of the beast have reached the status of full-scale lies (there is not a crew of assassins loose in the streets but merely one; there is not a carefully organized plan to terrorize the city but merely one beast, one humble, hard-working animal wreaking his justice) so it is to be said that as I throttle the lives and misery out of them, I often *turn them over* so that they can confront the beast, see what it is doing to them, and that I see in their eyes past the horror the heartbreak, the beating farewell signal of their mortality.

But beyond that I see something else.

Let me tell you of this, it is crucial: I see an acceptance so enormous as almost to defy in all of its acceptance because it is religious. The peace that passeth all understanding darts through their eyes and finally passes through them, exiting in the last breath of life as with a crumpling sigh they die against me. I must have killed hundreds, no, I do not want to exaggerate, it is not right, I must have killed in the high seventies. At first I kept a chart of my travels and accomplishments but when it verged into the high twenties I realized that this was insane, leaving physical evidence of any sort of my accomplishments that is, and furthermore, past that ninth murder or the nineteenth there is no longer a feeling of victory but only *necessity*. It is purely business.

All of it has been purely business.

Business in any event for the beast. He needs to kill as I need to breathe, that creature within me who I was always in the process of becoming (all the strangeness I felt as a child I now attribute to the embryonic form of the beast, beating and huddling its growing way within) takes the lives of humans as casually as I take my midday sandwich and drink in the local cafeteria before passing on to my dismal and clerkly affairs at the Bureau, accumulating time toward the pension credits that will be mine after twenty or thirty years. The beast needs to kill; he draws his strength from murder as I do mine from food and since I am merely his tenant during these struggles, a helpless (but alertly interested) altar which dwells within the beast watching all that goes on, I can take no responsibility myself for what has happened but put it squarely on him where it belongs.

Perhaps I should have turned myself in for treatment or seen a psychiatrist of some kind when all this began, but what would have been the point of it? What? They would not have believed that I was possessed; they would have thought me harmlessly crazy and the alternative, if they did believe me, would have been much worse: implication, imprisonment, fury. I could have convinced them. I know that now, when I became strong enough to will myself into becoming of the beast I could have, in their very chambers, turned myself into that monster and then they would have believed, would have taken my fears for certainty ... but the beast, manic in his goals, would have fallen upon those hapless psychiatrists, interns or social workers as he fell upon all of his nighttime victims and what then?

What then? He murders as casually and skillfully as I annotate my filings at the Bureau. He is impossible to dissuade. No, I could not have done that. The beast and I, sentenced to dwell throughout eternity or at least through the length of my projected life span: there may be another judgment on this someday of some weight but I cannot be concerned with that now. Why should I confess? What is there to confess? Built so deeply into the culture—I am a thoughtful man and have pondered this long despite my lack of formal educational credits—as to be part of the madness is the belief that confession is in itself expiation, but I do not believe this. The admission of dreadful acts is merely to compound them through multiple refraction and lies are thus more necessary than the truth in order to make the world work.

Oh, how I believe this. How I do believe it.

I have attempted discussions with the beast. This is not easy but at the moment of transfer there is a slow, stunning instant when the mask of his features has not settled upon him fully and it is possible for me, however weakly, to speak. "Why must you do this?" I ask him. "This is murder, mass murder. These are human beings, you know, it really is quite dreadful." My little voice pipes weakly as my own force diminishes and the beast, transmogrified, stands before the mirror, waving his tentacles, flexing his powerful limbs, and says then (he speaks a perfect English when he desires although largely he does not desire to speak), "Don't be a fool, this is my destiny and besides *I* am not human so this is not my problem."

This is unanswerable; it is already muted by transfer. I burrow within and the beast takes to the streets singing and crouching, ready once again for his tasks. Why does he need to murder? I understand that his lust for this is as gross and simple as my own for less dreadful events; it is an urge as much a part of him as that toward respiration. The beast is an innocent creature, immaculately conceived. He goes to do murder as his victim goes to drink. He sees no shades of moral inference or dismay even in the bloodiest and most terrible of the strangulations but simply does what must be done with the necessary force. Never more. Some nights he has killed ten. The streets of the city scatter north and south with his victims.

But his victims! Ah, they have, so many of them, been waiting for murder so long, dreaming of it, touching it in the night (as I touch the self-same beast), that this must be the basis of that acceptance which passes through them at the moment of impact. They have been look ing, these victims, for an event so climactic that they will be able to cede responsibility for their lives and here, in the act of murder, have they at last that confirmation. Some of them embraced the beast with passion as he made his last strike. Others have opened themselves to him on the pavement and pointed at their vitals. For the city, the very energy of that city or so I believe this now through my musings, is based upon the omnipresence of death and to die is to become at last completely at one with the darkened heart of a city constructed for death. I become too philosophical. I will not attempt to justify myself further.

For there *is* no justification. What happens, happens. The beast has taught me at least this much (along with so much else). Tonight we come upon the city with undue haste; the beast has not been out for two nights previous, having burrowed within with a disinclination for pursuit, unavailable even to summons, but now at four in the morning of this coldest of all the nights of winter he has pounded within me, screaming for release, and I have allowed him his way with some eagerness because (I admit this truly) I too have on his behalf missed the thrill of the hunt.

Now the beast races down the pavements, his breath a plume of fire against the ice. At the first intersection we see a young woman paused for the light, a valise clutched against her, one hand upraised for a taxi that will not come. (I know it will not come.) An early dawn evacuee from the city or so I murmur to the beast. Perhaps it would be best to leave this one alone since she looks spare and there must be tastier meat in the alleys beyond . . . but the creature does not listen. He listens to nothing I have to say. This is the core of his strength and my own repudiation is nothing as to his.

For listen, listen now: he sweeps into his own purposes in a way which can only make me fill with admiration. He comes upon the girl then. He comes upon her. He takes her from behind.

He takes her from behind.

She struggles in his grasp like an insect caught within a huge, indifferent hand, all legs and activity, grasping and groping, and he casually kicks the valise from her hand, pulls her into an alley for a more more sweeping inspection, the woman's skull pinned against his flat, oily chest, her little hands and feet waving, and she is screaming in a way so dismal and hopeless that I know she will never be heard and she must know this as well. The scream stops. Small moans and pleas which had pieced out the spaces amid the sound stop too and with an explosion of strength she twists within his grasp, then hurls herself against his chest and looks upward toward his face to see at last the face of the assassin about which she must surely have dreamed, the bitch, in so many nights. She sees the beast. He sees her.

I too know her.

She works at the Bureau. She is a fellow clerk two aisles down and three over, a pretty woman, not indifferent in her gestures but rather, as so few of these bitches at the Bureau are, kind and lively, kind even to *me*. Her eyes are never droll but sad as she looks upon me. I have never spoken to her other than pleasantries but I feel, *feel* that if I were ever to seek her out she would not humiliate me.

"Oh," I say within the spaces of the beast, trapped and helpless as I look upon her, "oh, oh."

"No!" she says, looking upon us. "Oh no, not you, it can't be you!" and the beast's grasp tightens upon her then. "It can't be you! Don't say that it's *you* doing this to me!" and I look upon her then with tenderness and infinite understanding knowing that I am helpless to save her and thus relieved of the responsibility but saddened too. Saddened because the beast has never caught a victim known to me before. I say in a small voice which she will never hear (because I am trapped inside), "I'm sorry, I'm sorry but it's got to be done, you see. How much of this can I take anymore?" and her eyes, I know this, her eyes lighten with understanding, darken too, lighten and darken with the knowledge I have imparted.

And as the pressure begins then, the pressure that in ten seconds will snap her throat and leave her dead, as the freezing colors of the city descend, we confront one another in isolation, our eyes meeting, touch meeting and absolutely nothing to be done about it. Her neck breaks, and in many many many ways I must admit—I will admit everything—this has been the most satisfying victim of them all. Of them all.

The Doll

JOYCE CAROL OATES

*Here is a classic horror fiction by a literary writer of the first rank, a penetration of reality by the shapes of the unsinkable, the slow rattling and tremors of the dropped bottom. Joyce Carol Oates's brilliant novelistic career (*Them, **National Book Award 1970**, Bellefleur, 1980, *almost a dozen others) has obscured her stature in regard to the American short story; this is ironic since no writer has ever appeared more often (seventeen times) or had more consecutive appearances (eight) in the annual O. Henry Prize anthologies than Ms. Oates. Her short stories have, since 1961, appeared in the full range of the great American magazines, from* Playboy, Esquire, Cosmopolitan, *and the* Atlantic *to the* Hudson Review, *the* Virginia Quarterly *and the* Southern Review. *"In the Region of Ice" (1967) and "The Dead" (1973) were awarded first prize in the O. Henry series; "Accomplished Desires" (1969) and "Saul Bird Says" (1972), second.*

Many years ago there was a little girl who was given, for her fourth birthday, an antique dolls'-house of unusual beauty and complexity, and size: for it seemed large enough, almost, for a child to crawl into.

The dolls'-house was said to have been built nearly one hundred years before, by a distant relative of the little girl's mother. It had come down through the family and was still in excellent condition: with a steep gabled roof, many tall, narrow windows fitted with real glass, dark green shutters that closed over, three fireplaces made of stone, mock lightning rods, mock shingleboard siding (white), a veranda that nearly circled the house, stained glass at the front door and at the first floor landing, and even a cupola whose tiny roof lifted miraculously away. In the master bedroom there was a canopied bed with white organdy flounces and ruffles; there were even tiny windowboxes beneath most of the windows; the furniture—all of it Victorian, of course—was uniformly exquisite, having been made with the most fastidious care and affection. The lampshades were adorned with tiny gold fringes, there was a marvelous old tub with claw feet, nearly every room had a chandelier. When she first saw the dolls'-

house on the morning of her fourth birthday the little girl was so astonished she could not speak: for the present was unexpected, and uncannily "real." It was to be the great present, and the great memory, of her childhood.

Florence had several dolls which were too large to fit into the house, since they were average-sized dolls, but she brought them close to the house, facing its open side, and played with them there. She fussed over them, and whispered to them, and scolded them, and invented little conversations between them; one day, out of nowhere, came the name *Bartholomew*—the name of the family who owned the dolls'-house. Where did you get that name from, her parents asked, and Florence replied that those were the people who lived in the house. Yes, but where did the name come from? they asked.

The child, puzzled and a little irritated, pointed mutely at the dolls.

One was a girl-doll with shiny blonde ringlets and blue eyes that were thickly lashed, and almost too round; another was a red-haired freckled boy in denim coveralls and a plaid shirt. It was obvious that they were sister and brother. Another was a woman-doll, perhaps a mother, who had bright red lips and who wore a hat cleverly made of soft gray-and-white feathers. There was even a baby-doll, made of the softest rubber, hairless and expressionless, and somewhat oversized in relationship to the other dolls; and a spaniel, about nine inches in length, with big brown eyes and a quizzical upturned tail. Sometimes one doll was Florence's favorite, sometimes another. There were days when she preferred the blonde girl, whose eyes rolled in her head, and whose complexion was a lovely pale peach. There were days when the mischievous red-haired boy was obviously her favorite. Sometimes she banished all the human dolls and played with the spaniel, who was small enough to fit into most of the rooms of the dolls'-house.

Occasionally Florence undressed the human dolls, and washed them with a tiny sponge. How strange they were, without their clothes . . . ! Their bodies were poreless and smooth and blank, there was nothing secret or nasty about them, no crevices for dirt to hide in, no trouble at all. Their faces were unperturbable, as always. Calm wise fearless staring eyes that no harsh words or slaps could disturb. But Florence loved her dolls very much, and rarely felt the need to punish them.

Her treasure was, of course, the dolls'-house with its steep Victorian roof and its gingerbread trim and its innumerable windows and that marvelous veranda, upon which little wooden rocking chairs, each equipped with its own tiny cushion, were set. Visitors—friends of her parents, or little girls her own age—were always astonished when they first saw it. They said: Oh, isn't it beautiful! They said: Why, it's almost the size of a real house, isn't it?—though of course it wasn't, it was only a dolls'-house, a little less than thirty-six inches high.

Nearly four decades later while driving along East Fainlight Avenue in Lancaster, Pennsylvania, a city she had never visited before, and about which she knew nothing, Florence Parr was astonished to see, set back from the avenue, at the top of a stately elm-shaded knoll, her old dolls'-house—that is, the replica of it. The house. The house itself.

She was so astonished that for the passage of some seconds she could not think what to do. Her most immediate reaction was to brake her car—for she was a careful, even fastidious driver; at the first sign of confusion or difficulty she always brought her car to a stop.

A broad handsome elm- and plane tree-lined avenue, in a charming city, altogether new to her. Late April: a fragrant, even rather giddy spring, after a bitter and protracted winter. The very air trembled, rich with warmth and color. The estates in this part of the city were as impressive, as stately, as any she had ever seen: the houses were really mansions, boasting of wealth, their sloping, elegant lawns protected from the street by brick walls, or wrought-iron fences, or thick ever-green hedges. Everywhere there were azaleas, that most gorgeous of spring flowers—scarlet and white and yellow and peach-colored, almost blindingly beautiful. There were newly cultivated beds of tulips, primarily red; and exquisite apple blossoms, and cherry blossoms, and flowering trees Florence recognized but could not identify by name. *Her* house was surrounded by an old-fashioned wrought-iron fence, and in its enormous front yard were red and yellow tulips that had pushed their way through patches of weedy grass.

She found herself on the sidewalk, at the front gate. Like the un-wieldy gate that was designed to close over the driveway, this gate was not only open but its bottom spikes had dug into the ground; it had not been closed for some time and could probably not be dislodged. Someone had put up a hand-lettered sign in black, not long ago: 1377 East Fainlight. But no name, no family name. Florence stood staring up at the house, her heart beating rapidly. She could not quite believe what she was seeing. Yes, there it was, of course—yet it *could* not be, not in such detail.

The antique dolls'-house. Hers. After so many years. There was the steep gabled roof, in what appeared to be slate; the old lightning rods; the absurd little cupola that was so charming; the veranda; the white shingleboard siding (which was rather weathered and gray in the bright spring sunshine); most of all, most striking, the eight tall, narrow windows, four to each floor, with their dark shutters. Florence could not determine if the shutters were painted a very dark green, or black. What color had they been on the dolls'-house. . . . She saw that the gingerbread trim was badly rotted.

The first wave of excitement, almost of vertigo, that had overtaken her in the car had passed; but she felt, still, an unpleasant sense of urgency. Her old dolls'-house. Here on East Fainlight Avenue in Lancaster, Pennsylvania. Glimpsed so suddenly, on this warm spring morning. And what did it mean . . .? Obviously there was an explanation. Her distant uncle, who had built the house for his daughter, had simply copied this house, or another just like it; no doubt there were many houses like this one. Florence knew little about Victorian architecture but she supposed that there were many duplications, even in large, costly houses. Unlike contemporary architects, the architects of that era must have been extremely limited, forced to use again and again certain basic structures, and certain basic ornamentation—the cupolas, the gables, the complicated trim. What struck her as so odd, so mysterious, was really nothing but a coincidence. It would make an interesting story, an amusing anecdote, when she returned home; though perhaps it was not even worth mentioning. Her parents might have been intrigued but they were both dead. And she was always rather careful about dwelling upon herself, her private life, since she halfway imagined that her friends and acquaintances and colleagues would interpret nearly anything she said of a personal nature according to their vision of her as a public person, and she wanted to avoid that.

There was a movement at one of the upstairs windows that caught her eye. It was then transmitted, fluidly, miraculously, to the other windows, flowing from right to left. . . . But no, it was only the reflection of clouds being blown across the sky up behind her head.

She stood motionless. It was unlike her, it was quite uncharacteristic of her, yet there she stood. She did not want to walk up to the veranda steps, she did not want to ring the doorbell, such a gesture would be ridiculous, and anyway there was no time: she really should be driving on. They would be expecting her soon. Yet she could not turn away. Because it *was* the house. Incredibly, it was her old dolls'-house. (Which she had given away, of course, thirty—thirty-five?—years ago. And had rarely thought about since.) It was ridiculous to stand here, so astonished, so slow-witted, so perversely vulnerable . . . yet what other attitude was appropriate, what other attitude would not violate the queer sense of the sacred, the other-worldly, that the house had evoked?

She would ring the doorbell. And why not? She was a tall, rather wide-shouldered, confident woman, tastefully dressed in a cream-colored spring suit; she was rarely in the habit of apologizing for herself, or feeling embarrassment. Many years ago, perhaps, as a girl, a shy, silly, self-conscious girl: but no longer. Her wavy graying hair had been brushed back smartly from her wide, strong forehead. She wore no make-up, had stopped bothering with it years ago, and with her naturally high-colored, smooth complexion, she was a handsome woman, especially attractive when she smiled and her dark staring eyes relaxed. She *would* ring the doorbell, and see who came to the door, and say whatever flew into her head. She was looking for a family who lived in the neighborhood, she was canvassing for a school millage vote, she was inquiring whether they had any old clothes, old furniture, for . . . .

Halfway up the walk she remembered that she had left the keys in the ignition of her car, and the motor running. And her purse on the seat.

She found herself walking unusually slowly. It was unlike her, and the queer disorienting sense of being unreal, of having stepped into another world, was totally new. A dog began barking somewhere near: the sound seemed to pierce her in the chest and bowels. An attack of panic. An involuntary fluttering of the eyelids . . . . But it was nonsense of course. She would ring the bell, someone would open the door, perhaps a servant, perhaps an elderly woman, they would have a brief conversation, Florence would glance behind her into the foyer to see if the circular staircase looked the same, if the old brass chandelier was still there, if the "marble" floor remained. Do you know the Parr family, Florence would ask, we've lived in Cummington, Massachusetts for generations, I think it's quite possible that someone from my family visited you in this house, of course it was a very long time ago. I'm sorry to disturb you but I was driving by and I saw your striking house and I couldn't resist stopping for a moment out of curiosity. . . .

There were the panes of stained glass on either side of the oak door! But so large, so boldly colored. In the dolls'-house they were hardly visible, just chips of colored glass. But here they were each about a foot square, uncannily beautiful: reds, greens, blues. Exactly like the stained glass of a church.

I'm sorry to disturb you, Florence whispered, but I was driving by and . . . .

I'm sorry to disturb you but I am looking for a family named Bartholomew, I have reason to think that they live in this neighborhood . . . .

But as she was about to step onto the veranda the sensation of panic deepened. Her breath came shallow and rushed, her thoughts flew wildly in all directions, she was simply terrified and could not move. The dog's barking had become hysterical.

When Florence was angry or distressed or worried she had a habit of murmuring her name to herself, Florence Parr, Florence Parr, it was soothing, it was mollifying, Florence Parr, it was often vaguely reproachful, for after all she *was* Florence Parr and that carried with it responsibility as well as authority. She named herself, identified herself. It was usually enough to bring her undisciplined thoughts under control. But she had not experienced an attack of panic for many years. All the strength of her body seemed to have fled, drained away; it terrified her to think that she might faint there on the sidewalk. What a fool she would make of herself. . . .

As a young university instructor she had nearly succumbed to panic one day, midway through a lecture on the metaphysical poets. Oddly, the attack had come not at the beginning of the semester but well into the second month, when she had come to believe herself a fairly competent teacher. The most extraordinary sensation of fear, unfathomable and groundless fear, which she had never been able to comprehend afterward. . . . One moment she had been speaking of Donne's famous image in "The Relic"—a bracelet of "bright hair about the bone"— and the next moment she was so panicked she could hardly catch her breath. She wanted to run out of the classroom, wanted to run out of the building. It was as if a demon had appeared to her. It breathed into her face, shoved her about, tried to pull her under. She would suffocate: she would be destroyed. The sensation was possibly the most unpleasant she had ever experienced in her life though it carried with it no pain and no specific images. Why she was so frightened she could not grasp. Why she wanted nothing more than to run out of the classroom, to escape her students' curious eyes, she was never to understand.

But she did not flee. She forced herself to remain at the podium. Though her voice faltered she did not stop; she continued with the lecture, speaking into a blinding haze. Surely her students must have noticed her trembling . . . ? But she was stubborn, she was really quite tenacious for a young woman of twenty-four, and by forcing herself to imitate herself, to imitate her normal tone and mannerisms, she was able to overcome the attack. As it lifted, gradually, and her eyesight strengthened, her heartbeat slowed, she seemed to know that the attack would never come again in a classroom: and this turned out to be correct.

But now she could not overcome her anxiety. She hadn't a podium to grasp, she hadn't lecture notes to follow, there was no one to imitate, she was in a position to make a terrible fool of herself. And surely someone was watching from the house. . . . It struck her that she had no reason, no excuse, for being here. What on earth could she say if she rang the doorbell! How would she explain herself to a skeptical stranger! I simply must see the inside of your house, she would whisper, I've been led up this walk by a force I can't explain, please excuse me, please humor me, I'm not well, I'm not myself this morning, I only want to see the inside of your house to see if it *is* the house I remember. . . . I had a house like yours. It was yours. But no one lived in my house except dolls; a family of dolls. I loved them but I always sensed that they were blocking the way, standing between me and something else. . . .

The barking dog was answered by another, a neighbor's dog. Florence retreated. Then turned and hurried back to her car, where the keys were indeed in the ignition, and her smart leather purse lay on the seat where she had so imprudently left it.

So she fled the dolls'-house, her poor heart thudding. What a fool you are, Florence Parr, she thought brutally, a deep hot blush rising into her face.

The rest of the day—the late afternoon reception, the dinner itself, the after-dinner gathering—passed easily, even routinely, but did not seem to her very real; it was not very convincing. That she was Florence Parr, the president of Champlain College, that she was to be a featured speaker at this conference of administrators of small private liberal arts colleges: it struck her for some reason as an imposture, a counterfeit. The vision of the dolls'-house kept rising in her mind's eye. How odd, how very odd the experience had been, yet there was no one to whom she might speak about it, even to minimize it, to transform it into an amusing anecdote. . . . The others did not notice her discomfort. In fact they claimed that she was looking well, they were delighted to see her and to shake her hand. Many were old acquaintances, men and women, but primarily men, with whom she had worked in the past at one college or another; a number were strangers, younger administrators who had heard of her heroic effort at Champlain College, and who wanted to be introduced to her. At the noisy cocktail hour, at dinner, Florence heard her somewhat distracted voice speaking of the usual matters: declining enrollments, building fund campaigns, alumni support, endowments, investments, state and federal aid. Her remarks were met with the same respectful attention as always, as though there were nothing wrong with her.

For dinner she changed into a linen dress of pale blue and dark blue stripes which emphasized her tall, rather graceful figure, and drew the eye away from her wide shoulders and her somewhat stolid thighs; she wore her new shoes with the fashionable three-inch heel though she detested them. Her haircut was becoming, she had manicured and even polished her nails the evening before, she supposed she looked attractive enough, especially in this context of middle-aged and older people. But her mind kept drifting away from the others, from the handsome though rather dark colonial dining room, even from the spirited, witty after-dinner speech of a popular administrator and writer, a retired president of Williams College, and formerly—a very long time ago, now—a colleague of Florence's at Swarthmore. She smiled with the others, and laughed with the others, but she could not attend to the courtly, white-haired gentleman's astringent witticisms; her mind kept drifting back to the dolls'-house, out there on East Fainlight Avenue. It was well for her that she hadn't rung the doorbell, for what if someone who was attending the conference had answered the door; it was, after all, being hosted by Lancaster College. What an utter fool she would have made of herself. . . .

She went to her room in the fieldstone alumni house shortly after ten, though there were people who clearly wished to talk with her, and she knew a night of insomnia awaited. Once in the room with its antique furniture and its self-consciously quaint wallpaper she regretted having left the ebullient atmosphere downstairs. Though small private colleges were, rather famously, in trouble these days, and though most of the administrators at the conference were having serious difficulties with finances, and faculty morale, there was nevertheless a spirit of camaraderie, of heartiness. Of course it was the natural consequence of people in a social gathering. One simply cannot resist, in such a context, the droll remark, the grateful laugh, the sense of cheerful complicity in even an unfortunate fate. How puzzling the human personality is, Florence thought, preparing for bed, moving uncharacteristically slowly, when with others there is a public self, alone there is a private self, and yet both are real. . . . Both are experienced as real. . . .

She lay sleepless in the unfamiliar bed. There were noises in the distance; she turned on the air-conditioner, the fan only, to drown them out. Still she could not sleep. The house on East Fainlight Avenue, the dolls'-house of her childhood, she lay with her eyes open, thinking of absurd, disjointed things, wondering now why she had *not* pushed her way through that trivial bout of anxiety to the veranda steps, and to the door, after all she was Florence Parr, she had only to imagine people watching her—the faculty senate, students, her fellow administrators—to know how she should behave, with what alacrity and confidence. It was only when she forgot who she was, and imagined herself utterly alone, that she was crippled by uncertainty and susceptible to fear.

The luminous dials of her watch told her it was only ten thirty-five. Not too late, really, to dress and return to the house and ring the doorbell. Of course she would only ring it if the downstairs was lighted, if someone was clearly up. . . . Perhaps an elderly gentleman lived there, alone, someone who had known her grandfather, someone who had visited the Parrs in Cummington. For there *must* be a connection. It was very well to speak of coincidences but she knew, she knew with a deep, unshakable conviction, that there was a connection between the dolls'-house and the house here in town, and a connection between her childhood and the present house. . . . When she explained herself to whoever opened the door, however, she would have to be casual, conversational. Years of administration had taught her diplomacy; one must not appear to be *too* serious. Gravity in leaders is disconcerting, what is demanded is the light, confident touch, the air of private and even secret knowledge. People do not want equality with their leaders: they want, they desperately need, them to be superior. The superiority must be tacitly communicated, however, or it becomes offensive. . . .

Suddenly she was frightened: it seemed to her quite possible that the panic attack might come upon her the next morning, when she gave her address ("The Future of the Humanities in American Education"). She was scheduled to speak at nine thirty, she would be the first speaker of the day, and the first real speaker of the conference. And it was quite possible that that disconcerting weakness would return, that sense of utter, almost infantile helplessness. . . .

She sat up, turned on the light, and looked over her notes. They were handwritten, not typed, she had told her secretary not to bother typing them, the address was one she'd given before in different forms, her approach was to be conversational rather than formal though of course she would quote the necessary statistics. . . . But it had been a mistake, perhaps, not to have the notes typed. There were times when she couldn't decipher her own handwriting.

A drink might help. But she couldn't very well go over to the Lancaster Inn, where the conference was to be held, and where there was a bar; and of course she hadn't anything with her in the room. As a rule she rarely drank. She never drank alone. . . . However, if a drink would help her sleep: would calm her wild racing thoughts.

There were acquaintances of hers here, and even two or three people who might consider themselves friends, but she could not ask them for help; the very thought was humiliating. And then of course word would get around afterward. Florence Parr this, Florence Parr that. She would make a fool of herself, she would be crushed and defeated. However: if she couldn't sleep, if the dolls'-house obsessed her all night, she might very well be incapable of giving her talk in the morning. "The Future of the Humanities in American Education." If she were as slyly sekptical as the former president of Williams she might begin by saying, "*Is* there a future of any kind in American education. . ." and everyone would laugh. One could say anything and an audience would laugh, gratefully. One could say almost anything. However: one could not break down, one could not stammer and falter and be forced to leave the podium.

Florence Parr this, Florence Parr that.

The dolls'-house had been a present for her birthday. Many years ago. She could not recall how many. And there were her dolls, her little family of dolls, which she had not thought of for a lifetime. She felt a pang of loss, of tenderness. . . .

Florence Parr who sufferd quite frequently from insomnia. But of course no one knew.

Florence Parr who had had a lump in her right breast removed, a cyst really, harmless, absolutely harmless, shortly after her thirty-eighth birthday. But none of her friends at Champlain knew. Not even her secretary knew. And the ugly little thing turned out to be benign: absolutely harmless. So it was well that no one knew.

Florence Parr of whom it was said that she was distant, even guarded, at times. You can't get close to her, someone claimed. And yet it was often said of her that she was wonderfully warm and open and frank and totally without guile. A popular president. Yet she had the support of her faculty. There might be individual jealousies here and there, particularly among the vice-presidents and deans, but in general she had everyone's support and she knew it and was grateful for it and intended to keep it.

It was only that her mind worked, late into the night. Raced. Would not stay still.

Sometimes when she believed she had been sleeping, or utterly absorbed in music, she discovered that her mind—her tireless frantic thoughts—had gone their own way, plotting.

Plots, possibilities. Speculations. If I do this, the consequence will be . . . . If I fail to do this, the consequence will be . . . .

Should she surrender to her impulse, and get dressed quickly and return to the house? It would take no more than ten minutes. And quite likely the downstairs lights would *not* be on, the inhabitants would be asleep, she could see from the street that the visit was totally out of the question, she would simply drive on past. And be saved from her audacity.

If I do this, the consequence will be . . . .

If I fail to do this . . . .

She was not, of course, an impulsive person. Nor did she admire impulsive "spontaneous" people: she thought them immature, and frequently exhibitionistic. It was often the case that they were very much aware of their own spontaneity. . .

She would defend herself against the charge of being calculating. Of being overly cautious. Her nature was simply a very pragmatic one. She took up tasks with extreme interest, and absorbed herself deeply in them, one after another, month after month and year after year, and other considerations simply had to be shunted to the side. For instance, she had never married. The surprise would have been not that Florence Parr had married, but that she had had time to cultivate a relationship that would end in marriage. I am not opposed to marriage for myself, she once said, with unintentional naïveté, but it would take so much time to become acquainted with a man, to go out with him, and talk. . . . At Champlain where everyone liked her, and had anecdotes about her, it was said that she'd been even as a younger woman so oblivious to men, even to attentive men, that she had failed to recognize a few years later a young linguist whose carrel at the Widener Library had been next to hers, though the young man claimed to have said hello to her every day, and to have asked her out for coffee occasionally. (She had always refused, she'd been far too busy.) When he turned up at Champlain, married, the author of a well-received book on linguistic theory, an associate professor in the humanities division, Florence had not only been unable to recognize him but could not remember him at all, though he remembered her vividly, and even amused the gathering by recounting to Florence the various outfits she had worn that winter, even the colors of her knitted socks. She had been deeply embarrassed, of course, and yet flattered, and amused. It was proof, after all, that Florence Parr was always at all times Florence Parr.

Afterward she was somewhat saddened, for the anecdote meant, did it not, that she really *had* no interest in men. She was not a spinster because no one had chosen her, not even because she had been too fastidious in her own choosing, but simply because she had no interest in men, she did not even "see" them when they presented themselves before her. It was sad, it was irrefutable. She was an ascetic not through an act of will but through temperament. What did it mean, really, for a woman to say that a man *attracted* her. . . . Erotic love, sexual relationships, were enigmatic, like riddles. What did it mean, why did anyone care, why was so much energy invested . . . ? Of course she had never talked about these matters with anyone, knowing that other people could not possibly know more than she, and most likely knew less; but a distraught woman professor at Swarthmore, many years ago, once confided in Florence that though she'd been married at the age of twenty-one, and divorced at the age of twenty-five, and remarried at the age of twenty-nine, and had had lovers too numerous to count, far less to recall, she herself, with all that extraordinary experience, did not know the first thing about love or sex or the "relationship between the sexes." Half-weeping, half-laughing (for the woman was breaking up with her current lover, a married professor of English whom Florence knew well, and whose liaison with the woman was utterly unsuspected by Florence) she had told Florence that all her lovers didn't really add up to one friend, and that her marriages and love affairs had the quality for her, in retrospect, of melodramatic second-rate films one sat through for a certain duration of time simply because one felt obliged to, having paid admission. I have never decided, the woman said, whether sex is a social thing, a socially conditioned thing, or simply a physiological drive that gets projected onto other people.

Florence had half-wanted to say, But what if one doesn't even have that physiological drive—but of course, wisely, prudently, she had kept silent.

It was at this point that she pushed aside the notes for her talk, her heart beating wildly as a girl's. She had no choice, she *must* satisfy her curiosity about the house, if she wanted to sleep, if she wanted to remain sane.

As the present of the dolls'-house was the great event of her childhood, so the visit to the house on East Fainlight Avenue was to be the great event of her adulthood: though Florence Parr was never to allow herself to think of it, afterward.

It was a mild, quiet night, fragrant with blossoms, not at all intimidating. Florence drove to the avenue, to the house, and was consoled by the numerous lights burning in the neighborhood: of course it wasn't late, of course there was nothing extraordinary about what she was going to do.

Lights were on downstairs. Whoever lived there was up, in the living room. Waiting for her.

Remarkable, her calmness. After so many foolish hours of indecision.

She ascended the veranda steps, which gave slightly beneath her weight. Rang the doorbell. After a minute or so an outside light went on: she felt exposed: began to smile nervously. One smiled, one soon learned how. There was no retreating.

She saw the old wicker furniture on the porch. Two rocking chairs, a settee. Once painted white but now badly weathered. No cushions.

A dog began barking angrily.

Florence Parr, Florence Parr. She knew who she was, but there was no need to tell *him*. Whoever it was, peering out at her through the dark-stained glass, an elderly man, someone's left-behind grandfather. Still, owning this house in this part of town meant money and position: you might sneer at such things but they do have significance. Even to pay the property taxes, the school taxes . . . .

The door opened and a man stood staring out at her, half-smiling, quizzical. He was not the man she expected, he was not elderly, but of indeterminate age, perhaps younger than she. "Yes? Hello? What can I do for . . . ?" he said.

She heard her voice, full-throated and calm. The rehearsed question. Questions. An air of apology beneath which her confidence held firm. ". . . driving in the neighborhood earlier today, staying with friends. . . . Simply curious about an old connection between our families. . . . Or at any rate between my family and the people who built this . . . . "

Clearly he was startled by her presence, and did not quite grasp her question. She spoke too rapidly, she would have to repeat herself.

He invited her in. Which was courteous. A courtesy that struck her as unconscious, automatic. He was very well-mannered. Puzzled but not suspicious. Not unfriendly. Too young for this house, perhaps—for so old and shabbily elegant a house. Her presence on his doorstep, her bold questions, the bright strained smile that stretched her lips must have baffled him but he did not think her *odd*; he respected her, was not judging her. A kindly, simple person. Which was of course a relief. He might even be a little simple-minded. Slow-thinking. He certainly had nothing to do with . . . with whatever she was involved in, in this part of the world. He would tell no one about her.

". . . a stranger to the city? . . . staying with friends?"

"I only want to ask: does the name Parr mean anything to you?"

A dog was barking, now frantically. But kept its distance.

Florence was being shown into the living room, evidently the only lighted room downstairs. She noted the old staircase, graceful as always. But they had done something awkward with the wainscoting, painted it a queer slate blue. And the floor was no longer of marble but a poor imitation, some sort of linoleum tile. . . .

"The chandelier," she said suddenly.

The man turned to her, smiling his amiable quizzical worn smile. "Yes . . . ?"

"It's very attractive," she said. "It must be an antique."

In the comfortable orangish light of the living room she saw that he had sandy red hair, thinning at the crown. But boyishly frizzy at the sides. He might have been in his late thirties but his face was prematurely lined and he stood with one shoulder slightly higher than the other, as if he was very tired. She began to apologize again for disturbing him. For taking up his time with her impulsive, probably futile curiosity.

"Not at all," he said. "I usually don't go to bed until well past midnight."

Florence found herself sitting at one end of an overstuffed sofa. Her smile was strained but as wide as ever, her face had begun to grow very warm. Perhaps he would not notice her blushing.

". . . insomnia?"

"Yes. Sometimes."

"I too. . . . Sometimes."

He was wearing a green-and-blue plaid shirt, with thin red stripes. A flannel shirt. The sleeves rolled up to his elbows. And what looked like work trousers. Denim. A gardener's outfit perhaps. Her mind cast about his garden, his lawn. So many lovely tulips. Most of them red. And there were plane trees, and several elms. . . .

He faced her, leaning forward with his elbows on his knees. A faintly sunburned face. A redhead's complexion, somewhat freckled.

The chair he sat in did not look familiar. It was an ugly brown, imitation brushed velvet. Florence wondered who had bought it: a silly young wife perhaps.

". . . Parr family?"

"From Lancaster?"

"Oh no. From Cummington, Massachusetts. We've lived there for many generations."

He appeared to be considering the name, frowning at the carpet.

". . . *does* sound familiar . . ."

"Oh does it? I had hoped. . . ."

The dog approached them, no longer barking. Its tail wagged and thumped against the side of the sofa, the leg of an old-fashioned table, nearly upsetting a lamp. The man snapped his fingers at the dog and it came no further; it quivered, and made a half-growling half-sighing noise, and lay with its snout on its paws and its skinny tail outstretched, a few feet from Florence. She wanted to placate it, to make friends. But it was such an ugly creature—partly hairless, with scruffy white whiskers, a naked sagging belly.

"If the dog bothers you. . . ."

"Oh no, no. Not at all."

"He only means to be friendly."

"I can see that," Florence said, laughing girlishly. ". . . He's very handsome."

"Hear that?" the man said, snapping his fingers again. "The lady says you're very handsome! Can't you at least stop drooling, don't you have any manners at all?"

"I haven't any pets of my own. But I like animals."

She was beginning to feel quite comfortable. The living room was not exactly what she had expected but it was not *too* bad. There was the rather low, overstuffed sofa in which she sat, the cushions made of a silvery white, silvery gray material, with a feathery sheen, plump, immense, like bellies or breasts, a monstrous old piece of furniture yet nothing one would want to sell: for certainly it had come down in the family, it must date from the turn of the century. There was the Victorian table with its coy ornate legs, and its tasselled cloth, and its extraordinary oversized lamp: the sort of thing Florence would smile at in an antique shop, but which looked fairly reasonable here. In fact she should comment on it, since she was staring at it so openly.

". . . antique? European?"

"I think so, yes," the man said.

"Is it meant to be fruit, or a tree, or . . ."

Bulbous and flesh-colored, peach-colored. With a somewhat tarnished brass stand. A dust-dimmed golden lampshade with embroidered blue trim that must have been very pretty at one time.

They talked of antiques. Of old houses. Families.

A queer odor defined itself. It was not unpleasant exactly.

"Would you like something to drink?"

"Why yes I . . . ."

"Excuse me just a moment."

Alone she wondered if she might prowl about the room. But it was long and narrow and poorly lighted at one end: in fact, one end dissolved into darkness. A faint suggestion of furniture there, an old spinet piano, a jumble of chairs, a bay window that must look out onto the garden. She wanted very much to examine a portrait above the mantel of the fireplace but perhaps the dog would bark, or grow excited, if she moved.

It had crept closer to her feet, shuddering with pleasure.

The redheaded man, slightly stooped, brought a glass of something dark to her. In one hand was his own drink, in the other hand hers.

"Taste it. Tell me what you think."

"It seems rather strong. . . ."

Chocolate. Black and bitter. And thick.

"It should really be served hot," the man said.

"Is there a liqueur of some kind in it?"

"Is it too strong for you?"

"Oh no. No. Not at all."

Florence had never tasted anything more bitter. She nearly gagged.

But a moment later it was all right: she forced herself to take a second swallow, and a third. And the prickling painful sensation in her mouth faded.

The redheaded man did not return to his chair, but stood before her, smiling. In the other room he had done something hurried with his hair; had tried to brush it back with his hands, perhaps. A slight film of perspiration shone on his high forehead.

"Do you live alone here?"

"The house does seem rather large, doesn't it?—for a person to live in it alone."

"Of course you have your dog. . . ."

"Do *you* live alone now?"

Florence set the glass of chocolate down. Suddenly she remembered what it reminded her of: a business associate of her father's, many years ago, had brought a box of chocolates back from a trip to Russia. The little girl had popped one into her mouth and had been dismayed by their unexpectedly bitter taste.

She had spit the mess out into her hand. While everyone stared.

As if he could read her thoughts the redheaded man twitched, moving his jaw and his right shoulder jerkily. But he continued smiling as before and Florence did not indicate that she was disturbed. In fact she spoke warmly of the living room's furnishings, and repeated her admiration for handsome old houses like this one. The man nodded, as if waiting for her to say more.

". . . a family named Bartholomew? Of course it was many years ago."

"Bartholomew? Did they live in this neighborhood?"

"Why yes I think so. That's the real reason I stopped in. I once knew a little girl who . . . ."

"Bartholomew, Bartholomew," the man said slowly, frowning. His face puckered. One corner of his mouth twitched with the effort of his concentration; and again his right shoulder jerked. Florence was afraid he would spill his chocolate drink.

Evidently he had a nervous ailment of some kind. But she could not inquire.

He murmured the name *Bartholomew* to himself, his expression grave, even querulous. Florence wished she had not asked the question because it was a lie, after all. She rarely told lies. Yet it had slipped from her, it had glided smoothly out of her mouth.

She smiled guiltily, ducking her head. She took another swallow of the chocolate drink.

Without her having noticed, the dog had inched forward. His great head now rested on her feet. His wet brown eyes peered up at her, oddly affectionate. A baby's eyes. It was true that he was drooling, in fact he was drooling at her ankles, but of course he could not help it. . . . Then she noted that he had wet on the carpet. Only a few feet away. A dark stain, a small puddle.

Yet she could not shrink away in revulsion. After all, she was a guest and it was not time for her to leave.

". . . Bartholomew. You say they lived in this neighborhood?"

"Oh yes."

"But when?"

"Why I really don't . . . . I was only a child at the . . . ."

"But when was this?"

He was staring oddly at her, almost rudely. The twitch at the corner of his mouth had gotten worse. He moved to set his glass down and the movement was jerky, puppetlike. Yet he stared at her all the while. Florence knew people often felt uneasy because of her dark over-large staring eyes: but she could not help it. She did not *feel* the impetuosity, the reproach, her expression suggested. So she tried to soften it by smiling. But sometimes the smile failed, it did not deceive anyone at all.

Now that her host had stopped smiling she could see that he was really quite mocking. His tangled sandy eyebrows lifted ironically.

"You said you were a stranger to this city, and now you're saying you've been here. . . ."

"But it was so long ago, I was only a . . . ."

He drew himself up to his full height. He was not a tall man, nor was he solidly built. In fact his waist was slender, for a man's—and he wore odd trousers, or jeans, tight-fitting across his thighs and without zipper or snaps, crotchless. They fit him tightly in the crotch, which was smooth, unprotrudent. His legs were rather short for his torso and arms.

He began smiling at Florence. A sly accusing smile. His head jerked mechanically, indicating something on the floor. He was trying to point with his chin and the gesture was clumsy.

"You did something nasty on the floor there. On the carpet."

Florence gasped. At once she drew herself away from the dog, at once she began to deny it. "I didn't—It wasn't—"

"Right on the carpet there. For everyone to see. To smell."

"I certainly did not," Florence said, blushing angrily, "you know very well it was the—"

"Somebody's going to have to clean it up and it isn't going to be *me*," the man said, grinning.

But his eyes were still angry.

He did not like her at all: she saw that. The visit was a mistake, but how could she leave, how could she escape, the dog had crawled up to her again and was nuzzling and drooling against her ankles, and the redheaded man who had seemed so friendly was now leaning over her, his hands on his slim hips, grinning rudely.

As if to frighten her, as one might frighten an animal or a child, he clapped his hands smartly together. Florence blinked at the sudden sound. And then he leaned forward and clapped his hands together again, right before her face. She cried out for him to leave her alone, her eyes smarted with tears, she was leaning back against the cushions, her head back as far as it would go, and then he clapped his hands once again, hard, bringing them against her burning cheeks, slapping both her cheeks at once, and a sharp thin white-hot sensation ran through her body, from her face and throat to her belly, to the pit of her belly up into her chest, into her mouth, and even down into her stiffened legs. She screamed for the redheaded man to stop, and twisted convulsively on the sofa to escape him.

"Liar! Bad girl! Dirty girl!" someone shouted.

She wore new reading glasses, with their attractive plastic frames. And a spring suit, smartly styled, with a silk blouse in a floral pattern. And the tight but fashionable shoes.

Her audience, respectful and attentive, could not see her trembling hands behind the podium, or her slightly quivering knees. They would have been astonished to learn that she hadn't been able to eat breakfast that morning—that she felt depressed and exhausted though she had managed to fall asleep the night before, probably around two, and had evidently slept her usual dreamless sleep.

She cleared her throat several times in succession, a habit she detested in others.

But gradually her strength flowed back into her. The morning was so sunny, so innocent. These people were, after all, her colleagues and friends; they certainly wished her well, and even appeared to be genuinely interested in what she had to say about the future of the humanities. Perhaps Dr. Parr knew something they did not, perhaps she would share her professional secrets with them. . . .

As the minutes passed Florence could hear her voice grow richer and firmer, easing into its accustomed rhythms. She began to relax. She began to breathe more regularly. She was moving into familiar channels, making points she had made countless times before, at similar meetings, with her deans and faculty chairmen at Champlain, with other educators. A number of people applauded heartily when she spoke of the danger of small private colleges competing unwisely with one another; and again when she made a point, an emphatic point, about the need for the small private school in an era of multiversities. Surely these were remarks anyone might have made, there was really nothing original about them, yet her audience seemed extremely pleased to hear them from her. They *did* admire Florence Parr immensely, that was clear.

She took off her reading glasses and continued without glancing at her notes. This part of the speech—a detailed summary of the consequences of certain experimental programs at Champlain, initiated since she became president—was more specific, more interesting, and of course she knew it by heart.

The night had been unpleasant, at least in the beginning: her mind racing helplessly, those flamlike pangs of fear, her insomnia. And no help for it. And no way out. Evidently she had fallen asleep while reading through her notes because she'd awakened suddenly, her heart quite literally hammering in her chest, her sides drenched with sweat—and there she was, lying clumsily back against the headboard, her neck stiff and aching and one of her legs numb beneath her. But afterward, after pressing a cold damp washcloth against her face, she was able to relax, and sleep: and so far as she knew her sleep was restful, without dreams.

And the speech went well, of course she had had nothing to worry about. After all she had given speeches like this many times before, and had always been applauded wholeheartedly.

Afterward everyone congratulated her. Coffee was being served.

Conversation, chatter. Good spirits. Gossip. Florence blushed with relief and pleasure. Why does one worry about anything, really, she thought, smiling into the friendly faces, shaking hands. These were all good people and she liked them very much.

There were artful bouquets of azaleas, and the coffee was fresh. Suddenly hungry, Florence found herself eating a glazed donut taken from a silver tray.

The discomfort of the night was fading, the vision of the dolls'-house of the previous afternoon was faint, dying. She could not attend to it, she hadn't time. How easily the night is banished, Florence thought, her face fairly glowing, as friends gathered around her. There were questions, provocative questions, there were even one or two amiable objections, all very welcome.

The conference went well, though in the end, on the very last afternoon, everyone grew weary, and anxious to leave. But that was only natural. That was always the case. Florence left Lancaster by a southerly route, in order to see countryside she had not seen on her way in, and she found it predictably beautiful. Of course this part of Pennsylvania is beautiful, as everyone says.

The conference went well, though after a week or two she forgot it, she forgot most of it; but that too was only natural. There were so many conferences, so many well-received speeches. Spring was always a busy time. And she must prepare for convocation at Champlain, which would be held the first week of June: always a busy time.

A check for three hundred dollars came, an honorarium for her speech. She experienced a moment of guilt, for perhaps she should not accept money for doing work she loved?—and she could barely remember, by then, the circumstances of the speech, or even where it had been given.

If Damon Comes

CHARLES L. GRANT

The pain acquires, every generation, a new terminology and a new set of journalistic labels or psychiatric appellation, but the pain is timeless and the consequence inevitable. Pain, seeping through the interstices of control, becomes horror; this is demonstrated as well as it ever has been in this story. Charles L. Grant, winner of two awards in short fiction from the Science Fiction Writers of America, and the author of many novels and short stories in several fields, is self-categorized as doing his best work in the horror genre. He is certainly one of the two or three best who have emerged there in the 1970's.

Fog, nightbreath of the river, luring without whispering in the thick crown of an elm, huddling without creaking around the base of a chimney; it drifted past porch lights, and in passing blurred them, dropped over the streetlights, and in dropping grayed them. It crept in with midnight to stay until dawn, and there was no wind to bring the light out of hiding.

Frank shivered and drew his raincoat's collar closer around his neck, held it closed with one hand while the other wiped at the pricks of moisture that clung to his cheeks, his short dark hair. He whistled once, loudly, but in listening heard nothing, not even an echo. He stamped his feet against the November cold and moved to the nearest corner, squinted and saw nothing. He knew the cat was gone, had known it from the moment he had seen the saucer still brimming with milk on the back porch. Damon had been sitting beside it, hands folded, knees pressed tightly together, elbows tucked into his sides. He was cold, but refused to acknowledge it, and Frank had only tousled his son's softly brown hair, squeezed his shoulder once and went inside to say good-bye to his wife.

And now . . . now he walked, through the streets of Oxrun Station, looking for an animal he had seen only once—a half-breed Siamese with a milk white face—whistling like a fool afraid of the dark, searching for the note that would bring the animal running.

And in walking, he was unpleasantly reminded of a night the year

536

before, when he had had one drink too many at someone's party, made one amorous boast too many in someone's ear, and had ended up on a street corner with a woman he knew only vaguely. They had kissed once and long, and once broken, he had turned around to see Damon staring up at him. The boy had turned, had fled, and Frank had stayed away most of the night, not knowing what Susan had heard, fearing more what Damon had thought.

It had been worse than horrid facing the boy again, but Damon had acted as though nothing had happened; and the guilt passed as the months passed, and the wondering why his son had been out in the first place.

He whistled. Crouched and snapped his fingers at the dark of some shrubbery. Then he straightened and blew out a deeply held breath. There was no cat, there were no cars, and he finally gave in to his aching feet and sore back and headed for home. Quickly. Watching the fog tease the road before him, cut it sharply off behind.

It wasn't fair, he thought, his hands shoved in his pockets, his shoulders hunched as though expecting a blow. Damon, in his short eight years had lost two dogs already to speeders, a canary to some disease he couldn't even pronounce, and two brothers stillborn—it was getting to be a problem. *He* was getting to be a problem, fighting each day that he had to go to school, whining and weeping whenever vacations came around and trips were planned.

He'd asked Doc Simpson about it when Damon turned seven. Dependency, he was told; clinging to the only three things left in his life—his short, short life—that he still believed to be constant: his home, his mother . . . and Frank.

And Frank had kissed a woman on a corner and Damon had seen him.

Frank shuddered and shook his head quickly, remembering how the boy had come to the office at least once a day for the next three weeks, saying nothing, just standing on the sidewalk looking in through the window. Just for a moment. Long enought to be sure that his father was still there.

Once home, then, Frank shed his coat and hung it on the rack by the front door. A call, a muffled reply, and he took the stairs two at a time and trotted down the hall to Damon's room set over the kitchen.

"Sorry, old pal," he said with a shrug as he made himself a place on the edge of the mattress. "I guess he went home."

Damon, small beneath the flowered quilt, innocent from behind long curling lashes, shook his head sharply. "No," he said. "This is home. It is, Dad, it really is."

Frank scratched at the back of his neck. "Well, I guess he didn't think of it quite that way."

"Maybe he got lost, huh? It's awfully spooky out there. Maybe he's afraid to come out of where he's hiding."

"A cat's never—" He stopped as soon as he saw the expression on the boy's thin face. Then he nodded and broke out a rueful smile, "Well, maybe you're right, pal. Maybe the fog messed him up a little." Damon's hand crept into his, and he squeezed it while thinking that the boy was too thin by far; it made his head look ungainly. "In the morning," he promised. "In the morning. If he's not back by then, I'll take the day off and we'll hunt him together."

Damon nodded solemnly, withdrew the hand and pulled the quilt up to his chin. "When's mom coming home?"

"In a while. It's Friday, you know. She's always late on Fridays. And Saturdays." And, he thought, Wednesdays and Thursdays, too.

Damon nodded again. And, as Frank reached the door and switched off the light: "Dad, does she sing pretty?"

"Like a bird, pal," he said, grinning. "Like a bird."

The voice was small in the dark: "I love you, dad."

Frank swallowed hard, and nodded before he realized the boy couldn't see him. "Well, pal, it seems I love you, too. Now you'd better get some rest."

"I thought you were going to get lost in the fog."

Frank stopped the move to close the door. He'd better get some rest himself, he thought; that sounded like a threat.

"Not me," he finally said. "You'd always come for me, right?"

"Right, dad."

Frank grinned, closed the door, and wandered through the small house for nearly half an hour before finding himself in the kitchen, his hands waving at his sides for something to do. Coffee. No. He'd already had too much of that today. But the walk had chilled him, made his bones seem brittle. Warm milk, maybe, and he opened the refrigerator, stared, then took out a container and poured half its contents into a pot. He stood by the stove, every few seconds stirring a finger through the milk to check its progress. Stupid cat, he thought; there ought to be a law against doing something like that to a small boy that never hurt anyone, never had anyone to hurt.

He poured himself a glass, smiling when he didn't spill a drop, but he refused to turn around and look up at the clock; instead, he stared at the flames as he finished the second glass, wondering what it would be like to stick his finger into the fires. He read somewhere . . . he thought he'd read somewhere that the blue near the center was the hottest part and it wasn't so bad elsewhere. His hand wavered, but he changed his mind, not wanting to risk a burn on something he only thought he had read; besides, he decided as he headed into the living room, the way things were going these days, he probably had it backward.

He sat in an armchair flanking the television, took out a magazine from the rack at his side and had just found the table of contents when he heard a car door slam in the drive. He waited, looked up and smiled when the front door swung open and Susan rushed in. She blew him a distant kiss, mouthed *I'll be back in a second,* and ran up the stairs. She was much shorter than he, her hair waist-long black and left free to fan in the wind of he own making. She'd been taking vocal lessons for several years now, and when they'd moved to the Station when Damon was five, she had landed a job singing at the Chancellor Inn. Torch songs, love songs, slow songs, sinner songs; she was liked well enough to be asked to stay on after the first night, but she began so late that Damon had never heard her. And for the last six months, the two-nights-a-week became four, and Frank became adept at cooking supper.

When she returned, her make-up was gone and she was in shimmering green robe. She flopped on the sofa opposite him and rubbed her knees, her thighs, her upper arms. "If that creep drummer tries to pinch me again, so help me I'll castrate him."

"That is hardly the way for a lady to talk," he said, smiling. "If you're not careful, I'll have to punish you. Whips at thirty paces."

In the old days—the very old days, he thought—she would have laughed and entered a game that would last for nearly an hour. Lately, however, and tonight, she only frowned at him as though she were dealing with a dense, unlettered child. He ignored it, and listened politely as she detailed her evening, the customers, the compliments, the raise she was looking for so she could buy her own car.

"You don't need a car," he said without thinking.

"But aren't you tired of walking home every night?"

He closed the magazine and dropped it on the floor. "Lawyers, my dear, are a sedentary breed. I could use the exercise."

"If you didn't work so late on those damned briefs," she said without looking at him, "and came to bed on time, I'd give you all the exercise you need."

He looked at his watch. It was going on two.

"The cat's gone."

"Oh no," she said. "No wonder you look so tired. You go out after him?"

He nodded, and she rolled herself suddenly into a sitting position. "Not with Damon."

"No. He was in bed when I came home."

She said nothing more, only examined her nails. He watched her closely, the play of her hair falling over her face, the squint that told him her contact lenses were still on her dresser. And he knew she meant: *did you take Damon with you?* She was asking if Damon had followed him. Like the night in the fog, with the woman; like the times at the office; like the dozens of other instances when the boy just happened to show up at the courthouse, in the park while Frank was eating lunch under a tree, at a nearby friend's house late one evening, claiming to have had a nightmare and the sitter wouldn't help him.

Like a shadow.

Like a conscience.

"Are you going to replace it?" He blinked. "The cat, stupid. Are you going to get him a new cat?"

He shook his head. "We've had too much bad luck with animals. I don't think he could take it again."

She swung herself off the sofa and stood in front of him her hands on her hips, her lips taut, her eyes narrowed. "You don't care about him, do you?"

"What?"

"He follows you around like a goddamn pet because he's afraid of losing you, and you won't even buy him a lousy puppy or something. You're something else again, Frank, you really are. I work my tail trying to help—"

"My salary is plenty good enough," he said quickly.

"—this family and you're even trying to get me to stop that, too."

He shoved himself to his feet, his chest brushing against hers and forcing her back. "Listen," he said tightly. "I don't care if you sing your heart out a million times a week, lady, but when it starts to interfere with your duties here—"

"My *duties*?"

"—then yes, I'll do everything I can to make sure you stay home when you're supposed to."

"You're raising your voice. You'll wake Damon."

The argument was familiar, and old, and so was the rage he felt stiffening his muscles. But this time she wouldn't stop when she saw his anger. She kept on, and on, and he didn't even realize it when his hand lifted and struck her across the cheek. She stumbled back a step, whirled to run out of the room, and stopped.

Damon was standing at the foot of the stairs.

He was sucking his thumb.

He was staring at his father.

"Go to bed, son," Frank said quietly. "Everything's all right."

For the next week the tension in the house was proverbially knife-cutting thick. Damon stayed up as late as he could, sitting by his father as they watched television together or read from the boy's favorite books. Susan remained close, but not touching, humming to herself and playing with her son whenever he left—for the moment—his father's side; each time, however, her smile was more forced, her laughter more strained, and it was apparent to Frank that Damon was merely tolerating her, nothing more. That puzzled him. It was he who had struck her, not the other way around, and the boy's loyalty should have been thrown into his mother's camp. Yet it hadn't. And it was apparent that Susan was growing more resentful of the fact each day. Each hour. Each time Damon walked silently to Frank's side and slid his hand around the man's waist, or into his palm, or into his hip pocket.

He began showing up at the office again, until one afternoon when Susan skidded the car to a halt at the curb and ran out, grabbed the boy and practically threw him, arms and legs thrashing, into the front seat. Frank raced from his desk and out the front door, leaned over and rapped at the window until Susan lowered it.

"What the hell are you doing?" he whispered, with a glance to the boy.

"You hit me, or had you forgotten," she whispered back. "And there's my son's alienation of affection."

He almost straightened. "That's lawyer talk, Susan," he said.

"Not here," she answered. "Not in front of the boy."

He stepped back quickly as the car growled away from the curb, walked in a daze to his desk and sat there, chin in one palm, staring out the window as the afternoon darkened and a faint drizzle began to fall. His secretary muttered something about a court case the following morning, and Frank nodded until she stared at him, gathered her purse and raincoat and left hurriedly. He continued to nod, not knowing the movement, trying to understand what he had done, what both of them had done to bring themselves to this moment. Ambition, surely. A conflict of generations where women were homebodies and women had careers; where men tried to adjust when they couldn't have both. But he had tried, he told himself . . . or he thought he had, until the dishes began to pile up and the dust stayed on the furniture and Damon said *does she sing pretty?*

It's always the children who get hurt, he thought angrily.

Held that idea in early December when the separation papers had been prepared and he stood on the front porch watching his car, his wife, and his son drive away from Oxrun Station south toward the city. Damon's face was in the rear window, nose flat, palms flat, hair pressed down over his forehead. He waved, and Frank answered.

I love you, dad.

Frank wiped a hand under his nose and went back inside, searched the house for some liquor and, in failing, went straight to bed where he watched the moonshadows make monsters of the curtains.

"Dad," the boy said, "do I have to go with mommy?"

"I'm afraid so. The judge . . . well, he knows better, believe it or not, what's best right now. Don't worry, pal. I'll see you at Christmas. It won't be forever."

"I don't like it, dad. I'll run away."

"No! You'll do what your mother tells you, you hear me?" You behave yourself and go to school every day, and I'll . . . call you whenever I can."

"The city doesn't like me, dad. I want to stay at the Station."

Frank said nothing.

"It's because of the lady, isn't it?"

He had stared, but Susan's back was turned, bent over a suitcase that would not close once it had sprung open again by the front door.

"What are you talking about?" he'd said harshly.

"I told," Damon said as though it were nothing. "You weren't supposed to do that."

When Susan straightened, her smile was grotesque.

And when they had driven away, Damon had said *I love you, dad.*

Frank woke early, made himself breakfast and stood at the back door, looking out into the yard. There was a fog again, nothing unusual as the Connecticut weather fought to stabilize into winter. But as he sipped at his coffee, thinking how large the house had become, how large and how empty, he saw a movement beside the cherry tree in the middle of the yard. The fog swirled, but he was sure. . .

He yanked open the door and shouted: "Damon!"

The fog closed, and he shook his head. Easy, pal, he told himself; you're not cracking up yet.

Days.

Nights.

He called Susan regularly, twice a week at preappointed times. But as Christmas came and Christmas went, she became more terse, and his son more sullen.

"He's getting fine grades, Frank, I'm seeing to that."

"He sounds terrible."

"He's losing a little weight, that's all. Picks up colds easily. It takes a while, Frank, to get used to the city."

"He doesn't like the city."

"It's his home. He will."

In mid-January Susan did not answer the phone and finally, in desperation, he called the school, was told that Damon had been in the hospital for nearly a week. The nurse thought it was something like pneumonia.

When he arrived that night, the waiting room was crowded with drab bundles of scarves and overcoats, whispers and moans and a few muffled sobs. Susan was standing by the window, looking out at the lights far colder than stars. She didn't turn when she heard him, didn't answer when he demanded to know why she had not contacted him. He grabbed her shoulder and spun her around; her eyes were dull, her face pinched with red hints of cold.

"All right," she said. "All right, Frank, it's because I didn't want you to upset him."

"What the hell are you talking about?"

"He would have seen you and he would have wanted to go back to Oxrun." Her eyes narrowed. "This is his home, Frank! He's got to learn to live with it."

"I'll get a lawyer."

She smiled. "Do that. You do that, Frank."

He didn't have to. He saw Damon a few minutes later and could not stay more than a moment. The boy was in dim light and almost invisible, too thin to be real beneath the clear plastic tent and the tubes and the monitors . . . too frail, the doctor said in professional conciliation, too frail for too long, and Frank remembered the day on the porch with the saucer of milk when he had thought the same thing and had thought nothing of it.

He returned after the funeral, all anger gone. He had accused Susan of murder, knowing at the time how foolish it had been, but feeling better for it in his own absolution. He had apologized. Had been, for the moment, forgiven.

Had stepped off the train, had wept, had taken a deep breath and decided to live on.

Returned to the office the following day, piled folders onto his desk and hid behind them for most of the morning. He looked up only once, when his secretary tried to explain about a new client's interest, and saw around her waist the indistinct form of his son peering through the window.

"Damon," he muttered, brushed the woman to one side and ran out to the sidewalk. A fog encased the road whitely, but he could see nothing, not even a car, not even the blinking amber light at the nearest intersection.

Immediately after lunch he dialed Susan's number, stared at the receiver when there was no answer and returned it to the cradle. Wondering.

"You look pale," his secretary said softly. She pointed with a pencil at his desk. "You've already done a full day's work. Why don't you go home and lie down? I can lock up. I don't mind."

He smiled, turned as she held his coat for him, touched her cheek . . .and froze.

Damon was in the window.

No, he told himself . . . and Damon was gone.

He rested for two days, returned to work and lost himself in a battle over a will probated by a judge he thought nothing less than senile, to be charitable. He tried calling Susan again, and again received no answer.

And Damon would not leave him alone.

When there was fog, rain, clouds, wind . . . he would be there by the window, there by the cherry tree, there in the darkest corner of the porch.

He knew it was guilt, for not fighting hard enough to keep his son with him, thinking that if he had the boy might still be alive; seeing his face everywhere and the accusations that if the boy loved him, why wasn't he loved just as much in return?

By February's end he decided it was time to make a friendly call on a fellow professional, a doctor who shared the office building with him. It wasn't so much the faces that he saw—he had grown somewhat accustomed to them and assumed they would vanish in time—but that morning there had been snow on the ground; and in the snow by the cherry tree the footprints of a small boy. When he brought the doctor to the yard to show him, they were gone.

"You're quite right, Frank. You're feeling guilty. But not because of the boy in and of himself. The law and the leanings of most judges are quite clear—you couldn't be expected to keep him at his age. You're still worrying yourself about that woman you kissed and the fact that Damon saw you; and the fact that you think you could have saved his life somehow, even if the doctors couldn't; and lastly, the fact that you weren't able to give him things like pets, like that cat. None of it is your fault, really. It's merely something unpleasant you'll have to face up to. Now."

Though he didn't feel all that much better, Frank appreciated the calm that swept over him when the talk was done and they had parted. He worked hard for the rest of the day, for the rest of the week, but he knew that it was not guilt and it was not his imagination and it was not anything the doctor would be able to explain away when he opened his door on Saturday morning and found, lying carefully atop his newspaper, the white-faced Siamese. Dead. Its neck broken.

He stumbled back over the threshold, whirled around and raced into the downstairs bathroom where he fell onto his knees beside the bowl and lost his breakfast. The tears were acid, the sobs like blows to his lungs and stomach, and by the time he had pulled himself together, he knew what was happening.

The doctor, the secretary, even his wife . . . they were all wrong.

There was no guilt.

There was only . . . Damon.

A little boy with large brown eyes who loved his father. Who loved his father so much that he would never leave him. Who loved his father so much that he was going to make sure, absolutely sure, that he would never be alone.

You've been a bad boy, daddy.

Frank stumbled to his feet, into the kitchen, leaned against the back door. There was a figure by the cherry tree dark and formless; but he knew there was no use running outside. The figure would vanish.

You never did like that cat, daddy. Or the dogs. Or mommy.

The telephone rang. He took his time getting to it, stared at it dumbly for several moments before lifting the receiver. He could see straight down the hall and into the kitchen. He had not turned on the overhead light and, as a consequence, could see through the small panes of the back door to the yard beyond. The air outside was heavy with impending snow. Gray. Almost lifeless.

"Frank? Frank, it's Susan. Frank, I've been thinking . . . about you and me . . . and what happened."

He kept his eyes on the door. "It's done, Sue. Done."

"Frank, I don't know what happened. Honest to God, I was trying, really I was. He was getting the best grades in school, had lots of friends . . . . I even bought him a little dog, a poodle, two weeks before he . . . I don't know what happened, Frank! I woke up this morning and all of a sudden I was so damned *alone*. Frank, I'm frightened. Can . . .can I come home?"

The gray darkened. There was a shadow on the porch, much longer now than the shadow in the yard.

"No," he said.

"He thought about you all the damned time," she said, her voice rising into hysteria. "He tried to run away once, to get back to you."

The shadow filled the panes, the windows on either side, and suddenly there was static on the line and Susan's voice vanished. He dropped the receiver and turned around.

In the front.

Shadows.

He heard the furnace humming, but the house was growing cold.

The lamp in the living room flickered, died, shone brightly for a moment before the bulb shattered.

He was . . . wrong.

God, he was wrong!

Damon . . . Damon didn't love him.

Not since the night on the corner in the fog; not since the night he had not really tried to locate a cat with a milk white face.

Damon knew.

And Damon didn't love him.

He dropped to his hands and knees and searched in the darkness for the receiver, found it and nearly threw it away when the bitterly cold plastic threatened to burn through his fingers.

"Susan!" he shouted. "Susan, dammit, can you hear me?"

A bad boy, daddy.

There was static, but he thought he could hear her crying into the wind.

"Susan . . . Susan, this is crazy, I've no time to explain, but you've got to help me. You've got to do something for me."

Daddy.

"Susan, please . . . he'll be back, I know he will. Don't ask me how, but I know! Listen, you've got to do something for me. Susan, dammit, can you hear me?"

Daddy, I'm—

"For God's sake, Susan, if Damon comes, tell him I'm sorry!"

home.

The Oblong Room

EDWARD D. HOCH

*A decade later it happened . . . the events of Hoch's horrifying story
were replicated in New York City. This neither increases the horror of
"The Oblong Room" nor lessens it; the terror comes from an internal
and consistent truth of the human condition which Hoch as an artist
perceived. This story won a Mystery Writers of America Award in 1967
as the best short story of its year; Hoch, the most prolific short-story
writer in America, wrote a masterpiece, and its resolution tran-
scends not only event but character to become in its flat and stark
timelessness, history.*

It was Fletcher's case from the beginning, but Captain Leopold
rode along with him when the original call came in. The thing seemed
open and shut, with the only suspect found literally standing over his
victim, and on a dull day Leopold thought that a ride out to the
university might be pleasant.

Here, along the river, the October color was already in the trees,
and through the park a slight haze of burning leaves clouded the road
in spots. It was a warm day for autumn, a sunny day. Not really a day
for murder.

"The university hasn't changed much," Leopold commented, as
they turned into the narrow street that led past the fraternity houses to
the library tower. "A few new dorms, and a new stadium. That's about
all."

"We haven't had a case here since that bombing four or five years
back," Fletcher said. "This one looks to be a lot easier, though.
They've got the guy already. Stabbed his roommate and then stayed
right there with the body."

Leopold was silent. They'd pulled up before one of the big new
dormitories that towered toward the sky like some middle-income
housing project, all brick and concrete and right now surrounded by
milling students. Leopold pinned on his badge and led the way.

The room was on the fourth floor, facing the river. It seemed to be
identical to all the others—a depressing oblong, with bunk beds, twin

548

study desks, wardrobes, and a large picture window opposite the door. The medical examiner was already there, and he looked up as Leopold and Fletcher entered. "We're ready to move him. All right with you, captain?"

"The boys get their pictures? Then it's fine with me. Fletcher, find out what you can." Then, to the medical examiner, "What killed him?"

"A couple of stab wounds. I'll do an autopsy, but there's not much doubt."

"How long dead?"

"A day or so."

"A day!"

Fletcher had been making notes as he questioned the others. "The precinct men have it pretty well wrapped up for us, captain. The dead boy is Ralph Rollings, a sophomore. His roommate admits to being here with the body for maybe twenty hours before they were discovered. Roommate's name is Tom McBern. They've got him in the next room."

Leopold nodded and went through the connecting door. Tom McBern was tall and slender, and handsome in a dark, collegiate sort of way. "Have you warned him of his rights?" Leopold asked a patrolman.

"Yes, sir."

"All right." Leopold sat down on the bed opposite McBern. "What have you got to say, son?"

The deep brown eyes came up to meet Leopold's. "Nothing, sir. I think I want a lawyer."

"That's your privilege, of course. You don't wish to make any statement about how your roommate met his death, or why you remained in the room with him for several hours without reporting it?"

"No, sir." He turned away and stared out the window.

"You understand we'll have to book you on suspicion of homicide."

The boy said nothing more, and after a few moments Leopold left him alone with the officer. He went back to Fletcher and watched while the body was covered and carried away. "He's not talking. Wants a lawyer. Where are we?"

Sergeant Fletcher shrugged. "All we need is motive. They probably had the same girl or something."

"Find out."

They went to talk with the boy who occupied the adjoining room, the one who'd found the body. He was sandy-haired and handsome, with the look of an athlete, and his name was Bill Smith.

"Tell us how it was, Bill," Leopold said.

"There's not much to tell. I knew Ralph and Tom slightly during my freshman year, but never really well. They stuck pretty much together. This year I got the room next to them, but the connecting door was always locked. Anyway, yesterday neither one of them showed up at class. When I came back yesterday afternoon I knocked at the door and asked if anything was wrong. Tom called out that they were sick. He wouldn't open the door. I went into my own room and didn't think much about it. Then, this morning, I knocked to see how they were. Tom's voice sounded so . . . strange."

"Where was your own roommate all this time?"

"He's away. His father died and he went home for the funeral." Smith's hands were nervous, busy with a shredded piece of paper. Leopold offered him a cigarette and he took it. "Anyway, when he wouldn't open the door I became quite concerned and told him I was going for help. He opened it then—and I saw Ralph stretched out on the bed, all bloody and . . . dead."

Leopold nodded and went to stand by the window. From here he could see the trees down along the river, blazing gold and amber and scarlet as the October sun passed across them. "Had you heard any sounds the previous day? Any argument?"

"No. Nothing. Nothing at all."

"Had they disagreed in the past about anything?"

"Not that I knew of. If they didn't get along, they hardly would have asked to room together again this year."

"How about girls?" Leopold asked.

"They both dated occasionally, I think."

"No special one? One they both liked?"

Bill Smith was silent for a fraction too long. "No."

"You're sure?"

"I told you I didn't know them very well."

"This is murder, Bill. It's not a sophomore dance or class day games."

"Tom killed him. What more do you need?"

"What's her name, Bill?"

He stubbed out the cigarette and looked away. Then finally he answered. "Stella Banting. She's a junior."

"Which one did she go with?"

"I don't know. She was friendly with both of them. I think she went out with Ralph a few times around last Christmas, but I'd seen her with Tom lately."

"She's older than them?"

"No. They're all twenty. She's just a year ahead."

"All right," Leopold said. "Sergeant Fletcher will want to question you further."

He left Smith's room and went out in the hall with Fletcher. "It's your case, sergeant. About time I gave it to you."

"Thanks for the help, captain."

"Let him talk to a lawyer and then see if he has a story. If he still won't make a statement, book him on suspicion. I don't think there's any doubt we can get an indictment."

"You going to talk to that girl?"

Leopold smiled. "I just might. Smith seemed a bit shy about her. Might be a motive there. Let me know as soon as the medical examiner has something more definite about the time of death."

"Right, captain."

Leopold went downstairs, pushing his way through the students and faculty members still crowding the halls and stairways. Outside he unpinned the badge and put it away. The air was fresh and crisp as he strolled across the campus to the administration building.

Stella Banting lived in the largest sorority house on campus, a great columned building of ivy and red brick. But when Captain Leopold found her she was on her way back from the drugstore, carrying a carton of cigarettes and a bottle of shampoo. Stella was a tall girl with firm, angular lines and a face that might have been beautiful if she ever smiled.

"Stella Banting?"

"Yes?"

"I'm Captain Leopold. I wanted to talk to you about the tragedy over at the men's dorm. I trust you've heard about it?"

She blinked her eyes and said, "Yes. I've heard."

"Could we go somewhere and talk?"

"I'll drop these at the house and we can walk if you'd like. I don't want to talk there."

She was wearing faded Bermuda shorts and a bulky sweatshirt, and walking with her made Leopold feel young again. If only she smiled occasionally—but perhaps this was not a day for smiling. They headed away from the main campus, out toward the silent oval of the athletic field and sports stadium. "You didn't come over to the dorm," he said to her finally, breaking the silence of their walk."

"Should I have?"

"I understood you were friendly with them—that you dated the dead boy last Christmas and Tom McBern more recently."

"A few times. Ralph wasn't the sort anyone ever got to know very well."

"And what about Tom?"

"He was a nice fellow."

"*Was?*"

"It's hard to explain. Ralph did things to people, to everyone around him. When I felt it happening to me, I broke away."

"What sort of things?"

"He had a power—a power you wouldn't believe any twenty-year-old capable of."

"You sound as it you've known a lot of them."

"I have. This is my third year at the university. I've grown up a lot in that time. I think I have, anyway."

"And what about Tom McBern?"

"I dated him a few times recently just to confirm for myself how bad things were. He was completely under Ralph's thumb. He lived for no one but Ralph."

"Homosexual?" Leopold asked.

"No, I don't think it was anything as blatant as that. It was more the relationship of teacher and pupil, leader and follower."

"Master and slave?"

She turned to smile at him. "You do seem intent on midnight orgies, don't you?"

"The boy is dead, after all."

"Yes. Yes, he is." She stared down at the gound, kicking randomly at the little clusters of fallen leaves. "But you see what I mean? Ralph was always the leader, the teacher—for Tom, almost the messiah."

"Then why would he have killed him?" Leopold asked.

"That's just it—he wouldn't!" Whatever happened in that room, I can't imagine Tom McBern ever bringing himself to kill Ralph."

"There is one possibility, Miss Banting. Could Ralph Rollings have made a disparaging remark about you? Something about when he was dating you?"

"I never slept with Ralph, if that's what you're trying to ask me. With either of them for that matter."

"I didn't mean it that way."

"It happened just the way I've told you. If anything, I was afraid of Ralph. I didn't want him getting that sort of hold over me."

Somehow he knew they'd reached the end of their stroll, even though they were still in the middle of the campus quadrangle, some distance from the sports arena. "Thank you for your help, Miss Banting. I may want to call on you again."

He left her there and headed back toward the men's dorm, knowing that she would watch him until he was out of sight.

Sergeant Fletcher found Leopold in his office early the following morning, reading the daily reports of the night's activities. "Don't you ever sleep, captain?" he asked, pulling up the faded leather chair that served for infrequent visitors.

"I'll have enough time for sleeping when I'm dead. What have you got on McBern?"

"His lawyer says he refuses to make a statement, but I gather they'd like to plead him not guilty by reason of insanity."

"What's the medical examiner say?"

Fletcher read from the typed sheet. "Two stab wounds, both in the area of the heart. He apparently was stretched out on the bed when he got it."

"How long before they found him?"

"He'd eaten breakfast maybe an hour or so before he died, and from our questioning that places the time of death at about ten o'clock. Bill Smith went to the door and got McBern to open it at about eight the following morning. Since we know McBern was in the room the previous evening when Smith spoke to him through the door, we can assume he was alone with the body for approximately twenty-two hours.

Leopold was staring out the window, mentally comparing the city's autumn gloom with the colors of the countryside that he'd witnessed the previous day. Everything dies, only it dies a little sooner, a bit more drably, in the city. "What else?" he asked Fletcher, because there obviously was something else.

"In one of the desk drawers," Fletcher said, producing a little evidence envelope. "Six sugar cubes, saturated with LSD."

"All right." Leopold stared down at them. "I guess that's not too unusual on campuses these days. Has there ever been a murder committed by anyone under the influence of LSD?"

"A case out West somewhere. And I think another one over in England."

"Can we get a conviction, or is this the basis of the insanity plea?"

"I'll check on it, captain."

"And one more thing—get that fellow Smith in here. I want to talk to him again."

Later, alone, Leopold felt profoundly depressed. The case bothered him. McBern had stayed with Rollings' body for twenty-two hours. Anybody that could last that long would have to be crazy. He was crazy and he was a killer and that was all there was to it.

When Fletcher ushered Bill Smith into the office an hour later, Leopold was staring out the window. He turned and motioned the young man to a chair. "I have some further questions, Bill."

"Yes?"

"Tell me about the LSD."

"What?"

Leopold walked over and sat on the edge of the desk. "Don't pretend you never heard of it. Rollings and McBern had some in their room."

Bill Smith looked away. "I didn't know. There were rumors."

"Nothing else? No noise through that connecting door?"

"Noise, yes. Sometimes it was . . ."

Leopold waited for him to continue, and when he did not, said, "This is a murder investigation, Bill."

"Rollings . . . he deserved to die, that's all. He was the most completely evil person I ever knew. The things he did to poor Tom . . ."

"Stella Banting says Tom almost worshipped him."

"He did, and that's what made it all the more terrible."

Leopold leaned back and lit a cigarette. "If they were both high on LSD, almost anyone could have entered that room and stabbed Ralph."

But Bill Smith shook his head. "I doubt it. They wouldn't have dared unlock the door while they were turned on. Besides, Tom would have protected him with his own life."

"And yet we're to believe that Tom killed him? That he stabbed him to death and spent a day and a night alone with the body? Doing what, Bill? Doing what?"

"I don't know."

"Do you think Tom McBern is insane?"

"No, not really. Not legally." He glanced away. "But on the subject of Rollings, he was pretty far gone. Once, when we were still friendly, he told me he'd do anything for Rollings—even trust him with his life. And he did, one time. It was during the spring weekend and everybody had been drinking a lot. Tom hung upside down out of the dorm window with Rollings holding his ankles. That's how much he trusted him."

"I think I'll have to talk with Tom McBern again," Leopold said. "At the scene of the crime."

Fletcher brought Tom McBern out to the campus in handcuffs, and Captain Leopold was waiting for them in the oblong room on the fourth floor. "All right, Fletcher," Leopold said. "You can leave us alone. Wait outside."

McBern had lost a good deal of his previous composure, and now he faced Leopold with red-ringed eyes and a lip that trembled when he spoke. "What . . . what did you want to ask me?"

"A great many things, son. All the questions in the world." Leopold sighed and offered the boy a cigarette. "You and Rollings were taking LSD, weren't you?"

"We took it, yes."

"Why? For kicks?"

"Not for kicks. You don't understand about Ralph."

"I understand that you killed him. What more is there to understand? You stabbed him to death right over there on that bed."

Tom McBern took a deep breath. "We didn't take LSD for kicks," he repeated. "It was more to heighten the sense of religious experience—a sort of mystical involvement that is the whole meaning of life."

Leopold frowned down at the boy. "I'm only a detective, son. You and Rollings were strangers to me until yesterday, and I guess now he'll always be a stranger to me. That's one of the troubles with my job. I don't get to meet people until it's too late, until the damage," he gestured toward the empty bed, "is already done. But I want to know what happened in this room, between you two. I don't want to hear about mysticism or religious experience. I want to hear what happened—why you killed him and why you sat here with the body for twenty-two hours."

Tom McBern looked up at the walls, seeing them perhaps for the first and thousandth time. "Did you ever think about this room? About the shape of it? Ralph used to say it reminded him of a story by Poe, 'The Oblong Box.' Remember that story? The box was on board a ship, and of course it contained a body. Like Queequeg's coffin which rose from the sea to rescue Ishmael."

"And this room was Ralph's coffin?" Leopold asked quietly.

"Yes." McBern stared down at his handcuffed wrists. "His tomb."

"You killed him, didn't you?"

"Yes."

Leopold looked away. "Do you want your lawyer?"

"No. Nothing."

"My God! Twenty-two hours!"

"I was . . ."

"I know what you were doing. But I don't think you'll ever tell it to a judge and jury."

"I'll tell you, because maybe you can understand." And he began to talk in a slow, quiet voice, and Leopold listened because that was his job.

Toward evening, when Tom McBern had been returned to his cell and Fletcher sat alone with Leopold, he said, "I've called the district attorney, captain. What are you going to tell him?"

"The facts, I suppose. McBern will sign a confession of just how it happened. The rest is out of our hands."

"Do you want to tell me about it, captain?"

"I don't think I want to tell anyone about it. But I suppose I have to. I guess it was all that talk of religious experience and coffins rising from the ocean that tipped me off. You know, that Rollings pictured their room as a sort of tomb."

"For him it was."

"I wish I'd know him, Fletcher. I only wish I'd known him in time."

"What would you have done?"

"Perhaps only listened and tried to understand him."

"McBern admitted killing him?"

Leopold nodded. "It seems that Rollings asked him to, and Tom McBern trusted him more than life itself."

"Rollings asked to be stabbed through the heart?"

"Yes."

"Then why did McBern stay with the body so long? For a whole day and night?"

"He was waiting," Leopold said quietly, looking at nothing at all. "He was waiting for Rollings to rise from the dead."

The Party

WILLIAM F. NOLAN

Although William F. Nolan is usually thought of as a science fiction writer (Logan's Run, Space for Hire), *much of his best work has appeared in the horrorssuspense field. He wrote the screenplays for film versions of* The Turn of the Screw *and of* Burnt Offerings, *and has had dozens of stories (including "Saturday's Shadow," a finalist for the 1980 World Fantasy Award) published in anthologies and magazines in the genre. Indeed, it was difficult to choose a story from his many excellent works, but "The Party" won out because, as you will soon learn, it is unforgettable.*

Ashland frowned, trying to concentrate in the warm emptiness of the thickly carpeted lobby. Obviously, he had pressed the elevator button, because he was alone here and the elevator was blinking its way down to him, summoned from an upper floor. It arrived with an efficient hiss, the bronze doors clicked open, and he stepped in, thinking *blackout. I had a mental blackout.*

First the double vision. Now this. It was getting worse. He had blanked out completely. Just where the hell was he? Must be a party, he told himself. Sure. Someone he'd met, whose name was missing along with the rest of it, had invited him to a party. He had an apartment number in his head: 9E. That much he retained. A number—nothing else.

On the way up, in the soundless cage of the elevator, David Ashland reviewed the day. The usual morning routine: work, then lunch with his new secretary. A swinger—but she liked her booze; put away three martinis to his two. Back to the office. More work. A drink in the afternoon with a writer. ("Beefeater. No rocks. Very dry.") Dinner at the new Italian joint on West Forty-Eighth with Linda. Lovely Linda. Expensive girl. Lovely as hell, but expensive. More drinks, then —nothing. Blackout.

The doc had warned him about the hard stuff, but what else can you do in New York? The pressures get to you, so you drink. Everybody

558

drinks. And every night, somewhere in town, there's a party, with contacts (and girls) to be made . . .

The elevator stopped, opened its doors. Ashland stepped out, uncertainly, into the hall. The softly lit passageway was long, empty, silent. No, not silent. Ashland heard the familiar voice of a party: the shifting hive hum of cocktail conversation, dim, high laughter, the sharp chatter of ice against glass, a background wash of modern jazz . . . All quite familiar. And always the same.

He walked to 9E. Featureless apartment door. White. Brass button housing. Gold numbers. No clues here. Sighing, he thumbed the buzzer and waited nervously.

A smiling fat man with bad teeth opened the door. He was holding a half-filled drink in one hand. Ashland didn't know him.

"C'mon in fella," he said. "Join the party."

Ashland squinted into blue-swirled tobacco smoke, adjusting his eyes to the dim interior. The rising-falling sea tide of voices seemed to envelop him.

"Grab a drink, fella," said the fat man. "Looks like you need one!"

Ashland aimed for the bar in one corner of the crowded apartment. He *did* need a drink. Maybe a drink would clear his head, let him get this all straight. Thus far, he had not recognized any of the faces in the smoke-hazed room.

At the self-service bar a thin, turkey-necked woman wearing paste jewelry was intently mixing a black Russian. "Got to be exceedingly careful with these," she said to Ashland, eyes still on the mixture. "Too much vodka craps them up."

Ashland nodded. "The host arrived?" *I'll know him, I'm sure.*

"Due later—or sooner. Sooner—or later. You know, I once spilled three black Russians on the same man over a thirty-day period. First on the man's sleeve, then on his back, then on his lap. Each time his suit was a sticky, gummy mess. My psychiatrist told me that I did it unconsciously, because of a neurotic hatred of this particular man. He looked like my father."

"The psychiatrist?"

"No, the man I spilled the black Russians on." She held up the tall drink, sipped at it. "Ahhh . . . still too weak."

Ashland probed the room for a face he knew, but these people were all strangers.

He turned to find the turkey-necked woman staring at him. "Nice apartment," he said mechanically.

"Stinks. I detest pseudo-Chinese decor in Manhattan brownstones." She moved off, not looking back at Ashland.

He mixed himself a straight Scotch, running his gaze around the apartment. The place *was* pretty wild—ivory tables with serpent legs; tall, figured screens with chain-mail warriors cavorting across them; heavy brocade drapes in stitched silver; lamps with jewel-eyed dragons looped at the base. And, at the far end of the room, an immense bronze gong suspended between a pair of demon-faced swordsmen. Ashland studied the gong. A thing to wake the dead, he thought. Great for hangovers in the morning.

"Just get here?" a girl asked him. She was red-haired, full-breasted, in her late twenties. Attractive. Damned attractive. Ashland smiled warmly at her.

"That's right," he said, "I just arrived." He tasted the Scotch; it was flat, watery. "Whose place is this?

The girl peered at him above her cocktail glass. "Don't you know who invited you?"

Ashland was embarrassed. "Frankly, no. That's why I—"

"My name's Viv. For Vivian. I drink. What do you do? Besides drink?"

"I produce. I'm in television."

"Well, *I'm* in a dancing mood. Shall we?"

"Nobody's dancing," protested Ashland. "We'd look—foolish."

The jazz suddenly seemed louder. Overhead speakers were sending out a thudding drum solo behind muted strings. The girl's body rippled to the sounds.

"Never be afraid to do anything foolish," she told him. "That's the secret of survival." Her fingers beckoned him. "C'mon . . ."

"No, really—not right now. Maybe later."

"Then I'll dance alone."

She spun into the crowd, her long red dress whirling. The other partygoers ignored her. Ashland emptied the watery Scotch and fixed himself another. He loosened his tie, popping the collar button. *Damn!*

"I train worms."

Ashland turned to a florid-faced little man with bulging, feverish eyes. "I heard you say you were in TV," the little man said. "Ever use any trained worms on your show?"

"No . . . no, we don't."

"I breed 'em, train 'em. I teach a worm to run a maze. Then I grind him up and feed him to a dumb, untrained worm. Know what happens? The dumb worm can run the maze! But only for twenty-four hours. Then he forgets—unless I keep him on a trained-worm diet. I defy you to tell me that isn't fascinating!"

"It is, indeed." Ashland nodded and moved away from the bar. The feverish little man smiled after him, toasting his departure with a raised glass. Ashland found himself sweating.

Who was his host? Who had invited him? He knew most of the Village crowd, but had spotted none of them here . . .

A dark, doll-like girl asked him for a light. He fumbled out some matches.

"Thanks," she said, exhaling blue smoke into blue smoke. "Saw that worm guy talking to you. What a lousy bore *he* is! My ex-husband had a pet snake named Baby and he fed it worms. That's all they're good for, unless you fish. Do you fish?"

"I've done some fishing up in Canada."

"My ex-husband hated all sports. Except the indoor variety." She giggled. "Did you hear the one about the indoor hen and the outdoor rooster?"

"Look, miss—"

"Talia. But you can call me Jenny. Get it?" She doubled over, laughing hysterically, then swayed, dropping her cigarette. "Ooops! I'm sick. I better go lie down. My tum-tum feels awful."

She staggered from the party as Ashland crushed out her smoldering cigarette with the heel of his shoe. *Stupid bitch!*

A sharp handclap startled him. In the middle of the room, a tall man in a green satin dinner jacket was demanding his attention. He clapped again. "You," he shouted to Ashland. "come here."

Ashland walked forward. The tall man asked him to remove his wristwatch. "I'll read your past from it," the man said. "I'm psychic. I'll tell you about yourself."

Reluctantly, Ashland removed his watch, handed it over. He didn't find any of this amusing. The party was annoying him, irritating him.

"I thank you most kindly, sir!" said the tall man, with elaborate stage courtesy. He placed the gold watch against his forehead and closed his eyes, breathing deeply. The crowd noise did not slacken; no one seemed to be paying any attention to the psychic.

"Ah. Your name is David. David Ashland. You are successful, a man of big business . . . a producer . . . and a bachelor. You are twenty-eight . . . very young for a successful producer. One has to be something of a bastard to climb that fast. What about that, Mr. Ashland, *are* you something of a bastard?"

Ashland flushed angrily.

"You like women," continued the tall man. "A lot. And you like to drink. A lot. Your doctor told you—"

"I don't have to listen to this," Ashland said tightly, reaching for his watch. The man in green satin handed it over, grinned amiably, and melted back into the shifting crowd.

I ought to get the hell out of here, Ashland told himself. Yet curiosity held him. When the host arrived, Ashland would piece this evening together; he'd know why he was there, at this particular party. He moved to a couch near the closed patio doors and sat down. He'd wait.

A soft-faced man sat down next to him. The man looked pained. "I shouldn't smoke these," he said, holding up a long cigar. "Do you smoke cigars?"

"No."

"I'm a salesman. Dover Insurance. Like the White Cliffs of, ya know. I've studied the problems involved in smoking. Can't quit, though. When I do, the nerves shrivel up, stomach goes sour. I worry a lot—but we all worry, don't we? I mean, my mother used to worry about the earth slowing down. She read somewhere that between 1680 and 1690 the earth lost twenty-seven hundredths of a second. She said that meant something."

Ashland sighed inwardly. What is it about cocktail parties that causes people you've never met to unleash their troubles?

"You meet a lotta fruitcakes in my dodge," said the pained-looking insurance salesman. "I sold a policy once to a guy who lived in the woodwork. Had a ratty little walk-up in the Bronx with a foldaway bed. Kind you push into the wall. He'd *stay* there—I mean, inside the wall—most of the time. His roommate would invite some friends in and if they made too much noise the guy inside the wall would pop out with his Thompson. BAM! The bed would come down and there he was with a Thompson submachine gun aimed at everybody. Real fruitcake."

"I knew a fellow who was *twice* that crazy."

Ashland looked up into a long, cadaverous face. The nose had been broken and improperly reset; it canted noticeably to the left. He folded his long, sharp-boned frame onto the couch next to Ashland. "This fellow believed in falling grandmothers," he declared. "Lived in upper Michigan. 'Watch out for falling grandmothers,' he used to warn me. 'They come down pretty heavy in this area. Most of 'em carry umbrellas and big packages and they come flapping down out of the sky by the thousands!' This Michigan fellow swore he saw one hit a postman. 'An awful thing to watch,' he told me. 'Knocked the poor soul flat. Crushed his skull like an egg.' I recall he shuddered just telling me about it."

"Fruitcake," said the salesman. "Like the guy I once knew who wrote on all his walls and ceilings. A creative writer, he called himself. Said he couldn't write on paper, had to use a wall. Paper was too flimsy for him. He'd scrawl these long novels of his, a chapter in every room, with a big black crayon. Words all over the place. He'd fill up the house, then rent another one for his next book. I never read any of his houses, so I don't know if he was any good."

"Excuse me, gentlemen," said Ashland. "I need a fresh drink."

He hurriedly mixed another Scotch at the bar. Around him, the party rolled on inexorably, without any visible core. What time was it, anyway? His watch had stopped.

"Do you happen to know what time it is?" he asked a long-haired Oriental girl who was standing near the bar.

"I've no idea," she said. "None at all." The girl fixed him with her eyes. "I've been watching you, and you seem horribly *alone*. Aren't you?"

"Aren't I what?"

"Horribly alone?"

"I'm not with anyone, if that's what you mean."

The girl withdrew a jeweled holder from her bag and fitted a cigarette in place. Ashland lit it for her.

"I haven't been really alone since I was in Milwaukee," she told him. "I was about—God!—fifteen or something, and this creep wanted me to move in with him. My parents were both dead by then, so I was all alone."

"What did you do?"

"Moved in with the creep. What else? I couldn't make the being-alone scene. Later on, I killed him."

"You *what?*"

"Cut his throat." She smiled delicately. "In self-defense, of course. He got mean on the bottle one Friday night and tried to knife me. I had witnesses."

Ashland took a long draw on his Scotch. A scowling fellow in shirt-sleeves grabbed the girl's elbow and steered her roughly away.

"I used to know a girl who looked like that," said a voice to Ashland's right. The speaker was curly-haired clean-featured, in his late thirties. "Greek belly dancer with a Jersey accent. Dark, like her, and kind of mysterious. She used to quote that line of Hemingway's to Scott Fitzgerald—you know the one."

"Afraid not."

"One that goes, 'We're all bitched from the start.' Bitter. A bitter line."

He put out his hand. Ashland shook it.

"I'm Travers. I used to save America's ass every week on CBS."

"Beg pardon?"

"Terry Travers. The old *Triple Trouble for Terry* series on channel nine. Back in the late fifties. Had to step on a lotta toes to get that series."

"I think I recall the show. It was—"

"Dung. That's what it was. Cow dung. Horse dung. The *worst.* Terry Travers is not my real name, natch. Real one's Abe Hockstatter. Can you imagine a guy named Abe Hockstatter saving America's ass every week on CBS?"

"You've got me there."

Hockstatter pulled a brown wallet from his coat, flipped it open. "There I am with one of my other rugs on," he said, jabbing at a photo. "Been stone bald since high school. Baldies don't make it in showbiz, so I have my rugs. Go ahead, tug at me."

Ashland blinked. The man inclined his head. "*Pull* at it. Go on—as a favor to me!"

Ashland tugged at the fringe of Abe Hockstatter's curly hairpiece.

"Tight, eh? Really *snug.* Stays on the old dome."

"Indeed it does."

"They cost a fortune. I've got a wind-blown one for outdoor scenes.

A stiff wind'll lift a cheap one right off your scalp. Then I got a crew cut and a Western job with long sideburns. All kinds. Ten, twelve . . . all first-class."

"I'm certain I've seen you," said Ashland. "I just don't—"

"'S awright. Believe me. Lotta people don't know me since I quit the *Terry* thing. I booze like crazy now. You an' me, we're among the nation's six million alcoholics."

Ashland glared at the actor. "Where do you get off linking me with—"

"Cool it, cool it. So I spoke a little out of turn. Don't be so touchy, chum."

"To hell with you!" snapped Ashland.

The bald man with curly hair shrugged and drifted into the crowd.

Ashland took another long pull at his Scotch. All these neurotic conversations . . . He felt exhausted, wrung dry, and the Scotch was lousy. No kick to it. The skin along the back of his neck felt tight, hot. A headache was coming on; he could always tell.

A slim-figured, frosted blonde in black sequins sidled up to him. She exuded an aura of matrimonial wars fought and lost. Her orange lipstick was smeared, her cheeks alcohol-flushed behind flaking pancake make-up. "I have a theory about sleep," she said. "Would you like to hear it?"

Ashland did not reply.

"My theory is that the world goes insane every night. When we sleep, our subconscious takes charge and we become victims to whatever it conjures up. Our conscious, reasoning mind is totally blanked out. We lie there, helpless, while our subconscious flings us about. We fall off high buildings, or have to fight a giant ape, or we get buried in quicksand . . . We have absolutely no control. The mind whirls madly in the skull. Isn't that an unsettling thing to consider?"

"Listen," said Ashland. "Where's the host?"

"He'll get here."

Ashland put down his glass and turned away from her. A mounting wave of depression swept him toward the door. The room seemed to be solid with bodies, all talking, drinking, gesturing in the milk-thick smoke haze.

"Potatoes have eyes," said a voice to his left. "I really *believe* that." The remark was punctuated by an ugly, frog-croaking laugh.

"Today is tomorrow's yesterday," someone else said.

A hot swarm of sound:

"You can't get prints off human skin."

"In China, the laborers make sixty-five dollars a year. How the hell can you live on sixty-five dollars a year?"

"So he took out his Luger and blew her head off."

"I knew a policewoman who loved to scrub down whores."

"Did you ever try to live with eight kids, two dogs, a three-legged cat and twelve goldfish?"

"Like I told him, those X rays destroyed his white cells."

"They found her in the tub. Strangled with a coat hanger."

"What I had, exactly, was a grade-two epidermoid carcinoma at the base of a seborrheic keratosis."

Ashland experienced a sudden, raw compulsion: somehow he had to stop these voices!

The Chinese gong flared gold at the corner of his eye. He pushed his way over to it, shouldering the partygoers aside. He would strike it—and the booming noise would stun the crowd; they'd have to stop their incessant, maddening chatter.

Ashland drew back his right fist, then drove it into the circle of bronze. He felt the impact, and the gong shuddered under his blow.

But there was no sound from it!

The conversation went on.

Ashland smashed his way back across the apartment.

"You can't stop the party," said the affable fat man at the door.

"I'm leaving!"

"So go ahead," grinned the fat man. "Leave."

Ashland clawed open the door and plunged into the hall, stumbling, almost falling. He reached the elevator, jabbed at the DOWN button.

Waiting, he found it impossible to swallow; his throat was dry. He could feel his heart hammering against the walls of his chest. His head ached.

The elevator arrived, opened. He stepped inside. The doors closed smoothly and the cage began its slow, automatic descent.

Abruptly, it stopped.

The doors parted to admit a solemn-looking man in a dark blue suit.

Ashland gasped "Freddie!"

The solemn face broke into a wide smile. "Dave! It's great to see you! Been—a long time."

"But—you can't be Fred Baker!"

"Why? Have I changed so much?"

"No, no, you look—exactly the same. But that car crash in Albany. I thought you were . . . " Ashland hesitated, left the word unspoke. He was pale, frightened. Very frightened. "Look, I'm—I'm late. Got somebody waiting for me at my place. Have to rush . . . He reached forward to push the LOBBY button.

There was none.

The lowest button read FLOOR 2.

"We use this elevator to get from one party to another," Freddie Baker said quietly, as the cage surged into motion. "That's all it's good for. You get so you need a change. They're all alike, though—the parties. But you learn to adjust, in time. We all have."

Ashland stared at his departed friend. The elevator stopped.

"Step out," said Freddie. "I'll introduce you around. You'll catch on, get used to things. No sex here. And the booze is watered. Can't get stoned. That's the dirty end of the stick."

Baker took Ashland's arm, propelled him gently forward.

Around him, pressing in, David Ashland could hear familar sounds: nervous laughter, ice against glass, muted jazz—and the ceaseless hum of cocktail voices.

Freddie thumbed a buzzer. A door opened.

The smiling fat man said, "C'mon in fellas. Join the party."

The Crate

STEPHEN KING

The author of Carrie *(1974),* Salem's Lot *(1975),* The Shining *(1977),* The Stand, *(1978),* Night Shift *(1978),* The Dead Zone *(1979) and* Firestarter *(1980) hardly needs an introduction. It is worth pointing out, however, that Stephen King is also (as is apparent in the introduction to this book) an acknowledged authority on horror fiction and its popularity. "The Crate" is one of his finest stories.*

Dexter Stanley was scared. More; he felt as if that central axle that binds us to the state we call sanity were under a greater strain than it had ever been under before. As he ulled up beside Henry Northrup's house on North Campus Avenue t at August night, he felt that if he didn't talk to someone, he really w uld go crazy.

There was no one to talk to but Henry Northrup. Dex Stanley was the head of the zoology department, and once might have been university president if he had been better at academic politics. His wife had died twenty years before, and they had been childless. What remained of his own family was all west of the Rockies. He was not good at making friends.

Northrup was an exception to that. In some ways, they were two of a kind; both had been disappointed in the mostly meaningless, but always vicious, game of university politics. Three years before, Northrup had made his run at the vacant English department chairmanship. He had lost, and one of the reasons had undoubtedly been his wife, Wilma, an abrasive and unpleasant woman. At the few cocktail parties Dex had attended where English people and zoology people could logically mix, it seemed he could always recall the harsh mule-bray of her voice, telling some new faculty wife to "call me Billie, dear everyone does!"

Dex made his way across the lawn to Northrup's door at a stumbling run. It was Thursday, and Northrup's unpleasant spouse took two classes on Thursday nights. Consequently, it was Dex and Henry's chess night. The two men had been playing chess together for the last eight years.

Dex rang the bell beside the door of his friend's house; leaned on it. The door opened at last and Northrup was there.

"Dex," he said. I didn't expect you for another—"

Dex pushed in past him. "Wilma," he said. "Is she here?"

"No, she left fifteen minutes ago. I was just making myself some chow. Dex, you look awful."

They had walked under the hall light, and it illuminated the cheesy pallor of Dex's face and seemed to outline wrinkles as deep and dark as fissures in the earth. Dex was sixty-one, but on the hot August night, he looked more like ninety.

"I ought to." Dex wiped his mouth with the back of his hand.

"Well, what is it?"

"I'm afraid I'm going crazy, Henry. Or that I've already gone."

"You want something to eat? Wilma left cold ham."

"I'd rather have a drink. A big one."

"All right."

"Two men dead, Henry," Dex said abruptly. "And I could be blamed. Yes, I can see how I could be blamed. But it wasn't me. It was the crate. And I don't even know what's *in* there!" He uttered a wild laugh.

"Dead?" Northrup said. "What is this, Dex?"

"A janitor. I don't know his name. And Gereson. A graduate student. He just happened to be there. In the way of . . . whatever it was."

Henry studied Dex's face for a long moment and then said, "I'll get us both a drink."

He left. Dex wandered into the living room, past the low table where the chess table had already been set up, and stared out the graceful bow window. That thing in his mind, that axle or whatever it was, did not feel so much in danger of snapping now. Thank God for Henry.

Northrup came back with two pony glasses choked with ice. Ice from the fridge's automatic icemaker, Stanley thought randomly. Wilma "just call me Billie, everyone does" Northrup insisted on all the modern conveniences . . . and when Wilma insisted on a thing, she did so savagely.

Northrup filled both glasses with Cutty Sark. He handed one of them to Stanley, who slopped Scotch over his fingers, stinging a small cut he'd gotten in the lab a couple of days before. He hadn't realized until then that his hands were shaking. He emptied half the glass and the Scotch boomed in his stomach, first hot, then spreading a steadying warmth.

"Sit down, man," Northrup said.

Dex sat, and drank again. Now it was a lot better. He looked at Northrup, who was looking levelly back over the rim of his own glass. Dex looked away, out at the bloody orb of moon sitting over the rim of the horizon, over the university, which was supposed to be the seat of rationality, the forebrain of the body politic. How did that jibe with the matter of the crate? With the screams? With the blood?

"Men are dead?" Northrup said at last. "Are you sure they're dead?"

"Yes. The bodies are gone now. At least, I think they are. Even the bones . . . the teeth . . . but the blood . . . the blood, you know . . ."

"No, I don't know anything. You've got to start at the beginning."

Stanley took another drink and set his glass down. "Of course I do," he said. "Yes. It begins just where it ends. With the crate. The janitor found the crate . . ."

Dexter Stanley had come into Amberson Hall, sometimes called the Old Zoology Building, that afternoon at three o'clock. It was a blaringly hot day, and the campus looked listless and dead, in spite of the twirling sprinklers in front of the fraternity houses and the Old Front dorms.

The Old Front went back to the turn of the century, but Amberson Hall was much older than that. It was one of the oldest buildings on a university campus that had celebrated its tricentennial two years previous. It was a tall brick building, shackled with ivy that seemed to spring out of the earth like green, clutching hands. Its narrow windows were more like gun slits than real windows, and Amberson seemed to frown at the newer buildings with their glass walls and curvy, unorthodox shapes.

The new zoology building, Cather Hall, had been completed eight months before, and the process of transition would probably go on for another eighteen months. No one was completely sure what would happen to Amberson then. If the bond issue to build the new gym found favor with the voters, it would probably be demolished.

He paused a moment to watch two young men throwing a Frisbee back and forth. A dog ran back and forth between them, glumly chasing the spinning disc. Abruptly the mutt gave up and flopped in the shade of a poplar. A VW with a NO NUKES sticker on the back deck trundled slowly past, heading for the Upper Circle. Nothing else moved. A week before, the final summer session had ended and the campus lay still and fallow, dead ore on summer's anvil.

Dex had a number of files to pick up, part of the seemingly endless process of moving from Amberson to Cather. The old building seemed spectrally empty. His footfalls echoed back dreamily as he walked past closed doors with frosted glass panels, past bulletin boards with their yellowing notices and toward his office at the end of the first-floor corridor. The cloying smell of fresh paint hung in the air.

He was almost to his door, and jingling his keys in his pocket, when the janitor popped out of Room 6, the big lecture hall, startling him.

He grunted, then smiled a little shamefacedly, the way people will when they've gotten a mild zap. "You got me that time," he told the janitor.

The janitor smiled and twiddled the gigantic key ring clipped to his belt. "Sorry, Perfesser Stanley," he said. "I was hopin' it was you. Charlie said you'd be in this afternoon."

"Charlie Gereson is still here?" Dex frowned. Gereson was a grad student who was doing an involved—and possibly very impor- tant—paper on negative environmental factors in long-term animal migration. It was a subject that could have a strong impact on area farming practices and pest control. But Gereson was pulling almost fifty hours a week in the gigantic (and antiquated) basement lab. The new lab complex in Cather would have been exponentially better suited to his purposes, but the new labs would not be fully equipped for another two to four months . . . if then.

"Think he went over the Union for a burger," the janitor said. "I told him myself to quit a while and go get something to eat. He's been here since nine this morning. Told him myself. Said he ought to get some food. A man don't live on love alone."

The janitor smiled, a little tentatively, and Dex smiled back. The janitor was right; Gereson was embarked upon a labor of love. Dex had seen too many squadrons of students just grunting along and making grades not to appreciate that . . . and not to worry about Charlie Gereson's health and well-being from time to time.

"I would have told *him,* if he hadn't been so busy," the janitor said, and offered his tentative little smile again. "Also, I kinda wanted to show you myself."

"What's that?" Dex asked. He felt a little impatient. It was chess night with Henry; he wanted to get this taken care of and still have time for a leisurely meal at the Hancock House.

"Well, maybe it's nothin," the janitor said. "But . . . well, this buildin is some old, and we keep turnin things up, don't we?"

Dex knew. It was like moving out of a house that has been lived in for generations. Halley, the bright young assistant professor who had been here for three years now, had found half a dozen antique clips with small brass balls on the ends. She'd had no idea what the clips, which looked a little bit like spring-loaded wishbones, could be. Dex had been able to tell her. Not so many years after the Civil War, those clips had been used to hold the heads of white mice, who were then operated on without anesthetic. Young Halley, with her Berkeley education and her bright spill of Farrah Fawcett-Majors golden hair, had looked quite revolted. "No anti-vivisectionists in those days," Dex had told her jovially. "At least not around here." And Halley had responded with a blank look that probably disguised disgust or maybe even loathing. Dex had put his foot in it again. He had a positive talent for that, it seemed.

They had found sixty boxes of *The American Zoologist* in a crawl-space, and the attic had been a maze of old equipment and mouldering reports. Some of the impedimenta no one—not even Dexter Stanley—could identify.

In the closet of the old animal pens at the back of the building, Professor Viney had found a complicated gerbil-run with exquisite glass panels. It had been accepted for display at the Musuem of Natural Science in Washington.

But the finds had been tapering off this summer, and Dex thought Amberson Hall had given up the last of its secrets.

"What have you found?" he asked the janitor.

"A crate. I found it tucked right under the basement stairs. I didn't open it. It's been nailed shut, anyway."

Stanly couldn't believe that anything very interesting could have escaped notice for long, just by being tucked under the stairs. Tens of thousands of people went up and down them every week during the academic year. Most likely the janitor's crate was full of department records dating back twenty-five years. Or even more prosaic, a box of *National Geographics*.

"I hardly think—"

"It's a real crate," the janitor broke in earnestly. "I mean, my father was a carpenter, and this crate is built the way he was buildin 'em back in the twenties. And he learned from *his* father."

"I really doubt if—"

"Also, it's got about four inches of dust on it. I wiped some off and there's a date. Eighteen thirty-four."

That changed things. Stanley looked at his watch and decided he could spare half an hour.

In spite of the humid August heat outside, the smooth tile-faced throat of the stairway was almost cold. Above them, yellow frosted globes cast a dim and thoughtful light. The stair levels had once been red, but in the centers they shaded to a dead black where the feet of years had worn away layer after layer of resurfacing. The silence was smooth and nearly perfect.

The janitor reached the bottom first and pointed under the staircase. "Under here," he said.

Dex joined him in staring into a shadowy, triangular cavity under the wide staircase. He felt a small tremor of disgust as he saw where the janitor had brushed away a gossamer veil of cobwebs. He supposed it was possible that the man had found something a little older than postwar records under there, now that he acutally looked at the space. But 1834?

"Just a second," the janitor said, and left momentarily. Left alone, Dex hunkered down and peered in. He could make out nothing but a deeper patch of shadow in there. Then the janitor returned with a hefty four-cell flashlight. "This'll show it up."

"What were you doing under there anyway?" Dex asked.

The janitor grinned. "I was only standin here tryin to decide if I should buff that second-floor hallway first or wash the lab windows. I couldn't make up my mind, so I flipped a quarter. Only I dropped it and it rolled under there." He pointed to the shadowy, triangular cave. "I prob'ly would have let it go, except that was my only quarter for the Coke machine. So I got my flash and knocked down the cobwebs, and when I crawled under to get it, I saw that crate. Here, have a look."

The janitor shone his light into the hole. Motes of disturbed dust preened and swayed lazily in the beam. The light struck the far wall in a spotlight circle, rose to the zigzag undersides of the stairs briefly, picking out an ancient cobweb in which long-dead bugs hung mummified, and then the light dropped and centered on a crate about five feet long and two-and-a-half wide. It was perhaps three feet deep. As the janitor had said, it was no knocked-together affair made out of scrap-boards. It was neatly constructed of a smooth, dark heavy wood. A *coffin*, Dexter thought uneasily. *It looks like a child's coffin.*

The dark color of the wood showed only a fan-shaped swipe on the side. The rest of the crate was the uniform dull gray of dust. Something was written on the side—stenciled there.

Dex squinted but couldn't read it. He fumbled his glasses out of his breast pocket and still couldn't. Part of what had been stenciled on was obscured by the dust—not four inches of it, by any means, but an extraordinarily thick coating, all the same.

Not wanting to crawl and dirty his pants, Dex duck-walked under the stairway, stifling a sudden and amazingly strong feeling of claustrophobia. The spit dried in his mouth and was replaced by a dry, woolly taste, like an old mitten. He thought of the generations of students trooping up and down these stairs, all male until 1888, then in coeducational platoons, carrying their books and papers and anatomical drawings, their bright faces and clear eyes, each of them convinced that a useful and exciting future lay ahead . . . and here, below their feet, the spider spun his eternal snare for the fly and the trundling beetle, and here this crate sat impassively, gathering dust, waiting . . .

A tendril of spidersilk brushed across his forehead and he swept it away with a small cry of loathing and an uncharacteristic inner cringe.

"Not very nice under there, is it?" the janitor asked sympathetically, holding his light centered on the crate. "God, I hate tight places."

Dex didn't reply. He had reached the crate. He looked at the letters that were stenciled there and then brushed the dust away from them. It rose in a cloud, intensifying that mitten taste, making him cough dryly. The dust hung in the beam of the janitor's light like old magic, and Dex Stanley read what some long-dead chief of lading had stenciled on this crate.

SHIP TO HORLICKS UNIVERSITY, the top line read. VIA JULIA CARPENTER, read the middle line. The third line read simply: ARCTIC EXPEDITION. Below that, someone had written in heavy black charcoal strokes: JUNE, 19, 1834. That was the one line the janitor's hand-swipe had completely cleared.

ARCTIC EXPEDITION, Dex read again. His heart began to thump.

"So what do you think?" the janitor's voice floated in.

Dex grabbed one end and lifted it. Heavy. As he let it settle back with a mild thud, something shifted inside—he did not hear it but felt it through the palms of his hands, as if whatever it was had moved of its own volition. Stupid, of course. It had been an almost liquid feel, as if something not quite jelled had moved sluggishly.

ARCTIC EXPEDITION.

Dex felt the excitement of an antiques collector happening upon a neglected armoire with a twenty-five dollar price tag in the back room of some hick-town junk shop . . . an armoire that just might be a Chippendale. "Help me get it out," he called to the janitor.

Working bent over to keep from slamming their heads on the underside of the stairway, sliding the crate along, they got it out and then picked it up by the bottom. Dex had gotten his pants dirty after all, and there were cobwebs in his hair.

As they carried it into the old-fashioned, train-terminal-sized lab, Dex felt that sensation of shift inside the crate again, and he could see by the expression on the janitor's face that he had felt it as well. They set it on one of the formica-topped lab tables. The next one over was littered with Charlie Gereson's stuff—notebooks, graph paper, contour maps, a Texas Instruments calculator.

The janitor stood back, wiping his hands on his double-pocket gray shirt, breathing hard. "Some heavy mother," he said. "That bastard must weigh two hunnert pounds. You okay, Perfesser Stanley?"

Dex barely heard him. He was looking at the end of the box, where there was yet another series of stencils: PAELLA/SANTIAGO/SAN FRANCISCO/CHICAGO/NEW YORK/HORLICKS

"Perfesser—"

"Paella," Dex muttered, and then said it again, slightly louder. He was seized with an unbelieving kind of excitement that was held in check only by the thought that it might be some sort of hoax. "Paella!"

"Paella, Dex?" Henry Northrup asked. The moon had risen in the sky, turning silver.

"Paella is a very small island south of Tierra del Fuego," Dex said. "Perhaps the smallest island ever inhabited by the race of man. A number of Easter Island-type monoliths were found there just after World War II. Not very interesting compared to their bigger brothers, but every bit as mysterious. The natives of Paella and Tierra del Fuego were Stone-Age people. Christian missionaries killed them with kindness."

"I beg your pardon?"

"It's extremely cold down there. Summer temperatures rarely range above the mid-forties. The missionaries gave them blankets, partly so they would be warm, mostly to cover their sinful nakedness. The blankets were crawling with fleas, and the natives of both islands were wiped out by European diseases for which they had developed no immunities. Mostly by smallpox."

Dex drank. The Scotch had lent his cheeks some color, but it was hectic and flaring—double spots of flush that sat above his cheekbones like rouge.

"But Tierra del Fuego—and this Paella—that's not the Arctic, Dex. It's the Antarctic."

"It wasn't in 1834," Dex said, setting his glass down, careful in spite of his distraction to put it on the coaster Henry had provided. If Wilma found a ring on one of her end tables, his friend would have hell to pay. "The terms subarctic, Antarctic and Antarctica weren't invented yet. In those days there was only the north arctic and the south arctic."

"Okay."

"Hell, I made the same kind of mistake. I couldn't figure out why Frisco was on the itinerary as a port of call. Then I realized I was figuring on the Panama Canal, which wasn't built for another eighty years or so."

"An Arctic expedition? In 1834?" Henry asked doubtfully.

"I haven't had a chance to check the records yet," Dex said, picking up his drink again. "But I know from my history that there were 'Arctic expeditions' as early as Francis Drake. None of them made it, that was all. They were convinced they'd find gold, silver, jewels, lost civilizations, God knows what else. The Smithsonian Institution outfitted an attempted exploration of the North Pole in, I think it was 1881 or '82. They all died. A bunch of men from the Explorers' Club in London tried for the South Pole in the 1850's. Their ship was sunk by icebergs, but three or four of them survived. They stayed alive by sucking dew out of their clothes and eating the kelp that caught on their boat, until they were picked up. They lost their teeth. And they claimed to have seen sea monsters."

"What happened, Dex?" Henry asked softly.

Stanley looked up. "We opened the crate," he said dully. "God help us, Henry, we opened the crate."

He paused for a long time, it seemed, before beginning to speak again.

"Paella?" the janitor asked. "What's that?"

"An island off the tip of South America," Dex said. "Never mind. Let's get this open." He opened one of the lab drawers and began to rummage through it, looking for something to pry with."

"Never mind that stuff," the janitor said. He looked excited himself now. "I got a hammer and chisel in my closet upstairs. I'll get 'em. Just hang on."

He left. The crate sat on the table's formica top, squat and mute.

It sits squat and mute, Dex thought, and shivered a little. Where had that thought come from? Some story? The words had a cadenced yet unpleasant sound. He dismissed them. He was good at dismissing the extraneous. He was a scientist.

He looked around the lab just to get his eyes off the crate. Except for Charlie's table, it was unnaturally neat and quiet—like the rest of the university. White-tiled, subway-station walls gleamed freshly under the overhead globes; the globes themselves seemed to be double-caught and submerged in the polished formica surfaces, like eerie lamps shining from deep quarry water. A huge, old-fashioned slate blackboard dominated the wall opposite the sinks. And cupboards, cupboards everywhere. It was easy enough—too easy, perhaps—to see the antique, sepia-toned ghosts of all those old zoology students, wearing their white coats with the green cuffs, their hairs marcelled or pomaded, doing their dissections and writing their reports . . .

Footfalls clattered on the stairs and Dex shivered, thinking again of the crate sitting there—yes, squat and mute—under the stairs for so many years, long after the men who had pushed it under there had died and gone back to dust.

Paella, he thought, and then the janitor came back in with a hammer and chisel.

"Let me do this for you, perfesser?" he asked, and Dex was about to refuse when he saw the pleading, hopeful look in the man's eyes.

"Of course," he said. After all, it was this man's find.

"Prob'ly nothin in here but a bunch of rocks and plants so old they'll turn to dust when you touch 'em. But it's funny; I'm pretty hot for it."

Dex smiled noncommittally. He had no idea what was in the crate, but he doubted if it was just plant and rock specimens. There was that slightly liquid shifting sensation when they had moved it.

"Here goes," the janitor said, and began to pound the chisel under the board with swift blows of the hammer. The board hiked up a bit, revealing a double row of nails that reminded Dex absurdly of teeth. The janitor levered the handle of his chisel down and the board pulled loose, the nails shrieking out of the wood. He did the same thing at the other end, and the board came free, clattering to the floor. Dex set it aside, noticing that even the nails looked different, somehow—thicker, squarer at the tip, and without that blue-steel sheen that is the mark of a sophisticated alloying process.

The janitor was peering into the crate through the long, narrow strip he had uncovered. "Can't see nothin," he said. "Where'd I leave my light?"

"Never mind," Dex said. "Go on and open it."

"Okay." He took off a second board, then a third. Six or seven had been nailed across the top of the box. He began on the fourth, reaching across the space he had already uncovered to place his chisel under the board, when the crate began to whistle.

It was a sound very much like the sound a teakettle makes when it has reached a rolling boil, Dex told Henry Northrup; no cheerful whistle this, but something like an ugly, hysterical shriek by a tantrumy child. And this suddenly dropped and thickened into a low, hoarse growling sound. It was not loud, but it had a primitive, savage sound that stood Dex Stanley's hair up on the slant. The janitor stared around at him, his eyes widening . . . and then his arm was seized. Dex did not see what grabbed it; his eyes had gone instinctively to the man's face.

The janitor screamed, and the sound drove a stiletto of panic into Dex's chest. The thought that came unbidden was: *This is the first time in my life that I've heard a grown man scream—what a sheltered life I've led!*

The janitor, a fairly big guy who weighed maybe two hundred pounds, was suddenly yanked powerfully to one side. Toward the crate. *"Help me!"* He screamed. *"Oh help doc it's got me it's biting me it's biting meeeee—"*

Dex told himself to run forward and grab the janitor's free arm, but his feet might as well have been bonded to the floor. The janitor had been pulled into the crate up to his shoulder. That crazed snarling went on and on. The crate slid backwards along the table for a foot or so and then came firmly to rest against a bolted instrument mount. It began to rock back and forth. The janitor screamed and gave a tremendous lunge away from the crate. The end of the box came up off the table and then smacked back down. Part of his arm came out of the crate, and Dex saw to his horror that the gray sleeve of his shirt was chewed and tattered and soaked with blood. Smiling crescent bites were punched into what he could see of the man's skin through the shredded flaps of cloth.

Then something that must have been incredibly strong yanked him back down. The thing in the crate began to snarl and gobble. Every now and then there would be a breathless whistling sound in between.

At last Dex broke free of his paralysis and lunged creakily forward. He grabbed the janitor's free arm. He yanked . . . with no result at all. It was like trying to pull a man who has been handcuffed to the bumper of a trailer truck.

The janitor screamed again—a long, ululating sound that rolled back and forth between the lab's sparkling, white-tiled walls. Dex could see the gold glimmer of the fillings at the back of the man's mouth. He could see the yellow ghost of nicotine on his tongue.

The janitor's head slammed down against the edge of the board he had been about to remove when the thing had grabbed him. And this time Dex did see something, although it happened with such mortal, savage speed that later he was unable to describe it adequately to Henry. Something as dry and brown and scaly as a desert reptile came out of the crate—something with huge claws. It tore at the janitor's straining, knotted throat and severed his jugular vein. Blood began to pump across the table, pooling on the formica and jetting onto the white-tiled floor. For a moment, a mist of blood seemed to hang in the air.

Dex dropped the janitor's arm and blundered backward, hands clapped flat to his cheeks, eeyes bulging.

The janitor's eyes rolled wildly at the ceiling. His mouth dropped open and then snapped closed. The click of his teeth was audible even below that hungry growling. His feet, clad in heavy black work shoes, did a short and jittery tap dance on the floor.

Then he seemed to lose interest. His eyes grew almost benign as they looked raptly at the overhead light globe, which was also blood-spattered. His feet splayed out in a loose V. His shirt pulled out of his pants, displaying his white and bulging belly.

"He's dead," Dex whispered. "Oh, Jesus."

The pump of the janitor's heart faltered and lost its rhythm. Now the blood that flowed from the deep, irregular gash in his neck lost its urgency and merely flowed down at the command of indifferent gravity. The crate was stained and splashed with blood. The snarling seemed to go on endlessly. The crate rocked back and forth a bit, but it was too well-braced against the instrument mount to go very far. The body of the janitor lolled grotesquely, still grasped firmly by whatever was in there. The small of his back was pressed against the lip of the lab table. His free hand dangled, sparse hair curling on the fingers between the first and second knuckles. His big key ring glimmered chrome in the light.

And now his body began to rock slowly this way and that. His shoes dragged back and forth, not tap dancing now but waltzing obscenely. And then they did not drag. They dangled an inch off the floor . . . then two inches . . . then half a foot above the floor. Dex realized that the janitor was being dragged into the crate.

The nape of his neck came to rest against the board fronting the far side of the hole in the top of the crate. He looked like a man resting in some weird Zen position of contemplation. His dead eyes sparkled. And Dex heard, below the savage growling noises, a smacking, rending sound. And the crunch of a bone.

Dex ran.

He blundered his way across the lab and out the door and up the ·stairs. Halfway up, he fell down, clawed at the risers, got to his feet, and ran again. He gained the first floor hallway and sprinted down it, past the closed doors with their frosted-glass panels, past the bulletin boards. He was chased by his own footfalls. In his ears he could hear that damned whistling.

He ran right into Charlie Gereson's arms and almost knocked him over, and he spilled the milk shake Charlie had been drinking all over both of them.

"Holy hell, what's wrong?" Charlie asked, comic in his extreme surprise. He was short and compact, wearing cotton chinos and a white tee shirt. Thick spectacles sat grimly on his nose, meaning business, proclaiming that they were there for a long haul.

"Charlie," Dex said, panting harshly. "My boy . . . the janitor . . . the crate . . . it whistles . . . *it whistles when it's hungry and it whistles again when it's full* . . . my boy . . . we have to . . . campus security . . . we . . . we . . ."

"Slow down, Professor Stanley," Charlie said. He looked concerned and a little frightened. You don't expect to be seized by the senior professor in your department when you had nothing more aggressive in mind yourself than charting the continued outmigration of sandflies. "Slow down, I don't know what you're talking about."

Stanley, hardly aware of what he was saying, poured out a garbled version of what had happened to the janitor. Charlie Gereson looked more and more confused and doubtful. As upset as he was, Dex began to realize that Charlie didn't believe a word of it. He thought, with a new kind of horror, that soon Charlie would ask him if he had been working too hard, and that when he did, Stanley would burst into mad cackles of laughter.

But what Charlie said was, "That's pretty far out, Professor Stanley."

"It's true. We've got to get campus security over here. We—"

"No, that's no good. One of them would stick his hand in there, first thing." He saw Dex's stricken look and went on. "If *I'm* having trouble swallowing this, what are *they* going to think?"

"I don't know," Dex said. "I . . . I never thought . . ."

"They'd think you just came off a helluva toot and were seeing Tasmanian devils instead of pink elephants," Charlie Gereson said cheerfully, and pushed his glasses up on his pug nose. "Besides, from what you say, the responsibility has belonged with zo all along . . . like for a hundred and forty years."

"But . . . " He swallowed, and there was a click in his throat as he prepared to voice his worst fear. "But it may be out."

"I doubt that," Charlie said, but didn't elaborate. And in that, Dex saw two things: that Charlie didn't believe a word he had said, and that nothing he could say would dissuade Charlie from going back down there.

Henry Northrup glanced at his watch. They had been sitting in the study for a little over an hour; Wilma wouldn't be back for another two. Plenty of time. Unlike Charlie Gereson, he had passed no judgment at all on the factual basis of Dex's story. But he had known Dex for a longer time than young Gereson had, and he didn't believe his friend exhibited the signs of a man who has suddenly developed a psychosis. What he exhibited was a kind of bug-eyed fear, no more or less than you'd expect to see a man who has had an extremely close call with . . . well, just an extremely close call.

"He went down, Dex?"

"Yes. He did."

"You went with him?"

"Yes."

Henry shifted position a little. "I can understand why he didn't want to get campus security until he had checked the situation himself. But Dex, you knew you were telling the flat-out truth, even if he didn't. Why didn't *you* call?"

"You believe me?" Dex asked. His voice trembled. "You believe me, don't you, Henry?"

Henry considered briefly. The story was mad, no question about that. The implication that there could be something in that box big enough and lively enough to kill a man after some one hundred and forty years was mad. He didn't believe it. But this was Dex . . . and he didn't *disbelieve* it either.

"Yes," he said.

"Thank God for that," Dex said. He groped for his drink. "Thank God for that, Henry."

"It doesn't answer the question, though. Why didn't you call the campus cops?"

"I thought . . . as much as I did think . . . that it might not *want* to come out of the crate, into the bright light. It must have lived in the dark fo so long . . . so very long . . . and . . . grotesque as this sounds . . . I though it might be pot-bound, or something. I thought . . . well, he'll see it . . . he'll see the crate . . . the janitor's body . . . he'll see the *blood* . . . and then we'd call security. You see?" Stanley's eyes pleaded with him to see, and Henry did. He thought that, considering the fact that it had been a snap judgment in a presure situation, that Dex had thought quite clearly. The blood. When the young graduate student saw the blood, he would have been happy to call in the cops.

"But it didn't work out that way."

"No." Dex ran a hand through his thinning hair.

"Why not?"

"Because when we got down there, the body was gone."

"It was *gone?*"

"That's right. And the crate was gone, too."

When Charlie Gereson saw the blood, his round and good-natured face went very pale. His eyes, already magnified by his thick spectacles, grew even huger. Blood was puddled on the lab table. It had run down one of the table legs. It was pooled on the floor, and beads of it clung to the light globe and to the white tile wall. Yes, there was plenty of blood.

But no janitor. No crate.

Dex Stanley's jaw dropped. "What the *fuck!*" Charlie whispered.

Dex saw something then, perhaps the only thing that allowed him to keep his sanity. Already he could feel that central axle trying to pull free. He grabbed Charlie's shoulder and said, "Look at the blood on the table!"

"I've seen enough," Charlie said.

His Adam's apple rose and fell like an express elevator as he struggled to keep his lunch down.

"For God's sake, get hold of yourself," Dex said harshly. "You're a zoology major. You've seen blood before."

It was the voice of authority, for that moment anyway. Charlie did get a hold of himself, and they walked a little closer. The random pools of blood on the table were not as random as they had first appeared. Each had been neatly straight-edged on one side.

"The crate sat there," Dex said. He felt a little better. The fact that the crate really *had* been there steadied him a good deal. "And look there." He pointed at the floor. Here the blood had been smeared into a wide, thin trail. It swept toward where the two of them stood, a few paces inside the double doors. It faded and faded, petering out altogether about halfway between the lab table and the doors. It was crystal clear to Dex Stanley, and the nervous sweat on his skin went cold and clammy.

It had gotten out.

It had gotten out and pushed the crate off the table. And then it had pushed the crate . . . where? Under the stairs, of course. Back under the stairs. Where it had been safe for so long.

"Where's the . . . the . . ." Charlie couldn't finish.

"Under the stairs," Dex said numbly. "It's gone back to where it came from."

"No. The . . . " He jerked it out finally. "The body."

"I don't know," Dex said. But he thought he did know. His mind would simply not admit the truth.

Charlie turned abruptly and walked back through the doors.

"Where are you going?" Dex called shrilly, and ran after him.

Charlie stopped opposite the stairs. The triangular black hole beneath them gaped. The janitor's big four-cell flashlight still sat on the floor. And beside it was a bloody scrap of gray cloth, and one of the pens that had been clipped to the man's breast pocket.

"Don't go under there, Charlie! Don't." His heartbeat whammed savagely in his ears, frightening him even more.

"No," Charlie said. "But the body . . ."

Charlie hunkered down, grabbed the flashlight, and shone it under the stairs. And the crate was there, shoved up against the far wall, just as it had been before, squat and mute. Except that now it was free of dust and three boards had been pried off the top.

The light moved and centered on one of the janitor's big, sensible work shoes. Charlie drew breath in a low, harsh gasp. The thick leather of the shoe had been savagely gnawed and chewed. The laces hung, broken, from the eyelets. "It looks like somebody put it through a hay baler," he said hoarsely.

"Now do you believe me?" Dex asked.

Charlie didn't answer. Holding onto the stairs lightly with one hand, he leaned under the overhang—presumably to get the shoe. Later, sitting in Henry's study, Dex said he could think of only one reason why Charlie would have done that—to measure and perhaps categorize the bite of the thing in the crate. He was, after all, a zoologist, and a damned good one.

"Don't!" Dex screamed, and grabbed the back of Charlie's shirt.

Suddenly there were two green gold eyes glaring over the top of the crate. They were almost exactly the color of owls' eyes, but smaller. There was a harsh, chattering growl of anger. Charlie recoiled, startled, and slammed the back of his head on the underside of the stairs. A shadow moved from the crate toward him at projectile speed. Charlie howled. Dex heard the dry purr of his shirt as it ripped open, the click as Charlie's glasses struck the floor and spun away. Once more Charlie tried to back away. The thing began to snarl—then the snarls suddenly stopped. And Charlie Gereson began to scream in agony.

Dex pulled on the back of his white tee shirt with all his might. For a moment Charlie came backwards and he caught a glimpse of a furry, writhing shape spread-eagled on the young man's chest, a shape that appeared to have not four but six legs and the flat bullet head of a young lynx. The front of Charlie Gereson's shirt had been so quickly and completely tattered that it now looked like so many crepe streamers hung around his neck.

Then the thing raised its head and those small green gold eyes stared balefully into Dex's own. He had never seen or dreamed such savagery. His strength failed. His grip on the back of Charlie's shirt loosened momentarily.

A moment was all it took. Charlie Gereson's body was snapped under the stairs with grotesque, cartoonish speed. Silence for a moment. Then the growling, smacking sounds began again.

Charlie screamed once more, a long sound of terror and pain that was abruptly cut off . . . as if something had been clapped over his mouth.

Or stuffed into it.

Dex fell silent. The moon was high in the sky. Half of his third drink—an almost unheard-of phenomenon—was gone, and he felt the reaction setting in as sleepiness and extreme lassitude.

"What did you do then?" Henry asked. What he hadn't done, he knew, was to go to campus security; they wouldn't have listened to such a story and then released him so he could go and tell it again to his friend Henry.

"I just walked around, in utter shock, I suppose. I ran up the stairs again, just as I had after . . . after it took the janitor, only this time there was no Charlie Gereson to run into. I walked . . . miles, I suppose. I think I was mad. I kept thinking about Ryder's Quarry. You know that place?"

"Yes," Henry said.

"I kept thinking that would be deep enough. If . . . if there would be a way to get that crate out there. I kept . . . kept thinking . . . " He put his hands to his face. "I don't know. I don't know anymore. I think I'm going crazy."

"If the story you just told is true, I can understand that," Henry said quietly. He stood up suddenly. "Come on. I'm taking you home."

"Home?" Dex looked at this friend vacantly. "But—"

"I'll leave a note for Wilma telling her where we've gone and then we'll call . . . who do you suggest, Dex? Campus security or the state police?"

"You believe me, don't you? You believe me? Just say you do."

"Yes, I believe you," Henry said, and it was the truth. "I don't know what that thing could be or where it came from, but I believe you."

Dex Stanley began to weep.

"Finish your drink while I write my wife," Henry said, apparently not noticing the tears. He even grinned a little. "And for Christ's sake, let's get out of here before she gets back."

Dex clutched at Henry's sleeve. "But we won't go anywhere near Amberson Hall, will we? Promise me, Henry! We'll stay away from there, won't we?"

"Does a bear shit in the woods?" Henry Northrup asked. It was a three-mile drive to Dex's house on the outskirts of town, and before they got there, he was half-asleep in the passenger seat.

"The state cops, I think," Henry said. His words seemed to come from a great distance. "I think Charlie Gereson's assessment of the campus cops was pretty accurate. The first one there would happily stick his arm into that box."

"Yes. All right." Through the drifting, lassitudinous aftermath of shock, Dex felt a dim but great gratitude that his friend had taken over with such efficiency. Yet a deeper part of him believed that Henry could not have done it if he had seen the things he had seen. "Just . . . the importance of caution . . ."

"I'll see to that," Henry said grimly, and that was when Dex fell asleep.

He awoke the next morning with August sunshine making crisp patterns on the sheets of his bed. Just a dream, he thought with indescribable relief. All some crazy dream.

But there was a taste of Scotch in his mouth—Scotch and something else. He sat up, and a lance of pain bolted through his head. Not the sort of pain you got from a hangover, though; not even if you were the type to get a hangover from three Scotches, and he wasn't.

He sat up, and there was Henry, sitting across the room. His first thought was that Henry needed a shave. His second was that there was something in Henry's eyes that he had never seen before—something like chips of ice. A ridiculous thought came to Dex; it passed through his mind and was gone. *Sniper's eyes. Henry Northrup, whose specialty is the earlier English poets, has got sniper's eyes.*

"How are you feeling, Dex?"

"A slight headache," Dex said. "Henry . . . the police . . . what happened?"

"The police aren't coming," Northrup said calmly. "As for your head, I'm very sorry. I put one of Wilma's sleeping powders in your third drink. Be assured that it will pass."

"Henry, what are you saying?"

Henry took a sheet of notepaper from his breast pocket. "This is the note I left my wife. It will explain a lot, I think. I got it back after everything was over. I took a chance that she'd leave it on the table, and I got away with it."

"I don't know what you're—"

He took the note from Henry's fingers and read it, eyes widening.

Dear Billie,

I've just had a call from Dex Stanley. He's hysterical. Seems to have committed some sort of indiscretion with one of his female grad students. He's at Amberson Hall. So is the girl. For God's sake, come quickly. I'm not sure exactly what the situation is, but a woman's presence may be imperative, and under the circumstances, a nurse from the infirmary just won't do. I know you don't like Dex much, but a scandal like this could ruin his career. Please come.

Henry.

"What in God's name have you done?" Dex asked hoarsely.

Henry plucked the note from Dex's nerveless fingers, produced his Zippo, and set flame to the corner. When it was burning well, he dropped the charring sheet of paper into an ashtray on the windowsill.

"I've killed Wilma," he said in the same calm voice. "Ding-dong, the wicked bitch is dead." Dex tried to speak and could not. That central axle was trying to tear loose again. The abyss of utter insanity was below. "I've killed my wife, and now I've put myself into your hands."

Now Dex did find his voice. It had a sound that was rusty yet shrill. "The crate," he said. "What have you done with the crate?"

"That's the beauty of it," Henry said. "You put the final piece in the jigsaw yourself. The crate is at the bottom of Ryder's Quarry."

Dex groped at that while he looked into Henry's eyes. The eyes of his friend. Sniper's eyes. You can't knock off your own queen, that's not in anyone's rules of chess, he thought, and restrained an urge to roar out gales of rancid laughter. The quarry, he had said. Ryder's Quarry. It was over four hundred feet deep, some said. It was perhaps twelve miles east of the university. Over the thirty years that Dex had been here, a dozen people had drowned there, and three years ago the town had posted the place.

"I put you to bed," Henry said. "Had to carry you into your room. You were out like a light. Scotch, sleeping powder, shock. But you were breathing normally and well. Strong heart action. I checked those things. Whatever else you believe, never think I had any intention of hurting you, Dex.

"It was fifteen minutes before Wilma's last class ended, and it would take her another fifteen minutes to drive home and another fifteen minutes to get over to Amberson Hall. That gave me forty-five minutes. I got over to Amberson in ten. It was unlocked. That was enough to settle any doubts I had left."

"What do you mean?"

"The key ring on the janitor's belt. It went with the janitor."

Dex shuddered.

"If the door had been locked—forgive me, Dex, but if you're going to play for keeps, you ought to cover every base—there was still time enough to get back home ahead of Wilma and burn that note.

"I went downstairs—and I kept as close to the wall going down those stairs as I could, believe me . . ."

Henry stepped into the lab and glanced around. It was just as Dex had left it. He slicked his tongue over his dry lips and then wiped his face with his hand. His heart was thudding in his chest. *Get hold of yourself, man. One thing at a time. Don't look ahead.*

The boards the janitor had pried off the crate were still stacked on the lab table. One table over was the scatter of Charlie Gereson's lab notes, never to be completed now. Henry took it all in, and then pulled his own flashlight—the one he always kept in the glovebox of his car for emergencies—from his back pocket. If this didn't qualify as an emergency, nothing did.

He snapped it on and crossed the lab and went out the door. The light bobbed uneasily in the dark for a moment, and then he trained it on the floor. He didn't want to step on anything he shouldn't. Moving slowly and cautiously, Henry moved around to the side of the stairs and shone the light underneath. His breath paused, and then resumed again, more slowly. Sudenly the tension and fear were gone, and he only felt cold. The crate was under there, just as Dex had said it was. And the janitor's ballpoint pen. And his shoes. And Charlie Gereson's glasses.

Henry moved the light from one of these artifacts to the next slowly, spotlighting each. Then he glanced at his watch, snapped the flashlight off and jammed it back in his pocket. He had half an hour. There was no time to waste.

In the janitor's closet upstairs he found buckets, heavy-duty cleaner, rags . . . and gloves. No prints. He went back downstairs like the sorcerer's apprentice, a heavy plastic bucket full of hot water and foaming cleaner in each hand, rags draped over his shoulder. His footfalls clacked hollowly in the stillness. He thought of Dex saying, *It sits squat and mute*. And still he was cold.

He began to clean up.

"She came," Henry said. "Oh yes, she came. And she was . . . excited and happy."

"What?" Dex said.

"Excited," he repeated. "She was whining and carping the way she always did in that high, unpleasant voice, but that was just habit, I think. All those years, Dex, the only part of me she wasn't able to completely control, the only part she could never get completely under her thumb, was my friendship with you. Our two drinks while she was at class. Our chess. Our . . . companionship."

Dex nodded. Yes, companionship was the right word. A little light in the darkness of loneliness. It hadn't just been the chess or the drinks; it had been Henry's face over the board, Henry's voice recounting how things were in his department, a bit of harmless gossip, a laugh over something.

"So she was whining and bitching in her best 'just call me Billie' style, but I think it was just habit. She was excited and happy, Dex. Because she was finally going to be able to get control over the last . . . little . . . bit." He looked at Dex calmly. "I knew she'd come, you see. I knew she'd want to see what kind of mess you gotten yourself into, Dex."

"They're downstairs," Henry told Wilma. Wilma was wearing a bright yellow sleeveless blouse and green pants that were too tight for her. "Right downstairs." And he uttered a sudden, loud laugh.

Wilma's head whipped around and her narrow face darkened with suspicion. "What are you laughing about?" She asked in her loud, buzzing voice. "Your best friend gets in a scrape with a girl and you're laughing?"

No, he shouldn't be laughing. But he couldn't help it. It was sitting under the stairs, sitting there squat and mute, just try telling that thing in the crate to call you Billie, Wilma—and another loud laugh escaped him and went rolling down the dim first-floor hall like a depth charge.

"Well, there is a funny side to it," he said, hardly aware of what he was saying. "Wait'll you see. You'll think—"

Her eyes, always questing, never still, dropped to his front pocket, where he had stuffed the rubber gloves.

"What are those? Are those gloves?"

Henry began to spew words. At the same time he put his arm around Wilma's bony shoulders and led her toward the stairs. "Well, he's passed out, you know. He smells like a distillery. Can't guess how much he drank. Threw up all over everything. I've been cleaning up. Hell of an awful mess, Billie. I persuaded the girl to stay a bit. You'll help me, won't you? This is Dex, after all."

"I don't know," she said, as they began to descend the stairs to the basement lab. Her eyes snapped with dark glee. "I'll have to see what the situation is. You don't know anything, that's obvious. You're hysterical. Exactly what I would have expected."

"That's right," Henry said. They had reached the bottom of the stairs. "Right around here. Just step right around here."

"But the lab's that way—"

"Yes . . . but the girl . . . " And he began to laugh again in great, loonlike bursts.

"Henry, what *is* wrong with you?" And now that acidic contempt was mixed with something else—something that might have been fear.

That made Henry laugh harder. His laughter echoed and rebounded, filling the dark basement with a sound like laughing banshees or demons approving a particularly good jest. "The girl, Billie," Henry said between bursts of helpless laughter. "That's what's so funny, the girl, the girl has crawled under the stairs and won't come out, that what's so funny, *ah-heh-heh-hahahahaa—*"

And now the dark kerosene of joy lit in her eyes; her lips curled up like charring paper in what the denizens of hell might call a smile. And Wilma whispered, "What did he *do* to her?"

"You can get her out," Henry babbled, leading her to the dark, triangular, gaping maw. "I'm sure you can get her out, no trouble, no problem." He suddenly grabbed Wilma at the nape of the neck and the waist, forcing her down even as he pushed her into the space under the stairs.

"What are you doing?" she screamed querulously. "What are you doing, Henry?"

"What I should have done a long time ago," Henry said, laughing. "Get under there, Wilma. Just tell it to call you Billie, you bitch."

She tried to turn, tried to fight him. One hand clawed for his wrist—he saw her spade-shaped nails slice down, but they clawed only air. "Stop it, Henry!" She cried. "Stop it right now! Stop this foolishness! I—I'll scream!"

"Scream all you want!" he bellowed, still laughing. He raised one foot, planted it in the center of her narrow and joyless backside, and pushed. "I'll help you, Wilma! Come on out! Wake up, whatever you are! Wake up! Here's your dinner! Poison meat! Wake up! Wake up!"

Wilma screamed piercingly, an inarticulate sound that was still more rage than fear.

And then Henry heard it.

First a low whistle, the sound a man might make while working alone without even being aware of it. Then it rose in pitch, sliding up the scale to an earsplitting whine that was barely audible. Then it suddenly descended again and became a growl . . . and then a hoarse yammering. It was an utterly savage sound. All his married life Henry Northrup had gone in fear of his wife, but the thing in the crate made Wilma sould like a child doing a kindergarten tantram. Henry had time to think: *Holy God, maybe it really is a Tasmanian devil . . . it's some kind of devil, anyway.*

Wilma began to scream again, but this time it was a sweeter tune—at least to the ear of Henry Northrup. It was a sound of utter terror. Her yellow blouse flashed in the dark under the stairs, a vague beacon. She lunged at the opening and Henry pushed her back, using all his strength.

"Henry!" She howled. "*Hen-reeeee!*"

She came again, head first this time, like a charging bull. Henry caught her head in both hands, feeling the tight, wiry cap of her curls squash under his palms. He pushed. And then, over Wilma's shoulder, he saw something that might have been the gold-glinting eyes of a small owl. Eyes that were infinitely cold and hateful. The yammering became louder, reaching a crescendo. And when it struck at Wilma, the vibration running through her body was enough to knock him backwards.

He caught one glimpse of her face, her bulging eyes, and then she was dragged back into the darkness. She screamed once more.

Only once.

"Just tell it to call you Billie," he whispered.

Henry Northrup drew a great, shuddering breath.

"It went on . . . for quite a while," he said. After a long time, maybe twenty minutes, the growling and the . . . the sounds of its feeding . . . that stopped, too. And it started to whistle. Just like you said, Dex. As if it were a happy teakettle or something. It whistled for maybe five minutes, and then it stopped. I shone my light underneath again. The crate had been pulled out a little way. Thre was . . . fresh blood. And Wilma's purse had spilled everywhere. But it got both of her shoes. That was something, wasn't it?"

Dex didn't answer. The room basked in sunshine. Outside, a bird sang.

"I finished cleaning the lab," Henry resumed at last. "It took me another forty minutes, and I almost missed a drop of blood that was on the light globe . . . saw it just as I was going out. But when I was done, the place was as neat as a pin. Then I went out to my car and drove across campus to the English department. It was getting late, but I didn't feel a bit tired. In fact, Dex, I don't think I ever felt more clear-headed in my life. There was a crate in the basement of the English department. I flashed on that very early in your story. Associating one monster with another, I suppose."

"What do you mean?"

"Last year when Badlinger was in England—you remember Badlinger, don't you?"

Dex nodded. Badlinger was the man who had beaten Henry out for the English department chair . . . partly because Badlinger's wife was bright, vivacious and sociable, while Henry's wife was a shrew. Had been a shrew.

"He was in England on sabbatical," Henry said. "Had all their things crated and shipped back. One of them was a giant stuffed animal. Nessie, they call it. For his kids. That bastard bought it for his kids. I always wanted children, you know. Wilma didn't. She said kids get in the way.

"Anyway, it came back in this gigantic wooden crate, and Badlinger dragged it down to the English department basement because there was no room in the garage at home, he said, but he didn't want to throw it out because it might come in handy someday. Meantime, our janitors were using it as a gigantic sort of wastebasket. When it was full of trash, they'd dump it into the back of the truck on trash day and then fill it up again.

"I think it was the crate Badlinger's damned stuffed monster came back from England in that put the idea in my head. I began to see how your Tasmanian devil could be gotten rid of. And that started me thinking about something else I wanted to be rid of. That I wanted so badly to be rid of.

"I had my keys, of course. I let myself in and went downstairs. The crate was there. It was a big, unwieldy thing, but the janitors' dolly was down there as well. I dumped out the little bit of trash that was in it and got the crate onto the dolly by standing it on end. I pulled it upstairs and wheeled it straight across the mall and back to Amberson."

"You didn't take your car?"

"No, I left my car in my space in the English department parking lot. I couldn't have gotten the crate in there, anyway."

For Dex, new light began to break. Henry would have been driving his MG, of course—an elderly sportscar that Wilma had always called Henry's toy. And if Henry had the MG, then Wilma would have had the Scout—a jeep with a fold-down back seat. Plenty of storage space, as the ads said.

"I didn't meet anyone," Henry said. "At this time of year—and at no other—the campus is quite deserted. The whole thing was almost hellishly perfect. I didn't see so much as a pair of headlights. I got back to Amberson Hall and took Badlinger's crate downstairs. I left it sitting on the dolly with the open end facing under the stairs. Then I went back upstairs to the janitors' closet and got that long pole they use to open and close the windows. They only have those poles in the old buildings now. I went back down and got ready to hook the crate—your Paella crate—out from under the stairs. Then I had a bad moment. I realized the top of Badlinger's crate was gone, you see. I'd noticed it before, but now I *realized* it. In my guts."

"What did you do?"

"Decided to take the chance," Henry said. "I took the window pole and pulled the crate out. I *eased* it out, as if it were full of eggs. No . . . as if it were full of Mason jars with nitroglycerine in them."

Dex sat up, staring at Henry. "What . . . what . . ."

Henry looked back somberly. "It was my first good look at it, remember. It was horrible." He paused deliberately and then said it again: "It was horrible, Dex. It was splattered with blood, some of it seemingly grimed right into the wood. It made me think of . . . do you remember those joke boxes they used to sell? You'd push a little lever and the box would grind and shake, and then a pale green hand would come out of the top and push the lever back and snap inside again. It made me think of that.

"I pulled it out—oh, so carefully—and I said I wouldn't look down inside, no matter what. But I did, of course. And I saw . . ." His voice dropped helplessly, seeming to lose all strength. "I saw Wilma's face, Dex. Her *face*."

"Henry, don't—"

"I saw her eyes, looking up at me from that box. Her glazed eyes. I saw something else, too. Something white. A bone, I think. And a black something. Furry. Curled up. Whistling, too. A very low whistle. I think it was sleeping.

"I hooked it out as far as I could, and then I just stood there looking at it, realizing that I couldn't drive knowing that thing could come out at any time . . . come out and land on the back of my neck. So I started to look around for something—anything—to cover the top of Badlinger's crate.

"I went into the animal husbandry room, and there were a couple of cages big enough to hold the Paella crate, but I couldn't find the goddamned keys. So I went upstairs and I still couldn't find anything. I don't know how long I hunted, but there was this continual feeling of time . . . slipping away. I was getting a little crazy. Then I happened to poke into that big lecture room at the far end of the hall—"

"Room 6?"

"Yes, I think so. They had been painting the walls. There was a big canvas dropcloth on the floor to catch the splatters. I took it, and then I went back downstairs, and I pushed the Paella crate into Badlinger's crate. Carefully! . . . you wouldn't believe how carefully I did it, Dex . . ."

When the smaller crate was nested inside the larger, Henry uncinched the straps on the English department dolly and grabbed the end of the dropcloth. It rustled stiffly in the stillness of Amberson Hall's basement. His breathing rustled stiffly as well. And there was that low whistle. He kept waiting for it to pause, to change. It didn't. He had sweated his shirt through; it was plastered to his chest and back.

Moving carefully, refusing to hurry, he wrapped the dropcloth around Badlinger's crate three times, then four, then five. In the dim light shining through from the lab, Badlinger's crate now looked mummified. Holding the seam with one splayed hand, he wrapped first one strap around it, then the other. He cinched them tight and then stood back a moment. He glanced at his watch. It was just past one o'clock. A pulse beat rhythmically at his throat.

Moving forward again, wishing absurdly for a cigarette (he had given them up sixteen years before), he grabbed the dolly, tilted it back, and began pulling it slowly up the stairs.

Outside, the moon watched coldly as he lifted the entire load, dolly and all, into the back of what he had come to think of as Wilma's Jeep—although Wilma had not earned a dime since the day he had married her. It was the biggest lift he had done since he had worked with a moving company in Westbrook as an undergraduate. At the highest point of the lift, a lance of pain seemed to dig into his lower back. And still he slipped it into the back of the Scout as gently as a sleeping baby.

He tried to close the back, but it wouldn't go up; the handle of the dolly stuck out four inches too far. He drove with the tailgate down, and at every bump and pothole, his heart seemed to stutter. His ears felt for the whistle, waiting for it to escalate into a shrill scream and then descend to a guttural howl of fury waiting for the hoarse rip of canvas as teeth and claws pulled their way through it.

And overhead the moon, a mystic silver disc, rode the sky.

"I drove out to Ryder's Quarry," Henry went on. "There was a chain across the head of the road, but I geared the Scout down and got around. I backed right up to the edge of the water. The moon was still up and I could see its reflection way down in the blackness, like a drowned silver dollar. I went around, but it was a long time before I could bring myself to grab the thing. In a very real way, Dex, it was three bodies . . . the remains of three human beings. And I started wondering . . .where did they go? I saw Wilma's face, but it looked . . .

God help me, it looked all *flat*, like a Halloween mask. How much of them did it eat, Dex? How much *could* it eat? And I started to understand what you meant about that central axle pulling loose.

"It was still whistling. I could hear it, muffled and faint, through that canvas dropcloth. Then I grabbed it and I *heaved* . . . I really believe it was do it then or do it never. It came sliding out . . . and I think maybe it suspected, Dex . . . because, as the dolly started to tilt down toward the water it started to growl and yammer again . . . and the canvas started to ripple and bulge . . . and I yanked it again. I gave it all I had . . . so much that I almost fell into the damned quarry myself. And it went in. There was a splash . . . and then it was gone. Except for a few ripples, it was gone. And then the ripples were gone, too."

He fell silent, looking at his hands.

"And you came here," Dex said.

"First I went back to Amberson Hall. Cleaned under the stairs. Picked up all of Wilma's things and put them in her purse again. Picked up the janitor's shoe and his pen and your grad student's glasses. Wilma's purse is still on the seat. I parked the car in our—in my—driveway. On the way there I threw the rest of the stuff in the river."

"And then did what? Walked here?"

"Yes."

"Henry, what if I'd waked up before you got here? Called the police?"

Henry Northrup said simply: "You didn't."

They stared at each other, Dex from his bed, Henry from the chair by the window.

Speaking in tones so soft as to be nearly inaudible, Henry said, "The question is, what happens now? Three people are gong to be reported missing soon. There is no one element to connect all three. There are no signs of foul play; I saw to that. Badlinger's crate, the dolly, the painters' dropcloth—those things will be reported missing too, presumably. There will be a search. But the weight of the dolly will carry the crate to the bottom of the quarry, and . . . there are really no bodies, are there, Dex?"

"No," Dexter Stanley said. "No, I suppose there aren't."

"But what are you going to do, Dex? What are you going to say?"

"Oh, I could tell a tale," Dex said. "And if I told it, I suspect I'd end up in the state mental hospital. Perhaps accused of murdering the janitor and Gereson, if not your wife. No matter how good your cleanup was, a state police forensic unit could find traces of blood on the floor and walls of that laboratory. I believe I'll keep my mouth shut."

"Thank you," Henry said. "Thank you, Dex."

Dex thought of that elusive thing Henry had mentioned —companionship. A little light in the darkness. He thought of playing chess perhaps twice a week instead of once. Perhaps even three times a week . . . and if the game was not finished by ten, perhaps playing until midnight if neither of them had any early morning classes, instead of having to put the board away (and, as likely as not, Wilma would just "accidentally" knock over the pieces "while dusting," so that the game would have to be started all over again the following Thursday evening). He thought of his friend, at last free of that other species of Tasmanian devil that killed more slowly but just as surely—by heart attack, by stroke, by ulcer, by high blood pressure, yammering and whistling in the ear all the while.

Last of all, he thought of the janitor, casually flicking his quarter, and of the quarter coming down and rolling under the stairs, where a very old horror sat squat and mute, covered with dust and cobwebs, waiting . . . biding its time . . .

What had Henry said? The whole thing was almost hellishly perfect.

"No need to thank me, Henry," he said.

Henry stood up. "If you got dressed," he said, "you could run me down to the campus. I could get my MG and go back home and report Wilma missing."

Dex thought about it. Henry was inviting him to cross a nearly invisible line, it seemed, from bystander to accomplice. Did he want to cross that line?

At last he swung his legs out of bed. "All right, Henry."

"Thank you, Dexter."

Dex smiled slowly. "That's all right," he said. "After all, what are friends for?"